By Peter V. Brett

Demon Cycle Novels

The Warded Man

The Desert Spear

The Daylight War

The Skull Throne

The Core

Demon Cycle Novellas

The Great Bazaar

Brayan's Gold

Messenger's Legacy

Barren

The Nightfall Saga

The Desert Prince

The Hidden Queen

The Demon King (forthcoming)

The Hidden Queen

THE HIDDEN QUEEN

BOOK TWO OF THE NIGHTFALL SAGA

PETER V. BRETT

DEL REY

NEW YORK

The Hidden Queen is a work of fiction.
Names, places, and incidents either are products of
the author's imagination or are used fictitiously.
Any resemblance to actual events, locales, or persons,
living or dead, is entirely coincidental.

Published in the United States by Del Rey, an imprint of Random House,
a division of Penguin Random House LLC, New York.

Published in the United Kingdom by Harper Voyager,
an imprint of HarperCollins Publishers Ltd.

Chapter opener and Ward artwork
designed by Lauren K. Cannon, copyright © Peter V. Brett
Family tree: design by Edwin Vazquez; texture map © NaokiKim

DEL REY and the CIRCLE colophon are registered trademarks of
Penguin Random House LLC.

Hardback ISBN 978-1-9848-1711-2
Ebook ISBN 978-1-9848-1712-9

Printed in Canada on acid-free paper

randomhousebooks.com

2 4 6 8 9 7 5 3 1

First US Edition

Book design by Edwin A. Vazquez

For the Phoenix and the Mermaid

CONTENTS

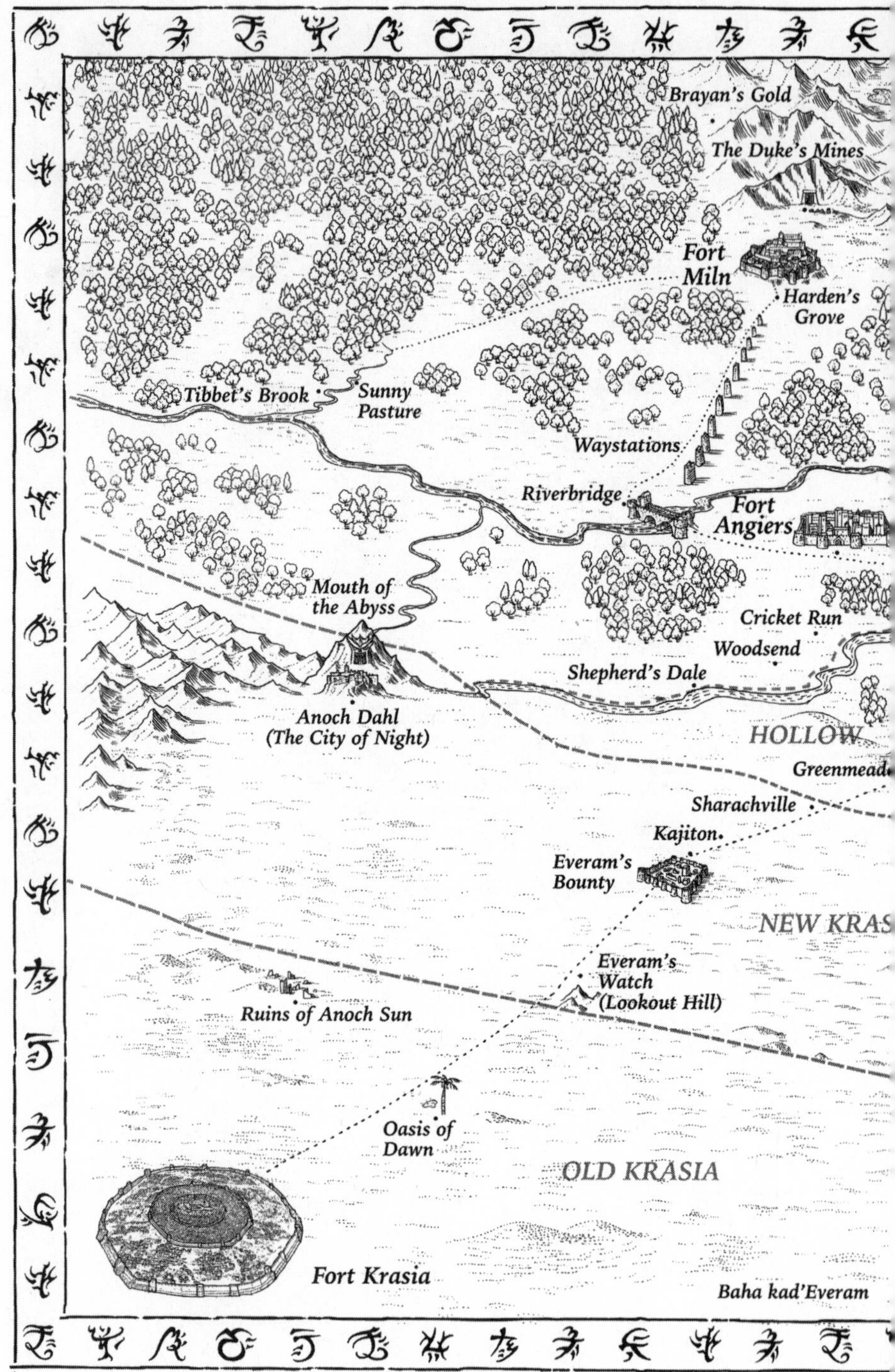
Brayan's Gold
The Duke's Mines
Fort Miln
Harden's Grove
Tibbet's Brook
Sunny Pasture
Waystations
Riverbridge
Fort Angiers
Mouth of the Abyss
Cricket Run
Woodsend
Shepherd's Dale
Anoch Dahl (The City of Night)
HOLLOW
Greenmead
Sharachville
Kajiton
Everam's Bounty
NEW KRAS
Everam's Watch (Lookout Hill)
Ruins of Anoch Sun
Oasis of Dawn
OLD KRASIA
Fort Krasia
Baha kad'Everam

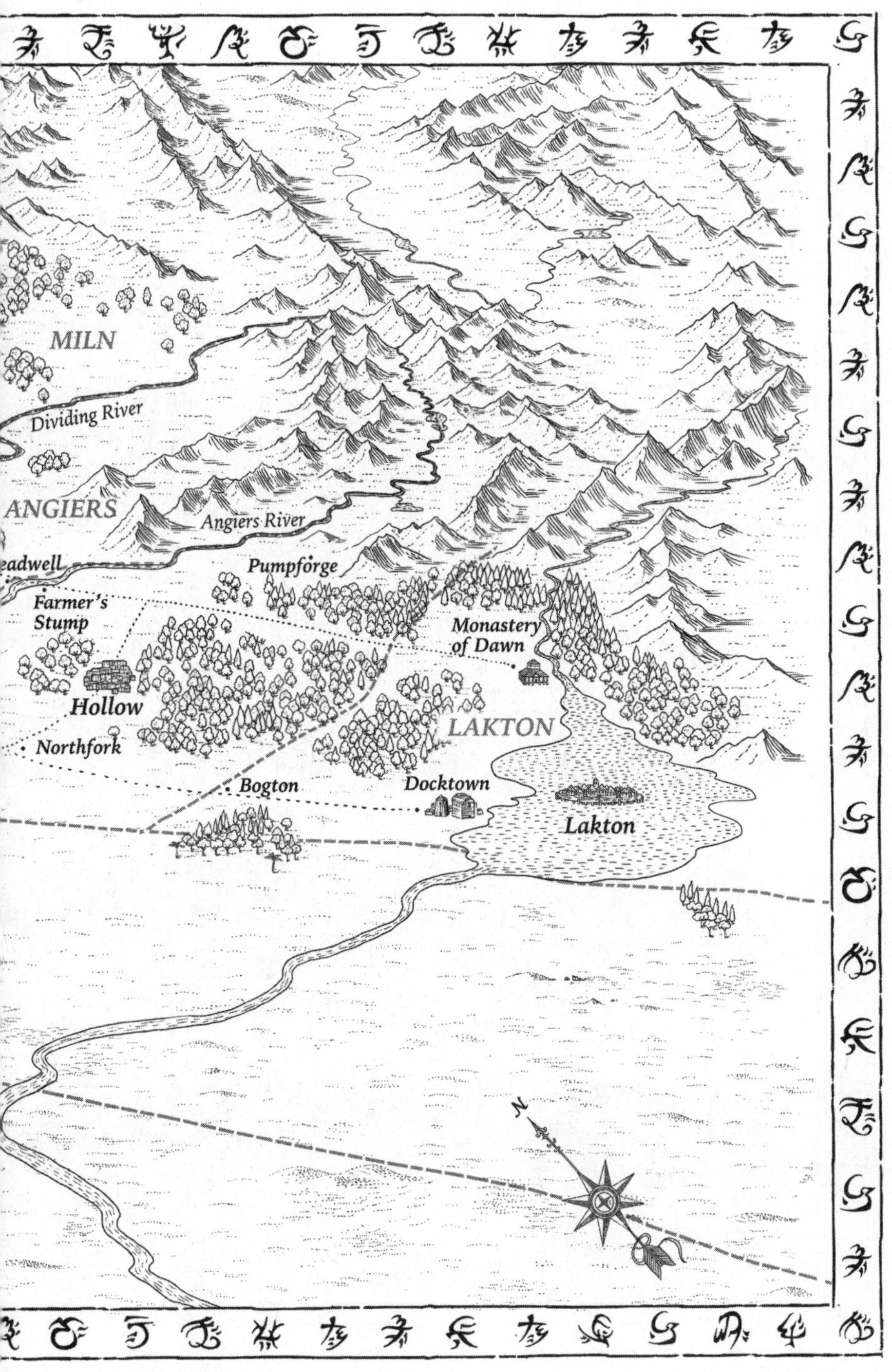
MILN
Dividing River
ANGIERS
Angiers River
eadwell
Pumpforge
Farmer's Stump
Hollow
Northfork
Monastery of Dawn
LAKTON
Bogton
Docktown
Lakton
N

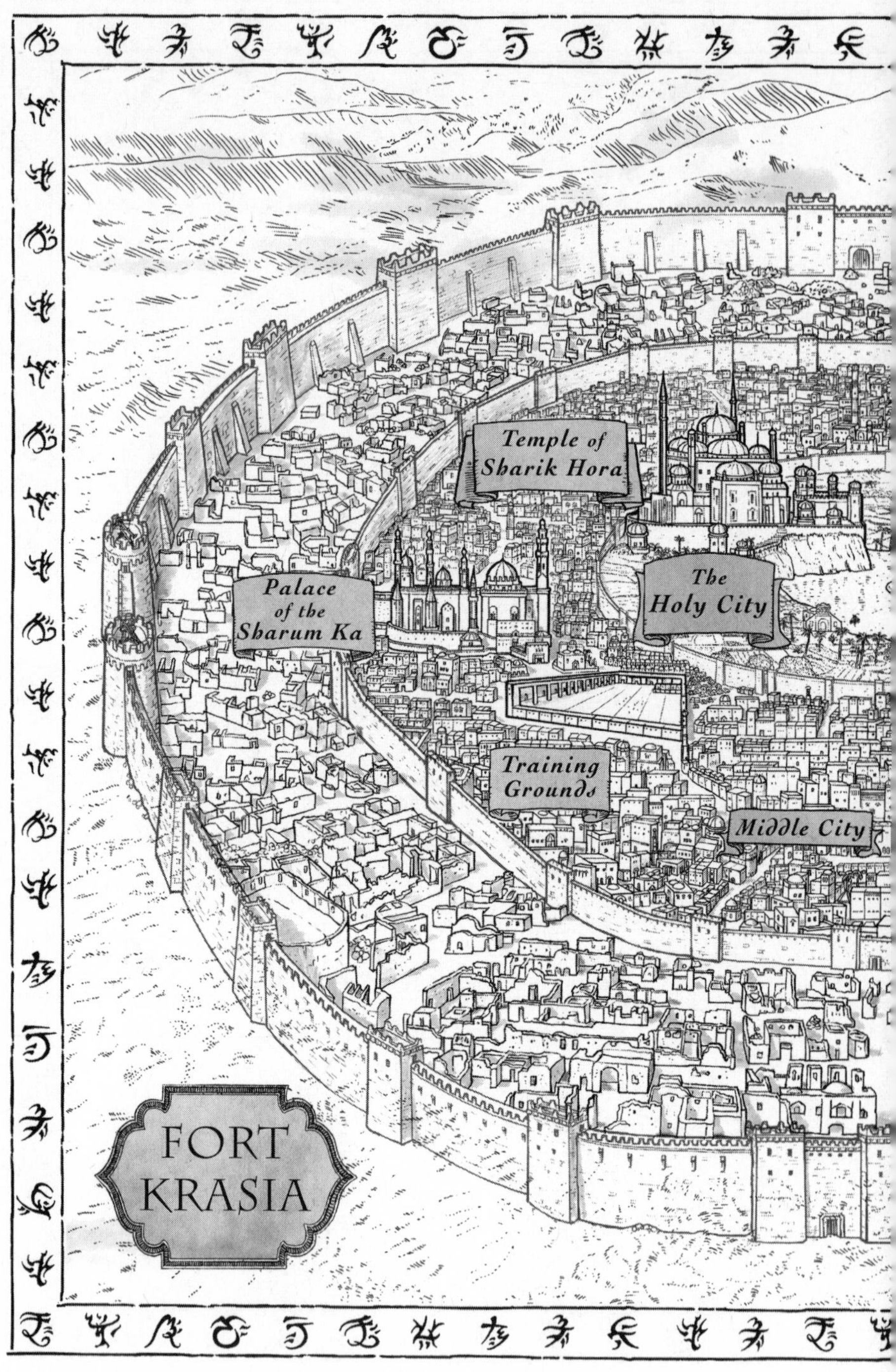
Temple of Sharik Hora
Palace of the Sharum Ka
The Holy City
Training Grounds
Middle City
FORT KRASIA

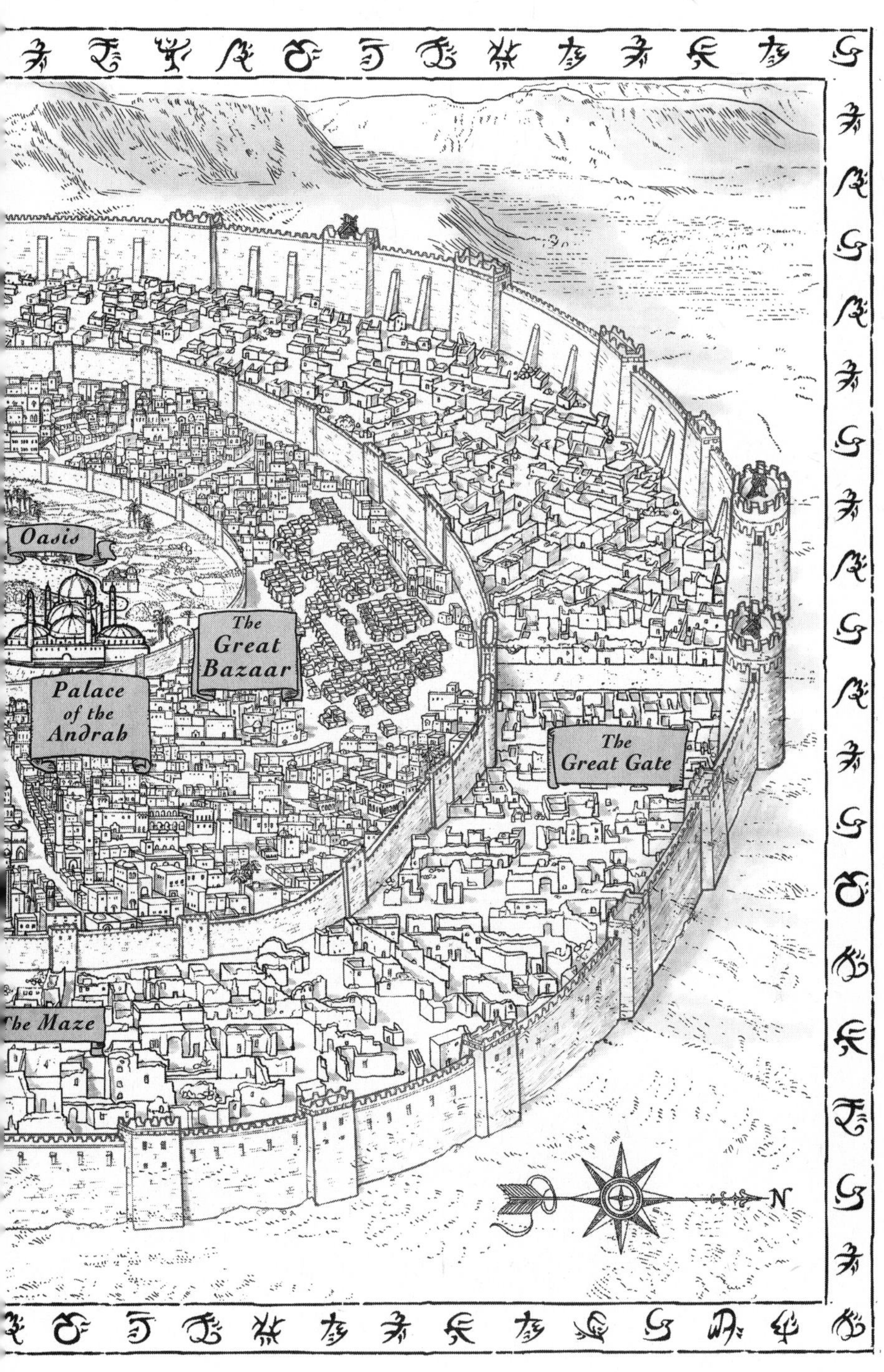
Oasis
The Great Bazaar
Palace of the Andrah
The Great Gate
The Maze
N

The Hidden Queen

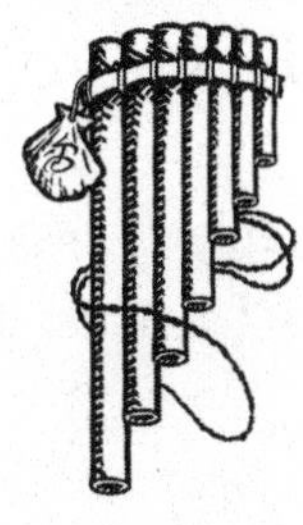

CHAPTER I

TEAR BOTTLES

349 AR

I'M DARIN BALES, and I'm looking for my mam.

Never knew my da. He died before I was born. Savin' the world, if you believe I'm telling honest word. Ask around if you like. Walk a hundred miles, and folk will all tell you Arlen Bales went down to the Core and sacrificed himself. How his last act was seen in the sky in the form of great, blazing wards that turned the tide of the demon war, burning the corelings to ash. Even those with him at the time say it. My bloodfather. My mam.

I was there, too, in a manner of speaking. Still in Mam's belly when he died, but she says I spilled out onto the stone floor of the demon hive just minutes later.

Missed my only chance to meet my da by minutes. Might as well be years. Goin' back a minute, a single second, ent any easier.

I'm starting to think folk were wrong, though. World still needs savin'. And if they're wrong about that part, why not the other? My aunt Leesha is a fortune teller. She cast her demonbones in my blood, and there was magic about the throw, to be sure. Her words have replayed in my mind so many times they've become part of me.

The father waits below in darkness for his progeny to return.

Might mean other things. Ent such a fool I'd trust a prophecy to say everything it seems to. But it ent crazy to wonder if something of my da is still down there, stuck halfway to the Core, like a cork in a bottle.

Is it?

But while my da *might* be alive, I *know* my mam is. And I know the thing that's got her is trying to fatten her up like a choice pig for a wedding feast.

Din't know my da growin' up. Saw other boys with theirs and knew I was missin' something, but it's hard to really miss someone you've never met.

Mam was the one who was always there for me. Who fed me and taught me and kept me safe. Mam, who felt strong as the sun.

Now she's gone. Taken. And I'm left to care for myself, best I can. It's good I got help, because I don't think I could do it alone. Since my first born day, folk have been trying to see something of Mam and Da in me, and they always go away disappointed.

And it ent just myself I need to take care of. All those years Mam looked out for me, what kind of son would I be if I din't come after her? Even if it means walking into the lair of a creature the Jongleurs have a dozen names for, each scarier than the last. The demon king. The Father of Evil.

Alagai Ka. He has some plan to hatch a new hive queen, and if he does . . .

What did Da even die for, if I let Alagai Ka bring it all back? If I let him feed Mam to a hatchling queen and repopulate the hive with a new generation of demons, just when folk were startin' to have a taste of what life could be without 'em?

I ent up to the job of stoppin' him, of course. I've got fifteen summers, and the demon king is older than a mountain. Got a bit of magic I can use—more by frightened instinct than control—but the Father of Evil wields power as easily as I play a tune on my pipes. Alagai Ka's got nothin' to be scared of, and I've never felt anything but. If I go alone, I'm more likely to die tryin' than put a rock in front of his plow.

But I'm not alone. Got a lot of friends, all of them better than me at one thing or another.

Olive Paper's got magic of her own—bound to her in the form of muscle and bone. Reckon she could pick up a milk cow and throw it through the barn wall. Demon's got her mam, too, and she's none too pleased about it.

Selen Cutter ent as strong as Olive, but she's a fair sight bigger'n stronger than me. Smarter, too. Don't know I would have dared any of this, trekking hundreds of miles through a desert to find Olive, if I hadn't known Selen would be around to keep me safe.

Arick and Rojvah, my cousins in all but blood, project confidence and assurance I can never have. Arick is built like a prize bull, and the best fighter I've ever seen short of Olive. Rojvah's music puts mine to shame, luring demons—and folk—in close and putting them under her spell.

I can't save our parents alone, but maybe all of us together can.

Want to get on with it. To get on the road and run at the thing I'm scared of, hoping the momentum, and not wanting to disappoint my friends, will keep pushing me forward when I get too spooked.

But first, we got some business left to attend.

THE FUNERAL ENT all that different from one of Tender Harral's Seventhday services back home in Tibbnet's Brook. Bunch of long, loud, boring prayers mixed with bits of half-sung lyrics, sandwiched between tedious sermons. Only here the prayers and lectures are all in Krasian, and instead of the little chapel up on Boggin's Hill, I'm in legendary Sharik Hora.

I've been in grand Holy Houses before. The Cathedral of the Deliverer in Hollow. The great Library and Cathedral of Miln. Even the new Sharik Hora in Everam's Bounty—which took my breath away, first time I saw it—pales in comparison with the *real* Sharik Hora, the temple of heroes' bones in Fort Krasia, or Desert Spear, as the locals call it.

There's magic here. Old magic, and . . . sleeping, but I can sense it, even if most folk can't.

It's different from what I'm used to. Ent like the demonbone magic Aunt Leesha uses, or the raw magic of the Core Mam used to Draw upon. Not like the magic inside me, born in darkness, or the demons themselves, saturated with magic from the dark below.

It's just past dawn, sun streaming through the stained-glass windows to fill the place with color and light. Sunlight burns magic away, but it has no effect on this place.

Not like it does on me. I'm as covered up as custom allows, showing nothing but my face and hands. Still the light hurts, and not just my eyes. It dizzies me, and makes my skin itch and burn. Magic comes out at night and clings to me like a stink until sunrise scours it off like sandpaper and a bucket of scalding water.

At night the Temple of Heroes' Bones comes alive, like it's got a will of its own. Reckon it does—shaped by the dying emotions of warriors who gave their lives defending humanity from the corelings.

That . . . purpose radiates from the bleached and lacquered bones that decorate every surface of the temple, a golden light that can only be seen by those with magic of their own.

Chandeliers made of hundreds of skulls stare down at us. I can sense every bone in a body, even if I ent got names for 'em all. Altar's got a bit of everythin', arranged like a jigsaw, floor-to-ceiling. Even the chalices and fonts pool blessed water in the tops of human skulls.

Alcoves around the room hold entire skeletons of great *kai*, captains of the demon war, holding spear and shield even in death. The pews are made of thigh and calf bones, lashed and glued together. Even through three layers of cloth between my bottom and the seat, I can feel the texture of bone. I squirm at the places where joints meet.

It's unsettling. Even a little scary. But I feel safe here, too. This is one place the demons can't touch.

Everything stinks of incense, and the chemics used to prepare the dead. For once I don't mind. Helps mask the smell of thousands of worshippers, their sweat and perfume and the clay dust on their sandals.

Like Seventhday services in the Brook, the pews in Sharik Hora are divided, with men stage right and women stage left. It's a bit old-fashioned—the Free Cities stopped the practice ages ago—and one of many reasons I used to skip services whenever I could get away with it, which was most of the time.

Here it means I'm on the men's side with Olive, Arick, and a few hundred *Sharum* warriors. Meanwhile, Selen and Rojvah are stuck across the aisle from us with the women.

Don't make a lot of sense to me, splitting up families across the aisle like this. And what about folk like Olive, who fit on both sides? Or maybe neither.

Not that she looks out of place. I'm the one who doesn't fit. Everyone in my row, Olive included, has at least six inches and a hundred pounds on me, not counting their armored robes, which puff them up even more. And it ent exactly subtle that I'm the only one not wearing black, or Krasian robes at all. Stand out like a sheep in a nightwolf den.

Across the aisle, Selen stands out just as much. She's taller than most men, and towers over the other women, thick with muscle and puffed by armored robes of her own. Like me, Selen refuses to dress Krasian, which has its disadvantages. Rojvah blends better in her clerical white, but I know she hates it.

Someone coughs, startling me enough that Olive spares me a glance.

"All right, Darin?" she asks, too quietly for others to hear.

My senses work differently from other folk's. *Nose like a hound and ears like a bat*, Mam used to say. Words whispered to the Creator are as clear to me as those shouted across a taproom.

But it's more than that. I can feel the heartbeats of the others in my row, vibrating the bones of the pew. I can taste the tea and spiced meat on their breath, and tell you which ones snuck a swig of couzi before services. A fly on the windows a hundred feet above our heads sounds like it's buzzing right in my ear. If I look up, I could count the facets of its eyes.

"Fine," I murmur, and Olive is happy to retreat to her own thoughts. Everyone's got a broken heart today, but Olive most of all.

Sometimes my senses come in handy, but mostly they're more trouble than they're worth. I hate crowds like this, but just like in the Brook, sometimes you can get away with skippin' services and sometimes you can't. Nothing for it now but to endure.

I focus on the loudest voice, Damaji Aleveran, speaking from a pulpit designed to use the acoustics of the great dome to project his sermon far and wide. It gives me a place to lay my attention, and that helps keep the other sights, sounds, smells, tastes, and touches from overwhelming me.

I don't pay much attention to his words—some tampweed tale about how everything is the Creator's will—my other senses tell me more. I know what kind of bleach was used on his pristine white robe, and catch the scent of parchment and ink on his fingers. I count the lines on his face and smell the years on him, but Damaji Aleveran is haler than most men his age. I can smell his strict diet, and see the calluses on his hands. Beneath the layers of robes I hear firm muscles bunch and shift against the cloth.

Aleveran's heartbeat is strong and steady. That and his scent tell me he believes what he's saying. Believes the Creator is up there in the sky, looking down on us and caring what we do.

Not every Holy Man does. Some give a convincing performance, but I ent easy to fool. The ones with doubts and good intention I can forgive, but not the ones who lie on purpose. But plenty of folk have real faith, and I envy that. Wish I could believe everything happens for a reason. That everything's gonna be all right.

Wish it was that easy.

At last, the main service comes to an end, and attention turns to the bodies lying in state at the front of the altar—two princes and a princess. Clerics file out of the front rows of pews and ascend the altar, with the men of the council of *dama* standing stage right, and the women of the council of *dama'ting* standing stage left as they speak prayers over the fallen.

Already the bodies of the other martyrs who fell on new moon have been turned over to clerics who specialize in boiling away flesh and bleaching bones to add to the power of this place. Selen says it's barbaric but if I'm to tell honest word, I think it's beautiful.

Still, it ent every day there's a set of royal bones to add, much less three. Prince Chadan, grandson of Damaji Aleveran. Prince Iraven, Olive's half brother. And Princess Micha, Olive's half sister.

It's hard to think of Nanny Micha as a princess, much less a famed warrior, but turns out she was both. Mostly I remember her as a stern but loving shadow, following along just out of sight as Olive, Selen, and I romped through the halls of Aunt Leesha's keep, oblivious to the dangers beyond the wards. Micha was more bodyguard than nanny, even if none of us knew it.

It's a bit of a scandal for her to be on the altar, even so. In thousands of years, no woman has ever had her bones displayed in Sharik Hora, but these days, heroes' bone magic is sorely needed. Desert Spear is a shadow of itself, the outer city destroyed, and sand demons still form storms out on the dunes. The Majah need all the protection they can get.

Krasians are good at letting pride get in the way of their decisions, but I hope they ent fool enough to turn up their noses at the bones of a powerful martyr just because she's a woman. I can sense Olive's tension about it, but there's not much I can do.

Like Micha, this Olive is different from the spoiled princess of Hollow I grew up with. Here she is *Prince* Olive, a famed *kai'Sharum* with a demon kill count to make many an older and more seasoned warrior green with envy.

Olive doesn't smell like she used to, either. Before coming here, don't think she ever went a day without a bath. Truer is, she was more likely to have two than skip a day, with soaps that smelled like a flower garden's sick-up. Not to mention all the paints and powders and fragrances she layered on the moment she was dry. Now she smells more like a man than I do—all sweat and dust and hava spice. So different, I almost didn't recognize her at first. Almost.

But same as back then, beneath it all, she still smells like Olive Paper, the first friend I ever had in the world. Magic quickened Olive and me faster in the womb than other children. We were walking in weeks, and chasing each other around the room for almost a year before Selen found her feet. I learned to smell Olive's moods before I learned to speak. Right now she's full of sorrow and anger in equal measure, and who could blame her? She's lost almost everything, and it din't have to be this way.

I expect someone who smells like that to be weeping, or raging, but Olive keeps her composure out of respect for the dead. It is not appropriate for *Sharum* men to cry in Krasia, or to question Everam's will when He calls His warriors back to Heaven, if you believe that sort of thing. Olive didn't used to, but a lot has changed, and I'm not sure how well I know her anymore.

To my right, Arick stands and smells much the same. Micha was not only Arick's aunt, she was his mother's spear sister, and perhaps the first warrior of renown who accepted him for who he was. Like Olive, he blames himself for much of what happened in the demon tunnels, even though it ent their fault.

Across the aisle on the women's side of the temple, emotion is not only allowed, it's encouraged. Rojvah is openly weeping, but it's more performance than true sorrow. Her sobs are carefully controlled in motion and volume, displaying her mourning without interrupting the services, or failing to keep up with the litany of prayers. And why not? She barely knew any of the deceased.

But her tears are real. I don't know how she manages to cry on purpose—or why anyone would—but even beneath her paints and perfumes, I can taste her tears on the air as she deftly catches each drop with the flat edge of a tear bottle before they can streak the kohl around her eyes.

Standing next to her, Selen ent one for powders, or for sobbing, but she loved Nanny Micha more than her own mam. Even in this crowd, I can pick out Selen's scent. I know it like my own. Her pain is real, silent tears leaving wet, salty lines glittering on her cheeks. I wish I was there to comfort her, but maybe it's for the best I ent. Never been good at that sort of thing.

I'm sad, too, but I've never understood the way other folk carry on about their feelings, trying to display what's right there in their scent. I worry folk think I'm heartless, sometimes. Reckon I could fake it like Rojvah, but it feels too much like lying.

The Krasians don't seem to notice. I am a man to them, and warrior class, though I don't look it. *Sharum* men are meant to embrace sorrow and joy alike, putting both to the side.

It's a small comfort, with everyone in the whole rippin' temple watchin' me.

Ent prideful to say it when it's true. Krasians think they're being subtle, but they're all stealing glances at our row while pretending not to. I hear their whispers. About Olive and the others, yes, but mostly about me. About how I'm the Par'chin's son, and what that means.

My father, Arlen Bales, has a reputation with the Krasians. Even in New Krasia, modern and at peace for fifteen years, folk have divided sentiments about his name. Creator only knows what it means to the Majah.

Could be worse. Least they ent talking about how I was born in the abyss and have demon blood, like Krasian gossips like to do up north. Still, don't like to be center stage if I can help it.

But Olive needs this, so I play my part. Ent much for prayer, but neither was Da. Wrote about it in his journals. Used to murmur *watermelon* over and over, so folk would see his lips moving and think he was praying along. That trick wouldn't fool me, but others can't see and hear like I do, especially while doing their best to pretend they ent paying attention.

"Chadan asu Maroch am'Majah," Aleveran booms, pulling my attention back to the altar as he sweeps a hand over the bodies. "Iraven asu Ahmann am'Jardir am'Majah. Micha vah Ahmann am'Jardir am'Kaji. Who bears witness to their glory?"

There are stirrings and murmurs throughout the pews, though it was all arranged in advance. The warriors who bore witness to what happened below were unanimous in who should speak for them.

Heartbeats are like faces to me. I know Olive's powerful beats as well as any. The solid rhythm when she's at rest, the heavy thumps when her blood is up. But now it's something I don't hear often, pounding fast like a hare with a hound at its heels.

Olive's da's name, like mine, carries weight—and not all of it good. The Majah used to believe Ahmann Jardir was the voice of Everam. Plenty of them still do, whatever their leaders say, which is why Damaji Aleveran and his councilors would be happy to never hear the name again.

But unlike me, Olive Paper ent one to run from a fight.

CHAPTER 2

EULOGIES

My name is Olive Paper, and I'm terrified.

I take a breath, embracing the fear. Chadan's armor fits me like a custom gown, making hardly a sound as I get to my feet.

Tazhan armor is made with the *alagai*-scale technique—countless tiny overlapping scales of sharp black steel. It flexes like a shirt, and protects like a shield. The scales are warded against demonkind, and when struck they ripple like water around a stone, distributing force and lessening impact.

Chadan's Majah sigil, a single spear, has been removed, replaced by my own. No gift from the Majah can ever pay back their debt to me, but there is something right to wearing my prince's armor, bearing the spear and olive crest we shared.

Over the armor I wear a simple black robe, open in the front—more cape than housecoat. It softens the sharp edges just a little, and protects the bone pews from the sharp metal scales. My helm is wrapped in a black turban, and a veil of pure white silk lies loose around my neck.

The Krasian raiment is as much protection against onlookers as the armor is against a blow, conveying a sense of belonging in this sacred place when I feel anything but. I am hundreds of miles from home, amid a tribe of my ancestral enemies, but I don't *look* out of place. My turban and veil are worn in the Majah style, like the cut of my robe and the lacing of my sandals.

I look like my captors.

It was only a few months ago that another room of this great temple bore witness to the most humiliating scene of my life. Forcibly taken from my home, I was carried here like freight and thrown to the floor like a prize of war. And when the *Damaji* found my tongue insolent, I was whipped until I collapsed weeping on the floor.

Now that same tormentor stands before me as I approach the altar.

I was known as the *push'ting* prince then, a "son" raised as a daughter by Duchess Paper out of cowardice—or perhaps cunning. But whether she was hiding me from assassins or maliciously plotting to steal my father's throne, the Majah took a dim view of Mother's actions, and of me. They did their best to make a man out of me, never minding who I actually was, or what I wanted.

And it worked. Better than any—myself included—could have expected. The Majah would not accept me as a woman, so I took the part of a man and made it my own, forcing them to accept me. Now I stand before them as Prince Olive, regal in my Tazhan armor, commanding as much glory as any warrior whose bones adorn this temple.

But much like that pampered princess, this isn't who I am. At least, not entirely. I'm still playing a role—one I've played for so long that I'm no longer sure who I'll be when I stop pretending. Certainly not Princess Olive, the girl who spent her days scurrying for Mother's approval, or going on vapidly about court fashion and gossip.

The desert made Prince Olive hard. Whether fighting demons in the Maze or Majah assailants where I sleep, I have never felt truly safe in Desert Spear, save when sleeping in the pillows beside Prince Chadan. Now my prince is gone, and I fear I may never feel safe again. But I can go home, and perhaps find something of what remains beneath Prince Olive's hardened shell.

I long to be rid of Desert Spear. Of its ghosts and demons and petty politics. I have shared blood and made bonds with my spear brothers, but their leaders have only ever dealt with me in bad faith.

Yet I must do this one last thing, see my sister and my prince to their afterlife, before that new life can begin.

I am no great believer that death holds secrets beyond oblivion, nor do I have faith in Everam, or the Creator the Tenders speak of in the North. Mother raised me to have a healthy skepticism for clerics and "sacred" text. *Respect the faith of others,* she would say, *but do not believe anyone who ascribes explainable events to the divine, or who is so fixed in their beliefs that they refuse to consider contradictory evidence.*

I don't think there really is a Heaven, and *abyss* is just a word for the magic-saturated world that exists beneath the surface of Ala. I have seen it with my own eyes and it is terrifying, but nothing about the experience suggested the influence of a greater power.

I've seen men come to blows over lesser blasphemy, but I am wise enough to keep such thoughts to myself.

My prince and my sister believed in Everam, even if I do not. The prayers and rituals meant something to them, and they in turn meant something to me. How can I honor those I loved without honoring their beliefs?

Even if I do not believe in the Creator, I do believe in magic. It is a quantifiable, measurable fact. The core magic that seeps up from the center of the world, and the bone magic of heroes. I've seen the power of Sharik Hora in wardsight. Mother herself was a ward witch, and I spent countless hours studying the art in the Chamber of Shadows, though I never had her knack.

Micha and Chadan spent their lives dreaming of dying with glory, and having their bones grace this sacred temple. And I know the sacrifice of their final hours will make the power of their *hora* potent and pure. What kind of sister, what kind of . . . friend would I be, if I did not stand up and see to it that they were honored as they deserve?

When I reach the altar, I offer Damaji Aleveran a shallow bow. Respectful—barely—but far short of the obeisance even the most powerful members of the Majah tribe show their *Damaji*. "I, Olive asu Ahmann am'Jardir am'Paper, will speak for the dead."

There are murmurs in the audience at the audacity of my shallow respect, but also at the sound of my father's name. All Majah once believed Ahmann Jardir was the Deliverer. Many still do.

Aleveran is within his rights to demand I kneel, but he knows better.

I will never willingly kneel before this man, and even if—and it is a big if—he could get the *Sharum* to force me to my knees, he would only lose face and support for doing so.

Aleveran wants me gone as much as I do. One last dance, and we can part ways forever. He returns an even shallower nod, still a public honor, especially after such a slight.

"Welcome, son of Ahmann." The *Damaji* stretches a hand out at me, and another to the Witness Pulpit. "Speak your truth, for Everam and all His children to hear."

I keep my back rigidly straight, standing as tall as I can as I ascend to the sacred Witness Pulpit—built from the ribs, spines, and shoulder blades of martyrs. It is said the bones will burn the hands of any who speak a lie from the blessed lectern. Part of me wonders if that is truth or legend, but I won't be finding out. Today I speak only truth, whatever the cost.

"Before you lies my grandson, Chadan asu Maroch am'Majah," Aleveran intones with all the emotion of a marble statue. "What glory does Prince Chadan bring, to earn his place in the Temple of Heroes' Bones?"

He gestures to the first of the three bodies on the altar. A turban hides the ruin of Chadan's head, making my prince appear whole. His powdered face is serene, as if he were peacefully sleeping and might wake at any moment. His armor hugs me like a Solstice gown, still smelling like him. I can feel his presence, even now.

The hurt of it threatens to overwhelm me, but I hear the steadying mantra of my old tutor in my head. *Fear and pain are only wind. Bend as the palm, and let them blow over you.*

I close my eyes. I had never seen a palm tree when Dama'ting Favah first spoke those words to me. A month later she came to me during a great storm, leading me to a window overlooking a willow tree on a small hill, whipped about by the winds and rain. It bent and swayed, weathering the storm without losing so much as a branch.

I picture that tree now, letting my spirit sway in time with the winds of sorrow. I am here as an advocate, not a mourner. As a man, to speak of Chadan's deeds and glory, not as a woman to weep over his body.

But I am a woman. Or part of me is. And why shouldn't I weep for Chadan? What does it matter, if I love as a man or as a woman? Will I ever love anyone the way I loved my prince?

I swallow a lump in my throat, afraid my grief will tie my tongue, but in the end, it is not difficult to speak of why I loved Prince Chadan.

"Chadan asu Maroch am'Majah was the bravest man I have ever known." I grip the lectern, unafraid of its supposed power. "We were blooded in *alagai'sharak* together, not in the Maze, but on the streets of the *chin* quarter, where he refused to leave even the lowest beggar to the *alagai* while there was breath in his body.

"Time and again, the *alagai* came for his charges," I say. "Women. Children. *Khaffit*. And let us not forget his spear brothers. Each time, the demons met instead the shield and spear of the son of Maroch!" I clench a fist, raising it for all to see. "I would be dead," I sweep my hand over the *Sharum* in the front of the men's side of the aisle, "all of us would be dead, if not for Prince Chadan. I saw this."

As one, my spear brothers stamp their feet, a sound that reverberates in the domed temple. "I saw this!" they shout in unison.

The refrain gives me confidence. Chadan's afterlife, at least, is secure. "When Waning came, and Alagai Ka walked the surface of Ala, even a brave man could be forgiven his fear. But the son of Maroch did not balk. Not when the Father of Evil sent his minions to tear down our walls. Not when the only way to end the threat was to venture down into the eternal night below, where Alagai Ka had corrupted the undercity and made it his own. I saw this."

"I saw this!" Again my brothers stamp their feet, this time joined by Arick and even Selen, though I imagine it is a scandal to hear a voice from the women's side of Sharik Hora.

"Grievously injured by the demon king, Chadan could have lain down and died with honor, his soul bright with glory. But doing so would have left me defenseless before the enemy, and that, my prince could not allow."

Again my throat tightens. I don't mention that Chadan's injury came not from a demon but from my possessed half brother Prince Iraven, or that he would have killed me, too, had my prince not ignored the blade in his lung to throw himself back into the fight. I do not mention that it was his own spear brothers, under the demon's control like Iraven, that finally brought Chadan down and dragged him before the demon king.

I swore to speak only truth, but that does not mean I must speak *every* truth.

"In the end, it was Alagai Ka himself who killed the son of Maroch. *Sharum* dream of a worthy death, and what could be worthier than to fall to the First Demon, Nie's hand on Ala? I saw this."

"I saw this!" my brothers cry, stamping, though in truth they did not. All were puppets to the demon's will when it feasted on Chadan's mind. But when we broke its control, they saw the horrid aftermath, and know my words are true.

Aleveran turns to his councils of clerics, but none are fool enough to contradict or offer question to my testimony. Aleveran gives them hardly a moment to nod their accord before raising his hands, signaling the *nie'dama* serving the altar to ring bells that signal acceptance.

"Everam, giver of life and light, accept the bones of Chadan asu Maroch to bless this great temple, in your eternal name."

Muscular priests bow to the altar, then lift the poles of Chadan's bier and carry it down to the undertemple for preparation.

When they are gone, there is a brief respectful moment of silence for Prince Chadan. I close my eyes, wishing his spirit well—whatever that truly means. All too soon, Aleveran's voice breaks me from the reverie.

"Before you lies Iraven asu Ahmann am'Jardir am'Majah." Aleveran's voice is equally flat as he introduces my half brother, a man who was an endless thorn in his side and threat to his power. "What glory does Prince Iraven bring, to earn his place in the Temple of Heroes' Bones?"

Unable to look at Iraven, my eyes flick to the council of *dama'ting*, where Iraven's mother Belina is watching, eyes full of hate. Jongleurs' tales are full of evil stepmothers, but there are few to match my own. Belina ruined my life without a thought to bring glory to her only surviving son. Now he, too, is dead. All that remains of her family is her daughter Linavah, supposedly held hostage by my father in the North, much as I was held here.

I know Belina fears what I will say—fears I will deny her son the one honor left to him. Creator knows, I want to. The *Sharum* chose their voice, and there is nothing Belina can do to prevent me from speaking my truth.

But she does not understand me as well as she believes.

"Iraven had a *Sharum's* heart," I say. "I stood on the walltop with him when the *alagai* breached the great gate three moons ago. He could have sealed off the Maze, sacrificing the men trapped within, but he refused to abandon his warriors. He could have ordered the gate retaken from the safety of the walltop, but he would not ask men to brave a battle he feared. The Majah son of Ahmann leapt into the courtyard and led the attack himself, retaking the gate and scouring the Maze. Hundreds of *Sharum* owe him their lives. I saw this."

Again the *Sharum* stamp their feet. "I saw this!"

"And when the demons tunneled below the *chin* quarter," I continue, "bursting from the streets, Iraven could have sacrificed the *chin* to conserve warriors. But all people are siblings in the night, and the Majah son of Ahmann would suffer none to die. He struck Drillmaster Chikga to the ground for suggesting otherwise. I saw this."

"I saw this!" my chorus of warriors booms.

I hope those words alone will be enough, but I see already they will not. While Chadan's petition was mere formality, Iraven's is more of a trial. Many powerful Majah clerics consider Iraven—and Belina—to be interlopers, and would deny him if they could. The venom is still in Belina's gaze as I decline to say more.

This time, when Aleveran looks to his council, his son Dama Maroch, Chadan's father, steps forward with practiced precision. "By your own words, son of Ahmann, much of the tragedy of the past Waning can be laid at Prince Iraven's feet. He betrayed us all, failing to seal the breach last Waning, and leading our best warriors into a trap beneath the city. Do you truly believe he is a worthy candidate to join Sharik Hora?"

There are gasps in the audience at this, and nods of assent from other *dama*. The council has already heard my testimony, and that of the other witnesses, but the gathered worshippers have not. This could have been settled behind closed doors, but Aleveran wanted Iraven's dishonor made public, to weaken the support of those who still believe my father to be the rightful ruler of all Krasia.

Politics. Even here. I grind my teeth at the ugliness of it.

But I will take no part in ugly politics. Not here, and not when I return home and it is my own power I need to maintain.

I raise my eyes, first meeting the gazes of Aleveran, Maroch, and the other clerics, before sweeping them over the gathered mourners. "It is true," I admit, to more gasping. "Alagai Ka took Iraven's mind before it was over, and forced my brother to betray us. He was not alone in this. Many *Sharum* turned on one another when their mind wards failed in the heat of battle. Possession is a weapon of the mind demons, no different from a sand demon's talons, or a flame demon's fire."

I turn and look at my brother, at last. Like the others, he is peaceful in state, but in his handsome face I see only the pain he has caused me. And I swore to speak only truth.

"I have no love for Iraven. My brother did more to destroy me than anyone alive, and not all of it was the demon king's influence. He sent warriors in the night to take me from my home with no more thought than stealing a well. He sent Drillmaster Chikga to his death. He killed my sister."

My hands begin to sweat as they grip the blessed lectern, and for a fleeting moment I wonder if it can sense a lie of omission. For again I leave unspoken that although it was the demon's will, Iraven was also the instrument Alagai Ka used to drive a knife into Chadan's lung. It is truth, but a truth that would tear what remains of this city, and the Majah, apart.

Instead, I continue to speak truth, though it hurts me to do so. "But so, too, did demons fall by the score upon the Majah son of Ahmann's spear. And when Alagai Ka fled the field and my brother had his mind back, Iraven chose to die with honor, rather than risk carrying the demon's taint back to his people in some dark corner of his mind. His last act was to martyr himself to protect Desert Spear and its people, and that is power the Holy City surely needs."

I deliberately raise my hands for all to see, then place them flat on the lectern, daring the holy relic to burn me if my words are untrue. "I saw this!"

Stamping feet is not enough for Iraven's personal guard, the Spears of the Desert. Drillmaster Zim raises an armored fist, punching it against the armor plate over his heart three times, echoed by hundreds of warriors. "I SAW THIS!"

Maroch's lips tighten. His objection was rehearsed, but he had not expected the *Sharum* to be ready for it with a rehearsed response of their own.

I hate politics, but I am not a fool.

I wait for more objections, but the clerics are no more fool than I. None wish to take the vanguard in alienating their warriors over Aleveran's personal vendetta. When the silence stretches long, Aleveran raises his hands again, signaling the bells.

"Everam, giver of life and light, accept the bones of Sharum Ka Iraven asu Ahmann am'Jardir am'Majah to bless this great temple in your eternal name."

After Iraven is carried away, only my sister remains. If my brother's acceptance was a trial, this feels more like walking into the abyss. No women warriors are interred in Sharik Hora, and old men fear little more than change.

But I have walked into the abyss for love before, and I no longer fear these old men. If they will not accept my sister as she deserves, I will carry her body home myself, and see her interred in the Cathedral of the Deliverer in Hollow. In my heart it is what I wish to do, but I know this is where she would want to be.

"Before you lies Micha vah Ahmann am'Jardir am'Kaji." At last a bit of disdain slips into Aleveran's voice, flat for his own grandson and his greatest rival. "What glory does the *daughter* of Ahmann bring, to earn a place among men in the Temple of Heroes' Bones?"

There are murmurs of assent from the *dama*. Elevating a woman is a direct challenge to their power. They will not give ground as easily as they did for Iraven, and my warriors did not know Micha as I do. They will not put themselves out for a woman's honor, nor would I ask it of them. This isn't their fight.

I look at my sister, lying so peacefully, and feel my heart breaking all over. Micha made up so much of my world, I don't know how I will function without her constant advice, love, and support.

Micha was my sister, but I did not truly understand what sisterhood meant until it was too late. Micha kept a whole side of herself secret for most of my life. I blamed her for that lie, but it wasn't fair of me. She gave up her own life, her limitless glory, her royal status, all to play nursemaid while guarding me from assassins' blades. Without Micha, I would be dead many times over, yet I had the arrogance to judge her.

There was so much Micha could have taught me—so much I wanted to explore with her. Now she's gone, and I have only her example to follow. Micha was a warrior without peer, but it was a woman's sacrifice she made for her infant sister. If that is what it means to be a woman—putting the needs of others before your own glory—it is as worthy as any feat of arms.

"My sister was born in Desert Spear," I begin, not knowing what words will sway these men, but knowing I must try. "The daughter of one of Shar'Dama Ka's lesser wives. Too common to take *dama'ting* white, too holy for *dal'ting* black, she was sent beneath this very temple with others of her kind, given to Drillmaster Enkido, to see if he could teach the spear to women."

There are murmurs in the audience at this, both the outrageous idea of women with spears, but also the name of their drillmaster. Micha's glory may have been hidden to provide cover in Mother's court, but Enkido's name is known far and wide. Even here, among the tribe of his enemies.

"Enkido was not gentle with his charges," I say. "I have been through *sharaj* as *nie'Sharum,* but the trials my sister spoke of are greater by far, for Enkido knew a woman must be twice as accomplished to earn half the respect of a man. There were five of them, then—Ashia, Shanvah, Sikvah, Micha, and Jarvah. Everam's spear sisters. *Sharum* blood of the Shar'Dama Ka. And all of them took glory to their name. Ashia took the white turban of Sharum'ting Ka, and killed the mind demon enslaving *Sharum* warriors and directing the assault on Everam's Bounty. Shanvah followed Shar'Dama Ka into Nie's abyss, and was martyred as they destroyed the *alagai* hive. Sikvah," I nod to Arick, her son, "was also martyred in Sharak Ka, defending the walls of Everam's Bounty against a demon horde. Jarvah is bodyguard to the Damajah herself. And Micha," I hold a hand out toward my sister, "killed a mind demon in Angiers."

"Hearsay," Aleveran scoffs. "Unworthy words from the Witness Pulpit."

"I beg the *Damaji's* pardon," I say loudly, "but it is not. These are documented historical facts."

Aleveran seems unimpressed. "Can you produce the documents and prove their veracity?"

I scowl, for of course I cannot. I bow, instead. "Apologies, Damaji. I fear we did not have time to visit the archives when your Watchers came in the night to kidnap us from our home."

Aleveran's face darkens at this, and I know I am playing a dangerous game. But I will not forsake my sister for an old man's pride.

I whisk a hand through the air like Grandmum used to, dismissing the thought like a bad smell in the air before placing my hands firmly on the sacred lectern for all to see. "But it does not matter. I saw my sister's spear punch through a wood demon that would have taken the life of me. Its ichor splashed my face. And when the rest of the pack attacked my friends, it was Sharum'ting Micha who saved us. I saw this."

I don't expect a response, but one comes anyway. "I saw this!" Selen's shout seems to echo in the room, and eyes turn her way, scandalized at a woman bearing witness. If Selen feels the weight of their gazes, she does not wither. She is looking at me, and in her eyes is all the support I need to carry on.

Aleveran whisks his hand, an imitation of my gesture. "The witness of a woman, for the deeds of another woman in the green lands, is not enough to earn a place in Sharik Hora."

Anger kindles in me. It seems Aleveran wants one last confrontation after all. One last flex of his power.

"You are correct, of course." I bow again. "Let us speak instead of her actions here, in Desert Spear, when she joined the *Sharum* on the path to the abyss beneath this very city, while the rest of you took shelter in the Holy City."

The *dama* do not like this, implying their honor is less than that of the *Sharum*, but none dare speak. I have the pulpit, and it is the gathered audience I need to convince, as much as the council.

"Alagai Ka had removed the helms of the *dal'Sharum*," I say. "Without their mind wards, they were little more than puppets at his command. But before he could infect their hearts, they were broken from his control by my sister's spellsong. And while they recovered, she joined me in the attack against the Father of Evil. I saw this."

I turn my gaze to my spear brothers. The warriors may not know my sister, and none care to be reminded of Alagai Ka's control, but they saw what they saw, and honor demands they support the witness. The stomp of feet is not as synchronous as refrains past, but it comes, with Darin, Selen, and Rojvah loudest of all. "I saw this!"

Again, Aleveran denies me. "Sharik Hora is for warriors, not singers. By your own admission, your sister fell to Iraven's blade, not *alagai* talons."

"Iraven," I say, "was under the direct control of Alagai Ka. He was sent to intercept her because the demon king feared her spear."

"Speculation," Aleveran sneers. "She was not killed by the *alagai*."

I want to shout at him the truth. That his beloved grandson Chadan fell to Iraven, too. His fatal wound came long before the demon king opened his skull.

But I will not rob others of their honor to satiate the *Damaji*. "Who then is responsible, when a warrior is ordered to kill, and does?"

The *Damaji* has no quick answer to that, and I give him no time to find one.

"Warriors die in the Maze every night, many without ever coming into contact with *alagai* talons. Crushed by rocks. Burned by fire. Knocked from the walltops. Blooded in battle, these men still died in *alagai'sharak* and are interred here."

"A technicality," Aleveran sidesteps. "You ask that we change three thousand years of tradition, interring a woman in Sharik Hora for the first time, on a technicality."

It takes all my strength to keep from baring my teeth at the words. I am considered a man by the Majah, but when I look at the all-male council of *dama* nodding their heads, it fills me with disgust. Hearsay. The green lands. A singer not a fighter. A blade instead of a talon. Excuse after excuse, deployed to deny a woman the glory they accord to men with little more than a formality.

"The *Sharum'ting* did not exist until after the exodus from Desert Spear," I remind the *Damaji*. "They were created when the Shar'Dama

Ka's forces needed every spear. Everam's spear sisters remained to fight in Sharak Ka, even when others did not."

If I was walking a dangerous path before, I am balanced on a wire above the abyss now. Under Aleveran, the Majah abandoned my father's armies at the height of Sharak Ka to return to Desert Spear, to the eternal shame of many. No Majah wishes to be reminded of that dishonor.

If I thought this might break Aleveran's resolve, I am wrong, for in his eyes I can see it redouble.

"*Sharum'ting* bones grace the temples of New Krasia," I say, "and in Hollow."

"Let our Northern brothers sully their temples with their liberal ways," Aleveran sneers. "Giving women the spear was one of many ways Ahmann Jardir strayed into heresy. We have reversed that mistake here, and Sharik Hora will remain pure."

"Demonshit!" Selen snaps, and my heart leaps. She's right of course. Without women with spears, the city would be under the demon's control. Still, she could be killed for such an outburst. My eyes flick to her and I see Rojvah has convinced her to be silent, but it is not quick enough.

"Tsst!" Damaji'ting Chavis hisses at Selen. So focused on Aleveran and his *dama* councilors, I had forgotten the mean old woman was on the altar.

Chavis takes a single step toward Aleveran and bows, but she does not kneel. Her power is not so great as Aleveran's, but he would be hard-pressed to hold on to his own without her support.

Aleveran knows it. It is practically unheard of for a woman, even the *Damaji'ting*, to speak in Sharik Hora. But Aleveran is wise enough to understand she does not do it lightly. "Speak your wisdom, Damaji'ting, for all to hear."

Chavis nods. "The *Damaji* is mistaken when he says there are no women interred in Sharik Hora."

Aleveran blinks. I don't know what he was expecting the ancient priestess to say, but clearly this is not it.

"The *dama'ting* have interred their own in the crypts below the temple for centuries," Chavis notes. "As have the *dama*, though few have fought in *alagai'sharak*."

Lines of tension appear on the *Damaji's* face. The words are a challenge, but not one Aleveran can easily refute, so he does not try. "Let the *dama'ting* take her then."

Chavis shakes her head. "Micha vah Ahmann was not *dama'ting*. She is *Sharum*. I witnessed them fighting, when the *Sharum'ting* made their debut. I watched a group of them, the daughter of Ahmann among them, take on a pack of field *alagai*. She is blooded in ichor. I saw this."

The challenge in the words is unmistakable, and suddenly the assembled council of *dama'ting*, little more than wall tapestries a moment ago, seem to loom outsize in the room.

Rights given are not so easily taken away, Mother used to say, and it seems—as with so many things—she was correct. The *Sharum'ting* brought honor to the women of the tribe, and it seems that is not something they will yield without a fight.

A stomp of feet from the women's side of the chamber booms all the way to the domed ceiling high above, and a lump forms in my throat. Not Selen, this time. It was the *dama'ting*, and their *dal'ting* bodyguards, women who answered my father's call to spears, only to have them taken away by Aleveran when they returned to old Krasia.

"The *dama'ting* accept Micha vah Ahmann into Sharik Hora." Chavis keeps her eyes on Aleveran, daring him to deny her. "And she will not be the last."

The words hang ominous in the air, a clear intention of the Majah *dama'ting* to resume training women to take the spear.

All made possible by my sister. I manage not to weep when Aleveran raises his hands and the bells ring for Micha, but there are tears streaming down my cheeks, and I make no effort to hide them.

"Everam, giver of life and light, accept the bones of Micha vah Ahmann am'Jardir am'Kaji to bless this great temple in your eternal name." Aleveran's voice is flat, but I can imagine the anger beneath. This is not a man accustomed to being thwarted, and that makes the victory all the sweeter.

CHAPTER 3

SNEAKIN'

When Olive disappeared, me and Selen ran away from Hollow to hunt her down. We were on the road for months, and it wasn't easy going. Both in a mood most of the time—worried, damp, tired, and hungry. But it was just the two of us, and we knew when to huddle up and talk, and when to give each other space.

Even after Arick and Rojvah joined us, it wasn't so bad. Everyone had their own problems to worry over, and the endless banter the twins were famous for in the palace died out in the waste.

But now the Majah are preparing a proper caravan to take us home, with *Sharum* guards and *dal'ting* workers, draft animals, and merchant carts. The caravan grounds are a cacophony of sounds and smells that threatens to overwhelm my senses. Casks of spice, grain, and dried meat, feed for the animals and the stink of their piss and droppings, merchants shouting at their workers, oil and leather and braying camels, people scurrying to and fro, breaking wind and breathing out their last few meals.

It makes my head pound and my stomach churn, and we ent even left yet. Don't know how I'm gonna last weeks on the road with all this stink and racket. Gonna have to keep my distance during the day. Ride out ahead, or drift back a mile or two behind. Ent like I could lose track of a rippin' parade like this.

Noise is worth it to get gone from this place. Da wrote about Desert Spear in his journals, and I always dreamed of visiting, but now that I have, I'd just as soon be back in the Brook. Been nothing but pain and heartache since I left.

Olive is making the rounds with the caravan guards and merchants, saying things that sound like requests, but ent, like Speaker Selia does back in Tibbet's Brook. She expects obedience, and gets it on the quick.

Selen is sticking close to her, like she's afraid Olive will disappear again if she looks away for a minute. That ent unusual. Olive and Selen always ran at a pace. I'm faster, but somehow I was always the one trailing behind.

Even so, something's off. After months of being constant companions, it feels like Selen's avoiding me, and it's like an ache under my skin.

They've given Rojvah a white canvas tent to wait out the heat and dust as the caravan readies, and she said I could hide there when I needed. Selen smelled annoyed when she said it, but right now it's the closest thing to respite I've got.

Last thing I want is to make things with Selen worse. Know she dun't shine on me the way I do her, but it ent like I can just stop. I'll take friends over nothing at all, and call it a bargain. Still, I'm careful she doesn't see me as I make my way to Rojvah's tent.

Folk call me a sneak. Not to my face—mostly—but when you can hear an ant sigh, you tend to catch what folk say when they think no one's listenin'. They think I got somethin' to hide, or that I'm spying on them at the swimming hole. Rabbit rustles a bush on someone's property at night, the next afternoon they're spinning an ale story about how they saw Darin Bales stalking the yard like a demon.

Truer is, I'm more scared of them than they ever were of me. Don't sneak to get the jump on anyone. Do it to keep my distance, so I don't have to process all the touches, tastes, sights, smells, and sounds of everyone I meet.

I know when they're sick. Sometimes before they do. I smell when they lie, or got somethin' to hide. See the flush of their skin when I unnerve them. I feel the vibration of tensed muscles and taste their fear when they're alone with me. Hear the tone in their voices, when they're disappointed I ent more like my da, but too polite to say it.

All that . . . noise multiplies with every person, until it's more'n I can stand. I'd love to just saunter around Town Square on Seventhday, but nothing makes my hands sweat like the thought of the crowds on market day. Rather be chased by a coreling.

So I sneak. To stay in the shade. To keep away from folk. To get a little peace, and somethin' closer to quiet, where I can hear my own thoughts above the din.

There's a pair of *Sharum* guards outside Rojvah's tent flap, looking sharp and alert. Can't say I'm glad to see them, but I ent surprised. Not only is she a princess of the Kaji, Rojvah is *nie'dama'ting*, a priestess-in-training, Betrothed to Everam.

It's a crime to lay hands on one of the Betrothed, or harm her in any way. Rojvah thought that would protect her when we arrived in Desert Spear, but Aleveran needed a flex to feel tough. He refused to recognize a half-blood Betrothed of another tribe, and stripped her of the white. Now, with Rojvah returning to the seat of Kaji strength, it is a move the Majah are falling over themselves to correct.

If I go right up to the tent, I'll have to talk to the guards. They'll have a bunch of questions, even though they know full well who I am. Then one will go in to announce me, but Rojvah will keep him waiting, and it will go on for half an eternity before I get inside.

Easier to sneak. Back of the tent is fetched up against a sandstone wall. The guards glance that way occasionally, but their focus is out front. It's easy to slip past the moment they look away and circle around back.

The tent canvas is opaque to normal vision, but my eyes don't work like other folk's. This time of day, with sunlight shining through the cloth, it's practically transparent to me. I can see Arick inside with his sister, pacing. Everyone's decent, so I slide along the back until I get to a small seam in the canvas where the sheets are lashed to a pole.

In the cool shade between the tent and the wall, a little seam is all I need to squeeze through, bones squishing and stretching like taffy as I push through the tiny opening.

Rojvah has removed her headscarf in the privacy of the tent, sitting with her back to me as she brushes out her long, silky cinnamon hair. "You could announce yourself before entering, Darin am'Bales."

I jump a little. "How'd you know it was me?" She ent even lookin' my way.

Arick stumbles in his pacing as he notices me. His scent turns embarrassed as he glances around to check if anyone saw, but it quickly blossoms into anger. Can't tell if he's angry at me, his sister, or himself.

All these senses, but I still can't read the room.

"Nie's black heart," Arick growls. "You could catch a spear, sneaking up on me like that."

I shrug. "You used to take a swing every time you saw me. Ent tagged me yet."

"One day, cousin," Arick promises. "I may not have your nose, Darin son of Arlen, but you have your own smell, and I know it in my tent."

"Smell like a person," I sniff, "not scrubbed in scented soap, rubbed in scented oil, and then covered in perfume and incense."

Rojvah laughs, keeping her back to us as she works the brush, keeping count with the barest whisper.

"Ent *nie'dama'ting* supposed to shave their heads?" I ask.

Arick snorts. "The Shar'Dama Ka doesn't have enough soldiers to force my sister to cut her hair. The other Betrothed hate her for it."

"I do not care what they think." Rojvah puts down her brush and turns at last. "Do they think I *want* to wear the white? Do they think I had a choice? At least here I was free of it."

"Ay, if you call bein' locked in the harem *free,*" I say.

"Given the choice between pillow silks in the harem and a white bido in the Dama'ting Palace, I choose the harem."

"Is it different for me?" Arick has resumed pacing. "I was forbidden the black at home, and here. But I took up the spear anyway, and claimed glory in the night. I will not give it up without a fight."

"Gonna fight your own people, Arick?" I ask.

Arick shifts his feet, and it ent hard to reckon why. It's a reminder of what happened in the dark below.

Most everyone who went into the coreling tunnels was possessed by

Alagai Ka at some point. Even Olive. But it's one thing for the mind demon to briefly snatch control of an unwarded mind and make their body little more than a stocking puppet. Mam says if a mind has time, it can implant suggestions that can lie dormant, unaffected by wards or the light of day, until a certain trigger occurs.

Iraven begged Olive to kill him because he had been the demon king's agent in the day, and could no longer trust his own mind.

When we found Arick in the tunnels, he was visibly warded and seemed much himself.

Then he kicked me off a cliff.

I forgave Arick. Wern't his fault. But I know he's haunted. Afraid he's tainted like Iraven, but too cowardly to kill himself.

Desperate for some sense of redemption.

I feel for him. Know what it's like to wonder if there's darkness inside you. Folk whisper about my demon blood, like they think I might turn into a coreling right in front of them. And sometimes, when I hear the magic callin', I worry they might be right.

Feel for Arick, but ent got any redemption to spare. Could use a bit, myself.

Arick mutters a reply, but I ent listenin' anymore. Caught the sound of marching feet—a dozen warriors at least. Arms of Everam, but the sound of it. The elite guard of the Holy City. I hear them stomp right up to Olive.

"The *Damaji* will see you one last time, before you depart," one of them says. "Alone."

"So close," Olive groans.

"Darin, what . . ." Rojvah begins, but I'm out of the tent before she finishes the sentence. All the attention is on Olive and the guards, and it's easy to close in without anyone noticing me.

"Core with that." Selen interposes herself between Olive and the temple guard. "You ent going in there alone. Not today."

The guard is briefly taken aback. It is not often the Arms of Everam are resisted. But then his eyes harden, and he takes a step forward. "The word of the *Damaji* is not a request."

"Oh, ay?" Selen mirrors him with a step of her own. He is six feet tall at least, but still she looks down on him, her bare arms thick with muscle. Immediately, two more white-sleeved guards step forward.

"Enough." Olive grabs Selen's arm and pulls her back, stepping in front of her.

Olive cows the guards with just a glare. "Wait here." She points, and the Arms snap to attention on the spot as Olive takes Selen aside to speak privately. I move to follow, keeping my focus on their conversation.

"It's all right, Sel," Olive says. "They've nothing to gain in killing me now, and I don't expect the gates will open for us until I go."

"Then I'm coming with you," Selen says.

"Absolutely not." Olive uses the same voice she uses for her soldiers. "They will not be candid with you in the room. I have to go alone."

"And what if things get *too* candid?" Selen asks. "Ent just them I'm worried about, Olive. You've got a temper of your own."

"Thanks, Aunt Sel." Olive rolls her eyes. Selen's technically Olive's aunt, but Olive only uses the honorific to mock.

Selen crosses her arms. "Fine. Darin, you'll follow her, ay?"

I'm startled again at the sound of my name when I thought I was being sneaky, though I reckon I shouldn't be. Like Rojvah, Selen always seems to know when I'm lurking in the shadows. Probably because I was always following her and Olive around when we were kids.

Some things never change.

I stick my head out from behind a cart. "Was gonna do that anyway."

Olive glares at me. "Darin Bales, don't you dare. If you get caught . . ."

Olive Paper's been giving me orders since we were in nappies. Most times it's easier to just go along with it, but then it gets her thinkin' she's really holding my bridle. It's kinda funny. "Ent one of your subjects, Olive. You don't get to tell me what to do."

"Darin's apparently a prince in New Krasia," Selen puts in. "Almost as close to the throne as you are. Funny how he never mentioned that, while teasing us 'princesses.' "

That catches Olive by surprise. She whirls on me, and suddenly I feel like we're eight years old again. "How's that?"

"Whose side are you on?" I ask Selen, but she just laughs.

Olive's still glaring at me. Ent scared of Olive Paper, exactly, but her stare makes my skin itch. "Your da is my bloodfather, you know that."

Olive's eyes widen. She smells of surprise, but also that scent folk get when it takes them a minute to figure out something obvious. Reckon *bloodfather* was just a word to her when we were kids, but now, after living among the *Sharum* for months, for the first time she really understands.

"That would put you in the succession after Father's bloodsons . . ." Olive's eyes flick to the side as her scent shifts to someone trying to remember something. Then her eyes snap back to me. "That places you forty-third in line for the throne."

I blink. She's right, but . . .

"Ay, how'd you do that?" Selen asks for me.

Olive just shrugs. "Mother made me memorize every member of every royal family in the Free Cities."

"Reckon it'll be forty-fourth now," I note, "with the Krasians callin' you prince."

Olive raises an eyebrow at that, and I take the opening to wink at her. "So you see why I gotta keep you alive."

Olive's mouth twists, and I can tell she's trying to decide if she wants to argue more. Finally, she just shrugs again. "Fine. I suppose it's not *impossible* the *Damaji* will try to have me killed. Just . . . unlikely."

"Ay, wonderful," Selen says as a knot of fear grows in my belly. After all, if they do try to kill Olive, what in the core am I supposed to do about it? When a fight breaks out, only thing I ever been good at is runnin' away.

BACK IN TIBBET'S BROOK, when it wasn't services, the Holy House up on top of Boggin's Hill was a quiet, solemn place. Folk would light candles and kneel in the pews to pray and have a think. I'd go there sometimes, to escape the noise and bustle of town.

Sometimes I'd hear people whispering confidences to the Tender—or the Creator—but seldom things I didn't already know. With ears like mine, you tend to learn everyone's secrets, like or not.

But most of the time, the Holy House stood empty, and I liked that just fine. I'd nap away the brightest hours of the day in the choir loft.

Sharik Hora ent like that. There's little pockets of quiet, ay, but mostly there's an army of folk tromping the halls all day, groups large and small. All of them focused on one another, their own thoughts, or getting wherever they're going.

None of them look up. Not even the guards.

And why should they? There are windows of stained glass everywhere, bathing the halls with light. The sun burns away magic, it is said, and who could flit about the ceiling without it?

But the light is directed down, at the floors abuzz with activity, at the reading rooms and gardens. The ceilings of Holy Houses are always high, meant to symbolize soaring toward Heaven or somesuch. Sharik Hora is no exception. Arched vaults, pillars, chandeliers, and monuments offer endless patches of shadow, and a patch is all I need to turn my fingers and toes sticky enough to climb along like an insect.

The squirrelly part is that almost every inch of the temple is covered in the dried and lacquered bones of fallen warriors. Reckon they wouldn't like me putting hands and feet on their skulls, but it ent like they can complain.

As I follow Olive I watch folk down below refuse to meet her eyes, only to stare at her back once she passes. They smell of fear, submission, envy, love, hatred . . . So many emotions it's impossible to sift them all from the stink, much less assign them to individuals. Olive's always left a cloud of emotions in her wake, but nothing like this. I don't like it. Selen's right to be worried.

Might not be much I can do about it, though. The guards outside the throne room are more alert than elsewhere, and there are wards on the doors that hum even in the light.

Magic burns off in sunlight, but there are workarounds if you got the knack. Krasian priestesses take charged *alagai hora*—demonbone—and cover it in warded metal, usually gold and silver, to protect it from the light and create magic than can endure, at least in part, in direct light.

Guards crack the door to admit Olive, but they got eyes everywhere, and quick as I am, I don't think I can climb through without bein' noticed. Then the moment is gone and the doors shut behind.

I concentrate, tryin' to listen in, but wards of silence are etched into the doors, and I can't hear a peep. Considering how much I hate noise, you'd think I'd like wards of silence, but they've always unnerved me. Like bein' deaf, and you only find 'em when someone wants to say things they don't want you to hear.

But while I can't hear inside, I do hear a . . . whistling. Too faint for others to hear, I expect. Olive's sister Micha told us she used to work in the throne room, guarding the Damajah. She said there were secret entrances for the *Sharum'ting*, and that they had *hora* jewelry that let them climb like me.

It doesn't take long to follow the sound to a shadowed nook beside a ceiling vault. I have to stick my fingers into the eye socket of some warrior's skull and pull, opening a hinged door into a tunnel no more than one foot square. Must be a real trick for most warriors to squeeze through there, but in the darkness I can turn slippery and glide through it like water.

The tunnel exits high on the wall overlooking the throne, in a shadowed nook no doubt meant for an archer to shoot down anyone who gets too close to the dais with ill intent. I don't have my bow, and don't expect I would be much help to Olive if she's attacked, but I can listen, and warn her if something's amiss.

Hope that's enough.

CHAPTER 4

BROKEN BONDS

Aleveran looks no happier to see me than I him as I enter the throne room. Darin is nowhere to be seen, but I am sure he's close enough to catch every word as I move to stand before the steps. It is seven steps to the Skull Throne. The *Damaji* is attended only by his son Dama Maroch and Damaji'ting Chavis, both standing on the sixth step.

Here, in private, I do not offer even the shallow bow I afforded Aleveran in the temple. The *Damaji* does not even twitch.

At last, we understand each other.

I wonder again if he might try to kill me. The guards outside took my weapons. At a glance, I would appear safe alone with three graying clerics, but I have too much experience with the secret martial arts of the *dama* to underestimate them.

Aleveran is old, but a *sharusahk* grandmaster in his own right. His family is legendary for their school of fighting, and I've seen the truth of it up close. Chadan was one of the greatest fighters I've ever met—more skilled than me by far—and by his own words, he was not yet deemed a master. But Damaji Aleveran is sixty years my senior. I have youth, strength, and speed to offset the difference in skill.

His son Dama Maroch, the next in line for the Skull Throne, is a different story. The grandmaster who instructed Chadan is still close to his prime, a true warrior-priest. I know the sting of the alagai tail coiled on Maroch's belt, next to a pair of fighting silvers—warded metal knuckles that can turn a fist into a sledge mattock. His staff of office is a *dama* whip-staff, a weapon I have only seen demonstrated once. It moved much too fast for my liking. Chadan's father still blames me for the loss of his son, and eyes me like a hound waiting to be loosed.

I take in my surroundings, but there is nothing in the nearly bare chamber to use as a weapon, apart from the bones of heroes I would rather die than desecrate. A rug runs from the main floor up to the dais of the throne. Perhaps I could pull it out from under Maroch's sandaled feet if he charges down the steps.

But no rug can protect me from Damaji'ting Chavis. Magic burns off in sunlight, but this early in the day the sun does not shine directly through the high windows of the throne room. I know from my studies there are limits to how magic can be used in half-light, but some of those methods can be no less potent when used by a skilled practitioner, and there are few more revered—and feared—than Chavis.

There is no softening of the *Damaji'ting's* gaze as the ancient woman looks down her nose at me. What happened on the altar, with my sister and the *Sharum'ting*, she did not do for me. The *dama'ting* have politics of their own.

"Welcome, Prince Olive, I hope for the last time," Aleveran calls.

I won't bow, but I give him a nod at this. "That is my hope as well, Damaji."

"What will Hollow do, upon your return?" Aleveran's tone is flat, but the very question betrays him. With his walls broken and much of the city destroyed by demons, Desert Spear is nearly defenseless should Hollow wish to retaliate for my kidnapping.

I don't have to speculate. With Mother missing, I will rule Hollow on my return, but the *Damaji* does not know that, and I want to keep it that way.

"Mother will be furious," I say, "but with my safe return, I do not think she will put more lives at risk crossing the desert for vengeance. In time, I can convince her to allow you to join the Pact of the Free Cities, forgiving past aggressions."

"You would advocate for this?" Aleveran seems doubtful. "Forgiveness?"

My throat tightens. I hate Aleveran. Like Maroch, I must restrain my urge to charge up the steps and put my hands around his throat.

But in this, as on the Witness Pulpit, I will not lie.

"For my part, yes," I lift my chin, meeting his eyes. "I forgive you, Damaji Aleveran, of your crime against me. We are all caught in the winds of *dama'ting* prophecies, and there are costs to everything a leader does. All of us have paid in full."

I look to Dama Maroch. "We make the best decisions we can with what we know at the time to protect our people. It is easy to look back and judge, harder to look forward." I take all of them in. "I claim no blood debt with Majah. If you petition in good faith to join the Pact of Free Cities, I will advocate for it, if for nothing more than to provide security for your people."

There is a pause as Aleveran considers. "What would your pact ask us to give up in exchange for this aid?"

"That is for the ambassadors to haggle," I say, "but expect the terms to include a chance for your greenland thralls to return to their homes in the North, if they wish it. No doubt many will choose to stay after so long a time, but they came here no more willingly than I."

Aleveran gives me a sour look that I am not sure is resignation or defiance, but he raises a finger, and Maroch thumps his staff on the stone step, sending a resounding boom through the chamber.

"I have chosen an ambassador who will join you on your journey across the desert," Aleveran says as a door to the women's side of the chamber opens.

"The *Damaji* is wise—" I begin, choking on the word as Belina enters the room.

Belina, who kidnapped me and brought me here. Belina, whose son I stabbed in the heart. Belina, who would kill me with her eyes, if she could.

"Absolutely not," I growl.

"Where is your forgiveness now?" Belina asks.

"Forgiveness does not make me a fool." I bare my teeth. "I will not have you in my caravan."

"You do not have a choice," Aleveran says. "Tradition gives me the right to send any emissary I choose, and your mother is not bound by your forgiveness. If she wishes to extract a price for the crime against her child and heir, who better to pay it?"

You, I think, but I know better than to say it. It is so easy for this man, safe on his seat of power, to offer a woman to take punishment in his stead. For a moment I wish they knew it would be me on the throne of Hollow, but Mother's disappearance is best kept secret until I am safely away from here.

For her part, Belina looks no happier than I. She is more exile than emissary, another complication to Aleveran's power removed. With both her Majah sons dead and her succession to Chavis' black scarf removed, Belina has no power left in Desert Spear.

"Then I'll have her *hora* pouch," I say. "And Rojvah will strip-search her when she enters the caravan grounds. She will not work magic or have *hora* in her possession for the duration of the journey."

Belina scowls, but Chavis is ready for the request, pulling a black velvet pouch from a deep pocket of her robe. "Her dice, *hora* stones, and jewelry. Anything else you find may be confiscated."

I see Belina's eyes follow the precious pouch through the air as the old woman tosses it down to me. She flinches when I catch it, no doubt remembering how she used its contents to torture me into submission. Does she fear I will visit the same upon her?

"If you wish to be rid of her sooner," Aleveran offers, "no doubt the Damajah will have much to discuss with her faithless *Jiwah Sen.* It will be in Belina's interest to broker a peace that benefits us all, if she wishes to keep her head."

It makes sense. The law prevents men from harming or laying hands upon a *dama'ting* in any way. Aleveran can't just kill her, but he can make her someone else's problem.

Mine.

I slip my fingers into Belina's *hora* pouch, probing for a certain cylinder shape. Rewarded a moment later, I pull out the tiny replica of the blood-locked armlet that served as my shackle in Desert Spear. Belina could use it to find me anywhere, and with a squeeze of her fingers, she could contract the metal until it threatened to amputate my arm.

I put the control in my own, smaller *hora* pouch, next to Micha's choker and marriage earring, and withdraw the armlet.

"And she'll wear this."

Belina pales.

I WANT NOTHING MORE than to be alone as I exit Sharik Hora, but there is a knot of warriors waiting outside. A score of my spear brothers from the Princes Unit, who have been conspicuously absent since the funeral ceremony. Faseek, Gorvan, Parkot, Montidahr, and Menin stand at the head of others who shared hardship with me in *sharaj*, bled with me in the city streets, and fought by my side in the Maze.

"Prince Olive." My spear brothers drop to one knee and bow in unison, putting fists to armored robes adorned with the spear and olive. "*Ajin'pel.*"

"Stop that," I snap before my throat can tighten. I reach out and grab Gorvan's wrist, pulling him up into a backslapping embrace. Then I do the same for the others. It is a break in protocol, but I do not think I will see these men again, and I am tired of holding my brothers at arm's length. "I had begun to suspect you were ordered to stay away from me."

"We were," Faseek says. He is small for a warrior, but quick and fierce. I did him a kindness once, and he has never forgotten, though it has been repaid one thousandfold. "But the drillmasters cannot keep us from hearing your final orders."

I shake my head. "I am no longer your *kai*, Faseek."

"The white can command we follow a new *kai*, but we have only one *ajin'pel*," Gorvan says. "You will need guards to escort you across the desert. Say the word, and we will replace those assigned to your caravan, even if we have to leave them bound in a fruit cellar."

"The *Damaji* would not be pleased on your return," I note carefully.

"*If* we return," Faseek says.

I shake my head. "Desert Spear needs warriors, now, more than ever."

Faseek looks ready to say more, but Gorvan, next in command after me, forestalls him with an outstretched hand. "Our spears will answer the Horn of Sharak, but not until we see you safely across the desert. You will not be left to brave the sand demon storms without the shields and spears of your brothers."

I could stop them. I should. But in my heart, I know they are right. The enemy is still out there, plotting, and there are demons in the dunes. If I must face them, I would prefer to do it with the Princes Unit at my back.

I nod. "You honor me. We leave in an hour, and will not wait for stragglers."

The men do not seem dissuaded. Each wears a *Sharum* gear pack, ready to go. They knew what I would say.

"Your will, Prince Olive." Gorvan punches a fist to his chest, turning to lead the men toward the caravan at a quick pace.

Only Faseek remains behind. "Will you not be coming, brother?" I ask.

I frown as Faseek kneels again, putting both hands on the ground and pressing his forehead between them in a sign of total submission. "As far as you will have me, my prince. To Hollow, and beyond, if that is where your path leads."

"Get up, brother," I say. "You shame us both with this display. I am not some insecure *dama*, needing to see your bare neck. Stand and look at me when you speak."

Faseek rises, and I see his eyes are wet as he lifts them to meet mine.

My sharp tone softens. "You wish to abandon your homeland?"

Faseek's eyes flick from side to side, as if he is concerned someone might overhear his next words. I don't mention Darin, no doubt still lurking somewhere out of sight.

I put a hand on his shoulder. "You are my spear brother, Faseek. Your burdens are my burdens."

"My mother lied when she had me entered in the full-blood *sharaj*," Faseek says. "My father was a greenlander she wed in secret before the Majah exodus."

Suddenly I understand his trepidation. Falsifying his bloodline was a serious crime, but the punishment would not fall on Faseek, a warrior with glory to his name. It would be laid upon his family.

"Is your father alive?" I ask.

Faseek shakes his head. "They were separated when the Majah left the green lands. He was taken as a thrall, and went willingly to be with his wife and unborn. At first they were able to pass messages in the chaos of the exodus, but one night he tried to escape the *chin* camp to visit her, and was killed by a *dal'Sharum* guard."

My hand throbs, and I realize my fist is clenched tight. I have to concentrate to loosen the fingers. "I'm sorry for your loss, brother."

Faseek shrugs, though his face belies the pain. "I was not yet born."

I think of Darin, still listening. "I didn't know my father, either, Faseek. It does not mean I do not mourn the empty place in my life where he should be."

Faseek nods. "That is so, my prince."

"What will happen to your mother if you disappear?" I ask.

Again, he shrugs, but this time his indifference seems real. "My mother remarried, this time to a full-blood *dal'Sharum*. She has new children to love, and I was never more to her than a weakling reminder of past shame. She was happy to see me off to *sharaj*, no doubt hoping I would never return."

"You have glory to do any warrior proud now," I say.

"Because of you," Faseek says. "I survived *sharaj* because of you. I have fighting spirit, because you gave it to me. I have glory, because I followed where you led. Why should I bring it home to a family that treated me . . ." He flicks a hand, as if to shake the filth from it.

"They are still your family," I tell him. "My own is no less fraught, but I accept the bad with the good. I gave you a bowl of gruel. Nothing more. You survived *sharaj* because you fought for it. I did not give you spirit, you found your own. Your glory belongs to you alone, brother."

"A bowl of gruel," Faseek laughs. "Perhaps that is how you see it, but you are not me. I was ready to give up that day, my prince. My spirit was broken. There was a knife that Tikka uses to cut vegetables. I meant to take it that night, and ensure I did not live long enough to be cast out and sent back to my mother in shame."

"You never told me." My words are gentle. Those of a friend and not a commander.

"It was not your burden." Faseek cannot meet my eyes. "It was mine. I tell you now only so you understand. You reached out a hand at the lowest moment of my life, even though the night before I had kicked you, just to impress my brothers. Every dawn I have seen since then belongs to you."

I nod. "Perhaps. But is it different from the debt you owe the spear brothers who have stood at your shoulders or covered your back? Who have saved or been saved by you countless times in the night? You are bound to them, and to Desert Spear, as much as you are to me."

"Your words are true, my prince, though I think our brothers would remain with you, too, should you but ask."

I shake my head. "If I must ask, then I have no right to ask."

Faseek nods vigorously. "Just so. If one of my bonds must be broken, it should be I who chooses which, and not you. My spirit fights for you, my prince, and before I die, I would like to see the green lands of my father."

I squeeze his arm, leaning my forehead to touch his. It is an intimate, feminine gesture, more motherly than fraternal, but Faseek does not question it. "Then you shall, brother."

CHAPTER 5

KISSY STORIES

I HURRY BACK THROUGH the tunnels and have to scurry a bit to keep up, but as Olive exits the building, I smell her brothers waiting for her. It's too bright out in the sun to stick to walls, so I hold back until their attention is on one another, then drop to the ground and flit behind a nearby statue of warriors triumphant. I climb the base and nestle into the shady hollow beneath the wings of a marble wind demon.

It's still a bit strange, seeing Olive in a suit of armor, slapping armed warriors on the shoulder and speaking to them in a voice deep as Hary Roller's cello. I don't wish to have any *Sharum* with us on our trek home, but I suppose if there must be, Olive's spear brothers are better than ones we don't know. If one of them meant her ill, I'd smell it. Quite the contrary, all I smell is loyalty. Ent one of these men wouldn't die for Olive, or her for them.

I feel a twinge of guilt as the others leave and Faseek's eyes pass over my hiding place without seeing me. Folk got a right to privacy, but my ears can hear a field mouse breaking wind. Secrets find them no matter what I do.

What I don't expect is for his story to cut me so. Know what it's like, to grow up without a da, and it sounds like he din't have much of a mam, either. I was the outsider in my family, too, but at least I had Mam.

"Run ahead and join our brothers," Olive tells Faseek at last. "I would have a few moments alone, before the bustle of the caravan."

That's my cue, and as Faseek turns a corner, I drop down next to Olive, matching pace with her, a step behind. It used to be a game between us, trying to sneak up on Olive and Selen and catch them by surprise.

"Sorry." I wonder if she will jump at the sound of my voice.

Olive doesn't miss a stride. "About what?"

"For thinkin' I had it worse'n you," I say, "because my da was dead, and yours was just far away. In the winter when the Brook got too cold, Mam used to skate us down south to your father's palace in New Krasia. Easy to forget you din't get to know him like I did."

The words have an effect on Olive, but I can tell from her scent she doesn't wanna talk about it.

"You're using past tense," Olive says, and I feel my blood turn to ice. "Do you think they're already gone?"

I don't have to ask who she means. Both our mams, and the closest to a father either of us has. Not to mention countless others gone missing.

Olive didn't see the aftermath of that demon attack, but I did. Saw it, smelled it, heard the crackle of burning flesh, the sizzling of hot fat. The air tasted of blood and ichor and demonshit, soaked into the dirt to make something akin to a swamp, buzzing with flies and skeeters. I start to gag, just remembering it.

Few of the bodies could be identified, but there didn't seem to be enough to account for a force of nearly a thousand Cutters and Warded Children. If they escaped, why hasn't anyone heard from them? Demons ent known for taking prisoners.

But this wasn't a random attack. We know this now. Alagai Ka, the Father of Demons, was behind it. Night, he was probably there himself. Must have been, for any horde of demons to be a match for Mam and Aunt Leesha, or my bloodfather.

"You're the one was in the demon's head," I say. "What do you think?"

A scent of revulsion wafts to my nose as Olive's eyes go distant. "It was only for an instant, though it felt longer. And it was just . . . flashes of memory, like sights glimpsed in a lightning flash at night. There was an image of them being fed live to a hatchling queen, but I don't know if it's fantasy or foretelling. All I know is the queen hasn't hatched yet."

"How long do we have?" I ask.

Olive shrugs. "Months? A year? Time enough to prepare a little, I hope. But that doesn't answer my question, Darin. Do *you* think they're dead?"

Scared to answer, if I'm to give honest word. Yes is a betrayal, and no feels like a fool's hope. Think it's why Selen and I never really talked about it. What was the point? So long as we didn't have to pick one, it could just be both, in my heart. Didn't change what I needed to do either way. Didn't give up, but I wasn't a fool.

But now Olive's waitin' for an answer, and I ent one to tell lies. "Dun't look good, that's for sure. But . . ."

"But what?" Olive prompts, when I do not go on.

I shrug. "Folk call Aleveran powerful—and maybe he is, here among the Majah. He tells folk what to do, and they do it, but he can't *make* 'em—not really. But Aunt Leesha, Mam, and Bloodfather were different. Magic hummed around them like glowing embers, flaring like the sun when they were roused.

"The night the demons first attacked me on Solstice, Mam came running when she heard. She was so mad, Olive. And the wards on her skin were so bright I couldn't even look at her. Went through those demons like hens in the slaughterhouse. Then she lost patience and started drawing wards in the air and demons exploded like festival flamework.

"Seen a lot of folk with my night eyes, Olive. Speaking honest word when I tell you I ent ever seen anyone more powerful than the three of them."

"Not even your da?" Olive asks softly.

The words sting, but I know that ent what she meant, so I shrug, much as Faseek did. "Never met him."

Olive isn't convinced. "If they're so powerful, why did they all disappear? Why haven't they come back?"

A chill runs down my neck. "Ent got an answer that's better'n what you saw in Alagai Ka's head."

"What if this is what the demon wants?" Olive asks. "For us to *think* they're alive, so we mount a rescue and charge right back off the safety of the greatwards into some trap?"

"Search my pockets," I say.

"Search yourself." Olive stops walking and looks at me. "What do you, Darin Bales, believe?"

Hate it when folk look me in the eye. Always have. Only Mam and sometimes Selen get a pass. When Olive gets like this, it's like lookin' at a twister that might come your way any second.

I flick my hair so my bangs fall over my eyes. Looking down I spy Mam's knife on my belt and reach for it. The heavy blade slips from its oiled sheath with a slick hiss. The handle might seem smooth to most folk, but I can feel thousands of little indentations, as well as the shape of Mam's hand, worked into the bone and steel.

I hold it up for Olive to see. "Knife was like a part of Mam's body. She used it for everything from pickin' her nails to cutting down rock demons, and anythin' in between. Every important moment of her life, it was in her hand or on her belt."

Olive nods, smelling impatient, but she does not press me.

"Item like that has emotions imprinted on it," I say. "Even here in the day I can feel them buzzing against my hand. Mam taught me how to pull magic through a print like that and Read it. Something like the flashes you had in the demon's mind."

Again, that scent of revulsion, but now Olive nods in understanding. "What did you learn?"

I shake my head, thankful for the hair in my eyes. "Haven't done it."

Olive cocks her head. "Why not?"

"Reckon it would be like readin' her diary." I shift my feet. "Personal stuff she might not want folk to see. Be the core to pay next time she saw me, I did that without permission."

Olive crosses her arms. "You overhear personal stuff all the time, Darin Bales. And what does that matter, if she's gone?"

"Dun't," I agree. "But maybe it says somethin' I ent been brave enough to risk it. All I know is, until I got real proof Mam ent alive, I'm gonna act like she is."

Olive looks at me a long time, and there's love in her scent. "I've missed you, Darin."

"Ay, well." I shift uncomfortably. "Your mam's dice said there was a city in the eastern mountains. That was where Bloodfather went looking for them, before he disappeared. If they're alive, reckon that's where we'll find them."

"*A mimic demon hungers beneath a city in an eastern mountain valley.*" A flash of anger enters Olive's scent, and I remember how Aunt Leesha questioned her like a schoolmam for hours, until Olive could read the throw herself.

"It didn't make sense then," Olive says, "but I saw it in Alagai Ka's mind. Mimics are shape-shifters. With the queen dead, Alagai Ka induced this mimic to become a sort of . . . proto-queen. It isn't a real queen, but it carries an egg for one. And if it hatches . . ."

". . . then my da died for nothin'," I finish, "and the rest of us won't be far behind."

"So we mount a rescue," Olive says, "and charge right back off the greatwards."

"Ay."

"Solstice is in six weeks," Olive says. "I mean to be back in Hollow building an army before the festival."

THE CARAVAN YARD is even louder than it was when we left. A disgruntled group of *Sharum* have been shunted off to the side, replaced by Olive's Princes Unit.

"Merchants ent happy about your men taking over," I say. "Hear Achman grumblin' the guards were hand-selected and loyal, and about this contract and that."

Olive shrugs. The merchants are *khaffit,* and in Desert Spear, *khaffit* who disobey the *Sharum* often don't live long enough to do it twice.

"They're all spies anyway," Olive says. "Achman worked for Belina when they stole me from Hollow. I don't trust them, and I certainly don't trust their hired spears."

"What if Aleveran finds out?" I ask.

"I think he'll consider twenty of my loyalists out of the city a bargain for getting rid of me," Olive says.

Selen and Arick lounge in the shade with a group of Olive's brothers, waiting for the order to move. Everyone's at their ease, laughing like old friends as Selen spins a story with the ease of a master Jongleur.

"So there I am, chatting up this tall farmer's son dressed up in his da's armor," Selen tells the rapt audience. "While Olive has snuck off to play kissy with the girl he shined on."

"Prince Olive?!" Gorvan is incredulous. The eyes of the other *Sharum* go equally wide and they roar, shoving one another in their delight. I cringe at the primitive display, but Selen and Arick just laugh and join in the shoving.

"So I take my helmet off," Selen continues when the shock has worn off, "and suddenly he's not so worried about what his little apple-picker's daughter is up to."

The warriors look scandalized—everyone is, when Selen tells one of her stories—but again they roar it away.

"But just when things were getting to a boil, up the hill tromps The Biggest Rock Demon. Big enough to blot out the stars! Picks up a stone the size of an outhouse and throws it right into one of the great wardstones! The ward shatters and demons pour into the camp. Suddenly kissy time is over and I'm fumbling for my spear."

I take a deep breath, inflating a chest suddenly gone tight. Selen Cutter's the only girl I ever played kissy with. Only one I ever wanted to. But that was a long time ago, and I see now I ent the kind of man she likes.

And why should I be? Selen's got more in common with warriors than she does with me. Olive Paper is six feet tall, and Selen's got inches on her. She's loud. Confident. Beautiful. The men are drawn to her like bees to a flower, and she soaks it in like sunshine. The pheromone stink from that pavilion is overpowering.

So it ent much surprise that Selen Cutter shines too bright to really see me, sneakin' in the shadows. Don't expect she'd be impressed even if she did.

"Prince Olive!" Parkot cries as we draw close. "Is it true you kissed an apple-picker's daughter?"

"Night, Sel," Olive snaps. "I can't leave you alone with my men for a quarter hour?"

"Sorry," Selen calls, but she smells delighted. Nothing Olive and Selen love more than embarrassing each other.

"All right, you lazy logs!" Olive barks as she moves toward the group, but her words are good-natured. "That's enough of Selen's kissy stories for one day! On your feet! We're leaving!" She smells as relaxed among the raucous men as Selen and Arick.

"What was her name?" Menin shouts, as the men start collecting their gear.

"Lanna." Olive crosses her arms, but I can see the muscles of her face twitching as she fights a smile. "She was pretty as a sunrise, and far too good for you, Menin! Now on the double, and tonight I'll tell the story of how Selen ended up in a dung stall to keep her father from catching her kissing the stableboy."

Again the men howl and start shoving, Selen laughing hardest of all. It's more than I can take, so I slip away amid the sudden bustle of activity, looking for shade and quiet. There will be too much noise and dust as carts and animals and people get moving. Better to wait it out and catch up to the caravan once they're on the move.

The sun beats down on me with an almost physical weight. It's the price I pay for my little magic tricks. Even with my hood up and layers of clothes, sunlight leaves me drained, dizzy, and sweaty. Any exposed skin feels like it's touching a hot skillet.

The nearest escape is Rojvah's white tent, though with Arick out in the yard, she'll be alone.

To tell honest word, Rojvah scares me a little. Hard to get a read on her scent sometimes, and I don't like how she looks at me. Like a bug that both fascinates and disgusts her, and she has half a mind to squash.

But anything's better than all the stink and noise and dust out here in the hot sun. I move to the shady side of the tent, where the direction of the light lets me see right through the canvas to make sure she's awake and alone.

I gasp, turning away quick as I can. As Olive promised, Rojvah is strip-searching Dama'ting Belina, and I glimpsed more than was proper.

I hurry away before anyone sees me, but there ent a lot of options as merchants and warriors break down temporary shelters from the sun and stow them on the carts. I find my horse, Dusk Runner, instead. Runner's a sturdy young courser, and like me, he doesn't like a crowd. I climb into the saddle and put up the sun shade. It's not considered manly, but I don't care. I pull my hood low and lift my pipes, creating a wall of music to drown out the noise as I ride on ahead, putting some distance between me and the rumbling caravan.

The guards at the gates to the Holy City do not hinder me. Why should they? The surrounding city, destroyed by corelings just a few nights past, is no welcoming place.

Many of the streets and buildings are structurally unsound, but still folk brave the ruins. Organized teams salvage building materials, families weep over lost homes and search for heirlooms, and scavengers roam the rest, seeking to loot whatever they can find to help build a new life in the Holy City.

My music turns mournful as I pass through, following the freshly cleared Messenger Road to the remains of the great gate, shattered from the inside out.

THE CARAVAN MOVES SLOW. I've got plenty of time to ride up ahead, and find a bit of afternoon shade to nap in. They stop early to set up camp, and I return just long enough to leave Runner with a groom and let myself be seen by enough folk that Olive and the others won't worry.

Ent exactly stealing the flat loaves of Krasian bread I snatch from the dinner cart, even though they weren't handing them out yet. I take the prize and move away from the dusty clay road, into the sands. I walk a mile or so, close enough to hear if there's a commotion back at camp, but far enough that I won't have to listen to any more kissy stories told by the fire.

I pull my hood over my eyes and doze through the glare of the setting sun, but I don't need a rooster to wake me when it finally slips beneath the horizon. I feel it in my whole body as magic begins to vent up from the Core, drifting along the sands until it finds me, clinging like bees on a comb. My night eyes come to life, and my other senses expand with them.

Easy to forget it's nearly winter during the day, but the temperature drops quickly with the setting of the sun. I can hear the crystals starting to form on the water in my bottle, but cold doesn't bother me when there's magic to keep me warm.

The desert is beautiful at night.

Folk say deserts are dead places, but they ent, if you know how to look and listen. In the light, rodents bound across the sand and reptiles skitter and slither after them. Hidden in the dust are dormant seeds and animals, ready to wake with the rain. There is water, too, if you know where to find it, and stubborn plants that cling to the outskirts of the moisture.

Demons rise with the flowing magic. I can see them out in the night, their auras bright pinpricks of light in the darkness, even as their scales blend into the surrounding sands. None are close enough for concern, and Mam's warded cloak, wrapped around me like a swaddle, would keep them from noticing me in any event.

But then I hear something, off in the distance. Ent the cries of a demon, or the quick feet of a desert animal shushing through the sand. Ent the wind, or the noisy warriors back in camp.

The sound's up ahead, away from Desert Spear, but I've got a bad feeling still. No reason Aleveran couldn't have sent an ambush to wait down the road.

I get up and breathe out slowly, turning slippery. It's a trick of magic that lets my particles slide a little farther apart. I'm lighter when I turn slippery, frictionless, and pliable.

Soft sand is as firm as clay under me now, and my feet glide across the surface as I run toward the sound. Don't expect Olive or Selen would want me going on ahead, but they'd just cause a ruckus coming along, and ruin any chance of surprise.

The buzzing gets louder as I draw closer, white noise coalescing into voices, then accents, then words. A mix of Krasian and Thesan not unlike what is spoken in Desert Spear. Could this be a Majah force, waiting in the right position to attack us on the road?

But then I hear a familiar voice, and crest a small hill, finally getting line of sight to the camp.

"Ay, you gotta be kidding."

CHAPTER 6

ESCORT

"SURE THAT'S MY DA?" Selen squints at the approaching riders, still too far for anyone but Darin to see clearly.

They spotted us this morning. Only one road in the desert, and we're both heading opposite ways on it. A smaller group has broken off from the main force to ride ahead and meet us. Still, they're close to our small caravan in number, with reinforcements not far behind.

Darin points to one, towering over those beside. "Know anyone else with a horse that big?"

Uncle Gared's Angierian mustang, Rockslide, is famous at twenty-one hands tall. Taller than any horse in Hollow, and too big for almost anyone save the general himself to ride.

Coveted as warhorses and draft animals alike, wild Angierian mustangs evolved to survive the naked night—bigger, stronger, and faster than horses bred in captivity. Heavy and powerful enough to flee, fend off, or outright stampede over the field demons hunting the grasslands. Mother surmised some of them must have eaten the meat or licked at the ichor of dead corelings after a stampede, growing larger and more powerful, and passing some of that on to their offspring.

"Ay, that looks like old Rocky." Selen squints at the silhouettes on the horizon. "But Da ent that . . ." she makes a vague gesture with both hands around her midsection, ". . . shape."

The laugh is welcome. Even with my own men posted around the camp and Belina shackled, it was difficult to find sleep, like there was an asp in my bedding. And now this new variable.

"Honest word," I agree. "But he's probably been out searching ever since I disappeared, four months ago. Been away from all those sugar cakes his chef likes to make."

Just imagining those cakes makes my mouth water and my stomach rumble to life. When was the last time I tasted sugar frosting? After nothing but Krasian food for months, I am suddenly craving Hollow fare.

Selen doesn't look satisfied. "Four months in the saddle doesn't turn a barrel into a beanpole."

"Perhaps not the saddle," Arick volunteers. "But if he's been off the greatwards, fighting *alagai'sharak* . . ."

I grunt at that. I've seen what feedback magic from fighting demons can do to a body, pushing it to its physical prime. None of my spear brothers—myself included—had found our full growth when we were thrust into combat. A short few weeks later we had put on inches and pounds of muscle as if five summers had passed.

My brothers gloried in the strength and reach of their new adult bodies, though mine presented problems, as well. Even now, my breasts are flattened and bound beneath my armor, lest someone see me remove it and ask questions I am not ready to answer.

But there is another effect of the magic, more coveted by the warrior class. Just as it pushes a young body into fullness before its natural time, magic can restore aging warriors to their fighting prime. "If he's been killing demons as they cross the desert . . ."

"Demons came to their camp last night," Darin says, "and they didn't leave it to the wards. Cutters put their axes right to work. Saw Uncle Gared strangle a sand demon with just his gauntlets."

The words exhilarate me. I would love to have seen that. To witness the general—the most storied warrior in Hollow—in action. To test myself beside him. I imagine what it would be like to choke a thrashing demon. The rush of power from the wards on my gauntlets. The . . . dominance of it. My fist tightens, and I feel my heart pumping.

But then I catch sight of Darin, and my blood cools a little. Darin looks more haunted than enthused at the memory. Like he's about to sick up. He's too gentle for this. Not for the first time, I wish he hadn't come, even as I love him like a brother for doing so.

"How many spears do they have?" I ask.

"Four hundred, countin' axes," Darin says. "And no hangers-on. Two hundred Cutters and a like number of *Sharum'ting*."

"So two hundred warriors," Gorvan laughs, "and a like number to cook their meals and warm their beds!"

Selen doesn't hesitate, turning and shoving Gorvan so hard he loses his feet entirely, crashing to his backside in the dust.

"Say that again," Selen growls as Gorvan scrambles back to his feet, glaring at her.

Such challenges were commonplace in *sharaj*, but rare for Gorvan, the largest and strongest boy in our class. Only Chadan, with his superior training, and I, with my enhanced strength, ever dared.

But Selen shows no sign of backing down. She's taller than Gorvan, but he outweighs her, all of it muscle and heavy bone. Gorvan is loyal, but he is a brute, and takes pleasure in dominating other men. I've been thinking of making him my drillmaster.

Men striking women is a crime in the North, but there are no such provisions in Krasia. Gorvan seems eager to return the blow, but he is not a fool. Selen is my mother's sister, and a princess in her own right. My spear brother glances at me for permission, and I know it will shame Selen if I refuse.

"Got this, Sel?" I ask, hiding the nerves in my voice.

"Stay out of it." Selen never takes her eyes off Gorvan.

I shrug and give Gorvan a nod. Selen isn't unnaturally strong like me, but she's about as naturally strong as one can be, and I know firsthand how she fights. She's got the edge in skill if not muscle.

The Princes form a circle, shouting, and the merchants, no fools when opportunity presents itself, start calling odds for wagers.

But when Gorvan turns and launches an attack, Selen doesn't bother with *sharusahk*. She slips a punch, sidesteps a kick, then launches herself at Gorvan's thigh, grabbing it and stealing his balance, slamming him back down into the dust.

Selen's got three younger brothers, all of them built like goldwood trees and taught to wrestle since they were old enough to run. She's been putting them in their place a long time now, and this is no different. Gorvan's weight and muscle aren't worth as much on the ground, and Selen is faster at getting a hold. Her arms redden as she begins to squeeze, and Gorvan bellows in pain as his shoulder threatens to twist free of its socket. More insidiously, Selen's forearm is pressed against the artery in his neck, cutting off the flow of blood to his brain.

Luckily for Gorvan, he was never one to fight with his brain. He bloodies Selen's nose with an awkward punch and gives a mighty flex, breaking the hold. But as he rolls away in an attempt to regain even footing, Selen remains on the attack.

My spear brothers wince as she puts a hard knee into his crotch, and the merchants change the odds even as a flood of new bets are called.

Gorvan shoves Selen back and finds his feet, but he's dizzied and in pain, and it's all Selen needs. A heel kick to his hip folds him in half and puts him on the ground for a third and final time. Selen falls on him savagely, pinning his shoulders with her knees as she pummels him about the face.

"Ay, if you're finished, we've got company," Darin says.

I look up, and see the riders have kicked into a gallop and are coming in fast. They're close enough to recognize now, and I see Darin was right.

The change in General Gared is startling. His long gray hair, balding at the top, has been cropped short, and decades seem to have fallen away with it. The sides remain tipped in gray, but there is gold beneath to match the fuzz sprouting on his crown.

Yellow, like the sun, Grandmum would say sometimes. I see now, for the first time, why her voice would grow wistful when she did.

He remains the largest man I have ever met, but he's shed his ale-fat, looking so much like his statue in the Coreling's Graveyard that I have to blink. A hundred pounds have moved upward to a chest that strains his wooden breastplate. Flabby arms have hardened into thick ropes of muscle that run from the pauldrons covering his great shoulders down to his famed warded gauntlets.

But it's more than just his appearance. The general's eyes are hard. Predatory. More nightwolf than hound. He's come to the desert looking for a fight.

He rides next to a *Sharum'ting* with a white turban, and they have half a dozen warriors each riding at their backs. I can see their main force on the road, but it is still some way behind.

Four hundred warriors isn't enough to conquer the Majah, but the gates of Desert Spear are shattered, warriors laid up in the hundreds, homes destroyed. Four hundred fresh warriors could do a lot of damage before Aleveran could stop them.

Gared rides in so hard I think he means to trample right through us, but he pulls his enormous stallion up at the last moment, rearing menacingly before vaulting down with grace I didn't know he had. That big axe he always carries is in his hands now, and he points it at Selen.

"Anyone dun't step away from my daughter and Darin Bales right quick gets split in two," he growls.

I can tell my spear brothers don't like that tone. Frankly, neither do I. Mother never would have tolerated it, and neither can I, if I am to earn this warrior's respect and fealty. I turn to face him fully as my men gather close, spears and shields at the ready.

"Uncle" Gared was always kind, if a bit bumbling. He had a tendency to misjudge his own strength and break things by accident—which I quite related to—and a carelessness about his appearance—which I did not.

Mother loved Gared like a brother, but her appraisal was even less flattering. *Gared was the person you wanted at your side when things got rough,* she told me once. *Anytime a demon tried to kill someone in Hollow, it had to get through Gared Cutter, first. Folk call him a hero, and he earned that. But being a hero doesn't get the paper made. When the war ended, Gared Cutter never figured out how to be anything else.*

I've only seen a fraction of the fights between the general and his wife Baroness Emelia that Selen has, but they were enough. Emelia is mean as an asp, and I will forever hate her for her treatment of Selen, but more than a little of the strain on his marriage is Gared Cutter's own fault.

Selen says her da isn't lazy and tries to be a good person, but he's a worker bee, not a baron. He's barely literate with no head for numbers, and after years of bungling, his only real responsibility was to sit in his office for an hour every morning before he was "allowed out," signing papers the baroness put in front of him without bothering to read them.

Sometimes, he went "hunting," and was weeks away from court.

The general grows impatient as I regard him, pulling the heavy warded machete from over his shoulder and clanging it against his axe. "You speak Thesan?!" he barks with the sound. "I said right quick!"

Before I was marveling at the change in the general's appearance, but now I find myself sizing him up as I would any foe, looking for strengths to avoid and weaknesses to exploit. I find too many of the former and few of the latter. One of many reasons not to let this confrontation escalate.

It isn't surprising the general has failed to recognize me. Why should he? Last time he saw me I was draped in silks and jewelry, face powdered and my hair long and flowing. Now I am unmade, hair shorn, in *alagai*-scale armor, with a man's biceps and a voice with far more bass than he remembers.

"You should have kept your saddle and waited for your full force, if you meant to make threats, Greenlander."

The general snorts as his men raise loaded crank bows, and the *Sharum'ting* ready slender throwing spears. "Don't need any help to chew up the likes of you and shit you back out. Best stow them spears and turn over my daughter and young Mr. Bales, you know what's good for you."

Darin snickers, and General Gared spares him a glance. "Somethin' funny, boy? Gonna be the core to pay when I get you and Selen back home."

I smile, taking off my turbaned helm and pulling away my white dust veil. "Don't you recognize me, General?"

It is most satisfying to see the general's eyes bulge out of his head. "Olive?!"

I offer a royal nod worthy of Mother.

"What in the core you doin' all git up like a sand . . ." The general glances around at his Krasian companions and my own warriors, thinking better of his next words. "Ay, well, dress-up time's over. Mount up. Time to get you home."

I cross my arms. "I think you're forgetting yourself, General Cutter. With my mother . . . away, *I* am in command here. Send riders back to your forces and tell them to start turning around. From you, I'll have a knee."

Ooooh, he doesn't like that. Not one bit. I see his face redden. "No disrespect, Olive, but I got hounds your age. You ent ready . . ."

"To lead?" I ask.

"You said it, not me," he says, thinking it will lessen the blow.

It does not. "Should I follow a general who abandons his post, then?" I demand. "Leaving the Hollow throne, *my* throne, unguarded while he runs off on some fool's errand?"

"Ent a fool's errand!" the general roars, but I can tell he's on the defensive now. "Came looking for you, Selen, and Darin, and here you are!"

"Ay," I agree. "Here we are, in command of an armed escort back to the court and responsibilities you fled. Tell me again what purpose your coming served?"

"Ay, ah," Gared blusters, but he doesn't have a quick reply to that.

I step forward. "Perhaps we can begin with you and your Cutters putting up your weapons," I say softly, "before my brothers and I lose patience?"

The general looks down at his hands, clearly having forgotten he still holds his axe and machete. He stows both with practiced smoothness into a harness on his back, and the men and women of his escort immediately do the same with their own weapons.

"Now send the riders." I make my voice just loud enough for others to hear. A quiet, dignified command. Again I feel myself channeling Mother, but I intentionally leave off the *please* she would have added. That soft power worked for Duchess Paper, but it would be seen as weakness by the *Sharum*.

"Tomm," Gared calls over his shoulder to Tomm Wedge, one of his oldest friends, and another graybeard restored to his prime, "send your boys back to tell the Cutters to start turning round."

"You heard him," Tomm tells his sons, three men who look more like his brothers. The Wedge boys punch heavy fists to their wooden breastplates as they turn and ride off.

I move closer, in easy reach of the general's long arms. *The kill zone,* Drillmaster Chikga had called it during our *sharusahk* lessons in *sharaj.*

"Ent apologizing for comin' after ya," the general says. "It was Selen missin'. And you. And Darin rippin' Bales. Ent interested in any post that means I ent protectin' you lot."

"Of course not, Uncle." I give him the honorific now. "You had to come, same as Darin and Selen did. Can we do any less for those we love?"

"Din't leave Hollow unguarded," Gared says quietly. "Arther's got the throne and Gamon's in command of the Hollow Soldiers. They're better at that business than I ever was. All I brought was the Cutters. Half-retired old warhorses like me, but we still got a bit of pepper in us."

Indeed they do. The Cutters are the most famous warriors in Hollow, many of them the original woodcutters from Cutter's Hollow, the small town of a few hundred souls that grew into the largest duchy in Thesa. I know all their faces from around Mother's keep, friends and neighbors from her childhood, but they've changed. Dug and Merrem Butcher were white-haired last I saw them, as were Samm Saw and Brianne Cutter. Now they could be thirty again.

I open my arms just a little, and Gared sweeps me into a crushing embrace that lifts me clear off the ground. I hear my men shift their feet at that, but then the general starts to sob. "Thought I'd lost you. All of you."

He releases one of his arms, beckoning. Selen is quick to join us, though Darin, who never enjoyed being touched, hangs back.

"Ent letting you go again," he promises through shuddering heaves and tears that feel like a goblet of water has been poured on my head. "So proud of you, both. Follow you to the Core and back, Olive Paper."

And there, hidden in that crushing embrace, I allow myself to cry, too.

WITH A NEW FORCE of loyal soldiers to guard me, I offer my spear brothers a chance to turn back, but none of them accepts.

"We promised to see you to New Krasia, at least," Gorvan says. "And we will keep that oath. No doubt your mother's warriors are formidable," he glances at the *Sharum'ting* escort, "but you will be in the company of a like number of Kaji, and they are not to be trusted."

"The Kaji say the same about Majah," I note. "And since when do you fear *Sharum'ting*?"

Gorvan smiles, displaying the split lip and bloodied teeth Selen gave him. "Every fight is a new lesson, Drillmaster Chikga said." I briefly worried he would bear a grudge, but if anything my spear brother seems to have developed a schoolboy crush on Selen instead.

We pitch a much larger camp as the sun begins dipping toward the horizon. General Gared throws another fit when Darin disappears, but that's just Darin's way. I sit close to the firepit with Selen, Rojvah, and Arick, warding off a bit of the night's chill. Faseek patrols a short way off, ensuring we are not disturbed without warning.

"Prince Olive!" my spear brother calls, and I look up to see the Sharum'ting Ka materialize out of the shadows. The Damajah's elite warriors all have *hora* jewelry that can silence their movements and bend the shadows to them like a cloak. No doubt she could have crept right past him, but she's being polite.

My spear brothers are less trusting, rushing out of the darkness to form up around me, hastily snatched-up spears in hand.

"Sharum'ting Ka." I give a deep, respectful bow. I have never met Ashia vah Ashan, but she is my first cousin and a warrior of legendary exploits, spear sister to my sister Micha. Ashia is nearly as royal as I am, and her white turban outranks my white veil.

But she is the Damajah's creature, and neither do I trust her as I did Micha. Mother would not allow me anywhere near my father's people, for fear they would kill me to end a threat to the throne.

"Prince Olive." Ashia's bow is deeper and longer than mine, a sign she sees a difference in our relative ranks. No doubt she is aware my mother is missing, and I am next in line for the throne of Hollow. "I hoped you would have a moment to speak."

"Of course," I say. "You honor me." I signal the men to stand down. They back away, but they do not disperse, fanning out instead to form a ring around us.

"It is good to see you safe," Ashia does not seem perturbed in the least, surrounded by a score of Majah spears, "and liberated from Desert

Spear." She glances back down the road, though the city is far from sight. "But I wonder if you can tell me the fate of our sister Micha. It is said she was taken the same night as you."

My throat tightens. I've been dreading this moment, and had hoped it would be a private thing, spoken behind the walls of my father's palace. My men and I looked at her with mistrust, but it was love that brought my cousin here tonight.

"She was." I nod. "Micha and I fought together against the Nanji Watchers who came for us, but we were outnumbered, and I . . . was not who I am today. We were taken, but twice on the trip to Desert Spear, she escaped and tried to free me. The Majah stripped her of the black, but she did not abandon them, or me, when Alagai Ka came to Desert Spear."

"Tsst!" Ashia hisses, drawing a mind ward in the air and glancing over her shoulder. "We do not speak the name of the Father of Lies in the night, my prince."

I lower my veil, spitting in the sand. "To fear a name is to fear its owner. Alagai Ka fled our spears, and if he is fool enough to come for us before we hunt him down, we will finish what my father started and end him once and for all."

Easy words. Truer is we survived as much by luck and surprise as any force of arms or will. I remember what it was like when the demon entered my mind—the enormity of his power. The memory fills me with terror, but I embrace the feeling.

Ashia nods. "You remind me of him, young prince. *Sharum* Blood of the Deliverer. I hope to be by your side when that day comes."

"Micha was there, when he came. I tried to leave her behind, safe in the Holy City, but my sister would not rest while I was in danger."

"Of course not," Ashia said sadly. "The honor of Micha vah Ahmann was boundless."

"Boundless," I agree.

"I take it she did not survive the encounter?" Ashia's voice is cold.

I shake my head. "Killed, when the Father of Lies took control of my brother Iraven, using him as a weapon."

"Tsst." Ashia's hiss is sad. "I knew Prince Iraven. He was . . . formidable. Is he . . . ?"

"Dead as well," I say. "Both will have their bones bleached and added to the power of Sharik Hora."

Ashia's serenity evaporates as her eyes go wide. "Impossible. No *Sharum'ting* has ever had her bones added to the holy temple."

I nod. "Micha will be the first."

"Aleveran agreed to this?" Ashia demands.

"The *dama'ting* gave him little choice," I say. "Chavis says Micha will be the first, but not the last."

Ashia stares at me for a moment, and then she does something I would not expect from a warrior, especially in the presence of enemy spears. Her eyes grow wet, and she falls to her knees, weeping.

Rojvah is on her feet in an instant, pulling from her robe one of the tiny bottles Krasian women use to collect their tears. My spear brothers nearly fall on themselves to get out of her path.

I think of how hard I work to keep my emotions in check in front of my men. It is unthinkable, in such a male space, to cry over news, however heart-wrenching. Warriors are not supposed to cry at all.

Rojvah moves toward Ashia, but I hold out a hand palm-out to forestall her, then turn my palm up. Rojvah understands, placing the vial in my hand.

Gently, I kneel before my cousin, reaching out a finger to lift her chin and catch a drop ready to fall. I scrape the edge of the bottle up to catch the rest, then move to the next. Ashia's tears do not slow. If anything, they fall harder, her face screwed up in anguish.

And then she looks at me, and darts a hand into her robes. At first I fear she is going for a weapon, but no, she produces a bottle, identical to the one I hold.

It is only then I realize I am crying, too.

When it's done, Ashia opens her arms, and we hold each other for a moment.

Then Darin clears his throat. "Demons are comin'." He inhales sharply through his nostrils, breathing a cloud of fog back into the cold night air. "Whole bunch of 'em."

CHAPTER 7

SANDSTORM

THE TENDER MOMENT evaporates with my words. Like sleepin' cats that heard a thump, Olive and Ashia are back on their feet, eyes sharp and alert as they peer into the darkness.

"How many?" I can smell Olive's frustration. She trusts my senses, but even with a warded helm to let her see in magic's light, she can't spot the enemy. Ashia ent looking in the right places, either, but the Sharum'ting Ka smells calm, focused, patient. She's ready to give orders, but wants to see what Olive does first.

I give a shake of my hair. "Can't get an exact count, but they're all around the camp. Woulda noticed sooner, but I got . . . distracted."

Olive scowls. "Not your fault, Darin. We all did. What can you tell me?"

"Buried in the sand to hide their auras. Creepin' in like they're late to Seventhday service."

Olive nods. "Dash over and let Uncle Gared know. Tell him to ready the Cutters but keep it quiet. Let the demons think they have surprise before we attack."

I feel ill at the words. I'll fight corelings if I gotta. Did that more than enough times on this rippin' trip. But maybe we don't need to pick a fight, every time?

"About that," I mumble, fingering the pipes on my belt and glancing at Rojvah, but Olive has already turned away, giving orders to her Majah brothers.

I raise my voice a bit. "Ay, I just . . ."

Olive spares me another look, harder now. "Now, Darin."

That gets my back up. Olive Paper may be next in line to rule Hollow, but Hollow's a long way off, and ent where I'm from in any event. I put my hands on my hips, and she turns to me fully, smelling of rising irritation. Olive was always bossy, but it's different now, like she doesn't want to seem weak in front of her brothers, and I ent got patience for that.

"I think what the son of Arlen means," Rojvah cuts in loudly, breaking the tension and drawing all eyes her way, "is that his skills—and mine—might be put to better use than messenger service." She touches the choker at her throat, a *hora* jewel that can amplify her singing like the little warded coin on my pipes. "Perhaps we need not fight at all. Why let the *alagai* approach us at a time of their advantage, and not ours?"

Olive looks down her nose at Rojvah. "Because too many *alagai* escaped the Deliverer's Purge, and I will suffer them in our lands no longer. I mean to eradicate them, not play them a lullaby."

"Idiot," Selen mutters. She doesn't contradict Olive, but I can smell that she wants to.

I see hurt surprise on Rojvah's face, and that's the last straw. I take the pipes off my belt and shake them in Olive's face. "That all this is to you? A lullaby? Your mam made you read all those histories of the war, and you din't learn a rippin' thing?"

Olive definitely doesn't like *that*. Mentioning the duchess is a last resort with dealing with Olive. As apt to set her off as it is to slap her out of acting the fool.

Can't help it, though. Rojvah and Arick's da is a bit of a hero of mine. Like my da, Rojer Halfgrip, the Fiddle Wizard, brought back a magic folk thought lost. Halfgrip figured out how to charm demons with his music, and wrote spellsongs other musicians could learn that gave them power to drive demons off, lure them in, or escape their notice entirely.

The final battles of the demon war were waged on many fronts, but the tales all agree the losses would have been far worse without Halfgrip's spellsongs.

"Ent sayin' we shouldn't hit 'em," I tell Olive, leaving out that I ent sayin' we should, either. "But Rojvah and I can do a lot more to keep the demons where we want 'em than asking the Cutters to tiptoe."

Olive wants to argue, but I'm not telling her anything she doesn't already know. She's just never needed to work my pipes into a battle plan before. She glances at Ashia instead.

The Sharum'ting Ka smells proud, as if Olive has passed some sort of test. "That is indeed how it was done in the war, cousin. And today."

Olive turns back and meets my eyes. "Sel?" she says over a shoulder. "Mind going to tell your da to ready the Cutters, and keep them quiet?"

Selen snorts, and I can smell her amusement. "Ay, he'll love that, getting orders from his teenage daughter."

"I know the feeling." Olive flashes a smile at me. "But we could all do with a lesson in humility now and again."

MY HANDS ARE sweaty as I reach for my pipes. I turn slippery and give them a flick to clear the moisture, then raise the instrument to my lips.

But my heart is pounding, and my chest feels tight. Maybe I had a moment of sack standing up to Olive Paper, but deep down, I know I ent ready for this.

I hesitate, trying to force my breathing to slow to a natural rhythm.

Behind me, Rojvah shifts. It isn't just my reputation at stake here, it is hers, as well. The longer I delay, the worse we both look. But Rojvah doesn't smell impatient.

Arick does. I can scent the emotions tearing at him. He wants to be out with the warriors, wants to prove himself to Majah, *Sharum'ting*, and Cutter alike, but he won't leave his sister unprotected.

"Fear is only wind, Darin am'Bales," Rojvah says too quietly for others to hear. "Let it slide off you."

The image is a calming one. I keep my hands firm, but let the rest of my body go slippery, imagining fear as a physical thing that cannot take hold of me.

And then I begin to play.

Slowly at first, like I'm testing the reeds, letting their resonance grow. The desert is quiet at night, and the sound carries far, even before

I begin to manipulate the wards on the pipes to activate the *hora* and amplify the music.

I fill the night with sound, projecting it everywhere, enveloping the demons stalking the sands. Rojvah adds her voice to my playing, offering a soft harmony at first, weaving in and out of my melody as she touches the choker at her throat, activating sound wards of her own.

We dominate the night air now, and I imagine the stalking demons, putting myself in their tracks. *Stay hidden,* I tell them with my pipes. *Your prey will flee if you move.*

Rojvah reinforces the command with her harmonies, growing in strength and complexity to match my melody. Our music intertwines, as intimate as any embrace.

I catch Olive's eye, giving her a nod.

Olive turns to Gared. "Take your Cutters out, General. Find the enemy and be ready to attack on my command."

Gared gives a signal, and the Cutters comply, taking their warded woodcutting tools out into the naked night. "Cutters know this game well as any. But I ent going anywhere."

Olive raises an eyebrow. "I thought this was settled, General."

"You want to give the orders, the Cutters will follow," Gared says. "But ent a corespawned thing you can say to get me to let you, Selen, and Darin out of my sight with demons at the wards."

Selen snickers. "Mum says Da's stubborn as a rock demon about things like this."

The general crosses his arms. "Even *your* mum's right once in a while."

Olive mashes her lips together, but she doesn't smell angry. Quite the contrary. "All right." She rolls the shield off her shoulder and lifts her spear. "Let's go."

Uncle Gared doesn't look happy at that, but those giant weapons come off his back, and he follows, towering over even tall Olive and Selen. "Demons will come out of the spell once the fighting starts, but it takes a few seconds for them to shake it off. Don't waste 'em."

Ashia's warriors slip short stabbing spears of warded glass from their backs. Each is three feet long, with threads on the end to screw together into a longer weapon. They keep them separate, leaving their shields on their backs. And then they do something unexpected.

They start to sing.

Ashia herself begins, weaving her song around ours like Micha did in the demon tunnels. But then all two hundred of her warriors raise their voices, joining in the song. Resonance wards on their armor glow softly, picking up their sisters' song and keeping it tight even as they separate to search for targets.

It ent easy. Music fills my senses, and even I have trouble spotting individual demons, but I know they're out there. If someone steps on one and causes a ruckus, it could break the whole spell.

Be still, my pipes appeal to their animal instincts. *Be silent. Wait.* Layered into that, I add a whine, rising in pitch, that winds coreling muscles like a spring. Rojvah and the *Sharum'ting* pick up on the change, filling the cold air with tension.

"Can't see a corespawned thing," Gared says. "Gonna need to jump 'em."

They are out of sight now, but I have my senses trained on Olive, Selen, and Uncle Gared.

"Ay," Olive agrees. "Now, Darin."

I break the tension in my music with an explosive burst of notes, made exponentially more powerful by Rojvah and our chorus of *Sharum'ting*. Shocked corelings leap straight up in a spray of sand. It would be funny, if they weren't here to kill us.

The fighters strike quickly, before the demons can collect themselves. Some score quick, decisive kills, but not everyone is lucky enough to be in position. Some strike glancing blows, but demon magic heals them quick. Anything that ent a quick kill or severed limb only buys you a couple minutes unless you can finish the job.

Most of the demons were hiding out of range from axes and spears. I hear wet thumps as Hollow archers pepper the next rank with warded crank bow bolts that sizzle as they continue to work their violent magic in the wounds.

But the sands have come alive with corelings, and the carnage shakes them free of my spell. They swarm like ants, charging with such ferocity I'm scared our lines'll be overrun.

Even now, I can drive them back. Folk are impressed by my little magic tricks, but it's only when I'm at my pipes that I truly feel powerful. Folk think it's the corelings I'm charming, because they don't have my night eyes. Truer is I'm charming the magic in the air around them, imparting my will onto it, same as drawin' a ward.

With a simple series of notes, amplified by the chorus, I could send the demons scrabbling back on their heels to turn and flee into the night.

But Olive wants to fight.

Deep down, I know she's right. We have power, and an obligation to use it to protect others, like our parents did in the war. But in my coward's heart, I am glad of the safety of the camp's wards as I change tune, drawing the demons in. They charge headlong, slavering through rows of sharp teeth.

Olive and the fighters give ground slowly, holding steady right before the wards. At the last moment, Olive signals and they all take a step back, letting the demons slam hard into the wardnet, filling the night with bright lines of magic. They flatten against the impenetrable net, stunned, and before they fall back, the warriors have struck again, scoring another brutal round of killing.

But still the sands crawl with demons, swarming in from what seems like every direction.

This ent a random encounter. It's a bushwhack.

Again I shift tone, driving the demons back on their heels.

"I see it too, Darin," I hear Olive growl, when I keep it up too long. "Stick to the plan."

I stop playing, and the demons stumble, unsure of their footing as they attempt to shake off the effects of the spell.

"Now!" Olive's command is amplified by Micha's magic choker, and carries all around the encampment.

There's a *tung!* sound Hollow crank bows make that hangs in the air like a stink. Fifty of them fire, and it feels like being grabbed and shaken.

It's made worse as Olive leads the charge of hundreds of screaming warriors. They slam into the disoriented demons, and I hear every grunt and shriek. The crack of breaking bones and the pop of punctured organs.

Mam would wash my mouth with soap if I ever said some of the awful things our warriors scream as they strike. Already I feel like I might sick up from trying to sort it all out. As the rush of magic takes them, it's going to get worse.

Our advantage is short-lived. Already, some of the corelings injured but not killed in the first round are staggering back to their feet, even as more skitter in from the darkness.

I lift my pipes before the chaos can overwhelm me, seeking that special clarity that comes when I play. Inside the music, I can create my own space and ignore the maelstrom of sensory input around me.

I begin *The Battle of Cutter's Hollow,* another of Halfgrip's famous spellsongs—this one designed for melee combat. I can hide in its rhythms, imposing them on the wildness of combat. My sick stomach fades away with the rest of the din.

The *Sharum'ting* chorus, unfamiliar with the Northern music, does not join me. Instead, the Cutters stop shouting curses, voices deep and resonant as they join the song in concert with the swinging of axes, sledges, and mattocks.

The Battle of Cutter's Hollow doesn't stop the demons' attack, but it keeps them on the back foot, like tryin' to fight with a headache that makes you dizzy. The giant Cutters take full advantage, cleaving into demons like they're clearing a stand of trees.

Arick has moved in front of us, staring hungrily at the magic flashing up the weapon handles of the fighters. That feedback makes them stronger, faster, tougher. It heals injuries and fills the recipient with the same wild energy that drives the corelings. A little makes you feel invincible. A lot makes you act like a demon, yourself.

Wasn't long ago Arick got drunk on that magic and tried to kill me. Wasn't in his right mind, but he did it, and we all know it can happen again.

That what's holding him back with us? Arick is usually the first to a fight. Hiding behind the wards was cowardice, to hear him tell it.

I can usually scent what folk are feeling, but with Arick it's like trying to figure out a soup recipe by licking the spoon. He glances back at us, eyes flicking to my pipes, and for a moment I smell longing.

I think I understand. Arick never loved music, but his father was Rojer rippin' Halfgrip, a Jongleur legend. In Krasia a man is expected to take after his father, and Arick was trained on the kamanj—the Krasian version of his father's famous fiddle—since birth.

But the morning after Arick first picked up a weapon and tasted feedback magic, he smashed his kamanj and threw it into the sands. He dedicated himself to the spear, only to find himself a pawn of Alagai Ka in our struggle. Does he want back what he cast aside?

The longing scent is gone a moment later, overpowered by the smell of suffering and self-loathing. Arick's Jongleur training lets him put any mask he wishes over his face, but he can't fool me. Arick is drowning in a bog. He needs help, but what can I give him?

The battle lines have merged now, and it is down to close fighting, where the demons have the advantage in numbers, speed, and agility. The voices of the Cutters begin to falter, as the song is compromised by labored breath and the screams of the injured and dying.

I've been sitting all this time, legs crossed, lost in the music. Now I get to my feet, wrapping myself in my Cloak of Unsight. Arick notices the movement and looks back at me.

I put on a mask of my own, hiding my fear as I grin and pull up my hood, then lead us out past the wards.

Arick and Rojvah have cloaks of their own, a subtle magic that makes demon eyes slide off us like water off a duck. Long as we don't make any sudden moves, we can walk right up to a demon, and it won't know we're there.

We move through the battle, seeking out places where fighting is thickest or people are down. Rojvah and I can't cover the whole camp with our music, but in a smaller sphere, we can still exert our will over the corelings enough to turn the tide of battle.

Arick keeps close, resisting the urge to join the battle fully, but anytime a demon wanders too close, he puts his spear to work, killing before the creature even knows he is there. His heart beats more rapidly as magic floods him, but Arick hums along with his sister, keeping his breath controlled.

The tide begins to thin, and I think we are holding, when a scrabbling sound echoes through my feet from the direction of the camp.

I look back, tracing it to the center of our portable wardnet, near where the animals are hitched. The ground explodes upward as the armored snout of a clay demon bursts free. More pour out of the gap, and I see one leap for Dusk Runner.

"Olive! The camp!" I scream as I drop my pipes and run.

I CAN'T PUNCH through a goldwood door like Olive, or turn demons to ash by drawing a ward in the air like Mam, but I'm fast. *Boy makes a rabbit look like a turtle,* Grandda used to say.

I suck in, making myself denser, tougher, and heavier as I leap. The clay demon's long claws have just begun to dig into Dusk Runner's flanks when I tackle it away. My horse's scream cuts through me, but I can hear his pulse, and know the damage ent serious.

I drive us to the ground, trying to wrestle my way into a hold on its back, away from its natural weapons. Clay demon claws are long and hard, perfect for tunneling and climbing. Their armored foreheads, ending in a sharp beak with incredible crushing power, can batter through a stone wall.

Quick as I am, I'm not quick enough to stop the snapping demon from catching my forearm in its jaws. They begin to squeeze, even as the demon uses the hold to twist and bring its talons into play. I may be tougher when I suck in, but I ent fool enough to test it. I turn slippery, popping from its grip like a muddy eel. I give the demon a second to orient, then I set off running.

More demons pour from the tunnel, scattering through the camp looking for prey. There's more than livestock to get their attention. Achman and his merchants are *khaffit* and women, both denied the spear. They run for emergency ward circles stationed around the camp, but one of Achman's sons, younger'n me, stumbles, and a demon bears down on him.

"Ay!" I shout at the demon, altering course to come between it and the boy. Once I have its attention I'm runnin' again, now with two demons on my tail.

I skid under carts and over piles of supplies, dashing into empty tents and then slipping out through the seams in another direction once I'm out of sight.

None of it much helps. The clay demons have my spoor and ent fooled by quick direction changes. What they can't climb over or under, they ram right through, splintering wood and tearing canvas.

More demons pick up the chase. I'm relieved to see most folk make it to succor in the emergency circles, but I'm starting to worry. Demons are coming at me from all around now, and it's all I can do just to keep from being cored. My pipes and cloak ent much good when I'm running around, but if I stop, the demons will have me before I have time to use them.

"Ay, Darin!" There's a loud *CLANG!* and I turn to see Uncle Gared waving his weapons in the air. "This way!" He stands shoulder-to-shoulder with Olive, Selen, and a wall of axes and spears. I hear Rojvah singing, laying something akin to a Cloak of Unsight over the fighters.

I'm light as a feather when I go slippery, and leap from cart to cart, landing on the ground in a tumble and rolling to my feet as I charge our lines, a shattering of clay demons right behind me. I drop and skid right between the general's legs as he puts his great warded axe to work, splitting a clay demon's skull.

Then it's all shouting and cursing and stabbing. Wet, horrible noises, and the sounds of hatred too great to contain. I feel battered by it. Sick.

"Done your part, Darin, but this ent a place for you!" Gared barks. "Git behind the wards!"

I want to argue, but in my heart I know he's right. The sounds of battle, the smell of blood and ichor and spilling bowels, the horrific sights and the slick, slimy ground are too much for me.

Olive's confidence was well founded. The demons would have overwhelmed our small caravan, but with the general's forces, they are beaten back. I can hear in their shrieks that they are ready to break and run.

The warriors roar with the final push, unified and proud. Arick is among them, his hesitance gone. Even Rojvah remains with the fighters as I slink off and hide like a coward, trying to shut it all out.

CHAPTER 8

LINAVAH

I'VE UNDERESTIMATED DARIN AGAIN.

I've always loved music, but have neither desire nor ear for making it. Mother's tutors drilled the history of spellsong into me like a thousand other subjects, but I'd never seen it in practice on the battlefield at scale. The Majah do not implement spellsong in combat, preferring to fight in the old ways. I learned to command warriors in the Maze with spear and shield, ward and wit, not this subtle art.

But now . . . applications are coming to me faster than I have time to consider in the heat of combat. This is a powerful weapon against the demons, and we will need every advantage in the months to come.

Still, for all his power, I am relieved when Darin finally takes cover. He's braver than he knows, but Darin's always been too sensitive for fighting. Even a benign crowd can be too much for him, much less the chaotic cacophony of violent melee.

Back when we were kids in Hollow, Darin had me and Selen to bully folk away from him whenever he had one of his . . . episodes. Out here, they're a liability that could get him killed.

Rojvah and Arick, on the other hand, make a great team. I can see *sharusahk* training in how she moves, but Rojvah doesn't fight. Doesn't need to. Her song does the work for her, keeping *alagai* confused and off balance for Arick and the other warriors to dispatch.

Selen warned me that Arick was at risk of losing control under the influence of feedback magic, but there is no sign of it in his focused, efficient protection of his sister. I've seen the look of men hungry for the rush of magic, and the wild actions of those caught up in it. Arick is anything but wild. His spear and shield move in perfect harmony as he rolls around Rojvah, driving off or killing any demon that ventures too close to her path. Rojvah strolls the battlefield with impunity, moving to bolster warriors wherever the fighting is fierce.

I, too, look for those hot spots, letting none falter where I can offer support. Gared and Selen fight at my right, and at my left, Faseek and Gorvan are ever present, guarding me with shield and spear as they relay my commands to our brothers down the line.

It feels right, my Princes fighting beside Hollow's finest warriors. For so long I've struggled to understand my place in the world, but perhaps I have found it at last. I can be a bridge between people, rallying us back to strength, if time enough remains.

Thanks to Darin, the clay demons that burrowed into the camp did not have time to mar the wards or cause too much damage before we came and swept them out.

The *alagai* sense the changing tide of battle and flee before they are completely destroyed, but we have done plenty of damage to the storm. All around, Cutters and *Sharum* finish off injured demons before they can heal.

It's a victory, but for all the glory of the fallen *alagai,* there is a price among our own. Brothers and sisters lie dead on the sands, and with the demons gone, the camp sounds of the familiar groans and rapid breath of warriors too proud to cry out.

"Gather the wounded," I tell my lieutenants. My hand drops to the healing pouch at my waist as I scan the carnage, wondering who to help first, but as the heat of battle cools, I realize that even with Rojvah's help, this is beyond my skills. I can stem a bleeding artery or cleanse and close a wound, but this . . .

Belina exits her tent as these thoughts run through my mind. The *dama'ting* has taken pains to avoid me thus far on the journey, but now she approaches boldly, meeting my gaze with a steady one of her own as she holds out a hand.

"I will need my *hanzhar*," she says, referring to the razor-sharp curved knife *dama'ting* use in both combat and surgery, "my herb pouch, and *hora*."

The words send a chill down the back of my neck, and I shiver inside my Tazhan armor. Even without *hora*, a *dama'ting* with herbs and her *hanzhar* is deadly dangerous. With demonbone to work magic, she could easily escape, or worse.

"Absolutely not," I tell her.

"Do not be a fool, son of Ahmann," she tells me. "I have seen your skill at healing, but this is beyond you. Will you sacrifice limbs and lives to keep your illusion of control?"

I draw a slow breath, embracing my fears, and blow them back out. She's right. I knew it as I spoke the words to refuse. Rojvah and I have some training, but neither of us has a fraction of the knowledge and experience of one who has taken the white veil.

If Belina escaped, where could she go? She would not be welcome in Desert Spear, even if she managed to cross days and nights of open desert to return. She wouldn't get far with the armlet on, in any event. She might attempt to kill me and take the control piece, but I don't see how it could end well for her even if she succeeded.

So I return her tools, and pray I haven't made a terrible mistake.

THE DEMONS DO NOT return in numbers again as we cross the sands. Alagai Ka's influence is limited between new moons, and we put the fear of the Creator into that storm. By the time the demon king can rise and exert control again, we will be safe in the summer palaces of my father's court in New Krasia.

I hear a sound in the distance one morning as we cross the seemingly endless clay flats at the outskirts of the desert. The cracked clay is easier for the horses and wagons, but somehow feels even more lifeless than the sands.

Darin points to a hill in the distance. "They've spotted us from Lookout Hill. Crack the reins and we'll be in Everam's Watch by nightfall."

I can't see this Lookout Hill even with a distance lens, but I trust

Darin. Indeed, the hill and town become clear by afternoon, when the clay flats have given way to spare vegetation and signs of life. By the time we reach proper green and the village at the desert's edge, I can see a formal escort waiting for us. Male *Sharum* warriors, outnumbering our entire force, Ashia's *Sharum'ting* included.

"Be ready for anything," I tell my lieutenants. The Princes gather close, surrounding me, and Gared similarly puts a guard of Cutters up front.

"Have no fear," Ashia says, pointing to a white turban on one of the warriors who rides to the fore as we come into sight. "That is your brother Hoshkamin, the Sharum Ka."

"That doesn't reassure me," I say, remembering my treatment at the hands of my brother Iraven.

"That is wise," Ashia says. "Not all of your siblings are to be trusted. But I know Hoshkamin well. If he is here personally, the Damajah must have foretold your return and sent him here to ensure we reach Everam's Bounty in safety."

I let it go at that, resisting the urge to loosen my spear in its harness. We are close to the assembled warriors when the *dama'ting* appears. Set against all the men in black, she looks like an apparition in her flowing white robes. The men give her a wide berth. It is a crime to lay hands on a Bride of Everam or hinder her in any way.

"Is Princess Olive among you?" Prince Hoshkamin asks as we pull up before the force blocking the road.

I lift the turban from my sweaty head, hanging it on the horn of my saddle. "I am Olive Paper, brother."

Hoshkamin blinks, taken aback. His eyes flick to Ashia, who gives the slightest nod.

"Of course." My half brother swallows his confusion, removing his own turban helm and dismounting with the grace of an acrobat, even with armor of warded glass over his *Sharum* blacks. He bows deeply to me. "We are relieved to see you returned safely to the lands of your father, Princess."

"Prince." I match his dismount and bow, showing equality, not deference. The word is no more accurate than *princess,* really, but I know how women were treated in old Krasia. New Krasia may be more enlightened, but it is still a patriarchy, and I will not cede the power I have fought so hard for among my southern relations.

The *dama'ting* glides up to me, her bow much shallower than Hoshkamin's but still a sign of respect. "Welcome . . . child of Ahmann. Is it true Dama'ting Belina travels with you?"

"Tsst." I turn to see Belina looking out the window of the carriage that serves as her makeshift prison. She is not allowed to leave it unescorted, but I let her have the view. The *dama'ting's* dignity would not allow her to climb through a carriage window to escape, even if her curves would allow it.

Linavah catches sight of her, as well. "Hello, Mother. The Damajah foretold you would return with Prince Olive, but I did not want to believe it."

Belina has a rare moment of speechlessness, but I can see her skin pale slightly at the words. Linavah's disgust is palpable.

She inclines her head, and a group of eunuchs detach from the other warriors, distinguished by the gold shackles at their wrists and ankles. The men are said to volunteer for the shackles of *dama'ting* guards, though the price is high.

The eunuchs move to push past the Princes I have guarding Belina's cart, and the men look to me before responding.

I don't know what drama is playing out between these two, but I know when someone is attempting to take power from me, and I won't have it. I gesture, and my men lock shields, barring the way. The eunuchs similarly raise arms, but show no further aggression. Both groups are well trained, waiting on further orders, and I breathe my relief at that.

I turn back to Linavah. "Belina is my prisoner, sister. Given to me by Damaji Aleveran in recompense for the blood debt she owes me."

Linavah does not react, but I recognize the artificial calm of a *dama'ting* in control. Favah tried to teach me the art, but I was never good at hiding my feelings.

"My mother is *ginjaz*." Linavah uses the Krasian word for "traitor." "She and all Majah cowards who abandoned their posts before the final battle of Sharak Ka."

My Princes are disciplined, but they are still men, and they chafe at being called cowards and *ginjaz*. I can feel their tension, hear their grumbles. Gorvan spits at the golden anklets of the eunuch facing him. This will erupt into bloodshed, orders or no, if it goes on much longer.

I turn back to Linavah and see her eyes crinkle condescendingly. "You see . . . sister, our blood debt predates yours."

Wisdom dictates I let this go. I don't want Belina. The Damajah can have her, for all I care.

But now my blood is up, too.

I spit at Linavah's feet, and everyone gasps. Even Ashia lets out a "Tsst!," but I need them all to know this is serious. "Belina is in my custody, sister. Sharak Ka is not over. I have seen this, and so declare your debt unfounded. The Majah are no traitors."

At last, a break in the vaunted *dama'ting* calm, as Linavah's brows tremble with anger. "I spent half my life among Majah, brother. They are zealots, minds still stuck in the sand even after our father, the Shar'Dama Ka, led them to the green lands. That is why Aleveran returned to Desert Spear. To strip women and *khaffit* of the rights our father gave them, and drag our people back into the past because they were too afraid to face the future."

More shifting from my men. This isn't going well.

I take a step toward Linavah. My hands are open and at my sides, but like her mother, she stands below five feet, and I am over six. I look down at her, and can feel her tension as she tries to maintain serenity.

"You're not wrong about Aleveran," I agree. "He is a man ruled by his grievances, and he punishes his own people for it."

Linavah nods. "Just as Everam left demons in the sands to punish cowards and *ginjaz*."

"Everam does not work His will through *alagai*!" My shout is manipulative. I don't believe in Everam, but I know most if not all of the assembled warriors do. I take another step forward. Linavah holds her shrinking ground, but around us I feel everyone tense. If I so much as touch her, there will be blood.

"I have shed blood with the Majah in *alagai'sharak*, sister. Night after night after night in the Maze. They are no cowards." I lean in closer, lowering my voice. "And if you call my spear brothers *ginjaz* again, *dama'ting* or no, I will put you down."

Linavah's eyes widen, and then she glares. Has anyone ever dared speak to her thus? Her mind must be racing now. The law forbids a man to lay hands on a *dama'ting*, but until this meeting, the world knew me as Princess Olive, daughter of Duchess Paper.

I see her veil bow inward as she takes breath to reply, and I cut her off. "Test me and see if I don't."

Before Linavah can reply, Hoshkamin breaks the tension. "We can encircle their entire force, sister. Your mother will not escape before the Damajah has a chance to greet her."

Linavah takes another breath, and then steps backward, giving a quick series of gestures in the finger language of eunuchs that makes them stand down. "The Damajah will hear of this."

I snort loudly. "I will tell her myself of the disrespect I encountered on my first visit to Father's domain."

Linavah turns and glides away, and I wonder if it is a mistake, to make an enemy of her when she would better be a friend. I have no allies in New Krasia, and do not know what the Damajah will say when I stand before the Skull Throne. But I entered Majah lands a prisoner, my rank and powers stripped away. I will not suffer that a second time.

THE REMAINDER OF the journey passes quickly, and in comfort. Scouts mounted on light-footed coursers race back and forth along the road, and the villages where we stop for the night open their finest inns and restaurants to our officers and royals. Even the rank and file billet in comfort in fallow fields with full bellies and fresh supply.

The coming winter strikes with less force in New Krasia than the freezing desert nights, or home in the North where snows will soon fall, but still I feel a chill as night descends. Massive obelisks, carved with wards of protection, stand in the village centers and enclose their perimeters. No demon is said to have set foot in New Krasia in more than a decade, but still my Princes and I keep our weapons close.

It is another week before we reach Everam's Bounty, the seat of my father's power. But Father is missing, like Mother and Mrs. Bales. The last time that happened, my brother Asome attempted a coup and tore our people apart. Ashia assures me that will not happen again, but I am less trusting these days.

We are met at the palace by another priestess, this one in the white robes and black headscarf of a *Damaji'ting*. Beside her, I am surprised to find a familiar face. Politics might have prevented my father from visiting Hollow, but Abban the *khaffit* visited often, as his emissary.

"Olive!" Abban steps forward, thumping one of his camel-headed crutches against the marble steps. "It is good to see you well!" He makes no mention of my change in appearance since I saw him last.

"Please allow me to present Damaji'ting Amanvah, who . . ."

I lay a gentle hand on Abban's shoulder, and he falls silent as I walk past. He is like an uncle to me, but it is Amanvah who holds my attention now. My eldest sister, who cut me from Mother's womb when I was too strong to birth naturally, perhaps saving both our lives.

Amanvah doesn't tense as I approach. Instead she does something unexpected, opening her arms to me, uncaring of my dusty armor and clothes. I accept the embrace even as the others look on in shock. "It is good to see you home, sibling," she whispers in my ear. "I am so proud of you."

It is my turn to look surprised. Of course Amanvah, who was there at my birth, knows my secret. But she, too, was the one whose foretelling cast me into the guise of princess for half my life.

"Everam's will cannot be denied," she answers my unspoken words. "You are who you were always meant to be."

She turns to regard Rojvah and Arick. "Of my reckless children, I am less proud. We will speak of this later."

The twins, so brave against a demon storm, immediately cast their eyes down. "Yes, Mother."

"They have earned honor and glory to make any parent proud," I dare to say.

"Perhaps," Amanvah agrees. "But that does not justify sneaking off into the night without a word."

I grit my teeth, wanting to argue, as I did with Linavah. My own mother did much the same when I similarly snuck off, but it wouldn't have happened if she had accepted me for who I was, and not who she wanted me to be. If she had prepared me better for the realities of the world.

But where Belina is my responsibility, I am not interested in inserting myself into this fight. It will be for Rojvah and Arick to fight for themselves.

Amanvah offers me a slight bow. "The Damajah accepts your claim of blood debt with Dama'ting Belina, sibling, but she wishes to meet in private with her errant sister-wife. I ask that you temporarily relinquish control of her for the meeting, with assurance that Belina will remain detained, and shall be returned to you when you are ready."

I bow in return, more relieved than frustrated. "Thank you for your respect, sister. Had Linavah spoken thusly, perhaps some . . . unseemliness could have been avoided."

"Forgive her, I beg," Amanvah says. "It has been difficult for Linavah, a Majah princess hostaged in Everam's Bounty, surrounded by her tribe's enemies."

The words strike harder than I expect. I know too well how hostage princesses are treated. Surely Amanvah knows that. Is this apology for Linavah, or a lecture for me?

"Exile forced Linavah to become hard," Amanvah continues. "She needed to do more than assimilate. Survival depended on proving her loyalty again and again, knowing it would never be enough."

Now I know the words are for me. "I see why you and Mother got along so well."

Amanvah laughs. "Is that what she told you? I would say we . . . found an accord, in time. Shedding blood together forges a different bond than friendship, but it is no less strong."

I nod. That, at least, is something we can agree on. "I am not Majah, but I will tolerate no disrespect of my Majah spear brothers, sister. I trust that has been made clear?"

Amanvah gives a slight nod.

"And if the Damajah's meeting with Belina does not go well?" I ask.

"You have my word she will not be killed," Amanvah says. "The Damajah believes there is value to extract from her still."

Perhaps the words are meant to reassure, but they have the opposite effect. I start to feel a bit of sympathy, but quash it back down. It's no less than Belina deserves. I whisk a hand back toward where Belina waits under guard. "Take her."

Immediately, a group of *Sharum'ting* detach from the waiting palace guards, their sleeves a dark crimson. The Damajah's personal bodyguard. She is taking no chances with Belina, which makes me all the happier to be rid of her.

I watch as Belina is escorted away like a prisoner to execution. Linavah appears to take control of the escort, and Amanvah's words have me feeling sorry for them both.

CHAPTER 9

BLOOD PRINCE

Amanvah is furious.

Can't tell to look at her. Her face is calm, body relaxed. Her heartbeat is slow and steady, like her breath. But it's all false face, like a Jongleur's mask. *Dama'ting* can hide a scowl, but not a scent. She's so far at the end of her rippin' patience, the smell burns my nostrils. The twins—Rojvah especially—are gonna have the core to pay.

Knew goin' in their mam was going to be steamed they snuck off on a dangerous mission across the desert. Still, it ent right, twins gettin' in trouble for doin' the right thing and standing by Olive when she needed us.

"Abban will see you to your chambers," Amanvah says. "The Damajah will receive you when you have had time to refresh." She turns on a heel, quick to follow Belina's entourage down the hall to the Damajah's wing of the palace. Her anger stink hangs in the air.

I don't like it. *A chance to refresh* in Krasia could mean an hour or it could mean a year. A silk prison, they call it. Just leave you to set until whoever's in charge decides it's time. Selen and I spent weeks in one on our last visit.

Ent much point in grousing about it, though. Expect Inevera's chomping the bit to hear what happened in Desert Spear, and none of us got much patience for setting with Mam and Aunt Leesha missing. If we're not back on the road soon, Olive and Selen'll cause a stir no matter what I do.

Abban gives Olive the closest thing to a bow his crutches will allow. "Seeing you in *Sharum* black reminds me of your father in his youth. Ahmann carried me through *sharaj* on his back."

His scent suggests Abban is worried for his friend, and that ent good news. Was half hoping my bloodfather would be back by now, and everything put to right.

"Then Prince Olive is much like his father," Faseek says. "For it was only by his strength that many of us survived *sharaj*."

"Nonsense," Olive says. "You stood on your own."

There is a rumble in the throats of Olive's Princes Unit at that. The men agree with Faseek.

Abban's eyes flick to regard Faseek, seeming to notice him and Olive's spear brothers for the first time. His gaze is cool, but he smells like Mam when I let a muddy dog into the house.

Abban is *khaffit,* the lowest caste in Evejan society, but he's rich beyond measure, and his whispered advice to the throne makes him one of the most powerful people in New Krasia. I can smell the fear of the servants, and even *Sharum,* when he passes.

Faseek and the others don't know this, though. The Majah are more conservative, and I saw no *khaffit* at court in Desert Spear.

Abban snaps his fingers, and a red-veiled *Sharum* drillmaster steps forward. "If your spear brothers will follow the drillmaster, we will see them billeted for the duration of your stay."

The Majah don't like that. I can smell the discontent.

"We are Prince Olive's bodyguard," Faseek insists before Olive can reply. "We will remain with him for his protection."

"Your loyalty does you great honor," I can smell Abban's patience fading, "but it is unnecessary. No harm will come to Prince Olive in his father's palace."

Olive's eyes flick between them. "Will there be guards outside my chamber doors?"

Abban bows. "Of course, Highness."

Olive nods. "Then I see no reason why they should not be my spear brothers. Billet the rest, and they can relieve in shifts."

Abban's scent gets . . . complicated, but he does not hesitate. "As you wish."

Other folk might be scared of Abban, but he's never been anything but smiles with me. He puts a big grin on his face as he turns to me, changing the subject. "It is good to see you well, son of Arlen! I trust the mount I provided was satisfactory?"

"Ay." I remember the fear I felt when the coreling leapt for Dusk Runner. I've got my cowardly moments, but it din't stop me from stepping in front of a clay demon to protect him. "Runner's like family, already."

"Good, good," Abban says as he escorts us to the family residential wing of the palace. "Never let it be said that Abban son of Haman does not pay his debts!"

"Anyone says that, I'll hear it," I tap my ear, "and give 'em a lesson."

Abban laughs at that.

"Highness." Servants bow and scrape as we pass, making me decidedly uneasy.

"Night, it's true!" Olive looks at me as we walk. "You really are a prince!"

"Of course," Abban says. "Arlen asu Jeph am'Bales am'Brook was *ajin'pal* to your honored father the Shar'Dama Ka. When the son of Jeph was martyred, he took Darin as his bloodson."

A rare grin breaks on Olive's face, and I catch a scent of amusement. "Please tell me you make him dress in court robes when he's here."

Abban laughs. "We try, Highness, but the son of Arlen is . . . stubborn."

Selen honks a laugh. "Ay, that's honest word."

It's amusing to them, but they don't hear the servants hissing quietly as I pass, whispering to each other about my "*alagai* blood." I may be a prince in Krasia, but foremost to the people here, I was the child born in Nie's abyss. Corrupted. Unclean. My powers, my sensitivity to the sun, only confirm what they fear—that I brought something of Nie's evil back with me.

In me.

Olive and Selen are given a suite of rooms to share, with Faseek guarding the door across from a pair of scowling Kaji guards. Kaji and

Majah hate each other, though I've never been clear on the why. When you ask, they're happy to spin some ale story about folk three thousand years ago not being neighborly, but truer is they been hating each other so long it's become a habit.

Already there is a stink of aggression in the hall that wasn't there before. I wonder if Olive might be safer without her spear brothers hovering nearby.

As USUAL, I end up in Arick's suite, which ent like having to share a bunk back in the Brook. Got my own room full of pillows to sleep in, and a shared common space.

Used to hate it when we were kids. Arick could be a bit of a bully, and I never got the sense he much liked me. Or Rojvah, for that matter. If I'm to give honest word, I'm not sure they do now. But I know they'd die to protect me, and me for them.

What else matters, really?

I take my first hot bath in months, letting the scalding water hug me tight and seep into my bones, rooting out the lingering feeling of all those frigid winter nights in the desert. I can stand the cold, but I don't like it.

A second steaming tub is filled for Arick, but he sits with his back to the water, showing no interest in getting in. I couldn't wait to take off my stinking travel clothes and clean up, but Arick is still wearing the same blacks he wore to cross the sands. They are rank even to normal folk, and worse to me. Arick himself smells just as bad, which ent like him at all. He's got his spear and shield with him, like he's expectin' a fight on the bath tiles.

"Everythin' all right?" I ask him.

"The warrior blacks were missing from my baggage," Arick says.

"Maybe they're in the warsh?"

Arick snorts. "I'll never see them again."

"Ay, likely." I'm no stranger to palace servants stealing my clothes when they are not up to court standards.

"This is Mother's doing," Arick says. "The blacks on my back are all I have left. The moment I remove them, or leave my spear and shield out of reach, they, too, will vanish, and I'll be left with nothing but Jongleur's motley and that cursed kamanj."

"Nothin' stopping you from just getting in the tub with your robes on," I say. "Warsh them and yourself at once."

Arick perks up at that, laying his weapons in easy reach and quickly removing the armor plates from the pockets in his robes. He lets out a sigh of relief as he splashes into the water. "Ahh, thank you, cousin."

"Doin' me a favor, too." I tap my nose, and Arick lets out a genuine laugh for what feels like the first time since we got to Desert Spear.

"No doubt the whole palace was scandalized when I returned home in black," Arick says. "I doubt Mother is alone in her feelings."

"She ent," I admit.

Arick's eyes had just started to slip closed, but now they're wide open. "What have you heard?"

I shrug. Don't really want to get into it, but Arick deserves to know. "Mostly just servants' gossip, like when they say I got *alagai* blood. Nonsense about how black robes shame your da, whatever that means."

"Perhaps my father was a great man," Arick says, "but I am not him, and cannot pretend to be, any longer."

"Honest word." I ease back into the water. "But you ent getting it half as bad as Rojvah."

Now Arick sits up, staring at me in his soaked robes. I wave him back down. "She and Amanvah are yelling at each other right now. Ent a corespawned thing we can do about it."

Arick nods sadly, submerging himself once more. "Amanvah takes responsibility for me, but she does not love me as she does Rojvah. Both our lives were plotted out before we were even born, but while Rojvah gets the honor of protesting to her mother's face, I just have servants stealing my clothes."

"We're all singin' the same song," I tell him. "Olive, Selen, you, me, Rojvah. Ent one of us got things easy when it comes to folk's expectations."

"What are they saying?" Arick asks.

I close my eyes, focusing on an argument two hundred feet and at least half a dozen walls away.

"How dare you put yourself at such risk?!" I do a fair impersonation of Amanvah's shout. "You are destined to be *Damaji'ting* of all Kaji! You are irreplaceable!"

"*Did the dice assign me that fate, or did you?*" My Rojvah voice is smoother, but no less fraught. I ent great at understanding emotions, but I can mimic them pretty good.

"Everam's beard," Arick breathes. "Take care, sister."

He's right. Amanvah's voice gets louder and shriller in response. "They said nothing of you dressing like a *heasah* and flaunting your sacred duties."

Rojvah spits, and I feel a twinge of fear at the anger in her reply. "*You strip Arick of his honor and the* Sharum *blacks he's earned to dress him in Father's motley, but when I want to honor Father, you call me* heasah *for not wasting my life in white!*"

I don't want to hear what comes next, taking a deep breath and sliding my head underwater for a few moments of blessed silence.

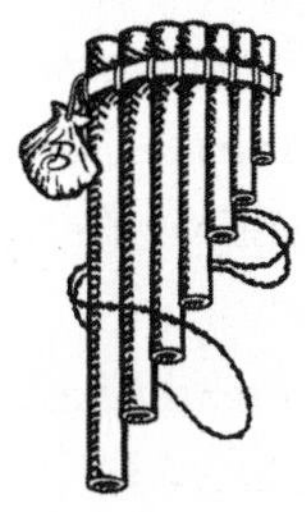

CHAPTER 10

CHALLENGE

Arick's blacks are barely dry when Inevera summons us.

"Must be in a hurry to hear what happened," I say.

Arick shakes his head. "The Damajah already knows what happened. Likely, she knew before it even happened."

I'm not so sure. Got more experience than most with wards for foretelling, and far as I can see, the dice might let you know something big's about to happen, but how it turns out is always a guess.

"We have been summoned to the throne, not a receiving room," Arick goes on. "This will be theater, that all Ahmann Jardir's many, many sons might take the measure of Prince Olive."

"Don't like the sound of that," I say.

"You shouldn't," Arick says. "I expect all of them would have preferred to see Olive remain a princess. The news that the Duchess of Hollow was hiding a prince has shaken the empire."

I look at him sharply. "Explain."

Arick raises an eyebrow, as if it should be obvious. "Prince Olive is a threat to the throne."

"Olive's the youngest one of them," I say. "Almost as far from the throne as we are. Forty people would need to die before Olive's claim meant a corespawned thing."

"Except Olive already leads a state almost as large as New Krasia," Arick says. "A claim to two thrones is dangerous, cousin."

I freeze. That really could shake the world.

"Olive's brothers might think it safer to kill him now, and have done," Arick finishes.

My skin crawls as we step into the hall and fall into line behind Olive. Selen and Rojvah are close at her sides, giving advice.

"You have to speak the words yourself," Selen says.

"I know." There's irritation all over Olive's response, but it's more than that. She's wound up tighter'n a fiddle string.

"Exactly as we practiced," Selen says.

"I know!" Olive smells like she's on her way to a fight, and might be she is. Sel ent helpin' keep her calm.

"She is right," Rojvah adds. "The request only has weight if you personally . . ."

I can feel the rumble growing in Olive's throat, and know this is going to get painful to be around if I don't nip it.

"Night, she rippin' knows, already," I snap.

Selen and Rojvah turn glares at me, but I glare right back. Olive offers an appreciative smile. "Thanks, Dar."

My senses come fully alive as the sun sets. Reckon that was the Damajah's plan all along, timing our summons for when her magic would be strongest. Could be a bad sign, but at least I can turn slippery if I need to.

Arick wasn't wrong about the crowded court. Too many princes and princesses fill the room for all to have places of honor. They cluster at the edge of the lush carpet path leading to the seven-step dais and the twin thrones of New Krasia. I start to get the shakes just looking at all of 'em. Not sure how long I can last in here. My eyes flick around the room, looking for cracks and crevices where I can make a quick exit if I need to.

The famed Skull Throne is built of human skulls, the bleached and lacquered heads of generals martyred in the war against demons. They bind the chair with powerful faith magic, like what protects Sharik Hora.

But unlike Aleveran's throne, the Skull Throne of New Krasia is coated in warded electrum and set with the skull of a mind demon. The demon bone is rich with core magic, Drawn and harnessed by the wards and protected from the sun by the electrum.

Every living thing shines with a little magic, like sun glitter on the water, but the Skull Throne is so bright it's hard to look at. The blending of faith and *hora* magic is beautiful, a wash of color that pulses and throbs in the air, casting protection for miles in every direction like a greatward.

I glance around the room, but only an elite few have wards of sight around their eyes. Most folk go their whole lives without seeing magic at all, and certainly not something grand as this. I pity them that.

The Pillow Throne reminds me of a great big four-poster feather bed, piled with pillows instead of a mattress. But beneath the colored silk curtains, I catch the glitter of electrum, and the throne hums with that same powerful magic. But while the Skull Throne projects it outward, this one holds it in, ready to loose like a loaded crank bow.

Ahmann Jardir, my bloodfather, had *Fourteen wives too many, and that ent countin' Leesha Paper,* as Mam used to say. One from each tribe, and a couple to spare. All of them delivered sons, with the eldest standing to the right of the throne in *Sharum* blacks with white veils, and the second sons standing left of the throne in clerical white.

Closest to Inevera's throne, a cluster of women, the black-scarved *Damaji'ting*—Amanvah among them—stand in front of a sizable number of princesses, bobbing up and down on tiptoes, trying to get a look at their new brother.

The whole rippin' royal family, leaders of every tribe's warriors and clerics, all glaring daggers at Olive.

Olive is the youngest by far—most were old enough to promise before Olive and I were even born. All are adults in their prime now, and many smell as mistrustful of one another as they do of Olive.

I catch whispers from all over the crowded court at Olive's appearance.

"The *push'ting* prince comes dressed as a Majah *kai,*" one prince whispers, his voice dripping with disgust at the style of Olive's black armor and the silk robes beneath.

Like when they call me *alagai* blood, Krasians have a name for Olive, too: the *push'ting* prince. *Push'ting's* a big word that can mean a lot of things. It can be kind when some folk say it, and downright unneighborly when others do. But the literal translation is "false woman," and that's what these folk see. A prince that Duchess Leesha hid away by raising him in dresses.

The truth is more complicated, but it ent my news to break. To Krasians, Olive presents as male, so that's how they see her. And why not? Olive is over six feet tall and ripples with muscle.

"That is Tazhan *alagai*-scale, fool," another of Olive's brothers says. "It is priceless. A raiment worthy of any prince."

"At his waist," another says.

"Is that a *hanzhar*?"

"A *dama'ting hora* pouch!"

"That womanly cloak!"

I linger a little too long, and the rest of the muttered comments start to seep in. I can't filter them all, and it starts making me twitchy.

Last thing I need is to have a fit with the whole royal family lookin' on, so I break my attention from the men entirely, focusing instead on the cluster of women.

There are sighs and stares from the gathered princesses, whispers about Olive's size and regal bearing that cast an imposing shadow on the room.

"Prince Olive may have been stolen from his home in colored silk," one princess breathes, "but see how he dominated his captors! He returns with Majah warriors under his command."

Next comment makes my cheeks burn. I focus on the clerics, but their whispers ent better.

"Did he dominate them? Or did they make him one of them?"

"The Majah are treacherous."

"We must be wary."

"No man should carry the *hanzhar*."

Again it gets to be overwhelming, and I need to jump again. In a crowd like this, it's all I can do. If I keep my attention in one place for too long, every sound starts to seep in until I can't sort any of it, and all I can do is cover my ears and close my eyes and curl up.

I force my attention back to Olive as she leads our group to the center of the floor before the thrones. Prince Kaji sits the Skull Throne in bloodfather's absence, straight as a statue but smelling decidedly uncomfortable. The diaphanous curtains of the Pillow Throne are down, but I can see through easily. Inevera, like everyone here, only has eyes for Olive.

Try as I might, I can't hear anything from the Pillow Throne. Wards of silence protect the Damajah's privacy, and I wish I had some of my own.

Kaji beckons Olive forward with a gesture. "Welcome, cousin."

Something ent right. Been to court enough times to know it's custom for a herald to shout everyone's name when they enter a throne room, and Olive is rippin' heir to Hollow.

"They want her to introduce herself," Selen whispers. I can smell the anticipation. Everyone's holdin' their breath on her next words.

I expect Olive to hesitate. I would. Night, I'd be ready to turn slippery and run. But bein' center stage is nothing new to Olive Paper.

"Wait here," Olive says, taking seven confident strides forward alone.

"I am Olive vah Leesha asu Ahmann Jardir am'Paper!" Olive projects to every corner of the room in the bass-heavy voice she uses in battle. "Crown Princes of Hollow!"

Everyone shuts up at that, but it's a tightening silence. Kind that's usually followed by shouting.

Olive doesn't give them time, looking to the women. "Olive, daughter of Leesha Paper. Heir to Hollow! Trained in *hanzhar* and the Chamber of Shadows at Gatherers' University under Dama'ting Favah."

Dama'ting Favah always scared me a bit, but the way the women in white breathe her name I get the feeling I wasn't nearly scared enough.

"Sisters," Olive spreads her blue cloak in something that's half bow and half curtsy, "I am honored to be one of you."

Olive turns to take in her brothers, from those in the cheap seats by the door all the way up to the throne. "Olive, son of Ahmann Jardir! Like my father, I learned *alagai'sharak* in the ancient ways, blooded in the Maze of Desert Spear! *Kai'Sharum* Olive, *ajin'pel* of the Majah Princes Unit. Hundreds of *alagai,* I have helped show to the sun. Brothers, I am honored to be one of you." The line of princes had begun to relax, but tension ramps back up at Olive's military credentials. Doubt many who came of age safe here in Everam's Bounty can match them.

"I do not seek the Skull Throne." Olive scans the faces of her prince brothers with a predatory stare. "But neither do I renounce my lineage!"

No one likes that. I hear muscles clench and teeth grind at the words. I've lingered too long on Olive, and now all the noise in the room is starting to creep in, hissing like the fuse of a thunderstick. Gonna get the shakes soon if I don't refocus, but there's no lookin' away.

"Brothers," Olive puts a fist to her armored chest in a warrior's salute, "I am honored to be one of you. I am sure we can learn much from one another in friendship and fraternity. I come to the court of my father in peace." Olive shows empty hands, yet smells anythin' but peaceful. "But if any wish to dispute my claim, challenge me with honor and there will be no shame in your death."

I blink.

"Ohhh, Olive, what did you just do?" Selen breathes.

"Tsst!" Rojvah hisses. Guess Olive didn't warn them about this, either.

Ent just us stunned. Don't think I've ever heard a room this crowded fall so quiet. Some of Olive's brothers had been softening, but this sobers the lot. Hard to pick out who is who with them all clustered together, but I smell anger, outrage, and honest offense.

Underneath it all, there is the rank stink of fear. But that doesn't make me feel any better. Fear's usually the last thing you smell before things get scrappy.

The scent that really worries me is Olive's. She *wants* someone to challenge her, here and now. Fixin' to set an example by putting anyone dumb enough to step forward down hard.

That's assuming she can. I see *hora* all over the room. Even the lowliest princes have demonbone worked into their armor or jewelry. If a fight breaks out, Olive ent the only one who will be unnaturally fast and strong.

Reckon Olive knows that. Maybe that's the point. Let 'em know she ent afraid.

But I am. Angry mutters start to break out, and it builds, like the vibration before a quake. I feel it humming through me, itchin', and know it's only gonna get worse.

Eyes flick to Prince Kaji on the Skull Throne. Kaji's only a year older than Olive, both young compared to the other heirs, but if there is to be a challenge, it should start with him.

Kaji's face is serene as he watches Olive and the posturing princes, but I reckon he's stunned as everyone else. With no leadership, the princes start growling and flexing, working up their courage, and maybe hoping someone else will step forward and give them Olive's measure.

Can't stand this much longer. Feel like I'm gonna crawl out of my skin. Just bein' here was all I could handle, and now Olive's got to go an' pick a fight.

I realize my hand is shaking only when Selen's fingers slide into mine.

"Steady, Dar." She squeezes, and Creator, it's something to focus on. I grip her like a line in the water, and Selen holds tight.

There's a quiet sniff, and I see Rojvah's eyes flick away from our hands. She wears too much perfume, but I can still smell the pity beneath.

Wish it din't sting, but it does. Ent a man to Rojvah any more than I am to Selen. Just a baby brother who won't stop cryin' during Seventhday services.

Arick doesn't notice, all his attention on Olive. He smells protective, like when he guarded his sister in *alagai'sharak*. Ready to leap forward and serve as Olive's second, if a challenge comes.

Just when it feels like things are about to snap, the curtains to the Pillow Throne open, and the cloak of silence around them drops. Everyone stops and turns, dropping to their knees. It's obvious who the real power atop the steps is.

Selen and I are left standing. She looks at me, and I offer a smile, pulling her down. "Like this," I whisper, sitting crisscross. "Mam was never one for kneelin', and we ent Krasian."

Selen gives my hand another squeeze, and I am grateful for it.

"Well spoken, Olive vah Leesha asu Ahmann," Inevera says. "Words worthy of your father. But violence is not tolerated before the throne."

Before the throne, she says. What about when Olive ent before it anymore?

"It pleases us to see you returned safely to your people," Inevera goes on. "You may ascend."

Olive bows. “I am honored, Damajah, but first I must formally invoke the Pact of the Free Cities,” Rojvah and Selen breathe a sigh of relief at that, “and ask for safe passage through New Krasia until I am across the border into Hollow.”

Inevera smiles and nods. “You are right to do so, of course. The peace between New Krasia and the green lands has been good for both our peoples. Sharak Sun is over, and *inevera,* will not come again in our lifetimes.”

Something about the way she says her own name winds me up. It’s a common Krasian word meaning “Everam’s will,” or “fate,” but here with my bloodfather missing, it is her will, not Everam’s, that holds power.

“Such escort will take time to arrange and supply,” Inevera notes.

“I already have an escort,” Olive says. “General Gared and the Cutters will be ready with only a short respite.”

Inevera smiles. “Of course. But the desert crossing is taxing, and there are many who will wish to know you better. I would invite you to accept our welcome and give your bodies time to recover before continuing on. Hollow will be immediately informed of your health and status.”

“One week to the day,” Olive says.

Inevera’s mouth tightens, but again she nods. “One week, to the day.”

Angry glares follow as Olive bows and ascends the steps to the Pillow Throne. The wards of silence activate again, sealing off their conversation from everyone in the crowded room.

Talk breaks out, then. Apparently, the Damajah is known for this. Folk keep their voices low, but settin’ on the floor I can hear all of it, too much threat and anger to process. I can smell seething outrage, and know the danger ent over.

Selen squeezes tighter, but it ent enough, anymore. I can feel myself starting to turn slippery. But then Rojvah finds my other hand. Her fingers are softer than Selen’s, but her grip is firm. Still I feel myself vibrating between them, and don’t think I can hold on much longer.

Rojvah cocks her head at Arick, who notices my shaking for the first time. I expect to smell pity or disgust, but instead it's the same steady protective smell he has for his sister, and Olive.

Then he does something amazing.

Arick starts tapping his leg with a finger. Just a whisper of skin against skin with a layer of silk between. Too quiet for anyone else to hear, it's like a heartbeat for me. A steady rhythm I can focus on.

Arick adds another finger, and another, building layers of upon layers of complexity in a perfect, even pattern. His skill and dexterity are amazing, and soon all ten fingers are thrumming in unison. It would be an impossible trick for most, but Arick has been training in music since he could first hold a rattle, and does it as easily as writing a letter.

I breathe in, becoming more solid as I let the rhythm fill me, become me, and take me out of the crowd's angry vibration.

CHAPTER II

DAMAJAH

I'M MORE NERVOUS ascending the steps than I was challenging my brothers. Men, I know how to deal with. The Damajah is something else, entirely. Like Mother, Inevera is a witch, with magic enough to blast me out of existence with a wave of her *hora* wand. Mother spoke of her with respect, but never trust. It was an open secret in Hollow that my father could never visit because of the animosity between the women, and Mother refused to let me off Hollow's greatward, much less visit Krasia.

Now I'm here, without Mother or Father to protect me, making threats in the Damajah's court to hide how frightened I am.

Most Jongleur's tales exaggerate, but Inevera is as beautiful as the ale stories say. She must have seen half a century at least, but the Damajah's skin is smooth as a woman of thirty, her lithe body draped in red silk that covers everything and hides nothing.

But it's her eyes that unnerve me, piercing from beneath a circlet of coins etched with wards. I know Inevera, like Mother in her warded spectacles, can peer past the surface and into my aura, gleaning information I might not even know myself.

The words of Favah, the teacher sent to me by Inevera herself, echo in my thoughts. *Keep your center before those with the Sight. Speak only truth, but offer nothing.*

I was never good at keeping my center, but I learned early that even Mother could be fooled if I was careful not to be caught in a lie.

Inevera regards me coolly as I offer a man's bow, carefully counting the duration. The Damajah knows Mother's throne awaits me, but I have still to claim it. We are not equals.

Yet.

Inevera touches a wardstone, and the sounds of the court vanish and there is only us. "Prince Olive?" Inevera asks. "Princess? You lay claim to both?"

I shrug. "Why not? Whether I wish it or not, I am saddled with the responsibilities of both, so why not twice the title? Olive Paper, Princes of Hollow."

Inevera laughs, a richer sound than I expect. "It's closer to the truth, I suppose." Her eyes flick down for a moment, taking in my body, but there's nothing to see. Clothes mean little to one seeing in wardsight, but my Tazhan armor offers protection even from the Damajah's prying Sight.

Still, the Damajah seems pleased with me, and warmer than expected. Like Mother when I've just passed some secret test. It immediately puts me on edge for more testing to come.

"You are welcome here, Olive Paper," Inevera says, "and safe from me, though I cannot promise as much from my sons, after your words of challenge."

I cross my arms. "In my experience, challenge is the only thing Krasian men respect."

Inevera leans back. "There is wisdom in your words . . . Princes Olive."

Offer nothing, Favah said, but I need answers.

"Princes was in Chavis' prophecy," I say.

Inevera's calm, pleasant demeanor turns suddenly serious. She leans in, voice harsher. "Chavis shared her casting with you?"

It was Belina, but I don't volunteer that information, keeping my face blank and aura flat. Prophecies are sacred things to the *dama'ting*, and they do not part from them easily.

The Damajah squints at me with those piercing eyes. "No. It was Belina who told you."

I curse inwardly. I need to get better at this. I cannot afford to let anyone with wardsight peer into my secrets.

"She will regret not volunteering that information," Inevera notes.

"She has little else to bargain with," I say. "Iraven is dead, and the Majah have stripped her of her title."

Inevera eases back into her pillows. "Perhaps. But Belina has the Sight, and that is power still."

"Is it?" I dare ask. "We cast dice, but seldom understand the prophecy in time to make a difference. Instead we tear ourselves and those around us apart in the guessing, and it does not save the ones we love."

I think of Micha, and Chadan, and my spear brothers, all lost to the demon king. I think of Mother and Mrs. Bales, gone off armed with Mother's prophecies, never to be seen again. Even my father benefited from the greatest seers of our age, only to disappear.

Dama'ting do not take it well when you question the *alagai hora*. Favah would have struck me across the knuckles and assigned a penance for such words, but Inevera only regards me coolly. When she speaks at last, her voice is calm.

"I was a palm weaver's daughter with a coward father," she says. "But the dice called me to the white, and the wards of prophecy . . . spoke to me. Guided me. I married a *Sharum* from a poor family with no great honor to its name. Now he is Shar'Dama Ka, and I am Damajah of Krasia. Your father and Darin's parents may have killed the demon queen, but without the armies I spent decades preparing, they would have come home to a burning grave, if they had lived long enough to face Alagai'ting Ka to begin with."

Inevera leans in. "The future is not set, Olive am'Paper. It is a living thing, like you. Full of potential and possibility. The dice seek our best hopes and guide us toward them. I am sorry if they do not tell you what you wish to hear, or put a burden of worry on you, but that is not a burden easily set aside by one who chooses to sit a throne."

"I did not ask to be born in line for any throne, much less two." The words are bitter and childish, but I cannot help them.

"None of us ask for the lives we are born to," Inevera says. "But taking a throne is a choice. A choice to take responsibility for your people.

To make their burdens your own. Not because you wish it, but because you are the only one strong enough to lift them."

"You sound like Mother." I don't know what I expect the Damajah to do at the comparison, but I am surprised when I see a hint of smile behind her gossamer veil.

"Leesha Paper is my *zahven,*" Inevera says. "Do you know this word?"

"Rival," I say in Thesan.

Inevera gives a little shrug. "Among other things. But the word itself means 'balance.' Forces that cancel each other. She would not have risen so far without being . . . formidable."

I nod. Mother was definitely that. "And now without that force?"

Again a shrug. "I am hoping you will be that force. I do not have a man's thirst for war, Olive vah Leesha. A strong and prosperous Hollow is good for a strong and prosperous Krasia. Our spears should spill demon ichor, not red blood."

I want to believe her, but by her own admission, this is a woman who makes plans that play out over decades, assisted by her prophecies. Am I being manipulated, even now?

"How did Chavis get your blood for a casting?" Inevera asks.

It's information I could hold back, but proof of veracity will make the prophecy more valuable.

"The Nanji Watcher whom Micha killed in my bedchamber when I was four," I watch Inevera closely, but there is no sign of surprise, "had a partner who escaped with a bandage from my scraped knee."

"Tsst." Inevera hisses at the latter half, which means she already knew about the Watcher Micha killed. Whoever Inevera's spy in Hollow was, Favah or Micha or Mother herself, Inevera seems privy to all my secrets, even those the dice choose not to reveal.

"Not taken from your flesh by force," Inevera notes. "The blood was untainted for prophecy, but you did not consent. Tribes have gone to war for less."

"I wish no war with Majah," I say. "Whatever blood debt they owed me was paid on *alagai* talons. When I am back in Hollow, I will open trade lines to them, and offer military aid, though I do not think Aleveran will accept my warriors in his lands."

"Certainly not," Inevera agrees. "What was Chavis' prophecy?"

The question is surprisingly blunt. A seer asking for another's prophecy is not forbidden, but it is . . . rude.

Still, the events have already come to pass—at least I believe they have—so I can think of no reason not to share the words with the Damajah now, save their value to her. I learned in Desert Spear that every boon of the Skull Throne comes at a price. I will not give this away for free.

"I want a prophecy in return."

"Tsst." Inevera's hiss confirms the rudeness of asking for a prophecy. "I can pry the information from Belina's lips. I do not need to pay for it."

I cross my arms, giving her a wry smile. "Belina, I know. She will not give you the information without extracting a price. Better to pay me for her prophecies, and leave her with nothing to bargain with."

Inevera smiles, noticing the emphasis I put on the plural. I feel I've passed another test. "What is it you seek?"

"The prophecy your daughter Amanvah cast in my birthing blood," I say. "In exchange for Chavis'."

"Your mother did not see fit to share it with you," Invera notes. "Nor did Amanvah herself. It is not my prophecy to give."

I roll my eyes. "I could say the same about Chavis'. *Knowledge, once claimed, claims the learner in turn with the responsibility to protect, or to share.*"

The words are from the Evejah'ting, the holy scriptures of Inevera's order. A reminder I am not uninitiated in the rules she is attempting to dissemble.

Another smile, this one more predatory. "I have Amanvah's dice pattern cemented in place. You are welcome to view them yourself, but I understand your studies in the Chamber of Shadows were . . . wanting."

The words confirm my deepest fears about her invasion of my privacy, but they are freeing, too. Inevera knows who I was, perhaps, but not who I am.

"What could I find," I don't bother to hide my fading patience, "that you, Mother, and my sister did not?"

"Very well," Inevera says. "Tell me."

"The exact words, as Belina related them to me, were, *The storms will end when the heir of Hollow joins blood with the Majah, and the princess stands in the eye,*" I say.

Inevera grunts, absorbing the words.

"But the symbol for 'princess' is not gendered, or necessarily singular." I can't help but editorialize. "It could be 'prince.'"

"Or 'princes,'" Inevera notes.

This is why I cannot put faith in prophecy. Each symbol has enough meanings to make a foretelling say almost anything.

"Princes Chadan and Iraven were with me when we entered Alagai Ka's greatward and faced him," I say. "Selen is a princess of Hollow, and Micha of the Kaji. Even my spear brothers are known as Princes Unit."

"But it was you, the Father of Evil fled before." Inevera is watching me closely, no doubt looking to confirm whatever version of events Rojvah provided before this audience.

I shrug. "Perhaps."

"Kneel with me, Olive vah Leesha." Inevera rolls to her knees before a small casting table affixed to the floor. The surface is pure white marble with a raised edge.

I glance back to the crowded court, still kneeling. How long will they wait like that?

Forever, I realize. Or at least as long as the Damajah wishes to meet. It is a display of power that makes me uneasy, but it would not be wise to show it. Instead I move to the table. My father's *Jiwah Ka* is already kneeling, and so there is no submission in kneeling across from her.

Inevera reaches into her *hora* pouch and produces her legendary dice. It is said they were carved from the bones of a demon prince, coated in precious electrum to protect their powers, even in brightest sun.

Inevera places one die on the table in front of me. "*Sharum*."

She sets another, at a precise angle to the first. "*Dama*."

I've seen this pattern before. "This is about my divided nature."

Inevera pauses before setting the next die, raising an eyebrow. "Why say you so?"

I regret the interruption. Not only was it rude, but now it may bias what Inevera says next. But it's too late to take it back.

"Another prophecy," I say. There have been so many. "The next symbol will be *domin*." The word means "two," and Belina supposed it was the two lives I lived, raised first as a princess, then trained in military *sharaj* as a prince. But there was much about me Belina did not know.

Inevera places the next die. "*Ka*."

I blink. The symbol for "one."

"*Sharum, Dama, Ka*." I may not be a seer, but I know enough to read that. "You think I am the Deliverer?"

This time Inevera seems less patient with the interruption. "Deliverers are made, not born, Princes. The *alagai hora* speak of potential. Of what may be, not what is."

I may be the Deliverer? The idea feels ludicrous. Laughable. "So this is a common pattern?"

"I have seen it before."

"Favah taught me to be truthful, but volunteer nothing," I note.

Inevera smiles. "Favah is fond of that lesson."

I hold my tongue while the Damajah sets the remainder of the dice with quick precision. This is a pattern she knows well. No doubt she and Mother have been studying it my entire life.

Favah often told me I would have been cast from the Chamber of Shadows for incompetence if I weren't a princess. Still, much of what I learned by rote remains. I know the symbols on the faces of the *alagai hora* as well as the letters of the alphabet.

Moravan.

Simikar.

Ala.

My heart thumps as Inevera places the last die.

Irrajesh. Death.

Inevera watches closely as I stare at the dice, reminding me so much of Mother it sends a chill down my spine. *Zahven,* indeed. Every moment a test.

It's powerful, to see at last the pattern that shaped my life. Mother has never shared it, but I know something in these dice made her decide to raise me as female.

There are seven dice, each with a different number of sides. Seventy-six faces in all, with one reserved on each for the ward of prophecy. The remaining sixty-nine faces have a large symbol at their center, and other, smaller ones at the edges.

The symbols are technically genderless, but in the Krasian language, words customarily default to male, unless the female *'ting* suffix is added. One of the lesser sides of the eight-sided die has a *Ting* symbol. I take a moment to find it, and cast my eyes in the direction the die points. Its trajectory misses *Irrajesh.*

"Mother thought I would die, if not raised female," I say.

Inevera clucks her tongue. "Perhaps Favah judged you too harshly."

She brings a manicured nail to the *Sharum* die, gesturing to how it intersects *Irrajesh* directly. "Amanvah and your mother read this as *he will die, if raised to the spear.*"

"And you?" I ask.

Inevera shrugs. "Those raised to the spear tend not to die in their beds. Your death does not concern me. Only what you may accomplish before you walk the lonely path."

Again, I wonder if I have judged Mother harshly for trying to guide me into a feminine role that never truly fit. What parent would willingly choose a path that would lead to their child's early death?

"My concern is this." Another flick of Inevera's nail, pointing to the die showing Ala—the world—and how it intersects with *Irrajesh* and the other dice.

I may have impressed her early on with my dice reading, but this is too much for me. "What does it mean?"

"*Death of Ala* is another term for Sharak Ka," Inevera says. Literally "the First War," Sharak Ka is the holy war between humanity and demonkind. "It means taking up the spear put you on a path whereby your actions may bring us victory, or utter defeat."

It feels like all the warmth leaves my body as I digest the words.

Then I take a breath and shake it off. "Again I must wonder at the point of all this. Mother did everything she could to keep me from the spear, and instead the spear came to me."

"Perhaps that is what was needed, to forge you into steel," Inevera says.

"That grouping," I say. "*Sharum, Dama, Ka*. How many times have you seen it before?"

Inevera meets my eyes and does not hesitate. "Twice. In your father, and in Arlen am'Bales."

The words are a punch to the gut. I expected a dozen at least, perhaps hundreds. Not . . . me and the two men everyone worships for saving the world.

"You are rare," Inevera says, "and powerful. What was the other prophecy you spoke of?"

I make my face a blank, casting my thoughts into a fire in hope it will clear my aura.

"You must trust me, Princes," Inevera says. "The Death of Ala concerns us all."

"It is hard to trust, here in your place of power," I say. "Surely you can understand."

Inevera nods. "I have nothing to gain by hindering your return to Hollow, and your own seat of power. You are the leader the North needs if they are to raise their spears in time. We must seize every advantage if we are to win Sharak Ka."

All my life, people—Mother in particular—have warned me not to trust the Damajah. The ale stories speak of a sorceress who seduces all with her beauty and leads them to her own ends. A manipulator who leaves you doing her will and thinking it was your idea all along.

Yet there are similar stories about Mother, and I know the real woman beneath them. The woman who gave everything to her people, and saved nothing for herself.

Can I do any less? If the demon king succeeds in hatching a new queen, it may well be the Death of Ala. What value have my secrets against that?

"Belina cast the dice before I was raised to the black," I say.

"In blood freely given?" Inevera asks.

"Yes," I say.

"Can you arrange the dice and show me?" Inevera flicks her fingers at the casting table a little too eagerly.

"I am not sure," I admit. The casting was memorable, but it was many months ago.

"Try," the Damajah urges, and I reach for the table, rotating *Ka* to *Domin,* and lifting the other dice, turning them over thoughtfully. I remember the face wards—air, sand, lightning, and mind—but their exact orientation, which brings the lesser symbols into play, is more difficult. It takes several minutes before I am at all confident.

"That is the best I can do," I say. Inevera, who watched with cool detachment, leans in now, examining closely.

"A storm," she reads. "With a prince of the abyss leading it."

"That much, at least, came true," I say.

"Perhaps," Inevera says. "Or perhaps it has only just begun. I will consult Belina and consider this."

She looks up at me. "What are your intentions toward my wayward *Jiwah Sen*? What gives your claim to Belina precedence over mine?"

"Did Belina lay hands on your royal person?" I ask. "Torture you? Throw you in a box and drag you halfway across the world? Did she cast you into the demon-infested Maze, with none but your blood enemies to set shields with?"

"She did not," Inevera agrees. "And so I ask again what your intentions toward her are."

"I have no intentions," I admit. "I did not expect Aleveran to give her to me. I did not want her given to me. I do not want her now. But she has a debt to me, and it must be paid."

Inevera nods. "Of course. Would you like her put to death after I am through . . . questioning her?"

The question is casual, as if putting a woman to death were no great thing. My response is anything but. "Creator, no!"

"Service, then?" Inevera says. "You will take her as a slave?"

"There are no slaves in Hollow." I do not intend to growl, but that is how the words come out. Is this what it means to be a leader? To not care at all for the lives of those below me? Do I have the strength for it, if so?

"Then what, in your estimation, would pay this debt?"

Inevera's question is fair, yet impossible to answer. How can I estimate the cost of my dignity? My body? My entire life?

Is there a cost, at all? Even if I could have that life back, I don't want it anymore. If, as a direct result of Belina's actions, I discovered my true self, and am left the better for it, am I owed a debt at all? Belina did not act out of malice. Like all these old witches, she was simply doing what she believed the dice were telling her to do.

"If Belina cannot repay her debt to you," Inevera says, "perhaps she can pay one of your father's."

"Ay?" I ask. "And what debt is that?"

"Prince Asome betrayed the Majah while your father was in the abyss with Arlen am'Bales," Inevera says. "I threw the dice the day they left, and the prophecy was clear. *If the gates of the Desert Spear close behind the Majah, they will not open again without bloodshed.*

"Your father had power enough to bring the Majah to heel at any time," she continues. "He stayed his hand because it was not worth the price."

"But now I have shed blood there." Understanding dawns on me.

"Yes." The word comes as a hiss. "The time to heal Krasia's wound is now. I have a solution that will bring Desert Spear back to us in peace, but it will require Belina."

"What solution?" I say.

"Think on this, while I . . . speak to Belina," the Damajah says. "If we come to accord, I will share my plans, and you can decide for yourself."

Again, I hear the Jongleurs' tales of the Damajah. No doubt when she presents me with the choice, it will feel like no choice at all.

"And if I wish a casting of my own?" Inevera asks. "What price would Princes Olive ask in return?"

I cross my arms. "Trust."

Inevera does not hide her frown. "What does that mean?"

"It means you have asked for trust again and again, but have given little in return. I will let you take seven drops of my blood, one for each die," I see her eyes glitter at the words, "after you let me take seven drops of your own."

Inevera leans back, and I wonder if anyone has ever had the audacity to make such a request of her before. "Why? You haven't the skill to cast and read them alone. Do you even have *alagai hora* of your own?"

She leaves unsaid what we both know. The blood does not just aid in casting. It would allow me to target her with other, blunter, spells if I wished.

I simply shrug. "What I do with the blood will be up to me. That is the price of my trust."

Inevera stares at me for a long time. "Very well. I will take three days to prepare my questions. We will exchange blood then, in trust and . . . sisterhood."

CHAPTER 12

CUPS AND STRING

NO ONE DARES a whisper while they kneel, waitin' for the Damajah's private audience to end. Quiet enough for most, but to me it's still more than a hundred folk sighing and breathing and shifting their weight. A hundred heartbeats, resonating in the air.

All save the Pillow Throne, where the Damajah's wards of silence have created a kind of bubble. Instead of passing through, sound skitters and bounces off its surface like rain on glass.

Arick keeps drumming his fingers as we wait, and wait, and wait. I close my eyes against the sights, breathe through my mouth to dull the smells. I focus all my touch into my fingers, feeling the strong protective grip of Selen's callused hand, and Rojvah's softer, smaller one, squeezing gentle support.

Then I filter out the sounds by focusing on Arick's beat. I doubt Arick himself can hear his fingertips strike the cloth, but his timing is perfect. Soothing as Master Roller's metronome. I wish I could take out my pipes and play along, but attention has finally drifted away from me. Last thing I want is to draw it back.

Slowly, I begin to feel like myself again.

How long have Olive and the Damajah been talking? Minutes? An hour? More? I've lost all sense of it. I know only that Arick has been tapping his fingers a very long time.

At last, I hear a whoosh as the Damajah deactivates her wards of silence and sound resumes its normal trajectory around the room. The curtains rise and everyone gets suddenly to their feet, leaving Selen and me scrambling to follow.

Amanvah is waiting at the bottom of the steps as Olive comes out of the pillows and descends from the dais. The curtains close behind her, and conversations resume around the room, over a hundred people all talking at once.

"The circus is concluded," I hear Amanvah whisper to Olive. "You and the others will follow me to a private hall before one of our brothers takes it upon himself to answer your foolish challenge." They walk purposely toward us, and we fall in line like ducklings as they pass. I'd follow anyone who gets me out of this room.

She takes us through one of the many side exits, this one belonging to the *dama'ting*. The door is wardlocked, but some item on Amanvah's person deactivates the lock long enough for us to pass through.

The floor slopes down immediately, and we quickly wind our way down into the underpalace, where daylight never touches, and the wards hum with permanent power.

I already know where they're taking us. The Chamber of Shadows, the Damajah's vault beneath the palace, where her magics are strongest. There, in a sound-warded room, is part of a great *hora* stone, with other parts of its whole in cities far distant, coated in precious metal and etched with wards of resonance. When the night is dark, a word spoken into the stone can travel hundreds of miles like two cups connected by string, bringing us voices from afar.

The last time I was in this room, it was for General Gared to shout at me and Selen from Hollow and threaten to come collect us. Now he's here with us, but there are other powers in Hollow, still.

Olive, Selen, Rojvah, Arick, Gared, Amanvah, Inevera, and I gather in the small room as the stone hums to life. No one has spoken yet, but I can hear shuffling cloth and scraping feet coming from the stone. Breath and heartbeats.

"This thing workin'?" Elona Paper's voice comes from the stone, and Selen curses under her breath.

"Favah." Inevera ignores the question. "Is all in readiness?"

"We are gathered as instructed, Holy Damajah," Dama'ting Favah replies. "Lord Arther, first minister and regent of Hollow, the duchess' parents, Ernal and Elona am'Paper, and Headmistress Darsy of Gatherers' University."

"Here stand Olive am'Paper—" Inevera clearly means to introduce everyone in turn, but Mrs. Paper cuts her off the moment Olive's name is spoken.

"Olive, are you there?" Elona demands. "Are you safe?"

"Is it possible Alagai Ka can intercept this conversation?" Olive quietly asks the Damajah.

Inevera shakes her head. "Unlikely, without a piece of the sympathetic *hora*."

Unlikely. It ent a no, but it's the best we got.

"I'm here, Grandmum." Olive's voice is softer and higher than I've heard it in a long time, more like the Princess Olive of old. "I'm all right."

Reckon that's what Elona Paper needed to hear. "Oh, thank the Creator."

"I'm all right too, Mum," Selen puts in, "if you care."

"Your backside won't be all right when I get my hands on it, girl," Elona snaps. "Ent gonna blame Olive for being kidnapped, but you ran off without a word of your own free will. Twice."

"Ent gonna be any punishments," Gared cuts in.

"Ay, what's that, Gared Cutter?" Elona's voice is sharp. A warning. "You were ready to strip the hide off her yourself, when you left Hollow to fetch her."

"Ay." Gared puts a protective hand on his daughter's shoulder. "But then I found her and Olive and Darin on the road, and know she done the right thing. Folk dun't need permission to help their kin when they need it."

Olive snorts quietly. Gared's as guilty of that as any.

"Proud of her." Gared runs his eyes over Olive and Selen, Arick and Rojvah, at last coming to rest on me, like a sack of potatoes across my back. "Proud of all of 'em."

"That don't—" Elona begins.

"Enough, Grandmum." Olive's voice has deepened again, becoming more resonant and assured. A voice accustomed to obedience. "There will be no punishments for *Captain* Selen when we return to Hollow, because in the absence of Captain Wonda, she will be taking command of the Paper house guard."

Even Elona Paper stops talking at that.

"Ay, it's news to me, too." Selen shifts uncomfortably as everyone turns to regard her.

"We have more important things to discuss." Olive has the floor now, and seems unwilling to yield it. I can hear her giant heart pumping blood, smell her adrenaline. "Has there been any news about Mother?"

There is a long pause, and then the voice of First Minister Arther. "I am afraid not, Highness. Our search parties have returned with empty pockets . . . when they have returned at all. We have identified what we could from the remains of the attack, but there are many still unaccounted for, including Her Grace the duchess, Mrs. Bales, Wonda Cutter, and Kendall Demonsong."

It's not the news anyone wants, but no one smells surprised.

"What about the Warded Children?" I could have kept quiet, kept the attention off me, but I need to know. "How many are left after . . . what happened?"

Warded Children are like family. Mum and I visited them often, and everyone snapped to attention like she was the queen bee. They were the only folk that came close to understanding me.

"Ah . . ." I hear the twinge in Minister Arther's voice, and he don't need to say the rest, but he does. "All of them answered your mother's call, I am afraid. None have returned."

Knew it. Mam was their leader, and they believe killin' demons is the purpose the Creator made for them. 'Course they all wanted to go.

I was the only one that din't. Too scared to argue when Mam told me to stay home.

Now I'm the only one left.

Selen's fingers slide into mine, squeezing to give me something to focus on over the sudden tightness in my chest. She was with me when we came upon that awful scene. How could any have survived that destruction?

"Has the Damajah informed you that my father went to search for them, and has gone missing, as well?" Olive asks.

"Tsst!" Inevera hisses, and that combined with the gasps from the other end of the string is answer enough.

"Either we are all on the same side, or we aren't," Olive says. "I have reason to believe they are alive, in any event."

All eyes turn to Olive. "How's that, girl?" Elona demands from the stone.

"Because I was in Alagai Ka's head," Olive says, to gasps on both sides of the string. "It wasn't for long and I didn't see much, but I know something of his plan."

"This is something you could have enlightened us about earlier," the Damajah notes, as if their secret talk didn't drag on long enough as it was.

"And you could have met us in a sitting room and had a normal conversation," Olive notes in return, "instead of parading me about in front of my siblings, and then bringing us here without warning."

They eye each other, and not for the first time, I'm glad no one ever expects me to do much of the talkin'. Ent good at cuttin' folk with words and dirty looks.

"The history books say my father and Mrs. Bales killed the demon hive queen," Olive says. "But not before she could lay a clutch of hatchling queens. They would have killed our parents and taken over the hive had Arlen Bales not destroyed them. With no queen, the hive could not replenish their numbers. Every demon killed after the purge was one step closer to eradicating them forever."

"So we prayed," Amanvah says.

"But Alagai Ka escaped," Olive goes on. "And somewhere out on the desert, out of range of the Deliverer's purge, was a single mimic."

"Idiot," Inevera whispers, too quiet for anyone to hear. I realize she's talkin' to herself, and my cheeks heat as she looks up suddenly, catching my eye. I can't meet that look, and give my head a shake to drape hair over my eyes.

"The mimic transformed into a queen," Inevera says aloud, perhaps to cover the exchange. "The *mimic who waits below* is a queen."

"Yes," Olive agrees, "and no. The mimic will lay a true queen egg, and soon. The hatchling queen will hunger, and Alagai Ka means for her first repast to be the minds and magic-rich flesh of their vanquished enemies, served live."

"Creator preserve us," I hear Headmistress Darsy breathe.

"Ay, and we're on the menu, too," I say.

Arick steps closer to me. "Only if we falter, cousin."

"When?" Inevera demands. "How much time do we have?"

"I don't know for sure," Olive admits. "The neo-queen has quickened, so it will not be long, but the demon king is patient and careful. I do not think he would have waited until the last minute to set his plans in motion. Months? Perhaps a year?"

"An eyeblink, for an immortal," Inevera says. "And not much time for us."

"Enough, perhaps," Olive says, "if we can work together. The snows will begin by the time I am back in Hollow, but I intend to have an army ready by the time the roads are clear."

"I will begin preparations immediately, Highness," Arther says.

"So Leesha is alive?" Elona asks.

"I don't know for sure if any of them are alive," Olive says. "But I felt the demon's intent, and believe most if not all are held captive."

"In a demon hive," Elona says.

"I never said it was good news," Olive says. "I don't want that information getting out. I expect folk would handle it poorly."

"Ay, that's undersaid," Elona grumbles.

"There is more news that should not leave these chambers," Inevera says. "The Spear of Ala has fallen silent."

The Spear of Ala is one of the great *csars*—walled fortress cities—of Kaji, the first Deliverer. It was the final base from which humanity struck out against the demon hive, three thousand years ago. Stood empty all that time, until my da found it, along with Mam and my bloodfather.

"What do you mean, fallen?" Olive asks. "Who's been living there all this time?"

"The *alamen fae*." Inevera's words send a chill through my spine. Mother used to speak of them. When the demons collapsed the tunnels and cut the fortress off from the surface, the captured inhabitants became livestock for the coreling hive, raised like cattle and shepherded by cave demons.

Expect they were blind at first, there in the deep dark below. But that was three thousand years ago. Can only guess how many generations that is, with nothing to do but eat and rut. A hundred? Two?

Two hundred generations, living and dying in the magic-rich eternal night near the Core. It changed them, like Mam and Da eatin' demon meat changed me.

"Mam says the *alamen fae* ent entirely human anymore," I say. "They been writin' you letters?"

The Damajah raises a brow at me, smelling bemused. "After your mother and bloodfather resettled them in the Spear of Ala, we sent their descendants, the Sharach tribe, to find what humanity remained to them."

"Did Mother know?" Olive asks.

"It is news to me, Highness," Arther says.

"And me," Darsy puts in.

She looks to Inevera, but the Damajah only shrugs. "It is a Krasian *csar,* its inhabitants descended from the same ancestors as our own. We were within our . . ."

". . . rights, ay." Olive smells irritated. "You and Mother both, keeping secrets within secrets. This is why the demons caught us with our bidos down last summer."

Inevera does not reply, so Olive crosses her arms. "And?"

"The youngest *alamen fae* we liberated from the hive can indeed read and write now," Inevera says. "The elders struggle even with speech, but they took to *sharak* as if born to it. Born in darkness, they are strong, like warriors charged with demon magic. Perhaps even stronger than you, Princes Olive, and there is other magic about them. They can scale sheer walls and walk silent and unseen when they wish."

Born in darkness, the words echo the prophecy cast about me before I was ever born, *and he will carry that darkness inside him*. Does it mean something, the Damajah using those same words now?

"Doesn't sound like they'd go down easy in a fight," Selen says.

"Indeed," Inevera nods. "The *csar's* walls are impregnable, patrolled by Sharach warriors and *alamen fae.* The wards of the Spear of Ala are the most powerful in the world, and the gates will only open from the outside for your father."

"But you've lost contact," Olive says.

"Lesser *csars* were built as waystations along the road to the Spear, each with resonance stones to keep the signal strong even across such vast distance," Inevera says. "One by one, they have gone quiet in the months since Alagai Ka set his plans in motion and your father disappeared."

Inevera smells scared at the words, and pained. Whatever her cold façade, she loves her husband, and fears for him.

"Why would the gates only open for Father?" Olive asks.

I know this one from Mam's stories. "The crown."

"Yes," Inevera agrees. "The Crown of Kaji is an artifact from ancient times, made, it is said, at the same time as the Spear of Ala. Its gems are cut from the same stones as those in the heart of the *csar*. Its *hora* cut from the same demons. Shar'Dama Ka could control the *csar* like a thing alive."

"*The father waits below in darkness for his progeny to return*," Olive repeats the prophecy her mother cast for me after the attack on Solstice. The words have repeated in my head for months. I thought they meant my da, Arlen Bales, but maybe they meant my bloodfather, Olive's da, instead. "You think Alagai Ka needs him to open the gates."

"If the demon hive is to live again . . ." Inevera begins.

". . . the Spear of Ala must fall," Olive finishes. "The demons can't have that on their doorstep."

"Impossible," Amanvah says. "The Shar'Dama Ka would never . . ."

"Tsst," Inevera says. "All things are possible for Everam, and for Nie. Ahmann Jardir would not help them willingly, but there might be a way to . . . pervert his magic, or find another capable of activating the crown. Perhaps that is what the demon king meant for Iraven, who was already his creature, and Blood of the Deliverer."

"So the crown is useless, unless worn by an heir of Kaji?" Olive asks.

"Hardly useless," Inevera says. "The crown is powerful. Unworn, its magics are still enough to hold an army of *alagai* at bay. Anyone wearing it would have a portion of those powers, but nothing like those a true heir could unlock."

A true heir like Olive. The words are unsaid, but we're all thinking it.

"I do not know that even Alagai Ka could take the crown from my husband," Inevera says. "After it was knocked from his head in battle, I added a blood lock to the strap. Only the Deliverer himself can remove it, and no demon can draw close, but that he wishes it."

"Reckon they could bury it in a cave-in," I say. "Make sure no one can ever use it."

Inevera nods. "Perhaps, but the crown is all but indestructible. It would remain. I do not think Alagai Ka would leave such a loose end, and it would leave the *csar* as a formidable base at their back."

"Can you ask your dice where the crown is?" Olive asks.

"I have." There is no lie in the Damajah's voice or heartbeat. "The answer does not help. In darkness, they say."

Dice ent ever much help, I think, but I'm smart enough not to say it aloud. In my experience, rippin' things cause as much trouble as they're worth.

"You will need to find your father," Inevera says to Olive. "Free him if he is alive, and take the crown if he is not."

"I need to find my *mother,*" Olive says. "If Father is with her I will free him, too. But take the crown? Why? I have more than forty older brothers, not to mention Prince Kaji. Ay, is there anyone in Krasia who *isn't* descended from Kaji?"

Inevera says nothing, her face serene, but her eyes bore into Olive and I can smell her frustration. She wants it to be Olive. Needs it to be, though she ent offering a hint as to why.

Arick drops to his knees, putting his hands on the floor and touching his forehead between them. "Damajah, it is said Leesha Paper helped nurse me when my own mother could not. If it is Prince Olive's quest to find her, I would, with your permission, offer him my spear and shield."

The Damajah smells bemused. "Your mother and the first of her spear sisters were the nieces of Ahmann Jardir, born of his *dal'ting* sisters. There were those who believed their common blood made them less than his heirs of more royal lines. But your mother Sikvah and her spear sisters earned another name in the *dama'ting* underpalace where they trained. Do you know what it was?"

Arick shakes his head, eyes still on the floor.

"*Sharum* Blood of the Deliverer," Inevera says, and I hear Arick suck in a sharp breath.

Amanvah smells suddenly angry. Dunno what those words mean to her, but it ent anything good. Never been good at readin' auras, but I can see hers cracklin' like a fire and even I know what that means.

"I saw you at Leesha am'Paper's breast, Arick, son of Rojer," Inevera says. "The bonds of milk can hold as tightly as blood, and I will not deny you a *Sharum's* rights in this. You may go north with Prince Olive."

Amanvah's heart is pounding, her breath sharp. I can hear her muscles tightening. Rojvah attempts to take a step forward to join her brother, but Amanvah latches onto her wrist and holds her in place with a sharp "Tsst!"

Inevera doesn't turn, but her ear twitches, and I know she heard. Rojvah smells as angry as her mother now, but when the Damajah does not offer leave to approach, it turns into resignation. She ent going anywhere.

Hard to say if it means Rojvah means too much to them, or Arick too little.

CHAPTER 13

PRINCE KAJI

SELEN'S HAD ENOUGH of everyone when we get back to our suite of rooms. I know the look and leave her be as she heads off to wash her face and fall into the pillows.

It's just as well. I'm in no mood for company. I feel like Darin when he has one of his fits. Too many fears and half-formed plans are running through my head for me to focus. I feel dizzy and sick with them.

I take off my armor and set it on the stand my hosts provided. After I rinse in my own basin I look in the dressing room, stunned at the selection I find. In an abundance of caution, the servants have provided full men's and women's wardrobes—solemn blacks and whites for outside, but also the colorful silks Krasians favor behind closed doors.

Tazhan armor like mine is legendary for its lightness, but even that becomes a weight after hours of standing at court. I choose for comfort, unwrapping the binding at my breasts and slipping into loose, feminine pants and a robe of airy blue silk. I don't need the veil behind closed doors, but I wrap it around my face anyway, enjoying the feel on my skin.

The front receiving room is large, if full of furniture. For all the ways magic separates me from people, there are benefits. I never need help to move a couch. I stack tables and chairs and luxury divans against the wall to clear space.

In *sharaj*, my brothers and I greeted every day with *sharusahk*. Over and over we practiced the *sharukin*—groups of precise movements designed to divert blows, or bring sudden deadly force to bear when applied with speed, power, and will.

After we took the black, Chadan and I continued the practice with our warriors each day. A time to clear our feelings and center our thoughts. To visualize death and failure and embrace them, preparing our souls should we suddenly be called to the lonely path.

But there was no time for *sharusahk* over the desert crossing, and everything has been a bustle since. I move to the center of the room and inhale deeply, moving into Camel Pose, a position of guarded strength that can transition into any number of attacks.

There is a knock at the door.

"Corespawn it," I growl. It is rude to come calling after dark, but it might well be one of my brothers come to kill me, so it seems petty to tsst over propriety. Part of me would welcome the challenge, if only to force my thoughts back into the now.

I open the door to find Prince Kaji waiting patiently. Even Faseek knew better than to hinder him. Kaji's eyes widen at the sight of me, and he immediately averts his gaze. "Apologies, I did not mean . . ."

I glance down, confused, and see the feminine blue silks I chose. Here in Krasia, dressed like this, I am an unchaperoned woman, and he a lone man.

"Not two hours ago you were sitting on the Skull Throne," I snap. "Now you're shy?"

Kaji gives a shallow bow, still refusing to look at me. "You looked different at court."

"The rules don't apply to family," I say. "Your father's my half brother, ay? That makes you my nephew. Pick your eyes up off the floor and come in."

"Half nephew," Kaji agrees, "and a cousin on my mother's side." Still, he lifts his eyes and comes in, closing the door behind him. He glances at the piled furniture and immediately grasps the reason. "Forgive me, I did not mean to interrupt your *sharusahk*. I can go."

"It's nothing," I lie. "I had yet to begin."

"Nothing?" Kaji strides to the center of the room, taking a Camel

Pose of his own. "*Sharusahk* is the union of body and mind. If there is a truer way to speak to Everam, I do not know it."

I move to face him, returning to the pose. "Show me."

He does, beginning slowly at first, with *sharukin* any novice should know. His poses are perfect, like a sculptor's masterpiece. He reminds me of Prince Chadan—seventeen, but with a body matured by magic and training, eyes full of wisdom. He is serene, but there is a steely competence about him.

The difficulty of his poses increases, but I match him move for move, even when he begins *sharukin* unfamiliar to me.

"There is more than blood that binds us," Kaji says as we flow from one move to the next. "Not many others can claim to have forced a mind demon out of their head."

"What?" I feel a twinge of fear at the words, wondering if my nephew is about to attack me, but he only continues to increase the difficulty of his *sharukin*.

"I was barely past my first born day," Kaji says. "I don't remember more than a blur of events before and since, but I remember the dark of the cavern. Too dark to see. There was a voice in my head, commanding me to hurt myself if my mother did not surrender."

"What did you do?" Still Kaji's poses grow more difficult. I've begun to sweat in my fine silks, and welcome the focus in my straining muscles.

"I told it no," he says, "and in that moment of distraction, my mother killed it."

That much I knew. Kaji's mother, Ashia, is a legend, but this part is new, kept from the histories. It is a sign of great trust that Kaji is telling me now. "Your will must be formidable."

"Perhaps," Kaji says. "Or perhaps it was just my child's mind, protected by innocence. It is nothing like your great deed, casting out Alagai Ka himself."

"Perhaps." I grit my teeth. "But like your encounter, doubts remain."

Kaji nods. "At first it felt like Everam's will, and I believed I was destined for even greater glories. Now I fear my Great Purpose was fulfilled when I was too young to understand what was happening."

I laugh. "You sit the Skull Throne. That is not glory enough?"

Kaji begins another *sharukin,* and the first pose stretches muscles I am not sure I have ever used before. "I sit the throne to keep my uncles from fighting over it, but I am only a mouthpiece for Grandmother while we await the Shar'Dama Ka's return."

"You think he will return?" Another pose that stretches me to my limits as Kaji bends like a taut Angierian longbow.

"The Deliverer disappeared once before," Kaji notes, "when he took battle to the abyss itself. I hold faith he will return, and will hold the Skull Throne from all challengers until he reclaims it."

As if to prove it, his next pose threatens to best me. I have to struggle to hold it without shaking. "And if he does not?"

Kaji's mouth becomes a tight line. "*Dama'ting* magic guards against the years like a shield against talons. The Damajah will still look a woman of thirty when my back is stooped and my beard long and gray. I will never rule Krasia in truth."

The words give me strength to hold the pose, and the next. "People who want to control you will always remind you of the power you don't have, in hope you will forget about the power you do."

"That is sound advice." Kaji slides into another pose, and at last, I begin to shake. "May I offer some in return?"

"Of course." My words are bitten off as my muscles twitch and strain.

Kaji continues to effortlessly hold the pose. "Do not underestimate your royal brothers. They resent you, and your mother, and fear you will attempt to skip ahead in the succession. You have given them invitation to kill you, and I do not doubt some are already laying plans to do just that."

He does not flow to another pose, standing like a statue on the toes of one foot, other limbs extended. His eyes meet mine, and no doubt he sees what we both know.

I cannot hold much longer.

"With me on the throne, the position of crown prince is open," Kaji says, never breaking eye contact. "By rights it will go to Prince Hoshkamin, the Sharum Ka, but Hoshkamin is *Sharum* to his core and cannot rule an empire at peace. Until I wed and produce an heir, the succession is in doubt."

My toes can no longer hold me, and I drop to the ball of my foot. My leg is shaking visibly now. Kaji sweeps into a kick, flicking a foot to simply tap my center, and it's enough to send me tumbling to the floor.

I roll quickly into Coiled Asp, another *sharukin* that puts me in position for a violent attack. Kaji does not pursue, returning to the pose I failed and holding it.

"There is more to fighting than *sharusahk*, cousin," I growl.

Kaji regards me coolly, refusing to return the aggression. "Capacity for violence is as important as training," he says, quoting from the battle wisdom of Kaji. "In battle against the *alagai*, we must find the savage within. Believe me now when I tell you all the sons of Ahmann can be savage, when they wish."

I nod. "I have stood in the Maze of Desert Spear. Savagery, I understand."

Kaji flows out of the pose and gives me a warrior's bow. "Grandfather often hoped aloud that you and I would marry one day."

I resist the urge to show visible disgust. Kaji is handsome, but . . . "You're my nephew on your father's side, and my second cousin on your mother's."

"Half nephew," Kaji notes again. "Thinner blood ties than my parents, who were first cousins."

"Royals in the North are known to intermarry as well," I say, "but if I should marry one day, it will be for love, not politics or a favorable bloodline."

"You will be lucky to have such liberty," Kaji says. "When I see my eighteenth born day, the Damajah will inform me who I am to wed."

"No one can make you take a vow you do not wish," I say.

Kaji shrugs. "I have already taken a vow, to do what is best for Krasia. I will find a way to love whomever she chooses, and be a true husband. The one to sit the Skull Throne can do no less."

"That is an impossible standard," I say. "How can you swear love and loyalty to someone you've never met? We are mortal. We make mistakes."

"I am mortal," Kaji acknowledges. "I am not the Deliverer. I will make mistakes. But they will not be things I know to avoid."

"Like choosing your own bride?" I ask. "What point is there to sitting the Skull Throne if you cannot control even that?"

"It was no different for Grandfather," Kaji says. "Ahmann Jardir was seventeen, as I am, when the Damajah informed him they were to wed. In the years that followed, she chose all fourteen of his *Jiwah Sen*."

"Except my mother," I say. "The Damajah hated Leesha Paper and forbid Father to marry her, but he made his own choice. Was it a mistake?"

"Everam wills as Everam will," Kaji says. "Should the Creator send me such passion that I am helpless to resist, then it will be so. But I have never felt its like, so why not trust in the Damajah, who saved us in our thousands during Sharak Ka?"

"You speak of Sharak Ka as if it is over," I say. "I think perhaps it has only just begun."

Kaji nods solemnly. "Perhaps. But Everam would not have chosen for us to live in such times of burden, if He did not think us capable of carrying it."

CHAPTER 14

HARMONY

Even a private meeting with the Damajah ent enough to quiet the chatter as I pass through the halls.

"Born in Nie's abyss."

"Sunlight burns his skin."

"*Alagai* blood."

Bad enough if it was just the servants, but it's royals, too, and the army of female clerks who make the palace run. All of them full of gossip about the Par'chin's half-demon son and the "corruption" he brings to these sacred halls. Reckon I could make any of them jump out of their skin with a sudden turn and a shout of *Boo!*

Arick's mood ent much better than mine. You'd think the Damajah's blessing would have pulled his thoughts from the bog, but he's back to sulking the moment we're in our rooms. I can tell it's about to get worse, because I can hear Amanvah and Ashia arguing down the hall.

"This is your influence," Amanvah hisses at her cousin.

"It is his blood," Ashia says. "The Damajah herself named it."

"And what of his father's blood?" Amanvah demands. "My blessed husband, shamed, because you chose to teach him the spear when I forbade it."

"If not me, he would have found some sympathetic *dal'Sharum*," Ashia insists. "It did not interfere with his Jongleur training."

"How can you say that, when he has abandoned his kamanj?!" Amanvah practically shrieks the words. I glance at Arick, but he's still oblivious. They're too far off for him to hear.

"I'll do it myself," Amanvah insists.

"No," Ashia says. "You will only drive him further away."

"He is my son," Amanvah growls, "not yours!"

"He is Sikvah's son," Ashia growls right back, and hers is scarier. "You did not want to admit that she, or I, were *Sharum* Blood of the Deliverer either, cousin. Do you need me to remind you how that went?"

Even down the hall, I can hear Amanvah's heart racing. She's scared of Ashia. "Don't you dare threaten me. The Damajah . . ."

"Named him *Sharum* Blood," Ashia says. "He won't listen to you, but perhaps he will listen to me."

Amanvah doesn't answer, but I hear her hand something over, and she walks away while Ashia approaches.

"Reckon I could use a nap." I'm halfway across the common before Arick can grunt his indifference.

I'm in my pillow chamber before Ashia knocks, letting myself go slippery silent. I should go farther—give them real privacy. Ent my business, what Ashia's got to say. But I can't help but feel protective of Arick. Know he'd stick around, someone came by to bully me.

Not that I can do much. Ashia scares me, too. Still, the walls in Arick's suite are thin, and I can hear like I'm right next to them. Even if I can't help in the moment, maybe there's somethin' I can do after she leaves.

"Enter!" Arick calls when Ashia knocks, too morose to even get up.

"Bloodson." I hear Arick scramble to his feet at the word.

"Sharum'ting Ka." His silk-covered knees hit the floor, followed by his hands.

"Your mother and I shared blood, Arick asu Sikvah," Ashia says, "and shed it together. Duchess Paper was not the only one who fed you from her own breast, after Sikvah was felled in glory with you in her belly. You may wear the black, but you need never kneel to me."

"You honor me." Silk scrapes the floor as he rolls back onto his feet.

"But you are leaving the lands of your mother," Ashia says, "to visit the homeland of your father. I would speak with you before you go."

"I have no doubt I will be as much a disappointment to the greenlanders as I am in the palaces of Krasia."

Ashia makes the dry spitting sound Krasian women favor when they are angry. "Self-pity does not befit your *Sharum* blood, boy. You have never disappointed anyone."

"Tell that to my stepmother," Arick says.

I hear Ashia move close to him. "You do not have your father's body, son of Rojer, but you have his face, his eyes and hair. No doubt that is what Amanvah sees when she looks at you. She was not married long, but she loved Rojer asu Jessum with a passion few wives ever know. She wants you to honor him, and does not understand why you do not wish it, as well."

"Because I have no wish to be a Jongleur." There is derision in Arick's voice. "To dress in the colors of a child, and dance to entertain *khaffit*. I wish to kill *alagai,* not make music for them."

"If you knock an *alagai* down for another warrior to spear, the kill is shared," Ashia says. "Your father's music did the same. He may not have wielded the spear, but he shared countless kills in the war, and brought joy when the battle was over. He is beloved in the green lands, and like her sister-wife, your mother Sikvah loved him fiercely. If he was worthy of her love, then he is worthy of yours."

"What if I am the one who is not worthy?" Arick asks.

Ashia lets out a breath, moving so close to him their hearts seem to beat together. "Something happened to you out on the sands," she whispers. "Something so painful you fear to give it voice, lest it consume you. But who can you trust, if not me, my bloodson? Did I not teach you the spear in secret, when your stepmother forbade?"

"Some secrets burn all who hear of them," Arick says.

Ashia laughs, though it is not a cruel sound. "You are all I have left of beloved Sikvah. You are bound to me by milk and blood and the spear. Your burdens are my burdens."

Arick chokes. I can hear him start weeping, and I feel bad for eavesdropping. Don't reckon I'd like it much if our positions were reversed.

I hear the little stopper pulled from a tear bottle, and the gentle scrape as Ashia collects the drops. "Tell me, my bloodson."

"Alagai Ka took me, in the darkness." Arick's words are low, garbled by sniffles and spit.

"He took nearly everyone, it is said." There is caution in Ashia's voice. She senses there is more to it.

"Indeed," Arick agrees. "He took our wards, and marched the others like puppets, and made them fight for him. But me . . ."

There's a pause as Arick collects himself, and I find I am holding my breath, wondering if he will have the courage to tell her. Ashia, for her part, gives time and space for him to steel himself.

"What the Father of Lies did to me was more insidious," Arick says at last. "There are gaps in my memory even now, and other times I thought I was in control, even as I did his bidding. The wards around my mind were restored when I betrayed my friends to him. I held blessed *sharik hora* in my hand, even as I threw the son of Par'chin from a ledge into the demon's den. There was a victory of sorts in the confrontation that followed, but the glory was not mine."

The words hang in the air for a long time before Ashia replies. I hear the sound of skin on skin, and know she is touching him, offering what comfort she can.

"I understand," Ashia says. "One of his princelings did the same to Kaji, when he was barely past his first born day."

"Below the Monastery of Dawn?" Arick asks. The story of Ashia's defeat of the mind demon is a legend of the war, but I've never heard this part.

"I have never admitted that to anyone, son of my heart," Ashia says, "and I will have your word you will not, either."

I squirm, knowing I've no business listening to Ashia's secrets, but there's nothing for it, now.

"On my honor and hope of Heaven, I swear it," Arick says. "What did you do?"

"What could I do?" Ashia asks. "Kaji is my son. I killed the mind, and put my faith in him, just as I do with you, Arick asu Rojer. There is ever only one path open to us in life. Forward."

"What if I am broken?" Arick asks. "What if this is a wound that cannot heal?"

"That, too, is the burden of *Sharum*," Ashia tells him. "All of us carry scars. Pains that linger long after the wounds have closed. All we can do is find a new goal, point ourselves at it, and put one foot in front of the other."

Arick sniffs hard to clear his voice. "I will . . . Bloodmother."

"I have no doubt," Ashia says. "I have brought you gifts, to help you on your path. Your mother's spear and shield, made of warded glass, laced with electrum. Stronger and lighter than steel, they will not fail you in the night."

Arick gasps in awe. *Sharum'ting* spears are bladed on both ends, and I can hear the blades slicing the air as he spins the weapon. There is a creak and a click as he detaches the center, and a new rush of air as he thrusts with the two short stabbing spears.

"I will honor them."

"You will," Ashia agrees, "as you will this."

There is a sound as she takes something from a silk bag, strings brushing against the cloth with a resonance I recognize immediately.

A kamanj.

Arick's heart beats faster, and there is annoyance in his tone when he speaks. "Did Stepmother put you up to this?"

"Amanvah may be *Damaji'ting,* but she can put me up to nothing, if I do not wish it," Ashia says. "I bring you this because when we worked the magic of your father out on the sands, your absence from our spell-song pained me. Sikvah's music did more than her spear to turn the tide in the demon war. I was but a shadow of her skill, but I would not have survived without it. A true warrior seeks every advantage, my bloodson. It does not shame a warrior to have powers beyond the spear."

"Perhaps," Arick's voice is morose again, "but I lack the talent of my parents, or even my sister."

"Nonsense," Ashia scoffs. "Too often we confuse talent and skill. Talent is ephemeral. It cannot be quantified, created, or destroyed. It is a gift from Everam. Skill is measurable, and accessible to all with dedication. Talent untrained will always fall to skill, for it is only when you master a skill that you have opportunity to understand yourself better and grow beyond it. You are a different man than you were when you left, Arick asu Rojer. The music can put you in touch with that."

"It can?" There is sudden hope in Arick's voice.

"Play for me, and I will sing," Ashia says. "Perhaps we can find something of what you lost, or something you did not know you had."

Arick blows out a breath, but he complies, and in moments his kamanj strings hum to life, filling the chambers with sound.

Arick is more skilled than I'll ever be, having held a bow from the moment he could close his fingers around one. His music is precise—perfect, like the steady beat of his fingers in the throne room. Ashia's voice, pure and high, rises to weave around his kamanj.

My hands twitch, aching to take out my pipes and join them, but I dare not reveal I have been listening. Instead I shove them in my pockets and close my eyes, letting myself drift on the sounds as Arick and Ashia find harmony.

I don't know how long it goes on, but I don't want it to end when the sounds finally die down. Even when I'm not part of the music, I can find peace in it.

"How do you feel?" Ashia asks.

"Different," Arick admits. "There is disharmony in me. The demon changed things. I can sense it, but I cannot say how. Even now, Alagai Ka's commands may be sleeping within me, waiting for him to put bow to my strings."

"Perhaps," Ashia says. "Nie will always try to turn us from Everam's path. But now that you sense the disharmony, you can explore it, learn it, and find a way to bring your spirit back in tune. The music can help you, if you let it."

I hear the press of her lips against his forehead, and the soft pop of the kiss. Then footsteps, and a closing door.

"I assume you heard all that," Arick says.

I feel my face heat, but I don't try to deny it, coming back into the common to join him. "Ay."

Arick lifts his new kamanj, a masterwork of craftmanship, worked with wards of resonance much like my pipes. "Perhaps you will help me then, as I try to find myself."

He dun't have to ask twice. I've got my pipes out in a moment, sitting beside him. He starts to play again, the *Song of Waning*. I play along, but unlike with Ashia, we struggle to find harmony.

Arick breaks off after a time, his bow screeching off the strings. "You keep changing the song. Can't you play it as it was written?"

I shrug. "Learned to play on my own, out in Tibbet's Brook. Cut my own reeds and taught myself to mimic what other folk were playing. Only took lessons when Mam decided my hobby might be a calling, and asked Master Roller to come teach me to read notes on paper. Always hated that. Sheet music's more a guide than a rule. I like to experiment, shaping the music to suit the mood. Don't think I've ever played a piece exactly the same way twice."

"I would have been beaten for such insolence," Arick says. "It is said Everam spoke to my father when he penned notes of the *Song of Waning.*"

"Ay, maybe." I don't much believe in the Creator, but I know better than to argue with folk who do. "Don't you ever get bored, just playing exactly what's on the page?"

"The page is how it was meant to be played," Arick argues.

I frown. "What about when you're fighting?"

"What do you mean?" Arick asks.

"See you practicing the *sharukin,*" I say. "Precise steps and moves. But when you fight for real, it ent precise like that."

"There is a difference," Arick speaks like I am a fool, "between fighting air on a smooth floor, and fighting *alagai* in the sands. The key to survival is adapting to the battlefield, and your opponent."

"Ay, and music's the same," I argue. "Master Roller knew your da, and said he changed things up all the time. Rojvah does, too."

I hear the bow creak in Arick's clenched hand, and worry I am pushing him too far. "Rojvah has talent," he says after a time. "Perhaps you have it, too. All I have is skill."

Don't know what to say to that. What even is talent? Ashia said it herself. Can't measure it. Can't even prove it exists. Arick thinkin' he's somehow less than us is stupid on its face, but if I tell him that, know he won't believe me.

"When the three of us played together, it was different," I say, remembering those nights. The power of our musical trio. "You felt it, too."

"Perhaps, but Rojvah will not be coming north with us," Arick says.

He's right. And we're not just going to Hollow. We're going to Safehold, where Alagai Ka has his secret lair. Together, the three of us might be able to cloak our approach with music, but without Rojvah, I don't much like our chances.

CHAPTER 15

ENEMIES AT TEA

Days pass in the palace without much event. Invitations come to visit my brothers in various parts of the city, but I remember Kaji's words, and view them skeptically. Here on royal grounds the Damajah's peace holds sway, but if I step outside her protection, who is to say what my brothers will do to eliminate a rival?

Part of me longs to tour my father's capital city, to meet my family, and compare modern Krasia with my experience in the ancient city of Desert Spear and the conservative Majah tribe. To rise to any challenges my brothers wish to bring.

But I have more important goals. To return home and take power, to find my mother and the others lost in the demon massacre, to stop Alagai Ka. This is not the time to indulge my personal pride and desires.

Instead Selen and I enjoy the luxuries of our chambers and the palace gardens. We try our best to ignore the stares, some half hidden and some bold as a predator, as we pass through the halls and garden paths. Hollow and Majah bodyguards trail us whenever we leave our chambers, far enough to give privacy to our conversation, but close enough to leap to our defense if we are threatened.

Darin checks in from time to time, but he is no more at ease than I am, and mostly keeps to himself. No one has seen Rojvah since our meeting with the Damajah.

General Cutter surprises me, more comfortable than any of us in the palace, despite his minimal grasp of the language and culture. Gared Cutter's reputation as a warrior is well known in Krasia, it seems, and friendly challenges abound. It would be unseemly for him to fight his hosts, but Gared is happy to compete in tests of strength, something he is known for in the North, as well.

There is something hopeful in seeing the games that arise between Gared's Cutters and the *Sharum*. The roars of laughter as they pull ropes against one another, or test their marksmanship.

If only the path to peace were so simple.

"Ay, Olive!" the general calls, waving me over to where he sits facing a line of *Sharum* attempting to best him at arm wrestling.

Abban is there, taking bets. "Would you care to place a wager, Highness?"

"Against General Gared?" I laugh. "I've seen this at Solstice Festivals my whole life, and no one has ever bested him."

"Of course, that would not be a fair wager," Abban agrees. "Instead we are betting on how many victories he can take in a row. Even the greatest warrior tires, with time."

"Still not a bet I wish to place," I say. "I am content to watch."

Ashia appears, heading toward me. Faseek moves to interpose himself, but I wave him back. Offering the Sharum'ting Ka a warrior's salute she returns in kind.

"The Damajah requests your presence for tea in the women's wing, Highness. Expect Belina and Linavah in attendance."

It's an unusual request, for a Prince of Krasia to be invited into the Damajah's gendered wing of the palace, but it seems she took seriously my claim to be a sister to the *dama'ting*. I look down at my armor. "I'll need to change."

"Of course, Highness," Ashia says.

Soon after, I am escorted into the Damajah's domain once more, feeling light and vulnerable without my armor, or the binding I usually wear to flatten my breasts' curve. My robes are fine black silk, loose and flowing, more akin to a woman's cut than a man's, especially with Mother's blue cloak around my shoulders. There is little I can do for my short-cropped hair, so I keep the hood up, giving the appearance of a woman's headscarf.

I've changed the powders on my face from the hard appearance I cultivated in the Maze. I couldn't grow a beard if I wanted to, but a little dark powder along my jaw went a long way to blend in with the other young warriors in the Princes Unit. I'm surprised at how much of a change comes just by removing it.

From there I need only a little kohl around my eyes and a few accents to soften my cheekbones and darken my lips. Micha taught me the Krasian powder kit before I'd even learned to read, and as always, my sister's teachings serve me well.

But my appearance is the least of my worries. I am going to sit with three powerful seers, all of whom have likely cast the dice for what to expect from the meeting. I have only my own guesses.

Gorvan, Faseek, and General Gared are allowed farther than I expect, but kept outside the Damajah's tearoom. An inner room of the palace, I know already it will have no natural light, allowing the witches access to their magic, while I will have little more than my wits, my strength, and the *hanzhar* at my belt.

"Don't like you goin' in there alone," Gared says.

"If the Damajah wants me dead, there are better ways to go about it than poisoning my tea with Hollow's general standing outside the door," I say, trying to reassure myself as much as him.

Inside, Inevera is already kneeling before a low table surrounded by pillows. The Damajah wears no scarf or veil, her long, flowing black hair oiled and bound with gold, face painted and almost ethereal in its elegance. The stories claiming her beauty was unmatched by any save Mother's may be hyperbolic, but if there are more portrait-perfect women in the world, I've yet to meet them.

On the table, a silver tea service is polished and steaming. Off to the side of the room, Belina and Linavah stand beside each other against one wall, no doubt waiting on my arrival. Belina's headscarf is white, but her veil is once again black.

"Princes Olive, welcome." The Damajah extends a hand to indicate pride of place, facing her across the table. "Please join me."

I kneel on the pillow provided. "By what right do you restore Belina to the black scarf the Majah stripped her of in shame?" Belina shifts uncomfortably. In part from my comment, but no doubt also from being made to wait for her place at the table. By seating me first, Inevera is sending a clear message about the hierarchy of power in the room.

"A better question is, By what right did the Majah take it from her," Inevera replies. "Whatever Chavis and Aleveran may wish, *Damaji'ting* are not called like *Damaji,* by blood or primitive combat. They are called by the dice, alone."

"Perhaps," I allow, "but a leader supported by the dice alone cannot remain in power, as Belina has shown." Linavah sniffs at that, earning a sharp glare from her mother, but Inevera only smiles.

"When another is needed, the dice will call her," Inevera says.

"As they presumably called Chavis," I note. "But you and Father forced her to abdicate before her natural death so Belina could take the black headscarf. Was that, too, in defiance of the dice?"

Inevera isn't smiling anymore. "Your father should have killed Aleveran's father honorably when Damaji Aleverak challenged his claim to the Skull Throne. He chose mercy, and paid a heavy price for it."

"So *primitive* combat has its place," I note.

"All things have their place, in Everam's great plan." Amusement has left the Damajah's eyes, as well. I am pushing the bounds of civility, but the point needed to be made. "The fact remains, Chavis had no right to take the scarf from my *Jiwah Sen.*"

"*Jiwah Sen?*" I ask. It means "sister-wife" in Krasian. "Rojvah proclaimed to Aleveran's court that you had divorced Belina."

"She proclaimed I *would.*" Inevera shrugs. "Rojvah spoke with authority at the time. Had Belina remained behind in Desert Spear, I would indeed have divorced her after learning what transpired. But instead, you returned my wayward sister-wife to me, and we have . . . resolved our differences. Sharak Ka is coming, and we must seize every advantage."

Linavah comes to the table, bowing as she takes up the teapot and serves first Inevera, then me, with a practiced pour. Tea politics were something Mother instilled upon me early. She bows again and steps back, and we both drink.

"Belina." Inevera gestures to her right, and Belina is quick to kneel at the table, removing her veil and headscarf. Like Inevera, her hair is immaculate, and she, too, is painted, powdered, and beautiful, with the ageless quality of a worker of *hora* magic.

Linavah's eyes are unreadable as she pours for her mother. Only then does Inevera gesture to her left. "Linavah." The priestess pours for herself, then wordlessly kneels and removes her own veil. She looks a more natural thirty, but it is strange, seeing her round face next to her mother's. They could be sisters, not mother and daughter.

"Are you enjoying your stay in Krasia?" Inevera asks. I know it is politeness, but the question grates on me.

"Respectfully, Damajah, I am not on holiday," I remind her, "and hardly free to walk the streets and see the sights."

"Indeed." Belina sips her tea. "Challenging one's brothers to open combat can curb one's liberty."

I turn to her, my patience eroding. "You wish to speak to me of lost liberty?" I see she still wears the armlet, and I lift the miniature version that controls it. "Shall I remind you what that truly means, as you so often reminded me?"

Belina stiffens, and Linavah's eyes tighten in what could be a suppressed smile.

"I have not forgiven our blood debt," I tell her. "I don't know what you and Inevera have schemed together, but I have yet to agree, and even if I do, I may yet ask for that arm in return."

Belina pales visibly at that, and I keep eye contact, letting her know I am not joking.

"Enough," Inevera says. "I had hoped for a civil discussion, but it appears there is too much *Sharum* in you, Princes, and too much asp in my Majah *Jiwah Sen*. So let us dispense with the pleasantries and move to business." She raises her scarf over her hair, and slips the translucent veil back over her face. The other women do the same.

Inevera claps her hands, and the doors to the tearoom open, admitting my bodyguards, though their weapons have been checked at the door. Gared, Faseek, and Gorvan shift uncomfortably in this women's space, but their presence is telling. It means three unarmed men are about to enter from the Damajah's side of the room.

Indeed, as soon as my men are settled, another set of doors open, admitting Ashia and a pair of *Sharum'ting*. They escort a group of three

Krasian Watchers, all bound wrist and ankle. They are without veil or turban, looking thin and haggard, but I recognize the lead warrior immediately.

"Kai Tomoka." The name comes out in a growl. I clench my fist. These are the Nanji warriors that broke into Mother's keep in Hollow and beat me and Micha senseless, stealing us away in the night.

Suddenly I regret not coming in armor. My heart is pounding in my chest as I feel a rush of adrenaline. Instinctively, my hand drifts to the *hanzhar* at my belt.

"Tsst." The Damajah's warning hiss is low but unmistakable. "We are not here for that. At least, not yet."

"Then why are we here, Inevera?" I have not been offered permission to use the Damajah's given name, but my patience is at an end. "I tire of games."

Tomoka drops to his knees, hands on the floor as wide as his manacles will allow as he presses his forehead between them. The other two mirror him, all three making obeisance to me.

"Prince Olive, Highness. I beg your forgiveness. We came to your home thinking you a helpless princess. Instead, we found a worthy warrior, but still, we did not truly understand. Everything about what happened was unworthy of us."

"That was you?!" Gared roars, and without turning, I hold up a closed fist, telling him to wait. A soldier to his core, he responds on instinct, but I feel his tension at my back.

"If your general cannot be silent when his betters are speaking," Belina sniffs, "perhaps he should wait—"

I reach into my *hora* pouch, squeezing the miniature armlet, and Belina's words are cut off with a howl. She drops to the floor, clutching her arm as the blood-locked armlet constricts until it must feel it will take off her arm. I know the pain well, and have half a mind to do just that, but my point is made.

I let go, and Belina lies there gasping, desperately trying to regain her vaunted *dama'ting* calm. "If you cannot be silent when your betters are talking, Belina, perhaps *you* should be the one to wait outside."

Belina's eyes bore into me with hatred and impotent rage, and I meet them hard.

"Breathe, sister." Inevera's voice is calm, unperturbed by the display. "Pain is only wind. Return to your seat and be silent."

I grasp my *hanzhar* by the sheath, pointedly removing it from my belt and setting it on the table before me in easy reach. "You are right, Damajah. There is *Sharum* in me. I am not the helpless Princess Olive those men assaulted, and I am not my mother, with her Gatherer's Oath. Do not mistake that."

Inevera nods. "We understand each other, Princes."

Slowly, so as not to provoke the armed and armored *Sharum'ting* bodyguard at her back, I take the knife by the sheath and roll back onto my ankles, getting to my feet. Kneeling with those men in the room was intolerable, and they will not catch me unarmed again.

No one will.

I stand over Tomoka as a man should over a vanquished enemy who might yet have teeth. "Why should I accept the apology of an honorless dog? Should it matter if you thought me man or woman? Perhaps such distinctions mean something to a backward savage, but they are spit and wind to me. You came into my home in the night, when all humanity should be united, and attacked unarmed women. Is that Nanji honor?"

Tomoka raises his head slightly, if only to pointedly put it down on the floor once more. "You are correct, my prince. I have no excuse, save following orders."

My grip tightens on the silver sheath of my *hanzhar,* and I feel the soft metal shape itself to my hand. "A man of honor does not follow orders to commit a crime against Evejan law."

Inevera sniffs at that, drawing my eyes back to her. Belina has recovered her seat and is massaging her arm. There are tears in her eyes, and I am ashamed that I enjoy the sight of them.

Inevera looks at Faseek. "You. *Sharum.* If your *kai* commanded you to steal a well in the night, would you ask who it belonged to, or why he wanted to steal it?"

Like Tomoka, Faseek drops to his knees and puts his hands on the floor when the Damajah addresses him. "If Princes Olive commanded me to put out the sun, Damajah, I would trust he had good reason, and do it if I could."

"Indeed," Inevera says.

The lesson is not lost on me. This is the loyalty of the Maze, the trust of spear brothers. When Faseek saw me break Drillmaster Chikga's neck, he didn't ask questions. He helped me hide the body. I do not doubt Uncle Gared would do the same. Or Selen. Or Darin.

Wouldn't I?

"The Watcher tribes have a different code," Inevera says. "Kaji the First Deliverer created the Krevakh and Nanji three thousand years ago to serve his eldest sons Kaji and Majah. The Watchers were secret warriors, skilled in stealth, infiltration, and the gathering of information. Their very purpose was to handle tasks that were beneath—or that would sully the honor of—the eldest sons of Kaji. It is the honor of Watchers to have no honor, save in service to their masters."

The Damajah gets to her feet, moving to stand before me. I can see flashes of rippling muscle in the flow of her loose silk robes. There is a *hanzhar* at her belt, inches from her hand. "I myself sent a pair of Krevakh Watchers to kidnap your mother in the night, when I first learned she had lain with my husband."

She holds my gaze, daring me to act, and it is not the bravado of a drunk *Sharum* in the harem. It is cold. An invitation, and a warning.

When I do not respond, she nods and returns to her tea, like Mother when I have passed one of her hidden tests. I look down, seeing I have crushed the delicately warded silver of my *hanzhar's* sheath. I hook it back onto my belt and let out a deep breath, looking down at Kai Tomoka and wondering how I can save face.

"I have not forgiven the debt you and your spear brothers owe to me, Kai," I say at last. "But I apologize for insulting your honor."

Again the men lift their heads just enough to put them back down, acknowledging acceptance of the apology. I go back to the table and kneel with the other women.

"Linavah," Inevera says. "Princes Olive's tea has gone cold." Linavah pours me a fresh cup, and the Damajah waits patiently for me to lift it and take a sip.

"Let us begin again," Inevera says. "You are here with Belina and these men because their fates are bound to each other, and to you. My sister-wife and I have found a solution to our Majah problem."

I was slow, but I've guessed it by now. "You will send them the Nanji."

"Like Belina's black scarf, it appears Nanji loyalty is not a thing that can simply be taken away by a *Damaji's* edict," Inevera says. "The Majah will not accept other warriors, but they will accept the Nanji. So we will allow them to rejoin their Majah masters and defend the Holy City from the *alagai*."

A hint of smile behind her translucent veil. "But years of peace and prosperity in Everam's Bounty have strengthened the Nanji. They have grown numerous, even as Majah numbers have dwindled, and they are wealthy, with extensive ties in the green lands. They fought with great honor in Sharak Ka, and have the respect of other tribes that the Majah lack. For fifteen years, they have been their own masters, and Aleveran will find he has no choice but to share power. Perhaps they can pull their wayward cousins back into the modern world."

"Or the Majah will make fanatics of the Nanji, as well," Linavah says.

"If that is Everam's will." The Damajah's voice is patient, though Linavah was not invited to speak.

"I will require Belina as an ambassador to facilitate this." Inevera nods to her sister-wife.

At last, Belina has learned to drop her eyes when she speaks to me. "The house of Jardir has followers among the Majah even now. Relations Iraven and I kept alive all these years, waiting to rejoin New Krasia. But my connection to those supporters was broken by Iraven's death. Only a new blood tie can reestablish it."

I feel my teeth grinding, and unclench my jaw. The last time the Majah needed a blood tie, they kidnapped me with the intention of forcing me to marry Aleveran's grandson.

"The dice say it is favorable for Linavah to marry Aleveran's son Dama Maroch," Inevera says, "and provide a son to replace Prince Chadan."

My jaw clenches again. "No one can replace Chadan."

Inevera offers me a bow of sympathy. "Indeed. I meant no offense. But the fact remains, Maroch is without an heir, and his *Jiwah Ka* too old to attempt another. Linavah can once again bind your father's blood to Majah."

I turn to regard Linavah. "No matter what her wishes?"

Linavah meets my eyes, bolder than her mother. "Do not mistake me, sister. If by living among savages I can bring unity to Krasia once more, then I do it without reservation."

Again, I am humbled. I thought I understood Krasian ways after months of immersion in Desert Spear, but it appears there is still much to learn. "Apologies, sister."

"You told me you wanted the Majah protected from the *alagai*," Inevera says. "And that you did not wish to carry a blood debt."

"I do not know that I have a choice," I say. "A blood debt is not a balance in a ledger, to erase with a handful of draki."

"Only Everam's forgiveness is infinite," Inevera says. "I ask only that you relinquish your claim on their lives, so they may serve a greater purpose."

She's right. Is forgiveness too high a price to protect the Holy City and broker peace in a conflict that has gone on since before I was born?

Mother would not have thought so. *Whenever forgiveness* can *be the answer,* she would say, *forgiveness* should *be the answer.*

Inevera knows she has me. "With their families and thralls, the Nanji will restore Desert Spear, and—"

"No," I cut in.

"Eh?" I can tell Inevera isn't used to interruption, and I do not want to lock stares with her again, but some things are worth a fight. Belina looks at me as if I am mad. Indeed, is this not everything I want? The innocent protected, and my enemies' power weakened?

"No thralls," I clarify. "The Nanji will take no greenlanders with them on their return to the desert. And the carts that bring them will return with any Majah 'thralls' who wish to return to the green lands. Those will be given lands and restitution to start anew in Everam's Bounty."

Inevera raises an eyebrow, but she sits back on her heels, a hint of smile beneath her veil now that the haggling has begun. "Why should I pay restitution for Majah thralls? I did not take them into the desert."

"Because you stole their land in the first place," I retort. It's the kind of impolitc language Mother taught me never to use, but I will not equivocate here. "And the Majah took them from Everam's Bounty while you sat the throne and did nothing. Even now, you speak of doing it again, letting the Nanji take the conquered Rizonans in their lands away with them like cattle. No."

"Fifteen years is a long time," Inevera notes. "A lifetime for some. Many will not want to return, and many of the greenlanders who bonded to the Nanji will wish to go with their tribe to Desert Spear."

"Allowances can be made," I say. "But Aleveran must agree to the exchange in good faith before any aid is given."

Inevera laughs. "He will agree to much more than that, before the negotiations are through."

"When I return to Hollow, I will send ambassadors to see that it is done," I say.

"You do not trust Belina to keep her word?" Inevera asks, nodding to her sister-wife.

She meets my eyes again, and then we both laugh.

Belina keeps her outer serenity, but I know she must be steaming right now. It's better than she deserves, but I appreciate the cut. I get the sense Inevera has no more forgiven her than me.

The Damajah claps. "Leave us."

Immediately, Ashia and her warriors retreat with the Nanji Watchers, and Belina rises, ushering out my bodyguard and closing the doors behind them. Linavah stays to clear the table, then she, too, is gone.

CHAPTER 16

A SPARE KEY

As soon as the doors close, Inevera produces her dice of clay, now cemented to a board, which she lays on the table beside her casting cloth. There are slight adjustments to my recollection of Belina's casting—no doubt the result of Inevera consulting her sister-wife—but I surprise myself with how accurate my reproduction was.

The Damajah shakes her true dice from their velvet *hora* pouch and draws her *hanzhar.* "Hold out your arm."

I cross them instead. "You first."

Inevera's eyes narrow, but she does not argue, holding out an arm. Her robes are attached at the shoulder and wrist, but slits along the length allow the robes to breathe, and grant access to her flesh.

Mother always took blood for the dice with a surgical lance to the fingertip, a precise ritual I witnessed countless times. But I am not my mother, and take Inevera's in the traditional *dama'ting* fashion, using my *hanzhar* to make a shallow cut to her forearm.

The Damajah does not flinch, holding steady as seven drops fall into my vial. When it is done, I move to put pressure on the wound, but it is not necessary. Already the bleeding has stopped, and even as I watch, the wound knits itself closed.

"I trust you are not so naïve as to leave that someplace unsecure," the Damajah says.

I slip the vial into my robes, in a pocket close to my heart. "Anyone who wants it will need to kill me first."

"If they learn you have a vial of the Damajah's blood, many will try," Inevera warns. "Now you."

This time I wordlessly comply, giving seven drops in exchange, one splashing on each of the Damajah's dice. She whispers a prayer as she shakes, a dialect of Krasian I do not recognize. There is a flash of light as she throws, and the spinning dice jerk to a sudden halt, forming a pattern, but without knowing the question, I can't even begin to decipher it.

"What did you ask?"

"Tsst," Inevera says. "I did not promise to share that with you, little Princes, any more than you promised to share your intent for the vial of my blood hidden at your breast."

I frown, though she's right. I was naïve not to be clearer in wording our agreement.

Inevera stares at the throw silently for a long time. At last, she grunts and returns her attention to me. "What do you know of the Spear of Ala?"

The question catches me off guard. "Just what Darin's mum told me. That she went there with my father, and it was abandoned, surrounded by demon dogs, and that Father . . . had power there."

Inevera snorts. "Had power. Like the sun has power. In the Spear of Ala, your father was the most powerful man in the world."

"Why?" I ask.

"Because the *csar* was built in the shape of a massive greatward," Inevera says. "And its Sharik Hora was built of the bones of martyrs, just like the Holy City in Desert Spear."

That, I understand. Mother used to Draw upon Hollow's greatward to work her greatest magics, but even that was nothing compared to the power of the Holy City in Desert Spear. Magic is drawn and shaped by emotion, and there is nothing to match the emotional power of a martyr in death. If the Spear of Ala is powered by both . . .

"But the power was tied to Father's crown," I say. "The Crown of Kaji."

"Indeed," Inevera agrees. "Seven points, each focused by a gemstone cut from a larger whole set in the heart of the Spear. The crown was the key to the city, and its wearer commanded vast, near-infinite powers in the environs of the *csar*."

I nod. "Yet Father is gone, and the crown with him."

"Not precisely." Inevera reaches into the pillows, producing an intricate, beautiful crown, pointed seven times, each set with a different gemstone, though I admit they are smaller than I imagined. Nevertheless, it is a masterpiece of wardwork, and from my time in the Chamber of Shadows, I immediately recognize the metal—electrum, a natural alloy of silver and gold coveted for its ability to conduct magic without loss.

"How did you get that?" I ask. "Has Father . . ."

"Your father remains missing." Her voice is calm, but I know the admission must pain her. "But I am not a fool."

"You copied his keys," I guess.

The Damajah smiles beneath her translucent veil. "Something like that. We could not risk losing access to the Spear of Ala once again, so I visited the *csar* myself and cut the sacred stones to link to a duplicate crown in case something befell the original."

That explains why the gems look so small. "So you can control the *csar*?"

Inevera shakes her head. "The replica is a key to the *csar's* power, not the power itself. I was forced to mimic the enchantment of the original. The crown gives power to any who wears it, but only a true heir of Kaji can unlock its full potential."

"Then give it to one of your sons," I say.

"Would that I could," Inevera says. "Do you think I wish to entrust it to you? The child of my hated *zahven*, and not one of my own? But Sharak Ka comes first. My eldest, Jayan, is dead. Asome is in exile and shamed. Hoshkamin is a competent Sharum Ka, but he will never be a great leader, and cannot be trusted with such power."

"Why not Kaji?" I ask. "He is the son of heroes, and you passed over an entire generation to put him on the throne."

"Because removing Kaji from Everam's Bounty threatens everything we have built," Inevera says. "The last time my husband disappeared, our son Jayan started an unwinnable war, and his brother Asome murdered the entire council of *Damaji* and his own father-in-law to take the throne. Your father has dozens of sons, and they are always one ill omen away from falling on one another like wolves."

She lifts an accusatory finger my way. "And you did not help matters, strutting about challenging them in open court. If you truly want to lead, you need to do it with more wisdom."

I put my hands on my hips, like Mother when she's run out of patience. "You were the one who walked me into that asp nest, Damajah. Would things have gone better if I had bared my neck?"

A puff of air through her veil. Amusement? "None of the other heirs are strong enough to hold the throne against their brothers. Without Kaji, Asome might return, and that would mean open conflict."

"Give the crown to one of Father's other sons, then," I say. "He has fifteen wives . . ."

"And I have cast dice in the birthing blood of all of their sons," Inevera says. "None of them have a reading like yours."

"Because you think I am Shar'Dama Ka," I say.

"Because whether you accept it or not, you have the potential to be," Inevera replies, "and that is more than the dice have said of any of your father's other get."

"Belina's reading implied I might not be Shar'Dama Ka," I remind her. "That my nature was a choice between *Sharum* and *Dama*, not their union in one."

Inevera raises an eyebrow. "*Now* Belina's words matter to you? You were ready to take her arm when they did not suit your purpose before. Regardless, one prophecy does not negate another. Both can be true."

"You're willing to risk that?" I ask. "Or could it be the dice just don't have the symbols to describe an aberration like me?"

"An aberration?" Inevera asks. "The ancient scholars say Everam created forty thousand species of spider. Thirty thousand species of fish. Five thousand of frog. Why would we think he wanted all humans to be rigidly the same? It is said we are made in His image, but Everam created Ala, the sun, and the stars out of nothing but Himself. No man or woman among us can create life alone, but you can. Who in all the world is more in His image than you?"

The line of reasoning makes me uncomfortable. "I don't believe in Everam." In Desert Spear, speaking such words aloud was tantamount to taking my life in my hands. Even here, I do not know how the Damajah will respond to such sacrilege.

"Too much your mother, even now." Inevera sighs. "It is a misconception, that Everam derives strength from our belief. Everam does not require your belief. Everam only requires that you stand against the *alagai*."

I nod. "That, I can do."

"Then you see that it *has* to be you," she presses. "No one else can harness the power of the *csar* in time to prevent Alagai Ka from returning to the hive with his new queen. If you go east to the mountains, you risk the doom of us all. You *must* go and secure the Spear of Ala."

My eyes flick for just a moment back to the dice on the tea table, wondering what they told the Damajah, and whether I can pry the information from her in some way.

I cross my arms defensively. "Let's say I consider it. What then?"

"The path will be dangerous," Inevera says.

"I've heard Mrs. Bales' ale stories," I say. "Fungus that infects the living and turns them into mindless defenders of the colony. Underwater worms that leach magic. *Gwilji*."

Once, that word just meant "dogs"—the hounds *Sharum* used in their hunts. But the animals fed on demon carrion from their masters' battles, growing stronger and more vicious until they could no longer be controlled. Like the *alamen fae*, countless *gwil* litters have whelped in the darkness, soaking in the constant flow of magic from the Core.

"Indeed," Inevera agrees. "And who can say what else lurks in the tunnels now that the *alagai* are no longer atop the food chain? Not all the *alamen fae* settled in the Spear of Ala. Many refused the city, preferring to remain nomadic and tribal. They are primitive and savage compared to their resettled cousins, but they are strong, and may not welcome an incursion into their territory."

"Just a stroll through the garden, then."

The Damajah doesn't see the humor. "I will send my cousin, Briar asu Relan am'Damaj am'Kaji, as your guide. The son of Relan has been to the Spear many times, and is known to you, I believe."

"I've . . . met him." I resist the urge to wrinkle my nose. Briar reminds me a bit of Darin, always skulking about, avoiding folk whenever he can, and speaking in short, clipped sentences when he can't. Always looking ready to flee at the first opportunity. And he stank. Like hogroot leaves gone rotten. Mother said the smell protected him from demons in the night, but even now I am not sure the trade was fair.

"Briar is no army of warriors and witches like your mother's retinue," Inevera admits, "nor is he a blazing star of fury like my husband. But there is value to him, still. More even than my *Sharum'ting*, the son of Relan is part of the night, more comfortable in demon-infested darkness than the light of day. He is also half Thesan, and has powerful friends and contacts in Hollow, Angiers, and Miln."

That, I believe. Briar had a tendency to appear without warning in Mother's office, which made the house guard crazy. Mother always greeted him warmly, with not a word for the hogroot resin he left on the rugs and furniture. Sometimes I would catch his stink on my way to her office and turn back, though he was always kind, and never failed to leave a gift for me from his travels.

"Of course the crown and a guide will not be enough for you to complete this task," the Damajah continues. "You will need an army. Your father's Spears of the Deliverer will—"

"I have an army," I cut in. "I will not march into Hollow with yours at my back."

"The only entrance to the tunnels to the Spear of Ala is the Mouth of the Abyss," Inevera says, "guarded by the city of Anoch Dahl. They will no more welcome Hollow Soldiers than your Hollowers would your father's *Sharum*."

I shake my head. "If I do this—and I haven't yet agreed I will—it will be me who decides how and with whom it is done, not you."

"Not if you wish my support." Inevera moves the crown in her hand farther from my reach.

I snort. "A moment ago you said I *must* take it. Now you want to pull it back? Do it. Give it to the Prince of Nothing, for all I care. I'll go find my mother."

Inevera moves her hand back, bluff called. "There is room to bargain, of course."

I thought so. "My spear brothers will be escort enough on my return to Hollow. If I move for the Mouth, it will be with Hollow Soldiers and more at my back. If they are mustered at Anoch Dahl when I arrive, and we are unhindered, I will take a like number of *Sharum* with me, if they swear to my command."

"They will fight for you," Inevera promises. "If need be, they will die for you. But they will be under the command of the Sharum'ting Ka. If you waste their lives needlessly, Ashia will countermand you, and the *Sharum* will obey."

"I am *kai'Sharum*," I growl. "I would never waste the lives of my spear brothers and sisters." The very idea is offensive, an insult from a woman who has probably never held a spear in her life.

Inevera only nods, as if I have passed another test. "Then we understand each other. Ashia will follow your lead, but you in turn will accept counsel, and brief your commanders. Ashia will relay what is happening to me, and speak with my voice in reply."

"I am not agreeing to anything," I warn. The Damajah speaks as if we are about to spit on our hands and shake on it, but all I have is her word that any of this is necessary, and not a ruse to remove me from power. "First I will go home and take my throne."

Inevera nods. "I trust that upon consideration, you will see the necessity of this task. Favah can help you on the journey. Your old instructor is powerful and can still teach you much, if you truly meant it when you called yourself a sister to the *dama'ting*."

"Even in Desert Spear, the Majah whisper the venerable name of Favah," I say. "Her teachings allowed me to save lives both on the battlefield and off. But she is ancient and cannot withstand the rigors of a trip to the Spear of Ala. Perhaps I could bring Jaia? Or Shaselle?" Jaia was the Krasian Studies teacher at Gatherers' University, and Shaselle ministered to the Krasians living in Hollow.

Inevera shakes her head. "Jaia is a child, and soft from living in the green lands. Shaselle trained with me in the Dama'ting Palace of Desert Spear, and she is competent enough, but Shaselle is not equipped even to understand the ancient magics at work in Kaji's fortress, much less manipulate them."

I frown. If this is truly so important, why is Inevera sending me and an old crone to do it for her? "Surely in all Everam's Bounty there is someone."

"Will you trust someone you don't know?" Inevera asks.

I shrug. "Respectfully, Damajah, I do not even know that I trust you."

She nods at that. "I will meditate upon the question."

"What did the dice tell you?" I ask.

Inevera looks at me for a long time, no doubt weighing her answer. She may not have promised to tell me under oath, but she wants something from me, even now.

"The debts of the father must be paid."

CHAPTER 17

DEBTS OF THE FATHER

Arick plays a soothing tune on his kamanj as Selen paces back and forth, but it doesn't much help. She's trampled a groove into the grass like Grandda plowing the barley field.

"What in the dark of night is taking so long?" Selen growls. "Darin, are you sure she's still in there?"

I'm perched atop a pear tree in the royal gardens. The palace encloses the gardens on all sides, so with an ear to the wind I can hear just about everything in the building and on the grounds. Too much for me to sort out normally, but here there is an advantage.

The Damajah's sound wards cover her entire wing, an unnatural bubble of silence easy to focus on amid the general bustle of the palace. When Olive emerges, I'll know.

I'm about to shake my head when the bubble bursts with a rush of air as the doors to the Damajah's wing open. For just a moment, I can hear inside, like peeking through a pinhole. But then Olive and her guards emerge, and it's all silent again.

"Darin," Olive says, knowing I will be listening, "find Selen and the others and meet me in my chambers."

I'm out of the tree quick as a squirrel who dropped a nut. Arick and Selen cut across the gardens to enter the guest wing, but I head back up the tree, running along one of its limbs and using it like a springboard to leap onto the roof. A quick sprint and I can drop over the far side and climb down to the windows of Olive's chambers.

I pause out on the sill, listening. Last time I was here, I didn't know what to listen for, but I've learned that lesson. Like I did with the Damajah's wing, I search not for a sound, but for the absence of it, a zone of quiet causing the sounds striking it to distort.

From there, it doesn't take me long to find them, Inevera's *Sharum'ting* guards, hidden in shadowy nooks all over the palace, spying. I don't let on that I've marked them, popping one of Olive's windows open just enough to slip through, then sealing it behind me.

Most of the royal chambers have hollow walls, ostensibly so servants can pass through unseen, though in practice it's as much for snooping as it is for delivering breakfast. I drum a little rhythm on the wall, listening for those telltale bubbles of silence, and find them here, as well.

Selen and Arick are the first to arrive. I touch a finger to my lips, tilting my head toward the walls. Arick nods, sitting on the floor and setting his kamanj. In moments he has filled the room with music, but I see him adjust the wardstone on his instrument. Another bubble of sound forms, only this time I am inside it. The noise of the palace without vanishes, and I hear only Arick's music.

Olive enters soon after. Can't hear her, but I'm a fair hand at readin' lips, too. She's telling her guards to stay outside. When she turns her attention to us, she sees Arick playing without hearing it, and quickly puts things together.

"Thank you, Arick," Olive says when she enters the bubble. "I was going to ask Rojvah to use her choker . . ." She looks around, noticing Rojvah is nowhere to be seen. "Where is she?"

"Rojvah ent been seen in days," I say. "Her mam's back was up somethin' fierce."

"Just as well, if we want a private talk," Selen says. "Anything we say with her around will go straight back to Inevera."

All eyes turn to Arick at that, but he only shrugs. "You do not know my sister as well as you think, but you are right that as *nie'dama'ting,* she is duty-bound to report to the Damajah."

"And you?" Olive asks, and I want to jump to Arick's defense, but he beats me to it.

"I shed blood with you in the night, cousin," Arick says. "And swore my spear to rescue your mother with you. Do you need more than that, to know where my loyalties lie?"

Olive puts a fist to her chest in a warrior's salute, but it looks out of place in her tea robes. "The Damajah doesn't want me to go in search of Mother."

Selen snorts. "Ay, well the Damajah can stick that idea up—"

"Where does she want you to go instead?" I ask, dread building up in my belly.

"The Spear of Ala." Olive confirms my fears. "Inevera thinks that's where I'll find my father."

"Dun't make sense," I say. "If Alagai Ka is lookin' to feed them to his new queen, wouldn't they all be together in Safehold?"

"Not necessarily," Olive says. "Inevera thinks the demon needs Father's crown to destroy the *csar* and secure the demon hive, and it only works when he's wearing it."

Makes sense. In Mam's stories, it's like Jardir and the mighty *csar* were one. Gates and doors opened at his whim, walls reshaped themselves to his will, and when the demon dogs came, he sent every spear in the city spinning in the air at them like leaves in a twister.

"She cast the dice again?" Selen asks, but we all know the answer.

Olive nods. "She said, *The debts of the father must be paid.*"

It's too much like my own prophecy for comfort. *The father waits below in darkness for his progeny to return.*

"Damajah herself said *father* could mean a lot of things," I remind her. "Could be my da stuck down there, or the Father of Demons lyin' in wait to pay us what he thinks we got comin'."

"Perhaps," Olive allows. "But why would your father's fate be tied to my blood? Ahmann Jardir is your bloodfather, and my father by blood. If it's the same father in both prophecies, stands to reason it's him."

"Or the demon," I say.

"Ay." Olive nods. "Or that."

"But what debt?" Arick asks.

"Both our das went to kill Alagai Ka, and failed," I say. "Reckon it ent a stretch that they need us to finish the job." Part of me wants to laugh at the absurdity of it. We barely survived our last encounter with the demon king. What makes us think the next time will go any better?

"Maybe your da is down there," I allow. "Maybe mine is, too, somehow. But we know our mams are at Safehold. Saw it yourself, in the demon's head. Dice or no dice, ent goin' anywhere until we get them first."

"You should go." Olive seems to agree, but I don't like that *you* when she should be sayin' *we*.

Can't believe what I'm hearin'. "So you'll just leave your own mam to get et?"

It was the wrong thing to say. Olive's scent turns angry, and her flesh darkens as blood rushes to her muscles. "You don't get to judge me, Darin Bales. With Mother gone, I have a duty to Hollow. You don't understand what it's like to have real responsibilities and people depending on you."

Usually I back off when Olive smells like that, but I can't let that comment go. "Like night I don't. You think we came to Krasia and rescued you by accident?"

Olive puts her hands on her hips. "I didn't need to be rescued."

"Core you din't." I don't like spitting to make a point like folk in the Brook, but Krasians just make the noise, and that works just as well. "You'd still be there, not for us, mooning over your desert prince."

I realize I've gone too far the moment the words leave my mouth. The tang of her anger turns sharp, and she balls a fist. I've been punched by Olive Paper before, and it's not something I ever care to repeat.

I tense, ready to turn slippery, but Olive takes a breath, calming herself. "You just don't get, it, Darin."

Selen comes over to me, and I worry they're going to gang up on me like they did when we were kids. Instead, she stands protectively before me as she wheels on Olive. "Then how about you explain it, Olive, because I'm having trouble understanding it, too. You of all people should know that every time the demon dice roll, lives are destroyed, and who knows if the world gets anything back for it. Tell me to my face you're thinking of turning your back on Leesha over anything that Krasian witch had to say."

Olive doesn't have an answer for that, and Selen bulls ahead. "And it ent just them. It's Mrs. Bales and Captain Wonda and Kendall Demonsong. Not to mention every other person lost in that expedition. You're gonna just leave them to rot?"

"Of course not," Olive snaps. "I'm thinking of trusting all of you to save them without me."

I feel sick at the words. Us? Olive is the leader. Always has been. Frankly, it was luck as much as anything that got me and Selen to her. Can't imagine doin' this without her.

"I haven't made any decisions," Olive says. "It may be Hollow needs me and I can't go anywhere. Or that I can support you better by taking some crown down to the ripping Core. Maybe you're right and you need me with you, or maybe we end up like everyone else that goes looking for Safehold. I don't know what to do, so I'm not ruling out anything yet."

Selen eases back at that, and I'm happy to back off and let tempers cool. Still think it's a mistake, but Olive is right to give it a think.

"Darin tracked you all the way from your mum's keep to the Desert Spear with just his nose," Selen allows. "If anything's to be found, he'll find it."

"Like it or not, you may need to stay in Hollow, Sel," Olive says. "You're next in line for the throne after me. We can't just toss off like Uncle Gared."

Selen crosses her arms at that. "Just you try and stop me, Olive Paper."

I can smell Olive's indecision. She doesn't want us going without her any more than we do, but we've already lost Rojvah. Without Olive, I don't see how we can succeed.

CHAPTER 18

INTENDED

Selen and Olive are still arguing when I quietly drift back to the wall and flit to the high window. As usual, I'm gone before anyone notices.

Never liked raised voices, and I know the signs when Olive and Selen get into it. This argument isn't going to end anytime soon.

For a minute back in the desert, it felt like we were a team, again. We all take the air out of each other when we're alone, but it used to feel like nothing could pull us apart from the outside.

But then Mam and Leesha Paper got into that fool argument over what Da would have wanted, if he was still around. Mam got her back up, and we didn't come back to Hollow for five years. I thought maybe things might go back to normal, and for a little while they did, but then Olive was taken, and now I don't think normal's ever coming back.

And if normal ent normal anymore, I need to find something to fill the hole. Can't do this with just Arick and Selen. Selen's strong, and brave, but she ent bringin' any magic to the table, and we're gonna need it if we want to sneak past Alagai Ka. Arick's got magic in his kamanj, but he's still apt to go for his spear in a fight, and he's got his own problems to figure out.

Without realizing it, I've started drifting toward the Damajah's wing of the palace. I tried to sneak in here once before and it din't go well, but

I've learned her guards' tricks now. The *Sharum'ting* rely on magic as much as skill for their unnatural stealth, and my night eyes can see magic like other folk see color. Like listenin' for wards of silence, there are trails in the air where they have used magic to cloak themselves in shadow, and residual prints on walls they used magic to climb or cling to.

Now that I know where they are, it's easier to slip by Inevera's guards. Their *hora* jewelry is a crude imitation of powers that come to me as naturally as breathing. A slippery finger is enough to unlatch a window, and I slip into the Damajah's bubble of silence.

The effect startles me. Not the pop of blending sounds when the bubble is pierced, this is the sudden cessation of all the sounds I'd been surrounded by, replaced instantly with an entirely new set. It's so disorienting I feel like I might sick up.

I find a hiding place and close my eyes for a bit, breathing deep and slow as I get used to the new sounds and give my stomach time to settle. After a few minutes, I am reoriented and start moving again. The protections tighten the closer I get to the Damajah's private quarters, but the residential floors where I'm headed are well away from there.

The Damajah's portion of the palace encompasses the harem, as well. Not so strict as the Majah, whose harems were effectively a prison for women, here they are free to come and go. The Damajah's harem is a retreat from men in the palace, where women can meet in private and even the most conservative women can walk about unveiled.

It is also a place where most of the unmarried palace women above a certain age reside. *Dama'ting* and young princesses not yet wed, for the most part.

Rojvah sang with me for weeks out in the desert, and it's easy to pick her voice out of the general din and head directly toward the sound. She ent alone, but I din't come all this way to leave without seeing her.

The sun has set and the palace chandeliers are lit, casting harsh shadows. I climb to the ceiling and slip into a dark patch close to Rojvah's door, focusing.

I didn't escape raised voices for long. Rojvah is arguing with her mother, and it sounds a lot like Selen and Olive.

"Arick is a man," Amanvah says, "and expected to throw his life away for honor. But you have sacred duties and cannot just—"

"Just stand by," Rojvah cuts in, "while my brother and cousins 'throw their lives away' in Sharak Ka?"

"Who will lead the women of Kaji if you die?" Amanvah asks.

"Someone else!" Rojvah shrieks. "I never asked to be *dama'ting*. Have another daughter to be your heir, if that's so important."

"And what will you be," Amanvah demands, "if I break my vow to honor your father by never bearing any child save his?"

"I will be honoring him, too!" Rojvah's voice has turned pleading. "I want to be like him—more than Arick ever did. I want to be a Jongleur and wear bright colors. I want to sing, and to dance."

"Your voice is a sacred gift," Amanvah says, "not a tool to entertain Northern princelings and crowds of commoners."

"Why not?" Rojvah demands. "Was that not exactly what Father did?"

"Your father brought glory to Everam." Amanvah's voice is low. Dangerous.

"As will I!" Rojvah swears. "I will be a diva, who ensorcels crowds with songs of glory to Everam by day, and enchants hordes of *alagai* by night."

"You will not," Amanvah says. "If your blessed father was here—"

"I wish he was!" Rojvah shrieks. "I wish he'd been here my whole life, so Arick and I could have one parent who was not ashamed of us both!"

"I am not ashamed of you!" Amanvah barks. "You shame yourself!"

Neither speaks for a long time after that, but I can hear their heavy breathing, their pounding hearts. Fights like this need a break now and then.

Amanvah is the first to speak again, her voice softer. "But you are right. Your father had a soft heart, and it was easy to soften in his presence. Even Sikvah and I wore colored robes when we performed with him."

"Truly?" There is disbelief in Rojvah's tone, but I seen paintings of Halfgrip and his wives in Hollow, and know Amanvah's giving honest word.

"But it was his soft heart that led to your father's death," Amanvah goes on. "He could not bring himself to be ruthless with his enemies, and they turned that weakness against him."

I hear Amanvah sob, and again I feel slimy for listenin' in on folk. "And if I had been more ruthless," she continues, "if I had not let my heart grow soft, I would have dealt with his enemies as a wife should, and he would be alive today."

Rojvah is crying now, too, and I hear the press of cloth and flesh as they embrace. They hold each other through it, hearts and sobs finding a harmony of sorts, until both ease, and a delicate peace forms in the room.

"Soon after, I was called home to lead the women of Kaji," Amanvah tells her daughter. "I returned with a hardened heart, and those liberties I took at my husband's side had to be sacrificed to the black veil."

"Perhaps," Rojvah says. "But even if you do not wish another child, you are young, Mother. Barely halfway through your fourth decade when most *dama'ting* live to see their ninth. Why can't I have a chance, as you did, to live and grow and see the lands beyond Everam's Bounty?"

"You have seen enough, sneaking off to Desert Spear," Amanvah says. "And it was different for me. I was a woman wed, traveling with my husband at the Deliverer and Damajah's command."

Rojvah is silent at first, but I can tell from her pulse she's got something to say. "What if I were intended to the son of Arlen?"

Amanvah doesn't reply right away. Night, it takes me a moment to realize I'm who she's talking about. Rojvah wants to marry . . . me? I nearly lose my grip on the ceiling.

"I do not think he would have you," Amanvah says at last. "The dice say he is not ready for a wife, or indeed if ever he will be, though the Shar'Dama Ka long desired to find a match for the son of Arlen among his heirs."

"But what if he did?" Rojvah presses. "What if he says the words of intention to me? Then it would be my duty to go with him, and Arick. Would the Damajah allow it then? Would you?"

Amanvah keeps her breathing steady, but her pulse is quickened. "The Damajah would allow it. Everam's beard, Mother would seize on it, if only to ease pressure from Father. And if Father has taken the lonely path, then it is another tie with the greenlanders we desperately need."

I hear her take Rojvah's hands. "But do you truly want to marry him? Or is this simply a ploy to escape your duty? His parents ate the flesh of *alagai,* it is said."

She leaves out the nickname, but I hear it in my head anyway. *Alagai* blood. *He will be born in darkness, and will carry it inside him,* the Damajah's dice said. Are they right? Am I unclean, somehow?

The words cut me because I know Amanvah's speakin' honest word. How could someone like Rojvah, brilliant and graceful and pretty as a sunset, with a voice like a seraph, and all that culture and royal blood, ever be interested in me?

"I do not want to marry anyone," Rojvah admits. It stings a little, but I ent surprised.

"But the son of Arlen is wise," Rojvah says, "and he is brave. I have never known a truer heart, and he is fair to look upon. He is unassuming, but that is just as well. I enjoy attention, and can shield him from it. And he is in desperate need of a woman's care."

I feel my face heat. Don't think I've ever been wise, or brave, but the rest . . .

Always thought I'd marry Selen Cutter one day, if I married at all. Sometimes I heard Brook girls gossip they shined on me, but it was only because I never let anyone get to know the real me. Selen and Olive were the only ones who really did, and liked me in spite of it. I shined on Selen all my life, and when we had ten summers and played that game of kissy . . . ent imagined myself with anyone else since.

But Selen dun't want me. Don't know much about women, but I know that. She's kissed plenty of boys since our game, and from the sounds of it, they were nothing like me. Big and tall and square-jawed. We were alone together on the road for months, and there wasn't even a hint of interest, not since that one time she teased me in her father's manse, half a year ago.

I realize I've stopped paying attention when the door opens, and Amanvah steps through. I have to scramble a bit to slip through before the door closes. Rojvah isn't looking my way, staring out the window at nothing.

"You heard everything?" Rojvah asks without turning. I freeze in place, even as she turns to face me.

"How did you . . ." I stumble.

Rojvah reaches into the velvet *hora* pouch at her waist, producing a set of seven dice, carved of demonbone and glowing bright with magic. "I have dice, too, Darin am'Bales," Rojvah says. "I finished carving my set in Desert Spear, though I have kept Mother from learning of it thus far. She will demand the test if she finds out, and nothing will keep me from the white, then."

"Secret's safe with me." I drop silently to the floor, coming closer, but not too close. Dice have caused enough problems in my life. Don't like the idea of adding another set.

Rojvah closes the gap from her side, until I'm close enough to feel her breath like a touch on my skin. "Will you do this for me, son of Arlen?"

Never noticed how big her eyes were, before. Be easy to lose myself in them and say ay to just about anythin'. But this ent a normal favor. "Said you din't want to marry anyone."

"I spoke the truth, because I knew you were listening," Rojvah says, "and you deserved to hear it. I will not lie and say I love you, but neither do I deny you would be a good husband, and there is more to marriage than love."

Again she ent wrong, but it stings to have it laid bare like that.

"You need not even commit fully," Rojvah says. "All you need do is indicate you wish to be intended. Mother and Grandmother will leap on it, and I can go north with you. Neither of us has reached our sixteenth year, so they cannot insist we marry before we go. We will go to Safehold, and if we survive and you do not wish to go through with it, make some excuse and you can refuse me, or I, you."

Sounds like she's got it all figured out. Dice probably helped. Bet she's been planning this a good while. Should've known it wasn't really about me. Just an excuse to clip her mam's apron strings. How could someone like her ever want me for me? This promise is just a scheme.

But so what if it is? Selen ent interested, and Amanvah wasn't wrong that I ent lookin' for anyone else.

Arick and I struggle to find harmony when we play together. He's too rigid about things being played the "right" way, and I'm all over the place. But when I play with Rojvah, she's not just deft and quick to keep up, she leads me to new places I could never have gone alone.

Yet somehow, when all three of us played together out on the desert, it worked. Arick was the foundation, and we were the builders. Ale stories said when Master Halfgrip played with his wives Amanvah and Sikvah, their trio could charm a demon into cutting its own throat with just their music. Playing with Arick and Rojvah, I really believed it, and that we could learn to do it, too.

Odds ent good no matter what we do, but if we're to have any hope of sneaking into Safehold without Olive, we need Rojvah.

And she's family already. Maybe not blood, but as good as. Rojvah went all the way to Desert Spear to help us find Olive. What kind of friend would I be, if I didn't help her when she needed it?

"All right," I say. "I'll do it."

The smile that splits Rojvah's face shines like a crescent moon. She takes a step closer, and another, until we are practically touching. Don't like folk getting this close, but I'm caught like a rabbit in a trap.

"You must demand I remove my veil before you speak the words of intention." She is so close I can feel the pressure of her full lips as they form the words. The moisture of her mouth. "And then you must kiss me."

I just stand there, stiff as a goldwood tree, frozen in place like I was that time with Selen.

Rojvah laughs. "Perhaps you wish to practice?"

"Ay, uh," I stumble, but she takes it for permission, leaning in quick and pressing her soft lips against mine. It's only the second kiss in my life, and like the last one, I'm the one being kissed, and not the other way around.

And I melt.

Literally. Tension I've been holding gives way and a deep part of me relaxes. Before I realize what I'm doing, I've turned slippery, our lips sliding apart.

Corespawn me. Din't mean for that. Din't want it to stop. She's still there, lips puckered. It's been less than a second. It doesn't have to end. All I need to do is suck back in and return her kiss.

But I'm scared, and I hesitate, and then the moment is gone. Rojvah steps back, but she is still smiling.

"Perhaps we should stand before the Damajah in sunlight, to do this."

"Ay." I laugh in spite of myself. "Reckon that's a good idea."

CHAPTER 19

HOLY MOTHER

"GENERAL," I SAY, when the servants grant Gared entrance to my chambers. "How go the preparations?"

"Core if I know for sure," Gared admits, "but Abban says Inevera will keep her word and things'll be ready for us to leave tomorrow."

"Excellent, thank you," I say. "I expect there are a line of men waiting in the garden for you to best them at arm wrestling?"

"Ay, reckon so." There's a twinkle in Gared's eyes I've never seen before. Not only has he shed years and pounds, there's a confidence and joy about him now that is a pleasure to see.

The Uncle Gared I remember from Hollow was always sad, or drunk. A warrior in a society that no longer had a place for him. Now he's the man I need, right when I need him.

"Then I shan't keep you longer," I say. Gared is the only one of us who seems to be enjoying his stay, so why not let him? Soon enough I may command him to follow me into the abyss, and I do not doubt he will do it.

As the general turns to go, the door cracks just enough to admit a servant, bowing before she's even in the room, eyes on the floor. "Excuse my interruption, Highness, but you have a message."

The servants are loath to enter when I have a guest, which tells me whoever sent the message outranks me. The Damajah perhaps, or one of the tribal *Damaji*. "Raise your eyes, Oshala vah Finela, and speak your message."

The servant starts a little. Krasian servants aren't used to their masters calling them by name and treating them like equals. Still, I have given a command, and she is quick to obey, straightening and meeting me in the eyes. "The Holy Mother, Kajivah, has summoned you to her palace for an audience."

"Summoned." Gared's voice is gruff. Protective. But he cannot protect me from this. "You're the leader of Hollow. Who's this Holy Mother think she is?"

I sigh. "My grandmother."

"Oh." Gared deflates. "Reckon the wrestlin'll have to wait."

WHEN I WAS growing up in Hollow, everyone was scared of my grandmum Elona. She could be sweet as honey when she wanted, and claw as unexpectedly as a cat. No one wanted to be on her bad side. Most folk avoided her entirely. But she was the duchess' mum, a position that came with power, and an army of sycophants looking to curry favor.

The only people who weren't scared of her were me and my sister Micha. I was her only grandchild, and Grandmum doted on me like I was the sun and moon.

Elona tried snapping at Micha once or twice, but my sister only regarded her coolly, seeming to take no offense, but neither giving way. Eventually, Grandmum backed off.

"Why aren't you afraid of her like everyone else?" I asked Micha once, while she brushed my hair.

"You have two grandmothers," Micha replied. "Elona Paper, and the one we share, Kajivah am'Jardir am'Kaji. Elona is like a tunnel asp, quick, sharp, and deadly. Kajivah is more frightening, by far."

The memory roils in my gut now. Rojvah always said the same, in our correspondence. Her letters were full of stories of Kajivah meddling in the lives of every one of her dozens of granddaughters. Rojvah described her as old, controlling, and deeply conservative, a nightmare there is no waking up from.

I can't deny I'm anxious about meeting her, but I'm curious, too. Spent two hours deciding what to wear. Should I come as a granddaughter, as a grandson? Or should I find something in between?

But then I think of Kaji's warnings, and Inevera's. Perhaps I didn't understand the ways of my father's people as well as I thought, when I made my challenge in the throne room.

I think of how I went to what I thought would be a peaceful tea, only to be faced with armed *Sharum'ting* and men who nearly beat me and my sister to death.

No. I will not go without armor again. Not here, where I cannot tell enemy from friend.

It's strange, traveling by palanquin. The Krasians see it as a sign of status, and power, to ride in a carriage borne on the backs of men, rather than pulled by animals. I'd just as soon be on the back of my own horse, able to run or fight as needed, but I am a royal visiting the Palace of the Holy Mother, and I do not wish to give insult.

The palanquin is armored and carried by my own spear brothers, surrounded in turn by burly Cutters in their enameled wooden armor. We draw stares as we move down the street, folk leaning from windows and a crowd of gawkers following down the street.

I have the same feeling I get in the Maze, when anticipating an ambush. Like there's demons around the next corner, and I need to be ready to fight. My spear is in easy reach, but it will do little good in the palanquin. Instead I grip the hilt of my *hanzhar,* ready to slash.

But there is no attack, and soon we are at the gates to the Palace of the Holy Mother. My escort stops, and I feel the palanquin lowered. I peek through the window and see a white-sleeved guard kneeling to greet me.

White-sleeved *Sharum* serve as temple guards of Sharik Hora and the Holy City in Krasia. It makes sense to find them here, as well. As I understand it, Kajivah isn't even a *dama'ting,* but she is mother to Shar'Dama Ka, the Deliverer. In the eyes of the people, that makes her as close to Everam as any who live.

A dozen paces up the road, a squad of white-sleeved guards outnumbering my escort two-to-one has taken a single knee, spears and shields in hand. Submissive to my rank, but prepared to fight, should they feel the Holy Mother threatened.

The guard kneeling to greet me has the white veil of a *kai,* but he moves to put his hands on the ground in submission.

The act offends me. Mother always hated folk bowing and scraping at royals, and for my part, no warrior who has fought the *alagai,* regardless of rank, should have to put their hands on the ground simply to greet me.

"Tsst." My hiss is that of a scolding Krasian mother, and the guard instinctively freezes, wondering how he has given offense. I should have just let the man bow. In trying to spare his honor, I may have bruised it further.

I deepen my voice to compensate for the womanly hiss. "Rise, honored Kai, and look me in the eye."

I do my best to imitate a Kaji accent, but it feels stilted, even to me. The Krasian Studies teachers back at Gatherers' University were Kaji, but it was only among the Majah that I was immersed in the language and truly became fluent.

The warrior seems mollified at that, rolling back onto his heels and standing in one smooth motion before raising his gaze. I punch a fist to my chest, the traditional greeting among *kai'Sharum,* and again he seems taken aback, though he mirrors the gesture on instinct.

"You honor me." This time he offers a warrior's bow. "Greetings, Your Royal Highness, Prince Olive asu Ahmann am'Paper am'Hollow. I am Kai Neven, and it is my honor to serve you. My men will be pleased to offer water and shade to your escort, for the duration of your stay."

"Of course, Kai Neven." We knew to expect this. The Palace of the Holy Mother is a women's space, and the temple guards do not allow other armed men inside the walls. There are stables and housing on the grounds outside.

At the gate my bodyguards and I give up our shields and the short stabbing spears—in Hollow they would be called fencing spears—we harness at our backs. Neven eyes the *hanzhar* at my belt, but he does not demand I turn it over.

The inner courtyard is vast, and abustle with activity. There are streams of servants and courtiers, but also *dama* and *dama'ting*. Like me, the priestesses wear *hanzhar* at their belts.

The clerics are trailed by acolytes carrying paper and writing kits, which tells me there is real power and influence here—if of a different sort than that of the Damajah's court. It reminds me a little of Mother's keep in Hollow, the courtyard dominated by a vast walled garden.

Separate from the main palace is a tall tower, ringed at its base by white-sleeved *dal'Sharum*, half of them facing outward to guard against attack, and half looking in, as if to keep someone, or something, contained. Occasionally, white-robed clerics and acolytes enter or exit the building. The guards eye them and what they carry carefully, but do not hinder them, otherwise.

"What is that?" I ask Kai Neven.

"That is the Tower of Nothing, Highness," Neven says. "It is the prison of Prince Asome."

Asome. My half brother, second son of Ahmann Jardir, who was called the Prince of Nothing, because he was set to inherit no title or power. Asome, who killed the council of *Damaji* in the night so he could ascend to the Skull Throne when Father disappeared with Arlen Bales fifteen years ago and was presumed dead.

Asome, who broke Father's oath to the Majah and tore the rift that sent them back to Desert Spear, even when they were desperately needed in Sharak Ka.

The rift that destroyed my life and forced me to build myself anew.

Suddenly I feel it was a mistake coming here, but it is too late to turn back now, and I hasten the pace.

"You are wise to keep your distance," Neven agrees. "Prince Asome has wealth, power, and influence still. He has spent his exile delving into *dama'ting* witchery and honing his *sharusahk*. It is said he is the greatest living master, save the Deliverer himself."

The words are meant to unsettle me, but instead they strike an unexpected chord. I, too, studied *dama'ting* magic in the Chamber of Shadows, and my last months have been nothing but *sharusahk*. Asome fathered a single son, Kaji, so he is technically not *push'ting*, but that word carries deeper weight than its definition in scripture. It is well known Asome prefers the company of men.

We're escorted to the gardens, where we are met by eunuch guards, wrists and ankles bound in gold to symbolize their servitude.

"Your men will need to wait here," Neven says. "Even I am not allowed into the gardens, save by appointment to visit my wife and children."

It seems the muscular eunuch guards, armed with clubs at their belts, are not considered bound by this rule. They bar the path of my bodyguards, and one has the audacity to reach for my *hanzhar.*

"Tsst!" Again that instinctive, scolding hiss, heard so many times from my sister Micha as I was growing up. The eunuch recoils as if burned, and I bare my teeth at him. "Eunuch or no, you are a man, and the *hanzhar* is not for your hands."

There is a pause as the eunuchs' fingers flit almost too quickly for the eye to see. Men guarding women of holy order often give up their tongues as well as their stones, and speak in a silent language of hand gestures that Micha only had time to teach me the rudiments of. Perhaps I can ask Favah to teach me more someday, but for now I can only guess at their meaning.

They are discussing, I expect, whether to allow me entrance with a weapon, refuse me, or, worse, go to the Holy Mother and ask. At last they wave me through, with one unlucky guard, the one who reached for my *hanzhar,* rushing ahead, no doubt to inform Kajivah of the irregularity.

The Holy Mother's gardens are a maze of hedges, meant to give privacy and layers of protection to the women within, that they might shed their veils and black robes in feminine company.

The *Sharum* in me, born in the Maze of Desert Spear, tenses as I enter. Once I would have seen only the beauty of the flowers, or the privacy offered by the secluded bowers. Now I see ambush pockets and choke points. Even as I try to shake the feeling off and see the garden for the plants, part of me is planning its defense.

The outskirts of the gardens are a kind of neutral area, where husbands may meet with their wives, or male children with their mothers or sisters. Not yet of marriage age and royal in blood, I am escorted deeper than other males, though still not into the center, where even eunuchs may not go.

I hear the Holy Mother before I see her.

"Fool!" I thought Rojvah exaggerated in her letters, but my cousin spoke honest word when she described Kajivah's voice as a sand demon's shriek. "Did they cut off your brains when they gelded you? You are lucky Prince Olive did not kill you where you stood, for attempting to put hands on your betters. Now begone, before you upset my grandson further."

The eunuch messenger comes darting around a hedge, nearly bowling me over. His eyes bulge at the sight of me and he moans, bowing so low his hands touch the grass. But he doesn't stop moving, and before the first slippered foot appears from behind the hedge, he has fled.

Here in her private gardens, Kajivah's veil and scarves are down around her shoulders like a shawl, over finely tailored silk robes in tones of orange, covered in elaborate wardwork stitched in thread of gold. I doubt this woman has ever as much as seen a demon in the flesh, yet here she is in the light of day, covered in more warding than a *Sharum* in the Maze.

I shake my head, thinking of the many similar dresses I have in Hollow. Most of them I made myself, back when I thought the *alagai* had all been destroyed in the Deliverer's Purge. Who am I to judge this woman? I know little of her trials.

Lowering the veil is supposed to put folk at ease, but Grandmother's face remains severe, pinched like she hasn't been to the privy in days. Her dark hair is streaked with white, like lightning splitting the night sky.

Like the point of a flight of wind demons, an entourage of women in brightly colored silks fans out behind my grandmother. Some have raised their veils, but many have not, and I recognize some of them from court.

My sisters. Like Micha, they are twice my age, but still in their primes, beautiful and vibrant. They cluster together at the sight of me, hanging back and whispering to one another as Kajivah approaches.

A pair of veiled women in *dama'ting* white trail the group. They have the look of servants, but I expect truer is they are the Damajah's spies. Part of Asome's coup was a failed attempt to assassinate his mother and replace her on the Pillow Throne with Kajivah. It is unclear if Grandmother was a pawn in that game, or if she knew full well what was happening and craved the Pillow Throne as much as her grandson did the Skull Throne.

"Olive!" Kajivah shrieks, opening her arms and rushing to me as if we have known each other all our lives. She embraces me warmly, kissing my cheeks.

Mother taught me to keep a smile painted on my face in circumstances like these, and the training serves me well. "Grandmother."

Kajivah waves the word away like a stink. "You will call me Tikka." The Krasian word for "grandmother," it is both a literal term and an honorific for respected elder women. She steps back. "Let me have a look at you."

I oblige, spreading my arms. Tikka rotates a finger in the air, and I turn dutifully for her appraisal.

"Handsome," she says at last, "and strong. But skinny. They must have starved you in Desert Spear. Majah cooking has always been offal. A warrior son of House Jardir should have more muscle on his bones." She turns to one of the veiled women at her side. "Have food brought to the gardens. Meat, and my special couscous."

I bow. "Thank you, Tikka, but that really isn't—"

"Phagh," Kajivah cuts in as the woman scurries off. "I cannot have my grandson looking thin as a pillow wife. Bad enough your *heasah* mother shamed you by raising you as *push'ting*."

I step forward, eyes cool but unyielding, like Micha's when she stared down Grandmum Elona. "I fear our visit will be short, Tikka, if you intend to speak ill of my mother." My tone is quiet. Calm. Firm.

Kajivah blinks, then laughs, kissing my cheeks again. "Of course, you are a dutiful son, whether it is deserved or not! How could a grandson of mine be anything but? They said I was cursed for bearing three daughters after your father, but I say Everam blessed me with a son so great, he needed no brothers."

Was Asome a dutiful son, when he tried to have Inevera murdered? I am wise enough not to ask the question aloud. Indeed, I might not like the answer.

Kajivah reaches out and takes my chin, turning my face this way and that as she examines me. "I worried you would have the greenlanders' look about you, but my son's line breeds true. We will have no trouble finding you a proper Krasian *Jiwah Ka.*"

"It will be months, yet, before I reach my sixteenth year," I say, hoping to deflect the topic. In New Krasia, weddings begin at sixteen, and Mother used that to keep their marriage brokers at bay.

"Indeed, it is late," Kajivah agrees. "You should already be betrothed, and your intended selecting sister-wives. But no matter!" She pinches her fingers together, smushing my cheeks. "Fifteen, and a hero of the Maze! Royal of blood and beautiful, with a throne all your own!" She turns to my sisters. "I do not think it will be hard to find this one a match!"

Dutifully, the women all laugh.

"No doubt the Damajah already has designs on you," Kajivah says. "Some *dama'ting* viper to keep you in line." At her back the two *dama'ting* in the entourage do their best to study the grass.

I cross my arms. "That won't be happening."

"Everam willing, it will not!" Kajivah agrees. "I will find you a proper bride, to keep your home and raise your children, as I raised Ahmann and his sisters. To pay your debts and warm your bed, not insert herself into matters that do not concern foolish women."

I blink, stunned. Why would I want that any more than some *dama'ting* viper?

"That's kind of you, Tikka, but I am afraid there is no time. I leave for Hollow on the morrow."

"Of course, of course," Tikka says. "Perhaps I should accompany you? I would like to see the palaces of the North, and I can bring candidates for you to consider . . ."

I bow. "You honor me, Tikka, but we must travel at speed, and I fear the mode will not befit the Holy Mother. You will need more than spears in your retinue. Perhaps you can visit in the spring, after the snows have melted?"

By then, whether it be to Safehold or the Spear of Ala, I will be long gone from Hollow. And if I should make it home alive, an overbearing grandmother will be the least of my fears. Perhaps she will lock horns with Elona and spare me entirely.

"A wonderful idea!" Kajivah shrieks. She turns to another of her veiled servants. "Begin making lists and preparations. And where is that food? Find that lazy chef and whip her if it takes any longer. Bring chilled nectar for Prince Olive, as well!"

As the second woman is sent running, one of the *dama'ting* bows to Kajivah. "Holy Mother, I do not believe the Damajah will think it wise for you to travel to the green lands . . ."

"Of course not!" Kajivah barks, uncowed. "Just as she did not think it wise for Ahmann to honor Prince Olive's *chin* mother by taking her as a proper *jiwah*. I will see to my grandson's matchmaking personally."

The priestess doesn't argue further. Like everyone in Kajivah's orbit, she seems to think it best to humor the volatile woman.

I'm no better, truly. I hope the priestess is right, and all this can be solved by simply warning Inevera of Tikka's plans.

"Walk with me, Olive." Tikka takes my arm, leaning symbolically—though she's still fit at what must be close to seventy winters—and steers me like a horse.

"You honor me, Tikka." I allow myself to be pulled along as we stroll past fountains and statues and manicured flower beds.

"We'll need to do something about that Majah accent," Tikka notes. "A prince of your stature should not speak like one of those savage *gin-jaz*."

Again, I am caught without a response. Kajivah laughs, tugging at my arm. "Oh, I don't blame you, my boy! It must have been difficult to live among the unclean, yet you return their master! Your father's blood runs true in more than your handsome face. We will find an instructor to remove the last vestiges of their offal from your princely tongue."

It's only been minutes, but she's managed to insult her own servants, my mother, my people, the Damajah, and now an entire tribe. I wonder how long I need to stay, in order to be polite.

"You must visit your brother, before you go," Kajivah says, as if reading my mind.

"I don't think . . ." I grasp for a response.

"Do not let rumor poison you against your brother without meeting him," Kajivah says. "Asome is a good man, and wise. Your father had disappeared and the *chin* were in revolt when he took power. We would have been unprepared for Sharak Ka, if not for his leadership."

That's not the version of the story I heard, but considering the low opinion Kajivah seems to have of her own gender, I suppose I shouldn't be surprised she can find no wrong in her eldest living grandson.

"Asome put his duty to Krasia first," Kajivah says. "A good prince does not have the luxury of doing otherwise."

The words are reminiscent of something Mother would say, and I wonder, not for the first time, where my own duty lies.

CHAPTER 20

TOWER OF NOTHING

THE SHADOWS GROW long before Tikka and my sisters are finished cooing over me. I exit the gardens and stand in the courtyard, staring up at the Tower of Nothing. It looms in the yard, rising high above the walls of the Palace of the Holy Mother to look out over the city of Everam's Bounty.

A prison, perhaps, but a princely one.

As with Tikka, I am curious about my disgraced half brother despite the warnings. Depending on who you ask, which histories you believe, Asome is a murderer and a madman, or a hero burdened by noble purpose. Some say he betrayed the Majah and caused the rift between the tribes, while others—most here in New Krasia—blame the Majah for abandoning Sharak Ka rather than submit to the Deliverer's son.

What drives a man to murder for a throne? To kill his uncle, his father-in-law, even sending assassins after his own wife and mother? I can make guesses, but that is all they will be if I don't have the stones to go and ask him directly.

"No weapons." The *kai* in charge of the temple guards ringing the tower crosses his arms, backed by a squad of armed and armored warriors. "No bodyguards. You must submit to a search on entry and exit."

"I fear we cannot be lenient in this," Neven says. "Our orders come from the Deliverer himself. There are no exceptions. If you fear to enter unarmed, you should not enter."

"I fear nothing." It's a lie, but I deliver it well. I take the *hanzhar* from my belt, wrap it in a scarf, and hand it to Neven. Then I step forward and raise my arms, empty palms toward the guards.

I tense as one of the guard pats me down, ready to break his arm if he should dare put hands where he shouldn't. But the *dal'Sharum* seems more scared of me than I am of him. I am a *kai,* and a prince. If I killed him on the spot for touching me improperly, there would be no penalty under the law.

I look at the dark, warded archway into the tower, and worry I am making a dangerous mistake, going in unarmed and alone. But now that I am here, I cannot bring myself to leave without at least looking my brother in the eye and seeing for myself if there is madness there.

The arched entrance to the tower is carved with powerful wards, not all of them meant to keep out the *alagai.* I wonder if the Damajah herself designed this wardwork to keep her son contained.

The rare and narrow windows of the tower are shuttered tight, blocking out the fading evening light. I see wardwork everywhere. The sigils on my helmet grant me the ability to see magic's flow, and my eyes follow veins of power running along the walls even now. Soon it will be true dark, and the magic will activate fully.

Mother's keep in Hollow is much the same, letting her Draw upon immense power when she wishes. But her wardings served other purposes, as well. In addition to standard defensive wards, they warmed in winter and cooled in summer, offering permanent lighting in active halls.

The wards along the wall spiral upward, Drawing magic toward the higher floors. What's it powering? It reminds me of Mrs. Bales' stories about the prison they built for Alagai Ka, back in the war.

I was in the demon's mind, and I know the shame of that imprisonment fuels his need for revenge now, every bit as much as his desire to repopulate the hive. Is Asome, too, planning his revenge inside some warded prison cell?

I am met by an acolyte in a white bido and sandals, a wide cloth of white silk draped over one shoulder. Acolytes are not allowed to speak in their first year, and this one only bows and bids me follow him with a gesture as he leads me up the winding stairs that climb the tower. Along the outer wall, the wardwork pattern climbs with us, still just Drawing power from the ground and pulling it upward. The glow brightens by the minute as night descends.

The tower has seven floors, all open and circular to make maximum use of the space. The lowest are functional, spaces for servants and visiting clerics to work. But as I rise farther, the Tower of Nothing looks less like a prison than a palace itself, with lavishly appointed visiting chambers, library, wardshop, and a bedchamber that would embarrass a princess.

Still the wards pull magic upward.

Finally we come to the seventh floor, a holy number. Each floor represents one of the seven pillars of Heaven—whatever that means. The Evejah, like the holy Canon of the Tenders, is full of long, beautiful figurative descriptions to spark the imagination without commitment in literal truth.

The acolyte bows, then turns and descends as silently as he climbed, leaving me alone atop the landing. At first my eyes are drawn by the wardwork, lit by magic's glow, climbing from the stairwell and circling the room, creeping like vines up the wall and out onto the floor.

A bright mosaic pattern of wardwork spins out from those vines, circling the room in intricate whorls. I follow the flow of magic to find my brother, kneeling at the center of the pattern, bathed in its power.

The men outside think they are his captors? It's almost comical. If Asome has even a fraction of Mother's or the Damajah's skill, this much power could set the entire Palace of the Holy Mother ablaze, or punch a hole in its walls. Asome is only a captive so long as he chooses to be.

But if the man before me has any ill intent, there is no sign. His aura is smooth. Peaceful. Controlled. Asome kneels in a perfect ward circle of polished white marble like a bull's-eye at the center of the floor. He peers at a pile of thrown silver sticks like a *dama'ting* at her dice. Wards etched into the precious metal glow with power.

"Welcome, sibling," Asome says without looking up. It's an uncommon word in the rigidly gendered Krasian language, and telling in its use.

"You've heard about me," I note.

Asome shrugs. "Nothing my sticks have not already told."

That is disconcerting. Enough of my life has been torn apart by the *dama'ting* dice. Now I have male seers to contend with, as well?

"I thought men were forbidden to use *hora* magic," I say.

"You of all people should understand the foolishness of that," Asome says. "What good comes from denying men *hora*, or women the spear? Does it help the *dama* rule more wisely, to hide behind wards at night while the *Sharum* fight and bleed? For the *dama'ting* to refuse to teach warriors to heal, or for *Sharum* to refuse any work not done with spear and shield?"

I can't argue with any of that. Krasian society—and Thesan—is hopelessly tangled in gendered rules that serve no real purpose save to divide. Proponents say it helps people understand their place in the world, but for those of us who do not comfortably fit in either box, it is more shackle than assistance.

"We limit ourselves with such rules," I say.

"Just so," Asome agrees, still staring at the sticks. "Tea?"

I don't think my brother has motivation to poison me, but the fact I'm considering it is reason enough to refuse. "Thank you, no." I pat my belly. "Tikka has been trying to put muscles on my frame."

Asome laughs at that, and his mirth seems genuine. "All Tikka's grandchildren are underfed in her eyes, and the servants and mothers take the blame."

"She doesn't care much for your mother," I agree, "or mine, for that matter."

"Her own daughters are spared no more of the lash than her daughters-in-law," Asome says. "There is no woman Tikka respects as much as she respects herself, but she loves us all, in her way."

I snort, again reminded of Grandmum Elona. The day with Tikka was tedious, and I had to bite my tongue the whole time, but I am glad I did it.

"And what do your sticks tell you about me?" I ask.

He turns to regard me now, eyes sharp and probing. "I will not lie like the *dama'ting* and tell you my seeings are Everam's will, or forbidden for me to share. But that does not mean you are ready for the knowledge, little sibling."

"And you decide what I am ready for?" I arch my back and cross my arms.

Asome does not appear impressed. Why should he be? I am no threat to him. Asome is a *sharusahk* grandmaster, said to be second only to my father. I haven't a fraction of his training or experience. If it came to blows here in his place of power, my brother could Draw upon his tower like a well, making himself stronger, faster, more resistant to harm. If he didn't just use the power to incinerate me.

Asome gestures to the floor before him, covered in mosaic wardwork. I trace their lines with my eyes and think of my training, trying to understand their purpose. I see wards of prophecy, but these aren't like any patterns I recall from the books of foretelling Favah had me study in Gatherers' University.

There are whorls of wardwork around the room with white marble at their centers, perfectly sized for a person to kneel. But I know if I step into one, I will be even deeper in my brother's power.

"Be at peace, Olive am'Paper. You are safe in my tower. By Everam and my hope of Heaven." Asome picks up an item next to him, a rolled carpet. In a smooth snap, he sends it unspooling, cutting across the wardnets on the floor and breaking their lines of power.

I nod and force my body to relax, moving to kneel on the carpet, facing him. Same position, same posture. Equals, though we are hardly that, even here in his "prison." Especially not here.

"Three of our brothers will answer your challenge." Asome speaks as if discussing nothing of consequence.

"Your sticks told you that?" I ask.

"They told me about one," Asome says. "The other two came here to ask my blessing to kill you."

I blink. "Who? And . . . did you give it?" It was clear Asome still had influence, but this . . .

Asome shrugs. "You made your challenge in open court. I would not dishonor you, or them, by telling my brothers they were not free to accept."

I don't know how to reply, so I grit my teeth and say nothing.

"Two swore an oath that they would accept your challenge openly, in front of witnesses, and offer seven breaths for you to prepare, as prescribed in the Evejah."

"That's something, I suppose," I say.

"The third will attack without honor," Asome says bluntly.

"So be it." It is my own fault, for making that challenge. "What do your sticks say about my odds of winning?"

Asome is not amused. "All our brothers are formidable, sibling. You would not do well to underestimate them. Everam will decide the victor, but do not be caught unarmed or unawares if you hope to survive."

It's not the answer I hoped for, but I am not surprised. "Do you even care who wins?"

"I bear you no ill will, sibling," Asome says. "The sons of Ahmann Jardir have ever fought like *nie'Sharum* in the gruel line for Father's attention and their place in succession. There was a time that struggle was everything to me. Now . . ."

Asome gestures to the mosaic floor, a breathtaking pattern of precious stones and marble that rivals anything I have ever seen, even in Sharik Hora itself. "This circle, and the secrets it unlocks, has become more my world than anything beyond."

"This is a . . . divination chamber?" I ask.

Asome raises an eyebrow. "Very good. It is said you were taught by the great seer Favah. What do you your trained eyes see?"

Trained eyes. I want to laugh. I was a passable student in surgery, but in the Chamber of Shadows, Favah spent more time scolding than praising my work. Not a session went by where she did not remind me that, princess or no, in Krasia I would have been cast from the Dama'ting Palace in failure.

Again my eyes run along the wardwork, not so different from patterns and designs I used to stitch onto silk garments back in Hollow. But where those were common protective wardings, these are designed to Draw magic from all directions, swirling around the kneeling spaces in the chamber before flowing inexorably to Asome, perched like a spider at its center.

"People you want to foretell kneel in the circles, so you can Draw magic through them and Read it," I guess.

"Indeed," Asome agrees. "The *dama'ting* need for blood is . . . primitive. Neither must I bind my throws to a specific question, and thus I see things the priestesses do not."

He points at wardwork climbing the walls like vines, then rises, gesturing for me to do the same. He backs to a wall with a heavy crank, and I find a similar wheel on my side. Together, we put our backs to work, and the wooden ceiling folds up like shutters, revealing the constellations rising above.

Seven crenels climb high above the parapet wall. I can see the wardings that flow up the walls of the divination chamber continue to rise unbroken to their points.

"The ward circles give a cleaner Read than the dice," Asome says, "and the crenels allow me to orient my throws to the stars."

"Who taught you this?" I ask. I've been around prophecy magic my whole life, but I've never seen anything like this.

"Clerics have attempted to find truth in sticks and the stars for thousands of years," Asome says, "but without magic to focus the throws, it was little more than guesswork. I learned the secrets of the *alagai hora* from a pair of the Damajah's *dama'ting*, eager to gain favor and aid me in my move to supplant her. My clerics studied their dice, but none of us could master the art. Instead, I turned to our own sacred texts and with the wards of foretelling brought some of that ancient magic back to the world."

"What do you use it for," I ask, "if you speak honest word when you say you do not care for the affairs beyond your tower?"

"To learn," Asome says. "To grow. My brothers in white, and those in blood, come for Readings and advice, and when I am moved, I do my best to help them find peace and fulfillment."

"And what moves you?" I ask.

"Untapped potential," Asome says.

"Well that I have in plenty," I say.

Asome laughs. "Remove the rug, then, little sibling. Kneel in a whorl, and I will cast the sticks for you."

I smile in return. "I do not know that you are ready for such knowledge, brother."

"You do not trust me." It's a statement, not a question.

"Is there a reason I should?" I ask. "I did not plan to come here, and I am not seeking advice. I only wanted to look you in the eye."

"And what did you expect to find?" Asome asks. "A gibbering madman, chained to the floor? A demon princeling, waiting to devour you? A penitent, broken by the failures of his past, forever begging forgiveness from a silent Creator?"

I shrug. "One of those, yes."

"Ah, but Everam made each and every one of us complex," Asome says. "Nothing is ever so simple. No one is fully villain, or hero, save perhaps Alagai Ka, and the Deliverer."

I snort. If that is so, I am no Deliverer.

"Why should you trust me?" Asome asks. "Because Nie is stirring once more. Because our father is missing, and Alagai Ka stalks the land at Waning."

None of these things is common knowledge, but Asome does not pretend to be in the dark. Are these things he learned from his sticks, or his spies?

"The last time Father was missing, you murdered the entire court," I note, "in the night when all men are brothers against the *alagai*. You broke faith with the Majah, costing the armies of Krasia their second-strongest tribe while Sharak Ka raged. You killed the man on the Skull Throne, your uncle and father-in-law, with your bare hands, and sent assassins after your own wife and mother."

If the words cut Asome, it does not show through the veil of calm Krasian clerics are taught to hold. I am not skilled at reading auras as Mother and the Damajah are, but Asome's is smooth and even, a steady glow and not a crackling fire.

"I did what I thought best for Krasia, at the time." Asome's voice is placid as a still pond. "I watched the Par'chin toss Father off a cliff, and did not think he would return. The *chin* took the opportunity to rebel. My brother Jayan was recklessly charging across the green lands, pillaging without humanity and exposing our forces to greater and greater risk in an attempt to win glory enough to take the throne. I could not allow that to happen. It was my right to challenge for the throne, but instead Mother handed it to my uncle Ashan, not because he was the strongest contender, but because she could control him."

I cross my arms again. "And now?"

Asome spreads his hands. "I was a fool. Impatient, and with delusions of grandeur no less blinding than those of my elder brother." He gestures to his sticks. "Long have I pondered that choice, and the divergence it created. And do you know what I see?"

"Please enlighten me," I say, knowing he is going to tell me regardless.

"If I had simply done nothing the night Jayan was killed, I could have had it all. The sticks and stars are clear about that. I had the love of the people and the loyalty of the men. If I had simply been patient, I would be heir, and not Kaji. If I had just been a little wiser, I would be on the Skull Throne this very day, not trapped in a tower, reading the stars.

"But in my impatience to see my honor satisfied, I struck out at those who would have supported me, in my turn. I killed in cold blood, and bade my younger brothers to do the same, cheating with *hora* in the night to ensure their own victories against the *Damaji*."

I try to keep my face as serene as my brother's, but there's a twitch at that.

"I could have presented Father with a unified Krasia when he returned, but in my arrogance, I presented him an empire fractured, instead. What could Mother and Father do, save remove me from power and public life? I am fortunate they did not kill me. In many divergences, they do, and who could blame them? It is what I would have done in their place."

I can't sense a lie in his words, but they don't ring of truth, either. "So do you regret your actions because they were wrong, or because they didn't get you what you wanted?"

Asome shrugs. "The stars do not care about right and wrong. They only burn."

"And that's how you see yourself?" I ask. "A star, beyond such things as good and evil?"

My brother offers me a smile. "I oppose Nie. Even you are not so naïve as to think victory over Her can come with no blood on your hands."

I think of drugging Wonda the night of the borough tour. Clutching the bodies of Chadan and Micha. Pressing a punch dagger into Iraven's chest.

When I do not respond, Asome nods. "But while I was put in a tower, my cousin Asukaji was pardoned for the same crimes, and serves as *Damaji* of the Kaji to this day. At first he kept his bed here with me, but more and more, his own palace called him, and could I blame him? To ask him to spend his life in a cell, because his lover could not leave? No. He has wives now, and children of his own."

"I'm sorry," I say. I don't know if it's worse to have a lover die or slowly abandon you.

Asome inhales deeply, blowing a long breath from his nose. "I let him go. I let everything go. And I am at peace. I took the throne, but it did not make our people stronger. If I could go back and repair the breach with Majah, or resurrect my father-in-law, I would. But we always see clearest when we look backward."

He moves back to the center of the divination chamber. "And so I have devoted myself to finding a new way to look forward. And that is something you sorely need, little sibling. You are thrusting your spear in the dark."

The condescension burns me, but he isn't wrong. I've been in over my head since demons first struck the borough tour on Summer Solstice. Winter Solstice approaches now, and my footing is no firmer.

"What did you mean, Nie is stirring?" I ask.

"Everam's battle with Nie is as eternal as night and day." Asome gestures to the sky above. "We do not see the stars in the day, but they are still there. So, too, the *alagai*. Father and the Par'chin may have won us a respite fifteen years ago, but the enemy is regrouping."

I've heard this all before. "Can you tell me how many? Where they are? When and how they will strike?"

Asome shakes his head, unsurprisingly. Of course not. Creator forbid a seer actually offer anything useful.

"I can tell you a convergence is coming," Asome says. "That futures once clear soon become clouded by the Void."

"When?" I press, though I know the answer will be more meaningless vaguery.

"The new moon before Summer Solstice," Asome says, "there will be a . . . birth."

Asome watches closely as the words register. I keep my face calm, but no doubt he can see it in my aura. This feels dangerously close to a real answer.

"Have you told the Damajah this?" I ask.

Asome chuckles. "My mother has not spoken to me since I was banished here to my tower."

"I cannot imagine why."

Asome nods, accepting the rebuke. "Even if she did, I do not believe she or any *dama'ting* would put faith in a man's Sight."

He's right. *Dama'ting* look down their noses at men in general, and would be more likely to burn a *dama* caught performing magic for heresy than trust his visions.

But Inevera said it herself. I must seize every advantage. If Asome knows something . . .

"Not a birth." I can hear Inevera's *tsst* in my head, but I ignore it. "A hatching."

"Of course." A shock runs through Asome's aura, there and gone like a flash of lightning. "I can help you, Olive. But you must trust me." His eyes flick to the mosaic floor.

I have no illusions about the enormity of the request. Asking me to kneel in one of his divination circles is tantamount to Inevera asking for my blood. To calculate my chances, to glean anything useful, I must give my half brother access to everything I am, to my deepest secrets and privacies, to things I don't even know about myself. I must do this, and trust him not to abuse the power. Not to turn it against me. And to be truthful about what he sees.

I must put all this trust in Asome, who admits to murdering dozens in his bloody coup for the throne, and carries no burden on his aura for it. Asome, who can look back on killing his uncle with bare hands, shrug, and say, *It seemed like a good idea at the time.*

Even mentioning the hatching is more trust than I should have for this man, who was the ruin of so many lives. I look at the glowing wards climbing the crenels, blending into the brightening stars filling the night sky.

But he knew a birth was coming in the forces of Nie, and that it would herald change. I thought we might have a year or more, but if my brother is right, there's even less time than we thought.

"And what will you give me in exchange?" I ask.

Now it is Asome who crosses his arms. "Must we play games like *dama'ting*? You claimed at court to be a sister to them, but it is said, too, that you have the heart of a *Sharum*. *Sharum* do not haggle favors with their spear brothers when they are in the Maze."

He's right, but he's got some stones to say that to me. "What would you know of it, Dama Asome? Have you even set foot in the Maze? My brothers would not hesitate to bleed for me, and I for them. What do you sacrifice, here in your private tower?"

Surprisingly, Asome offers a shallow bow. "You are correct. I apologize. Like you, I was denied the spear as a child. *Dama* were not allowed to fight the *alagai*. I changed that, for a time, but it is nothing compared to the sacrifice of countless generations of *Sharum*."

Honest word, or a political apology? His aura tells me nothing.

My brother spreads his hands. "I have nothing else to offer you, Olive am'Paper. Wealth? Power? You have your own, no doubt far exceeding anything I can offer. I am trapped here, and cannot stand at your back in the night. Information is all I can offer, but I cannot give it without trust."

"Corespawn it," I mutter, and roll up the carpet Asome cast across the floor, revealing the wards. I kneel in one of the whorls of wardwork. The moment the lines are unbroken, they fill with power, casting the room in beautiful patterns of wardlight to match the constellations above.

Like a cool breeze, the magic tingles and pimples my skin as Asome Draws it through me. Just a fraction of what I feel when I put my spear into a demon, but still a rush of pleasure.

Barely a moment later, I feel that breeze move on, flowing into the circle surrounding Asome. He is chanting quietly, not a question like a *dama'ting*, but a rhythmic prayer that builds resonance in the air until suddenly it breaks, and with a shout, Asome casts his sticks.

Around the room, prophecy wards flare briefly, and there is a clatter as the sticks rearrange themselves in midair before falling to the ground.

"You are strong," Asome says, peering at the throw, "but divided. You will not unlock your full strength until you understand yourself and your place in the world."

Again, not wrong, but nothing I don't already know. "Does anyone truly understand themselves and their place in the world?"

Asome ignores my acerbic tone, his eyes following the directions the sticks point to their corresponding vines of wardwork climbing the crenels. He pauses, staring at the constellations splayed across the sky. "Your heart pulls to the east, but that path leads to destruction."

I tense at the words. Such things were spoken only in the strictest confidence of the Damajah's casting chamber, and under Mother's wards of silence. There is no way he could have known about Safehold.

"Why?" I dare ask.

Again Asome consults the sticks, their orientation, the stars. "You are too . . . blunt to accomplish what must be done there."

Alagai Ka will see me coming, he means. Darin may have the knack of sneaking into places unseen, but I tend to kick in doors, not skulk in shadows.

"And the task your mother set before me?" I ask, without hinting what that might be.

Asome peers at the sticks, and the wards, and the sky, and at last at me. "I do not know," he says, "but I do know my mother. She is a true enemy of Nie, and believes that makes her impartial, but she is not, and that is dangerous. Do not doubt for an instant that she will sacrifice you, your mother, or even Hollow itself, if it will benefit Krasia or return her husband to her."

CHAPTER 21

TRIO

SELEN WHITTLES WHILE Arick and I practice. It's a habit she picked up from her da, and she ent bad. Top of the stick she's working on is already a passable nightwolf head, getting clearer with every flake her blade coils away.

Whittlin' ent as quiet as most folk like to think. I hear the scrape like she's sawing a log, and it's a challenge to keep tempo with the distraction. But I can hear how the simple hobby keeps her blood calm and her heartbeat steady. Ent gonna ask her to stop when I know it helps keep her from worrying every time Olive is out of sight.

The struggle to keep in sync with Arick ent entirely Selen's fault. We're getting better, but it's slow going. Arick lays down a deep sound I can build off and improvise around, but I smell his irritation every time I do something he doesn't anticipate. Tried to do it his way, but Arick's playing is always perfect. Even when I'm at my best, it ent good enough for him.

A knock at the door makes us all jump. Selen is on her feet and moving while sound still hangs in the air. Night has fallen, and Olive still ent come back from her grandmam's palace.

I sniff the air and smile at the scent. "Ent Olive," I call. "It's Rojvah!"

Selen opens the door, and Rojvah gives a cry of delight, throwing her arms around Selen, who stands frozen, smelling uncomfortable.

"It sounds like two cats deciding if they should mate in here," Rojvah laughs. "I knew you two couldn't get along without me."

"I fear you are right." Arick is the next to embrace her.

Rojvah smells positively delighted. "I am what, brother? I don't think I quite heard."

"Once was enough for your ego, sister," Arick says. "Don't expect to hear it again soon."

Rojvah laughs again, turning to me with a twinkle in her eye that scares me a little. I step back, and she pouts her lips, still smelling delighted.

"Darin ent much of a hugger." Selen smells amused, too.

"That's all right." Rojvah smells triumphant. "His kiss of intention before the Damajah this morning said more than any embrace."

"His what of what?!" Selen whirls on me, and I know the smell of her anger the instant it hits my nostrils. Usually when I catch that scent, it's time to turn slippery and find a quiet place to hide for a few hours.

But this time, I got nowhere to run.

Arick looks at his sister, incredulous, and then over at me. "You can both do better."

Rojvah laughs a third time, and it's enough to make Selen boil over the pot. "Will someone rippin' tell me what in the core is goin' on?"

"Rojvah's mam wouldn't let her come with us," I remind her.

"Know that," Selen says. "I was right there."

"Agreed to change her mind," I say, "if we got promised. Damajah blessed it and everything. Now that we're intended, it's only proper for her to come."

"And you agreed to that?" Selen barks. "Are you a rippin' idiot?"

"When last we asked," Rojvah's voice is sharp, her scent shifting from amused to protective, "you likened a betrothal to the son of Arlen to 'marrying your brother.' If you have changed your mind, perhaps I will consider taking you as *Jiwah Sen*."

"Ay, that tears it!" There is rage in Selen's scent as she balls her fists and stalks in. Rojvah doesn't flinch, sliding a foot behind her in what looks like a *sharusahk* stance.

"Not in my chambers, thank you." Arick steps between them.

Selen pulls up short. "Stay out of this."

"Yes, brother," Rojvah agrees. "If the daughter of Gared wants to settle her problems like a dog, I will treat her like one."

"Ay, that's enough!" I bellow. Don't think I've ever been that loud in my life, and everyone stops and looks at me like I've turned into a demon.

"Nobody's puttin' hands on anyone!" I shout at Selen, and she instinctively opens her fists and puts her hands down.

"And enough with the teasin'!" I tell Rojvah. "Askin' to get stung, poking a hornet's nest for a laugh. Can always go see the Damajah and call that promise off, you make me regret this."

I expect a fight, but Rojvah backs down immediately, taking a step back and . . . bowing? That ent the Rojvah I know, and I don't much like it. "Of course, Intended. I did not mean for things to get so heated." There's sincerity in her scent. She was just playin'. Din't expect Selen's kettle to whistle so fast.

I look back at Selen. "Ent real. Just a Jongleur's show so Rojvah can come with us. We make it back from Safehold, we can just call it off."

"Ay, that's what she wants you to think." Selen shakes her head. "Gives her time to put her claws in you."

Now Arick smells protective, taking a step forward. "Perhaps you should leave, Selen am'Cutter, before you say something we all regret."

Selen eyes him a moment and nods. "Honest word." She's out the door a moment later, stomping all the way back to the chambers she shares with Olive.

"She was just surprised, Intended." Rojvah's voice is calm. Soothing. "And perhaps offended you did not share our plan with her, before going to the Damajah."

"Ay, maybe." That does sound like the kind of thing Selen would get steamed about, but not so much she'd go around hitting folk. Thoughtfulness in Rojvah's scent suggests she ent told me all her guesses.

Corespawn me if I can understand what either of them are thinking. Ent like I'm some great catch. Arick's right that Rojvah could do better, and if Selen wanted me, I been there for the takin' all this time. Heard enough kissy stories to know she ent shy.

Even if one of them really did think I had what it took to be the man in her life—whatever that even means—I ent sure what I want, myself.

Krasians call me a prince, and to the Hollowers the son of the Deliverer is as good as, but truer is my lifestyle ent got much in common with the palaces and pampering Selen and Rojvah are used to. I don't want to spend the rest of my life at court any more than they want to climb trees in Tibbet's Brook. Anyone thinks they got a fancy catch marryin' me is in for a lifetime of disappointment.

WITH AN EAR TO THE WIND, I hear Olive's escort long before they make it to the palace. Rojvah's long gone and Arick's fast asleep, so there's no one to see me flit out the window, down to the ground, across the yard, and over the wall. I scale one of the houses across the street and run like wind across rooftops until I find their procession.

I turn slippery and leap from the roof. Light as a feather, I drop silently onto Olive's palanquin. Menin rides beside the door, eyes scanning back and forth, alert for threats. I time it so he's looking away, sliding through a gap in Olive's window before Menin's attention comes back to front.

There's a hiss as a knife comes from its sheath. Sunny thing I'm already slippery as I twist out of its path. I slide by the next slash, and the one after that. "Olive, it's me, corespawn it!"

"Night, Darin!" Olive's voice is a harsh whisper. "You couldn't wait for us to get back? I could have killed you."

"Ay, sorry," I say. "But I took a demon by the horns today, and I need some advice."

Olive calms at that. "Well that's got my attention. I've been on the receiving end of unasked-for advice all day. Happy to offer some, for a change."

I quickly fill her in, and Olive makes a face. "Selen's got a point, Darin. It was foolish to agree without at least talking to us, first."

"Ent foolish to help folk in need, Olive," I say.

"Ay, I didn't mean it like that," Olive says. "This was just a bit . . . impulsive. Even for you."

"Reckon it was my turn," I say, "after you challenged half the court to a duel."

Olive laughs, and we both relax a little. "I just worry you're being taken advantage of. I see how this serves Rojvah, but I don't see what you get out if it."

She smells protective now. She's giving honest word, but . . . "Don't see why everyone always needs to get somethin' out of everythin'. Can't we just stand by each other without writing debts in the ledger?"

Not sure why that one lands, but Olive gives herself a little shake at that. "You're not the first person to say something like that to me tonight. And you're right. I don't think that's why Selen's mad, anyway. She's always had a soft spot for you, Dar. I imagine this hurt her feelings."

"A soft spot?" I ask. "What's that even mean? Sayin' she likes me? Or am I just part of the crowd she plays kissy with?"

Olive sighs. "Core if I know, Darin. I'm just saying she wouldn't be mad if she didn't care about you."

That don't make a lick of sense. "Gettin' mad's a funny way of showing you care."

"How would you feel," Olive asks, "if Selen suddenly told us she was engaged to Arick?"

Reckon I'd feel like I was punched in the gut. I don't say it, but I don't need to.

"You can't put it all on her," Olive says. "You could have opened your mouth and told her you shined on her a long time ago."

"Ay," I snap. "And when was I supposed to do that? While we were chasin' you across Thesa, and the desert besides? In between her kissy stories, with all your spear brothers laughing along? Ay, maybe I shined on Selen, but it's all just a joke to her, ennit? Teased me about it right in the hall of her da's manse the night you were took. Made like she was gonna kiss me, then said *you* were the jealous one, and walked away smelling smug."

Olive frowns, and I can smell her annoyance. "I didn't know that part."

"Ay, reckon she had good laugh about givin' my head a spin," I say. "Knew she was makin' fun, but didn't know if I should be excited or angry. Then you disappeared and . . ."

"Oh, so it's my fault, now?" Olive's scent changes from annoyed to indignant. "Need I remind you I was fighting for my life while you two were playing kissy games at Baron Cutter's manse?"

"Know it ent your fault." I put my hands up. "But you got no business tellin' me it's mine. Rojvah needed help and we need her if we want to sneak into Safehold without you. There's your trade, Olive. Fair and square.

"And even if Selen did shine back on me, can you see her coming to live in Tibbet's Brook?"

"Of course not," Olive says. "You would live in Hollow with us."

"And what if that's not what I want?" I ask. "You and Selen gonna tag along as I play the hamlets with my pipes?"

Olive rolls her eyes. "We both know you're never going to be a Jongleur, Dar. Night, you can't even stand in a crowd without having a fit."

The matter-of-factness of her tone, her scent, cuts deeper than the words themselves. Like she's just been humoring me all these years when I told her and Selen my dreams. Reckon Selen feels the same. Look at little Darin, dreaming of sitting at the grown-ups' table.

"Stood in a lot of crowds, Olive Paper, comin' to fetch you out of Desert Spear." Tears start welling in my eyes. Can't hold 'em back for long. "Rojvah wants to be a Jongleur, too, and no one's got her back, either."

I turn away quick, before she sees me cry.

"Darin!" Olive reaches for me, but I'm already slippery, and her fingers slide right off as I squeeze out the window. Menin gives a shout at my sudden appearance, but he recognizes me and doesn't try to stop me as I climb to the roof.

Olive leans from the window, looking up at me. "Darin Bales, you come back here!"

I ignore her, leaping to a windowsill. I go from slippery to sticky, and run up the wall like a squirrel runs up a tree. I'm halfway to the palace when she calls a second time, and atop the wall by the third.

I don't head back to Arick's chambers. Instead I scale one of the minarets. The tiny chambers atop the towers are empty, save when the *dama* sing the call to prayer.

Alone at last, I curl up and let myself cry.

CHAPTER 22

DARIN BALES IS MAGIC

THE PALANQUIN CRAWLS ALONG, even as Darin vanishes into the night. I know better than to think I could catch him, or find him if he doesn't want to be found, but I'm ready to be back in my rooms, packing up so we can put this place behind us. If Asome is right, we haven't a moment to lose.

"Enough of this demonshit." I open the door, startling Menin.

"Prince Olive?" Menin asks.

I offer him a bright smile. "Have you ever ridden in a palanquin?"

A moment later, I am atop Menin's horse, and Gared, Faseek, Gorvan, and Jow Cutter break off my escort to gallop the rest of the way back to the palace with me.

The palace guards are surprised, but they do not hinder us. We move freely until we reach the entrance to the hall where my chambers are set. The hall seems empty at first, but the shadows to one side bleed out and detach, coalescing into three men, two *dal'Sharum* and one *kai*.

The magic is similar to what my sister Micha used, *hora* jewelry to draw shadows and silence footfalls. Assassination magic. Yet here they are, making themselves seen.

It puts my bodyguards on edge. I am used to seeing magic at work, but Gorvan and Faseek are not. To their credit, they do not panic, but they are quick to ready spears and shields, though the men have made no threatening moves.

The *kai* takes a step forward, giving a proper, if shallow, warrior's bow. A bow of equals. "Greetings, Olive asu Ahmann am'Paper am'Hollow, I am your brother, Vuxan asu Ahmann am'Jardir am'Krevakh."

That explains the shadow magic. Like the Nanji, the Krevakh are a Watcher tribe. Trained in special weapons and combat, the Krevakh serve the Kaji tribe—my father's tribe—as scouts and infiltrators, doing the dirty work needed to keep the Kaji dominant, and their hands clean.

Faseek and Gorvan do not relax at the introduction. The Majah and Krevakh are blood enemies, going back through centuries. No doubt my spear brothers see battle as inevitable, though there is no sense of fear about them. The Maze beat that fear out of all of us.

I raise two fingers, and my bodyguard reluctantly raise the tips of their spears to the ceiling. Not quite standing down, but at least a bit further from things escalating.

"What can I do for you, brother?" I already know the answer, but I hold out hope.

"I have come to accept your challenge." There is no emotion in Vuxan's voice, like he was accepting an invitation to lunch, and not mortal combat.

"At night." I blow out an exasperated breath. "I hoped the Krevakh had more honor than the Nanji. They, too, struck me at night."

Vuxan's eyes tighten. Inevera told me the purpose of the Krevakh and Nanji was to be without honor, but I know a little of tribal rivalries now. They might not care about brother killing brother in the night, but they do care about being compared to their blood enemies.

Vuxan bows again. "We have been waiting for many hours. We expected you to return before sunset." I don't know if it's a lie, but neither is it a denial. If I were willing to fight, Vuxan would happily oblige.

But I'm not in the mood. I offer a return bow, precisely mimicking Vuxan's. "I am sorry, then, that you will have to wait a few hours longer," I say. "Nanji may be willing to attack brothers in the night, but we carry more honor than that."

Vuxan bows a third time. There is tension in the three men, but I can tell when a person is wound up, and when they're ready to fight. "We will return at dawn."

I keep eye contact, cool and measured. "I look forward to it. Weapons?"

"If you wish." Vuxan smiles. "I will kill you with *sharusahk*, alone. I do not wish to bloody the palace of the Shar'Dama Ka."

"You are wise, brother." He's a fool. "Our seconds can search us to ensure we bring no weapons or *hora* to the fight."

Selen opens the door to our chambers, noticing me down the hall. "Heard voices," she says loudly. "Everything all right?"

"Ay, Sel, nothing to worry over," I call back, not looking away from Vuxan. "We're done here."

"How can you be so calm," Selen asks, "when someone's coming to kill you in the morning?"

"He's agreed to fight in daylight, without *hora*," I say. "They don't know how strong I am, Selen. Vuxan thinks his *sharusahk* is better—and he's probably right—but Micha says the Krevakh like to get in close and grapple. He's in for a surprise when he does."

Selen puts her hands on her hips. "Don't get swollen, Olive. Wonda always said strength ent as important as having leverage and a good hold. You might be strong as a bull, but you choke like everyone else."

She would know. Selen made me tap out enough times, back in the practice yard at Gatherers' University. "I've had months of intense training since then, Sel, and wrestled live demons in the Maze. I know how to use what I have."

I hold up my hands when she looks ready to argue further. "But you're right. I'll fight smart. I won't take anything for granted."

"You could just not fight at all," Selen says. "We're leaving in the morning. Don't answer the door for a quarter hour and Da will show up with a team of Cutters and we'll be on the road."

"Can't do that, Sel." I harden my voice. "Maybe it wasn't my best decision to run my mouth in the throne room—"

"Ay, you think?" Selen cuts in.

"But now that I have, my honor is on the line," I say. "I'm about to take the throne of Hollow. I can't have them thinking I'm weak or a coward, or I don't respect their customs."

"Should you," Selen asks, "when the custom is siblings beating each other to death over a throne neither of them is likely to inherit?"

"I don't intend to kill anyone," I say.

"And Vuxan?"

"Can't speak for everyone." I shrug, though I know full well none of my brothers would accept my challenge if they didn't intend my end. I will sit a throne of my own in a month, if I am not stopped now. "I'd rather talk about what happened here."

"Here?" Selen asks.

"Darin paid me a visit in my palanquin," I say.

"Oh, ay, did he now?" Selen's already on the defensive, which isn't a good sign. "That woodbrain tell you what he did?"

"He did," I say. "And why. It isn't the brightest thing he's ever done, but it was his decision to make."

"Like night it was!" Selen snaps. "You think his mam would have allowed it, if she was around?"

It's not hard to imagine Mrs. Bales putting the fear of the Creator into poor Rojvah, but it's beside the point. "You aren't his mother, Selen. And you're not acting like his friend. He told me about your little game after Seventhday supper with the general. What are you playing at with him?"

"I'm not 'playing' anything, Olive Paper." Selen looks ready to spit.

"Demonshit," I say. "We were friends with Darin all our lives with nary a problem. Everything changed, after you kissed him."

"Ay, what of it?" Selen demands. "I've kissed a hundred since."

"At least," I laugh. "But he's the only one who put you in a spin."

"You're one to talk." Selen puts her hands on her hips. "Every kiss puts you in a spin. What makes you think Darin is so special?"

"Because Darin Bales isn't some stablehand that's sunny to look upon," I snap, tired of her dissembling. "Darin Bales is ripping magic and we both know it. Always was."

"So are you!" Selen snaps back. "Or do you think everyone can bend iron with their bare hands?"

"Not like Darin," I say. "You remember what he was like when we were little? Flitting around the nursery like . . ."

Selen smiles. "Some kind of fairy pipkin." We both laugh, and a little of the tension eases.

"Darin's got feelings for you, Sel," I say softly. "Any fool can see it."

"Ay, what am I supposed to do about it?" Selen asks. "He's been following us everywhere since we learned to walk."

"And we liked the attention," I say. "We liked our little pipkin. But then you kissed him, and it was just you he was following. Now he's a man, and maybe doesn't belong to either of us, anymore."

"The core he doesn't," Selen growls. "You went missing, and you should have seen him, Olive. Nothing was going to stop Darin from coming for you, and he'd do the same for me. Just like we would for him. If that ent belonging, then I don't know what is."

"He's family," I agree. "But so are Arick and Rojvah. You think Darin wouldn't do the same for them? What you're feeling is something else."

The hands go back to her hips. "Ay? Tell me."

I shrug. "I can't. Only you can answer that question, Sel. You and Darin were alone on the road for months. What does he mean to you?"

"Ent like we played kissy on the road, Olive," Selen sighs. "First we were chasing after you, and then Darin's mam and Leesha were gone, too. Didn't really set the scene for romance."

"Fair and true." I nod. "And now?"

"I don't know," Selen says. "But can't shake the feeling that witch Rojvah is using him."

"What if he's letting himself be used?" I ask. "What if it's like he said—she asked for help, and he gave it?"

"That's just it!" Selen cries. "Darin's openhearted and trusting enough to get married just to help someone out. Doesn't make it right for her to take advantage.

"What can I offer him, anyway?" Selen demands. "Darin is magic, and so are you. I'm the odd one out, always trying to keep up with you two."

"What are you talking about?" I mean the words. "You've always been better than me at everything!"

"Because you were holding back!" Selen shouts. "Don't you think I knew that?"

"Only in the practice yard. Would you prefer I ripped off your arm because I misjudged a hold?" It's the wrong thing to say, an admission of the lie, even if we both know it to be true.

There are tears in Selen's eyes. When's the last time I saw that, outside a funeral service? Maybe never.

"Ent angry at you, Olive," Selen says. "Don't hate who I am. Just sayin' what we know to be true. You and Darin inherited magic powers and grand destinies, and what did I get? A scandal that leaves everyone in my family miserable, and legs so long even the tall boys have to look up at me."

"Demonshit, Selen." I know she's in pain, but I won't tolerate this false picture she's painting. "You're the one everyone wants to be around. You're the one everyone loves. The life of the party. Darin and I were the ones who didn't belong. It was all I could do not to break everything I touched! More often than not, Darin couldn't handle the party at all. Stuck by himself in an attic, listening to everyone laugh at your jokes and kissy stories."

Selen pulls back, but I reach out, taking her hand and holding her fast. "And you're a princess of Hollow. Crown princess, now. It will fall on you to take the throne while I'm away."

"The core you say!" Selen yanks her hand from mine. "What makes you think I have any business sitting a throne?"

"As much as I have," I say. "We've been side by side at every lesson. What do I know that you don't? And you're the duchess' sister. Apart from me, you may be the only one in Hollow with a stronger claim than Elona." I love Grandmum, but no sane person would want that woman on a throne.

"No." Selen spits on the floor. "Core with that. Ent staying behind and warming a chair while Darin goes off with that witch and her demon-addled brother, and you abandon us to march off to Creator knows where."

I TRY MY BEST TO SLEEP, but despite the bravado I showed Selen, I can't stop thinking about Vuxan and the fight to come. I keep waking with a start, thinking it is time to prepare, only to find it still deep in the night.

Bells mark the hours, and I calculate how much rest I could get if I managed to drift off now, or in ten minutes, but in my heart I know that if I was going to sleep, I wouldn't be doing math in my head.

I give up when the sky begins to lighten, pacing the room a bit, before opening the doors and admitting Faseek and Gorvan.

"Do either of you know how this works?" I ask.

Both men shrug. "Your seconds will perform searches to check for weapons, and then you bow and fight," Gorvan says. "Either you kill Vuxan, or he kills you."

I tighten my lips but don't comment. "Faseek, you will be my second."

Faseek starts to kneel, but stops at the look I give him, offering a warrior's salute instead. "Gorvan would be a better choice, my prince. Your second will need to fight, if you are not able."

Not a good answer. Gorvan is a better fighter than Faseek, at least in terms of size, strength, and reach, but no match for a Krevakh prince. Faseek is wiser and more cunning. "That will not happen. Faseek will be my second, and search Vuxan for weapons and *hora*."

"And if the Watchers are hiding something?" Faseek asks.

"Then we all fight."

I look back and see Selen is awake and in her armored robes, a grim look on her face.

Precisely at dawn, there is a knock at the door. I wonder if my brother and his men really did just wait in the hall for the sun to crest the horizon.

We let them in, and Vuxan glances at Selen, then back at me. "It would be best to dismiss her. *Domin Sharum* is not for the eyes of women."

Selen snorts and crosses her arms. "Not going anywhere."

Vuxan looks at her again, then at me, but when I say nothing, he shrugs. "She can stand between sides and judge."

I nod, and he removes his armor, then we both raise arms, letting our seconds perform a search for hidden items. I've told Faseek what to look for, and he does well, making my brother remove the *hora* jewelry from his wrists, fingers, and ankles. My brother does so with calm confidence, and I remember Selen's words.

You choke like everyone else.

Everyone warned me, but here I am, muscles all in a knot as I move to face my brother. Vuxan is of an age with most of my siblings—on the sunny side of thirty-five summers. That makes him twice my age, but still in his prime, with twice my experience, at least. Can I really beat him?

"Begin," Selen says.

My brother wastes no time, darting forward, hand chopping like a hatchet. I swat it aside, but he follows quickly with more attacks, each flowing smoothly into the next, leaving little exposed as he thrusts open palms and stiffened fingers. All the while, his feet move like a dancer's, trying to position me for a takedown.

I keep my defenses in close, blocking and accepting minor hits without committing myself to an attack that might leave one of my limbs vulnerable.

"I expected better, brother," Vuxan says. "Do you fear to strike?"

"The *chin* prince has a coward's heart," one of the Krevakh says, and his partner laughs.

They're baiting me. I know it. And yet it works. I throw a tight punch, and Vuxan flows around it like a viper, threading his arm through my armpit and latching fingers onto my neck, even as he kicks out one of my legs and I slam painfully down onto one knee.

There's a hole in my guard then, and Vuxan has another hand around my neck, locking his fingers, even as his legs pump to drive me to the ground.

It's a strong hold, powered as much by my brother's weight and my own struggles as it is his muscles. Already I can feel my face swelling as he cuts off the flow of blood to my head.

"Olive!" Selen cries, and I know she won't hold to honor if it means watching me die. I flail a hand gesture her way. *Hold.*

I slap my hands atop Vuxan's. "There is no quarter here, brother," he growls, misunderstanding the gesture.

I wasn't tapping out, I was locking my own grip. The tight hold, bolstered by weight and struggle, means it's muscle against muscle, bone against bone. I pull with all my strength, twisting as soon as I feel a shift.

My brother's wrists break with audible snaps, but to his credit he does not cry out. I let go one arm and throw myself forward as I yank the other. Vuxan flies over my shoulder to land on his back on the floor. His arm is locked, and I twist before he can recover, driving my elbow down hard. The arm shatters, and while Vuxan is too disciplined to scream, his eyes droop, and I finish the fight with a simple roundhouse punch that lays him out on the floor.

"Winner," Selen says loudly.

Vuxan's second shakes his head and pulls his mouth shut, but he still looks stunned. "Finish it, and have done."

I shake my head. "What is your name?"

"I am Obun asu Obun am'Akeera am'Krevakh, Kai Olive." The warrior has more respect in his tone now.

"My brothers may wish to kill me, son of Obun," I tell him, "but I do not wish to kill them. Remind Vuxan of that when he wakes, that he may reflect upon it over the weeks while his bones heal."

Obun doesn't question further, he and his compatriot moving quickly to pick up their *kai* and carry him off before I have a chance to change my mind. I've shamed Vuxan, I know. He might have preferred death, and by my denying it, he may become an even greater threat. Or he may indeed reflect, and realize I do not have to be his enemy.

Always choose peace. This time it's Mother's voice in my head, but the more I see of the world, the more her sayings feel like lessons hard-earned, and not the platitudes I used to hear them as.

Gared appears in the doorway, eyeing the *Sharum* as they hurry past. "Everythin' all right, Olive?"

"Ay, Uncle Gared." I keep my voice sunny. "One of my brothers just stopped in to say goodbye."

"Looks like he got more than he bargained for." The general seems unperturbed. "He dead?"

"Just broken bones," Selen tells him. "Olive was feeling generous."

"Attagirl." I can't remember the last time anyone called me girl, but there is pride in the general's voice, and even I am not immune to it.

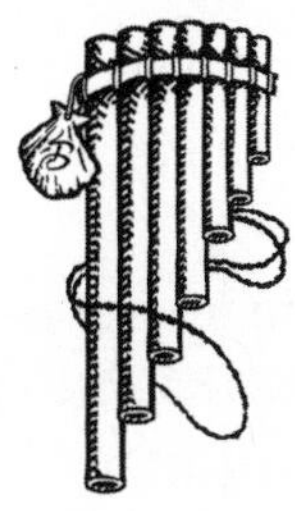

CHAPTER 23

MESSENGER ROAD

I FEEL DAWN COMIN'. Even when I'm asleep, the sense is enough to wake me up, like the heat and pressure in the air right before a summer storm.

Just as well. I'll be exposed to the sun if I don't get off the minaret balcony, and soon the *dama* will begin the climb to sing the call to prayer. Want to be gone by then. Everything goes to plan, we're leaving today. Can't just hide like I could some other day.

Don't much feel like seein' anyone, I'm to tell honest word. Selen's mad at me, core only knows why, and Olive's takin' her side, even if she can't explain it. Arick and Rojvah are fine when we're making music, but I don't know what to do with them, rest of the time. Arick's haunted and Rojvah ent tellin' me everything.

Night, Rojvah and I are *promised*. Never really expected I'd promise anyone, and if I did, always thought it would be Selen. Maybe Olive's right. Maybe I don't know what I'm getting into.

But I don't reckon Olive does, either. What did the Damajah say behind those wards of silence, to make her consider heading down into the dark, in the opposite direction from us? What's she thinkin', leaving finding our mams up to me, of all people? Ent got a clue where to look. Olive's the one who saw Safehold in the demon's mind. And what do I do if I find it? Might be able to sneak in, but I can't exactly bend prison bars and fight off coreling guards like she can.

As my senses come out of slumber, I notice a presence. Someone's on the balcony with me.

Immediately I go slippery. I open my eyes to find a man perched on the rail, staring down at me. His skin is similar to Olive's—dark for a greenlander, but light for a Krasian—and his scent is . . . confusing. He mostly smells like hogroot, a weed that grows wild just about everywhere. So common I normally filter it out, here it swallows the man's natural smells in much the same way as the alomom powder Watchers use when they want to sneak.

"Do not be afraid, Darin am'Bales," the man says. "I mean you no harm."

He gets points for using my name and not just my da's, but still I slither back from the balcony. Slippery like I am right now, I can give one good kick and fly down the steps like a mudslide. "Funny way of showin' it, sneaking up on a body like that."

The man smiles. "Some of us can't help but sneak, brother. You of all people should understand that."

I reach down, feeling the bone handle of Mam's knife at my belt. Ent a sharper blade in all the world. "Not feelin' very understanding at the moment. And I ent your brother."

"Are you not?" he asks. "So far as I know, you and I are the last of our people."

I grip the handle now, fighting the urge to pull the knife out. Ent ever been one for fighting when I've got room to run, but already I can hear the *dama* stirring in the courtyard. They'll cross the yard and be on their way up the steps soon. "What people?"

He pulls the wrappings from one of his hands, holding it up to show a pressure ward tattooed on his palm. "Wardskins."

The skin on my scalp tingles where Mam tattooed a mind ward, so long ago. I shiver and break out in gooseflesh. Uncle Gared said all the Warded Children were missing, which means . . .

I sniff again, and this time the hogroot smell reminds me of a story Hary Roller used to tell, about a little boy who escaped the demons that killed his family by spending ten years hiding in a bog. "You're Briar Damaj."

The man nods. "I am to accompany you to the green lands, and Princes Olive into the dark below, if that is her path."

"And if it ent?" I ask.

Briar shrugs. "Then I will guide whoever the Damajah sends, instead."

I swallow a lump in my throat. Briar left the Warded Children not long after his initiation, but they never stopped spinning tales about him. Ella Cutter said it was because Stela kissed him once, and then mucked it up by kissin' someone else.

Ent that a thing.

Used to be more than a hundred Warded Children. Some of them new blood—tatted but untested—and others, like Stela Inn and Brother Franq, who ate demon meat in the war and were nearly as strong as Mam.

But it seems none of them was strong enough to escape Alagai Ka's trap. Found a bloody bit of Stela's hair at the scene of the ambush. It smoldered and stank, but not enough to fool me. Wasn't much more left of Brother Franq. Just a foot that must have gone flying when the demons tore him apart and ate him, landing under some debris.

Ella Cutter was mostly in one piece. Reckon she lasted till close to dawn, and there wasn't time for demons to eat her. Din't make it any easier to look at.

Memories of that day start flashing through me, faster than I can absorb. The smell of demonshit, the taste of my friends' cooked flesh on the air. Their torn and gnawed bodies, the muck that sucked at my feet, churned wet with their insides.

I take three quick breaths and focus on the only thing at hand to break me out of it. Briar is waiting patiently, keeping his distance, giving me time.

"How did you find me?" I ask.

Briar smiles. "I don't like palace walls any more than you, brother, but I do enjoy balconies." He turns, sweeping a hand at the view from the railing. The palace is on the highest hill in the area, and from atop the minaret we have an unobstructed view of the entire city. "I didn't find your hiding spot, little brother, you found mine."

I hear the *dama* enter the minaret far below and start to ascend the steps. They like to get to the balcony well before dawn, so they can catch their breath and be ready to sing as soon as the sun crests the horizon.

"Come," Briar reaches out with his warded hand, pulling me to my feet, "fetch your things, and we can talk on the road."

We're long gone before the cleric reaches the balcony. Briar has no more need of stairs than I do, and we climb down the sheer wall of the minaret like others might let themselves down a rope.

BRIAR BREAKS OFF, promising to see me shortly, and I make it back to Arick's room before the sun comes to burn my powers away for another day. I slip in one of his windows and away from the growing light, but Arick's got a visitor, and I take care not to be noticed.

"You cannot stop me from going," Arick says.

"I am not here to try." Amanvah smells anxious and afraid, but she's come herself, this time.

Amanvah's always looked after Arick like he was her own son, but he ent, and the distinction is clear in the difference between how she treats Rojvah and Arick. Rojvah gets all the attention and judgment. Arick's always needed to chase her attention, and never been able to win her approval when he does.

"I swore to your mother Sikvah that I would love and raise you as my own," she says quietly. "And for my part, I thought I did. Your father was a great man, and deserved a worthy heir. I gave you the best of everything, so you could claim his power as your birthright, and honor his legacy."

She drops her eyes. "But perhaps, if you had been my own, I would have sensed your pain sooner. Perhaps . . ." She trails off, shaking the thought away. "There is nothing for it, now. It is the spear you live for, and the Damajah has done what I could not, and given it to you."

Arick's scent is confused, half expecting a trap in these penitent words. "I thought I lived for the spear, but that, too, comes with a price." He doesn't say more, but the weight in his words is unmistakable.

Amanvah does not pry, but I smell sympathy. "No life's path is an easy one." She nods toward the kamanj. "It pleases me to see you will take that with you, and to hear you and your sister playing with the son of Arlen. Your fathers were the best of friends. It is right that you should be as family."

I get a lump in my throat, at that. Arick's da is a hero to me. Ent much like my own da, but if he loved Rojer Halfgrip, maybe he'd have found a way to like me, too.

Amanvah steps close and reaches out, hand shaking just a little. She smells afraid, and it ent hard to see why. Arick stiffens as she pulls away the black veil hanging loose at his throat, but Amanvah still has a mam's power over him, and he does not resist.

"It was wrong to keep you in colored robes when you deserve a man's black." Amanvah lifts a silk veil streaked with colors. "But that does not mean you should forget who you are. Your mother Sikvah came from a long line of warriors, and you honor her, but your father, too, helped turn the tide of Sharak Ka. It does not diminish Sikvah's sacrifice to honor him, as well."

Arick stands as tall and stiff as a soldier in a parade as she wraps the veil about his shoulders, but he smells like he's fixing to cry.

Amanvah kisses his cheek. "Carry your spear and shield with pride, but do not forget your kamanj, and your father's motley cloak. I pray you the wisdom to know when to choose between them. Whatever your blood, you are my son, and I would see you return to me."

Corespawn it.

Now I'm fixin' to cry again, too.

I CUFF AT my eyes while I climb the wall and collect my cloak and satchel, hidden behind a loose ceiling panel. Servants already packed and loaded the rest.

Didn't come to Krasia with much more than the clothes on my back, but I'm considered royal in Krasia, or as good as, and folk at court get itchy when one of their own shows up in a stained shirt and torn britches. Got a whole wardrobe of clothes I'll probably never wear now, but leavin' it behind would offend all sorts of people. Easier to take it all and unload it in Hollow.

Everyone's waitin' on me when I make it to the caravan, but I know better than to come early and sit with all the noise. I keep an ear out until I hear the general head over to Olive. "All set to go once we find Dar . . . ay, there he is!"

I pull up on Dusk Runner, but Olive barely notices. She smells wary, mixed with sweat and adrenaline. Face and arms are flushed. She's been fightin', and worries it ent over.

"'Bout time he found the stones to show his face." Selen's mutter is low, but she knows full well I can hear it.

Ent fair. She was the one stormed off in a snit yesterday, but I'm the coward? Funny how easy it is, to get folk to show what they really think of you. 'Specially when you can hear them casting shadows at you from half a mile away.

Was planning to ride up front with them, at least for a bit. Reckon it would make Olive feel better if I was on lookout for whatever it is she's fretting over, but it seems I ent welcome, and that's just as well. I don't want to be around Selen any more than she wants to be around me.

Arick's crowd ent much more inviting. His multicolored veil ent a *Sharum* rank, exactly—like a drillmaster's red or a *kai's* white—but Olive's Majah bodyguards seem to take it as one. They seem drawn to him, but they don't get too close. I can smell their deference, and his pride. Happy for him, I guess, but I don't want to ride in the middle of all that.

Morning sun's brighter than I'd like, but my saddle has a canvas top I can take shade under. Rojvah's got a whole carriage, and I bet it's nice and quiet inside. But the thought of being alone in a carriage with Rojvah is more nerve wracking than riding between Olive and Selen.

But then I notice Briar, still on foot, keeping pace off to the side as the caravan gets moving. He gives a wave, and I hitch Dusk Runner to one of the carts so I can drop down and join him.

Briar doesn't seem to fit in to the crowd any more than I do. He's in *Sharum* robes, but they're green and brown, rather than black. Means he's *chi'Sharum*, a warrior with greenland blood. A lesser caste, if you believe in that sort of thing. I can hear folk in the caravan murmuring about him, callin' him names. Mudboy, mostly. A Northern word for half-bloods, and not a nice one. One of the Warded Children said it about Olive, once, and Mam practically smacked his cheek off.

I even hear Uncle Gared call him Stinker. Voice makes it sound like he's teasing, but that don't make it less mean.

Briar *does* smell a bit. He's chewing a tough stalk of hogroot, not as food, but to fill his mouth with the juices. Demons don't like hogroot—avoid it when they can—so the precaution makes sense. A lot of the Warded Children used to do it, and Mam says Briar's the one that taught them the trick.

But everyone smells a bit to me. Hogroot breath's better than a lot of the stinks other folk carry around in their personal clouds. Briar's is consistent, and absorbs a lot of his natural smells. Makes him harder to read, but easier to talk to, if that makes sense. I can just pay attention to the words, without my nose feeding me a whole other conversation.

"Ent got a horse?" I ask.

Briar snorts. "So I can get stuck in that crowd? It will take them two hours just to reach the city gates, and even then, they will move slower than my legs."

That gets a real smile out of me. "Fair and true."

He points to a small side street. "On foot we can be outside the city in twenty minutes, and scout the path ahead. So long as we let ourselves be seen taking a loaf of bread at mealtimes, no one will ask any questions."

Feels like he's talkin' right to my heart. "Don't like people much, do you?"

Briar straightens to his full height and puts a hand to his chest like he might be offended, but he ent much taller than me, and after so much time around Olive and Selen and Gared, it ent intimidating. "I like people perfectly well." He waves a hand at the procession, and the crowd surrounding it. "I just like them over there."

My laugh surprises us both, and we're off running. Soon we're out of the city and into the countryside, ranging far ahead of the caravan. Sometimes we walk together and sometimes we split up, getting the lay of the land, and exploring anything that looks interesting.

Even so, there's time to climb a shady tree and let my legs dangle while we wait for the others to catch up. Briar ent the chatty type, and I like that just fine. Easy silence, like I used to have with Selen. Reckon there'll be plenty of silence next time I see her, but it won't be easy.

WE BREAK FOR THE NIGHT, and while most of the troops put up tents in a fallow field, Olive and "ranking officers" get rooms at an inn. Guess Arick and I count as officers, because we're bunking together again. I drop my satchel on the bed and have a flop, not eager for dinner in a crowded common room.

"Shall we practice tonight?" Arick asks as he sets down his kamanj case.

I stare at the instrument for a moment too long, and he nods, waving me away. "I can practice alone, but take care, son of Arlen. You cannot avoid my sister forever."

He turns without waiting for a reply, which is just as well. I follow him down to dinner, and we sit at the far end of the table with the *Sharum*. Think Olive's men are a little scared of me, but I like that fine. Means they give me space. Rojvah ent at the table, and I hear one of the servants say they're bringing food up to her. Ent like her, but maybe it's for the best.

"How come Darin ent sittin' with us?" the general asks, peering down the table at me.

Selen throws me a glare. "Because that woodbrain went and got promised to Rojvah while none of us were looking."

"Oh, ay?" Gared lifts his cup at me. "That's nice. Din't think he had it in him." Olive snorts, and Selen's got a glare for her, too.

And they wonder why I don't want to sit with them.

Selen's up to her old tricks after that. She takes her drink over by the fire, and before long she's got a crowd roaring with laughter at her stories. Even the general is slapping his knee and sloshing his drink, though every story inevitably includes some boy she stole away with for a kiss.

Soon as I'm done eating I'm on my feet, moving quick to drop my plate at the bar and get out. Arick tries to do the same, but Selen catches his arm as he passes by.

"What's your hurry?" Her voice has that smooth, inviting tone I know so well. The one that's gotten me into trouble more times than I can count. "Come share stories with us by the fire."

Expect Arick to give in like I always do, but he simply bows. "I have no tales to match the ones you spin, daughter of Gared."

Selen wrinkles her nose at him. "Ay, maybe we can fix that." Her eyes flick to me for just an instant when she says it.

Arick takes a step back, but Selen is undeterred, pursuing him until he backs into a wall. "Why so shy? Princes are supposed to be bold."

Arick raises a hand, creating a barrier between them. "Perhaps some princes, but not me."

"Why, are you *push'ting*?" There's a laugh in her voice when she says it, but then she sees his face. "Oh, night! I'm sorry. I didn't mean . . ."

Arick waves it away. "I do not have the luxury to be *push'ting*, if I am to carry on my father's name. My stepmother will select a bride for me when I am of age, and I will give her children, if I can."

Selen smiles again. "Hear it's an easy recipe. In the meantime, I know a few handsome young men I can introduce you to once we're back in Hollow."

She's trying to be friendly, but Arick smells even more uncomfortable. "I've never actually . . ." He shakes his head. "It doesn't matter. I am not fit to be with anyone, now."

Selen reaches out to touch his shoulder, her tone softening further. "None of us had it easy out on the desert, Arick. But that's all the more reason to keep living."

"Perhaps," Arick says. "But not tonight." He bows again and moves for the stairs.

Selen's eyes flick back to me, standing frozen at the bar. Her words are too low for anyone else to hear, but she knows I can. "Suppose you already knew he din't like girls, and let me make a fool of myself anyway."

She turns for the stairs herself, smelling angry and embarrassed. Know following her's a mistake, but I do it anyway.

"Go away, Darin," she growls.

I ignore her. I don't know what's happening between us, but I can't stand it. Got to at least try to make things right.

"Din't know," I say. "Ent surprised, but I din't know. And it ent like I ever 'let' you do anything. Only thing Selen Cutter's ever done is exactly what she wants."

"Ay, well, see where that's got me." Selen puts her hands on her hips. "Go on and have a laugh. Know you think I have it coming."

The words sting, but they ent fair. "Never laughed at you, Selen Cutter. Not to be mean. Not ever."

That hits, maybe harder than I wanted it to. I can smell her tears coming as she turns away. "Well ent you just perfect." She stinks of shame and humiliation and anger.

"Wait." The word feels like begging and I hate it, but Selen only picks up speed, heading for her room.

"Go away, Darin," she says again.

I could flit past her before she knows I've moved. I could stand in front of her door and demand she talk to me. But I don't. She slams the door shut behind her and buries her face in her pillow. She refuses to cry, but I can hear her rapid breathing, and the moisture on the cloth.

I head to my room, but not for long. Arick is already practicing his kamanj and says nothing as I open the window and slip out onto the roof.

I spot Briar immediately, wind carrying his hogroot smell from up a tree, too high even for that weed to grow.

"Took you long enough," he says. "What did they have for dessert?"

"Sugar cake." I reach into a pocket for the piece I wrapped in a napkin. "Saved you a slice."

Over the next week I let myself be seen once every day or two—just enough so no one thinks I've gone missing, but I was downright social on the road out of the desert by comparison.

One night while we're passing through the Laktonian wetlands, Briar waves me off the main road, and I follow as he runs at speed through peat bogs full of rotten logs and hidden sinkholes. I can smell corelings out here in the wetlands. Not many—just a handful of bog and swamp demons that were lucky enough to be out of range when my da purged them from the cities. Easy enough to avoid.

Still, I put up the hood of Mam's Cloak of Unsight. Might be even these stragglers wandering the wetlands report back to Alagai Ka at new moon.

We come upon a small village. Used to think Tibbet's Brook was small compared to Hollow or Everam's Bounty, but this place makes the Brook look like one of the Free Cities. Just a little cluster of modest houses, made more from sod and mud than wood and stone.

I like it. Most towns dominate their area, built on high ground on big clearings of land. This place blends into the bogs instead.

"This is Bogton," Briar says. "I was born here. Come."

There's a small Holy House that ent got room for more'n a hundred in the pews, but it's got good strong wards. Briar climbs up to the bell tower and then slips down inside. He sneaks up to the altar and lifts the silver cover to the offering, a fresh-baked loaf of bread. He takes it, sniggering to himself as he leaves a sprig of hogroot in its place like it's some secret joke.

"It's not sugar cake," he tells me, "but Tender Heath missed his calling as a baker."

We take the prize out of the town proper, sharing it as we walk a dark and winding path to what smells like the town dump. It's mostly bigger refuse—folk compost the food waste—but there's still plenty of stink. Even amid all of it, I can smell something else.

I put a hand on Briar's arm, pointing up ahead with my chin. "Bog demon."

Briar nods. "If one gets close to town, the folk come out with bows to drive it away, but no one comes to the dump at night."

I follow him up a tree and we string our bows, waiting for the demon to step out of cover. When it does, I take aim, but before I can loose, Briar has already put a warded arrow in its chest, dropping it as we watch the ground around it grow wet with ichor, bright with magic.

Briar drops down and moves to retrieve his arrow, laying his warded hand on the coreling as he does. Immediately, the demon's fading glow is Drawn to Briar's tattoo, and I seen his own aura brighten in response, even as the bog demon's grows dim.

His eyes glow like a cat's at night, and I know his other senses have come alive as well. He's experiencing the world like I do. He stands still, reaching out to see if any other corelings have gotten close.

They haven't. I flit down to join him as he cleans the ichor from his arrow and puts it back in the quiver.

"Ever get to be too much, all the sights and sounds and smells?" I ask.

Briar looks at me, sympathy in his eyes. "Sometimes. But I've learned to filter some of it out. Like skimming my eyes over the page of a book without reading."

"Never been much good at that," I admit.

"It's about finding harmony with the world around you," Briar says. "Becoming part of the night, instead of passing through it. Making its sounds and smells yours."

He leads me to a great patch of wild hogroot, growing on a pile of trash near the center of the dump. I follow him right into the weeds, and he rolls a tabletop out of the way, revealing an entrance to a cozy hiding hole inside. It's tight, but I can sense this is a special place for him, and I don't complain as we squeeze in.

"I used to stay up all night, in here, listening," Briar says. "Frightened. Paranoid. Jumping at every sound. But those feelings keep you alive in the naked night. Don't ever forget that."

"Why did you stay here, when the dawn came?" I have no right to ask, but I need to know.

Briar's eyes drop to the floor. "It was my carelessness that caused our wards to fail, and my family paid the price. We were the only mixed-blood family in the village, and I did not think any would take in one mudboy stray. Better I live here, among the trash, than among those who would only remind me of loss."

Having shown me this place, he seems eager to be gone, crawling out the way we came and standing back up to look at the stars and moon above. "It feels safe to hide, to not get involved in people's problems. But it's empty and lonely and will slowly drive you mad. I was adrift until I found people again."

"Sometimes I feel more adrift around people," I admit.

Briar nods. "We create patterns for our own sanity, but we don't need to be slaves to them. Wherever you go, you can make a new pattern." He waves to the hogroot patch. "I created dozens of briarpatches like this one while I was scouting during the war. Places to retreat, find my center, and emerge strong once more."

"Ent ever been strong," I say. "Running away to hide's the only thing I ever been good at."

"You and I both know that isn't true," Briar says.

Slowly, he reaches for my shoulder. Don't like being touched, but he's showin' trust by giving me time to step back, and so I allow it. His hand comes to rest and squeezes. "It is easy to feel small, Darin am'Bales, when the enemy is vast. But the tiniest point can pierce a bubble, and let its own power destroy it."

SOON AFTER, we cross the border into Hollow, and the hubbub when we left Krasia is nothing compared to the reception we get once we start passing through the boroughs. Word traveled ahead of us, and it seems like every hamlet's taken it as an excuse to throw a party.

Even when we're just passin' through, Olive and Selen have to get down and shake hands with the grayhairs on every town council, and let every Herb Gatherer ask after their health. There are tears and hugging and praises to the Creator, and I don't want any part of it.

Arick's and Rojvah's names are on everyone's lips, and talk of their father, Halfgrip, the famed fiddle wizard. They see Arick's kamanj case on his back and he doesn't even need to play it before they are falling over themselves in praise.

Rojvah handles it better. Her carriage and regal bearing, not to mention her *Sharum* guards, keep folk on their best behavior, especially in the hamlets where folk ent used to royals passing through. But she seems energized by the attention, whether she's waving from her carriage window, bestowing blessings on Town Speakers, or asking a group of wide-eyed children to teach her the local songs and dances.

Even Briar is sucked in. An experienced guide, he has contacts he needs to maintain in most of these towns. But the check-ins are never just a *How d'you do.* There's more hugging and kissing and usually a meal with the whole family crowding the table.

I stay away from all of it, hovering just at the range of my senses. I watch our caravan get a little bigger with each town. Local militia volunteer to escort us through their lands, but never seem to turn back at their borders.

It shouldn't be surprising. Hollow thought Olive and Selen lost, and the duchy with them. Now they are returned, and layer by layer, the Hollowers are creating a protective shell around them.

I get it, but I don't like it. It's suffocating, and I wonder what it's going to mean when we need to sneak off, again. Folk ent gonna like that. But right now, it's all *Creator be praised!* and spontaneous cheering.

Ent like they don't got cause. I just like my celebrations . . . quieter. I keep my distance until one afternoon, a day out from the capital city of Cutter's Hollow, when Olive calls me on it.

I'm half a mile from the road, too far to smell, but Olive raises her voice just a bit, and the irritation in her tone hits me like a cat scratch. "Enough sulking, Darin. These people are scared, and grieving, and they need to see you and know that you're safe."

None of us are safe. But I blow out a breath, knowing she's right. I make sure I'm seen as I rejoin the procession.

Dusk Runner perks up the moment he smells me. I make time for him every day, but it's nothing like it was in the desert, when we were all but inseparable. He's happy to be unhitched, and I don't weigh much to the likes of him. I put up the awning on his saddle and take out my pipes, letting everyone know I'm about.

No one wants to interrupt my playing, so they keep their distance out of respect. I get to smile and nod and that's enough, no need for hugging. All I have to do is play continuously, which is a fair deal, you ask me.

But pipes ent enough in Cutter's Hollow. People are gathered in the thousands, packing every side street and lining every avenue with barely enough room for us to pass. They are singing, cheering, crying, and sometimes just . . . shrieking.

Even I can't hear my pipes, and I'm the one playing them. It's daytime, so I can't use the magic coin to amplify my pipes, or turn slippery and flee. I'm stuck, and the noise envelops me, cutting from all sides until it feels like I can't breathe.

There's only one place I can go, and it can't possibly be worse than this.

I slip from Dusk Runner and flee to Rojvah's carriage.

Know I ought to knock, but it hurts too much. I bounce right up onto the step and open the door, rolling inside and pulling it shut before the guard even fully realizes I am there.

Rojvah is alone by the window, waving to folk, but she doesn't so much as yelp as I tumble past her and pull down the shade on the opposite side. I curl up in that shaded corner, arms over my ears and eyes. I expect the guard to give a shout, but he doesn't.

Someone in the crowd does, though. A man bellows my name, and others take up the call.

It's quieter, inside. Not quiet, but . . . quieter. The carriage walls are thick, and lined with stuffing and velvet and layers of paint for just this purpose. The inside is just a wide and thickly carpeted floor, covered in pillows that muffle everything, helping me filter some of the noise from outside.

Rojvah smells amused. "I was wondering when I would see you again, Intended."

'Course she's amused. All a joke to her. Some whisper of the ripping dice so she can clip off her mam's apron strings.

Folk are chanting my name now, and it's like a drumbeat fixing to split my skull open. I moan and grab a pair of pillows, stuffing them into my face. Rojvah's got a window cracked, letting in sound and light and smells like a lash. I start digging. Maybe I can bury myself in the pillows.

"Oh, Intended." The amusement is gone, but now it's worse. She smells like pity, and it makes me wish I'd never left Tibbet's Brook.

She closes the window and draws down the shade. Helps a little. But then she pulls a rope and thick velvet blackout curtains drop, bathing the inside of the carriage in complete darkness.

"This is a *dama'ting* carriage, Intended," Rojvah whispers, "designed to let my sisters use *hora* in the day."

My eyes are shut tight, but I hear as she dials the gem on her choker, changing the alignment of the delicate wards around it. The *hora* stone within activates, casting a bubble of silence around us.

I take a full breath for the first time in what feels like hours, but I am still shaking and clenched, gritting my teeth not to cry. The sounds are gone but I still hear them, over and over in my head.

I try to pull away when Rojvah reaches for me, but I'm not in control of my body anymore, and can do little more than twitch as she pulls my head into her lap, and begins to sing.

Slowly, at first. A hum that rises into notes that wrap themselves around me like my mam's arms, pushing out the echoes of the crowd. Then rising in power to make it my whole world.

The smell of her perfume is everywhere. Never much liked perfumes. They tend to give me a headache, just hanging in the room, covering up everything else. But right now, it's something to focus on other than the competing stinks of the thousands in the crowd, and by itself it smells . . . nice. Somewhere between a flower and a spice.

Her hand is cool as she strokes my cheek in time with her song, a Krasian lullaby. I crack my eyelids, and the inside of the carriage is so dark my night eyes come to life, seeing in magic's light. Rojvah is painted in a wash of colors, prettier than a sunset.

I don't smell pity anymore, and at last, I start to relax.

There's a bang at the door, and I close my eyes against a flare of light as it's yanked open. Catch a glimpse of Selen standing on the step of the moving carriage. "You okay, Darin?"

"Nie's black heart!" Rojvah throws a pillow that I hear thump against Selen's head. "He was, oaf, before you pulled open the door!"

"Ay, sorry!" I hear Selen say.

"Get out!" Rojvah throws another pillow, but it hits the door as Selen withdraws and shuts it tight, reestablishing the dark and quiet.

She doesn't start singing again. That spell is broken. But neither does she press, as I crack open my eyes and adjust to the inside of the carriage. She gives me water to drink, and a honey cake to nibble, and after a little while, I feel like myself again.

"Do not be vexed at the daughter of Gared," Rojvah whispers. "No doubt she believed she was running to save you."

"Maybe I don't need savin'," I say.

"Everyone needs saving sometimes, Intended," Rojvah says. "We are all of us connected, and there is no shame in it."

"Well it's only going to get worse once we get to the keep," I say. "Everyone's going to want a piece of us. I'll try to spare you having to save me twice in one day."

I start to get up, but Rojvah lays a gentle hand on my chest, and I stay where I am, head still in her lap as she strokes my hair. "There is no counting between intended. I will save you a thousand thousand times, as you have done for me. Do not fear what is to come at court."

"You've never even been to court at Hollow," I say. "How can you know what there is to fear?"

"Phagh." Rojvah waves a hand. "The night is your place of power, Intended, but court is mine. Stay close and let me do the talking. You will think you have gone slippery, with the polite ease I slide us past the servants, penitents, and well-wishers, and parry away even the most powerful and banal."

I blink. "You mean that?"

"Did I not promise you as much, Intended?" she asks.

"Ay," I say.

"Then trust in me." She slides soft fingers over my brow, gentling my eyelids closed, and then she begins to sing again.

CHAPTER 24

HOMECOMING

NEAR THREE WEEKS on the road, and there's still no sign of the other challengers Asome foretold.

If someone was going to take a shot at me, there were countless opportunities before now. Why wait until I was surrounded by countless loyalists, and nearly to Mother's keep—as secure a place as any in the world?

It knots my muscles, as I become more and more sure an attack is imminent. But from where?

I am surrounded by my closest friends, family, and spear brothers. General Gared's Cutters are the original inhabitants of Cutter's Hollow. Most of them watched Mother grow up, and me.

Messengers have galloped up and down the road, a steady stream of communication from Minister Arther over the course of the journey. Fresh horses and provisions have been waiting in the larger towns, always with an armed and armored "honor guard" from the local militia. Loyalists and veterans eager to take up a spear to defend Princes Olive on the journey back to the capital.

For the first time in months, I am home. I can feel Hollow's power thrumming at my fingertips in ways I never imagined. My brothers would be fools to challenge me now. But if Asome's foretelling is wrong about this, can I trust any of it? Should I?

We come around a bend, and Mother's keep comes into sight. The flag of Hollow flies steadily in the breeze, but for the first time I can remember, Mother's mortar and pestle does not fly the pole next to it.

Mother is not in residence.

I knew to expect this, a footnote in the endless lists of preparations for my arrival. But knowing a thing is different from experiencing it.

Up until right this moment, a tiny part of me felt that if I could just get home, everything would be all right. That we'd find Mum and Mrs. Bales and my father at court, having a laugh as they divide Alagai Ka's body for the *hora*.

But Mum is gone and even now I don't know if she is alive or dead. Inside Alagai Ka's mind, I *felt* his hatred of her, and experienced for myself how mind demons feed on our deepest pain and insecurities as much as they do our flesh. Alagai Ka made me relive the worst moments of my life, over and over.

If Mother is alive, the demon is torturing her. Part of me hopes she isn't, and I hate myself for it.

A knot forms in my throat as a new banner climbs up the pole, emblazoned with the spear and olive. My spear brothers cheer, for they, too, wear the symbol. It is the emblem of the Princes Unit, commanded by Princes Chadan and Olive. Chadan's family symbol was a spear, and I combined it with an olive, ostensibly to give the men something to rally around.

But also, if I am honest, I made it to tell Chadan I loved him, when I dared not speak the words, even to myself.

His voice was as bound as mine, but when he pinned our symbol over his heart, I knew.

Tears fill my eyes as I watch that banner fly atop the Royal Keep of Hollow. It is my crest alone now, but it will always remind me of Chadan.

As we pass through the gates, the house guard, a majority-female force I've known all my life, flow in to surround me. With no time for new uniforms, they still wear Mother's colors, but each wears an armband with the spear and olive on a patch.

Built by Count Thamos during the war with Krasia, the keep was designed to be a fortress capable of withstanding any assault, human or corespawn. Mother worked hard to make it a welcoming place, full of green spaces and bright colors. The gates were closed at sunset, but never during the day.

But the moment I am safely in the courtyard, they close behind us with a resounding boom.

A CROWD WAITS by the courtyard fountain. This close to Winter Solstice, the air is chill, and has only gotten more so as we journeyed north. I am used to it after so long on the road, but all the courtiers wear fur-lined coats over their fine formal attire.

"Can't we do this inside?" Selen says. "Maybe after we stretch our backs and put on something that doesn't smell like horse?"

"I asked for that," I say, "and was told it wasn't possible."

"Why in the core not?" Selen asks. "Ent you the one in charge?"

I snort. "Not when your mum is around. Elona insisted on waiting outside to be the first to greet us."

"And Mum doesn't do anything without an audience," Selen moans as we dismount. "Might as well get it over with."

Indeed, I can see my grandmother, waiting at the forefront of the crowd of officials and advisors who will no doubt all try to slip some bit of business into their few moments of face time.

I want it over with, too, but I put a hand out to hold Selen back. "Wait for Darin and the others."

I don't know what she saw in Rojvah's carriage when she went to check on Darin, but Selen came back red-faced and sullen. She throws me a look, but I match it until she backs down. She casts her eyes around, noticing Perin, the handsome stablehand who features in one of her funnier ale stories. She throws him a wink, and now it's his face that reddens as he hurries to lower the steps of Rojvah's carriage.

When Darin, Arick, and Rojvah catch up, Selen signals the house guard, and they snap to attention, opening a path to the fountain.

Grandmum Elona waits until we draw close, then rushes forward the last few steps to throw her arms around me. "We were so worried!"

I've been worried, too. Throughout my life, my most feminine traits were encouraged not by Mother, but by Grandmum. Fashion. The powder kit. How to be the center of attention and envied for my beauty.

But even with regular baths and changes of clothes at inns along the way, I feel filthy and unkempt after weeks on the road. My armor and dress are that of a man. I wear no paints or powder, and I suddenly remember my hair, cropped short from the long tresses she must remember, and matted to my head.

Indeed, Elona takes a step back to have a good look at me, and gasps. "Well ent that a thing."

After all that's happened these last months, it's ludicrous to feel stung at something so small, but disappointing Grandmum Elona has always been my greatest fear.

"Always thought you'd make a pretty boy, but I was wrong for once," Elona says. "Turned out to be one core of a handsome man."

She smiles and gives me a slap on the cheek. "Going to have to beat the girls off with a stick."

I laugh, but it chokes on the lump that's returned to my throat. Even when I was young, Grandmum was always there for me. Some things, at least, don't have to change.

Selen crosses her arms. "Ay, Mum, I'm fine, too."

"'Course you are," Elona says, embracing her in turn. "Only you disappeared on purpose, so don't expect a party for coming home after what you put us through."

Selen hasn't changed as much as I have, but neither is she the same young woman who left Hollow. Still, Grandmum barely gives her a glance before looking past.

"Darin!" she cries, throwing her arms wide. Selen and I take the opportunity to step quickly past as Grandmum catches sight of Rojvah and lets out a shriek.

My grandfather Erny is next, the small man attempting to embrace us both at once. He isn't Selen's father, but he's never treated us differently, and Selen and I are happy to wrap him in an embrace.

First Minister Arther follows. My mother's most trusted advisor, the man seems to have kept Hollow together in our absence. He's at the head of a group of officials including Shepherd Jona of the Tenders, and his wife Gatherer Vika. Headmistress Darsy and Dama'ting Favah represent the university. Even Hary Roller is back in Hollow, returned to serve as royal herald, with Kendall Demonsong still missing after the attack that took Mother and Mrs. Bales.

All of them bow and scrape and rattle off speeches no doubt practiced in front of the mirror. I fall back on the training Mother gave me, making each one the center of my attention for just a few moments before excusing myself to move down the receiving line.

Selen's stepmother Emelia is there, as well, like an asp among flowers. Selen moves to put me between them, but the baroness shows little interest in her, instead marching up to Uncle Gared like a kettle about to steam.

But Gared isn't the same aging, overweight war hero he was when he left Hollow. Months on the road, killing demons and absorbing feedback magic from his weapons, have not only grown his muscles and trimmed his waist, they have restored his sense of self-respect.

Her face is one about to launch into what I do not doubt is a long-practiced verbal lashing, but when he takes off his helmet and she finally has a good look at him, she hesitates.

It's all the opening Gared needs. He sweeps her into a crushing hug, and she does not resist when he kisses her, seeming to melt in his arms.

All around the fountain, there are cries of happiness and embraces, and for a time we're swept up in it all.

When I finally think to cast about for Darin, he's nowhere to be found.

CHAPTER 25

RECEPTION

I'M ALREADY FEELING drained as the carriage door opens. One of the stablehands unfolds the steps, and Rojvah takes my arm. Somehow she makes it look like I'm helping her, but truer is it's the other way around.

She's the center of attention, anyway. Already the prettiest one in any room, she's dressed in the Northern style—a crimson silk dress that complements her cinnamon hair, wide-skirted with long sleeves and a low neckline. Her shawl is lined and trimmed with soft brown fur, and she's powdered and painted her eyes in the Krasian style, and her lips in the way Hollow courtiers favor.

All the white marble in the courtyard is reflecting the sunlight, making everything so bright I need to squint. The guards standing at attention aren't saying anything, but I can hear their heartbeats. Their every breath and pinched fart. After the controlled environment of the carriage it takes a minute to get used to. I feel dizzy, and reckon I'd sway like a drunk without Rojvah's support.

I'm steadier as we reach the bottom of the steps. The stablehand is on one knee, but his heart is beating fast. His skin is flushed, and he smells a little scared, but also . . . smitten. I think he must be under Rojvah's spell, but then he lifts his chin a little, and I see his face.

A memory flashes in my mind. Worse, the memory ent mine. It was

Selen's, from the night all those months ago when Olive was taken. I Drew power through Selen to give us the strength and speed to run down the trail. I'd never done that before, and without meaning to, I Read her.

Maybe it's my own fault. Maybe I was thinking about the time we kissed. But a flood of images came to me of all the people Selen's kissed since, and it ent just a few. Remembered it from her point of view, like I was her.

I don't even know his name, but remember kissing this stablehand like I did it myself. I glance at Selen, and see her eyeing him openly. No wonder he's blushing.

Is she already planning their next encounter? Can't blame her. As we pass, the hand gets to his feet, and he's everything I'm not. I'm barely as tall as Rojvah, and he towers over us, broad-shouldered with the thick arms of a Cutter and a jaw fit to grind rocks.

Rojvah doesn't even notice him. She tightens her grip on my arm, pulling me forward, speaking in a bare whisper only I can hear. "Be at peace, Intended. When someone greets you, speak their name aloud, and immediately introduce them to me. I will handle the rest."

"Ay, all right." Seems too good to be true, but ent got much choice but to trust and go along.

"Darin!" Elona's shriek makes my teeth ache, but I manage to keep from flinching. Can't go slippery in sunlight, so all I can do is hold my breath as she hugs me against her low-cut gown. The duchess mum always sprays perfume between her paps, and it clings to my face when she finally lets me up for air.

"Duchess Mum Elona Paper," I say, "you remember Rojvah?"

I'm ready for the shriek this time, but it still feels like a lash. Before Elona can try to suffocate her, Rojvah rushes in with an embrace that she controls. Elona is surprised for a moment, then melts.

Suddenly, Rojvah pushes her back. "Oh, you must meet my brother!" Still in control, she spins Elona around and pushes her in front of Arick.

Elona shrieks again, but Rojvah grabs my arm. "Quickly now, Intended."

Incredibly, by the time Elona is done getting perfume on Arick, we're past Erny Paper and into an open area, well out of range.

But there's folk all around, eyeing us like the bowl of potatoes at suppertime while Grandda says the blessing.

Even before they come at us, they're already talking to my nose, even with Elona's perfume still clinging to my face. Selen's stepmam Emelia is angry. Lord Arther had garlic. Shepherd Jona was burning incense this morning and his robes reek of it. His wife Vika's pocketed apron holds enough dry herbs to brew a dozen cures on the spot.

But there's bigger smells, too. Relief. Joy. Resentment. Worry. All of them mixing into a cloud. Too much for me to sort out.

But Rojvah keeps pulling me along, whispering to me even as she greets and laughs and soaks up all the attention. "You're doing fine, Intended. Who is that Jongleur by the steps?"

I look up, surprised he escaped my notice. "That's Hary Roller, my old teacher from back in Tibbet's Brook."

He ent the Hary I remember. This Hary smells of paints and powders and cologne. There's scented wax in his beard and mustache, and oil in his hair. Hary never bothered with more than mustache wax back in Tibbet's Brook unless he was doing a show, and even that was a dull whiff compared to the stink of the cloud around him now.

I love Hary. He's one of the few people I could ever relax around. I knew he used to be a court Jongleur, but I never really thought about what that meant. This person, with manners as silky as his fine clothes, is not the man I know. Somehow he puts me more on edge than ever.

But Rojvah gives a tiny squeal and squeezes my arm tight. "The first Jongleur I meet, and he is both your teacher and a friend of my father! We must speak with him, but not before we greet Favah."

I lift an eyebrow. "Olive's teacher from school?"

Rojvah snorts quietly, but she doesn't elaborate. "Who is that woman beside her?"

I follow the flick of her eyes. "That's Headmistress Darsy of Gatherers' University."

Rojvah nods, pointing us toward them like an arrow. "Favah's lesser, then."

I don't know if the Hollowers see it that way, but core if I know how these things work. Happy to leave Rojvah in charge.

"Honored Favah." Rojvah spreads her arms, sweeping into an elegant bow.

"Welcome to Hollow, Highness." Favah uses Rojvah's title, but she offers only a slight nod. "Is your mother aware you have abandoned your whites?"

I can tell she means to intimidate, and I'm a bit surprised when it works. For once, Rojvah ent got a quick reply. She smells scared, and I don't like that one bit.

"Her mother is not here." Mam took me to Krasia every winter when I was knee-high, and I can speak like a native when I want to. I make my voice deep, an imitation of the arrogant way Krasian princes speak. "My Intended is visiting the home of her father, and it is her wish to honor him by dressing in the style of his people."

Darsy sucks in a breath, and Rojvah turns to stare at me, wide-eyed, but I know a staring contest when I'm in one, and don't turn away from Favah. Maybe her white robes mean she can bully Krasians around, but it don't work on me.

After a moment, the ancient *dama'ting* seems to realize that, and breaks the stare with another of her slight nods. "As you say, son of Arlen. Everam spoke to Rojvah's father, and it does her no shame to honor him."

The words are tight, clipped. Know this fight ent over, but it's over for now, and that's enough. Like Rojvah did with me, I take her arm and start walking. "If you'll excuse us, I need to greet my master."

"I cannot believe you did that," Rojvah whispers, smelling incredulous. "No one speaks to Favah like that!"

"Ay, she ent so scary," I lie. Already the flush of adrenaline is wearing off, and I feel sick to my stomach. "And she had no business talking to you like that."

Rojvah puts her free hand over mine on her arm, squeezing gently. For a moment, it makes me forget about my queasy stomach. "She did, in truth. And she will tell Mother."

"So throw the white robes away before she gets the chance," I say. "Oops, they fell in the brook! So sad. I'd wear the spares, but my horse trampled one set in the mud, and the dog et the other."

Rojvah laughs, and it sounds like music. I wish she'd keep on, and drown out every other sound with it.

Then Hary sees us heading his way, and steps up to close the distance. Folk give ground like he's a royal himself.

He's the embodiment of grace as he slides down to one knee. "Princess Rojvah vah Rojer am'Inn am'Kaji, it is my honor to make your acquaintance. I am Hary asu Regnal, known as Roller, herald of Hollow Duchy."

Hary is using a formal Hollow court accent, which ent at all how he talked in the Brook. I know accents are just a Jongleur's trick to make folk comfortable, but it makes me feel all the more like I don't know this man. Maybe I never really did.

However I feel, Rojvah's excitement is genuine. She wants a connection to her father, and Hary Roller was as close to Rojer Halfgrip as anyone alive.

Rojvah's bow is deep and low. More than I've ever seen her give anyone. "The honor is mine, Master Roller. Mother speaks of you with great respect. She says you are a man of boundless glory."

While they have their moment, the rest of the party starts seeping in. Emelia is grousing about what Selen's put everyone through by running off. Elona says something mean to Erny and then barks a laugh like it was a joke. I jump at the sound.

More choked voices, tears, gasps, and exclamations. Everyone's breath, and sometimes their behinds, tells me the last things they et or drank. Some of the women think their thick petticoated dresses muffle the sound, and pass wind like they're on the privy.

"All right, Darin?" Hary puts a hand on my shoulder. He knows what crowds are like for me. Or the real Hary does, anyway.

"Just . . . busy out here," I manage, trying to stand up straight.

Hary lowers his voice, shifting back to the accent he used back in the Brook. "I played the hamlets on my way back here, Darin. Folk have been worried with no sign of Leesha, Renna, or all of you. Know you don't like parties, but you need to let folk have a look at you and see that you're all right."

"Olive said the same thing," I agree glumly.

"Indeed," Rojvah's voice is bright. Cheery. She lets go of my arm and moves beside Hary, taking his arm instead. She flashes him a smile, and he's caught.

"Go, Intended," she breathes so softly only I can hear. "Go now and be at peace. I will offer your regrets, accept well wishes, and assure all of your good health."

I blink, but I'm moving before Hary can take his eyes off Rojvah. There's a servant with a tray of glasses and I take one, dancing around to use him as a shield as I slip out of the crowd. I empty it on the stones and hand it to the first guard I come to.

"Where's the privy?"

The guard blinks, taking the glass reflexively. She points to the steps, and I'm up them in a flash.

"Where's Darin?" I hear Olive ask as I reach the doors.

"My intended apologizes," Rojvah answers, "but there was a matter requiring his attention."

"Intended?" Elona asks.

"Should've known better than to take my eyes off that boy," Hary mutters.

"Ay, that's our Darin," Selen says. "He'll show up again when he's ready. Probably scare the core out of us when he does."

"Back in Tibbet's Brook they wanted to bell him like a cat," Hary says, and everyone laughs.

It's a good joke. I put on speed to get through the doors and out of earshot before someone says something about me that's less funny.

CHAPTER 26

MY OLD ROOM

THE CHILL WORKS in my favor, as even Grandmum decides after a short while that she's seen and been seen enough to make her point.

"Highness," Arther says as we move up the steps into the keep, "once you have time to refresh yourself, there are some urgent matters . . ."

The request is not surprising, but the minister's tone surprises me. I am used to Arther speaking with Mother's authority. Firm. Decisive. Now he sounds tentative, like he is stepping carefully out of fear that I will replace him as easily as I installed Selen as captain of the house guard.

He needn't fear. I desperately need Arther and the stability he creates, if I am to take my forces and leave Hollow once more, regardless of whether I go east or west.

"In the morning, Minister," I say. "First I need a hot bath and a night's sleep in my own bed."

"Ah," Arther breathes, and I turn to regard him as we walk.

"The keep is yours now, Highness," Arther says. "I took the liberty of freshening your mother's chambers."

The minister swallows hard at the sour look I give him. Mother is alive. I believe that deep down, and moving into her rooms feels disrespectful, and an admission that perhaps she will never return. I don't know if I want to give that signal, to others or myself.

But then we reach my old chambers, and I cringe at the sight.

After months in Desert Spear and on the road, everything looks so . . . garish. So bright and polished and pristine, every surface smooth, every fabric silk or lace or delicate fur. The rug alone is so soft I feel like I am sinking into the floor.

The guest rooms in my father's palace were equally lavish, but I was a visitor there. These are the rooms I grew up in. They used to be my succor, my place of power. Now they feel like they belong to someone else.

Mannequins around the room hold the dresses, gowns, and more practical outfits I designed and made myself. Beautiful feminine garb that was once my pride and joy. It's alien now. The figures stand around the room like ghosts of who I once was, ready to haunt me.

Rojvah, however, gasps at the sight, losing a bit of her dignified façade as she rushes in for a better look at one of the frillier gowns. "This is your work? Cousin, they are beautiful."

"The dresses are yours," I say, making the decision. "My chambers, as well, for the duration of your stay. I'll sleep in Mother's bed." There will be ghosts there as well, but perhaps they will push me forward rather than pull me back. "We'll send someone to collect my most personal effects and the few clothes I will keep."

"Cousin, that is too—" Rojvah begins.

"Nonsense," I cut in before I can rethink the decision. "I doubt much of this still fits in any event."

It's true, if not the truth. I'm taller and thicker with muscle than I was just half a year ago, but that's not why I won't be wearing dresses anytime soon. When the Watchers came for me half a year ago, I had to fight in a wide-skirted dress stuffed with crinoline. I won't be caught by my brothers at that kind of disadvantage.

Arther nods at the words. He raises a finger at one of the maids setting fresh towels by the bath and whispers instructions before setting her off and running.

Rojvah's face lights up, and she gives an uncharacteristic squeal as she runs around the room, examining each outfit in turn. Selen rolls her eyes at me but is quick to square her expression when Rojvah looks back at us. "I wish to try on everything."

"Might take a while," Selen says. "Ent even seen the closets. Olive's got more clothes than there are leaves on a tree."

Rojvah claps her hands. "I want to learn everything about greenland fashion! Is it true you wear dresses without sleeves in summer?"

She doesn't wait for a response, running into one of my closets with a cry of delight. By the time we join her, Rojvah's dress is stripped and she is laughing as she twirls the skirts of her first selection before the angled mirrors I had installed to see all sides of an outfit at once.

"Night," Selen says. "You think she really means to try them all?"

It certainly seems so. Rojvah is already making a pile of dresses to model before the mirrors, the most colorful rising to the top. Her current pick is an orange gown so garish even I wouldn't wear it. A gift from some distant noble, Selen dubbed it "the tangerine" and it's hung forgotten in my closet ever since.

But Rojvah wears it well. She would make anything look good, I think. She splays her cinnamon tresses over one sleeve. "How does it go with my hair?"

"Beautifully," I say, and mean it, but I am already backing toward the door. There was a time I would have enjoyed nothing more than helping my cousin try on everything I owned. But that Olive died in the Maze.

"I'm . . . going to stay in my rooms at Da's manse tonight," Selen announces, joining my hasty retreat while Rojvah is still admiring herself in the mirror.

I LOOK AROUND Mother's private rooms, but they are not a familiar place. They say I was born in the bedchamber, but I haven't spent much time here since I was weaned.

Neither did Mother, really. The duchess was always working, often late into the night. When she wasn't holding court, Mother lived in the garden and her office, and often only retired under pressure from Tarisa, her lady's maid and head of the household staff. The bedchamber is luxurious, yet cold. Utilitarian. The only space that speaks of her is the desk, full of carefully organized ledgers, papers, and writing materials.

The duchess' work never ceased, and I wonder if the same fate awaits me. Already Arther has pressing matters, and I haven't even washed off the smell of horse and saddle oil. Mother was explaining tax law as soon as I had numbers, and taught me how to command a table of unruly advisors, but given the choice between facing demons in the Maze and endlessly sitting meetings with sanitation committees and merchant associations, I'll take the Maze every time. I'm exhausted just thinking about it.

My Tazhan armor is lighter than anything short of the warded wooden armor the Cutters favor, and more flexible besides. But it is still steel, and I've been bearing its weight all day. I undo the fastenings and remove the scaled shirt, laying it on a table and taking a deep breath as I unbutton my sweaty, stained undercoat, steeped with the smell of metal and kanis oil.

But as I am about to pull off my shirt, I catch a flash of movement deeper in the chambers, and think again of the three challengers Asome predicted. I am not crowned yet, and my brother foretold one would strike without honor.

I bolt across the room, *hanzhar* in hand, and leap through the doorway where I saw the movement. Tarisa screams as I land in front of her, weapon raised.

For a moment, we both stand frozen in shock. Then Tarisa's face darkens into a familiar scowl. "Olive Jardir Paper, just what in the core has gotten into you?!"

I jump at the sound, and suddenly I am ten summers old again. Tarisa wasn't my nanny—it was worse than that. She was the woman—perhaps the only woman shy of the Damajah or Mother herself—that Nanny Micha was afraid of.

I make the blade disappear even faster than I drew it. "Sorry! I just . . . It's been . . ." I falter, having no words to explain brandishing a knife at a woman five times my age for turning down the linens on Mother's giant four-poster canopy bed.

Tarisa cannot hold her scowl long. Her thin lips quiver, eyes filling with tears. "Olive, dear. Is it really you? Are you home?"

"Ay," I say, holding out empty hands. "It's me, Tarisa. I'm home."

And then she is in my arms, or perhaps I am in hers. Tarisa, the iron rod of Mother's household, whose back is always straight, whom I have never seen lose composure, sobs into my shoulder.

"Tsst," I whisper, hugging tighter and rubbing her back.

"Apologies, Your Grace." She takes a step back, whisking a kerchief from her sleeve to dry her tears. "I swore I wouldn't spoil your homecoming with tears, but with you and your mum gone all these months . . ." She sobs into her kerchief.

"Tsst," I say again, louder this time. The sound Micha used to reprimand me as a child, now turned about.

Tarisa has seen seventy-five winters at least, and served my mother since before I was born. Home was a distant thing while I was fighting for survival in Desert Spear. I hadn't given Tarisa a thought, but she must have been devastated to lose us both.

I should be devastated, as well. It was easy enough to avoid thinking of Mother too much in recent months. Now that I am home, everything reminds me of her.

But Mother is alive, though I cannot risk telling Tarisa that. She needs to be rescued, not mourned. What's the point of crying when there's work to be done?

Again, I think of Inevera's urging to go west, away from Alagai Ka's Safehold, and the failure Asome foretold if I went east. To not go would be a betrayal of Mother, of the bond between us, to say nothing of the fraying bond that ties me to Selen and Darin. They will see it as betrayal, too.

But can I go in good conscience, knowing my very presence may doom the endeavor from the start? Or that by not going below, I may doom Thesa and Krasia both?

Tarisa collects herself, back arching once more. "I've turned down the linens, Your Grace, and heated a bath."

"A moment ago I was Olive Jardir Paper," I say, "and now it's Your Grace?"

"You are duchess now," Tarisa says.

"Duch," I say. "And no one's crowned me yet. It's Olive to you, Tarisa. Always."

"As you say." Tarisa says. "It's time for your bath, Olive."

I bark a laugh. "Now you sound like Tarisa."

"Let's get you undressed." She reaches for my belt.

I take a quick step back. "I can undress myself. I'm not a child, and I'm not a lady. I don't need a lady's maid."

"Well someone needs to look after you," Tarisa says, "with Micha . . ." She looks sad again but bulls ahead before it overtakes her. "Would you prefer a valet?"

"No," I say. "I'd prefer to bathe myself."

Tarisa crosses her arms, all pretense at deference gone. I am in her place of power now. "Olive Paper, I have bathed you a thousand times. And your mother. And Prince Thamos before her. You've grown while you were away, but I assure you it's nothing I haven't seen before."

I frown, but I see that I will need to remove her bodily if I want my privacy. Tarisa was the same with Mother, when she fell into her work and forgot self-care.

I give in. There is fruit and cheese and bread by the bath, along with chilled water and wine. I slide into a deliciously hot tub, thick with scented foam, and sigh, feeling the dust of the road wash away. Tarisa takes the brush to me vigorously, scouring a layer of skin off with the sweat and filth, and I love every moment of it.

"They don't have baths in Desert Spear," I murmur.

"How do they keep clean?" Tarisa massages my shoulders with surprising strength until I feel something unclench and my muscles go slack, letting the hot water soak in.

"They don't have bathwater to spare," I say, "so they gather in a tiny room, ladling water over hot coals, then scrape off the sweat."

Tarisa shudders. "So you just . . . sit there in one another's stink?"

I laugh. "It's nicer than it sounds. The heat relaxes you, and if you sweat long enough, the stink scrapes away, mostly."

I stretch my legs, looking at my wrinkled toes. "But more than anything else, I missed my bath."

Tarisa washes my short hair and trims it with skillful snips of the scissor. While she works, Tarisa talks, filling me in on the keep's workings and gossip, as seen through her omnipresent staff. For a moment I thought I didn't need her—what a fool I was. What greater font of knowledge is there for Hollow's Court, and what Mother might have done?

"Arther wants to see me first thing in the morning," I say.

That's all the opening Tarisa needs. "Lord Arther is as happy to see you returned as I am. He's managed to hold power as regent, as much because Elona abhors paperwork as any politicking. She makes a stink when she's not treated like a duchess, but she has little interest in council meetings."

"And how has he managed?" I ask.

"Arther is a good man," Tarisa says. "And competent, if a bit stiff. He did his best to continue Duchess Leesha's policies and govern as he thinks she would have wished, but he doesn't have your mother's wisdom."

Neither do I. We both know it, even if we don't say it aloud. "What does that mean?"

"It means he avoids big decisions," Tarisa says, "especially those that might upset the barons and make them question why they are taking orders from him. He could bully them when executing Leesha's vision, but he's grown timid in her absence."

"So he needs me to knock a few barons' heads together?" I guess.

Tarisa smiles. "Perhaps just a reminder there's a Paper standing behind him. You should write to Duchess Araine, as well."

I raise an eyebrow at that. Araine is Duchess of Angiers to the north. She and Mother are friends, but I've only briefly met the woman.

"She owes your mother more than you can ever know," Tarisa says, "and she and Princess Melny held you when you were in swaddling with more love than a woman can feign. If you ask it, they will help you."

"With what?" There is indeed something I want from Angiers, but I haven't spoken the need to anyone.

Tarisa shrugs. "With your mother gone, there is no wiser and more experienced leader than Duchess Araine. It is my job to guess at your needs in the home, but I cannot advise you on what your needs will be at court."

Court is not where my needs lie, but Araine has something even Mother didn't—or wouldn't—have. "That's good advice, thank you. I will take it to heart."

"What are your immediate needs from the staff?" Tarisa has left me to soak, fetching towels and one of Mother's robes. Her eyes flick to the plate every time I go too long without putting something in my mouth, and I fear she will try to hand-feed me if I don't keep at it.

"Rojvah needs a maid who knows about fashion," I say. "I gave her all my dresses, and she'll need someone who can do alterations."

Tarisa nods. "I'll see to it."

"And a valet for Arick who knows armor and can introduce him around the practice yard. Make sure both have appointments with Hary Roller, as well."

"Of course."

The more I speak, the more things come to me. "Selen will need a captain's uniform. I'll make some sketches for the seamstress. Have someone sent to the general's manse in the morning to get fresh measurements."

"And for you?" Tarisa holds open a towel as I step out of the bath. "You've given away all your clothes. I can't imagine you want to continue dressing as a Krasian now that you're back in Hollow."

"I won't give up my Krasian armor," I say. It is how I keep Chadan close, even now. No suit of Hollow craft can make me feel as protected. "But you're right. I need a uniform, as well."

"A . . . uniform?" Tarisa asks. "Your mother never—"

"I am not my mother," I cut in. "I am back, but Hollow is not out of danger. I will be taking a more direct hand than Mother did in the defense."

"Your mother walked the front lines more than you know," Tarisa says, but she nods. "Something along the lines of the uniforms Angierian royals wear?"

I shake my head, pulling on one of Mother's warm robes and going to her writing desk for a pen and paper. "I'll have designs ready by morning. In the meantime, here is a list of things I will need from Rojvah's closets."

Tarisa takes the paper, and soon maids are scurrying in with my favorite boots and leggings, my riding gear, and other pieces I can work with. I find Mother's sewing kit, and barely notice when Tarisa retires herself.

I work late into the night. I used to stay up all night often, when feeling inspired with the needle, but it's been a long and draining day. When I have something to wear in the morning, and silk sleepwear I can fight in, I turn to face the ghosts in Mother's bed.

I half expect her spirit to haunt me as I crawl into the giant, feathered monstrosity Count Thamos built to share with Mother. I wonder if Mother actually likes this bed, four-posted with thick curtains, or if she keeps it because it reminds her of the man she lost, like I keep Chadan's armor.

Regardless, after months of sleeping on the hard ground of *sharaj* without so much as a blanket, I sink into the soft mattress like a pit filled with dust. It's suffocating, and the curtains make me feel as if enemies are sneaking up on me from all sides.

I pull back the curtains, but it's not enough. If someone attacked, I would be vulnerable, trying to fight on a floor of stuffing.

I thought it would be Mother's ghost to drive me from the bed, but it's sheer instinct. I take a pillow and blanket, rolling out of bed to look for a defensible corner of the floor where I can put my back to the wall and see all the windows and doorways.

But even the blanket makes me feel tangled, and I toss it aside despite the night's chill. The pillow goes next, and I curl up on the floor, wishing for the warmth of my spear brothers as sleep takes me.

CHAPTER 27

WATCHTOWER

In Jardir's palace, I hid in the minaret tower. Here in Aunt Leesha's keep, I like the archer's nook atop the western watchtower. Comin' here since I was knee-high, anytime the noise of the keep got to be too much for me.

Ent much reason to come up here, unless the keep's surrounded. Nook's barely big enough for one person, accessible only by a steep, narrow, spiraling stair. Ent much going on this far from the gates, so there's usually only one bored guard keeping watch downstairs. It's the shadiest spot in the courtyard, with a good view all around.

Looked in on my usual room in the keep after I fled the party, but it was full of maids, kicking up dust and laying fresh sheets. They were readying for two, so I reckon Arick's bunking with me again.

Took one look at that busy beehive and was out the nearest window and up the tower before anyone knew I was there. Spent the whole night here, not counting a little excursion to steal a snack from the pantry and take care of my necessaries. Everything got busy again come morning, so I'm fixin' to spend the day here, too.

Or I was, until I see Hary Roller cross the yard, and hear him enter the tower when he leaves my line of sight. Reckon Selen or Olive must've told him I like to hide up here. But Hary is old, and slow, and there are a lot of steps. Maybe he won't come looking all the way to the top.

I don't usually need to hide all day, but everyone's makin' such a fuss, and as usual, I'm the only one who can't handle it all. Olive and Selen are in their place of power, and Rojvah's thrilled to be talk of the town. Even Arick, however dark he gets when he's alone, can put on a party mask and chatter about nonsense when the situation calls for it.

I can still hear most anything in the keep, if I focus on it, and I've kept watch over my friends. Folk keep invitin' Rojvah and Arick to things that sound all right, like "tea," but I learned the hard way that in Hollow tea means three hours trapped in a room with fifty people I don't know, all their scents mixed with as many perfumes, and a dozen varieties of stinky potpourri steaming in hot water. Fifty people, all talking at once, and I hear every one like they're leaning into my ear.

I'd rather wrestle a field demon.

Can't say Rojvah hasn't kept her end of the deal. Kind of envious of how effortlessly she lies, making my apologies and giving out my kind words and well wishes a lot more freely than I ever have. She deflects questions about where I'm hiding, quickly making every conversation about her. Folk are giddy to gossip about us bein' promised. Seems like everyone in Hollow wants to help plan the wedding.

Thought I might hide among Olive's Majah brothers, but they're so moon-eyed about their first visit to Prince Olive's palace, the chatter from their barrack is constant. Sounds like most of them are planning to go down to see the "bazaar" in Corelings' Graveyard.

Hary makes it to the watch guard, spinning an ale story about how he wants to see the view from the archery nook for some song he's writing. Guard's too busy saluting the royal herald to argue.

Hary sighs as he puts his hand on the rail of the long spiral stair. "Listen to my knees, boy. I'm too old for this, so you'd best still be up there when I get to the top."

He ent lyin'. A lifetime of tumbling has worn away most of the cartilage in Hary's knees. I can hear the bones grinding against each other with every step and feel a bit of an arse, putting my master through this.

Ent just his knees. Hary's got a heart problem, too. I hear the way it gets out of rhythm when he strains himself. Asked Mam about it once, back in Tibbet's Brook. She already knew. Said she talked to Aunt Leesha about it before Hary left Hollow to come teach me. Aunt Leesha said it was a little hole in his heart—too small to risk surgery or even magic on.

Hary was born with it, and magic only helps a body heal itself. His body "thinks" it should be that way, so there's nothing to be done without cutting him, and it wan't worth the risk.

Mam warned me not to push my master. Said Hary came a long way and gave up a lot to teach me music, and he deserves respect. Reckon she's right, and this ent doing right by him. Just din't expect him to come climbing towers to find me.

Hary is huffing when he reaches the tiny archer's nook. Ent much space for one, much less two. I can hear the tiny hole in one side of his heart widening just a little with the more powerful beats, making a squirting sound as it leaks a bit of blood from one side of his heart to the other. It forms a little pool in the next chamber, throwing off the rhythm.

Hary peeks over the ledge at the cobbles a hundred feet below, and his heart starts racing even faster, coupled with a scent of fear.

He wobbles, and I catch his wrist to steady him as I throw my backside onto the ledge to make space. He glances at me perched on the lip and I smell his worry. "'Sall right, Master. Ent gonna fall and I won't run off. Set on the floor and take your ease."

Hary sits, taking a drink from a waterskin and breathing hard. I wait patiently, listening as his heart flushes and calms, returning to something close to its normal beat. All the excess paint and powder is gone from his face, as is the smelly fragrance. He's still dressed a lot fancier than he did in the Brook, but to my senses, he's my master again.

"I'm sorry about your mam, Darin." All trace of his court accent is gone, as well. "Know I'm not your grandda, but I lived at the Bales farm a long time, and think of you as family. Cuts me, too, having her missing."

He's right, and it makes me feel even worse, actin' like my pain is something special even while others are hurtin', too.

I could tell him Mam's still alive, but I don't know that for sure, so it ent a lie to stay silent. Tell a Jongleur a secret, and you might as well tell the whole town. Hary's no exception.

My master knows I don't like to be hugged, but he reaches out, putting a hand on my foot. Just a gentle weight and warmth. "Know she'd be proud of you, boy, for going off and rescuing Olive."

There's a sudden lump in my throat, but I swallow it. "Had a lot of help."

"Ay, maybe," Hary agrees, "but I also know you never give yourself the credit you're due."

He wasn't there, and I don't want to argue, but truer is Olive did her own rescuing. We just . . . gave her a kick.

"Not just me in mourning," Hary says. "Folk are wearing black and making statues of her. Pews are full in the Holy Houses, and folk in the taprooms go from toasting her honor to fear of a world without her."

I shake my head. "Know you're gonna tell me to go out and make folk feel better, Master, but I ent the one for the job." Just the thought of the crowds on our way to the keep has me sick to my stomach.

"Don't know there's anyone else," Hary says. "Your mam hated this sort of thing, too, but even she knew to show her face sometimes, because if she didn't, people start using her name to justify whatever they want."

Hary leans in, seeing me unconvinced. "Know you ent a people person, Darin, but you can pretend to be. Just a stage role, like any other. You want to be a Jongleur, you'll need to learn to play them."

Olive's words return to me, unbidden. *We both know you're never going to be a Jongleur, Dar. Night, you can't even stand in a crowd without having a fit.*

She ent wrong, but does that make her right? "Don't rightly know if I want that anymore," I confess. "Going from town to town, seeing all the places my da wrote about, it was a simpler dream from a simpler time. The pipes still have me, but the rest . . . Hunting for Mam doesn't leave a lot of time to practice juggling and mummery."

Hary sighs. I can smell his doubt. He thinks there ent much point in hunting. "Not every Jongleur does it all, Darin. Some just pick a focus, like you with your pipes. But all need to know how to work a crowd. You used to do it with me, at festivals back in Tibbet's Brook. How can you handle that, but not going to tea?"

"You worked the crowd," I say, "I just repeated what you said and passed the hat. And we always played outside, so I could set myself upwind and have the breeze wash most of the crowd's stink away."

Hary laughs, but I ent joking. "When you're performing, folk keep their distance. Whether it's a stage or just the tumbling zone, people keep back, like demons at a warded circle. But more, you manipulate the crowd with your performance. They laugh when you want them to laugh, cheer when you want them to cheer, cry when you want them to cry. Same as charming a demon. A shrieking crowd I can't predict or control is like a knife in my brain, but when it comes at my command, it's like a warm bath."

"Ay, that I understand," Hary says. "It's the trick that Rojer struggled so hard to teach. Only a Jongleur at heart can even see those levers, much less pull them with any consistency."

"I can see the levers with corelings," I say. "People are still a bit of a mystery."

"Sometimes," Hary says, "pretending to do a thing is the same as doing it. I was a street performer who worked his way up to guildhouse music teacher before I was sent to Hollow during the war. Creator knows I'm not a trained herald. But I've been faking it for years, and no one has figured it out."

I smile at that. "Nice to know I ent the only one who feels like I don't know what I'm doing."

"Far from it," Hary laughs. "There must be some way for you to fake your way through this, Darin. Some way to let yourself be seen, some person you need to visit anyway, some ceremony you can attend so folk can see you, even if there's wards to keep them from getting too close."

That gives me an idea. A way to help a friend, and let myself be seen. "Ay, maybe."

After I make sure Hary gets back down all right, I head over to Olive's old rooms just as Arick and Rojvah return from some luncheon that went on far too long. It's close to Solstice, and the sun is already close to setting.

"Intended." Rojvah doesn't seem put out at all to find me lurking in her chambers. She smells pleased.

"Thought you'd made your escape and were halfway back to Tibbet's Brook," Arick says.

"Ay, there's a sunny thought," I say.

"I never doubted your return." Rojvah curls up like a cat on one of Olive's divans, relaying in a few sentences the handful of interesting things she must have sifted from hours of meaningless chatter. She gives me greetings from lords and ladies I've never even heard of, and asks a few follow-up questions she can no doubt spin into an endless conversation with anyone who asks after me.

"Don't be cross," Rojvah's smile is disarming, "but I did promise the three of us would perform in Hollow's famous sound shell for the Solstice Festival next week."

"All right," I say. That stage is a good buffer to the crowd.

"Then we'll need to start practicing again." Arick turns, reaching for his kamanj.

"Ay, but not tonight," I say. "Let's go see our das, instead."

CHAPTER 28

BARONESS

TARISA THROWS OPEN the curtains, and we both startle. Me at the sudden sound and light, her at the sight of me leaping to my feet, hands up in a *sharusahk* stance.

Again, I feel the fool. Throwing open the curtains was Tarisa's favorite way of passive-aggressively waking a body attempting to sleep past the eighth hour, no matter if it be your born day or the morning after the Solstice Festival. She's done it to me—and Mother herself, I have no doubt—a thousand times. Perhaps that's why I didn't wake at the sound of her entering.

"Olive Paper, did you spend the night on the floor?!" Tarisa gasps.

"Bed was too soft," I mumble, knowing how I must look. Hollowers have felt safe for so long, they've forgotten what it's like to leap at shadows.

Tarisa huffs over to the pull rope and gives it a yank. "That's why you have this, *Your Grace*." In seconds, there is a butler at the door. "Have a team remove Duchess Leesha's bed to storage," she tells him. The man nods and vanishes.

"What kind of bed do you want," Tarisa asks, "or did your time in the south train you to sleep on a pile of pillows?"

"Creator, no," I say. "They shift around and you fall into the crevices."

"Then what?" Tarisa asks. "I won't have you sleeping on the floor in your own chambers."

She calls them mine and gives orders in the same breath. I would protest, but truer is this is the most normal part of the entire homecoming. "Low to the ground. Narrow. Flat stiff mattress. One pillow. No curtains. Set in a corner where the head and one side are against a wall."

The answer doesn't please her, but Tarisa dips slightly. "I'll see it done."

"One other thing," I say, with not a little guilt. But soon after I am in my second hot bath in a dozen hours, and it is worth it as Tarisa lays out my schedule for the day while I soak.

Mother's powder kit is as equipped as mine ever was, though she always kept the paints and powders to a minimum. I follow her example, adding just a bit of color to hide the lack of sleep, and subtle highlights.

After that I dress in the riding gear I spent the night modifying. I originally designed it to give freedom of movement while being as feminine as possible—back when that meant everything to me. The leggings were soft, flexible suede, with a fine cotton blouse that flared into a short overskirt, open in front, to accent my hips. The long tails of my stiff wool riding coat flared around me like a dress when I dismounted, embroidered wardwork running along the seams.

I've removed Mother's crest and replaced it with my own. I hadn't fully realized just how much muscle I put on in recent months until I had to let out the arms and shoulders of the coat. The leggings are tight, but they will stretch with a little use.

I sling my herb pouch and *hanzhar* from the belt, and admire myself in the mirror. It feels strange but familiar to be in my own clothes again. The person looking back at me isn't the Princess Olive of old, but neither do I see Prince Olive of Krasia. I am someone new. Both, and neither.

I look up at a knock on the door, but Selen doesn't wait for a response, coming right in and closing the door behind her. "Well that was a mistake."

"What was?" I ask.

"Slept at Da's to avoid Rojvah's fashion show, and got a show of my own. Da and the baroness had a shouting match that everyone in the manse heard."

"I'm sorry." Selen's always hated her stepmother, and with fair cause. The woman has always been awful to her and Gared, both.

"Ent the worst of it." Selen looks ill. "Once they were good and worked up, they were on each other like rabbits, and everyone heard that, too."

Tarisa sniffs and glides out of the room without another word. Selen, who hadn't noticed her at first, snorts, and we both laugh as the door shuts behind her.

ALL TOO SOON, Selen and I finish breakfast, and Lord Arther appears at the door to escort me to our meeting.

"Baroness Cutter is waiting for us in your office," Arther says, causing Selen to look up from her third breakfast plate.

"I had thought we were meeting alone," I say.

"I would like to begin with financial reports to provide context for some of the issues of the day," Arther said. "Baroness Cutter—"

I feel Selen's eyes on my back. Mother may have tolerated the way Baroness Emelia treated Gared and Selen, but I will not. "Get someone else to give the reports."

Arther clears his throat uncomfortably, taken aback at the sudden force in my voice.

"I beg pardon, Highness, but on matters of finance, there is no one else. Your mother and the baroness built the Hollow's economy together. I can advise you and verify her tallies, but I cannot present the picture she does. If you prefer a written report, I will have it made, but . . ."

"Best I hear it from the coreling's mouth," I say. Arther gives a pained smile, and nods briefly as Selen lets out a low growl.

"OLIVE!" THE BARONESS holds her arms out to me like Elona had in the courtyard, lips already puckering.

I sidestep smoothly without making contact. "Cut the demonshit, Emelia, and address me as Highness or Princes."

The baroness blinks. "Have I offended you in some way, Highness?"

I cross my arms. "A lifetime spent making Selen miserable offends me, yes."

Emelia tilts her head at that, and a little smile quirks at the edge of her mouth. "Direct. Just like your mother. I like that. Arther, will you give us the room for a short while?"

"By all means." Arther looks visibly relieved as he turns to me. "With your permission, of course, Highness."

I flick a hand, and he all but scurries out of the office as the baroness walks over to the refreshment service and fills a glass with wine, as if it's not the tenth hour of morning.

Emelia takes a seat on one of the small plush divans Mother preferred for more intimate audiences, whisking her hand toward the other. "Leesha was even blunter when she had Amanvah cast the bones in my blood before allowing me to marry Gared."

My own blood goes cold at the words. It's easy to think I'm the only one whose life has been twisted by the *alagai hora*, but the *dama'ting*—and Mother, it seems—were doing this to people long before I was born.

I take the opposing seat. "What did they say?" It's the height of rudeness to ask such a thing, but I don't think the baroness would have brought it up, otherwise.

"That I would be loyal," Emelia tosses back half the glass, "to Gared and to Hollow, and that Gared would marry no other."

"That doesn't sound so bad," I venture.

Emelia drains the rest of her cup and fills it again. "They said I would bear him strong sons, but it would be his daughter who succeeds him."

And just like that, I understand.

Gared's affair with Grandmum came before he met Emelia. "Elona was already pregnant with Selen when the dice were cast."

Emelia extends a finger to point at me as she raises the glass again. "But of course, I could not have known that at the time. No one asks the *man* to give blood to the dice before promising."

It's true enough, in my experience. I effortlessly claim rights and freedoms as a man that were denied me as a woman.

"Even when I found out, I held hope," Emelia tops off her glass again, "that the prophecy was wrong, that his bastard might be a boy, or I have a girl."

Something about that grates on me most of all. It seems Selen and I both were born with fates tied to gender. Why should our lives be tethered to something so . . . fluid? Why should so much ride upon what's between our legs at birth?

"From the moment she was born," Emelia says, "Selen only had eyes for her da, and he for her. She was his world, and my sons and I might as well be guests in our own home."

"That isn't true," I say. "Gared taught all his kids to fight, to cut trees and build things from the lumber. To plant new trees and respect the wood. He took them hunting, camping, fishing . . ."

"He took *her* hunting and camping and fishing," Emelia says. "The boys he grudgingly allowed to come one year, after we spent a night screaming about it."

There's fire in the baroness' eyes, and I don't think it's because she's lying. I think it's because she's kept the truth bottled up too long.

"Everyone knew it," she says, "gossiped about it all over court. Elona made sure of that. I felt like I was being humiliated anew every time Selen was around, or spoken of."

I can't deny that sounds like Grandmum. Elona isn't exactly fond of Selen, either, but she loathes Emelia, and would delight in rubbing the baroness' nose in the fact that her sons are also-rans.

"None of that is Selen's fault," I say. I never had a father and couldn't help but envy what Selen and Gared had.

"Perhaps not," Emelia agrees, "but it was hard to love her for it. Your mother was the only one who understood that, and the trials the general caused us both, even as he took credit for our work."

"What?" I ask.

"Did you think Gared Cutter runs the barony of Cutter's Hollow?" Emelia laughs. "I've done every tally, made every decision, written every law and decree, but Gared gets to sign them. Baron Cutter, the great war hero! No matter that he nearly bankrupted the entire duchy before I took over his ledgers. Leesha and I built Hollow's economy together, but ask anyone on the street and they'll thank Gared's axe for any prosperity they enjoy."

I pour myself a glass of water, if only to give myself time to think. I remember Mother and Emelia were nearly inseparable, working in this very office until all hours of the night. She was always kind to me, and why shouldn't she resent having neither credit nor heredity to show for all her work?

And yet for all that, I cannot easily forgive the core she made Selen's life—trapped between a mother and stepmother, each taking out her hate for the other through Selen.

Yet I still love Grandmum. Can I make room for the baroness as well? Should I?

"Selen says the whole manse heard you make peace with Gared last night," I note.

"Peace was the last thing we made!" Emelia laughs, not seeming ashamed at least. "But I let him touch me for the first time in years, ay. I'm not made of stone."

"Mother said peace is not kind to the baron," I say. "But Hollow is no longer at peace, and I need his axe as well as your ledgers."

Emelia nods. "Gared is at his best when he has something to fight."

"Perhaps you can make an attempt with Selen for the first time in years as well," I say. "Now, before it's too late." The words are phrased as suggestion, but my tone makes them an order, and Emelia does not miss it.

"Ay, Highness." Emelia looks like she's eaten a lemon, but she nods, lifting a pinch of skirt to imitate a curtsy from her divan.

It's not friendship, but it's a peace of sorts, and I call Arther back in as Emelia sets down her empty glass and begins producing charts and reciting numbers with cool sobriety. It's easy to understand what Mother saw in her.

And to understand what they fear. The Hollow economy, robust under Mother, is already faltering.

"How is that possible?" I ask.

"The duchess had the treasury print and spend vast sums, pumping klats by the million into the reconstruction and building of Hollow after the war." Arther might as well be reciting a history text. "The duchess was a Gatherer at heart, and would let none in her duchy go without food or shelter or medical attention. She was constantly juggling debt with the needs of the people."

"Much of that spending was loans to individual baronies that repaid themselves over the ensuing years of prosperity," Emelia notes, "and Leesha's dice guided investments that assured sufficient returns."

"But Mother is gone," I say.

"Disappeared," Emelia agrees, "along with both her heirs. The resulting uncertainty has roiled the financial markets and caused a run on some of the smaller banks and treasuries. The seams of her carefully stitched economy are threatening to tear."

"The central bank has stabilized the klat for now," Arther says, "propping it up with cash from the royal treasury, but that won't last forever. The markets need stability only *you* can give them."

"Me?" I say. "What can I do?" I've studied economics in Gatherers' University, but I can't just wave my hand and create money from nothing.

"Just news of your return has brought a turn in trade," Emelia says. "The bank of New Krasia is strong, and right on the border, with ready loans for Hollowers feeling the strain. If we're not careful they'll soon own swaths of Hollow the way they do Lakton."

"If they don't attack outright," Arther says.

I roll my eyes. "The Krasians are not going to attack us, Minister."

Lord Arther looks at me patiently, like one might a child. It makes me angry, but not so much that I don't realize what a foolish thing that was to say.

The Krasians hold to the Pact of the Free Cities because my father commanded it, and he did that as much because of his love for me, Mother, and Mrs. Bales as the goodness of his heart.

Again, I hear Asome's words in my head. *My mother thinks herself impartial, but she is not. Do not doubt for an instant that she will sacrifice you, your mother, or even Hollow itself, if it will benefit Krasia or return her husband to her.*

With no one left to challenge her, who is to say Inevera isn't sending me to my doom on purpose, to prime Hollow for invasion? That Belina wasn't working for her all along?

"Hollow remains strong," Arther says, when I have the decency not to argue further, "but it has been difficult to keep the barons and merchants and people united. Your mother was . . . beloved. Worshipped, even. Leesha commanded barons, Gatherers, Hollow Soldiers, Warders, and commoners alike, and they followed her with equal devotion."

I realize now—too late, always too late—why Mother pushed me so hard. Why she forced me on a path of books and diplomacy, doubling the pressure every time I was less than perfect. She could break every council deadlock because she understood everyone's job better than they did themselves.

I always thought Mother was trying to force me into an identity that didn't fit, but perhaps it had less than I thought to do with my gender, and more with what Hollow needed. Duchess Paper put her people ahead of her own needs, and made that choice for me, as well.

She had no right to, but she was *right* to. I thought Mother was sheltering me from danger, but looking back I see she was making me into the leader Hollow required, and I would not wish it another way. Would not wish to be just a vapid princess, or a wood-brained warrior.

She wanted me to be an Herb Gatherer, like her. I will never be that, but I have stitched the bloody bodies of my friends and spear brothers back together, and closed their eyes when they could not be saved. I know the value of a Gatherer's art.

She had Captain Wonda train me to fight, so I would understand conflict, as well. I didn't feel called when studying *sharusahk* when I was young. It wasn't until the fighting moved from the university's safe and sterile practice yard to the life-and-death struggle of the naked night that I discovered where my talents truly lay.

I despised the endless, oppressive hours in Favah's Chamber of Shadows, studying magic. Yet those lessons and my own imprisonment by Belina's armlet gave me understanding and respect for the power of *hora*, and its dangers.

What am I now? A healer? A warrior? A witch? Can I be what Hollow needs? *All* the things Hollow needs? And what of Inevera's warnings, if I stay here in Hollow to stabilize markets while our enemies mount?

"What do you need?" I ask. "What will set Hollow right?"

"The Winter Solstice Festival is only a week away," Arther says. "We'd like to make it into a coronation."

ARTHER IS ALL too eager to fill my calendar with appointments. Already a crowd of courtiers, pages, and supplicants is gathering at court, all hoping for just a chance at an audience.

I knew to expect this. All the time I spent as Mother's shadow at court has paid off, as I recognize familiar players, and her whispered words of advice. Who I could trust, and with what. Who would seek to take advantage of me, and who would be afraid to ask for what they truly need.

This is not the way I would spend my first day back at home, but Arther and Emelia were right. It doesn't matter what I say. My very presence is a signal that the system they have come to depend on will continue to operate.

I smile and comfort and console, equally pleasant to those truly devastated by Mother's disappearance and those feigning while they seek advantage on the new political battlefield. I deflect any questions about my time in Krasia, and they all know it would be unwise to press.

I meet so many advisors and leaders it's perfectly natural when I meet with the one person I truly wish to speak to, Lord Commander Gamon.

Another hero of the demon war, Gamon was captain of the Hollow Lancers, Mother's prized cavalry—another way she honored her lost love. The lancers had the highest kill rate of all Hollow's armies, but so too had they taken the greatest losses. Mother loosened her normally tight purse strings to see them restored to glory.

It shows in Lord Commander Gamon, whom I have always adored for his bold fashion sense. His uniform is always crisp and flamboyant, just a hair short of garish in its rainbow of medals.

Gamon is in his fifties, but he took a lion's share of demon feedback magic during the war, and even now, when his lance has likely not touched ichor in ten years, he looks to be the sunny side of forty. The touch of silver in his hair just adds to his flair.

Where peacetime softened General Gared, who had no patience for military ceremony, Gamon thrived, and rose through the ranks to lord commander even as Gared eased into semi-retirement. He remains fit and muscular, training his men from the saddle daily.

Hollow's forces will look to Gared, now that he is again the man they remember from the war. But as Emelia has reminded me, Gared has no head for logistics. He can assure me of the loyalty of the troops, but he can't give me the information I need.

Gamon and Arther can.

"Highness." Gamon snaps his boots together with a sharp click, his jaw pointed up at the perfect angle as he punches an immaculate white-gloved fist to his chest. "I am here to personally vouch for the strength of your armed forces. Hollow is secure, and we stand at the ready, should you seek retribution against the desert rats."

There is venom in his tone, and I am not surprised. Not all wounds from the war have healed. Gamon was like a brother to Count Thamos before my half brother Jayan slew him at the Battle of Docktown.

"There will be no retribution with Krasia, Lord Commander." I put bass in my voice, an order he will not miss. "We have greater foes to worry about."

"The corelings." The venom in Gamon's voice is deeper, and I am pleased to hear it. "General Gared told me they still roam the sands. I'd hoped we'd seen the last of their scum."

"More than sand demons survived," I tell him, "and they have a mind. This will not be solved with a single charge. How many active forces does Hollow have, and how they are equipped and provisioned? How many could you field tomorrow? A month from now? By Spring Equinox?"

Arther fetches his ledgers as he and Gamon begin reciting numbers, companies, divisions. Active forces and reserves for each barony, down to the number of pack mules in the stables, which barons meet their military requirements, and which have fallen slack.

"And how many do you think we could recruit, train, and equip over the winter if I put out a call to all able bodies on Solstice?" I ask.

Both men stare at me a moment, but then Gamon snaps back to attention. "Is that your intention, Highness?"

"I haven't decided," I say, and it's honest word.

"I feel compelled to mention, Highness," Arther flexes a sudden tension from his fingers, "the cost would strain an already—"

"I understand your concern, Minister," I cut in. "But our choices may be to strike at the corelings now or wait for them to come to us in numbers not seen since I was in nappies. I'm giving you warning to prepare the tallies so I can make an informed decision, but this is not to be discussed outside this room for any reason."

Arther's bow is deeper now, and Gamon clicks his heels again. "Of course, Highness."

After that it's back to shaking hands, patting backs, settling disputes, and avoiding questions about where I've been. They all remember the pampered princess I was, and see me now, riding into Hollow in Krasian armor, with a unit of hard *Sharum* warriors at my command.

No doubt the salons and taprooms of Hollow are filled with rumors even grander than the truth, and why should I spoil them. I'll need every bit of glory the Jongleurs spin into their tales for what I may need to ask of my people.

The sun has already set when I finally exit Mother's office, wondering how I will find the strength to do it all again tomorrow. Wondering how Mother managed it day after day, season after season, year after year.

Mother gave up everything on the path to the throne of Hollow. She loved three men and lost them all. She buried her mentor, her best friends, and the dreams of her own future. Refusing to be cowed, she worked magic on the front lines of the demon war even as I rode in her belly.

Sharaj made me think the Duchess Paper who raised me was soft, and that in raising me as a girl, she had made me soft, as well.

Now I think perhaps Mother was the hardest of us all.

Faseek is waiting outside the office, enduring the glares from Hollowers as he stands in Majah armor, with spear and shield on his back, so close to their seat of power.

Selen assigned Becca, one of my mother's house guards, to me as well. I've known Becca all my life and told her Faseek was my trusted spear brother. Still, she eyes him suspiciously, treating him as more threat than ally.

Mother's chambers are chill when we return. A draft turns my eyes to the billowing curtains of the balcony overlooking the keep's inner courtyard gardens.

"Apologies, Highness," Tarisa says from over in the corner where I'd spent the night. The bed she's placed there remains larger than one person needs, but it's much more modest and functional than Mother's monstrous four-poster, or even the one in my old chambers. A pair of maids are making up the linens under the head maid's watchful eye.

"It took longer than expected to remove your mother's bed. It wouldn't fit through the door, and so we had to lower it from the balcony. I'd thought to let the chamber air out and stoke the fire when we finished . . ."

"It's all right." I inhale deeply of the cold air, feeling refreshed after spending the day confined in Mother's heated office. The guards follow as I move to the balcony, looking out over Mother's gardens. She did love them so. Even in winter, they are beautiful.

There's a sudden hiss by my cheek that ends in a thump as Faseek stumbles behind me. I turn and catch him, seeing the arrow embedded in his shoulder. From the tear in his shirt, and the dent in the armor plate beneath, it seems to have skittered off the armor over his heart to reach the nearest seam. The shot should have killed him.

I turn back to look along its path. I don't have night eyes like Darin, or my helm with its wards of sight, but like my strength, my senses have always been sharp. Moonlight and window lamps are enough for me to spot the shooter, perched on the opposite rooftop of the inner courtyard, nearly invisible in *Sharum* black.

Already they have another arrow in the air.

I don't know if it's meant for me or Faseek, but my brother takes no chances, launching himself in front of me and taking a second hit.

There's a flare of wardlight, and this one strikes with a bang, punching through armor and a lung. My brother coughs blood in my face as I ease him to the floor.

The arrows are embedded deep. It would be foolish to remove them now, without proper equipment and a safe space to work. Looking at Faseek's blood-soaked robes, I realize why the assassin shot him and not me. In Krasia, I wore only my Tazhan armor and *Sharum* blacks. The shooter must not have recognized the new attire, and mistaken my bodyguard for me. Likely they still haven't figured it out.

Tarisa and the maids are shrieking. Becca is racing across the chamber, but she's not fast enough. I grab the spear from Faseek's shoulder.

"Sound the alarm and fetch a Gatherer!" I shout, racing onto the terrace.

I do not know if the shooter has realized their mistake or is simply responding to a new threat, but as I charge out, they raise their bow for another shot. I throw first, with little time to aim. It costs me my weapon, but I have no harness to stow it anyway, and will need my hands.

My aim is true enough for my purpose—causing the archer to fumble the shot as they dodge. I spin round as I hop onto the marble railing of Mother's balcony, running two strides before I leap. My first two steps connect with the vertical wall, propelling me higher. I coil and spring on the second, catching the lip of the roof, twenty feet above the terrace.

Another arrow shatters against the stone, missing by scant inches as I kip and flex, swinging up onto the roof. I land in a roll, keeping low among the crenels. Unlike Faseek, I have no armor to blunt the impact. My stiff riding jacket looks quite dashing, but it might as well be a sheet of paper against a powerful Krasian short bow.

Another mistake. I thought here of all places I could feel safe, but perhaps the time has come to accept I will never be safe again. Any court garb will need armor pockets like the Krasians use, and I'll need more than just my *hanzhar* about my person.

I catch sight of the shooter again, perched unnaturally on a sheer wall, bathed in shadow. He's got *hora,* and the sun has set. I won't have the advantage, as I did against my Krevakh brother.

But I do not hesitate, Faseek's blood still wet on my face. I do not know if my spear brother will live, but I will not let his attacker escape.

I keep low as I charge along rooftops to circle around to him in the skittering, irregular steps we use in the Maze to confuse wind demons.

The assailant does not waste his shots, but twice more, arrows shatter on stone, inches from my head or chest.

They do not flee, perhaps thinking me a fool as I make it to their side of the roof and emerge into their line of sight. Perhaps I am, but I have the archer's measure now. The next arrow comes straight for my heart, but I am quicker, batting it aside with my *hanzhar*.

The assassin's nerve breaks then, and they turn to flee as I pick up speed. They have a man's build, but they move like a dancer, racing along what is no doubt a practiced escape route.

But I grew up running the rooftops of Mother's keep with Darin and Selen. I know every inch of them, from the patrol areas to the rooftop gardens, every chimney and water tower, every slope of warded tile.

He disappears over a steep tile crest, but I know the wraparound terrace on the other side and take a shortcut, leaping onto one of the guest balconies and smashing through the doors to race through the thankfully empty chamber to the terrace doors on the other side. I fling them open just as the assassin drops down.

Somehow, he manages to turn and shoot one more time before I reach him. I twist, feeling the arrow punch into my side, but I am so full of fury I barely feel it as I tackle him into the marble railing.

We hit hard, but the archer is armored, and the blow does not break bones as I intended. He is strong, too, no doubt aided by *hora* jewelry under his clothes. He drops his bow and grabs me, lifting me clear off the terrace floor as he seeks to redirect the force of our rebound to throw me over the railing—a sheer drop of more than forty feet to the stone courtyard below.

I have to sacrifice my weapon as well, dropping my *hanzhar* to grab a rail post and heave, bungling the throw. The arrow in my side screams to life, so I pull it out and stab it into the armor gap on my attacker's inner thigh.

He grunts and kicks me away as we both hit the floor and roll to our feet.

"Who are you?" I demand. "An assassin, or one of my brothers, too cowardly to state his name and fight with honor?"

I expected a moment to regroup with the assailant's bow fallen over the rail, but his hand whips back and forth to a bandolier, flinging sharpened triangles of warded glass, like those my sister Micha favored.

I throw up my arms and duck, protecting my face and torso, but there's nothing to do but take the hits. I feel the throwing glass thunk into my arms and stick. I bull through the pain and charge before he can throw more.

I thought rushing back in would take him by surprise, but my attacker is prepared, setting his feet as we exchange a quick series of blows. He's undeniably skilled, but he's given me a new weapon as I block with forearms studded with razor-sharp glass. He punches one of his own triangles of throwing glass and breaks away with a hiss, fist covered in blood.

I take the offered pause, studying my opponent as we circle. I recognize the Mehnding cut of his robe, and things click into place. Known as the far-reaching tribe, Mehnding specialize in ranged weapons, from artillery and missile fire to throwing weapons.

Again his hands slip into his robes, pulling out a dart and silk. An elegant weapon, the dart is a small throwing knife made of indestructible warded glass with a loop at the end for a long cord of lightweight, braided silk.

I pivot out of the path of his first throw, but am cut across a shoulder as he yanks the dart back to his hand, spinning it for fresh momentum. All around, the keep is coming to life with shouts of alarm. Guards are racing through the courtyard with lanterns, but none of them will reach me in time to make a difference.

I keep moving, but the spinning blade makes it difficult to get in close. I grab a heavy flower pot and hurl it his way, but it's a clumsy missile and he sidesteps it easily, launching the dart at me before I can recover.

I think it a miss, but then the silk hits my leg, sending the blade whipping around to catch the limb in a twist of cord. He tries to yank me from my feet, but I am quick, too, closing the gap to slack the line before he can heave.

That, he didn't anticipate, and I strike my first real blow, a punch to the chest that would have caved in the ribs of a normal man. But my fist hits armor, and not the clay plates of lesser *Sharum* that shatter upon impact. These, like my assailant's weapons, are made of warded glass, and hurt my hand as much as my opponent.

Warded glass is fabulously expensive to make, and its presence tells me much, even if my opponent offers me little more than a grunt as he stumbles back.

"It is said the Mehnding are all cowards," I growl. "The Majah call you gray robes, for you lack the courage of the black. Until today, I did not believe it . . . Prince Ramm."

It's a guess, but an educated one. I know the names of my siblings, if not much more. Ramm asu Ahmann am'Jardir am'Mehnding is Father's firstborn Mehnding son.

My opponent does not reply, but his eyes narrow, and it feels like confirmation enough. A powerful tribe, the Mehnding are numerous, in part because they do not put themselves in range of *alagai* talons when they fight.

But that can be a weakness, too. The Mehnding are not known for their close-quarters *sharusahk*.

Again, my brother spins and launches the dart from a new angle, but this time I am ready. The cord wraps around the arms I had raised invitingly, and my assailant spins, wrapping the silk around his shoulders to keep tension as he reels in his catch.

I stumble along for a moment, allowing myself to be drawn in close before I pull my arms apart, using the sharp, embedded glass in my forearm to shred the cord and free my hands. I catch the dart before it falls and launch myself the remaining distance. My attacker recoils from the lost tension, and for a moment his armpit is exposed—a notoriously difficult place to armor. I slam the dart into the gap.

The blade isn't long enough to reach his heart or lungs, but the shock and pain are enough to break his defenses momentarily. I sweep his legs and bear us to the floor, pummeling him about the head. I land a punch on his throat, and he seizes up as I pull off his helm, recognizing my brother's face from the crowd at the foot of the Skull Throne.

One will attack without honor, Asome had predicted.

Another opponent would have been crippled—if not killed—by that throat-crushing blow. Indeed, there is fear in Prince Ramm's eyes now.

But my brother is charged with *hora* magic and continues to struggle, threatening to dislodge me. He reaches behind his back and produces a small metal tube with a wooden handle. I stare at it in confusion for a moment, then my eyes widen as I remember where I've seen it before.

I throw us into a roll, sacrificing my dominant position to bungle his shot. There is a deafening bang, and a chunk of marble explodes beside my head.

I can't hear anything, the air cloudy with an acrid smoke, but I see Prince Ramm raise the weapon again and I grasp his arm, pulling it away as I curl up and smash my forehead into his nose.

My ears start ringing, loud enough to split my skull, but I focus the pain into action, rolling again as my stunned brother attempts to recover. On top once more, I put a knee into his arm to pin the weapon hand, and keep him stunned with a punch to his unprotected head, followed by another. I hit him again and again, refusing to let him get his bearings.

And then the house guards are pulling me away, my fists bloody and Ramm's handsome face swollen beyond recognition. He lies limp, and I wonder if I've killed him. The guards—many of whom remember me as a child scampering through this very place—look at me like I've become a coreling.

I gasp, trying to rein in my anger amid the endless ringing in my cranium. As I breathe, all the pains I embraced during the battle seep into the edges of my consciousness. My blouse and silk jacket are soaked with blood from the arrow wound, and there are still blades in my arms. My shoulder burns from the dart cut, and contusions make themselves known all over my body from the desperate race across the rooftops.

But the most disturbing feeling is relief. Asome's prediction came true. There will only be one more to follow, and I can at least take comfort that he will announce himself honorably and give me time to set my feet before trying to kill me.

CHAPTER 29

HOLY HOUSE

WE SEND A RUNNER AHEAD, and he's back to let us know all will be ready on our arrival before Perin sets the steps on Rojvah's warded carriage. I catch Selen's scent on his collar, and wish there was a ward for scents as well as sound.

There's a steady stream of folk heading to evening services when we reach the Cathedral of Hollow, a sprawling structure connected to an abbey that spans several blocks, enclosed by its own wall, intricately carved with the beautiful script of church warding. Sunset services are still an hour away, but I've seen the place with my night eyes enough to know that if someday the greatward fails, there's no safer place in all Hollow than the cathedral.

We're able to enter by a gate not open to the public and pull up in a private courtyard where Inquisitor Hayes and Dama Halvan are waiting to greet us.

Hayes, clad in fine brown robes with the crooked staff of the Tenders of the Creator emblazoned on his surplice, is the second-highest-ranking Tender in Hollow, ministering to a flock in the hundreds of thousands. Clad in robes and turban of pristine white, Dama Halvan ministers to the much smaller Evejan minority. But Duchess Leesha decreed the faiths share the cathedral's nave, so the men are equal under Shepherd Jona in rank, if not power.

It ent frictionless. I can smell how much the graybeards dislike each other, even if they're too proud to show it.

"Mr. Bales." Hayes bows as I step out of the carriage.

Hate it when folk call me that. Mr. Bales is my da, and the less I'm compared to him, the better. Folk are only in for disappointment.

"I cannot tell you how pleased we were to hear you would be attending sunset services with us," the Inquisitor goes on. "Your mother was . . . not one to attend mass."

"Ay, that's undersaid." Mam never trusted Holy Men. *Even if there is a Creator,* she'd say, *He's got better things to do than worry about our problems. Can't trust anyone to do what you won't do for yourself, or tell you what the Creator wants.*

Hayes clears his throat. "There was some bad blood between us, I fear."

"Blood?" Arick is the next to step from the carriage, waiting halfway down the steps as he holds a hand out to steady his sister as she emerges.

When she heard where we were going, Rojvah had something close to one of my fits. She ent a priestess-in-training anymore. Not in her heart, at least. Her name's still in the books. What to wear to a greenland temple? How can she respect the Creator while refusing His service?

In the end she had one of Olive's green gowns pinned to suit her slimmer figure, taking a long scarf of matching green silk and draping it over her hair and to cover her shoulders and the gown's immodest neckline. Her veil is made of at least a hundred glittering gold coins, each etched with wards, connected to a lattice of spun gold atop her head. She'll have night eyes like mine when the sun sets.

I can smell how eager the clerics are to greet the newcomers, but Hayes does the courtesy of answering the question first. "It used to be my honor as Inquisitor to root out false Deliverers. I was sent to Hollow to expose a false Deliverer, your father, Arlen Bales, only to find he was who I was searching for all those years. But in those early days, I fear the . . . rigor of my inquisition was offensive to your mother. Nevertheless, I was honored to perform their wedding ceremony when they asked it of me, and to stand with them when the night tried to claim Hollow."

"Ay, fair and true," I tell him, but I don't relax. Hayes wants something from me. I can smell it. Ent hard to guess what. Mam never liked this Deliverer business, and says Da had even less patience for it. Just lettin' myself be seen here is giving the Tenders a boost.

"Prince Arick. Princess Rojvah." Halvan doesn't put his hands on the floor, but his bow is deep and long. I can smell competitiveness. "You honor us with your presence. I am Dama Halvan. It was my honor to train with Shar'Dama Ka in Sharik Hora."

Rojvah blows a breath as she offers a shallow nod of her head in return. Behind her veil, she whispers, "*Trained with* is what *dama* say to save face. What they mean is Grandfather pummeled them in the *sharusahk* circles."

I snigger, and both clerics narrow their eyes at me.

THERE'S AN OLD Holy House at the center of the cathedral grounds. A tiny structure, it ent got room for more than a few hundred in the pews. It's a protected landmark now, so out of place with the newer and more modern structures in the surrounding abbey. Out front is a statue of Da standing ten feet tall, appearing to float in midair. To either side is Duchess Paper with her *hora* wand, and Rojer Halfgrip—Arick and Rojvah's da—with his fiddle.

Don't have any more faith than Mam did, but I can't keep my throat from tightening at the sight. It was here the elderly, children, and infirm of the original Cutter's Hollow huddled in fear the night my da first came to town and taught folk to fight the corelings.

Used to come here at night when the clerics had gone to bed, just to stare a bit at Da. Mam caught me at it more than once. She never scolded, just sat with me. *Din't really look like that, Darin,* she'd say. *Wasn't that big, or muscly, or square in the jaw. Din't look that different from you, in fact. He just . . . carried himself big.*

So I've got a bit of an idea of what Rojvah and Arick are feeling as they step forward, staring at their father's likeness. Mam says that's exaggerated, too. *Rojer wasn't a big man, but they've got him looking like he's got less summers than you. Only thing they didn't need to exaggerate was Leesha's paps.*

Took her word on that. Aunt Leesha I knew was a lot more modest than the woman in the statue.

They closed the place to the public for our visit, but clerics gawk and whisper just like everyone else as the three of us enter the little chapel.

The inside has become a museum, of sorts. Da used to go around in a worn brown Tender's robe to hide the wards on his skin. Now it's on display behind half an inch of warded glass, illuminated by lectric lights. Night, there's kneeling pads in front of it.

There's weapons on display, too. "Blessed" axes, spears, and shields Da warded with his own hand, donated to the temple or acquired by the Tenders. I know my da's script at a glance, and can confirm the pieces are authentic, even if I can't follow the complexities of the wardings without my night eyes to cheat.

Around the chapel are heroes' bones, like in Sharik Hora, but rather than decorating out of the bones, Hollowers keep their fallen together, embedding their skeletons in the walls like silent guardians, commemorating with gold plaques the names of those who fell in the Battle of Cutter's Hollow.

The sun has not fully set, but there is darkness enough here in the chapel for my night eyes to come to life, along with the wards of sight on Rojvah's headdress and Arick's turban.

As with the martyr's bones in Sharik Hora, the greenland skeletons glow with that same golden magic, like and yet unlike the energy I can see drifting up from the Core, or in the auras of living things. These people died protecting their loved ones, and that final act shaped their magic into something . . . purer. Anathema to the corelings.

I know what to expect when we reach the front of the chapel, but Rojvah and Arick ent expecting it. To the right of the altar in a place of honor is another illuminated case of warded glass. But this is no robe or warded mattock. Within is the polished skeleton of their da, Rojer Halfgrip, here at the very center of the cathedral grounds.

Halfgrip is a hero of mine, and I'd sneak in here sometimes late at night to have a look, but I hear Rojvah and Arick gasp as they see it. With our night eyes, the golden glow of Halfgrip's bones is unmistakable. Overpowering. Even if you removed every other relic from the chapel, no corespawn could set foot inside while Halfgrip was here.

I can hear Arick's heart thumping in his chest. He lets out a moan and I can smell his anguish as he ignores the pad and falls to his hands and knees on the floor. "Forgive me, Father. I did not understand. I did not see!"

He weeps, but Rojvah kneels at his side, putting an arm around her brother with one hand as she scoops his tears into a tiny bottle with the other. All along she whispers soothing words.

I hate crying. Like your body's betraying you, making itself sick right when you need it most. And it ent got rhythm, so you can't predict it, or grow used. Arick's sobs cut at me, and I want to put distance between us, to lessen the discomfort.

But what kind of friend would I be if I did that? "There was no undercity for the Hollowers to flee to, that first night," I say instead. "Soot from the fires had marred every ward left in town. Folk were defenseless, and not everyone could fight. Sickness laid out half the town, and others had burns and breaks and demon wounds. They hid here in this little chapel, the last place standin', while the few who still had their feet under them faced the corelings come to feed. Ent a soul to say those who did the fightin' ent heroes, but it was Halfgrip that kept the demons from getting in here."

Arick's still shaking, but I can tell he's hanging on my every word. "Don't just take it from me."

"Young Mr. Bales speaks honest word," Shepherd Jona says from behind us. I smelled him coming. "I was there when the demons came. This chapel was my Holy House. The Hollowers, my flock. I believed in the Creator's love, but even I expected to die, that night. Without your father, even if the Cutters had won the battle, they would have lost.

"I never saw Rojer Inn touch a spear," the Shepherd continues. "He could thread a needle at thirty paces with one of his throwing knives, but I never saw him kill a demon with them. And yet he saved as many lives that night as any short of the Deliverer himself."

Even without night eyes, Halfgrip understood the effect music had on magic. He rippin' invented it, or as good as. Mam says he could march a line of unsuspecting demons right into the spears and axes of a waiting ambush, trick a wind demon into thinking the ground was lower than it was and crashing, or play so fast and loud that the resonance could shatter a stone demon's armor.

It wasn't just the sound. It was the emotion he put into the music, and how it affected those that heard it, how it shaped the magic in the air. Arick and Rojvah ent the only ones who wish they'd got to meet Rojer Halfgrip. Reckon he might've understood me, even when other folk din't.

"Services will begin in a few minutes," Jona notes. "We would be honored to have you participate? Perhaps a blessing?"

It seems like he's speakin' to all of us, but he's looking at me. I hold my breath, hoping Rojvah will step in and give my regrets like she did at the party, but she hangs back, breathing silent words into her veil. "This is for you to decide, Intended."

I suck in a breath and put up my hands. "Just here to pay our respects, thanks. Ent got any business handin' out blessin's."

"Indeed," Rojvah adds. "I have yet to take the veil, and I think my brother would prefer to pray privately." She's right, there. Arick's still on his knees before his da, and I can smell his relief.

Jona nods at that, his scent and aura calm, but I smell irritation from Hayes and Halvan.

"You are the Deliverer's son," the Inquisitor presses. "Who has greater right to give his blessings?"

"Never met him," I say. "How do I know what he'd want?"

"You think he would not wish to bless the people of Hollow and give praise to Everam?" Dama Halvan demands. "You dishonor his memory."

I clench up. This is why Mam never liked Holy Men. They're all sunshine, so long as you agree with them.

"Honest word?" I ask. "Reckon you're the one dishonoring him. You talk about my da, but what you really want is me to stand up and give the Creator credit for what he done."

"How dare . . ." Halvan balls a fist.

Arick is on his feet at that. He doesn't speak, but he's quick to put himself between me and the *dama*.

"You ent got any more proof than I do the Creator is even real, much less what He wants," I say, "but you talk like He sends you parcels every Messenger day."

Hayes thumps the leatherbound copy of the Canon that hangs from his belt. "He sent us His book."

I snort. Know I ent bein' polite, but I think Mam would forgive it. "Book written by men like you, who claim to speak for a Creator they don't even know is real."

Both Holy Men are equally offended at that. Looks like I've finally found something they agree on.

"You sound like your father." Shepherd Jona remains serene. Ent fakin' it, either.

"Mam, too," I say.

"But is that not the essence of faith?" Jona asks. "To believe something so strongly in your heart that you don't need proof to know it is true? And there is power in faith." He gestures to the glowing bones of heroes. "What do you believe, Darin Bales?"

The question hits harder than I expect, because I ent got an answer. "How do I know the difference between what I believe and what I want to be true?"

Jona shrugs. "Sometimes they are one and the same. The only way to know is to take a leap of faith."

That ent exactly a comfort. "Sometimes you take a leap and end up cracking your head on the cobbles."

Jona nods. "And sometimes, you fly. When the flux came to Hollow and the demons burned the wards, we didn't stop struggling, but hope was in short supply. Then Mistress Leesha returned that very day with two strangers in tow, offering their own lives to protect a tiny chapel of sick and injured, and asking folk to have the faith to stand with them in the night. In all my life, I have never felt a miracle as clearly as I did then. It does not steal from their heroism to know it was part of the Creator's plan."

A bell chimes, and there's a break in tension.

"Come, come," Jona says. "The sun is setting and services are about to begin." An acolyte appears, and the Shepherd instructs him to show us to our seats.

I listen in as we walk to a private entrance to the cathedral.

"Insolent," Halvan growls. "I expected more from the son of the man even Shar'Dama Ka called Deliverer."

You and everyone else, I think.

"The boy is lucky to be offered such an honor," Hayes agrees. "How dare he refuse?"

"Darin Bales refuses to speak words he does not believe true in the House of the Creator." Jona does not raise his voice, but it shocks the other men like the sting of a lash. "Perhaps the two of you should meditate upon why this strikes you as insolence."

I smile a bit at that. Mam says Jona's as much a fool as any Tender, but he's a fool with a good heart.

WE'RE ESCORTED TO the front-row pews, roped off from the other congregants, but right where all of them can have a good look at us. I wonder if just bein' here is as bad as standing on the altar and givin' a blessing.

There are wards cut into the wood pews, forming a net more complex than I could easily follow in daylight, but with my night eyes, it is alive with power, Drawing from the heroes' bones and the Hollow greatward, forming an impenetrable web of protection over this place.

I glance around the great nave, overwhelmed by images of my da.

Tenders don't have idols on the altar, but there are stained-glass windows, friezes, chapel nooks, and statues, all showing Arlen Bales performing his miracles.

Mam used to find me in here, too, late at night when the clerics had gone to bed. Don't know what I was looking for. Some kind of link, I reckon, to a father I never knew.

Artists never knew him, either, Mam said.

My eyes pass over the great stained windows depicting the time Arlen Bales floated in the sky. There's a halo of power around him, coming down from above as he wields fire and lightning to destroy demons by the thousand.

Mam tells that story differently. *He floated in the sky and threw lightning at the corespawn, ay, but he was pulling power from the greatward, not the heavens. And then the corespawned fool forgot to breathe and nearly got himself killed when he tried to pull too much.*

There's more bells and a choir and acolytes with stinky incense burners as we all stand to watch Jona's procession head to the altar.

"Before we begin," the Shepherd says, "I would like to dedicate tonight's service to Rojer Inn, in honor of his children's first visit to his shrine."

There's applause at that, and I can hear everyone talking about the three of us as Arick and I wave weakly in response. Only Rojvah scents of pleasure at the attention.

Reminds me a bit of the funeral back in Sharik Hora. The service seems to go on forever. Pews are packed, folk gathered to give thanks for Olive's safe return. In some ways it's okay. So many people in a tight space can be overwhelming to me, but it's easy to push all of it into the background, like playing my pipes by a waterfall. All I need to do is focus on Jona, who stands at a pulpit that blends wardings with plain old acoustics to amplify his speech and dull sounds from the pews.

But the Shepherd's service is as boring as any other. Jona might be kinder than the other clerics, but it ent a comfort that he thinks my da was Heaven-sent. I'd like to believe things are as simple as his sermon, but the stories of my father floating in the sky give lie to that. Everything can look like a miracle—or a curse—from the right point of view.

Still his question sticks with me.

What do you believe, Darin Bales?

What *do* I believe?

I believe Mam is alive, and I can save her. Gonna make a leap of faith, let it be that.

At last the service ends, and they open the great cathedral doors, letting in sounds from the outside.

And I hear alarm bells from Olive's keep.

CHAPTER 30

FAVAH

There is a crowd in front of the keep's infirmary. My spear brothers have gathered at the news of Faseek's injuries, spurring the house guard to outnumber them decisively. All of them take one look at my face and part with military precision to clear my path.

Selen is waiting inside with Lord Arther and Tarisa. She takes my shoulders, looking me over. I must look a sight, covered in blood and makeshift bandages. "You all right?"

"No," I don't stop moving and Selen moves to clear my way to the surgery, "I'm a ripping far sight from all right."

There is always a Gatherer on call in Mother's keep, though the duchess was apt to see to anything serious personally. But the duchess is not about, and the Gatherer on call wrings her hands, still staring at the arrow in Faseek's chest. She's cut away the robes and armor, but the arrow remains embedded, my brother breathing in short, ragged gasps.

I turn to the Gatherer. "Why haven't you prepped for surgery?"

She shrinks from my glare. "There's nothing I can do, Highness. The arrow is barbed and warded. It's unbreakable, and I cannot pull it clear in either direction without causing further damage. Even if we did, his lung has collapsed."

I want to shout, but then I truly see the woman, young and frightened. A night Gatherer used to fevers and broken bones, not battle surgery. She's out of her depth.

I turn to Selen. "Send a runner to the university. Have Favah meet us in the surgery."

Arther clears his throat. "Favah is . . . not a young woman, Highness. She will have retired."

He isn't wrong. If Favah has not seen a hundred winters, she is close to it. Mother thought her older still, her life unnaturally extended by her use of *hora*.

"Wake her," I say. "Tell her if my spear brother dies, I am sending Prince Ramm's head to his mother in a box."

"That could start a war," Arther says, but Selen is undeterred, already out of the room and shouting.

"All this for a desert rat," one of the house guards murmurs.

No doubt she did not expect me to hear, because the big woman nearly jumps out of her armor when I turn my eyes on her.

"He took an arrow for Olive, Manda," Becca says.

Manda tries to press herself into the wall as I move in to stand nose-to-nose with her. She's taller and broader than most women, but I've got inches on her still. "You guarded Mother as well, Manda. What do you think she would have said, if you told her a Krasian patient is worth less than a Hollower?"

Manda swallows hard, and it's all the response I need. I turn to Tarisa on my way out the door. "Find some chamber pots for Manda to empty while she considers if she wants to remain in our employ."

"Of course, Highness." Tarisa turns her hard eyes to the woman, and I trust she will reinforce the lesson as I stride to the door.

"Brothers!" I shout. "Extraction!"

Immediately, my spear brothers march into the room and load Faseek into a stretcher with practiced precision. "We're moving!" I order the moment they have him secure, marching at the head of the procession to ensure the way is clear as we head out of the infirmary. The house guard scrambles to form an honor guard around us.

Dama'ting Favah is waiting in the surgery with the much younger Dama'ting Jaia to assist. I cannot say if my venerable teacher, unreadable as always, is vexed at the disturbance. The *dama'ting* stand washed and prepped beside with Headmistress Darsy, who must have heard the commotion and come running.

"Tsst," Favah hisses as she examines the wards on the arrow shaft jutting from my spear brother's chest. "These wards are designed to pierce Krasian armor, not that of the *alagai*. Leave it to the Mehnding to create something so devious."

Wrinkles become deep fissures as she narrows her eyes at the symbols. With a huff of breath that billows her veil, she holds out a hand. "Brush."

Jaia has the item ready, putting a slim warding brush smoothly into Favah's hand, the bristles already wet with ink. Favah paints wards around the arrow shaft in a quick hand, though the symbols are too small for me to see. With a grunt she holds out the brush and Jaia takes it. Then the old woman reaches out to grasp the shaft on either end of her work, breaking it with a quick snap and a flash of magic.

Then she looks at me. "Step back."

"I can assist—" I begin.

"You're filthy, and still bleeding yourself." Favah cuts me off with none of the deference others have shown since my return. "Have Darsy tend you before you infect and I need to treat two."

She's right, of course. I'm used to stitching up my brothers on the floor of the Maze, but this is a sterile room in Gatherers' University, the greatest hospit in the world. There's nothing I can do Jaia cannot do better.

Reluctantly, I let Darsy lead me from the table as Favah resumes her work.

"You shouldn't be running around like this," the headmistress scolds, looking at the torn bedding hastily wrapped around my midsection and arms after I pulled out the throwing triangles.

But as she removes the bandages and clothes to clean the wounds, she's surprised to find the pressure alone has stopped the bleeding and closed most of them. Even my bruises have gone yellow. The healing of a full day in less than an hour. "Olive, what . . ."

"Mother's magic did more to me in the womb than bond me to my sibling," I say quietly.

Darsy nods, eyes flicking around to see if anyone overheard even that small bit of information. Mother is gone, but we are all still bound by her secrets.

The wound in my side still seeps blood, and Darsy needs to put me on a table and open it further to stitch and cut. She offers to put me to sleep, but that's the last thing I want. Instead I embrace the pain as I watch over my spear brother across the room.

Favah has painted wards around the entry and exit wounds in Faseek's chest, as my friend breathes in long, faint wheezes. He doesn't have the strength to resist as Jaia braces him and Favah takes the arrowhead in her forceps, pulling with surprising strength.

Faseek thrashes as the barbed head is drawn clear, but Jaia has leverage, and he does not skew the work. I wince at the blood and flesh that coats the arrow as Favah tosses it into a bowl.

Faseek has gone limp again. Jaia holds gauze under pressure on both wounds. Favah produces *hora*—rare and valuable in Hollow, where no one has encountered a demon in more than a decade. She brings the charged demonbone close to the ward circles she has painted on Faseek's flesh, and they begin to glow as they draw power from the *hora*.

The wards seem to spin, growing brighter and brighter. So bright they obscure the wound as I squint from the glare, finally needing to look away as the spell reaches its climax and the wardlight fades once more. The demon bone in Favah's hand crumbles to dust, its power spent.

"Why isn't he breathing?" I croak through my surgical veil.

"The breath was trapped inside his chest when the lung collapsed." Favah does not look at me as she and Jaia roll Faseek onto his back. "We will need to give it a path to escape before the lung can reinflate. Needle."

Jaia hands Favah a long, hollow needle, and my teacher does not hesitate, driving it between my spear brother's ribs. Trapped air escapes with a hiss, and Faseek gasps his first full breath since the arrow struck. Soon he is breathing normally, and Favah turns to the shaft still jutting from his shoulder.

"Glory in your breath, Sharum," Favah soothes. "Embrace the pain and be still, if you wish to ever hold a spear again."

Faseek tenses at that, and I can see fear in his eyes. He was considered a weakling in *sharaj* and would have been cast out, if not for me. But when he was put to the test in the night, Faseek showed the heart of a hero.

Wounded veterans are celebrated in Hollow, but in Krasia, a warrior who can no longer fight shames himself and his family. Warriors are meant to spend their lives on *alagai* talons, not limp home and burden their families. Countless *Sharum* have taken their own lives rather than surrender to such a fate.

But even in Desert Spear, Favah's name is spoken in respectful whispers among the *dama'ting*. Her threat is meant to keep Faseek still while she works, but now that he is breathing again, I've stopped worrying. So long as the arm remains attached, anything Favah cannot heal with surgery can be repaired with magic.

Favah continues to speak as she works, explaining what she is doing, and why. Not for Jaia's benefit, but mine.

Still teaching, even now.

Darsy's work is long done by the time Favah finishes stitching the wound. She turns to look at me. "He will need two Wanings to heal, and it may be months of therapy before . . ."

I shake my head. A small gesture, but Favah takes my meaning. I need Faseek fighting fit, and soon. She lets out a sigh but does not argue, painting another set of wards around neat row of stitches on Faseek's shoulder. With the benefit of surgery, less power is needed, and Jaia produces a much smaller bit of *hora* to power the spell. Again the wards glow, turning the swollen and ugly wound into a thin scar in mere moments. Even that fades, as the bone crumbles, and Favah cuts and removes the stitches with quick flicks of her *hanzhar*.

My ancient teacher turns to me once more. "And Prince Ramm?"

"He will live," I say.

Favah raises an eyebrow. "Does he require healing?"

"He does not deserve it," I say.

"He is your brother," Favah reminds me. "Blood of the Deliverer."

"Who attacked me in the night rather than challenge me to my face," I growl.

Favah nods. "And you were within your rights to kill him. But you did not. Now he is your prisoner. Do you know what your mother would do with an injured prisoner, regardless of their crime?"

I frown, because I know the answer, and I don't like it. "I'll have a Gatherer tend his wounds, but no *hora*. He can heal the natural way."

"Of course." Favah gives me a shallow bow. "It is late, Highness. Come again in the morning, and we will speak more."

The invitation is polite, but it is as much a summons as my Tikka's. Still, I bow in response, deeper and longer than the venerable *dama'ting*. This is not how I imagined our first meeting on my return.

Our relationship will change tomorrow, but for now I remain her student, and she my teacher. "Of course. Apologies for disturbing you after hours, honored Favah."

THERE ARE GUARDS everywhere as I finally return to my rooms. In the hall, on the terrace, some even in the room with me, spear brothers and house guards I have known my entire life. Arick and Selen were waiting in full armor when I emerged from the university surgery, and even Darin Bales allowed me to glimpse him, letting me know he was keeping watch.

I might once have found so many spears around while I try to sleep disconcerting, but I grew used to sleeping with my spear brothers in *sharaj*, and seeing trusted faces all around finally lets me relax enough to close my eyes.

It's morning when I next open them, sunlight streaming in through the curtains. I stretch, and last night's wounds are little more than tightness and a dull ache. A good night's sleep for me is a week's healing for most folk.

But there is a cost to the healing. Even magic cannot not create new flesh from nothing. I eat breakfast like a pregnant woman, and continue snacking as Selen brings in an assortment of wooden breastplates from the armory.

Tarisa was right that my Tazhan armor, black steel designed to mimic the scales of a demon, sends the wrong message at court. For every fool like Manda who speaks their prejudice aloud, there are others who quietly share the sentiments. The Krasians were not kind when they conquered southern Thesa.

The ache in my side is proof I cannot walk unprotected, even in my most private spaces. Hollow wooden armor is light and thin, carved with wards and bonded to glass enamel. Charged by the city's greatward, it is strong as warded glass. I find a breastplate snug enough to fit like a vest, invisible beneath my peplum blouse and surcoat. I sling a shield on my back and cover it with the warded cloak Mother made for me.

I ride my own horse to the university, refusing to hide in an armored carriage. My honor guard keeps the folk from my path, but I remember Arther's words and put on a smile I do not feel, waving to the crowds that spontaneously form along the streets.

I need no guide through the halls of Gatherers' University, but it is surreal entering Favah's classroom, even so. I am no longer the nervous girl who walked these halls, fretting over test scores and hours in the Chamber of Shadows.

Favah kneels serenely in the same place she always did when I would come for lessons. The door shuts behind me, wards of silence activating around the room, and I am alone with my teacher for the first time in more than half a year.

I leave my spear and shield at the door, sweeping my cloak back to kneel across from her. Then, for the first time in my life, I put my hands on the floor and press my forehead between them, as the Krasians do in supplication.

"Teacher." My voice is tight. "I apologize in sincerity for the insolence of my youth. I deeply regret that I did not offer the respect you were due. How could I have known that your honored name is spoken with awed whispers even now in the court of my father, and half the world away in Desert Spear?"

I rise, kneeling with my back up straight, meeting her eyes at last. But Favah surprises me, putting her own hands and forehead to the floor with surprising limberness for one so ancient. "Olive asu Ahmann vah Leesha am'Jardir am'Paper, it is good to look upon the real you at last."

"The real me?" I ask as she rises.

"Your mother and the Damajah both demanded an oath that I instruct you as *nie'dama'ting,*" Favah tells me. "I do not give oaths lightly, or when my own foretellings disagree. The dice told me it was not your fate to wear the white veil, but that I should pass on what wisdom I could to the leader you would become."

Again the dice, but this time I cannot fault this casting. Indeed, I am thankful for it. "By your training I was able to save many of my brothers from crippling or death, sometimes even as the fighting still raged."

Favah nods. "It is one thing operate in a pristine theater on a sedated patient, and another to stem the flow of blood from a man screaming and thrashing in the dust. You have honored what you were given. There is no feud between us. I, too, was insolent in my youth."

I find that hard to believe, but I do not argue. "There is more wisdom I need from you, if you will give it, but not as it was before. As student and teacher, we knelt together in this chamber." I roll back on my heels and stand, extending a hand. "Now I ask you to stand with me. To offer me truth and not obeisance. Advice and not instruction. To be my ally, not my subject."

Favah takes the offered hand, though she puts no weight on it as she rises. "You're a lot like him, you know."

I cock my head. "Like who?"

"Your father," she says. "Ahmann despised sycophants. He was literate, but not a scholar. Pure of heart, but not a cleric. Humble, but not a fool. His first language was that of the spear, but he guided the blade with a surgeon's hand by respecting seer and merchant's tally alike, and led with his heart as much as his head."

She squeezes my hand. "You will not be the leader he was. Or your mother. You will be the leader *you* are. But that does not mean you cannot exceed them both."

A difficult climb, but I will need to prove it true, if I am to navigate the path ahead. "And what wisdom would you offer, to help me get there?"

"First you must survive, little Princes." Favah points to the *hanzhar* on my belt. "It is time you learned how to use that."

I brush my fingers against the new sheath I had made to replace the one I crushed. "I know . . ."

I don't have time to finish the sentence as Favah's hand darts out, grasping the hilt and spinning the blade through the air to rest cold against my throat.

"A *nie'dama'ting* first must learn to use her *hanzhar* to heal," Favah says, "before she is taught to use it to harm."

COUNT THAMOS BUILT dungeons beneath the keep, but Mother hasn't used them since the war. The walls and floors are rough unfinished stone, and it is filthy, smelling of must. Spiderwebs hang from ceiling beams, and I can hear the squeak of rats. Mother would be horrified. Rats spread disease.

The one thing that has not fallen into disrepair is the wards Mother carved into the rock, creating a constant magical Draw. After a night here, whatever excess magic my brother Drew from his *hora* has been drained away.

Ramm has been stripped to his bido, and all of his possessions have been searched. The guards found more throwing blades and powerful *hora* jewelry, but that was not the most interesting item on his person.

A Gatherer has seen to Prince Ramm's wounds, but, denied magic, he will have a slower path to recovery. Still, when I reach his cell, my brother is exercising, using the steel bars of his cell to pull himself up over and over, despite the heavy chains at his wrists and ankles.

"Brother," I say, as he meets my eyes with a coldness that is unsettling even now, when I have every advantage. "I apologize for the filth. These chambers have not been used in many years."

Ramm only grunts, dropping to the floor and limping to his cot. A rat, startled by the move, scurries out from beneath. My brother flicks a wrist, sending a wave through his chain that cracks into the rodent like a whip, breaking its back. "Your *chin* prisons are soft. If you lack the strength to kill me, it will not be long before I make my escape."

"I wouldn't be so sure of that," I say. "My mother's prison may be soft, but I assure you her wards are not."

I hold up the flamework weapon he used as a last resort when the battle turned against him. "Where did you get this?"

Ramm laughs. "We are not fools in the Mehnding tribe. When Jayan's army was destroyed by your greenland fire chemics, we sent spies into the ruin of Angiers to learn of them. They came away with one of the mountain spears that launched the deadly projectiles, though it took some time to unlock its secrets."

It makes sense. Mother, too, had the secrets of fire and diagrams of the weapons of the old world. She outlawed their use in Hollow, even as they became more common in the militias of Angiers and Miln after the war. It was only a matter of time before the Krasians added them to their arsenal.

You must seize every advantage, Inevera had said. Good advice, even if I do not entirely trust the advisor.

I tuck the weapon away and look at him again. For all his bravado, Ramm has little to bargain with if he hopes to ever see his home again.

It isn't difficult to guess why Ramm would come for me. With the Majah returned to the desert, the Mehnding are the second most powerful tribe in new Krasia. As their crown prince, Ramm has spent his entire life just heartbeats away from the Skull Throne.

"You and Vuxan failed to kill me," I say. "Who will be the third prince to accept my challenge?"

Ramm shrugs. "Your information network is better than mine, little brother, if you know of another."

"Demonshit," I say.

There are teeth missing from Ramm's smile, but it only makes him more unsettling. "Why should I help you, even if I knew?"

I cross my arms. "To keep the courts from executing you for attempting to assassinate the heir to Hollow?"

Ramm laughs again. "The courts are an extension of your will, brother. You did not have the courage to kill me when I came for you in the night. I do not think you will find it now, or be so weak as to hide behind your pitiful 'courts' to absolve your cowardice."

The words needle at me, mostly because I know he is right. Capital punishment is another thing Mother outlawed in Hollow. None would challenge me if I made an exception, but I do not think I can find it in myself to kill another of my brothers. Iraven's eyes still haunt me.

I offer my brother a smile. "I don't have to kill to destroy you. I can simply let you rot in your cell while every Jongleur in Thesa sings of your shame. Prince Ramm the coward, who struck in the night and dared not face his youngest sibling in fair challenge, yet still failed the contest. At least our Krevakh brother kept something of his honor in defeat. Will your tribe's *Sharum* even follow you after this, without Father's shadow for you to hide in?"

Ramm's mouth tightens, and for once he does not have a laugh or retort at the ready. "Why on Ala would one of our brothers confide their plans in me?" he asks instead. "If Father is truly gone, then Prince Kaji will not sit the throne for long."

I feel my skin go cold. "What is that supposed to mean?"

"It means," Ramm speaks slowly, as if to a child, "the bloodshed has only just begun."

ARTHER IS WAITING as I emerge from the dungeons, and from there it is another long afternoon of meetings, tallies, and politicking. The first minister does his best to ease the burden, telling me who to flatter and who to bully, whispering names and relevant laws, proclamations and agreements as I need them.

Still, there is much to learn. I trust Arther, but simply acting on his word grates on me. Mother knew all these things herself, and was more powerful for it. *Even an honest baron can get a tally wrong,* she would say.

The last meeting of the day comes unexpectedly, as Grandmum arrives without an appointment. None of Hollow's barons intimidate Arther, but he is quick to excuse himself when Elona appears.

"Olive!" Grandmum is all hugs and kisses. Her cloying perfume clings to my coat even as she withdraws to take the most comfortable chair in the sitting area, the one usually reserved for Mother.

"Took my advice, I see," Grandmum says.

"Ay, how's that?" I ask, my mind still on mining contracts in New Rizon.

"Not hiding who you are, anymore," she elaborates. "Princes Olive! I love it!"

It's true Elona counseled this course moons ago, but I didn't do it for her. "I didn't have much choice when I was thrown into *sharaj* with the men in Krasia," I say. "I don't know that I would have had the courage to take your advice on my own, but I am glad it's done."

"Ent done by a long sight," Grandmum says. "You're off to a good start, but the folk still don't quite know what to make of this 'princes' business. They're used to seeing you in jewelry and gowns, not arms and armor."

"What does it matter?" I say.

"It matters if I ever want great-grandchildren!" Elona says. "How are we going to get you married if folk don't know if you're man or woman?"

"I'm both," I say, "and I'm not looking to get married."

"Doesn't matter what you're looking for," Elona says. "You owe it to Hollow to give them an heir."

I used to dream of having children of my own. I would have done it in a heartbeat with Prince Chadan. But now . . . "I don't even know what that would look like. Mother believed I could carry a child to term in my own belly, or father one on a woman."

"I expect you have a preference by now." Elona winks.

I wince and shrug in reply. "I've only ever kissed two people, a girl and a boy, and I liked them both."

"Take one of each, if you like!" Elona laughs. "Wouldn't that be something? Why should your da be the only one to marry more than once?"

The idea isn't as appealing to me as it seems to be to Grandmum. I wanted to marry for love, not duty. Now she's talking about taking a harem like a Krasian prince.

"Regardless, it's best we spell a few things out for the marriage brokers and the common folk," Elona says. "Not just this princes business."

"What do you mean?" I ask.

"I mean, they've as many questions about what happened out in the desert as they do what's happening under your skirts," Elona says. "And when folk have questions and no answers . . ."

I remember the rumors in Everam's Bounty about me. "They make the answers up."

"Ay," Elona says. "You need an official story, and to spread it far and wide."

I cross my arms. "And how do you propose we do that?"

"We bring in Hary Roller," Elona suggests. "Get him to write a song about the twins in the duchess' womb, and how they joined. About why the princess they knew dressed as a man on that infamous borough tour. About why the Majah wanted you, and how you came back their lord."

"I'm not their lord," I grouse.

"Details." Elona waves my words away again. "Jongleurs always embellish. All we need do is give folk time to wrap their heads around who you are, and what it means. Why they've got princes instead of a princess or prince. Why a duch and not a duchess or duke."

I purse my lips, thinking. She's not wrong. I won't go back to being one or the other, but I don't want to have to explain it to everyone I meet. With a few songs and whispers to the right people, Hary can spread the news faster and wider than I ever could.

Still, there is a cold animal squirming in my gut at the thought. Hary might make folk understand what I am, but there is no guarantee they will accept it.

I blow out a breath. "Do it."

DEEP BELOW WHAT is now Rojvah's chambers there is a hidden training room. It was once my sister's sanctuary, and the site where she delivered the most brutal beating of my young life, at a time when I desperately needed it.

Now Dama'ting Jaia stands over me in that same spot, *hanzhar* in hand.

Jaia, whom I always knew as the Krasian Studies teacher at Gatherers' University. Jaia, who taught young girls the foods and dances and tongue of our southern neighbors; and taught the pact of peace between us. Jaia, who married a Hollower and bore him six children. Jaia, whose eyes were always crinkled by the smile behind her white veil.

Jaia, who could have killed me half a dozen times in the scant few minutes we've spent in today's practice circle, had she not spared me the edge.

"Tsst!" Favah hisses from the edge of the circle before I can even draw a fresh breath to replace the one I lost on impact. "You keep favoring your right hand."

"My right hand is stronger," I say.

"If it is, you have no one to blame but yourself," Favah snaps. "We strengthen the side of us we use. You of all people should understand that, Princes."

She draws her own *hanzhar,* twirling it in her fingers like a Jongleur. The blade seems to dance from one bony hand to the other, moving faster than I can clearly see.

"The *hanzhar* is most dangerous when your opponent doesn't know where it is." The blade seems to vanish from Favah's hands, until she rotates an arm to show me the blade hidden behind one of her forearms. In a blink, it has jumped to the other hand.

Favah begins the spinning blade dance again, slowly this time. I lean in, watching closely. This is today's true lesson.

I memorize the *sharukin,* knowing she will not repeat it. I watch every flick and roll as she tosses the curved knife from one hand to the other. There are no lunges or cuts, no defenses or moves to realign one's opponent.

A child's *sharukin.*

Still I have to knit my brow in concentration as I perform the slow series of moves. Twice, I drop the blade and scramble to catch it. Once, I cut a line across my palm, catching the blade instead of the hilt. I stop and bandage it, making sure there is no stray blood.

Favah nods in approval. "Never be so foolish as to leave anyone with your blood."

Again and again I toss the blade, doing nothing else for the remainder of the hour. By the time I hear the chime of Micha's water clock, my left arm is aching from the effort, but the knife is moving faster.

"Practice." Favah slides her knife back into its jeweled sheath. "Whenever you are alone. A thousand times a day."

"A thou—" I begin, but I bite my lip before I can finish the word. Instead I offer a polite nod. "Of course, Honored Favah."

The old priestess grunts. "You are formidable, Highness, but do not mistake that for having nothing left to learn. I expect twice the speed by tomorrow's lesson."

My arm aches the rest of the day, as I sign papers and read reports, trying to glean from a thousand disparate tallies the true state of the duchy, and quietly strengthen our forces without causing alarm.

The Solstice Festival provides a perfect cover. All I need do is voice a desire for a military parade in front of a group of advisors, and I have all the excuse I need to increase drilling, hire recruits, and divert funding to equipment and supply. Only Arther, Gared, and Gamon know the truth as they quietly help me reposition our forces.

Every time there is a break between meetings, I steal a little time to flick my *hanzhar* from hand to hand. My fingers and palms are crisscrossed with tiny cuts, but I pay them little mind.

I'm getting faster.

MY LEFT HAND ROLLS the *hanzhar* along my fingers, even as I go through Mother's desk with my right.

The top drawers are familiar. I remember rifling through them as a child. Blank papers and writing implements, her blotter and her wax sealing kit. Warding tools. The lower drawers held files and were of little interest to young me.

Now I tug on one, and it resists my pull. Arther gave me the keys for the desk, but while one seems to fit the ornate, warded lock, it refuses to turn. "What's in here?"

Arther glances up, and I practice making the *hanzhar* disappear behind my forearm before he sees it. "I do not know, Highness. Personal papers, I expect. The key is not among the copies Her Grace provided, and I have not been able to open it in the months since her disappearance. With so many wards around the drawer, I assume your mother locked it with magic."

The words remind me of Belina, and I examine the lock more closely, immediately understanding when I see what looks like a red decorative gem in the molded wards. One of the symbols is carved in relief, with the strokes of the ward ending in sharp points.

It's a blood lock.

Blood locks are powerful magic, but they are fickle. The magic is keyed to the blood of the last person to let the spike draw blood, and in theory will open for no other. In practice, however, close relatives are enough to fool the spell.

I insert the key again, this time pressing my thumb against one of the spikes. Immediately, the color begins to drain away from the gemstone, going from red to pink to milky white. I turn the key with an audible click, and the drawer pops open.

"I must have tried that key a hundred times," Arther breathes. "How did you . . ."

"Mother must have meant it for me." I give the minister a pointed look as he leans in eagerly.

It takes a moment, but Arther remembers himself and straightens. "Yes, of course, Highness. If you will excuse me . . ."

I wait for the door to shut behind him before opening the drawer. There are heat wards lining the inside. If anyone attempted to force the drawer open, or break the wood, the contents would incinerate.

It's full of handmade books—personal journals—all written in Mother's smooth, rolling hand. Over time they become more uniform, but the earliest have flowers pressed into the paper like Grandda Erny taught me to make in his paper shop when I was little. I sniff one, decades old, and it still has a faint perfume.

I thumb it open to a page where Mother is shining on none other than Gared Cutter. I heard stories of how they once courted, but it's different to see it in Mother's own excited script. This isn't the Mother I knew. She speaks of the general as if the sun rose and set upon him, and how she cannot wait for them to marry so she can . . .

I snap the book shut. If Mother is still alive, this is not my business, and even if she isn't, I'm not sure I'm ready to know her every secret. I scan the dates written on the spines, choosing another from after my birth. I thumb through, glimpsing my own name far too often.

I close the book. Another thing I'm not ready for.

It's the last one I want. The one that covers Mother's plans to seek out the city in the mountains. I find one with an open end date, but it isn't the last book in the drawer. There's one more, its leather spine worn but unmarked.

I take both, opening the unmarked one first. I read through a list of names and case studies from other Gatherers—sometimes annotated by Mother herself, when she was able to examine the patients—and correspondence about the cases.

It doesn't take long to determine what ties them all together. A blacksmith living in New Rizon, born female, now living as a male. A mother of three in Lakdale, born with a vestigial penis. A school headmistress and two women working in a brothel near Stallion's Ranch who were all born men.

She was looking for others like me.

There are more—few enough to be noted in a single journal, but more than I could have imagined. People from all walks of life, soldiers, Gatherers, Warders, and simple tradesfolk. All occupying some space on the line between the points of female and male. I used to think I was the only one who questioned themselves. Now I see I wasn't alone at all.

Mother had mentioned this research to me in vague terms, saying only that there were no cases quite like mine, but it is something else entirely to look at her neat rows of notes in the margins and replies to local Gatherers. She offered advice where she could, and did not hesitate to use her influence to aid a patient in a difficult situation or protect their privacy.

This was personal for her. Important. A Gatherer's quest for knowledge blended with a mother's love and a healing hand.

Mother does not appear to have given up the search, but a line in one of the last entries of the journal sticks with me.

Can it be that Olive is indeed unique?

I put the book back in the drawer, keeping only the journal that might offer clues to find Alagai Ka's hidden city. There will be time over the winter to consider the rest.

I'm about to reseal the blood lock when a thought occurs to me. I reach into my pocket for the bottle of Inevera's blood. Like Mother's secrets, the tiny vial offers me a window into the Damajah's privacy I do not want, and dare not share.

I haven't felt safe to keep the vial anywhere save on my person until now, but my battle with Prince Ramm is a reminder of the risk there as well.

A weight lifts from me as I add it to the drawer and press my thumb into the blood lock, activating the wardnet and sealing some of my burdens inside.

CHAPTER 31

HAVIN' IT OUT

Solstice is coming up fast, but our trio has been practicing every night, and playin' better than ever. Arick still plays like a machine and Rojvah's still a diva who needs the spotlight, but we've figured out how to work together, finding rhythm at last.

Got to admit it comes from practicing reels and party music instead of spellsong. Having a setlist gives us common footing. There's need to improvise when you're playing for a crowd, speeding songs up or slowing them down, taking a request or letting someone solo so the others can take a drink or tune an instrument, but it ent the frantic improvising you sometimes need to get an angry demon to do what you want in the middle of a fight.

The rises and falls of a concert are things you can plan and practice for, and if you make a mistake, the audience doesn't eat you.

My night eyes can see the glow of magic, and how our music shapes the flows around us. Even here in the keep where Aunt Leesha's wardings have magic under a tight leash, we Draw power and bend it to our will. Folk won't just want to dance 'cause the tune is catchy, the very air around them will whisper their toes into tappin'.

With the wards of sight on Arick's turban and Rojvah's jewelry, they can see it, too—now that I've shown 'em what to look for. These little ditties we're practicing are just the beginning of what we can do now that we're finally finding our sync. With enough practice, even some of Halfgrip's "miracles" will be within our reach.

Just hope it will be enough.

Arick holds the last note, even after Rojvah and I fade out. When he finally takes bow from string, I feel the wood of his kamanj vibrating a few moments more.

It's our best practice yet, but there ent anyone to clap. Selen always used to put her hands together when we finished a set, but other than when Olive was attacked, she ent spoken to any of us in days.

She's been busy, ay. I hear her giving orders to the house guards, going over reports, and meeting with Olive. She's been makin' excuses to visit the stables, too. I play my pipes while she's there so I don't hear anything by accident, or get tempted to listen on purpose.

But Selen's got her own rooms in the keep, right down the hall. I hear her in there plenty of times. She ent too busy to see us. She just don't wanna.

Know I should leave it be. Don't like folk crowdin' me when I ent ready to talk, and I don't reckon she does, either. But knowin' she's right next door and won't even check in makes my brain itch. If we've got any hope of sneaking into Safehold, we all got to be in rhythm, not just the players.

"Are you all right, Darin?" Arick has that big-brother voice again. Been taking it a lot with me, even though I'm his elder by more'n two months.

Can't say I don't like it, though. Feel as safe with Arick and Rojvah as I used to with Olive and Selen.

"Just got a lot on my mind," I tell Arick. Never been a good liar, so I keep it vague as I look out the windows. "Reckon I just need a little fresh air."

"Intended." Rojvah's voice pulls me up short as I open the terrace doors.

"I'll . . . be in the privy." Arick hurries out of the room as his sister approaches.

I give ground instinctively as Rojvah presses in close, backing out onto the terrace until I fetch up against the railing. The night air is chill, but Rojvah doesn't seem to notice.

"Just go to her, Intended," Rojvah says quietly.

"Ay, what?" The response is clumsy on my lips. Ent a good liar, and we both know who she's talking about.

"The daughter of Gared," Rojvah says patiently. "I cannot see for miles as you can, but even I can see that her absence pains you."

I shrug. "It's what she wants, or she'd be here."

"Why do you do that, Intended?" Rojvah asks quietly.

This time I really am confused. "Do what?"

"Put everyone's will before your own?" Rojvah asks. "Act as if their needs are more important that your own? As if they are above you?"

"Ent they?" I ask. "I'm the one who can't ride through a crowd without havin' a fit. Who can't get close enough to folk to talk about the weather, much less make friends."

Rojvah takes another step toward me, and I ent got anywhere to go unless I want to hop the rail. "You are close to me, Intended."

She's right. Anyone else, and I would have vaulted the rail in a heartbeat. Now I can feel my heart thumping in my chest. She lays a hand atop it. "You are not less than Olive or Selen, Intended. You are not less than anyone. Where would either of them be, without you?"

I swallow, but I ent got an answer.

"Olive would still be with the Majah at best," Rojvah says. "More likely in the belly of Alagai Ka. And Selen," she waves a hand, "would never have left, sitting still while the world moved around her."

"Ent that simple," I say.

"Is it not?" Rojvah asks. "You think everyone takes care of you, Darin, but you never take your own measure."

I snort. "Reckon I'd just come up short, like always."

"Tsst." I can smell Rojvah running out of patience. "Do you want to kiss me?"

"What?"

"Even I can tell Selen is visiting the stables to see her horse groomer," Rojvah says, "so do not pretend you haven't noticed."

"Ent my business who Selen kisses," I say, as much for myself as her.

"Then why the wistful sighs and longing stares?" Rojvah demands. "We've been intended for weeks. Am I so repulsive that you would rather envy the dung shoveler who sets the carriage steps beneath your feet than kiss me?"

"No!" I don't know what I was expecting, but this ent it. "That's crazy."

"Indeed it is," Rojvah agrees. "So you do want to kiss me?"

"A-ay, course I do," I say. "But said yourself we're just playin' a game, so your mam will take a step back. Ent gonna take advantage . . ."

She takes it as permission and leans in, her lips soft and slick against mine. I can feel her warmth, and the pulse of her blood. She's taken to wearing less fragrances, but that just makes her own smell stronger, and right now her scent's going right past my head to tell my body all kinds of things it ent used to.

Never been one for hugs, but I can't help it now, putting my arms around her and pulling her close, wanting this moment to last forever. In a way, it seems to. Then it is over, Rojvah pulling back until I hear the sound of our lips peeling apart with a burst of breath.

"Stand tall, Intended," Rojvah whispers. "You are not less than anyone. And next time we say good night, do not wait for me to kiss you first."

With a smile, she turns away, going in out of the cold and shutting the doors. I'm left alone on the terrace. I feel like I'm floating as I scale to the roof, and it takes me several minutes to catch my breath and shake off the fog so I can think again.

Ent easy to believe Rojvah would really want me, but I felt her pulse quicken with that kiss, too. Reckon she's got as little experience with kisses as me.

Harder to believe what she said about me. Been disappointing folk my whole life. I can smell it even if they're too neighborly to say it out loud.

But she's right about one thing, at least. Time's come for me and Selen to have it out, as Mam would say.

I TILT MY HEAD, inhaling. Selen's alone, and she ent in the bath or the privy. There's a slight rustle and a scent of paper. Not the rough parchment the guard uses for reports. I hear cushions compress as she shifts.

She ent workin'. She's on the couch, prob'ly readin' a Jak Scaletongue story or somesuch.

Selen's pulse changes. "Know you're lurking up there, Darin Bales, so you might as well come out."

Dunno how she does it, but Selen's always been good at knowing when I'm around. I drop off the roof onto her terrace. The doors are locked tight, but there's a tiny gap between them, and it's all I need as I turn slippery and squeeze through. "What gave me away?"

Selen puts her book facedown on the couch and gets up. "What do you want, Darin?"

She smells angry. Ready for a fight.

And I'm sick of it.

"Ent we friends anymore?" I ask. "Shown up at your window a hundred times. Used to call it comin' to set and visit. Now it's *lurking,* and I ent welcome?"

I can see the words hit her aura and there's a whiff of uncertainty, but Selen ent one to budge when her back is up. "What do you need to visit with me for? Got your little 'intended' for that now, ay?"

I move deliberately into the room, going to my favorite chair. It's padded and quiet, with a view of all the windows and doors. It's where I always set, and I make a point of plopping down. "What do you care if I'm promised? Both know you got other prospects."

Her scent is even madder now. "Just because your nose tells you all my secrets doesn't mean I need to explain myself to you, Darin Bales."

"Honest word," I agree. "So why do I have to explain myself to you?"

Selen pauses for a response, but I don't give her time. "Tell you why. Because you and Olive treat me like a child. Always have. Gotta help little Darin wipe his bum! He'd be lost without big sister!"

Selen's muscles unbunch, and she rubs her face a moment before going back to the couch and flopping down with a scent of resignation. "Ent like that, Darin. We just care about you, and some things are . . . hard for you."

"Some things are hard for you, too, Sel," I say. "I been at your da's house for Seventhday supper. Ent I always been there for you, when I can? Don't mean I get to tell you what to do."

Selen sighs, her muscles going limp, but she doesn't reply.

"Don't know what's happened to us, Sel," I say, "but I hate it. Don't care if you'd rather kiss Perin than me."

"Never said that, Darin," Selen says.

"Not with words," I say. "But I ent as wood-brained as you and Olive think."

I can smell fresh irritation and push forward. "Point is it dun't matter. Rojvah dun't matter. You're my best friend, Selen Cutter. I got to give that up, just because someone wants to kiss *me,* for a change?"

Selen looks at me, and her body starts giving off all the signs she's gonna cry. Muscles in her neck and face tighten, and I can smell saltwater collecting in her tear ducts.

Quick as a blink, I snatch a silk handkerchief from my pouch of Jongleur's tricks, crossing the floor and putting it in her hand. I'm back in my chair before she realizes I've moved.

Selen starts, staring at the kerchief. It did the trick like it usually does. Nothing stops Selen from cryin' quicker than handing her a hankie.

"I'm sorry, Darin," she says at last. "Feels like everything's changing so fast. Olive used to be my best friend, but lately it feels like I don't even know her anymore. Then it was just us, alone on the road all those months, but now that's changed, too."

"Nothing important's changed," I say. "Still cross a desert, if you were on the other side and needed me."

Selen nods. "Me, too. Darin. Always."

Now it's me that feels ready to cry. I push the feeling down before it becomes a distraction. We're so close.

"Now Olive's in her office all day, with everyone bowing and scraping," Selen says, "and I've got guards that have seen me get my bum paddled asking my permission to use the privy."

I nod. "Olive wants it that way. Heard her tell Arther she wants folk used to you givin' orders."

Selen looks up at that. "Why?"

"Know why," I say. "You're princess of Hollow, too. Someone's got to stay home and be in charge while she goes off to the Spear of Ala, or wherever the Damajah is sending her."

"Like night I'm staying behind." Selen looks ready to spit. "Already told her that."

"'Course not," I agree.

"And I got a message for Olive," Selen says, "if she's going on that witch's errand over rescuing her own mam."

"Hold your glove for you," I say, "you want to slap the fool out of her. Don't think it will change her mind. And maybe it don't matter. Might be Inevera's right, and we're better off without Olive on this hunt."

"Oh, ay," Selen rolls her eyes. "Why would we need someone who can arm-wrestle a wood demon?"

"Because we need to sneak," I say, "and after Prince Ramm's little stunt, Olive ent going anywhere without a briarpatch of spears around her."

"She could *sneak*." Selen throws my own word back at me.

"Folk would lose their minds, she disappeared again," I remind her.

"Ay, but no one would miss me?" Selen asks.

"'Course they would, but I got thoughts about that," I say. "Maybe we can do without Olive, but I can't do it without you."

Selen cocks her head at me. "Why's that? I ent got special magic, and I can't carry a tune. What can I do the others can't?"

"Thought about leaving you behind, that night after Olive was taken," I tell her. "Reckon I could have run those horses down, I'd really leaned in."

"Why didn't you?" Selen asks.

"'Cause I was scared," I admit. "'Cause I might be able to run them down, but what was I going to do, then? Ent a fighter like you."

"You'd have figured something out," Selen says. "Ent always about fighting."

"Ay, maybe," I say, "it's about heart. And I ent got any when I'm by myself. Never would have made it to Olive, you hadn't been there with me."

Selen looks at me for a long time. Then she gets up and holds out her arms. "Know you don't like hugs, Darin, but . . ."

I'm in her arms before she can finish the sentence.

CHAPTER 32

SOLSTICE

BARELY PAST SUNRISE on a cold Solstice morning, the streets are lined with cheering crowds, packed behind the barricades as we pass. Any building with a terrace or flat roof is covered with folk, and more lean out of windows, all vying for a view of the parade.

I look back at the seemingly endless line of horses, riders in military dress uniforms, spears pointed at the sky. They stretch all the way up to Mother's keep, winding down the hill to the Corelings' Graveyard, the market center of Cutter's Hollow.

The graveyard was so named because it was on that very spot Arlen Bales first taught the Hollowers to kill demons. If there is a place more sacred in all Hollow, I don't know of it. Mother was crowned onstage at the graveyard's famous bandshell, and Arther wants the same for me.

The parade has been an excellent reason to get to know the infantry and cavalry captains, and drill with the Hollow Soldiers. They are more formal than Gared's Cutters, but if there is one place I am at home after my time in Krasia, it is the training grounds.

The Hollow Lancers all ride Angierian mustang, giant animals that make the full-sized coursers we rode from Krasia look like ponies. After escorting us to the city center, the lancers will ride out to the larger fields outside the city to perform drills for cheering crowds.

There are Solstice Festivals happening in all the boroughs of Hollow, with music and dancing and the traditional bonfire against the longest night. Folk give small gifts, especially to children, as friends and family gather from afar to celebrate. Winter Solstice was always my favorite day of the year, sweeter for its shortness. I would spend months working on my Solstice dress, and trying to find a dress Selen would consent to wear.

Neither of us wears a dress today. Not out in the open, so soon after Prince Ramm's visit. Not on coronation day. There are guards everywhere and Favah herself cast the dice and saw no threat to my life. Still, I cannot deny my unease. Asome said there would be three, and it stands to reason that none of my brothers would be fool enough to wait for me to take power.

Riding at my side, Selen looks radiant in her new wooden armor, glittering with warded enamel. I tested the breastplate myself when it arrived, thrusting a practice spear so hard the steel tip shattered without leaving a scratch on the surface.

I remember the sound of the arrow striking Faseek, and am relieved that Selen will be protected if someone aims for me and misses.

Over the suit she wears a captain's tabard with my house colors and sigil, and the warded cloak that was Mother's last gift to her. The rounded shield slung from the saddle of her giant mustang carries the sigil of House Cutter, a two-headed axe crossed with a machete before a goldwood tree.

I wear Chadan's Tazhan armor, but I know the black steel scales—so distinctly Krasian—unsettle some folk. My house tabard matches Selen's, covering my chest and falling around my legs like a skirt. Mother's blue warded cloak softens my shoulders.

The helm is slung in easy reach from my saddle, but I cannot afford to hide my face from the people. It has only been three moons since I stopped shaving my head, but the royal hairdresser made the most of the scant inches he had to work with, affixing it in place with a jelly that dried hard as cement, while giving the appearance of hair slick with oil. At my brow is one of Mother's warded diadems, a brilliant sapphire at its center.

From the cheers of the folk and ribbons of paper that rain down upon us, it appears we have struck the right note. The armor sends a less-than-subtle message, but it's a needed one. I don't want panic, but now is not the time for Hollow to become soft.

There are still dangers in the night.

Hary Roller likes to make jokes at his own expense, but I am coming to understand the value of a skilled royal herald. In one meeting, I told him what I wanted my people to know about me, about what happened out in the desert, about what's to come. He began composing *The Ballad of Princes Olive* on the spot, stroking his bow against the cello strings as he plucked the most emotional elements of my tale and began humming them into lyrics.

It took him three days, but I could tell Master Roller was inordinately pleased with himself when he sat down to play us the final piece. Hary took some . . . liberties with the truth, lionizing not just me, but all my companions, and glossed over the uglier and more sensitive bits. But in its entirety, it's a fair summation of what happened, and who I am. Plus it has a nice melody.

Hary has set Jongleurs along the parade route, all of them playing the ballad loud and often throughout the parade. We hear it fade in and out as we wind through the streets of Cutter's Hollow.

There's a verse about my ill-fated borough tour with the young folk from Apple Hill, and the next time it comes up, there is a great cheer up ahead.

"Ay, look!" Selen points to a group of familiar faces crowded at the parade barricade. I see a flag with a red-appled tree atop a verdant hill. I wince as I glance down and see it rises from the back of a wheeled chair. Boni is there, waving at me like an old friend, but for a moment, all I can see is my memory of her screaming until she passed out as I frantically tried to tie her arteries in time for Micha to amputate her leg.

But I wave, and the folk of Apple Hill cheer again. I see Tam, who had nearly been eviscerated by a demon talon, walking with the aid of a cane. Cayla stands beside him, offering support. Six from Apple Hill died that night, nine more injured. All because I was stupid and impulsive and left Mother's greatward, drawing demons to our camp.

Yet still they are here, cheering the sight of us when they have every reason to cast shadows and blame.

"Ent that a sunny sight," Selen breathes as we catch sight of Oskar.

"Guess we weren't the only ones who found a calling on that tour." I remember the tall boy with arms like a blacksmith standing side by side with Selen, bathed in glory as they attacked a rock demon with their spears. Now Oskar stands in the dress uniform of a Hollow cadet.

I have to swallow a tightness in my throat. "Oskar is your *ajin'pal*," I say. "Your blood brother."

"Ay?" Selen asks.

"You fought side by side the first time you shed demon ichor in the night," I say. "In Krasia, there is no greater bond between warriors."

Thoughts of the battle bring other sights to mind. Gyles, lifeless on the ground. Elexis, still shrieking as she was eaten alive.

Selen sees my eyes go distant and gives me a shove, keeping me in the now. "Any rules in Krasia against kissing your blood brother?"

"Ay, I hope not." I force myself to smile and wink. "Kissed mine." Selen honks a laugh.

Oskar leans back, and I catch my breath as another familiar face appears, round and soft with bright eyes and full lips. The top button of her dress is still undone, even in the winter air, and I feel my face heat as another memory comes to mind.

Lanna.

She waves, bouncing up and down with excitement, pretty as a sunrise. I wave in reply, and we reach hands toward each other as I pass, but from atop my giant mustang we might as well be separated by a chasm.

There's no way to stop a parade, but I glance down at the footman pacing my horse. "Have the Apple Hill delegation escorted to the graveyard and given a place of honor in the royal section."

"Of course, Highness." The man steps smoothly out of the procession, quickly disappearing behind us.

The festival stretches all through the town, with special sales, storefront games, and decorations on every street. The main attractions will be at the bandshell in Corelings' Graveyard, where already teams of Jongleurs provide music that wafts down streets like a gentle breeze.

The market pavilions have been cleared from the center of the great cobbled plaza, but vendors work the crowd with warm food, noisemakers, and banners bearing the spear and olive. There are games to play, prizes to win, and classes in dance, singing, and crafts.

The coveted tiered benches near the bandshell are crowded when we arrive. Likely they filled the moment the plaza opened. Guards limit the crowd size, but folk crowd the barricades, hoping for a chance to be let in as others exit.

Next to the bandshell on the opposite side from the bleachers is the royal section, walled on three sides and roped in front, with alert guards on patrol and stationed atop buildings around the city center.

There's a raised viewing platform with shade and comfortable seating around Mother's wooden throne, where she would sit to witness the games and performances, occasionally coming out to kick off a contest, or inviting folk in to stand before the throne as she bestowed awards.

I remember years of playing on that platform with Selen, and years more sitting next to Mother, clapping and cheering.

Now I'm expected to sit on that throne and be Mother. To cut ribbons and toss ceremonial horseshoes, to bless folk and settle their disputes with a word that is law.

Selen and I ride up to the central fountain, the space around it cleared with ropes for special events. The fountain is dry this time of year, and an oil fire burns in the bowl held aloft by its twenty-foot-tall statue of Arlen Bales. In densely populated Cutter's Hollow, the fire is only symbolic, but in the outer boroughs, folk chop sacrificial trees for Solstice and build massive bonfires to ward against the long night.

The crowd cheers as we dismount. Without thinking, I revert to Mother's training, giving the crowd a moment to revel before I raise my hands for silence.

"Good folk of Hollow!" I boom, as the hubbub dies down. "I know I have been away, but I have never missed a Winter Solstice Festival in Cutter's Hollow, and I don't mean to start!"

Again the crowd explodes with cheering, noisemakers, and applause. I let the wave crest, as Mother would say, and then speak again, welcoming, thanking, blessing, and formally opening the festival.

Darin, Rojvah, and Arick are already in the royal section. I know Darin struggles on festival days. So many folk crowding the plaza and cheering at irregular intervals—not to mention the noisemakers, festival crackers, and toss bangs—gave him fits when we were kids until we started packing his ears with wax. Even then, he appeared late and vanished early.

Darin has his hood up against the morning sun and looks a little drained, but he seems regulated. Nevertheless, Rojvah hovers by him protectively. Among Hollow's elite, everyone wants a little time with the mysterious son of the man whose statue stands just a few yards away.

But every time some noble or courtier ventures over to offer greetings, Rojvah interposes herself, smiling and charming and doing most of the talking. Most folk might not notice, but I do.

I feel torn. Selen is my best friend, and instinctively I want to take her side in any dispute. But looking out for Darin Bales is a direct path to my favor. Whatever her motives, Rojvah seems to take their relationship seriously, and that's what Darin deserves.

"Princes Olive!" a voice cries behind me. I turn, already raising fists, and see guards and my spear brothers tense. But then Lanna throws her arms around me and presses her soft mouth into mine.

Faseek laughs, clashing his spear against his shield. "Olive!"

My spear brothers and Selen join the cheer, clashing their spears and chanting my name. They are joined by the folk on the bleachers, and soon almost everyone in the plaza is roaring and clapping. Lanna giggles at the sound, but does not pull back until she's left me breathless.

"Still shy?" Her eyes glitter as she watches my face turn red. All I can do is smile dumbly, but the response seems to please her.

Oskar is more formal approaching Selen, dropping to one knee and punching his chest in a salute befitting their respective ranks.

"Core with that!" Selen cries. "If Olive gets a kiss, I'm getting one, too!" She hauls him up and kisses him as boldly as Lanna did me. Everyone is watching now, and again the crowd roars. I glance at Darin, but he's stomping and hooting along with everyone else. Selen told me they worked things out, but I didn't really believe it until now.

Even Rojvah has joined in the merriment, cheering and then grabbing Darin, planting one right on his lips. I know the look when Darin tries to turn slippery, but he's got no powers here in the sun, and flails helplessly in her embrace as everyone cheers a third time.

I spare a look at Selen. She's cheering, but it hasn't reached her eyes. Maybe Darin's worked things out, but I'm less sure about her.

But then the festival begins in earnest, and there are games and entertainment to hold our attention. Gared Cutter proves he can still split wood faster than anyone in Hollow, and swings the sledge on the strength test so hard he knocks the bell off the pole and it takes an hour to repair. He gets a kiss from his baroness anyway, as Grandmum glares at them and my grandfather pretends not to see it.

Darin and Arick take over the sound shell, though the other Jongleurs remain onstage, instruments ready to support.

They aren't needed. Boosted by the shell's acoustics, Arick's kamanj lays down a steady rhythm as Darin's pipes weave their spell over the crowd. I wonder where Rojvah has gone, but then a voice from backstage heralds her appearance.

My niece has changed from her frilly and rather conservative festival dress into what the Krasians would call pillow silks—thin, colored robes that flow about her like smoke.

In Krasia, pillow silks are reserved for the harem, where no men are welcome, or the privacy of a marital bedchamber. To wear them in public would be a scandal, and even in Hollow, where female Jongleurs often dress in revealing clothes while they perform, they are daring.

Rojvah plays tiny cymbals bound to her fingers in rhythm with her song, and a lattice of warded coins around her waist jingles as she sways and spins across the stage, taking folk's breath away with each snap of her hips.

When her performance is over, the crowd explodes in cheering and applause, and Rojvah bows, basking in the attention. Oskar has an arm around Selen, but she seems to have forgotten he's there, staring at Rojvah like a spider eyes a fly.

"I am told it is tradition for Princes Olive to lead the first dance!" Rojvah needs no magic to carry her voice with the bandshell at her back. "Shall we invite her out of hiding?"

"Ay! Ay!" the crowd bellows, clapping hands and stomping feet.

Rojvah isn't wrong. I've led the first dance for years, but it was always in twirling skirts, on the arm of Uncle Gared or Darin Bales or some hopeful young nobleman. Now I stand in a man's armor, and cannot conjure that girl again.

I turn instead to Lanna, holding out a hand. "Dance with me?"

Her face is aglow as I lead her out into the plaza and Darin begins a slow soulful melody, doubtless delighted to make someone else the center of attention. I have to concentrate, not used to leading a dance, but Lanna and I have done this before. I look in her eyes, and the months melt away to that night not so long ago when my biggest worry in life was whether or not we would kiss.

Soon we are joined by other couples from the royal section, and then the guards let others in. Lanna beams at me, holding my gaze, making her my world, if only for the short while before Darin strikes up a reel that has everyone laughing as women spin from one partner to the next.

When the dancing is over, Darin's trio performs more famous pieces, the ancient *Song of Waning* and *The Battle of Cutter's Hollow.* There are wet eyes all around for that one. There are comparisons to the legendary trio of Rojer Halfgrip, but that was before my time, and I have no basis to weigh them against each other.

Hary Roller joins them onstage, Darin and the others playing backup as my herald sings *The Ballad of Princes Olive.* I keep my back straight as folk turn their eyes my way, refusing to melt under the scrutiny. It only gets worse as Lord Arther takes the stage holding aloft a warded crown. He beckons and I kneel before him, voice amplified as I pledge myself to Hollow until Mother returns, or my death.

"Olive Paper," Arther booms as he sets the crown on my brow, "Duch Regent of Hollow!"

The crowd's reaction to Lanna's kiss was nothing compared to the roar that comes in response.

I SHED THE WEIGHT of my Tazahn armor after the coronation, feeling safe enough under guard to slip into something more comfortable—warm leggings under a silk peplum blouse.

My new surcoat has pockets for armor plates in the Krasian style, but the plates themselves are made of Hollow warded wood—light, easy to shape, and hard as steel. The order helped restore my reputation with the Warders' Guild, who were not pleased by my decision to keep my Krasian armor in active use.

The day goes by in a bit of a haze. I used to wonder why Mother always had such a headache on festival days, but I understand it now. Even with the coronation done, there are endless duties. Each performer begs my permission to begin, and my favor at the end. Mother always set aside time on festival days to meet with locals from the crowd who would not otherwise have access to court. I wanted to beg off, but Arther was firm.

"Festival supplications were a tradition your mother began to keep trust with her people, even as she became increasingly ensconced at court. This year, of all years, we must show the people that your mother's commitments remain unbroken."

I don't like it, but he's right. So I sit as a line of supplicants come before me, asking for royal loans to start or save livelihoods, land bequests, property disputes, and in one instance a divorce. In most cases, Arther has already vetted the pleas and readied generous recommendations that require little from me save a ruling, though that last came as a surprise to everyone, including the husband.

They were on Arther's roster to ask for a loan, but the moment they entered, the woman ran to me, kneeling at my feet. "Please, Your Grace. I beg your protection, and a divorce. My husband told your minister we lost our crop to flood, but truer is he spent our seed money on drink and . . ."

"That's ridiculous!" the man shouts. "She's lying!"

The *hanzhar* at my belt has become almost part of my hand under Favah's tutelage, deadlier in close quarters than my spear. My hand itched to twirl it in my fingers while petitioners gave evidence, made accusations, and begged for boons, but I resisted the urge.

Now, when I see the husband ball a fist and the wife shrink back in response, even here in my presence, the knife finds its way into my hands.

Arther clears his throat. "Your Grace, perhaps . . ."

I ignore him, spinning the knife so fast it becomes a blur that draws every eye in the room. "Choose the words you speak in my presence carefully," I say. "The investigator I send will not be a fool, and if you bear false witness before me . . ." The spinning knife comes to a sudden stop, ready to strike.

Arther offers me leave after that, handling the remainder of the petitioners personally. I take the steps down into the platform, disappearing from view so I can enter unseen one of the private tents in the royal section, heated against the chill and stocked with refreshments.

Lanna is waiting downstairs, and I don't resist as she pulls me into an empty tent. "Alone at last."

Lanna does not seem interested in food or drink. She moves close, and this time I take her in my arms and kiss her. It's impulsive. I feel like I have no control over myself, and for just a moment, the kisses let me forget all my fears and worries. I haven't kissed anyone since . . .

I see Chadan's face in my mind and pull back suddenly.

"Your Grace?" There is concern in Lanna's voice. "Are you all right? Was I too forward? I apologize if . . ."

"It's nothing like that," I say. "I like your kisses."

"Then what is it?" Lanna asks.

"Master Roller's ballad did not tell all," I say before I have time to think better of it. "Out on the desert, I . . ."

I swallow hard, and Lanna lays a gentle hand on my shoulder. "I was in love," I blurt. "I was in love and he . . . died."

"I'm so sorry." Lanna puts her arms around me, squeezing me tight, her body warm and soft. "I do not expect anything from you, Your Grace, but I promised you as many kisses as you like after you saved my life, and I do not think it a betrayal of your love for you to take comfort in them."

"I saved your life, ay." I've lived in terror of this conversation for two seasons, but now that it's here, I won't spare myself. "But only after I put it in danger. The demons were hunting *me,* Lanna. The moment I left the greatward, they were tracking me, and I led them right to our camp. Six dead, their blood on my hands. Boni in her wheeled chair, Tam still needing a stick and Cayla's support to walk. All the others carrying scars to this day. It's all my fault."

I try to look away, but Lana takes my chin in her hand, turning me to face her with a surprisingly strong grip. "Nonsense. Do you think I don't mourn those lost and wounded? They were my friends. We grew up together. We were all so proud to go on tour. We laughed at the warnings as we stepped off the greatwards. We treated it like a game. You didn't make the corelings real, Your Grace. Or make them want to kill us. But when they came, you stood between us and the demons. Again and again. That's all I remember. All any of us do. You didn't kill anyone that night, but those of us that survived did so because of you."

Lanna takes one of my hands in both of hers. "My mam says it does no disservice to the dead to celebrate life, especially on Solstice. I know I ent a suitable match for Duch Olive to marry, but that doesn't mean we can't dance."

Outside the tent, as if he'd been listening all along, Darin starts playing a lively jig on his pipes, and I smile as Lanna pulls me by the hand to the tent flap to join the dance.

IT'S EASY TO lose myself in Lanna and my friends for a time. Darin keeps to his pipes, but Rojvah and Selen join the dancing with the young folk of Apple Hill. I lift Boni from her chair, effortlessly supporting the girl as we twirl and dance. She laughs for the joy of it, and weeps when I call Mistress Darsy over and make an appointment at Gatherers' University to have her fitted with a proper prosthetic.

Darkness falls early, but we are safe on the greatward, even on this darkest of nights. Lanna keeps finding excuses for us to slip out of sight for a few moments. Each kiss is hungry for the next, but I have duties still, as the night's entertainment begins.

We watch mesmerized as festival flamework explodes in the sky. Mother understood the power of Prince Ramm's secret flamework weapon, but preferred to turn it into tools, and flashes of light and color and beauty to give her people joy.

My eyes start to see spots from the flashes, but one light remains, even as others come and go. It seems farther away than the others, and I realize almost too late that it is not flamework, but the glow of magic in the wardsight of my crown.

It's a demon, flying so high above the greatward that it skates along the forbiddance, causing a streak of light, like the splash of a fowl skidding across water to snatch up a fish.

"Eyes!" I point, and my spear brothers all snap on target, spotting the flare of wardlight.

Captain Gamon produces a distance lens and passes it to me, but Darin doesn't need it.

"Wind demon," Darin says. "It's alone, but . . . LOOK OUT!"

He seems to blur, moving so fast I can only follow the path of his wind as he runs up to the platform and grabs Lord Arther, throwing both of them off the stage just as a heavy stone splinters Mother's throne.

They hit the dirt hard, but Darin has gone slippery, putting himself between Arther and the ground. They skid some distance from the wreckage, absorbing the impact, and seem unharmed.

Warded arrows streak into the air, but I already know the demon is out of range. "Gorvan. Hunt."

My spear brother punches his chest and is off, signaling a handful of Princes to follow. They will track and kill the demon.

"Don't bother," my grandfather Ernal says, pulling an electrum pen from his pocket. Grandda Erny is master of the Warders' Guild. He's seen almost eighty winters, and is the gentlest man I have ever known. I have never seen him so much as kill an insect or raise his voice, no matter what fresh torment Grandmum lays upon him.

But Grandfather is angry now. I see it crackling along his aura as he lifts the pen.

Electrum pens are a common enough Warder's tool in Mother's keep. They look like ordinary fountain pens, but they contain a demonbone core, encased in warded electrum to contain the power and protect it from sunlight.

The devices allow the holder to Draw upon that store of magic, powering minor wardings inscribed with the pen. Opening the nib wider or closing it tighter controls the flow of power, but the items were used sparingly, for the store of demonbones was depleted after the war.

I don't understand what he means to do, but then Grandfather draws a glowing silver wind demon ward in the air in front of him, brightens it by opening the nib, then sends it off with a flick of his wrist.

Faster than my eyes can follow, the ward streaks through the air, swatting the demon like a fly. It crumples and drops, skittering along the forbidding for a moment, but on its death, it passes through the shield, bursting into flames as it enters into free fall.

Grandfather draws another quick warding, snuffing the flame, and there are screams from the street where it crashes down onto the cobbles.

Shouts of alarm come from all sides as folk witness the wreckage of Mother's throne. In seconds, panic will spread and the festival crowd will become a stampede.

I grab my spear and race to the sound shell, leaping atop the stage. In the day, it is a masterwork of acoustics, but at night Mother's wardings make it something more.

"Take heart, people of Hollow!" My voice is amplified a hundredfold, filling every ear, cutting through the noise of rising terror. I look to the statue of Arlen Bales in the fountain, and shout perhaps his most famous phrase. "It is not we who should fear the corelings! It is they who fear us!"

Everyone freezes, staring at me, fear held in check for a moment that I must extend. "Was it so many years ago the corelings came to this very place, seeking to destroy Hollow?" I demand. "General Gared! What did we do then?"

"Stomped 'em!" The big man doesn't need wards to carry his voice. "Chopped 'em down like trees!"

There's a cheer from the crowd at that, and I raise my spear to the sky. "What do they call this place?"

This time, it is more than Gared Cutter who replies. It is the crowd, latching on to our defiance. "Corelings' Graveyard!"

"Ay!" I shout. "The demons are gathering once more, but they are weakened still by the Deliverer's Purge. They do not have the strength to attack our greatwards, so they hurl stones like children!"

I hop down from the stage, striding purposefully over to the wreckage of the royal viewing platform. The stone at the center of the ruin is larger and heavier than any normal wind demon should be able to carry. I doubt even Uncle Gared could budge it. Still I reach down and take a firm grip, gritting my teeth. I refuse to let out a groan as I pull it free of the pulverized wood and heave, lifting it over my head.

I turn and see the wide-eyed faces of my subjects, staring in wonder.

All my life, I've had to hide my strength from them. To feign weakness, lest someone discover I was more than I seemed. Mother lived in terror of that day, and in truth, I did, too.

I see it in their eyes. There is awe, but also fear. I look over at Lanna, and she unconsciously takes a step back.

I put it aside, flexing to raise the stone higher, for all to see. "But anything they can hurl at us, we can throw back, a thousandfold!"

I toss the stone aside, careful not to crush anyone. It lands with a boom, the impact smashing cobblestones into gravel.

Folk are still gaping as I leap back onstage. "Should we quake in fear from a lone wind demon with a stone, when we stood against everything the Core could muster and cast them back?"

"NO!" the crowd roars.

"No!" I echo. "We will exterminate them, once and for all!"

Again the roar, louder this time. Loud enough to drown doubt. Loud enough to draw eyes away from the wreckage of Mother's throne. I feel panic washing away, leaving determination in its place. "Hollow!" they cry. "Hollow! Hollow!"

This wasn't an attack. It was a message from Alagai Ka. A reminder he is out there. A reminder he knows where I am, and can strike at me when he chooses. It is a promise, and a dare.

And I intend to answer.

I MAY HAVE quelled the fear, but no one much feels like celebrating after that. I dispatch soldiers to keep order as the crowds disperse. They start with the folk of Apple Hill, and Lanna rushes over to me as my bodyguard prepares to sweep me back to the safety of Mother's keep.

My hands are filthy from hauling the stone, but she takes them in hers, squeezing. "Some of us are staying in Cutter's Hollow," she whispers. "At the Sunny Inn, on Garden Street. In case you . . ." Her face colors, and she steals a last peck on my lips before running off to join her friends.

I don't want her to go, but I am not ready to ask her to stay. Tonight was a clear reminder of that.

But even if I had time for such distractions, I cannot help my feelings of guilt about Chadan. I don't love Lanna—not like I did Chadan—but our intimate moments predate him, and somehow she reached a part of me I thought covered in armor.

I expect my prince would understand, but it still feels like betrayal. I thought I might never love again after his death, but now I see how naïve that was. I haven't yet seen sixteen summers. If I survive whatever the Father of Demons has planned, should I expect to be alone the rest of my life? Eventually I will need to marry, if only to secure the throne. I would have married Chadan, borne his children happily, but now that he's gone, who is to say I should marry a man and not a woman? Perhaps Grandmum's suggestions aren't so bold, after all.

Mother wanted me to grow beyond the boxes society tries to force me into, but even I don't entirely understand what that means.

How do I best serve my people? By staying here, offering stability to Hollow and providing an heir, as Arther and Emelia suggest? By going to rescue Mother, and restoring Hollow's true leader?

Or by taking an army and putting my spear into the heart of what would destroy us?

Alagai Ka wants me to come to Safehold. He expects it. All part of the plan I saw in his mind.

And all the more reason to do otherwise.

Inevera thinks Darin better suited to sneak into Safehold than me, and I can hardly argue. I am more inclined to break doors down than pick their locks. If Darin and the others can find Mother and Mrs. Bales, freeing them before the queen hatches, it could change everything.

But if Asome is right and the hatching is just a few months away . . .

The moment the new queen hatches, they will make for the hive. The image of their swarm was clear in Alagai Ka's thoughts.

The hive is Alagai Ka's seat of power. His life's work. That is where the true fight will be. Not Safehold.

That's where I have to go, even if it means my friends and perhaps my own mother will never forgive me.

CHAPTER 33

LOYALTIES

350 AR

WE'RE ALL WORRIED, but I know things are really serious when Olive calls me, Selen, Arick, and Rojvah to her office and activates her mother's wards of silence around the room.

Always made me uneasy when Aunt Leesha used to do it—usually because she was more worried about me listenin' in than some spy. She and Mam knew about my senses, and anytime they wanted to talk private, there was a little pop, and it was like they vanished. Like the office and everythin' inside was dead.

From the inside, it's even worse. Whole world outside slips away. Might think this would be something I like, but truer is, it scares me. I'm used to hearing everything. Every footstep, every creak of floor, every turning hinge. It's how I orient myself with the world, and how I keep anyone from sneakin' up on me.

But now there's no sounds to get my bearings, like I'm in the dark under water. There could be a pack of demons at the door, and I'd never know unless they broke it down.

"I'm going to the Spear of Ala." Olive ent one for preamble. "In the spring, once the snows melt and I've gathered forces."

"So that's it," Selen says. "You're going to choose that sand witch's dice over your own mum?"

"Tsst!" Rojvah hisses. Inevera's her grandmum, and as legend as anyone left in the land.

Olive doesn't seem to care about that, but she's got a ready head of steam. "Cut the demonshit, Sel." She raises a balled fist and smells ready to use it. "You try to tell me this means I don't love my mum, Creator my witness I will black your eye."

I can smell Selen's anger, but she ent ready to take it that far. She crosses her arms, refusing to escalate. "Loving your mum doesn't mean you ent wrong."

Olive lowers the fist, putting it on her hip. "You've got some stones, judging me for doing exactly what Mother would have done."

"You think if Alagai Ka had you, Leesha wouldn't come?" Selen is incredulous.

"Not if the dice told her it was a bad idea," Olive says.

"You can't know that," Selen snaps.

"I do." Olive makes no effort to argue, but I don't need convincing. I heard every whisper in this keep growin' up, and if Aunt Leesha had a religion, it was those dice.

"Alagai Ka wants me to go to Safehold," Olive continues. "He's baiting me. It's a trap. If I take an army and go east, there will be countless opportunities for him to strike, and it will end up the same as Mother's force."

Can't really argue that, either. Mam was a force of nature, and Leesha the strongest ward witch this side of the Damajah. They had cavalry and flamework and the Warded Children, all with magic of their own. Tougher than anythin' we got.

What I remember most about findin' them was the smell. Blood and ichor and demonshit, smoke and mud, but most of all somethin' I never smelled before, and never want to again.

What folk smell like, spitted over a fire like a Solstice pig.

"Spear of Ala could be a trap, too," I note. "Maybe Alagai Ka made it go silent on purpose, knowing it would send you runnin'."

"I don't think so." Olive shakes her head, and her scent ent lyin'. "I saw his plan, plain as a portrait on the wall. He wants all of us in Safehold, to feed to the new queen when she hatches."

I shudder in spite of myself. Da was the most powerful person in the world, but when he was stung by a demon queen, even he couldn't heal from her venom.

"It's not just the Damajah and Belina whose dice cast us on this path," Olive says. "Mother had two foretellings. The city to the east, where the mimic sleeps . . ."

"And the father waiting below," I say.

"You thought that was your da, Darin," Olive says. "But I think it means the hive. Alagai Ka wants to repopulate it, and we have to stop him at all costs."

"Maybe it is a trap," I say. "Doesn't mean we shouldn't spring it. This mimic queen's in Safehold. Said it yourself. Might be we can slip in and kill her before her egg even hatches."

"Ay," Olive agrees. "But if you fail, the demon queen will make for the hive, taking Alagai Ka and every last demon in Thesa with her. Someone's got to be there to meet them. Perhaps I cannot sneak an army into Safehold, but nothing less will be able to reclaim the Spear of Ala and stand guard over the hive."

"Doesn't matter," I say. "None of it matters. Maybe you got what it takes to put the greater good over kith and kin, Olive Paper, but I don't. If Safehold's where Mam is, then that's where I'm goin'."

"Ay," Olive agrees. "You're better at slipping into places you ent welcome than I am, Darin Bales. If you can't get in there without being spotted, it can't be done."

She's flattering me. I can smell it. "Two weeks ago you were tellin' me I couldn't be trusted to go to market without havin' a fit. Now you're sayin' I got what it takes to trick the Father of Demons?"

Olive shrugs. "You're going no matter what I say, aren't you?"

"Corespawned right."

"But not alone," Rojvah says. "Where my intended goes, I will follow."

"And me," Arick puts in.

"Ay, and—"

Selen cuts off as Olive raises a finger. "Not you, Sel."

"I don't care if you're duch or king or the ripping Shar'Dama Ka, Olive Paper," Selen growls, "you can't just order me to sit your throne while you run off and play Inevera's puppet."

That sets off an angry scent from Olive, but it's nothing compared to the rage stink on Selen. Olive may be stronger, but I wouldn't take this fight, I was her.

"Hollow needs a leader," Olive says. "We can't both go."

"Then *you* stay!" Selen snaps. "You're the one with the crown."

"Dice say I'll bungle Safehold, but there isn't anyone else who can bring the Hollowers and Krasians together to march on the Spear," Olive says. "You can't do that, and . . ."

Selen puts her hands on her hips. "And what? I'm no use on the road to Safehold because I can't lift a big rock, or carry a rippin' tune?"

Olive holds up her hands helplessly. "You're the one who said it."

I hear Selen's teeth grinding together. Her bones creak as tendons and muscles tighten. Her heart is pounding, and it ent gonna help anyone if they start fightin'.

"Selen needs to come," I say, turning them both to notice me.

"Stay out of this, Darin," Olive says.

"Core I will," I say. "Ent a Hollower, Olive. Don't get to tell me what to do any more than Selen, and I can't do this without her."

"If you need another spear, take someone else," Olive says. "Gorvan, or Faseek. Lots of fighters to choose from."

"Don't need a spear," I say. "Need Selen Cutter."

"So does Hollow," Olive says.

"Hollow needed your mam," I point out. "Didn't stop her from going to war when she was needed."

"Oh, ay, and look at how that turned out," Olive says.

"Don't matter," Selen says. "There's a time to sit on a throne and talk about taxes, and there's a time to go out and fight what's trying to end you. Hollow economy don't mean spit if there's no Hollow."

"The forces of Nie cannot be bargained with," Rojvah says. "Nie cannot be satiated or appeased."

"Nie can only be fought," Olive agrees. It was the speech she and her spear brothers recited every night before going into battle, and seems to reach her when other arguments can't.

"Folk of Hollow are tougher than you give credit for," Selen says. "If they can't last until we get back, here safe on the greatwards, then things are worse than we thought."

"And if neither of us comes back?" Olive asks.

"Then they got bigger problems than who decides the sanitation tax," Selen says.

Olive seems to deflate at that.

"Question now is how we find Safehold," I say. "Olive, you saw the place when you and Alagai Ka were linked. Anythin' you can tell us?"

"I think it's a city," Olive says. "A human city, I mean. The minds call them larders—breeding grounds to fatten us up like cattle for slaughter. He's been marching folk right into the mimic's mouth like spoons full of porridge."

"The Father of Demons will have protections over his private stock," Rojvah says.

None of us sits well with that idea. Remember what the demon's greatward was like in Krasia, sucking the strength from us.

"If it's magic, it won't work in sunlight." Olive moves to a map on the wall, pointing. "And the city is near a natural reservoir, fed by the same snowmelt that becomes the Angiers River. If you follow the river upstream, you will at least get in close."

"I dunno," I say. "That's a long way, and there are a lot of little lakes in the mountains. Like lookin' for a pea in a silo of beans. Might hunt for months and not find it."

"You won't have months," Olive says. "Best guess I have says the queen hatches on Summer Solstice."

"How can you know that?" Selen demands.

"A foretelling." Olive smells evasive.

"Whose?" Rojvah demands. "Not my grandmother's or she would have told me. Favah?"

Olive shakes her head. Her scent tells me we ent gonna like the answer. "Asome."

"Tsst!" Rojvah hisses. "Tell me you do not listen to my uncle's heretical prophecies."

Olive shrugs. "I watched him cast in wardsight. Heresy or no, there is real magic in his foretellings. Already they are coming true."

"Sure about that, Olive?" I ask. "My experience with prophecies is you never really know if they've come true, or not."

A tinge of doubt enters Olive's scent at that, but she shakes it off.

"He knew things he should not have. Things he could not have. He knew about the queen, and when she was laying."

"And you did not inform Grandmother?" Rojvah asks.

Olive puffs up at that. "I am not Inevera's creature, Rojvah. Even now, can you swear she tells *me* everything *she* sees in the dice?"

Rojvah stares back at her a long time. I can tell she wants to argue. That she thinks Olive's an idiot for keepin' this to herself. But there are some lies so big that tellin' 'em means no one's ever gonna trust you again.

"Of course the Damajah . . . has secrets—" Rojvah concedes.

"Mother had secrets, too," Olive cuts in. "Our families are full of them, and I am finished letting them rule my life. I am Duch of Hollow and will keep my own counsel."

"Ay, that's how it is?" Selen's voice is irritation, but her scent is . . . hurt. "Just called us to hear the duch's decrees? Ent got a say in all this?"

Olive spreads her hands. "If that was the case you'd be staying in Hollow, Sel. Would you do it, if I wrote a decree?"

Selen ent so crass as to spit on the fine carpet, but she makes the noise, and it's answer enough.

"Ay, thought not," Olive says. "So let me help you."

I can smell the secret on her, and her eagerness to share it. "Help us, how?"

"Mother and Mrs. Bales aren't the only ones unaccounted for," Olive says. "We've identified most of the dead from the massacre, but several prominent names are missing from the roster, including Wonda Cutter and Kendall Demonsong."

"Kendall," Rojvah whispers.

Kendall Demonsong was Aunt Leesha's herald. She traveled from town to town and court to court, speaking with the authority of Hollow. But she was also the apprentice—and some say lover—of Rojvah's father. Amanvah had meant to take Kendall as a sister-wife before Halfgrip died. Reckon she still liked the idea, because a few years later, she married Olive's sister Micha.

Rojvah's always been in awe of Kendall. Remember it from when we were kids. Kendall called Rojvah and Arick niece and nephew, and lavished them with gifts and affection whenever she visited Jardir's court.

But it was her Jongleur's motley Rojvah could not tear her eyes from. Even in modern Krasia, a woman wearing bright colors in public was a rare sight, and often a sign of power. Messengers were sacred in Krasia, and that allowed Kendall to get away with dressing outrageously, in trousers and bright colors.

"I don't have a way to track Mother, or Wonda," Olive says. "Might be a way to use Mrs. Bales' knife to find her, but that's beyond anything I was able to master in Favah's Chamber of Shadows."

I touch Mam's knife at my belt, feeling it tingle with power. She might be right. Mam's knife is full of magic, but it ent got any demonbone in it. The magic is more like a twisted version of Sharik Hora. Knife's been in my family a long time. The bone handle is imprinted with the emotions of its history, and Draws magic like ants to an apple core. But it ent the pure golden glow of heroes' bones. It's darker, bloodier, painful. The power makes the weapon formidable, but it's always scared me, I'm to tell honest word.

Using the knife to find Mam would mean opening myself up to that power, and Drawing it through me to Read it. Reckon it would be like rummaging through my family history for the most painful and awful things I can find, and living 'em myself.

Ent ready for that.

"You think you can track Kendall," I guess, instead.

Olive nods, reaching into the black velvet *hora* pouch at her waist. "When Micha died, the Majah returned her possessions to me." She lays them on the table. A velvet choker with a gem at its center. Two bracelets and two anklets, woven of thick links of gold, and a delicate earring with a dangling golden ball.

All are stitched or etched with delicate wardwork, and glow to my night eyes. The flows of the bracelets and anklets are familiar. They are how Inevera's elite *Sharum'ting* can mimic my powers, summoning shadows, climbing walls like a spider, and Drawing strength and speed as needed.

The choker, too, is familiar. Rojvah wears one that is nearly identical to focus the power of her spellsong.

"The earring . . ." I tilt my head, looking closer. Its magic is similar to the choker, but not the same.

"It is a marriage earring," Rojvah says, "and a resonance stone, allowing spouses to communicate over distance."

"Meaning Kendall has its mate," I say. "We find her, maybe we find the others."

"Ay," Olive says. "Belina used my armlet to make a compass to find me. Rojvah, can you . . ."

Rojvah takes the earring reverently, running a sensitive finger over the wardwork. "Yes, I can fashion something like that. But marriage earrings are meant to allow wives to listen in on their husbands over short distances. I can prepare *hora* to boost its range, but even that has limits. We will need to get very close before it's much help."

"How close?" Selen asks.

Rojvah shrugs. "A few miles?"

"So it will be a bigger pea in the silo of beans." Selen's right, but she ent helpin'.

"Ent as much help as we were hopin' for, but it's more than we had," I say. "Selia Barren always said havin' a hundred problems ent much different than having two. Still need to solve them one at a time. We'll figure out a way to get close enough, and with a point in the right direction, maybe I can sniff out the rest."

"And if the ring's stuck in the middle of a pile of demonshit somewhere?" Selen asks.

"We'll bury it and say a prayer." I'm annoyed now, and don't bother to hide it. "Won't be any worse off than before."

Never known Selen to shy away from a fight, but she ent got it in her this time. She drops her eyes. "Ay, you're right."

"What's our plan for sneaking off?" I change the subject quick. "I can slip off anytime I want, but getting the rest of you out of the keep with the new security, supplied and equipped for a long trip . . ."

Olive gives me a knowing look. "When Darin Bales says *What's our plan*, it means he's already got one and is too shy to share it."

"Go on then, Dar," Selen says. "You're the expert at sneaking."

"Don't clomp around like a herd of mustang like you two," I admit. Selen snickers, and some of the tension leaves the scents in the air.

"Can't go now," I say. "Snows are on their way, and we won't find anythin' if we freeze to death."

"Agreed." Selen rubs her arms. "So when?"

"Reckon Olive should throw another big festival for Equinox," I say, "and make sure we're in the bandshell. Let everyone get a good look at us, then sneak off while they're all drinkin' and dancin'. Be a while before anyone notices we're gone, and then Olive tells 'em we went off to Tibbet's Brook to introduce Rojvah to my family, now that we're promised. Say Selen and Arick came for support, and to see a bit of the world. Round trip takes months. Folk won't ask questions."

"He's right," Selen says. Night, twice in one talk! "Plenty of folk make the pilgrimage out to the Brook to see the birthplace of the Deliverer."

"Ay, then they take one look at the place and turn right back," I say. "Brook folk ent unfriendly, exactly, but they like bein' left to their peace, and nothing spoils peace like a pack of wide-eyed city folk trampling your fields and puttin' up tents on your property."

"It is a good plan," Rojvah agrees. "I should like to see your home in truth some day."

I can tell from her scent she means it, and it makes me think of Olive's dismissal of the Brook—her casual assumption Hollow must be preferable, and that if I got married I'd have to stay, because of course no woman would want to go there.

"I would see your homeland too, cousin." Arick surprises me. "It cannot be coincidence when a place produces so many heroes."

"Make you a deal," I tell Arick and Rojvah. "We live through this next year, I'll take you there for real." Rojvah takes my hand, her scent delighted. Selen's . . . ent. Not angry, just a little sad.

I turn and hold a hand out to her. "Used to say you'd visit one day, too. Still mean that?"

Selen looks at the hand. "Ent that many of us going to disturb folk's peace?"

"Reckon it will." I grin. "Grandda always used to fret I din't have any friends. I come home with a pair of pretty girls, he'll throw a party that keeps the whole town awake for a week."

That forces a laugh out of her. "Corespawn it, Darin Bales," Selen grouses, but she matches my grin and her sad scent dissipates as she takes my hand.

I WALK ROJVAH back to her rooms. It's easier knowin' a kiss is coming. It's become a ritual, and I like rituals. When my senses are chaos, rituals help me focus. Easy to kiss even someone pretty as Rojvah, when it's expected of you.

We go out onto the terrace like we do every night to say goodbye. I still feel a burst of magic when our lips touch. Rojvah always smells nice. More I smell her, the more I want to. Her mouth is warm and she squeezes me so tight I never want it to end. But it has to. That's part of the ritual. Even as I melt in her arms, part of me is counting breaths until it's time to step back.

"Your kisses are improving," Rojvah whispers, and she smells pleased. "But you need not pull away so soon."

"Don't want to be improper," I say. "Ent married, yet."

Rojvah rolls her eyes, smelling amused. "If you wish. I could dance for you, if you prefer."

"Dance?" Suddenly I'm all tensed up again.

"I learned the pillow dance in Sharaj." Rojvah's voice is low, reverberating in the air. Mischief in her scent. "It is written a bride may perform it for her intended, if they leave space for Everam between them."

"What's that mean?" Images of Rojvah dancing are swirling in my head. I feel drunk, like Hary stumbling around after he's had too much wine.

Rojvah steps in close. "It means you can look, Intended," she's so near I feel her breath, the heat of her body, the way she shapes the air, "but you cannot touch."

She drifts back to the doors, leaving me standing there like a tree shaking in the wind. "Good night, Intended."

I force myself to climb the wall with shaky fingers, then lie on the roof a short while until my breath is back under control.

Arick is putting on a nightshirt when I get back to our rooms. "Did you enjoy kissing my sister, son of Arlen?"

"It was her idea to get promised." Arick doesn't smell mad, but it's hard to tell with these things. "Know you don't like it . . ."

Arick waves for me to quiet. "I like you better than the other suitors Mother was considering for her, and this way I don't . . . lose her."

"She's your sister," I say. "Ent ever gonna lose her."

"Here in the North, perhaps," Arick says. "In Krasia, when a woman marries, she goes to live in her husband's house. Rojvah and I have been together every day of our lives. I do not know that I could bear to be without her."

"What if you find someone, too?" I ask.

Arick shrugs. "Perhaps someday. But I have no right to be with someone until I understand what the demon did to me, and show him the sun, so he can never do it again."

I nod, though it ent that simple. Alagai Ka got in Arick's head, ay, but it's only a piece of what's eatin' him.

I can smell he dun't want to go on about it, so I let Arick head to bed and slip back onto the terrace. Rojvah got me saying good nights and sleeping in a bed, but Arick and I don't keep the same hours. Night is when my senses and body truly come alive. Daytime feels like the sleepwalk.

I usually haunt the keep until everyone's turned in. Olive's taken to working late in her office, and usually only goes to her bed when the maid scolds her. I wait till she's settled, and then go explore. Into town some nights, but more and more I find myself wandering the Gatherers' Wood. Place reminds me of Mam, and the Warded Children. Ent one for cryin', but I can set up a tree with a pretty view and think sad thoughts all night long.

Don't head back inside until I feel dawn comin', like that gentle pressure you get in your skull an hour before a headache hits. Aunt Leesha made me a special bed when I was little, and I love it still. Sat on a thick carpet, the four-poster is canopied and surrounded by thick layered curtains that block out all the light and most of the sound, givin' me just enough peace to sleep through the heat of the morning.

By the time I slip into the covers, Arick is already up and dressing, heading down to the practice yards to drill with anyone and everyone who can hold their own against him in a fight, or teach him something he doesn't already know about fightin'. Ent a long list, but he's just as happy to practice *sharukin* alone, with the same diligence as when he practices the kamanj.

Arick's strength at music is repetitive precision. Skill, not talent, he says. But if talent's a thing, it's clear where his lies. He treats fightin' like I do my pipes, and it ent an exaggeration to call what he does an art. Ent heard tell of anyone takin' him down twice with the same move. Next time they spar, he turns the move back on them, oft as not.

Sometimes, though, I catch him staring at his spear, and he smells scared.

I draw a cold breath as I climb to the roof. I've got my night eyes, but they don't tell me as much on Hollow's greatward, which sucks in all the ambient magic and smooths it out, destroying all the currents I might try to Read.

Doesn't matter. Don't need them. I can tell where folk are and what they're doing from the tastes and smells in the air, the way sounds echo off the walls, the vibrations in the stone I cling to.

So I ent surprised when I find Briar Damaj sittin' in a crenel, waitin' for me.

"Where d'you go?" I ask, climbing atop the merlon next to him. Ent my business, really. Briar's been close enough to meet with Olive more than once, but I lose track of him once he leaves the keep. Spent more'n one night sniffing around, failing to pick up the trail. Ent used to that. Briar smells more of hogroot than anything, and that grows all over Hollow.

"Briarpatch in Gatherers' Wood," Briar says. "Been working on it since before you were born."

"Wander that wood a lot," I note. "You had a patch out there, reckon I would've found it."

Briar laughs. "Did you look beneath the hogroot patch?"

"Hogroot patches all over the wood," I say. "Reckon it's near trees, too?"

"Briarpatches are no use once folk know where they are," Briar says.

"Don't suppose you got any briarpatches out east?" I ask.

Briar shakes his head. "Never got out to the mountains. But I can show you how to make your own."

"Be real grateful," I say.

Briar holds up his hand, showing me his warded palm. "Anything to aid you in your quest, brother."

"Need all the help we can get," I admit.

"You can lead them through it," Briar says.

I laugh. "I ent the leader."

"Are you not?" Briar asks. "Who, then?"

I open my mouth to say Olive, but Briar knows as well as I do she ent coming. I think for a minute, and a deep chill of fear forms at the center of me. Selen won't take orders from Rojvah, and Rojvah won't listen to Selen. Arick gets along with both of them, but he's got his own problems and ent lookin' to tell folk what to do.

But night, no one listens to me.

"We're an ensemble," I say at last.

"Of course," Briar agrees. "But you're the resin that binds them together."

"Olive is the glue," I say, on surer footing now. "She's the one related to everyone under the sun. Arick and Rojvah wouldn't be here if they weren't blood. Selen wouldn't have crossed the desert with me if Olive wasn't blood."

"Family is more than blood, Darin am'Bales," Briar says. "You of all people should understand that. You share no blood with any of them, but it was you who drew them into your ensemble."

"We're in a whole mess of trouble, then," I say.

Briar shakes his head. "The Damajah walks in futures we cannot see, and she has faith in you. That is no small thing. Your ensemble makes you stronger, son of Arlen, but they draw more strength and courage from you than you know. You will need to guide them, as I must guide Duch Olive into the night below."

It's a scary thought, and Briar doesn't press, giving me space to think it through. "Come," he slips off the crenel and begins climbing down, "I will take you to Gatherers' Wood and teach you to build a briarpatch."

CHAPTER 34

ALONE

I HEAR ARTHER COME IN, but I'm deep in a ledger, hunting for something that doesn't add up.

Baron Orchard is avoiding some of his taxes. That, in and of itself, is nothing new. The baron had been skimming for years, as Mother was well aware. The baron was powerful, and clever. Orchard knew the cost for Mother to audit and enforce the law was far more than the margin he was underreporting.

But since Mother's disappearance, the baron has grown bolder, reporting whole crops as losses even as he quietly sells them to New Krasia for twice the local rate, using the excuse to cut funding to schools and hospits in his barony.

Mother would never have tolerated that, and neither can I. The baron needs a reminder—they all do—that Hollow's laws have not changed.

Arther clears his throat. It's so quiet that from anyone else I would think nothing of it. From Arther when he sees me occupied, it is practically a shout.

I pause, holding three numbers in my head while I search for a fourth that will prove my suspicion. "I'm a little busy, Arther. Can it wait?"

"That is for you to decide, Your Grace." Arther offers a shallow bow. "There is a Miss Lanna Apple asking to see you."

Just like that, all the numbers flee my head.

"I think Baron Orchard is corrupt," I say.

Arther nods. "Almost certainly."

I close the ledger and shove it a few inches in his direction. "The proof is in there. Have an auditor find it, and summon the baron to court."

"Of course, Your Grace," Arther says.

"And escort Miss Apple to my sitting room," I say. "Perhaps you could give one of your wonderful, informative tours on the way?"

Arther smiles, knowing full well what I think of his tours. "Would an hour suffice?"

"WHAT ARE YOU DOING HERE?" I sweep into the room casually, as if I hadn't just run to my chambers and spent an hour at the mirror.

Lanna is carefully to one side of a divan made for two, wearing her Seventhday best, the same dress she wore to the festival. It's not what women wear at court, but it takes my breath away still. I see the soft hollow where her neck meets shoulder, and remember how soft it was against my lips.

"It snowed again last night," Lanna says. "We're going back to Apple Hill tomorrow, before the next storm comes, or we might be here all winter."

Would that be so bad? I wonder.

"Of course," I say. In truth, I thought them already gone. "I'm sorry I didn't . . ."

"Oh, you don't have to apologize!" Lanna seems scandalized. "Know you must be busy. It's just . . . Oskar wanted to see Selen one last time, and we decided to go to the gates and just ask. Worst they could do is say no, ay? But then the guard squints at me and she says, 'Ent you the one kissed Duch Olive at Solstice?' Next thing we know we're surrounded by statues and paintings and . . ."

She looks at me, blushing, and I feel my face heat in return. "Hope that's all right? Just thought, maybe you might want to see me, but it ent . . . appropriate for you to visit a commoner in town."

"I don't care about that," I say. "Everyone at the festival saw us kiss. I'm not ashamed to be seen with you."

"Festival's one thing," Lanna looks around the lavish room, "palace is somethin' else. Know I stick out like an onion in the apple cart. Don't belong here."

"Nonsense." I sit beside her, taking her hand. "Can I tell you a secret?"

Lanna's fingers curl around mine. "Of course."

"Mother says no one belongs in a palace," I say. "And when you begin to think you do, it's time to leave it. I never did. That was why I ran away and joined the borough tour. This place can be . . . stifling."

Lanna nods, leaning in closer, lips parting slightly, and I realize it doesn't matter what we say, and I don't feel like talking in any event.

I can't be with Lanna. She isn't wrong about that. It's not that I'm scared to scandalize the matchmakers, or to marry a commoner, or a woman. It's that all we have in common is kisses, and I'll be lucky to live through next Solstice. But when she's near, it dulls some of the hurts inside, and that's worth some time no matter how busy my schedule.

I forget work for the rest of the day and into the night, enjoying her company. We send Lanna and Oskar back to the inn where the others from Apple Hill are staying with a warm carriage to escort them home, laden with gifts for them and their village.

But I don't ask her to stay. There is work to be done, and every moment I spend with her is a moment I am not focused on my goal. Every kiss could be a robber baron I let escape. Every embrace a missed drill in the yard.

Everyone used to wonder why Mother never married. When I was little, I thought the duchess—the most powerful woman in the North—could do whatever she wanted, and it was *my* life that was stifled.

Watching their carriage recede in the distance, I understand too late that in some ways, Mother was the least free of us all.

Faseek and Gorvan fall in behind me as I march back inside. They are my brothers. Giant Gorvan was my trusted lieutenant in the Maze. Ferocious Faseek's loyalty is without question. He's hidden bodies and taken arrows for me.

But I find myself confiding in them less and less. In truth, I never confided in them much to begin with. Chadan and I were *kai* and kept our own counsel. We presented Gorvan and the others with plans, and they executed.

I trust them, but they cannot advise me in this place. Barely educated, they speak only the Majah dialect of Krasian, and a smattering of the trade pidgin of the greenland thralls in Desert Spear. They shadow me everywhere, but understand little beside threats to my person.

All my life I had friends I could rely on to keep my secrets and tell me theirs. Selen, Darin, Micha, Chadan. People I knew in my heart could never betray me. Now, suddenly, I have only my own confidence to keep. It's no wonder Mother always seemed so tired, beneath the armor of her practiced appearances.

"Your Grace." Baron Orchard bows as he enters my office. He does not take a knee, but that is to be expected. Mother never cared for such shows of submission, and neither do I.

The baron is a big man. Six and a half feet tall and thick with muscle, even if there are streaks of gray in his hair and beard. A veteran of the demon war with his own militia, as loyal as my spear brothers.

Orchard had been a Rizonan lord with vast holdings, forced to burn his own orchards and flee his lands when my father conquered Fort Rizon. When his people arrived in Hollow, they were ragged and penniless, but Lord Orchard's banner was still a rallying point, his hierarchy intact.

Mother assigned them land when they arrived, provided food, water, and blankets, shelter from the elements, and firewood. Loans for seed and materials to build anew on a Hollow greatward. All of it given freely, to be paid back in taxes and local services based on output once the barony was on its feet. It took some time for his neatly cultivated orchards and vineyards to begin fruiting, but now they supply the entire duchy, and Orchard is wealthier and more powerful than any other baron save perhaps Uncle Gared.

"My lord, welcome." I don't get up from behind the desk, but I gesture to the chair in front of it. "Please, take a seat."

Mother always took private audiences in the tearoom in her office. Guests would be invited to relax on soft couches and chairs, offered tea and refreshment. Uncle Gared famously has a fresh keg tapped daily in his office, and plies visitors with local ale.

I don't offer the baron so much as a water.

"Duch Olive!" The baron shakes his head at me. "I remember when you were this high," he pats his knee, "running around your mother's keep in your frilly dresses. And look at you now."

I smile. "What do you mean by that, Baron?"

"I just . . ." the baron sputters. "I meant only . . ." He waves a hand in my general direction and trails off.

I don't press the question. I don't really care what the baron thinks of me. "I called you here to discuss your barony's loss of revenue. It is truly so bad you've needed to cut funding even to local services?"

"Ay." The baron nods gravely. "An infection in the trees of my northern orchards destroyed an entire crop."

"How terrible!" I say. "Shall I contact the university? They can send a team of Gatherers to examine the orchard, and . . ."

"No need to trouble yourself, Your Grace." Orchard's smile is tight behind the screen of his beard. "Our Gatherers have already come upon a cure, though it may take seasons for the trees to recover fully. Until then, their fruit is not safe to eat."

I nod. "Did you mention that to the Krasian merchants you sold the crop to?"

The baron blinks, caught between lies. "I don't know what you mean, Your Grace. My men were ordered to destroy that crop. If such a sale occurred, it was without my knowledge. I would certainly never condone selling tainted fruit to our neighbors in the south."

"And yet in these grim times, you made an investment of nearly the same value as that sale to develop lands for a new series of orchards," I note.

"The loss made clear to me I need to diversify and separate my holdings so such pestilence cannot easily spread," Orchard says. "The investment was a loan . . ."

"A loan from your duchy's own central bank," I say, "whose ledgers did not shift, even with the outlay of such a vast sum, and who have no record of you making payments."

The baron shrugs. "If there is some clerical error, I will have my clerks . . ."

The baron talks smoothly, effortlessly dissembling and spinning a web of lies and obfuscations nearly impossible to verify without months of investigations, by which time the baron will have formulated even more excuses and bribed or threatened witnesses.

He knows I am onto him, but he keeps smiling as he talks, knowing the strength of his hand. *Of course I am stealing,* his eyes tell me. *What are you going to do about it?*

Mother would have taken those months, smiling in return as she slowly built a case. Likely Orchard would not have known she was onto him until it was too late, had he even dared make such a bold move under her watch.

But I don't have months, and I am not my mother.

Fight, Micha taught. *It is the only thing men respect.*

I vault over the desk in one easy motion. The startled baron stumbles over his chair in his rush to back away. He puts out a stiffened arm to keep space between us, but I bat it aside and advance, backing him up toward the wall.

Baron Orchard is no stranger to violence. He takes one look in my eyes and realizes he is in real danger. Instinctively, he reacts with his fists.

I'm ready for it, slipping his left jab and seeming to walk into the path of a right cross that likely would have put down a smaller man. Instead I catch his wrist in my left hand and pull, using his own force to twist and lock the baron's right arm as I seize his collar with my dominant hand, squeezing tight.

Mother always made me hide my strength. She said it would unnerve folk to know the princess of Hollow could bend an iron fire poker and tie it in a knot. Even in *sharaj,* Micha told me to keep my strength secret, and I did, never truly letting loose in the practice yard, or anywhere else.

Baron Orchard has inches and a hundred pounds on me, but it's not enough to keep me from lifting him off the floor. His face reddens as the tightened collar cuts off precious air and blood. One-handed, I raise him to the full extent of my arm, feet kicking and scrabbling, inches from the thick carpet.

He throws a punch with his free hand, but I drive forward, twisting the arm away and bashing him against the wall.

The impact loosens my grip just slightly, and the baron draws a sharp breath and lets out a shriek quite unlike his usual baritone.

Uncle Gared almost breaks my office door down at the sound, barreling in with Arther, Faseek, and Orchard's burly bodyguard.

"My lord!" The guard rushes forward to help his baron, but Gared grabs him by the shoulder, controlling the big man as easily as a willful child. "All right, Olive?"

"Baron Orchard has been stealing from his people, and from the duchy," I growl, but I loosen my grip, allowing the baron to breathe.

"And now he has a choice." I turn and meet Orchard's eyes again. There is no mockery in them now. "Either you accompany me to court, where you announce your clerks have made an error, and you welcome a royal auditor to help you correct the records, or you accompany me to the balcony, and I introduce you to the cobblestones below."

"You cannot be serious." Orchard isn't able to hold my gaze, desperately looking around the room for sympathy. He sees Arther, wringing his hands anxiously. "Arther . . ."

I squeeze my fist again, and the baron's words choke off. "Uncle Gared, am I the kind of duch who tells ripping jokes to people who steal money from schools and hospits?"

Gared tosses the bodyguard to Faseek. He outweighs my spear brother by fifty pounds at least, but Faseek is quick to put him in a submission hold as my general comes over. At seven feet tall, he can look the baron in the eye, even with his feet off the ground. "Wouldn't respect you if you were."

I ease my grip again, and the baron gasps another breath. "What would happen, Uncle, if Orchard returns to his barony and refuses to pay his taxes, or takes up arms against Hollow?"

Gared tsks. "Don't like his chances if the Cutters come callin', but it'll be messy for everyone. Say the word and I'll just put him over the railing and have done for you."

Arther takes a half step forward. "Your Grace, your mother would never . . ."

"Is my mother here, Minister?" I ask.

"Of course not," Arther agrees, eyes flicking side to side as he chooses careful words. "I meant only . . . as you say, perhaps this is a matter best left to the auditors. The baron's cuts can be renegotiated, with no loss of face . . ."

"A-ay!" Orchard's voice is a rasp. "My forecasts can be amended, of course."

I nod, letting go and dropping him back onto his feet, still coughing and gasping. "Put it in writing before court this afternoon, where you will publicly invite Arther's auditors."

Now the baron takes a knee, punching a fist to his chest. "Your will, Duch Olive."

A tilt of my head in permission, and the baron is quick to exit the office. Uncle Gared's men will see he does not leave until his proclamation is made.

"AY, THAT WAS FUN," Gared chuckles, watching from the window as Baron Orchard and his retinue ride out from the keep, accompanied by a royal auditor and an escort of Hollow Lancers. "Think he knew we were playin' him?"

"Is that what we were doing?" I wonder aloud. The scene and the parts the men played were all orchestrated in advance, but if the baron had balked, I don't know how far I would have taken things.

Arther clears his throat. "If he did, he was wise to play along. I daresay Baron Orchard won't steal so much as an apple from his own trees after this."

"Now that the spies at court have the story, none of them will," I say. "We can't audit them all, and they need to know where the wards end while Selen and I are away."

"Away?" There's alarm in Arther's voice. "Both of you?"

"I will issue decrees to strengthen your powers in my absence," I say. "Darin will be taking Rojvah to Tibbet's Brook to meet his family in the spring. I want Selen to go with him."

"Why?" Gared asks.

"Because if she's in Hollow when we march she will want to join us," I tell him. "And it's too dangerous. I want her out of harm's way."

"Ay," Gared nods. "Best keep her and little Darin safe. Reckon they won't find too much trouble in the backwoods."

The words have unexpected sting, for of course I am lying. Selen's path is as dangerous as mine, and I'm promising her father I will keep her safe.

"And where will you be marching?" Arther asks.

I look at the minister a long time, wondering just how far I can trust him. Mother could read what was in a person's heart, know if they told lie or truth, with just a glance of her warded spectacles. I have the same wardsight, but there's little I can glean from the pulsing rainbow of a person's aura.

Arther is Angierian. Mother trusted him to put Hollow above his birth duchy, but can I? Or will a man who saw me in nappies never keep the same faith with me?

My eyes flick to Uncle Gared. I know he will not hesitate to follow where I am going. Night, I expect he'll ride in front as he did in the desert, proudly protecting me with his own body.

Gared's loyalty is beyond question, but his wisdom is not. Uncle Gared is many things, but canny is not one of them. Can I trust him not to tell Baroness Emelia, or his most trusted Cutters? Can I trust either of them? The moment my plan leaves my lips, there is a chance Alagai Ka will hear it whispered by the night. That chance grows with every person who learns. The seer's art is a child's game compared to what the demon king can Read on the currents.

If I hold my designs, I protect the secret, but I will not be able to have my forces in position. Parades and festivals and increasingly implausible lies can only do so much. I have to trust someone, or I will fail as surely as if I told the Father of Demons my plans personally.

At last I go to the desk, unlocking the drawer where Mother kept her wardstones.

Arther and Gared don't need instructions, moving immediately to close the heavy curtains and bathe the room in darkness. I set a few of the stones into a pattern of wardwork on Mother's desk, and a net activates around the room, bathing us in wardlight and a bubble of silence.

"North to Angiers first." I unlock another drawer, removing a bundle of oilcloth. "We can't face whatever . . . took Mother, Father, and Mrs. Bales with just spears and axes." I open the cloth on the table, laying out Prince Ramm's pistol. "I want flamework weapons."

"About rippin' time." Uncle Gared's response surprises me. "Been sayin' that for years. Miln and Angiers could come cut us down any day with those corespawned things, but Leesha wouldn't allow it."

"Miln and Angiers are our allies," Arther reminds him.

"Ay, for now," Gared says. "But I seen a lotta thrones change hands in my day."

"It was Duchess Leesha's belief that the weapons of the old world were more evil than good," Arther says. "They are not effective against the corelings. Flamework is used for men to kill other men."

"Is that what she said?" I ask, reaching for the hidden release at the back of the drawer. It slides open, revealing a worn volume, heavily annotated by Mother. "Because she solved that problem long ago, according to her notes. Bullets thrown in warded glass will not shatter or flatten on impact, keeping their wards intact when they strike *alagai* . . . coreling armor. I can have the Warders' Guild . . ."

Gared shakes his head. "Known Erny Paper a long sight, Olive. Your mum got her bleedin' heart from him. Your grandda ent gonna help you put flamework in soldiers' hands any more than she would."

I curse inwardly, because of course he's right. "Then we'll find someone who will."

"If you are sure, I can send coded messages to Duchess Araine," Arther says. "Her Grace owes Hollow a great debt, and I do not think she will balk at even this request."

"Do it," I say. "Quietly. I will need as many arms as she can provide by Equinox."

I can see anxiety spawn across the first minister's face. He didn't expect it would be so soon. "And after Angiers?"

I look to Gared, then back to him, and let out a breath. "Into the demon's lair."

It's the truth, and more than enough to put both men on their back foot, but even now, it isn't the whole truth. I say nothing of the Damajah's warning, or her mission, or even which "lair" I mean.

Better to carry that burden alone than risk its compromise.

CHAPTER 35

LIKE A *GWIL* IN THE NIGHT

The snows come in force not long after Solstice, and a peace falls over Hollow. The nights are long, and I like that, sleeping away most of the day and emerging when the light is already on the wane.

During the short days we discuss and lay provisions for the spring journey. In the evenings I practice with Arick and Rojvah, and then she walks me to her terrace for our kiss. I'm less skittish now, but still it's my favorite part of the day. My senses are alive, and the night beckons, but I stay as long as I can, only breaking off when it starts to feel improper. Rojvah's mouth, her touch, her heart rhythm and scent, all invite me to linger, perhaps even to come inside and stay.

But I ent ready for that.

So I break away, though it gets a little harder to go each night, a little more tempting to stay. Sometimes I scale the wall in a hurry, like I'm worried about what I'll do if I don't.

Hollow folk stay active after dark, secure in their greatwards, but the winter streets are empty after sunset, and it feels like the night is mine, alone. Cold never much bothered me, nor heat, unless it comes with the draining light of the sun. I pad barefoot over snow and ice, exploring more and more of the land as I collect my thoughts.

Olive marks her sixteenth winter, and there are celebrations throughout Hollow. I can hear matchmakers clamoring at court, doing anything and everything they can to secure an audience with the duch. Olive's condition is common knowledge now, but it doesn't seem to have cost any prospects. If anything, it's made it worse, with men and women both being proposed.

Olive ent got time for any of it. Don't blame her. I can hear the matchmakers bemoaning how Rojvah and I are already promised, and I'm happy to be spared the attention.

Selen and Arick ent so lucky. Got folk pesterin' them so much Selen's got the house guard on notice, but they still get notes slipped into their hands, or calling cards left in their rooms, for all the good it does. Arick ent interested, and Selen seems happier hunting for a match—or just a night's kisses—on her own.

Equinox seemed a long wait to get started, but the weeks of peace seem to fly by, and it's upon us quicker than a fly on stink. Days are getting steadily longer, and will outlast the nights for the next two seasons. Less time the demons can be out lookin' for us, the better our chances.

It's now or never, we want to go hunting for Safehold.

I SEE MORE colors than other folk, even during the day. Din't know it, most of my life. Even now, it dun't help much to know. Impossible to describe colors, really, and talkin' about it only makes folk smell jealous. Like the jealous smell even less than when they feel sorry for me.

But it makes for pretty sunsets, washing across the sky in a vast rainbow that goes far beyond the seven colors others around me see.

I love sunset. My flesh tingles as the magic inside me, protected from sunlight by my skin, begins to bubble to the surface, seeking to link to the magic beginning to seep up from the Core.

I watch a bit longer, breathing deep and at peace, looking forward to a few hours of practice with Arick and Rojvah, and the kiss at the end.

Then I hear Rojvah shout, and I'm moving before the words even register, vaulting across the roof and skittering down to her terrace, even as there's a crash of breaking pottery.

I already know it's just her and Arick in the room. They ent fightin', and neither is hurt. Arick's on one knee, pickin' up pieces of broken crockery, and Rojvah's over on the bed . . . cryin'.

"Everythin' all right?"

Know it ent. Never seen Rojvah cry, except the kind Krasian women do on command, where the tears are real, but the sadness never reaches their scent. This ent that. Rojvah's upset for real, and it's makin' me upset, too.

Arick shrugs. "My sister would rather break things than tell me."

I nod, moving slowly toward the bed. Arick takes the cue, throwing the broken pieces on a tray and slipping out of the room.

Olive's old bed is a four-poster like mine, but . . . frillier, with lacy curtains that don't hide anythin' or hold back the light. They haven't been let down for the night, and Rojvah is facedown on the silk sheets.

Ent ever been this close to Rojvah's bed, and I feel my heart beating faster as I approach. Dunno if it's from her sobbing, or the way her scent clings to the bedding. "Rojvah?"

She dun't answer, and I hope it ent too bold as I sit on the bed next to her and try somethin' new. "Intended?"

The word feels awkward on my lips, but Rojvah pauses at it, and turns, eyeing me through her hair.

"Turn away," she croaks at last. "Do not look at me like this."

"Seen you cry at the funeral," I say. "Still prettier than any other girl at her Seventhday best."

Nevertheless, I turn away and Rojvah sits up, drying her eyes and fixing her robes, scarves, and hair. "All right."

I look back, and my breath catches. There's little sign of tears now, and she's carefully arranged herself, curled up in a way that makes me all too aware I'm on her bed.

I stand, taking a step back. Leavin' room for Everam, as the Krasians say. I wait for her to say something, but the quiet stretches. "Somethin' upset you?"

There is fear, doubt, and worry in Rojvah's scent. Not things I'm used to smellin' from her. "I cannot put off meeting with Favah any longer."

"That's supposed to help me make sense of things?"

"My dice," she says, and that's enough for me to get the gist.

Rippin' dice. They've got real power, but my experience is they hurt folk a lot more than they help. Ent much in the world that scares me more than prophecies.

"Mam says when you're afraid of something, better to run right at it than hide and wait for it to corner you." I laugh a little. "Easier said than done."

I put a hand over hers, feeling her rapid pulse. "Maybe we can do it together."

There's a jump in Rojvah's pulse. "Would you . . . ?"

"'Course," I say. "Go just about anywhere, long as it's with you."

Her pulse slows, and some of the fear leaves her scent, replaced by that smell she has when we're sayin' our good nights.

IT'S FULL DARK by the time we get to the university, but no one's off to bed. Like my own powers, *dama'ting* magic is strongest at night.

You'd think we were expected, the way Favah's Kaji attendants receive their princess and her intended. Maybe we were.

Ent long before we're seen to Favah's office. There ent any chairs, just pillows on the floor to kneel on. The old crone kneels at the center of the room, acting like she don't know we're here.

Favah's interesting. Probably the oldest person I've ever met who looks their age. Folk say Jeorje Watch has six score winters, but he killed so many demons during the war, it doesn't show.

Favah's body is withered by comparison. Just wiry sinew and bone, with thin skin sagging around it. She has that smell graybeards get when their bodies start to sour.

But her aura is strong. Usually old folk's auras dim with age, but Favah's is bright, probably from a lifetime of casting the dice. She's got the power under tight control, like winter freeze on a pond. No tellin' what's beneath.

"Princess." Favah does not open her eyes as she gestures to the pillow across from her. The only one on the floor. "The son of Arlen may wait outside."

Rojvah's scent is full of fear and deference, but she shakes her head.

"He is my intended, Honored Dama'ting. My questions will affect his life as well as mine."

Don't much like the sound of that, but I ent here for me. Here for Rojvah, and nothing else.

"Very well," Favah concedes, though her scent is less than pleased. She doesn't offer a pillow as I kneel next to Rojvah. "The dice said you would not speak until you came to me, but I did not expect it to take all winter."

Rojvah puts her hands on the floor, bowing until her head nearly touches the floor. "Apologies, Honored Dama'ting. I . . . was afraid."

"And what could make the crown princess of Kaji fear me?" Favah wonders.

There's panic in Rojvah's scent. I don't look at her, but I lay my hand on the floor, touching hers just a little.

"I do not wish to be *dama'ting*!" Rojvah blurts. She pauses and pulls in a fresh breath, her words growing stronger. "I will not do it. I cannot. If put before the oath, my words will ring false in my aura, and even the Damajah would have no choice but to cast me out."

Like someone who just sicked up, Rojvah seems both relieved and exhausted by the effort. She sets back on her folded legs and breathes as her heart tries to find its rhythm.

"Then why come at all?" Favah smells irritated, and Rojvah flinches at the lash of the words. "To approve your blasphemy? To forgive your rejection of duty and your betrayal of Everam?"

Each accusation hits Rojvah, rippling pain across her aura like stones skipped on a pond. You'd think Favah was coming at her with a knife from the way she smells. Rojvah opens her mouth, but nothing comes out.

She asked me not to speak. To respect the venerable *dama'ting*. Olive, too, talks about Favah like she's some kind of livin' legend.

But I've had people sayin' I was worthless and a disappointment all my life, and no matter what mask I put on to hide my feelings, it hurt every time. Sometimes it hurt so much I didn't think I could take it.

Corespawn me if I'm gonna let someone make my promised feel like that.

"Ay!" I snap, drawing all the attention in the room. Favah's glare is sharp, her scent stunned at my audacity, but that just makes me angrier.

"Ent *betrayal* when folk try to force you to do something you don't wanna," I growl. "Ent *betrayal* to not be everything your parents wanted. And it ent *blasphemy* to not want to put on white robes and pretend you're better'n folk."

Favah ent stunned anymore. My words hit her aura like a hammer on ice, each one cracking away at the pond to reveal red lines of anger pulsing beneath.

Rojvah's holdin' her breath, even more scared than before. Thinks I'm makin' things worse—and maybe I am—but I'm too steamed to care.

"My promised went into the undercity to hunt Alagai rippin' Ka," I say. "While the *dama'ting* schemed and judged from the safety of the Holy City, Rojvah was singin' pain right into his knobby skull."

I lean forward. "You may not 'approve' of Rojvah's choices, but you got no call for disrespect."

Favah stares at me a long moment. When's the last time anyone spoke to her like that? Night, has anyone ever? Her aura is unreadable, the ice melted into a cloud that could be a cooling fog, or steam fit to scald my skin off.

Favah flicks her sleeves back, and I wonder if she's fixin' to cast a spell. But then she puts her hands on the floor, bowing without lowering her eyes.

Now it's my turn to be stunned. To Krasians, this is the sincerest form of apology short of submission.

"You are correct, son of Arlen." Favah's voice is flat, but for the first time I smell real emotion on her. Humility. "Everam is watching always, and will weigh my words against me in Heaven." She looks to Rojvah. "I apologize, Honored Rojvah. Indeed, your glory is boundless, and it was wrong of me to speak to you so."

She sits back up, sleeves wafting gently down to cover her gnarled hands. Still, she holds Rojvah's gaze. "Why have you come, if not about the white?"

Even with Favah putting her teeth away, Rojvah smells more scared than ever. Her hand drifts down to the *hora* pouch at her waist, beside a *hanzhar* carved of hero's bone. She reaches into the thick velvet bag, bones rattling as she lifts her hand to Favah.

"Because white robes or no, if we are to survive the trials to come, I must know if these speak true." Rojvah's fingers open, revealing a set of seven dice, carved from polished demonbone and glowin' bright with magic.

"Tsst!" Favah hisses. "How long, girl?"

Rojvah's eyes flick to the floor. "I finished them in the desert."

"Before your return to New Krasia." Favah sounds like a school-mam at the end of her patience. "But you did not tell your mother. Or the Damajah."

Rojvah keeps her eyes down. "No."

"Because you feared they would press the white on you," Favah says, "and keep you from your chosen path."

Rojvah's yes is barely a squeak.

"Better to sneak off like a *gwil* in the night," Favah says, "than face your destiny."

Now Rojvah looks up. "I am here, now, Dama'ting." She raises the dice again. "Test them. If they are not true, I will show them the sun and walk away, my heart the lighter for it."

"And if they are?" Favah says. "It is forbidden to See without the white."

"Everything is forbidden, until it is not," Rojvah says. "Did you yourself not teach Leesha Paper to See? I do not recall her taking the white."

"I did not approve of that," Favah says.

"Ay, but you did it," I say.

"On the Damajah's command." Favah's scent is dismissive. Like I got no business sticking my head in. And maybe I don't, but that's when it's the most fun.

"What do you think is *inevera*, right now?" I ask.

EVEN AT NIGHT, Favah takes us down to her underground Chamber of Shadows, so not even moonlight can reach us.

"No man has witnessed this rite in three thousand years," Favah advises me, but I can tell from her scent she wants me to turn my back, like when someone's changing clothes.

"Lucky me," I say, and stay right where I am.

For all the solemnity of this "rite," it's a little boring, if I'm to tell honest word. Favah starts with cards, dealing hidden hands and making Rojvah guess them with the dice. She asks things Rojvah could not possibly know the answer to, and notes her responses.

Finally, she flicks her hand for Rojvah to put away her dice. "I will meditate on this."

Just like that, Favah closes her eyes, and I hear her heartbeat slow as her breath falls into a deep, steady rhythm. The emotions in her scent fade, still as a statue.

Rojvah's hand finds mine as we kneel in wait. She squeezes tighter'n I'd like, but I just squeeze back a nice, even pressure.

Here in the darkness, the touch of our skin makes a link between our auras, like a straw I could suck on, Drawing a bit of her aura through mine and Reading it.

Readin' someone's aura ent the same as looking at it. It's about the most intimate, personal thing you can do. You can see hopes and dreams, live memories like they happened to you, learn things they don't even know about themselves. I could do it as easily as takin' a breath.

And I want to. I want to know everything about Rojvah. Want to know if I mean to her even a tiny fraction of what she's come to mean to me. To know if our promise is real, or just a means to an end.

To know if she really likes me for me.

Only, it ent my business, how she feels. Read Selen Cutter once by accident, and I felt . . . dirty after, like I'd been thumbin' through her diary, only a thousand times worse.

Won't do that to Rojvah. All she needs right now is someone to hold her hand, so I cap the link, like using my tongue to cover the tip of the straw.

At last Favah's eyes snap open. "Your dice speak with Everam's voice, Rojvah, daughter of Amanvah."

Rojvah squeezes so hard her nails dig into my skin.

"The Damajah will ask after you," Favah says. "I will not bear her false witness."

"Then do not," Rojvah says. "Tell her I passed the test, but did not take the oath. That I *will* not take it. But I will go into the demon king's lair once more, for Everam, and all Ala.

"That, I will do."

Favah puts her hands on the floor again as she bows. "May your glory be as boundless as your spirit, Princess. Everam loses a powerful Bride, this day. It will be on you to exceed that fate."

ROJVAH'S BACK TO her old self after that. Almost giddy, even knowin' where we're headed. When we finally kiss good night, it makes my head spin.

For once I go to bed, pulling the curtains tight and sleeping as much as I can with the night whispering to me. Ent much, before the Equinox Festival starts causing a ruckus.

Worst of winter's freeze has receded. Snow lines the roads and some of the tracks are muddy, but Hollow's paved streets are clear.

Still chilly, but folk are getting psyched up for planting season, so a lot of people have cause to come to town for supplies, or just to poke their heads out after the cold months. Equinox ent usually as big a holiday as Solstice, but Olive wants the excuse to move soldiers and horses around, and opens the coffers to throw a barn burner that folk will be sleepin' off for a week.

Another day of seeing and being seen, waving at crowds even as their press and irregular bouts of cheering feel crushing. It gets louder and louder as the day goes on into night.

And then it's time. Try not to listen in as Olive and Selen say their goodbyes with tears and a crushing embrace. Selen's got work to do while the rest of us are onstage.

Selen's eyes are puffy as she emerges from the private tent. "Your turn, Dar. See you soon."

Olive has composed herself better, but folk can't hide their smell the way they can fix their face. This ent easy on her. "You got this, Dar?"

Even Olive, who all but told me I couldn't keep it together enough to be a Jongleur, is acting like I'm in charge on this trip. "Core if I know. But I ent comin' back without Mam and Leesha, or proof they been et."

"Spoken like a true *Sharum*," Olive says, but I ent that, and she knows it.

"What about you?" I ask. "You ent shared your plans. You got this?"

Olive shrugs. "As much as you. I have a direction, and a task. I'll figure out the rest as I go."

"Ay."

Olive lifts her arms for a hug. Don't usually like hugs, but Olive Paper ent just anyone. I'm in her arms before she's fully extended, squeezing tight. "Don't get et."

Olive gives a little chuckle, as I feel her tears wet my hair. "Good advice for us all."

We're all fake smiles as we emerge, Jongleur's masks for the cheering crowd as Arick and Rojvah take their places and I tumble onto center stage, practicing Jongleur's tricks to warm the crowd.

The acrobatics have always come easy, and at night my hands move so fast the random assortment of items I juggle crawl through the air, giving me all the time I need to catch and hurl them back up into the pattern.

Some folk cast nervous looks skyward, but looking out from the stage I can see scorpion teams lining the rooftops, alongside senior Warders with their electrum pens. No demon's going to sneak up on us tonight.

Hary gave me a Jongleur's bag o' marvels, full of toss bangs and wingseeds, colored balls and scarves, magic tricks and musical instruments. I pull out a set of shackles, and Arick and Rojvah make a great show of chaining me up. Rojvah sashays across the stage with confidence, calling folk from the audience to test the bindings before they toss me in a box. It's effortless to turn slippery and free myself, leaping out with a flourish. It isn't the polished act of a Master Jongleur, but Hary Roller says it dun't take much to impress the bumpkins.

By then, Arick's sitting with his kamanj, and Rojvah is dancing in a dress strung with scarves of colored silk that tinkles with webs of warded coins. My pipes are resting on a stool behind her, and as I take my place, she touches her choker and begins to sing.

We've practiced this set dozens of times, syncing it with Selen's movements out in the dark while everyone is watching us in the sound shell. Even the encores are planned and scheduled. Toward the end of the final song, Olive holds up a hand to me, and I wonder if I'll ever see her again.

Then I take a carefully prepared pouch from my bag o' marvels, holding my breath as I cast it down with a bang and a flash, filling the stage with smoke as the crowd shrieks and cheers.

All the noise should be too much for me, but I knew it was coming, orchestrated it, and the noise rolls over me with little effect.

For now.

Behind the screen of smoke, our trio drops through a hidden trap in the stage, appearing to vanish as Hary Roller himself appears out of the smoke, seamlessly keeping the party going.

Beneath the stage are rough disguises, and I turn my back as Rojvah trades her bright performance dress for something less likely to draw the eye. Arick and I change, too, putting on plain clothes, hats, and scarves that will draw little attention in the chill night as we slip out into the throng.

No one, not even the other performers onstage, sees us go, and the crowd is the last place anyone will expect us. They'll assume we've gone someplace backstage, or been spirited back to the royal section.

This is the worst part of the plan for me, enveloped by the crowd. Smells and sounds and sights and tastes press at me from all sides, cheering and shouting and conversations, the stink of alcohol and vomit, the smell of the temporary privies that fills the air.

It's the worst part, but it's my plan. Hary knows he's creating a distraction, and gives a performance that puts mine to shame. He opens with *The Battle of Cutter's Hollow*, a favorite that always pulls in the crowd. I focus on its rhythm and familiar cadence, blocking out the other input as best I can as the three of us filter out of the crowd and flee Corelings' Graveyard.

Once we're free of the crowd, we race through the night streets, still too busy for horses, but clear enough to move at speed. Soon we reach streets that are all but empty, keeping away from the wardlights as we head for the spot where Selen waits with the horses and pack animals.

I take a moment with Dusk Runner, putting my hand on his great head and feeding him a carrot as I Draw a touch of magic through him, Reading his love and devotion.

"Ent goin' to a sunny pasture, boy," I say, knowing he cannot understand. "Thank you for taking me."

Then I saddle up with the others, and we ride off, disappearing into the darkness like a *gwil* in the night.

CHAPTER 36

RHINEY

You ask for a lot, child,
and offer little in return.
Pray come look me in the eye,
so I can see for myself which Olive Paper
I am dealing with.
—A

THE HANDWRITTEN NOTE arrived under separate seal from a formal invitation to visit Angiers. The venerable Duchess Araine, too old and frail for the journey, wished to pay her respects to Hollow's new duch, in hope that their special relationship continue.

It's a relationship that served both duchies well. Hollow was once a vassalage of Angiers, but the war reversed that balance of power. Hollow's forces—Mother and my unborn self among them—took Fort Angiers back from the demons, and returned the exiled duchess Araine and her infant grandson to power. Mother and Araine had been very close. Not just allies, but friends. Family.

Yet despite Tarisa's assurances, it seems a thousand flamework weapons, ammunition, and training in their use is too great an ask to pass without scrutiny.

The wording of Araine's note keeps rebounding in my mind. *Which Olive Paper I am dealing with.* What did the duchess mean by that? Is she worried my time in Krasia has left me compromised? Or is it about my dual gender, and her own designs?

Mother told me once that Araine was eager to arrange a marriage between me and her grandson Rhinebeck. Rhiney and I have been exchanging letters since we first learned the pen. Many times over the years, I wondered if he was handsome, like the painting of his uncle Thamos that hangs in Mother's keep. I wondered what it would be like to fall in love with a prince.

But now I know. It is pain, and heartbreak, and grief. If Araine thinks she can parlay my request into a political betrothal, she is mistaken.

I ride out the morning after Equinox with a thousand Hollow Soldiers. Arther worried so large a military escort might make the Angierians uneasy, but I need as many warriors as I can take without raising suspicion.

We put on a bit of a show for the Angierian herald. Me acting put upon at such a large bodyguard, and Gared loudly insisting Hollow won't risk losing me again.

While the folk are still sleeping off the indulgences of the festival, we ride north, a loud and raucous distraction as Darin and the others slip away to the east.

At the same time, Lord Commander Gamon used the cover of the festival parade to take thousands of foot soldiers, archers, and Hollow Lancers west, overland and away from prying eyes, to meet Inevera's *Sharum* at Anoch Dahl.

I sent my spear brothers with them, all save Faseek, who refused to leave my side. Krasians are not welcome in Angiers, not since my mad brother Jayan attempted to sack the capital. I've stowed my Tazhan *alagai*-scale in favor of the wooden armor worn more commonly in the North.

Commissioned over the winter, the wooden plates offer full protection—lighter than Tazhan steel, and just as strong, etched with powerful wardwork. Over the suit I wear a tabard of fine wool with a feminine cut that flares like a dress when I dismount. It's beautiful and functional, but it doesn't hold Chadan's blessing. Good enough for a political message, but not what I will wear when we enter the night below.

Even Faseek, riding at my left, consented to wear the uniform of my house guard rather than his *Sharum* blacks. The order pained him, but his sharp uniform and neatly trimmed hair do little to lessen the intimidation he projects.

Like Gared's Cutters, my brother rides with spear and shield still on his back, rather than secured to his saddle like the Hollow Soldiers and members of my house guard. Wisdom says they will be better rested if we are attacked, but Faseek will already be killing while they still fumble at clasps.

General Gared looms at my right like a mountain. The general's transformation is complete as he rides in his full regalia. His armor is polished to a sheen, his tabard awash in the color of his many commendations, but I've seen him wade into a pack of sand demons in that armor and scatter the lot. Gared's hair and beard are cropped close, all signs of gray shorn away by thick golden-blond hair. Grandmum said it looked like the sun when he was young, and she wasn't wrong.

More, Gared's regained his pride and self-respect. "Still at it like they're on their honeymoon," Selen said of her father and Baroness Emelia, after a recent Sixthday dinner.

I feel safer, knowing Gared and my spear brother are close.

Briar travels on foot, yet he roams far ahead of our mounted forces, scouting the territory and meeting us each night at caravan grounds placed at intervals along the seven-day journey up the Messenger Road to Angiers.

Sometimes in the camp I notice Oskar—one of many sharp-eyed recruits who volunteered for this mission, not knowing what they were signing up for.

Part of me wants to send him home, back to Apple Hill. Back to his family. I cost his village enough lives already. But another part of me remembers the look in his eyes when he and Selen charged the rock demon that was attacking his friends. Oskar has steel in him, and I need that where I am going.

His eyes slide by whenever we pass, careful not to meet mine. I do the same for him, respecting his desire to earn his place, not find favor in knowing the duch. He will make a fine officer one day.

As in the Krasian court, General Gared does not put on airs, laughing and eating with his soldiers when we make camp. I tend to get a headache when I stare too long at people's auras, but I swear I can see the love the Cutters have for him vibrating in the air. They would die for him.

Cutters and Hollow Soldiers take turns challenging the general to feats of strength or wrestling, and the challengers do their best. Some are faster, or more skilled, but no one is stronger. Gared shrugs off blows that would have shattered the bones of weaker men, and even I would balk before attempting some of his feats of strength in front of an audience.

I watch, laughing and cheering with the crowd, but there is a hungry part of me that longs to challenge him. That relishes the idea of facing a hero of the demon war in his prime, pitting my strength and skill against his. If I am who the Damajah believes I am, who Mother believed I am, then it isn't enough to have the strongest warriors at my back. I need to *be* the strongest warrior.

"Could beat him, you kept your wits," a voice beside me says. I turn in surprise to see Briar. How did he get so close without me noticing him?

"But why?" he continues. "To shame your general in front of his men? The Hollowers will not love you more for it."

"I am not sure they love me now," I say. "They loved Mother, and they love General Gared, but do any of them truly know me?"

"Does anyone truly know anyone?" Briar asks. "They will love you until you give them reason not to. They love your mother and Gared because time and again Nie came for Hollow, only to find Leesha Paper and Gared Cutter standing in Her way. Would you do any less?"

I lift my chin, looking hard in his eye. "Of course not."

"Then you are worthy of their love, Olive Paper, for you give it in return."

———

"Wooden Soldiers," Briar advises, moments before we hear the thunder of their approach.

The Angierian force is smaller than our own, in both number and stature. There are perhaps two hundred unarmored soldiers mounted on light, fleet-footed coursers. Angierians on the whole tend to be shorter than their southern cousins, and Gared's Cutters, mounted on huge mustang, seem giants by comparison.

The Angierians carry no spears or shields, no axes or mattocks or bows. There are large knives on their saddles, but nothing of use while fighting atop a horse. Instead each has a long-barreled flamework weapon harnessed in easy reach, and a smaller pistol, similar to Prince Ramm's weapon, at their hip.

Their leader is taller than the others, his horse an almost perfect white. His tailed green-and-gold surcoat is crisp and sharply pressed, helm polished to a sheen, but I am not fooled into thinking this is some foppish dandy. He handles his stallion expertly, seeming to fly down the road to us until I feel he will not have time to pull up.

Instinctively I reach for my shield, but Gared and Faseek are already moving their horses in front of me as the rider yanks the reins so hard his stallion rears, hooves kicking so close to Rockslide that I see Gared's biceps bulge as he pulls the bridle to keep the surly animal from responding in kind.

"Ay, ya ripping fool," Gared growls, "what d'ya think you're—"

The rider ignores him, raising a hand to signal his escort to pull up. He turns a circle to ride off the rest of his animal's momentum and sweeps off his helm.

He's beautiful. Tall and broad-shouldered, with a waxed mustache above an angled jaw. His thick black hair springs back to fullness when the helmet is removed, dark waves above eyes as blue as my own.

But it's his smile that stands out, bright and wide within a shadow of beard as he meets my eyes. "Olive!"

I blink. Ally or no, who is this man to use my first name like he . . .

"It's me, Rhiney!" he cries when I do not react.

That startles me. Is it possible? Prince Rhinebeck and I have corresponded all our lives, but he's six months younger than I am, while the man before me is in his full growth. I'm used to the effect in my spear brothers—feedback magic pushed our bodies into their physical primes—but Thesan lands are largely clear of corelings, and it's surprising to see this far north.

I think again of the painting in Mother's keep. This isn't the same man, but the resemblance is unmistakable. "Rhiney!"

We mirror each other, throwing legs over the saddle and jumping down to embrace. He's taller than I am, muscular without being bulky. He meets my eyes like a warrior when we pull apart, but the sweeping leg he makes is Angierian etiquette for greeting a woman of royal blood. "Your Grace."

"Highness." I cannot help but smile, spreading the "skirts" of my tabard in something like a shallow curtsy. I outrank Prince Rhinebeck, but likely not for long. He is the only blood heir to the wooden throne of Angiers, and his grandmother has seen close to ninety winters. Soon he will be duke, and I can see his men already defer to him.

"You're a bit young to be leading a company of soldiers," I note.

"I could say the same of you." Rhiney offers me a wink that no doubt makes the girls at court swoon. "There has been an increase in coreling activity in the borderlands. We've been hunting them."

This is news, and it isn't good. The greatward system in Angiers is not as ambitious as Hollow's, leaving many of their surrounding hamlets with only traditional warding. Since the Deliverer's Purge, that has usually been enough. If demons are returning in numbers, it could mean Alagai Ka is drawing them back to the hive. Or it could mean he knows my plans, and is hunting me.

I shake the thought away. "You hunt them with flamework weapons?"

"They're called rifles." Rhinebeck reaches into the harness on his saddle, pulling free the weapon. "Mother told me you had an interest."

"Flamework don't work on demons." Gared has dismounted as well. "Saw it myself in the war. Them little pellets shatter or flatten, ruinin' the wards. Even thundersticks dun't do much more than make a coreling dizzy."

Rhinebeck reaches into one of the pouches on his belt, holding up a clear bullet. "Warded glass. A marksman can take down a lesser coreling with a single shot, though the larger ones can require a few hits before they fall."

"Don't they just heal up?" Gared asks. It's a fair question. Demon magic can heal anything short of a severed limb or mortal wound in minutes.

Rhinebeck reaches for his saddle again, this time sliding free a heavy knife with a foot-long, warded steel blade. Suddenly his unnatural growth makes sense.

"You finish them off with that," I say, "once they're already down."

Rhinebeck smiles. "The ale stories say Princes Olive wrestles corelings with bare hands, but I find killing them at a distance much more sensible."

I laugh. "You aren't wrong. Are you returning from a hunt?" Rhinebeck's soldiers look too fresh and clean to have been out in the borderlands.

"Of course not," Rhiney laughs. "I am here to escort you to Grandmother! Apologies for crowding the road. *Got to keep up with the dance,* as Grandmum always says. You brought a thousand warriors, so politics demand I meet you with an equivalent force."

Gared snorts, and I can't help but share the feeling. "Two hundred Wooden Soldiers against a thousand Cutters is an equivalent force? I don't know if I should laugh or feel insulted."

Rhinebeck shrugs. "You don't have rifles. Your horses are slow. The terrain here would make it difficult to leave the road. That wooden armor may hold off a rock demon, but a glass bullet would punch right through."

"Demonshit," Gared says.

Rhiney gives Gared an appraising look. Is it confidence I see, or arrogance? "Care to wager on that, General?"

It feels like a trap, but Gared only smiles. "Ay, all right. Got a keg of my best ale on a cart back there. Say, against a cask of Angierian brandy? The good stuff, not that apricot business."

Rhiney shows his teeth, and the trap is sprung. "General, if you win, I will take you to Mother's vineyard personally, and let you taste them all and pick your favorite."

Gared still looks confident, going over to Rockslide's barding and removing a thick wooden armor plate, enameled in warded glass. It's thicker than my own breastplate, and the wardwork is exquisite, as befitting a general's mount. Even I am skeptical Rhiney's weapon can damage it.

Rhiney slides his glass bullet into the rifle and works the bolt to chamber the round with a loud *ka-chak*. "Tell your men to hold tight to the reins," he says loudly. "The sound will startle animals if they are not used to it."

The prince moves to the side of the road, where he can raise the barrel of his weapon pointed away from everyone. "Whenever you're ready, General."

Gared grunts, throwing the armor plate high into the air. Quick as Prince Ramm with his bow, Rhiney puts the weapon to his shoulder, sights down its length, and lets fire with a gout of smoke and flame.

Indeed, there is a ripple through our ranks, animals of war suddenly gone skittish as the deer that have begun to repopulate since the purge. Soldiers work to calm animals as they kick and stomp and rear, even as the armor plate comes crashing back down to the ground.

"Excellent shot, Highness." One of Rhinebeck's attendants, Corporal Taler, runs to retrieve the plate, holding it up so all can see the sunlight streaming through the bullet-sized hole at its center.

Gared lets out a low whistle. "Owe you a keg."

"The glass enamel on wooden armor is thin," Rhiney says, "which is why the armor is so light. Proof against an arrow or spear, and the wards offer protection from corespawn, but in modern war, armor is . . . obsolete."

Gared's smile is a little pained, now. "Reckon those fancy weapons are great when you have space, but sooner or later, every fight gets in close."

"Wise advice," Rhinebeck nods, looking to his men. "ARMS!"

Moving as one, the Wooden Soldiers draw rifles from saddle harnesses, ready to shoot in seconds.

"BAYONETS!" Rhiney calls, and this time the soldiers pull those thick warded hunting blades, affixing them to the end of the rifles, turning them into warded spears.

I look at my soldiers, and sense their worry. Even Gared looks more respectful in the face of so many flamework weapons.

In spite of it all, I find myself smiling.

Seize every advantage.

"BEAUTIFUL, IS IT NOT?" Rhiney asks, seeing my eyes drift over his lands, up to the walled city in the distance.

Cutter's Hollow wasn't much of a place before the war. A town of hundreds, devastated by demons and plague. When refugees began to pour in from the south, the only choices were to expand rapidly or be consumed.

Mother chose the former, designing a series of interconnected greatwards into the layout of Hollow before new ground was broken. Some are small as single farmsteads, others so large they can only be seen by the clouds above, the very roads and lines of buildings in a town or entire barony forming symbols of protection against corespawn.

But Fort Angiers is an older place, protected by a great wardwall with buildings that have stood for hundreds of years and immutable streets. With most of the demons purged, there was little incentive to wipe the slate and start fresh. Forced out of Hollow entirely, it makes sense that any remaining demons would gather in Angiers. But we ride through lush pastures, rich farmland, orchards, and hunting grounds, unspoiled by demons or the engines of industry.

"Beautiful," I agree. "I fear I look like a bumpkin, staring at everything. I've never been so far north."

"I would see Hollow one day, if I can," Rhiney says. "Even in peacetime, our mothers couldn't cease work long enough to take a holiday and visit."

I think of Arther and his endless papers, and know he's right. Mother didn't know the meaning of holidays. But it's more than that. "I think it was us, more than them."

"Ay?" Rhiney asks.

"My sister killed an assassin in my nursery," I say. "Not the first, nor the last. I don't think she would ever have let me off the greatwards by choice."

Rhinebeck nods. "All my uncles dead in the war, and Grandmum in her dotage, I don't think she would have risked me on the road, either."

"But she lets you hunt the borderlands in your sixteenth summer?" I ask.

"The first time, I ran off," Rhiney laughs. "Came back inches taller, and with stubble on my face. And now Grandmum isn't the . . . force of nature she once was."

"Is she well?"

"You'll learn soon enough not to underestimate her," Rhiney says. "Still sharp as a spear, but she tires quickly now, and isn't faking anymore when she holds my arm to walk across the room. She's still the power in Angiers and the people love her fiercely, but more and more she delegates the day-to-day running of the city to me and Minister Pawl."

CHAPTER 37

DUCHESS ARAINE

RHINEY HAS ARRANGED lodging for my warriors, and escorts Gared, Briar, Faseek, and me into the palace—grander by far than Mother's keep, if less defensible—and through to a lavishly appointed sitting room with a table heavily laden with food.

"I warned you not to get fat, Baron," a voice checks Gared as he reaches to tear a drumstick from the roast fowl. I look over to see an old woman, wrapped in a heavy shawl, sitting across the room. Her thin wisps of hair are oiled and pulled back beneath the wooden crown, carved into a circlet of ivy, set with precious gems.

Gared straightens like a student when the headmistress comes to inspect their work. "Ent fat, Mum."

"You've shed it well enough," Araine says, "but my birds tell me it's a recent change."

"Ay, Mum," Gared says. "It . . . ah, won't happen again."

"See that it doesn't," Ariane says. "Now, run along and find an organ to move. I'd like a private word with Olive. You, too, Rhiney."

The men hop to her command so quickly it reminds me of Mother, but the withered crone has more of Favah's look about her—frail of body, but with fierce eyes that miss nothing.

The tea service on the table before Araine tells me all I need to know.

Tea politics is something Mother made sure to teach. I set a cup before the duchess, pouring with a practiced hand.

By pouring and serving, I assume a subservient role. Since my coronation, Araine and I are effectively equals, but this is her duchy and her palace, and a reminder that right now, I need her more than she needs me.

"Your mother was always stingy with the honey," Araine notes, "but I've earned it."

"Of course, Your Grace." I smile, adding a generous dollop to her tea.

"Thank you dear," she says, taking the cup. "Please, sit."

I pour a second cup for myself, ignoring the honey as I take a seat across from the venerable woman.

"Duch Olive," Araine says. "Rhiney says General Gared calls you she, and your Krasian bodyguard calls you he. What should I call you?"

"Olive?" I ask.

Araine does not reply, simply raising an eyebrow.

"What feels right?" I ask. "The general saw me grow up as Princess Olive, and so I am she to him. My spear brother was introduced to me as Prince Olive, and knows me as he."

"I've known your condition longer than you have," Araine says. "But Rhiney and I have always known you as Princess Olive, though we know it isn't that simple."

"Mother told you," I say.

"Of course," Araine says. "I lived in her keep while you were still in swaddling. Saw for myself more than once."

"Does Rhiney know?" I try to make the question casual, but it feels anything but.

"Your own Jongleurs have seen to that well enough," Araine says. "But I never kept it from him, when he was old enough to understand."

"Even I don't understand it fully," I admit.

"Settled, then," Araine says. "I've a fondness for women of power, so if it's all right with you, I will continue to use the feminine and have Rhiney do the same."

"He can make his own decision," I say.

"Indeed," Araine agrees. "He's grown into a dashing lad, hasn't he? Takes after his uncle Thamos, the only one of my sons who was worth a damn. I daresay he'll be ready for the crown when it comes, but I mean to keep its weight from him for as long as I can bear it."

She leans in. "Long enough to find him a feminine bride, I hope."

I lean back. "That isn't what I've come for."

"And why not?" Araine asks bluntly. "Rhiney is a worthy catch by any woman's standards. Handsome, brave, intelligent. Kindhearted, but not a fool. And let us not forget, with our duchies combined, your child could be king."

"I don't want that," I say.

"Neither did your mother," Araine says, "but what you want and what the people need are not always the same."

I cross my arms. "Not interested."

"Do you have a preference for girls?" Araine asks. "My little birds saw you kissing a peasant girl at your coronation. They say you spent the night with her."

I feel my cheeks heat. "That is none of your . . ."

The old duchess waves my anger away like a cloud of gnats. "I don't care who you kiss, or take to bed. My boy Pether snuck young men to his acolyte chamber in the monastery nearly every night. I had birds there, too. Yet I loved him as much as any of my idiot sons. I am simply asking that you do me the courtesy of not letting me go on and on, making a fool of myself, if Rhiney is not to your fancy. So I ask again. Do you have a preference for girls?"

I think of Lanna. And Chadan. And, try as I might not to, Rhiney. "I don't."

"So you prefer men?"

"I don't have a preference," I clarify, realizing it's true even as I speak the words aloud. "Rhinebeck is handsome enough, and I don't think of him as a brother, as I do Darin. But neither do I have feelings for him, and I will not lie to you. Who I marry is of little importance to me right now."

"You are a duch," Araine says. "You have a duty to secure your line."

"Duch regent," I say. "There is no proof Mother is dead." It isn't the whole truth, but it is true enough.

"Is that why you want my guns?" Araine's eyes grow sharp. "Some rescue mission? Do the Krasians have her, as they did you?"

I consider the story. I don't want to lie, but neither do I trust her to know—or support—my true intentions. This might get me what I want, but there are too many chances I could be caught in the lie. "No. The official story is correct. Her caravan was attacked by demons, but Mother's body was never found."

Araine's face grows sad at that. "The young have the luxury of hope, dear, but it can be a bitter companion as the winters pass."

She thinks I am lying to myself. That Mother is gone and I simply cannot let go. Best, perhaps, she continue to believe that.

"What, then?" Araine demands. "What enemy are you willing to forsake your mother's oath for? If Leesha had wanted you to have the weapons of the old world—"

"She would have left me their secrets," I cut in. "And she did. Make no mistake, Your Grace. Two princes now have shown me the power of flamework weapons. I do not think Hollow can survive in generations to come without accepting their inevitability. But I cannot build factories overnight, and would keep the weapons off the streets of Hollow as long as I can."

I sit back, deliberately taking time to sip my tea as I breathe out my tension. "As for my mother's oath, I am no Gatherer, and not bound to their oaths. But I can assure you I don't mean to turn the weapons on anything . . . human."

Again no lie, but not the whole truth.

"One could say Hollow is vulnerable like it has never been before, or likely will be again," Araine notes. "Your mother claimed her magic protected Hollow from flamework weapons, but she never said how. I wonder if those protections survive her?"

The tension returns instantly, but I resist the urge to put my back up, to loom and intimidate as I would when challenged by a man. Araine is watching me, judging. The duchess has been overly blunt, poking at my defenses and looking for a reaction.

But I am used to women like that, and give her no free energy. "That almost sounds like a threat."

"Simply an observation." Araine sips her own tea. "Magic isn't what it once was, and the most powerful users are passing on."

I understand she's fishing, trying to get me to give something away. But I am asking for something, as well. Perhaps it's a fair trade.

"Mother could use Hollow's greatward to render the chemics of your flamework inert," I say. "And like the secrets of fire, the power was not lost with her."

"Powerful magic." Araine takes a biscuit, dipping it in her tea and taking quick bites. "Not many left who could work such a spell, even in Hollow. And there would be unintended side effects that could cripple your industries."

I shrug. "More than an army with flamework weapons?"

Araine raises her cup to me before taking another sip. "Your mother hated violence, but that was what made her so terrible, when she saw no other course."

"Hard to imagine Mother hurting anyone," I say.

Araine snorts. "Your mother crushed an assassin's spine right in my throne room with a stomp of her heel."

I gape at her. "Impossible."

"Swear it by the sun," Araine says. "You were even there, after a fashion."

Araine sets her cup and saucer on the table. Her thin hands shake a little as she does. The duchess may have a *dama'ting's* will, but she's used no *hora* to extend her life past its allotted span.

"Your mother's violence saved my life and my line," the old woman says. "I owe her everything. Your father, on the other hand, brought with him a war that killed three of my sons, and many I called friend. Who, then, are you?"

"Neither," I say. "And both. But I was raised by Leesha Paper, and wear the crown of Hollow. You know my father better than I, and I make no claim to his throne."

"But neither did you renounce it," Araine notes. "I have little birds everywhere, dear. If you truly have a Thesan heart in your breast, why not renounce your father and your claim? Why not take the opportunity to remind your allies who you really are?"

"Because I have been called upon to pay my father's old debts already," I say. "So why should I show my neck to my spoiled brothers, and renounce what none of them have earned?"

"There it is," Araine whispers.

"There what is?" I am losing patience, and I know it will not end well if I do.

"That dangerous spark," Araine says. "The same as Arlen Bales. The same as your father. Both stirred folk into a froth around them."

"And then my father and Arlen Bales saved the world," I remind her.

"Indeed," Araine agrees. "Is that your plan as well? Five hundred flamework weapons shattered your brother's army like a hammer on glass. You want me to give you a thousand of them, without even the courtesy of telling me why?"

"Because enough demons survived the Deliverer's Purge to attack my mother's caravan and destroy it, despite all her protections," I say. "I intend to track and destroy them once and for all. But if I am to succeed, I need something they didn't have."

That, Araine understands. "And when it is done?"

I look at her a long time, understanding the question beneath. "And then if I am still duch, I will consider . . . other matters."

"FIRST LINE, LOAD!" Rhiney's voice booms across the practice yard, and my Hollow Soldiers are quick to respond, lowering the long poles they carry and mimicking the action of inserting shells and working bolts.

"Second line! Point and advance!" Rhiney calls, and a line of warriors raise their poles and step past those loading, ready to fire. "Third line, advance!"

The third line steps forward, poles resting on their shoulders, ready to point and step forward to cover the second line as they reload.

I watch as the prince of Angiers puts them through drills like a seasoned drillmaster. Across the training yard, there is a popping sound as others train with live ammunition.

Spotting me, Rhiney smiles and signals one of his men to take over directing the drill so he can join me.

"Your Grace." He makes another leg, every bit the charming noble, even as his eyes dance at me. "Are you ready for your lesson?"

I smile in spite of myself. Rhinebeck may be a fighting man, but he carries none of the swaggering bravado of my brothers that makes me want to test myself against them. Even his display on the road seemed geared more to impress me than to challenge.

I have no intention of marrying Rhiney, but I had always been feminine in our correspondence growing up. Unlike with Chadan and Lanna, when I'm with Rhiney, I find myself wishing to be seen as feminine still.

I've softened my appearance, dispensing with my "obsolete" armor here in the palace, though I keep a few strategically placed plates in my tight surcoat. The skirts of my peplum blouse fall around velvet leggings that hug close, retaining freedom of movement, but with a more feminine shape. My thick black hair isn't long as it once was, but it's been eight months since my head was shaved, and there is enough to toss when I want to catch an eye.

He presents me with his own rifle as we get to the range, standing perhaps closer than necessary as he shows me its workings, adjusting my grip and repositioning the stock against my shoulder.

"Good," he breathes, so close his mustache brushes my cheek. "Now close one eye and sight down the distance lens."

I don't mind the attention, but neither do I lose myself in it. The lens makes aiming simple. I steady myself and squeeze the trigger, grateful for the wax in my ears as the weapon bangs and kicks against my shoulder, and the bullet hits the center of the target with a satisfying thump.

"Well done!" Rhiney cries. "Do it again."

I work the bolt a little awkwardly, chambering another round. Again I sight, and hit the target.

"Again," Rhiney says. "Faster."

This time I am smoother with the bolt, but I am overconfident, firing before the weapon is perfectly steady. I still hit the target, but wide of center.

"Excellent," Rhiney says nevertheless. "You've truly never held a rifle before?"

It's hard to judge his sincerity—we both see I missed the final shot, but it's true I haven't done this before. My experience with ranged weapons is limited to things I can throw, and a few turns with the crank bow with Selen and Uncle Gared when Mother wasn't around.

I turn, looking at my soldiers drilling in the yard with plain wooden stocks. "How long before they are fit to fight?"

Rhinebeck lets out a long breath. "Months."

I turn to him in surprise. "Months?"

Rhiney raises his palms helplessly. "If Grandmother gives you the weapons before then I cannot stop it, but I would not think it wise."

"I held a rifle for the first time today," I remind him, "and hit the center target twice out of three."

Rhinebeck raises an eyebrow. "Does spearing a practice dummy mean a warrior is ready for the Maze?"

"Of course not," I say. "But my soldiers are not *nie'Sharum* still in their bidos."

"Nevertheless," Rhinebeck says, "there is more to a cohesive rifle unit than hitting stationary targets on a closed range. In the heat of battle, untrained soldiers are more likely to shoot one another than the enemy."

I frown, handing the weapon back. "Show me."

Rhiney looks at me a moment, then nods. He turns to Corporal Taler, who takes his meaning and steps behind a device that looks like something between a crank bow and a scorpion.

"Ready," Rhiney says, and the man aims seemingly at random, pulling the lever to send three small clay discs spinning high into the air.

Rhinebeck's fingers are a blur as he loads three rounds into his rifle, lifts, sights, and fires. One of the clay discs shatters, and then another. I watch the speed at which he works the bolt before destroying the last disc still high in the air.

All three, starting from an empty weapon, in less time than it took me to take my final, quickest shot.

There is no gloating in his eyes when he turns to me. "Months."

"I don't have months," I say.

"Why?" Rhinebeck's voice drops as he moves in close. "What is the hurry? Do you even know where the demons you hunt are?"

Araine must have told him my plans, or at least the dissembling I shared with her. "I . . . know where they will be," I say. "And there isn't time to wait."

"Then perhaps I should take a company and go with you." Rhiney doesn't look at me, striking a pose of boyish insouciance. "We can drill the men on the road."

"You don't even know where we are going." I barely know myself, and I am sure it is not a place the duchess would want her only grandson, even if I cannot tell him so.

"It doesn't matter," Rhiney says. "Hollow and Angiers have been allies since before we were born. If demons took Duchess Paper, Grandmother wants to see them destroyed as much as you."

He looks at me now, eyes piercing. "And it is not only Grandmum's wish. Our friendship has been one of paper and Messengers, but it is no less real to me for that.

"Besides," his mustache twitches as his mouth curls into a smile, "if I am not safe beside the great Duch Olive, then where am I safe?"

CHAPTER 38

NIGHTWOLVES

WE MOVE MOSTLY at night the first week. Can't risk being seen. Anyone who knows where we're going is a risk, another chance the demon will learn we're coming. Hopin' he's got his eye on Olive, and dun't think we're fool enough to go huntin' him without her.

Might be it's fool's hope. In Mam's stories, the demon king boasted the dice were primitive things. Magics that just scratch the surface of a sense that is as innate to him as my sense of smell. How much of the future can the demon see? Can he shape events so our own foretellings show us only what he wants us to see?

The greatwards are concentrated in the crowded center of the duchy. There, the protections overlap, ensuring no demon can come within a hundred miles of the capital . . . or a couple miles straight up, turns out.

Selen had that first week all planned. Even sneakin', she had us traveling in style. Hideouts stocked with fresh supply and feather beds to snooze away the days.

For once, everyone was on *my* schedule. Sleepin' the sun away and goin' out all night.

Never really got to share the night with anyone. Not the demony parts, but the beauty. The hidden world day folk don't even know is there. Ran the night a few times with Briar, and Mam when I was younger, but they wern't new to it.

My friends are. Gettin' to show all that beauty to Arick, Selen, and Rojvah makes me feel full in a place I never knew was empty. Maybe that's how day folk feel all the time, with plenty of people to share their lives with, but I ent ever had that before. Know things are dire, but I'm to tell honest word? Reckon it was the best week of my life.

While it lasted. We're a lot more than a hundred miles from the capital, now. Here in the outskirts of Hollow, only the lines of the greatwards themselves are safe from corespawn, forcing communities to carefully build villages at the thickest parts of the symbols, and farm irregularly shaped fields.

The roads likewise twist and turn, sometimes doubling back for no reason, curving in on themselves, or ending abruptly. Sometimes you need to go off road a bit to get to the next line.

Shorter to cut overland, as the wind demon flies, and leave them entirely, even if it means traveling in the naked night.

We've had months to prepare and have layers of protection—wards of unsight and confusion stitched into the canvas of our tents and the barding of our animals, much like our warded cloaks. Traveling at a steady pace, we could ride right by a copse of wood demons or a reap of field demons and they'd just stumble around, sniffin' the air but unable to find us.

Still, it ent smart to move too much at night. Off the wards, Alagai Ka's spies could be anywhere. He can only control surface demons directly on a new moon, but that dun't mean he can't have them on lookout. If we're spotted by even one, it could be the end of us.

Fortunately, there ent much sign of corelings. Uncle Gared's Cutters swept these lands personally after the Deliverer's Purge, killin' every demon in the borderlands.

Ent caught a whiff of demon since we left the greatward, and there are other signs. Olive's mam set deer and other wild animals loose after the lands were swept clean, after being hunted near extinction by corelings. Little more than a decade later, and they're everywhere. I can tell the lands are safe because not only are the animals alive, they don't smell scared.

Still we play it safe, putting out warded circles and making camp at sunset. Everyone goes back to sleepin' at night and I'm left alone again when twilight fades.

We keep playing our music, but it's more practice than protection. Demons tend to cluster near populated areas. They'll gleefully kill deer if they find them, but it's us they really want. An instinct to kill humans that goes beyond hunger. Even if there were a few Wanderers in these lands, they'd drift toward the border towns we've left behind.

Without demons to charm, there's no way to know if our spellsongs even work, but more and more we shave down the rough edges of our trio and polish our act. When it comes time to enter the demon's den, spellsong will be our real defense.

Going overland has its own challenges, with all manner of natural snags for the animals. Silty rivers to ford, stinking bogs and steep ridges to skirt around, overgrowth too tangled and thick to pass.

There's predators, too. Demons did for most animals out in the night. Ones that survived either got good at hidin', or grew tough enough to encourage demons to look for easier prey.

Those ent the kind of animals you want to meet, 'less you're lookin' to get et.

It's painful, movin' at a crawl like this. None of the obstacles in the undeveloped land could even keep me from runnin' at speed. I can skate across water when I'm slippery, and climb over anything I can't squeeze past. Every time I slap a skeeter off my neck, part of me thinks about how easy it would be to just . . . go.

On foot, with the night filling me with power, reckon I could have run to the mountains by now. But to do that I'd have to leave everyone behind, and I'm too craven for that.

So I force myself to go slow, inching like a snail around hitches I could just hop over.

At dusk, I take care of the animals while the others unload and make camp. Animals and I usually get on. After Arick takes the baggage off I make my way through the ponies, and can tell with a sniff and a listen who's hungry and who's thirsty, whose back hurts and who's getting a sore. I take care of the neediest first, and that helps keep the lot of them calm.

As slow as the ponies make us, it would be worse if we had to spend half the day just lookin' for food. I let 'em know I'm grateful.

With the shadows grown long, I can get the drudge work done fast, though I slow down when I bring oats and water. Horses and ponies both like their food right quick, but they spook if there's a sudden blur and it just appears in front of them. Brushin's another story. Ent met an animal yet that don't like it when I brush them down at speed.

Selen and Rojvah lay out the portable circles. Wards of unsight are worked in among the defensive symbols, making us invisible to core-spawn and barring them entry. Setting them properly so the plates all align is a two-person job, and I never been good at it.

Things seem better between them. I hear them joking and laughing, and don't smell a lie to it.

Reckon it don't hurt that Rojvah and I stopped playin' kissy. Got a girls' tent and a boys', and that's better for everyone. Need to stay sharp on this trip, and nothing spins my head like Rojvah's hugs and kisses.

I get to Dusk Runner last. He dun't mind the wait 'cause he knows it comes with extra time and special care. Feed him treats out of my own hand, and brush away every ache and pain.

Three years old, he's still a colt at heart, nimble and strong. All the animals have had some of the fear of the dark trained out of them, but I've been takin' Dusk out at night for months, runnin' side by side. He loves it, and so do I. Ent many times I'm happier than when the two of us race around like a boy and his hound.

Da wrote a lot in his journals about his own horse, a bay courser named Dawn Runner. Da feared for Dawn because he was riding out into the naked night and doing reckless things that could have gotten both of them killed. Said the guilt was apt to tear him apart sometimes. He loved Dawn as much as anything in the world, but not enough to leave behind the wards. Dawn was the key to a larger world.

Dawn did end up stranded, and I hope had a good life in the Krasian bazaar. Can't help but wonder, though, if it means the same for Dusk. If bein' Darin Bales' horse means he'll end up in a demon's belly, or hitched someplace dangerous with me not comin' back.

"Sorry, boy." I put my forehead against Dusk Runner's and he leans into it, fur soaking up my tears.

WE HEAD NORTHEAST until we find the Old Hill Road. Fort Hill was its own duchy once, big as Angiers or Miln. Been more than a hundred years since demons cracked its walls and got inside. Now it's just another ruin of the old world.

Exploring ruins of the old world was my da's passion. It was how he brought back the fighting wards and ignited the demon war, but before all that, he used to seek old forgotten places out in the naked night before they faded off the maps forever.

Da's journals were the closest thing I had to knowin' him, and I read them over and over. Memorized every word. Means I know a few secrets about Thesa, and one is a way to cross the river without having to answer questions at the main bridge.

The Old Hill Road is a relic that predates even the fort—a wide stone avenue hundreds of years old that ran north along the woodland before turning west to Fort Angiers. The road's fallen into disrepair, cracked and pitted and overgrown in places, but the path remains unmistakable. Olive's brother Jayan used it to sneak his army up north to try and sack Angiers.

That din't end well for them, but there's a fork in the road before it turns west, continuing due north to an ancient stone bridge over the River Angiers. *So thick and sturdy,* Da wrote, *it will still be there a thousand years after I'm dust.* Da crossed it once, just to prove it.

It had better be. This time of year the river will be swollen with spring melt, current enough to wash the lot of us away like a rock demon swatting a fly.

Da followed the road on the northern side as it wound up into the mountains, but he never found anything. *Another ghost road, I expect,* he wrote. A road that just fades out, its purpose forgotten. Like Fort Hill, there's nothing but ruins up there.

Or so we thought.

"WE'RE BEIN' FOLLOWED," I say.

It's been two weeks since we left Hollow, and we ent seen a soul in ten days at least. I can hear the river up ahead, close, but still too far to reach before night falls.

"Followed by who?" Arick asks. "It cannot be the *alagai*. It is daylight still."

I inhale deeply, sifting the smells on the open air. Every once in a while, I catch a hint of movement among the trees to the left of the road, or along the ridge to the right, but they melt away when I turn my full attention their way.

"Nightwolves," I say.

"Corespawn it," Selen spits.

Arick seems less perturbed. "We fight *alagai* in the night, cousin. What have we to fear from wolves?" Rojvah tsks at her brother, but doesn't say anything.

"Nightwolves ent the kind of wolves you read about in fables," I say. "Used to be pretty rare, but they got more common after the demon war. Normal wolves ate carrion from battlefields, and the coreling meat . . . changed them. Made them like me. They run like the wind, and heal quick like a demon. Some of them have even learned to mist."

"Like *gwilji*." It's Arick's turn to spit. "Feeding on the tainted flesh of the *alagai*. Disgusting."

Rojvah's eyes flick to me, and I grind my teeth. She knows, even if Arick don't, that my parents ate demon meat. It's why they had powers others who warded their skin din't. Powers they passed—at least in part—down to me.

Alagai blood, they call me in Krasia, whenever I hiss in the sunlight, or unnerve someone with my senses. Ent far from the truth. Would Rojvah still want to be promised to me if she knew?

Again, Arick shrugs. "Still no worse than demons. If they are so powerful, why haven't they attacked?"

He doesn't get it. "They're nocturnal. Pack hunters. What we've got is a couple scouts following us. Come nightfall, they'll start howling, and their packmates will come streaming from all around to herd us into a bushwhack."

"So we hide," Selen says. "The circles have wards of unsight and confusion. Maybe . . ."

I shake my head. "Ent demons. Wards of unsight ent gonna faze them, and they'll step right over the circles. Nightwolves are smarter than corelings, and they work together. Might be we don't even see 'em until we're surrounded."

I take a deep breath before sharing my real fear. "Or they might be workin' for you know who."

"Said yourself they weren't demons," Selen says.

"Don't quite know what they are," I admit. "But mind demons can control people. Why not animals? What if he's got them out sniffin' for folk wandering through these parts?"

"You sure about this, Dar?" Selen asks. A whiff of hope enters her scent, and I know I have to crush it.

I stare hard into the shadows under the trees to the side of the road, scanning back and forth until . . .

"There." I point.

"Where?" Selen holds up a hand to shield it from the brightly setting sun.

"I do not see anything, cousin," Arick says.

I look to Rojvah, but even she shrugs and shakes her head sadly.

"The you're gonna have to trust me," I tell them. "We're in real trouble."

"So what do we do?" Selen asks.

"Fight," Arick says, even as his sister says, "Flee."

"Bit o' both, I reckon," I say. "Gonna need to crack the reins and hurry for the bridge. River's full to bursting this time of year. I can hear it from here. Might be the wolves'll be too spooked to cross."

"That's a lot to gamble on *might*, Dar," Selen says.

"No, he's right." Arick surprises me. "If we can reach the bridge, funneling them into a narrow crossing is favorable for defense, and will allow us to fall back in safety."

"Unless there's demons on the other side," Selen says.

Rojvah strokes her choker. "Demons, we can handle."

WE DRIVE THE PONIES HARD.

If it was just the horses, we could have crossed the bridge long before night fell and hopefully lost the wolves on the far side. But ponies ent half as fast as coursers, and they got a lot strapped to their backs. I can hear their panting breaths, smell the sores forming under their saddle straps. One of them's got something stuck in her hoof. I can hear it clacking against the road, and the little cry she gives with each step.

Ent nothin' for it but to keep pushin' them. Know what to do for an infected hoof. There's no cure for bein' in a nightwolf's belly.

All the animals stink of fear. They can smell the wolves now, same as me. There are even more than I feared in these parts, and the howling of the scouts has them all come runnin'.

The bridge is in sight just as the last of twilight disappears, and my night eyes take over, seeing the world not with light but by its magic.

This far from the greatwards, magic is everywhere, a glowing fog rising from the ground that clings to everything, highlighting the world. It is reflected in the auras of every living thing, from the animals to the trees to the scrub grass growing in potholes on the road.

Water doesn't conduct magic, but the cold river is full of life, and blazes with kinetic energy. I see it like a black sky teeming with stars and streaks of lightning as it rushes past.

The stone bridge, surrounded by water, is nearly magic-dead as well. My night eyes see it mostly as a silhouette against the water and sky, highlighted only by some clinging slime with a dim glow of life.

The others see it, too, with their warded eyes. But the animals are all but blind now, hearing only the roar of water and smelling the wolves.

There's a last stretch of open ground from the road to the bridge. It's their last chance to surround us, and they have the numbers to do it. I can see them gathering, like some leviathan rising from the depths.

"I'll lighten the load!" I thrust Dusk Runner's reins at Selen. "Run on!"

Selen's lips bunch up to start shouting, but I'm moving too fast. Out of sight before she gets any sound out.

Mam's knife is in my hand and I move among the ponies, lookin' for things I can cast off to get the animals moving faster.

Water's my first choice. It's the heaviest thing we carry, and the easiest to replace with all the mountains in spring melt. Not that we'll have anything to put it in, as I slice open skins and cut the straps holding casks in place, rolling them back in our wake.

Rojvah's giant trunk of clothes? Don't need it. The armor plates that go in my robes? Hate wearing 'em, anyway. Four of us can share a tent. Bedrolls are overrated.

There are wolves on the road now, barking and howling as they dart around or leap over the debris of our cast-off baggage. I'm lightening the load much as I can, but at this rate they're still going to run us down before we can get to the bridge.

I cut open sacks of flour and meal, throwing up a thick cloud in our wake. I can hear wolves choking and blinking, but the cloud don't reach all of 'em. I split a sack of apples and throw it at a group coming in from the side, scattering them as they dodge, lose footing, or stumble into one another's paths.

One makes it through, but I rush in to meet it, turnin' slippery as I do. Not much can hurt me when I'm slippery, but it doesn't make things less scary. Up close the nightwolf, average among its packmates, is huge. Four hundred pounds if it's an ounce, almost half the size of the ponies, all tooth and claw and matted fur.

I keep Mam's knife solid, and hold it out as we slide by each other. The wolf crashes to the ground on its next stride, one foreleg lopped off above the knee.

But then I feel a sting of pain and look down to see a jagged tear in my coat, wet with blood. One of the nightwolf's claws cut me, even while I was slippery. Din't think that was possible for a mortal creature, but nightwolves ent exactly that. Not a deep cut, but this is serious business.

I put on speed to rejoin the group as Arick and Rojvah fall back, shouting curses and lashing the animals with straps. The ponies cry out, but they leap forward, running for their lives. Their pain cuts at me, but I join the others, slapping flanks with the flat of Mam's knife, drawing stinging lines of blood. "Ay, move it!"

My tears are cold in the wind. I wonder if the animals will ever trust me again. Hope we're lucky enough to find out.

I hate myself, but forcing the animals to run seems to work. The path to the bridge is still clear, and the nightwolves aren't pressing their charge. If anything, they're slowing as we get closer to the roaring water.

"Keep going!" I shout. "They're fallin' back!"

As Da's journal said, the bridge is pitted and cracked, but still sturdy. Once my bare feet touch its surface, I can attest to that. I can feel the vibrations in the stone, and know we can cross without fear, if we avoid potholes and the places where the raised lip has broken away. Cold spray fumes endlessly as the river rushes beneath us. I can feel its power thrumming against the stone, and it's as scary as anything I've ever felt. Like when Da touched the Core, no one could survive falling into the River Angiers in spring melt.

I scamper onto Dusk Runner's back and kick ahead, leading the way. It's easy enough to pick a path around the potholes, even in the dark. They're full of stagnant water, brimming with life that illuminates them in wardsight. The bridge is wide enough for four horses to comfortably fit side by side, or two and two in different directions. I keep us close to the center, moving fast as we can up to the height of the span, until there's a clear view of the far side.

And that's when it hits me. I pull up hard, causing Dusk to rear and kick. "It's a bushwhack!"

Everyone tries to stop short, with similar results. The ponies, not understanding, come driving into them. My friends manage to ride off the impact and keep their seats—barely—but more than one of the smaller animals goes down in the tumble, neighing in pain. One tumbles off the bridge, his screams lost in the roar of the current.

No one pays them much mind, eyes fixed ahead. Nightwolves have thick shaggy fur that hides the magic in their auras, like some demons. Makes 'em hard to spot, night or day. But they can't hide their eyes, glowing fierce with magic.

Where's the line? I wonder. How much magic can you carry inside before you become a demon yourself? Is that even how it works? Other creatures fed on the battlefields of the demon war. Carrion birds. Rodents. See 'em sometimes, even back in the Brook. Bigger'n they had a right to be, and dangerous.

A dozen nightwolves wait on the far end of the bridge. There's a howl as they catch sight of us, and the pack leader sets her paws onto the bridge.

I look back, and it's worse'n I thought. The nightwolves that chased us here have already started flowing onto the crossing like a creepin' shadow. They weren't trying to run us down before we got to the bridge, they were herding us onto it. Ent scared of the river at all. They're using the bridge like a spiderweb, and we're the rippin' flies.

"Music?" Even Arick is having second thoughts about fighting our way out, with the enemy on both sides.

I shake my head. "Tried it on a nightwolf den once, back in the Brook. Some sounds they like and some they don't, neither so much they won't eat you."

I take a warded arrow from the quiver on Dusk's saddle, holding the tip between my fingers until I feel the cutting and piercing wards Draw a little of my magic and activate.

I'm a fair shot at things that are standing still, or moving at steady speed. Not so much when something is chargin' in to kill me. But the wolves are still creepin' up like barn cats, and it ent hard to stick an arrow in one.

Nightwolf fur might tangle a normal arrow, but the enchanted head cuts through so easy it punches into the lead wolf and out the other side. With a yelp, she drops to the ground, but the glow doesn't leave her eyes. As one of her packmates licks the wound, the wolf starts twitching, already trying to get back her feet.

"Anything other than a killing shot's just gonna be temporary," I say.

Selen leaves her spear in its harness, taking up a long-handled axe like the one on the Cutter coat of arms. "Da says they can't heal what you chop off."

"Ahead or back?" Rojvah asks. "We cannot stay here."

"Din't come all this way to turn back at the sight of a few wolves," I say. "Got some tricks to play still. We'll charge the center and try to bust through. Lose 'em in the hills on the other side."

I don't mention I have no idea how to do that. Nightwolves are fast as horses, and don't tire as easily. "Might be I can give 'em a scare when we get close. Help us break through."

We get the ponies to their feet and untangle the leads. One has a broken leg, and Arick puts it down with a quick thrust of his spear. He looks at me as if expecting challenge, but what can I say? Anything can't run is gonna get a lot worse.

Then he lashes with his strap, and we charge.

I fire my bow into the press of wolves in the center of the road in front of us. We're moving fast and I'm scared, but they're all bunched together and it's hard to miss. I hear yelps and see wolves stagger, but it's only buyin' us a minute.

Piercing neighs of pain pull my attention from the front. I look back to see three ponies with wolves on them, teeth and claws biting deep. I leap off Dusk and run across the backs of animals until I can cut the lead and let the other ponies run free. Ent much I can do for the last three. They go down quick, and the wolves swarm in to feed. The ponies' cries are blessedly short, but I can hear the rending and tearing of flesh, the squelch and pop of organs, and try not to sick up at the blood smell.

The wolves caught in the feeding frenzy leave off pursuit, but still more nightwolves charge forward to take their place. I have to run full speed to catch back up to Dusk, scrambling back onto the galloping horse. Ponies are scattering now, unbound by the leads. A wolf's jaws close on the leg of one, and it goes down and stumbles right off the bridge, taking the still-biting wolf and one of its fellows with it into the frothing water.

The wolves make short work of the other ponies as our faster horses pull ahead. With most stopping to feed, I can focus in front, trying to lose the sounds of screaming ponies in the thunder of the current below.

The wolves up ahead haven't charged. What's the point, with us comin' right to them? I see them tamping down, ready to pounce when we get in close.

Stole some festival flamework before we left Hollow. Nothin' powerful, but lots of crackers and a few rockets, in case we get separated in the mountains. One string has twenty crackers, all designed to go off one after another. Soon as we're in range I light the fuse with a spark of magic and throw.

The crackers go off with bangs, flashes, and puffs of acrid smoke. Nightwolves jump like puppies and skitter back from the continuing display. They don't clear the way entirely, but there's a weak point. We ride into the gap just as last little roll of paper explodes, and I know we have only seconds before the wolves close back in.

Arick lays about with his spear, wielding the foot-long blade at its tip like a butcher's knife. Opposite him, Selen's axe is a cleaver, choppin' bits off any wolf gets too close. I see feedback magic shock up the weapon hafts, filling them with strength, and charging their weapons and armor.

The alpha, bigger'n the rest, stands right in our path with another giant—probably her mate. I put my head down and kick Dusk's flanks, hoping we can blast by on sheer weight and momentum.

Rojvah gives a piercing cry, holding up a flame demon skull, black-boned and slick like obsidian, no bigger than my fist. I can see glowing wards etched into the surface, and Rojvah's fingers slide over them, revealing some and covering others.

A burst of flame spits out from the skeletal jaws, striking the larger wolf. The blast isn't large, but my eyes can see heat, and this makes my vision go white, if only for a moment.

It's more than enough to ignite the alpha nightwolf's thick black fur, a blaze that has engulfed her almost entirely when I can see again. She howls and crashes into her mate, setting his fur on fire as well. Both of them break, running off the bridge and down toward the water's edge.

Rojvah holds the skull above her head and lets out a gout of flame above us, keeping the nightwolves back in fear as we thunder past.

My relief doesn't last. The remaining wolves collect themselves quickly and move to pursue.

There's a road ahead, leading away from the water and into the mountains, but I can already tell what's up there.

I hear the cries of corelings, drawn by the sounds of our fight.

There's a cracked stone structure on the shore beside the bridge. Maybe an old gatehouse? The roof is broken in and the door long lost to the elements, but the walls are intact. I race Dusk up the steps, thinkin' it might be a place to hide, but we're turned and runnin' before the others try to follow.

It's the nightwolves' den. I can hear the mewling and barking of cubs, smell the older wolves who ent got energy for the hunt. We go in there, the whole pack'll be on us.

Rojvah uses her skull to spray a line of fire across the road behind us, pulling the wolves up short for a moment before they think to cut around it.

"Up here!" I ride up a steep ridge to where there's an outcropping we can put our backs to. The others follow, Rojvah setting two more wolves alight and careening into those around them. She sprays another line of fire across the slope, putting up a brief wall of flames.

And that's it for her flame demon skull. Glowing fiercely a few moments ago, it's gone black now, and crumbles away like a log gone to ash in the fire, but kept in shape until you hit it with the poker.

"It won't last long!" Rojvah says of the flames.

"We can't stay here!" Selen shouts, but I'm not paying her any mind. I've got my pipes in hand, activating the ward that amplifies the sound as I begin to play.

Rojvah takes my meaning, touching her choker and immediately joining me in song.

Arick fumbles at his kamanj case, but then a nightwolf leaps over the lowering flames, launching itself at Selen. She gets her shield up in time, bashing it with her axe, but the weight of the animal pulls her from the saddle.

Arick leaps from his own mount and spears the wolf in the eye, twisting the blade before pulling it free. He stands over Selen as she collects herself, guarding her with spear, shield, and his own body as more of the beasts tamp down to spring over the dying flames.

I want to go to her, too, but I know it won't help. I can still feel the sting where the nightwolf clawed me, and I don't have Arick's reach, strength, or skill with weapons. All I have are my pipes and Rojvah's voice as we send a call out into the night.

Prey.

In moments, we hear demons shrieking in response. A wind demon swoops in, but Rojvah and I have a cloak in place, and its attention slides off like we're all slippery. It sinks long talons into a nightwolf instead, carrying the thrashing beast off with a great snap of its leathern wings.

The rest of the pack scatters from the spot, snouts turning up to look for more. For the moment, the skies are clear, but over the roar of the river, I can hear the footfalls of hill and stone demons tumblin' down the slope like an avalanche.

Nightwolves hear it, too. There's a howl, and they turn like a flock of birds. I wish they'd flee, but most of them make for the den to guard their young. I remember all the mewling and high-pitched little barks. Don't want to get et, but it doesn't feel right, siccing the corelings on anything.

Demons don't need any more encouragement. I drop the insistence from my call and focus on strengthening our musical cloak. The corelings go racing by, oblivious, even as they instinctively avoid us.

I focus on my music as we hustle up the road, tryin' not to hear the sounds as the nightwolves and demons face off. Wolves have the numbers, but corelings are stronger. Honest word I don't know who's gonna come out on top, but there ent gonna be many left to celebrate.

"THINK WE LOST THEM?" Selen asks.

I give a long listen. "Ay. And I don't hear anything bigger'n a badger close by."

"It means little," Arick notes, "if the Father of Demons knows we are coming."

"Might be I was bein' paranoid," I say. "Ent new moon, so Alagai Ka couldn't have been lookin' through the nightwolves' eyes, and the spellsong hid us from the demons. Most of the evidence about us went in the river or the wolves' bellies, and scuffles between corelings and nightwolves been known to happen."

I can tell they ent satisfied, and I don't blame 'em. It's a hopeful spin, but with all our stuff lost and us no closer to even findin' Safehold, hope's in short supply.

We find a dry spot where we can put our backs to a rock face and lay out our circles. Portable warding circles are too precious to keep on pack animals. We each carry one, and can link them to form a circle big enough to all bed down in peace.

Only we ent got any bedding. We all have food in our saddlebags, but it's the sort that keeps a long time, not the sort that tastes good and is easy to chew. We're soaked from river spray, and it's still winter this far north. Cold never much bothered me, and I can dry off just by turning slippery and givin' myself a shake, but everyone else's got the shivers.

"I'll look for firewood," Selen volunteers.

"No," Rojvah says, though she hugs herself against the cold. "We cannot risk being seen tonight."

"Better we risk freezing to death?" Selen asks, and she's got a point. Ent got much more than saddle blankets and the clothes on our backs. "Maybe we can shield the light . . ."

Rojvah shakes her head. "Gather stones. The bigger the better. Make a pile in the center of the circle, and more around the perimeter."

Arick immediately sets to work, and after a moment Selen shrugs and complies, hauling rocks while I try my best to calm and care for the horses.

Arick and Selen make a pile of brick-sized stones in the center of the circle like a firepit, and then lug in bigger ones for the perimeter. A couple are so heavy they have to carry them together.

Rojvah reaches into the *hora* pouch at her waist and produces a slim electrum pen on a thin but sturdy chain. The same kind of pen Erny Paper used to knock a wind demon right out of the sky. I can see the intense glow of magic at its core, kept sealed away by the precious metal and etched wardwork.

"A gift from the master of the Warders' Guild," Rojvah says. "It has a limited well of power stored, but unlike the flame demon skull, this can be refilled."

Rojvah's slender fingers slide across the wards etched on the pen, opening the nib to release a steady stream of power as she traces heat wards in silver light across the stones. The light throbs and the wards dim as the stones heat up like coals, givin' us something to gather round.

She moves around the circle, heating the larger stones as well. I can smell the horses' relief as they gather by the largest rock. They're closer to the wards than I'd like, but they're trained not to step over them.

"Tsst!" Rojvah hisses as she tries to ward the last stone, but the pen has gone dim, its power spent. Camp's warmer now, but a cold draft sneaks in through the gap.

Rojvah moves a slider on the pen, reversing the nib to activate a Draw. Ambient magic starts flowing to the pen, but only slowly—most of it sucked up by the wards on our portable circles. At this rate, it will take more than one night to refill it.

"Nice trick," Selen says, rubbing her hands in front of one of the stones. "Hope you've got a few more up your sleeve?"

"The Damajah saw fit to provide me with considerable *hora* to aid us on our journey," Rojvah says. "Too much to carry on my person. Most of it was in my trunk of clothes."

One of the first things I cut off the baggage train. "Din't go in the river, at least," I volunteer. Dunno why I feel guilty. Trunk was going to get lost one way or another. "Don't reckon we ought to go back for it, though."

"Certainly not," Rojvah agrees. "Beyond that, I have only my *hora* jewelry, and . . ." She rests her hand on the pouch again. "Brother, I need your shield."

Arick fetches his shield, and seein' what she's up to, Selen does the same, angling them to create a wind break. Rojvah's casting cloth is still pristine white, stitched wardwork encouraging the cloth to shed stains like our warded cloaks, even as every other bit of cloth we have is damp and spattered with blood and filth.

Rojvah kneels, and I hear her whisperin' to the dice. Same prayer all the *dama'ting* use. "Everam, giver of light and life, your children seek answers . . ." I wonder if the prayer part really matters, or just the question they add at the end. That's when the dice flash with light, and Rojvah casts them down.

Little *whumps!* of air, too quiet for the others to hear, mark the dice jerking unnaturally out of their spins to form a pattern. Rojvah leans in, her scent a mix that's hard to sort. Cold and scared and battered about like all of us, but hurting a different way, too. She hates the dice. Hates that cloth. Hates the whole life it represents.

But she's doin' it anyway, because it's what's to be done. Wish I was half as brave.

I look at the symbols carved into Rojvah's dice. Wards do the same thing as spellsong. They pull at the ambient magic, Drawing and shaping it to their will. But the squiggles and scrawls never made sense to me the way music does. Magic is shaped by emotion, Mam says. The symbols are imbued with the emotion and belief of both the ones who trace them, and the generations that have gone before.

It's hard for me to put emotions on paper. Different for everyone, ent they? Can't see 'em or smell 'em. Ent got a taste or sound. Gotta be felt.

Learned to draw the basic wards in school, before I started skippin'. Mam made sure of that. I can draw 'em if I need to, and align 'em so the lines connect if I keep them to a circle or something with right angles. But for Rojvah, there's a whole language written on the faces of her dice.

"I do not think the Father of Lies saw us," she says after a time. "His eye is on . . ." She hesitates, reaching out as if stroking the air above the dice. ". . . Shar'Dama Ka."

That gets everyone's attention. "Bloodfather?" I ask.

"There is no other," Rojvah says, but that ent exactly right. There's my da, missing almost sixteen years now. Folk thought he was the Deliverer, too.

The father waits below, Aunt Leesha's dice said, and I wonder again what they really meant.

"If you've got dice," Selen says, "can't we just ask them where Safehold is?"

Rojvah shakes her head. "Every divination affects the currents of magic. If we seek the place directly, the magic will connect us, and give the Father of Evil our exact location."

"Ay, well then," Selen says. "Don't do that."

"Perhaps there is a way." Rojvah takes out Micha's earring and pierces her finger with the pin to draw blood for the dice. She whispers another prayer, seeking its mate, but this time I can smell her frustration even before she speaks. "Nothing."

"Nothing, nothing?" I ask. "Or nothin' that made sense?"

"The dice cannot sense the ring's mate on the currents," Rojvah says. "It could be out of range, destroyed, or shielded in some way."

"Ay, well, let's worry about it tomorrow," I say. "Everyone get some rest. I'm on watch till mornin'."

The hot stones keep everyone from freezin' to death, but not much more than that. Ent enough to dry their clothes, and the cold wind blowing through the hills steals the heat. The magic fades over time, like a fire burning low, and Rojvah makes another pass, draining the magic from her bracelets and anklets to keep our teeth from chatterin'.

Selen and Arick have thick padded coats under their armor. Their body temperatures ent in a danger zone, but Rojvah, shivering on the ground as she clutches a damp blanket around her, is turnin' blue at the edges. I can see the cold seepin' toward her chest.

I glance at Selen, and find her staring right at me as she lies with her head propped on her saddle. Her words are quiet as a puff of breath. "Go, you woodbrain."

I drift over and lie down beside Rojvah, laying the blanket over us both. I don't say anything, and neither does she, but she rolls into me and lets me put my arms around her, willing my own heat into her as much as I can.

After a time, the chill damp of our clothes becomes a warm humidity under the blanket, and her shivers slow. Rojvah drifts off to sleep, as do the others. Her steady heartbeat is a warm comfort, but I can't sleep like the others. Not when a fresh pack of nightwolves, or Creator only knows what else, could be comin' from over the next hill.

CHAPTER 39

DETOUR

INNS AND SMALL VILLAGES have cropped up along the Messenger Road from Hollow to Angiers, but nothing to accommodate a thousand Hollow Soldiers and the two hundred in Rhinebeck's Flamework Corps.

I take us west as soon as we cross the bridge over the Angiers River, avoiding the road entirely to move our forces over undeveloped grasslands, just waking from their winter slumber.

"Where are we going?" Rhiney asks.

"Detour," I say. "Seeing so many soldiers on the march will make folk uneasy. Best we leave everyone in peace."

Rhinebeck looks doubtfully at the thick mud sucking at the horses' hooves and spattering his boots. He doesn't argue, but I know he isn't satisfied.

He's blunter at dinner. Rhiney and I have taken to eating together in my tent, a ritual expected of our rank, but one that reminds me all too much of the meals I shared with Chadan before we went into the Maze. The prince has brought along his personal chef, who somehow manages to deliver meals on the road that rival what was served in the palace.

But where Chadan was serene, reserved, and proper, Rhiney is . . . flamboyant. His stories are like a Jongleur's show, replete with funny voices and pantomime that have me laughing until my cheeks ache from it. Chadan ate with quick, efficient snaps of his sticks, never spilling so much as a grain of couscous. Rhiney eats with more gusto, calling out flavors, insisting I try things, and gnawing bones like a nightwolf in its den. He'll speak at length about the origins of a dish or how the sauce is made.

I would tell Chadan of my life in Hollow, but Rhiney has heard it all, asking after my friends and family. We've corresponded all our lives, and yet for the first time, we are truly getting to know each other.

Tonight I see a different side of him.

"I'm not a fool, Olive," Rhiney says the moment we're alone in my tent. "There's no gain in heading this far west. We're not headed for Hollow, and we're not headed east, to the foothills where your mother disappeared. New moon is tomorrow, and we're making portable circle camp in a field. So again I ask, where are we going?"

He doesn't sound angry. He isn't trying to pick a fight. But he's staring at me with those blue eyes, and I know he won't accept half an answer like I gave in front of the others.

And I don't want to give one. I don't want to be alone anymore. Rhiney has a right to know where we're going. "We're going to Anoch Dahl."

I pause, letting that sink in. Anoch Dahl, the City of Night, is Krasian territory, and Angierians harbor an earned mistrust of Krasians.

But Rhinebeck isn't just anyone. The Krasians are why his grandmother sits the throne; they killed his father and two of his uncles. Rhiney's been raised to take that throne, and Araine isn't the sort of person who would turn her duchy over to a fool. He'll have intelligence on Anoch Dahl, a once massive city, now part military junction and part archaeological dig. Anoch Dahl stands over the Mouth of the Abyss, the entrance to . . .

"The hive," Rhiney swallows hard as he pieces it together. "You're going to the Core to assault the hive."

"I hope it doesn't come to that," I say. "I am going to secure the Spear of Ala."

"The lost fortress in the tales of the Deliverer?" Rhiney asks. "The one full of the demon-blooded?"

"The *alamen fae* are not demon-blooded," I say, perhaps a little too forcefully. After a lifetime of hiding my strength, and seeing folk distance themselves from Darin, who couldn't so easily mask his powers, it's a sensitive topic. The *alamen fae* were Krasian warriors taken prisoner three thousand years ago, raised in the demon hive as livestock.

"Three thousand years," Rhiney says, as if reading my thoughts. "How many generations is that? A hundred fifty? Two hundred? Born, raised, and dying in utter darkness, bathed in the magic of the Core. What would you call them?"

I don't have an answer. "It doesn't matter. The Krasians have lost touch with them, and Mother's prophecy warned of what waits below. I need to get to the fortress and take command."

Rhinebeck looks at me a while, then nods. "And you think you can do that with a thousand Hollow Soldiers, and two hundred of my Flamework Corps? Why didn't you say something sooner? I could have taken ten times as many! Night, if it's that important, why not run a Messenger to Miln? Duke Ragen would send an army of Mountain Spears . . ."

I shake my head and he drifts off. "What do you know of mind demons?"

Rhiney pales a little at that. "I know one of them took my uncle's mind. Forced him to beat his wife and unborn child to death. Would have done for Grandmother, as well, had she not found a way to flee."

He looks at me with wide eyes. "But the Deliverer killed them all . . . didn't he?"

A shrill whistle cuts off my reply. Both of us spring to our feet, rushing for the tent flap.

"What is it?" I demand, looking around for the source of the alarm. I see no threat, but several of Rhiney's men have their weapons pointed to the sky, looking through their distance lenses.

Rhiney takes his own weapon, putting the lens to one eye as he searches the sky.

"Wind demons," he says, passing the weapon to me. "A flight of them."

I lift the weapon and close one eye, looking where Rhinebeck indicates. The lenses are warded, and I can see magic's spectrum through them. Wind demons are not the most powerful of demons, but still their bright auras are easy to spot against the sky unless they find cover in the clouds. There's more than a dozen of them, and I know from experience that they can swoop in and carry a man off in their talons before he even realizes what's happening. Worse, I see the stones they are carrying.

Hollow's greatwards can protect against specific types of bombardment, but even then, the Father of Demons found a weakness for his strike on Solstice. Our portable circles and other defenses are proof against corelings entering the camp, but they will not protect us from mundane attack.

But a dozen wind demons are not a significant threat. I lower the weapon, scanning the horizon, but suddenly Rhinebeck grabs the barrel, lifting it high and spoiling my vantage.

"What—" I begin.

"Never point your weapon at your own troops," Rhiney cuts in. He detaches the distance lens and passes it to me.

"Sorry," I mutter, taking the device. My embarrassment at my own lack of discipline fades a moment later as I spot reaps of field demons approaching rapidly. Farther out, more slow and lumbering, rock demons follow to finish what the lesser demons begin.

"Kill the wind demons!" I shout, remembering the uncanny accuracy of the attack on Solstice. "Now, before they can loose their stones and foil the wards! Gared! Ready the Cutters!"

Rhinebeck gives a signal, and his men open fire, dropping wind demons from the sky long before they are in range of a Hollow crank bow. Most are taken down in the first volley, stones falling short of the mark. The remaining wind demons scatter, performing dizzying maneuvers before launching their stones.

I expect the stones to be aimed at the wards around the soldiers' camp, or perhaps even my tent. Instead, they take out the protection of the circle containing the animals and supply.

Wise. Without animals and supply, the journey to Anoch Dahl would be difficult, if not impossible. We'd need to turn back to Hollow or Angiers, losing precious time. Already I fear we may be too late. Even after we reach the Mouth of the Abyss, the accounts of my father and Renna Bales describe a journey of weeks at least.

But while the demons have an opening, exploiting it is another matter. Spear and shield in hand, I take my place in front of Gared and his Cutters, ready to meet the charging field demons head-on.

We needn't have bothered. Rhinebeck himself puts down the last wind demon, then turns his attention to the demons in the grass. "Turn!" he calls, and the Wooden Soldiers take two choreographed steps to face the horde. "Load!" The corps chamber new ammunition. "Aim!" The rifles go up, and Rhinebeck's eyes narrow as the demons draw closer, moving so quickly I tense, ready to leap in front of the young prince before he's eaten.

"Shoot!" The flamework weapons go off as one, a deafening sound as each coughs a gout of smoke and flame.

Field demons shriek and fall immediately, causing those behind to stumble or leap out of the way.

KA-CHAK! The Angierians work the bolts on their weapons, firing another round into the off-balance foe. And again, a third time.

"Break!" Rhiney calls, and the Flamework Corps break their line in the center, smoothly stepping aside.

"Now!" I cry, and race forward without waiting to see if any follow.

With a roar, my warriors follow, just like in the Maze. We tear into the field demons, putting an end to those twitching on the ground as their magic attempts to heal the bullet wounds, as well as those still on their feet. This is where Gared and his fighters are at their best, trampling over a disoriented foe.

Seeing them come over the horizon, it felt like there was an endless stream of demons, like the storms out in the desert, but either Alagai Ka doesn't have the same numbers to draw upon this close to protected lands, or he is simply testing our defenses. There were barely a hundred field demons, now hacked apart and twitching. The rock demons, advancing a moment before, draw back, vanishing into the darkness.

We return to camp covered in spattered ichor and sweating in the cold night air. Rhiney and his Flamework Corps are still fresh and pristine, but no one can say they didn't pull their weight. I punch a fist to my chest at them, and the men visibly stand taller as they return the salute.

"You continue to impress," I tell Rhiney, and his eyes glitter as he sketches a bow that feels both sincere and teasingly mocking. "But this was only a taste of what we will face in the eternal night below. We need to arm my soldiers, and soon." Thus far, Rhinebeck won't even let the Hollow Soldiers use live rounds in training, and he collects the rifles when drilling is done.

That sobers him. "Each bullet is precious, Olive. A silver moon apiece just in the making, and all the more valuable because we cannot replace them now that we have left Angiers. I won't turn them over to your soldiers until I can be sure they will not be wasted."

I have no argument, so I turn my attention to the camp, making sure the circle of protection around the animals is restored, and additional guards are posted on watch with warded distance lenses.

"I've never seen so many corelings in one place," Rhiney notes.

"This was a weak showing," I say again. "A test to see what your new weapons are capable of, perhaps. The real test will be when we go below."

I KEEP OUR forces on alert through new moon and the dark night that follows. We sleep in shifts, not daring to remove our armor, but Alagai Ka does not strike again.

Did he only want information on Rhinebeck's flamework? If so, I was a fool to show our hand so soon.

Or is this a sign of weakness, at last? There was no strategy to the attack, none of the precision that let a lone wind demon smash my throne from miles above Cutter's Hollow itself. If Alagai Ka was in full control, the demons could have circled safely out of range, dropping boulders on supply carts and warriors alike as they took out the ward circles.

I learned in Chamber of Shadows that *hora* magic dilutes and weakens over distance. Why should the same not apply to the demon king's mental control over his drones? We are far from the mountains where Alagai Ka keeps his Safehold, and I do not think he can leave the queen's side so close to a laying. Perhaps we are at the limit of his reach at last.

Or perhaps he is simply running out of drones. Unlike the sands of Krasia, these lands were swept clean of any lingering corelings by the armies of Angiers and Hollow while I was still in the nursery.

We see little sign of demons over the following nights.

CHAPTER 40

ANOCH DAHL

I'D HOPED TO make better time. The spring grasses are long enough to graze the horses, but not so much they hinder us. But it's melt season, and the carts—particularly Rhiney's, laden with heavy ammunition—keep getting stuck in the mud. Even the horses need to step gingerly in places, so they don't lose footing or break an ankle.

Gradually, the mountains come into view. Not a proper range as in the east where Darin and Selen have gone, these peaks look spat violently from the plains, as if rejected by the Ala itself. They stand like a wound, at their center a gateway to evil my ancestors named the Mouth of the Abyss.

It was into the Mouth that my father and Mr. and Mrs. Bales took a captive Alagai Ka, forcing him to guide them to the hive like a hound. It is a humiliation the Father of Demons has not forgotten, and can only forgive by feeding us all to his new queen.

Even in the foothills, I can see the increased flows of magic after sunset, venting from the Mouth—a direct open-air path boring down into the living Ala, all the way to the demon hive, and from there to the Core itself.

We don't need a map to follow those currents. A few days later we crest a rise and get our first glimpse of the City of Night.

Anoch Dahl sits within an ancient ring of warded obelisks, towering structures that look lain by giants. The stones are pitted with age, but their wards are in fresh repair, much like the city they protect.

Like Desert Spear, Anoch Dahl's outer city is in ruins, a once vast metropolis, shattered by corelings and the weight of untold ages. But in the center is a thriving town, new masonry and buildings melded to the skeletal remains of old. Part garrison and part archaeology dig.

Anoch Dahl is ostensibly controlled by the Shunjin—one of Krasia's larger and more powerful tribes—but Father has invested heavily in its revival, drawing merchants and artisans in search of profits, as well as *dama* scholars of all tribes and their entourages, hoping to unlock something of the history of our people.

Most exciting of all, a significant percentage are said to be *alamen fae,* the descendants of the armies of Kaji, the first Deliverer. The *fae's* ancestors were taken prisoner by the demons thousands of years ago and kept as livestock until they were freed by my father and brought back into our fold.

I have never met an *alamen fae,* though I've read about them in books and seen illustrations. What stands out most in my memory are Mrs. Bales' bedtime stories about them. *Like humans out the corner of your eye,* she used to say, *but look right at 'em and they . . . ent.*

I flex my fingers to relieve their sudden tension as I look down at the encampments in the ruined parts of the city. There lies Hollow's army—a thousand of Lord Commander Gamon's lancers and four thousand foot soldiers billeted directly across from an equivalent Krasian force sent from Everam's Bounty.

Even from a distance, the distrust hanging in the space between them is palpable. Blood debts and grievances run deep on both sides, and now in addition to my own bodyguard I am adding two hundred Angierians with flamework weapons to the mix.

My stomach churns painfully, but I embrace the feeling, giving no sign to the others. What right do I have to command these people to put aside their pain and unify behind me, apart from an accident of birth and a throw of the dice? Is such a union even possible, with Mother and Father lost?

I need a combined force capable of storming the Core itself. What I have is a divided army, with no trust or joint training, and the demon king watching. The journey into the endless night below has yet to begin, and already I feel set up for failure.

I wonder if Darin and Selen are all right. I wonder if they need me—if Mother and Father and Mrs. Bales need me—and I let the Damajah manipulate me into abandoning them. I wonder if all of this is just Inevera taking the chance to rid herself of rivals.

But then I raise my gaze and lay eyes for the first time upon the Mouth of the Abyss.

Even miles away it's visible to the naked eye, like an open wound on the mountainside. With the aid of a distance lens, I can make out its true horror. Like the *alamen fae,* the Mouth of the Abyss is an illustration. A bedtime story, now come to life.

The gateway stands above the city, a road leading to a pair of warded pillars thirty feet high, cut into the living rock. Their arch is carved into the shape of a demon's head, eyes full of malevolence, jagged teeth ready to close upon any foolish enough to enter. Freshly built gates seal the entrance, as strong as any I have ever seen, but no mere gate can hold back what is coming.

I looked into Alagai Ka's mind, even if it was only a glimpse. He's bent on restoring the hive, and that will spell doom for everyone. The moment the new queen hatches, she will send out a mental command that far outstrips the limits of Alagai Ka's power. When that happens, every demon that survived the purge will dematerialize and skate to the hive fast as lighting.

Once the queen and king are ensconced in the hive's greatward with thousands of demons to guard the tunnels, there will be no dislodging them. Whatever Inevera's manipulations, I need to get there before that happens. And to do that, I need to march my forces through that gate, and into darkness.

BRIAR WENT ON ahead to prepare for my arrival, and I see him now, pacing the horse of Anoch Dahl's leader, Dama Daisu of the Shunjin.

The old cleric has brought a personal guard, but they are flanked on one side by Lord Commander Gamon and an equal number of Hollow Lancers, and on the other by Ashia and a matching force of Sharum.

"Dama," I greet the priest, nodding politely while offering no deference, as befits my rank.

The *dama* is not pleased by that, I can tell. I am half *chin* and half woman. His eyes flick up and down, taking in my Tazhan armor—a product of the traitorous Majah tribe—and my lack of turban or headscarf. Behind me, Faseek has changed back into his Majah blacks, and General Gared towers over my shoulder.

But I think it's the warriors to either side, led by Gamon and Ashia, that have the most to do with Daisu slowly climbing down from his horse. A *nie'dama* helps him, quickly laying out a thick carpet over the muddy ground as his master eases down onto his knees and puts his hands on the ground. Normally I don't like such shows of obeisance, but here, in front of troops from all sides, the display is important.

"Prince Olive," he does not acknowledge my Northern title at all, "we are honored by your visit to Anoch Dahl. The . . ." his eyes flick doubtfully to Ashia, ". . . Sharum'ting Ka informs us you mean to enter the Mouth of the Abyss and attempt to restore contact with the Spear of Ala. Of course, if our humble village can aid your mission in any way, it would be our honor."

He does not lower his eyes, but it is always gratifying when a Holy Man is forced to acknowledge objective reality over chauvinist dogma. Ashia commands the *Sharum* no matter what Daisu thinks of women generals. No doubt he fears my *chin* blood will sully the sacred fortress of Kaji as well, but with the forces we have massed, vastly outnumbering his small garrison, there is little he can do to stop it.

We're escorted into the city, and again I am reminded of the Krasian Maze. Inside the protection of the great pillars I feel small and vulnerable, riding through the skeletal remains of the ancient city. In Desert Spear, those ancient remains were fortified into cover, traps, and ambush pockets for *alagai'sharak*. Here, they are a colder reminder that nothing in this world is permanent.

But there is rebirth. The city center bustles with activity. Our coming has stirred the attention of everyone, and *Sharum* are out in force to keep the streets clear for my escort.

I see Shunjin crests on most of the *Sharum* shields, but now that I know how to look, I see the distinctive cut and style of many tribes represented in the crowd. Daisu may lead, but he does not dominate in such a holy place as this.

More interesting are the *alamen fae*. The don't look like the brutish creatures illustrated in books, but despite many of the Core dwellers having taken to wearing Krasian blacks, they stand out even at a glance.

They are larger than most of their surface cousins, even with their backs and shoulders stooped as if they are used to moving around on four limbs as often as two. Their eyes and ears are overlarge, no doubt to compensate for their lack of sight in the eternal night below the surface. Few of them wear shoes, even in the windy cold of the mountains, and their long fingers and toes look designed to probe in darkness.

Are they like me? I wonder. Mother's use of magic changed me in the womb, making me stronger and quicker to heal than normal folk. What is it like for these people, who spent centuries living and dying in a place suffused with raw core magic?

Mother's herald, Kendall Demonsong, spent countless hours with me in front of a mirror, practicing expressions for moments like this. I paint my face with an air of benevolent dignity and meet as many eyes as I can as we ride past.

Inside I am tense as a bowstring. I doubtless have half brothers among the *kai* in Ashia's forces, and perhaps the many *dama* in the city. Asome's warning still hangs over me. There will be a third attempt on my life, and here among the ruins, cut off from my full forces and surrounded by Krasians, I am particularly vulnerable.

Daisu's attitude does not reassure me. The cleric looks like he would smile and bow as he held open the door to a room of full of assassins.

But whatever malice the *dama* might have toward me, I do not see it reflected in the eyes of the citizens of Anoch Dahl, or the *Sharum* keeping order. I see fear, and hope. The fallen waystations on the road to the Spear of Ala might seem a distant problem in Hollow or Everam's Bounty, but for those who guard the Mouth of the Abyss, they are very real. Krasians are taught to put faith in great warriors, and in my Tazhan armor atop an enormous mustang with eleven thousand spears at my back, I don't need lessons from Kendall to project that.

None of the permanent structures befit my rank, so Daisu escorts us to a richly appointed pavilion for me to meet with my commanders. His smile and bow at the entrance to the tent flap is so like my daydream from moments earlier that my hand itches to grasp my *hanzhar.*

There are no assassins within. At least, none who plan to strike immediately.

Three *dama'ting* await within, led by a woman in white with a black headscarf and veil. Northerners might find that an effective disguise, but I know at a glance who it is, and the sight—as perhaps intended—reinforces my sense of Inevera's sincerity. It is Amanvah, the Damajah's eldest daughter, Rojvah's mother, and *Damaji'ting* of the Kaji—Krasia's most populous tribe. Amanvah is my half sister, who swore a blood oath to Mother that she would protect me, always.

If I cannot trust her, can I trust anyone?

And yet . . .

Two of my half brothers have already tried to kill me. I claimed to be a sister to the *dama'ting,* and my father is Kaji. If Amanvah were to die, I would have as much of a blood claim to her title as any save Rojvah, whose chances of survival are not much greater than mine.

That isn't enough to supplant her, of course. Privately, *dama'ting* follow who the dice chooses, regardless of blood, but outsiders do not know that. And if the Krasians really are worried I may try for the Skull Throne, Amanvah might well prefer one of our other brothers over me.

My fears are not alleviated when the rest of my commanders file in and the tent flap closes. Ashia produces a thick bag of black velvet, like a *dama'ting hora* pouch, and my heart sinks as she reaches in and pulls out Inevera's replica of the Crown of Kaji.

Natural electrum, a rare alloy of silver and gold, is often mistaken for other metals, but after years in the Chamber of Shadows, I have come to recognize it on sight. Just the base elements of the crown could feed whole towns for years.

I know the lore of the Crown of Kaji, and I do not expect Inevera scrimped for the internal materials, either. Each point will have a mind demon horn to power its wards, and the gems to focus that power, cut from those in the central keyward of the Spear of Ala, giving me control over the *csar's* formidable greatward.

At least, in theory.

But here, that is the least of my concerns. Greater is my fear of what it will mean if I don it before the assembled *Sharum*. I might as well declare myself Father's heir here and now.

More frightening still is the milky white stone on the strap beneath the crown. I learned a harsh lesson about accepting jewelry with Krasian blood locks in Desert Spear, and it is not one I wish to repeat. Who knows what magics Inevera might have worked into the crown, to bind me to her will.

"No," I say reflexively, before Ashia has a chance to present the crown to me.

"Sister," Amanvah says quietly, "you must."

I shake my head. "Not here. Not now. I will put it on when we reach the Spear, if I must."

"The *Sharum* may not follow you into the night below without it," Ashia warns.

I spit in the Krasian fashion, all sound and no moisture. "They are *Sharum*, cousin. I offer them death on *alagai* talons in defense of the Ala itself. If they refuse because I will not wear a crown, then they should give up the black."

Gorvan seconds my words with a punch to the chest. "Crown or no, I will follow Prince Olive to the Core itself."

"You do my heart glad, brother," I say, "because our mission is nothing less."

I look back to Ashia. "Do your warriors lack the fighting spirit of the Majah?"

"Of course not." Ashia frowns.

Amanvah steps close, her words a whisper meant for my ears alone. "You are being foolish, sister," she advises quietly. "The crown is irreplaceable, and you will need its power to face the challenges below."

"Perhaps," I say. "But I have not earned it, and wearing it here is an open declaration of intentions I do not have. Will the *Sharum* follow me if I don it, or will they revolt, and doom our mission before it begins?"

Neither my sister nor my cousin has an answer for that, but Ashia thrusts the crown back out of sight, and my tension eases just a little.

When we have refreshed ourselves, the true council begins, with leaders of all factions present as we discuss our plans.

I made the decision not to bring Jongleurs on this mission. Hary is too old and frail to come, and better back in Hollow where he can spin tales of my disappearance into something positive. But my plans require teams of Warders, and no army dares march without Herb Gatherers. I notice Gatherer Roni—an old apprentice of Mother's—and approach her.

"Your Grace." Roni's curtsy is quick and smooth. She wears the wide divided skirts Hollow women favor for riding and fighting. Roni is young, strong, and fit, decorated from the war, when she was no older than I am now. Her reputation as a surgeon in the university hospit is so great even Favah speaks of her with respect, but it's her festival flamework I always loved.

I nod in return. "Gatherer Roni. As the Krasians say, your glory is boundless for leaving the safety of the university to take this journey with us."

"The honor is mine, Your Grace," Roni says. "I will speak for the Gatherers, and take responsibility for the chemics we carry into the dark."

I nod. "Who speaks for the Warders?"

Roni's eyes widen. "You don't know?"

"The master of the Warders' Guild," a familiar voice says from behind me, before I have time to process Roni's surprise.

I whirl around. "Grandda?!" After a day of holding a benevolent mask on my face, I'm unprepared to contain my surprise as my aged grandfather enters the tent. "What are you doing here?"

"Nice to see you too, Olive." Grandda's voice is as warm and kind as ever, but his eyes catch me, and I feel a compulsion to sit up straight and eat my vegetables.

Grandda is in his seventies. Magic use has preserved him somewhat, but he still looks older and more frail than Hary Roller.

"Don't shake your head at me," he says, still in that light tone. I hadn't even realized I was doing it. "You can stitch needlework wards well as anyone, Olive, but you don't have the craft for this. You need a Warder who knows their business."

"Ay," I agree. "But I also need one who can march and climb and fight . . ."

Erny waves the thought away. "We're bringing carts for wardposts, materials, and tools. I don't need to march."

Grandda complains his back hurts when he sleeps on a feathered mattress. Does he have any idea what weeks in jostling carts will do to him?

"As for the rest . . ." Erny pointedly opens his coat and taps his breast pocket, where his stylus hangs on an electrum chain like a pocket watch. I remember the calm, measured way he slapped the wind demon out of the air on Solstice, and remind myself not to underestimate him.

"Got a point." Gared steps over. "This ent the place . . ."

Erny raises a finger at him, and the general's mouth shuts mid-sentence. "I don't think you're in any position to lecture me about where I belong, Gared Cutter."

Gared blinks, and his cheeks color. "Ay. Sorry, sir."

"Besides." Erny fixes me with that kind look I remember so well. "What kind of grandda would I be, if I let you come down here alone?"

My throat tightens, and I embrace him. "Elona must be furious."

Erny chuckles. "It was her idea, even if she didn't expect me to actually do it."

When we draw back, I notice Briar has entered the tent with two *alamen fae*—one larger and thicker with muscle than even Gared, the other a female elder who looks older than Favah, but still needs to stoop to make eye contact with Briar. I try not to stare as Briar brings them over.

"Your Grace, I am honored to introduce you to Elder Kriva and her great-grandson Jaavi."

The hairy old woman narrows her wrinkled eyes, regarding me. She smells like a Gatherer, pockets stuffed with herbs and cures. She carries a gnarled staff carved with wards and hung with bottles, but it seems more a symbol of office than an aid to her strong steps.

Her great-grandson looks as old as Gared. I wonder how many winters this woman carries. Ninety? Two hundred? Either is possible, for one who spent most of her life bathed in the magic below the surface of

Ala. I wish it was night so I could read her aura, but we hold our council while the sun is still in the sky, for secrecy.

"You are the son of Erram?" the old *fae* asks bluntly. Her Krasian is heavily accented, but easily understood.

I hesitate. *Erram*. The name the *alamen fae* gave my father, believing, like many in Krasia, that he is Everam on Ala. The Deliverer.

I have my doubts Everam exists at all, and I am certainly not his son. "Ahmann Jardir is my father."

I don't expect the parsing of words to draw attention, but she cocks her head at me, eyes flicking up and down. She sniffs the air like Darin Bales. "You are *doveen*."

Jaavi looks at his mother sharply, then at me.

"What is *doveen*?" I ask.

Kriva frowns. "I do not know the word in your language. A son, and daughter, too."

"Intersex," I say in Thesan.

The old woman grunts, nodding. "Powerful. A good omen."

"There are . . ." I hesitate. "Other . . . *doveen* among the *alamen fae*?"

"Some." Almost too quick to see, her wrinkled eyelid winks at me.

Before I can say more, Dama Daisu clears his throat, shuffling a sheaf of papers as he waits on our attention to give his presentation.

"Shar'Dama Ka rebuilt the roads to the Spear of Ala," Daisu begins. "Wide and tall enough at even the narrowest points for four horses to ride comfortably abreast."

That's enough to set Mother's voice in my head, lecturing on supply lines and baggage trains. The vast majority of our force will be infantry, but we'll need some cavalry to properly defend the *csar,* presuming it still stands, not to mention pack animals for supply and ammunition carts. If the path forces us to leave it all behind and proceed on foot I will, but it's a last resort.

"We cut new paths where the *alagai* had caused collapses," Daisu goes on, "drained water from flooded tunnels, rebuilt bridges, and kept the predators of the abyss at bay. Seven *csars,* one for each pillar of heaven, were built evenly along the road. The Evejah says it took Kaji's army three times seven days to reach the Spear of Ala from Anoch Dahl. For a time, it was the same for us."

He pauses. "Then one by one, Nie reclaimed the waystations. We lost contact first with the great fortress, and then the smaller *csars* in turn. Any we sent to investigate, be they *dal'Sharum* or Watcher or *ala-men fae,* did not return."

I suppress a chill of fear. I remember going into the demon's lair out in the desert. It is one thing to die on *alagai* talons. It is another to die alone in the dark, where your body will never be found.

"The final *csar* was lost," Daisu says, "when a powerful group of warded tunnel supports suddenly failed, caving in the passage."

"So you do not know the final fate of any of the *csars*?" I ask.

"We do not," Daisu admits. "Shar'Dama Ka made sure the *csars* were powerfully warded and well supplied, with seasoned warriors at the walls. We pray they still fight, but if Nie is truly rising again, as the *Damaji'ting* says . . ." He shrugs. ". . . *inevera*."

"Have our sisters been able to divine anything more?" I search Amanvah's face as I refer to the *dama'ting* as *our sisters,* but there is no break in her serenity. I am flinching at shadows.

My sister shakes her head. "The resonance stones in our listening devices have gone dead, and the dice have been . . ." Her eyes flick around the room. "Unreliable."

I can tell the admission pains her from Daisu's rueful smile. The news is grim, but *dama'ting* have a long history of bullying the *dama* with their prophecies and knowledge of the future. It is not often that one of them admits fallibility in her Sight.

"Unreliable how?" I ask.

Amanvah shrugs. "The flows of magic increase in power the deeper one delves into the Ala. Perhaps that is why the dice show too many divergences to glean answers."

"What about the closest *csars*?" I ask. "Where the flows are weakest."

"*Onvaria,*" Amanvah says. Not a word for those uninitiated to the Chamber of Shadows, *onvaria* describes the metaphysical state of balance between life and death, material and void, from which all divergences flow. The *csars* are both dead and alive until experience reveals their fate.

I take a moment to digest that.

"Our engineers believe the cave-in is a minor problem," Gamon notes, when the silence draws on too long. He nods to Roni. "The Gatherers believe we have sufficient flamework to blast through in no more than a week, while keeping some in reserve for the journey."

Another week lost. We left Hollow after Equinox, with thirteen weeks until Solstice, and the queen's hatching. Now we have less than ten remaining, not counting a week of blasting with thundersticks. Under ideal circumstances, it will still be a minimum of three weeks from there to the Spear of Ala, and Creator only knows how much longer to the hive itself.

And circumstances are never ideal.

"Have the dice revealed anything that may aid our planning?" I ask Amanvah carefully.

"Fragments, only," Amanvah admits. "Pairings of symbols I have never seen before. Warriors of decay. Soul drinkers. *Kai'alagai*. And the hand of Alagai Ka."

There are shudders at the words. And why not? *Soul drinker* is enough to give even the bravest Sharum pause, and the Father of Demons is quite a bit worse. But it is the pairing in the middle that draws my attention. "*Kai'alagai?*"

"A caste we have not seen before, I think," Amanvah says.

"Or one that did not exist," I say. In the desert, the *alagai* evolved, it was said, and we could see it in their tactics. Too wise for sand and clay demons, even when the moon was full and Alagai Ka was unable to control them directly. Without mimics to act as his lieutenants, perhaps the Father of Demons is imparting some new intelligence on those who remain.

"We have extensive maps." Daisu bows, presenting me with some papers Faseek takes on my behalf. "But we do not know if the enemy has . . . altered them further."

Kriva steps forward. "Jaavi knows way." The old *alamen fae's* voice is as rough as her wrinkled skin. "And I will go." Her accent is thick, sentences clipped short, but there is authority in her voice.

"Just you two?" I ask in surprise. "We need . . ."

"Two." The woman thumps her staff with finality. "We have lost too many. When he led us to the surface, Erram promised we would never be forced to return. Erram cannot be forsworn."

At least, not without being replaced. Perhaps if I had accepted the crown, I might command the *fae* to obedience, but have I any right to? These people suffered for thousands of years as little more than livestock for the demon hive. Who am I, to order them back down into the dark?

"I, too, know the way," Briar notes. "And perhaps Dama Daisu can provide a few *Sharum* who have made the journey, as well."

My eyes flick to Daisu, who looks less than pleased at the volunteering of his own warriors, but he bows. "Of course."

I return my attention to Kriva, with a bow of respect. "Thank you, honored elder."

I find myself pleased she will be joining us, but my stomach churns. If those who know the night below best are refusing to risk a return, what chance do the rest of us have?

GAMON'S ESTIMATE OF a week proves conservative. It only takes five days of blasting and hauling to clear a path through the blockage. Five days of unease, listening to explosions echo from the Mouth of the Abyss like it is roaring its hatred upon us.

Everyone is on edge by the time we assemble before the Mouth of the Abyss the morning of the sixth day. Behind me in their legions comes a combined force the likes of which has never been seen. More than eleven thousand Krasians and Thesans—counting Rhiney's corps and my personal escort—prepared to march on the Core itself. Unified in purpose at least, if not with each other. Will the dangers below strengthen their bonds, or will they tear us even further apart?

I stare at the yawning Mouth, its great gates swung wide to admit my army. The midmorning sun shines directly on the entrance, but it penetrates only weakly, swallowed by the blackness within.

It reminds me of our march into the demon greatward in Desert Spear, and the pain and loss that decision brought. Micha dead. Chadan dead. Iraven dead. Arick broken. So many of our spear brothers lost.

What will it cost, this time?

There is no need for me to ride in first. I could send a few thousand foot soldiers to march in first and ensure the path is secure. It is what any wise leader would do. But if I wish to lead, I cannot ask of others what I am not willing to do myself.

"There is no courage without fear," Ashia says, but I am not sure if she is speaking to me, or herself.

Gared grunts. "Da used to say, *Yur scared of somethin', put your head down and run right at it. Sometimes it's scared of you, too.*"

Rhinebeck blows out a breath. "Mum used to say, *Get down from there! It's too dangerous!*"

We all laugh at that, but it doesn't reach the eyes. Like mine, Rhiney's face is a Jongleur's mask, but his hands are shaking as he grips his reins.

Between my thighs, my horse feels no less tense than I am. As we all are. Rather than dwell on it, I give him a kick, riding through the great gates and into darkness.

CHAPTER 41

THE WEB

"ADMIT IT, DARIN," Selen says. "We're lost."

"Lost is when you can't get back to where you started," I say.

"Ay, sunny," Selen snaps. "How's that get us any closer to where we're going?"

She's right, of course. I just don't want to admit it. So much of this whole plan hinges on me somehow sniffin' out Safehold the way I sniff out everything else.

But finding a city that's been hidden in a mountain range for hundreds of years ent the same as tracking Olive when she was kidnapped. Had the spoor, then. Only so many places they could run.

And we still din't catch them in the end.

It's been weeks of wandering through the mountains. Hard, punishing terrain, still cold even though it's full spring by now in Hollow. There's graze for the horses and sometimes I can track a critter or some eggs we can cook up. Rojvah magics up hot couscous that takes the hunger away, but we're all looking thinner. Air's thinner, too. Makes it hard to catch a breath, and harder still to catch a faint scent . . . if I even knew what I was smelling for.

We find ruins here and there. A broken bridge, a bit of archway or pillar. Nothing that's been used in centuries. Nothing that points the way to anything else. Any other time, I'd love to just wander and explore, but we got business to attend.

Mountains are full of predators. Not just nightwolves and demons. Some have a bit of magic from feeding on demon. Others got there naturally, culled by the corelings until only the toughest were left. Panthers quick and strong enough to tear the face off a hill demon with a swipe of their claws. Bears with the weight and muscle to shove a rock demon off a ledge.

Hard to kill a demon that way, but all it takes is licking a little ichor off their claws and they start to become somethin' unnatural. Like me.

Been able to keep us out of their way more often than not. The rest of the time, Selen and Arick have shown them the spear. The animals we drive off, or run from. The demons we charm with spellsong and kill, leaving them to feed the other predators in hope our passage remains unnoticed.

I'm always too spooked to be much use in a fight, and Rojvah can't afford to waste even a bit of the magic she's got left. The loss of most of her *hora* hit hard. She's got a good mask on most of the time, but I learned long ago that my eyes don't tell me near as much about a body as my ears and nose. Rojvah's used to luxury. Attention. Influence. She's tired and hungry and dirty and scared for maybe the first time in her life.

But she'll be corespawned before she admits, even to herself, that she doubts me.

Sometimes my senses tell me more than I want to know. Arick's as frustrated as Selen, though like his sister, he ent complained.

"We're getting closer. Gotta be." Do I say the words because I believe them to be true, or because I need them to?

"Why?" Selen demands, and I can feel everyone's eyes on me, waitin' on an answer.

"'Cause every day that goes by, there's less places we ent looked!" I snap. Selen blinks and pulls back a bit at that, but I know if I don't keep the pressure on, she'll come right back in, and harder.

"Ent got any answers for you, Selen Cutter," I say. "Don't even know what it is I'm lookin' for, so you'll excuse me if I ent found it yet. Knew before we started this wasn't gonna be easy."

I turn, briefly meeting Arick's and Rojvah's eyes. "Ent forcin' anyone to be here. Want to turn back, go right ahead. I ent goin' home until I find my mam."

That takes the fight out of everyone.

"No one's saying that, Dar." Selen's voice is soft, but firm. "But we're in this together, and we've got a right to talk about it."

"Ay, all right. Let's talk." I pull out the map tube and find a place out of the wind to open it. "Here's where Aunt Leesha's dice said to look." I put my thumb down on the parchment. "Might not look like much, but that's this whole cluster of mountains. Hundreds of square miles. Ent many noses better'n mine, but even I can't smell that far."

"Night, Darin!" Selen says. "When you said sniff, we all thought it was a figure of speech. Got to be more you can do than just put your nose to the wind."

"I've cast the *alagai hora* every night, Selen vah Gared," Rojvah says. "There is still no sign of the earring."

"Not talking about that." Selen whisks a hand my way. "Talking about him."

"Got ears like a bat, Sel," I say, "but even I can't hear what's over the next mountain."

"What about your night eyes?" Arick asks. "Is that not how you followed us through Alagai Ka's greatward?"

"Ay, that's right," Selen agrees. "Said you could find the demon just by looking at the way the magic blew, or whatever."

"Ay, but I can't just . . ." I trail off. Can't I? Ent like I've tried.

I hand the map to Arick and take out my pipes. Everyone starts calling after me as I dash to the edge of the camp's warding circle, but my thoughts are racing, and they're easy to tune out as I search for the best vantage.

I play a little ditty on my pipes to keep the corelings away as I cross the wards and hurry to a tall tree. I scamper up quick as a squirrel, poking my head from the highest boughs. We're halfway up a mountainside, and the view is somethin' else. Any other time, I'd have liked to just play my pipes and enjoy the scenery, but Selen's given me an idea.

Maybe the demon's wards around Safehold are like the wards of silence on the Damajah's guards. Even if we can't sense what's there, maybe we can find what ent.

I find a comfortable perch and close my eyes, breathing like Mam taught me for when I get too activated. Heart's beating quick, muscles clenched. I want to flap my hands or rub them together—anything to get the pent-up energy out—but Mam's words come to me on the chill night air. *You control your body, Darin, not the other way round.*

So I relax instead, letting my hands rest comfortably in my lap as I breathe and breathe till my body calms.

Then I lift my head and look at the world with my night eyes.

This time I ignore the landscape, focusing instead on the flows of ambient magic drifting over the mountains and valleys.

Magic is constantly drifting up from the Core by little natural vents that occur almost everywhere on undeveloped land. Sunlight burns it away during the day, but at night it pools and drifts like a low fog, glowing faintly with power.

I let my eyes drift over the flows, trying to find some sense or pattern to them. Magic is drawn to life, particularly emotion, but there ent much of the latter out here. Just millions of trees shaping the currents. Like clouds, some of them move quick, and others so slow you need to stare a good while to notice which way they're going.

Alagai Ka ent stupid. Olive says Safehold's built on a powerful greatward, but he wouldn't be so obvious as to let the glow of the greatward's power be a beacon folk can follow to his hideout.

But the demon is greedy. All this ambient magic, just rolling uselessly along the hills, is too tempting. And he certainly ent going to let any of the magic he's already gathered drift off.

And that's when I see it. A gentle tug on the magic, drawing the flows toward a gap between two mountains. I look around, and see it happening from almost every direction. It seems natural at a glance, but I can't think of any reason for it all to be drifting to that one way if there ent something there.

I climb back down and return to the camp.

"What in the core was that all about?" Selen asks.

"It is dangerous to leave the wards unaccompanied, Intended," Rojvah notes.

I look to Arick, waiting for his two klats, but he only stands with his arms crossed, smelling confident. He trusts me, and knows I've found something.

"You were right," I tell Selen. "We're going the wrong way."

"You sure about this, Dar?" Selen's voice is low this time, meant just for me. "Ent looking to pick a fight, it's just . . ."

Can't blame her for being uneasy. Everyone other than me is. We're back on my schedule—traveling at night to follow the flows, and sleepin' through the days. Sight wards let the others see in the dark, but wardsight spooks the horses, and they pick their path carefully, following their riders' direction more than their own senses.

Our wards of unsight are usually enough to keep demons from noticing us, but we ent takin' chances. Arick, Rojvah, and I take it in turns to cast a protective cloak of music over our small party. Demons are more numerous than they should be, this far from anythin'.

Still, we been at it a week, with nothin' to show for it.

"Not like followin' a scent," I say, "where I can tell how old the trail is, or where the quarry slept and made its necessaries. This is more like followin' a river, because you know folk like to build towns close to fresh water."

"So even if we're going the right way, you have no idea if we're getting close," Selen says.

"We're gettin' close," I assure her.

"How can you know?" she asks.

"'Cause these hills are crawling with demons," I say, "and I ent scented a bear or a nightwolf in days."

I lift a finger, pointing. "And the flows are moving faster."

Selen hasn't had my practice with night eyes, but even the sight wards on her helm are enough to follow the drift of the ambient magic. When we started it was so slow I didn't even notice until Selen made me think. Now it feels like we're in a whirlpool heading for the tub drain.

GOT THE FULL trio playing, now. Can't throw a rock in these parts without hittin' a demon, but we have them caught in our spell. Selen rides with her shield slung on her shoulder, ready to drop onto her arm, and her spear in hand.

Ent necessary. Countless hours of practice have brought Rojvah, Arick, and me to a harmony I din't know existed. Like the three of us are talkin' without ever sayin' a word, following and trusting one another's instincts. The ambient magic around us is quick to respond, forming a cloak around us the corelings can't penetrate. The ones in our path step aside, thinking it's their own decision, never knowing why.

Growin' up, everyone thought my da killed all the corelings, or as good as. That his . . . suicide in the Core paved the way for a new future.

"Deliverer swept all the demons away like the Creator's hand!" folk like to say, but it ent exactly true. Mam and Aunt Leesha think he just reached out to the Free Cities to keep them safe. Demons were swarming the gates by then, and when Da gave his life, I expect the explosion of magic that burned them away did look like the Creator's hand.

Reckon it must've hurt like nothing ever has. Not just his body, his very aura, bursting like a popping log in the fireplace. Giving up his life. His wife. His son.

Maybe it's just as well. Don't expect he'd be too proud of the result.

Arick seems to sense my thoughts drifting, and puts an extra thrum in his next stroke of the kamanj strings to bring me back to myself. Too many demons about to start getting distracted.

What Da did was dramatic. Paintings of it all over Thesa. But it didn't kill anything close to *all* the demons. There're thousands out here in the mountains. I can sense them all around us.

Corelings tend to come in two types. Wanderers and Regulars. Wanderers don't like to sit still. They'll haunt an area with good huntin', but unless there's prey right in front of them, any ruckus will draw their attention, and they'll wander off to have a look.

Regulars find a spot they like and just keep rising there, lyin' in wait, until something to eat comes along. There's lots of old ruins in the mountains, the remains of towns and villages the corelings likely destroyed hundreds of years ago after the Return. The Regulars must've kept on hidin' in the same spots all that time, waiting for dinner to come back.

And now it has.

Corelings seem just as caught in the strange flows of magic as us. They patrol the currents like guards on a walltop. Our music nudges them out of our path, but we can't risk sending them running. If I'm right, these currents flow right to Alagai Ka himself, and I expect he's readin' them like a book. Can't risk anything that draws too much notice.

The drift takes us deep into the mountains where even the low points are high enough for air and vegetation to thin. Snow still tops some trees, and the peaks are covered in it. All four of us sleep in a huddle under the blankets now, any awkwardness lost in the need for warmth.

The road we're on is nearly invisible, but now that I know where to look, I see hints of it jutting from the dirt and scrub, bits of crete and masonry that likely spanned all the way to Angiers, once upon a time.

But then the road, and the flows, take us to a sheer cliff face, formed where two mountains smashed together in some violent event long ago. Doubt the others could climb it without ropes, and it would mean leaving the horses. Don't think that would end well for them with so many demons around, warded barding or no.

"We'll have to go around," Selen says.

I can't talk while playing my pipes, which is just as well, 'cause I don't have an answer. Selen's right, but I don't understand why. The magic doesn't go around. I can see it just flowing into the stone, even though that's impossible. And what's that noise, like distant thunder?

I pull up, adding power and rising volume to my pipes. Arick and Rojvah follow without question, and as my eyes flick to Rojvah, she knows what I need without havin' to say anything. She touches her choker, lifting her voice until it echoes from the peaks.

I realize I'm staring. Even here, when we ent had a good-night kiss in weeks, just lookin' at her too long puts my head in a spin.

I close my eyes and turn my attention back up front, listening carefully for the echo of her voice against the cliff.

I ease my playing, and Rojvah dials her choker back down. I lead us in the other direction, lower and lower until our song barely shields us from notice. In the relative quiet I can filter it out, searching for that distant thunder. It's beneath us, something I feel as much as hear.

Fault lines, books of the old world call 'em. Great plates of stone that separate the surface world from the molten Core, still grinding against one another, thousands of years after spawning these mountains.

Yet even that sound and vibration does not echo as it should. I can see the cliff at the end of the road with my own eyes, but the rest of my senses are telling me part of it ent there. I give Dusk Runner a kick, heading right for the gap.

"Darin!" Selen's voice is a harsh whisper. "What are you . . ." Her voice trails off as I ride right into the wall and keep on going, enveloped by the illusion. Everything goes black for a bit, and then it's a web of magic too complex for me to understand.

Fear grips me. This is Alagai Ka's web I've just stumbled into like a wood-brained fool. For a moment I think the wardnet will kill me, or react to my presence in some way. A shock, or a barrier, like the circles we use to keep the corelings out.

But I keep playing my pipes, and the magic seems to flow around me like I'm slippery. A moment later things go black again before I come out the other side, finding a narrow pass, about as wide as the old road. I turn around, once more seeing sheer rock.

I turn back, reaching out with my senses along the path ahead, but things have changed, this side of the net. The breeze blowing over me is warm and fresh and doesn't smell like coreling at all.

"Darin Bales!" Selen shouts.

"It's a magic trick!" I call as loud as I dare. "Keep playing and just ride right through!"

"Corespawn it, Darin," I hear Selen mutter, but Rojvah's voice and Arick's kamanj draw closer, and then the three of them slip out of the stone like ghosts.

Arick looks back at the rock face. "Do you suppose that's what it's like for the demons, when we charm them into thinking we're not there?"

It isn't quite the same, but it's not all that different, and that scares me. Wonder what we're riding into as we press through the narrowest part of the pass, headin' down, down, into a little sliver of a valley, like a wound between mountains that hasn't had time to heal.

A mimic demon hungers beneath a city in an eastern mountain valley, Aunt Leesha's dice told us, almost a year ago.

This is the problem with dice. Can't rippin' understand them even when they're right, and there's no way to know when they are and when they ent.

But this has got to be the place. Reckon that pass is hard to spot even in the day, and we still can't see what lies below. Magic rises from the Core in gaps and natural paths on its way upward. Here, where the plates grind against one another not far below, there must be vast amounts of magic venting to the surface.

But where is that power? All the magic in the area is being sucked back down instead.

The demon hive was a massive three-dimensional greatward made of tunnels, not unlike what we saw Alagai Ka build beneath Desert Spear. A mind demon tried to build one right under Tibbet's Brook, until my aunt Selia put a stop to it.

Mam told me Alagai Ka called the Free Cities breeding grounds. Her imitation of the demon's laugh used to scare the piss out of me.

Reckon if I was a demon that din't want to be found, I'd build one of those greatwards up in the mountains where there's a big magic vent, and hide my breeding ground where no one would think to look.

No watchtowers, guards, or signs anyone's been here recently at all, but the dice, and my gut, say there's people down below. A larder for the demon king and his expecting queen. But what will the folk in the larder be like? Will they be like the *alamen fae,* kept so long as livestock they forgot how to be human?

The path widens, but still it goes steadily down. I signal the others, and we move off the road to a spot sheltered a bit by jutting stone. It's warmer still down here, and there's a crop of spring grass for the horses to chew as we wait for sunrise.

"Should we set up the circles?" Selen asks.

I stop playing and let my pipes hang from my belt. "Can't hurt, but if there's any demons this side of that net, I can't sense them."

Arick and Rojvah tentatively cease playing and help set up the circles. "Perhaps that wardnet was not demon-made," Rojvah ventures. "Perhaps there are people here."

"Ay, maybe," I say. "Reckon we should wait for sunrise to go have a look."

Rojvah nods, but she takes out her casting cloth, Micha's earring, and the dice. This time, when she casts the bones, she gives a gasp, turning to look down the path ahead.

"What is it?" Selen asks.

"The earring's mate," Rojvah points, "is down there. I'm sure of it."

"Could be the wardnet we just passed was blocking the signal," I say. "Can you . . ." I shrug, "ring it, or whatever?"

Rojvah shakes her head. "Not without boosting its power more than I dare, if we wish to remain unseen. Even at its normal power, there is risk, if it is not in Kendall's possession."

"The jewel could be riding in a demon's belly," Arick notes.

"Or in a pile of treasure Alagai Ka sleeps on at night," Selen says.

"Someone could have taken it from her," I say. "Even if there's people down there, we've no reason to expect they're friendly."

"Ay," Selen agrees. "That's why we should wait here a bit while you . . ." She waggles her fingers.

"While I what?" I ask.

"While you go be Darin," Selen says. "Skulk. Turn the color of paint. Listen in and learn secrets."

I scowl. "I don't do that."

Everyone laughs. "Of course you do, cousin," Arick says.

I blow out a breath, knowing they're right, but scared to go on alone. But that's my problem, ent it?

"Give me the day," I say. "I'll come back at nightfall."

Then, before I can talk myself out of it, I set off at a run.

CHAPTER 42

SKULKING

Got to admit Selen was right. Been so used to keepin' with the group, I've forgotten how much they hold me back. Might be like other folk when the sun is on me, but here in the dark I'm as fast as I want to be, and can jump and climb like a squirrel.

Got my warded cloak and pipes, but I don't need them to move unseen, even if someone's lookin' with night eyes. Plenty of rocks and crags and crevices to hide me, though I ent sure what from. There's animals about, but just the regular kind. Ent seen a demon track or smelled their stink anywhere.

Smell of people's getting stronger, along with signs of habitation. The air grows warmer and warmer as I breeze past grazing fields with low fences to keep animals from wandering. Herds of sheep, goats, and cattle left to spend the night with little fear of thieves or predators.

Steps begin to appear, cut into the rock where the slope must have been too steep. Long use has worn the grooves of cart wheels into the stone. There are no walls, gates, or wardposts. No wards of any kind. Either these people have never seen a demon, or they ent afraid of them.

The steps get wider and more frequent, until they become a complete road, zigzagging down a steep cliff to a verdant valley floor. Ent surprised when I come to an outcropping with a panoramic view and get my first look at Safehold, but the sight stuns me nevertheless.

It's beautiful. If I'm to tell honest word, it may be the most beautiful place I've ever seen.

The city is cut right into the cliff face, soaring façades carved into the stone that imply great depth within, running along the long, wide steps beside aqueducts that carry snowmelt from above down to feed a wide pool on the fertile valley floor.

I smell flowers and orchards and fruiting fields below, seeing their auras as a soft green glow. Crops're further along than they ought to be this time of year. Safehold is unnaturally warm, with no sign winter ever truly comes.

As with most places, it looks like the rich folk live up at the top of the caldera, where the view is breathtaking. Bigger façades grace the top steps, ornately carved and luxurious. Things get more crowded on the way down, with smaller homes mixed in with warehouses, shops, and gathering halls.

Everyone's asleep, at least for a little while longer, but this is no small hamlet. My senses tell me there are thousands and thousands living here in the caldera walls, even if you'd never see them from above.

The valley floor is wider in the center, narrowing on either end. I'm on one side of the fissure, and as I run my eyes over the crevasse, I see it, nestled at the far end of the valley.

The rock face is carved into the likeness of a demon's head, with a great gate at the center of its open maw.

AFTER MAM'S TALES of the *alamen fae*, I expected any folk in the demon's Safehold to be primitive, but this place looks . . . regular. Maybe not sophisticated like Hollow or Everam's Bounty, but the level of craft and artistry in this beautiful tiered city speaks of a people that are more than simply cattle for a mind demon.

I find the prints of sandaled feet, and they ent much bigger'n mine. Give me hope we might be able to blend in and have a look around without drawing too much attention.

The sky lightens, but the sun takes its time creeping into the little valley. Folk are beginning to stir now. I can hear them stretching and groaning, filling chamber pots and pulling on clothes. Mumbled words, but I can't make out what's being said.

I flit down the steps as fast as I can, sometimes forgoing the path entirely and simply jumping or climbing straight down to the next tier. Folk start coming out of their homes, opening shops, putting out wares, starting their day. Their clothes are a little different, but not so much they would seem too out of place at any busy marketplace in Thesa.

Their talk's gibberish at first, but after a minute I realize they're speaking Ruskan, or a dialect of it. Ruskan's a dead language—or so we thought—but I learned a little from Hary Roller. He had me practice the accent for hours to play supporting roles as my master acted out scenes from classic Ruskan theater, or sang Ruskan songs. I can ask about the weather, recite King Waldomir's soliloquy, and cuss to make Mam threaten to wash my mouth with soap. That's a fair sight from understandin' these folk, but it tells me somethin' about 'em.

It's not hard to keep from being noticed when I can hear, smell, and see folk long before they can me. The only road is these long, irregular steps, but there are plenty of places to hide as I make my way to my destination.

I can smell lye soap a mile away. Nose leads me right to a laundry shop and I slip inside. It's steamy, with a line of water from the aqueduct to fill the vats, and piles of clothes, clean and dirty.

I got a good look at what folk on the street were wearing. Most just had on a loose robe and pants with simple sandals, all of it woven by hand. The colors and cuts vary, but I think more for style than a sign of station. Likewise, some men had beards, and others were clean shaven.

Doesn't take long to find a set that fits. I hear the launderer comin' and change quickly. By the time he enters the shop, I've slipped back out the door, looking much more like the other folk on the steps. I keep my head down and move quick, and no one seems to take especial note of me.

The sun's full on the western caldera now, and people have come out in droves to greet the day. The eastern side remains in shadow, but I see movement there, as well.

If I'm to tell honest word, Safehold seems like a nice place. Everyone seems to be in good health, with plenty of shops, markets, and friendly faces. There's laughter, and an ease about them, even as they go about their chores. Kids play, adults watching them with one eye as they cook and gossip and play at table games in the sun. There are men and women with staves who make rounds, but no one shies away when they pass. Reckon they don't have a lot of call to keep the peace.

No beggars. No homeless or hungry. No one truly old, sickly, or infirm.

It's what towns ought to be, but I ent ever seen one that really was. I want to relax, but something still feels off.

Downright hot down near the bottom, where the rich soil of the valley floor feels warmed from below. Ent a spot wasted, the lands around the central pool are full of crops, all flourishing despite the weak light. Ent an expert, but I grew up on a farm, and that don't seem right.

This place . . . this perfect idyll, safe from coreling claws without ward or wall, didn't happen by accident. Time may have weathered it into something almost natural, but I can see Alagai Ka's hand in it.

Ducking into the cornrows, I make for the gate at the far end of the valley. It's set into the cliff face, surrounded by a wide plaza of white stone. At its center . . .

"Night," I breathe aloud in disbelief. There, plain as day, is a statue of rippin' Alagai Ka, standing benignly over the statue of a kneeling woman.

Friendly folk, but they worship a demon. Folk are here prayin' already, laying flowers by the statue, and bowing in the direction of the demon mouth gate. The main doors are thirty feet high, but there's a smaller, human-sized door at the center.

Don't see hinges, a bar, or a lock on either gate. Reckon they only open from the inside, and I don't think it's going to go well for this town when the big one opens.

I've seen paintings of the Mouth of the Abyss, and heard Mam's stories. Always assumed it was the ancient Krasians who carved that gate to look like a demon, but maybe it wasn't? Maybe the demons themselves had a hand in it.

We can hunt all we want, but I reckon one way or another, the trail's going to lead us here. If Mam and Aunt Leesha are alive, that's where they'll be.

I get closer, examining the seam around the door. Come nightfall I could turn slippery, maybe squeeze inside, but I ent fool enough to do it alone. Maybe I can get in and then open it from inside to admit the others?

Or maybe it's a trap. Demon ent stupid. Might not know when we'll show up, but he knows we're comin'.

I'm so focused on the door, it takes me a moment to catch the scents behind me. There're big stone plinths on either side of the gate to hold ceremonial braziers, smelling of lamp oil and old flame. I duck behind one quick, before I'm seen.

CHAPTER 43

THE GATE

"Get me an axe and I'll just chop the corespawned thing down," Wonda grouses.

"You really think it'll be that simple, Won?" Kendall is sketching the gate and its surroundings in a notebook with a charcoal stick. She even takes a few moments to draw the plinth I'm hiding behind. They're dressed in robes and loose pants like the rest of the Safeholders.

"Ay, maybe not," Wonda agrees, "but less a risk than tryin' to get through that crowd without bein' spotted and torn apart."

"What crowd?" I ask, coming out of my hiding spot.

Wonda gives a yelp, and Kendall quickly slaps a hand over her mouth. The worshippers laying flowers by Alagai Ka's statue are looking our way. There's a whiff of irritation at our disrespect, but no alarm.

"Darin Bales, what in the core are you doing here?" Wonda demands in a harsh whisper when Kendall takes her hand away.

"Reckon I could ask you the same thing," I say.

Kendall's eyes scan all around us. She takes both of us by the elbow, steering us out of earshot of the others in the plaza. "Are you alone?"

"Not exactly," I say. "Are you? Do you know . . ."

Kendall puts a finger to her lips. "Not here. Not now. Let's get you inside."

INSIDE PROVES TO be a small three-room domicile on the shadowed side of the caldera, too high for convenient access from the valley floor, but too low to afford a fine view. Most of the tier is empty.

"No neighbors to get nosy." Kendall puts a hand on Wonda's shoulder. "Wonda and I pretend we're a couple who moved from the other side of the valley for a place of our own. Isn't that right, dear?"

"Ay," Wonda says. "Kendall speaks enough Ruskan to get by, and I just grunt and act dim. Plenty of space here on the shadow side. Folk here love making babies, but even they can't keep up with the disappearances."

"Disappearances . . . ?" I start to ask, but it's like picking up a book and starting in the middle. "Who are these people? Why are you here? What happened to Mam and Aunt Leesha? Are they here with you?"

Wonda shakes her head sadly. "Demons took Leesha in the middle of the fight. One minute she was drawing wards with her wand, smashin' corelings like she was stompin' ants. Next minute something hit her and she went down like a chopped tree. Windie swooped in, picked her up, and carried her off. Yer mam took off after them, but somethin' . . . slapped her out of the sky."

I blink. "What?" I seen Mam's wards flare so bright she burned a pack of demons away just standin' there. What could have the power to slap her down?

But it ent what. It's who. And I know who. "She dead?" Now that the answer's in front of me, I'm not sure I want it.

"Don't know for sure," Wonda says. "Wind demon came and took her, too. Kendall and I left the battle to go after them."

"You tracked 'em all the way here?" I'm more than a little doubtful. The place they were ambushed was on the other side of the river. Hundreds of miles from here. A wind demon might fly that far in a single night, but on foot it would take months.

Wonda reaches into her robe and pulls out a large locket on a heavy chain. I sniff and catch the scent of electrum, and a bit of Aunt Leesha's blood in the red gem at its center. The round face is covered in wardwork, etched in the duchess' flowing script.

At the click of a release, the locket opens to reveal a compass, a delicate electrum needle floating in a vacuum of warded glass.

"At night this points to Mistress Leesha," Wonda says.

"Or what's left of her," Kendall notes.

Wonda stiffens, and the look she gives Kendall ent somethin' I ever want fixed on me. "Don't wanna hear that kind of talk, Kendall."

"Ay, sorry, Won." Kendall smells like she means it.

"Took us months to follow it all the way here," Wonda continues. "Got lost more'n once."

"So she's here?" I ask.

Wonda shrugs. "Compass says she is."

I don't have to guess where. "On the other side of the gate."

"Ay," Wonda agrees. "It's magicked shut, and only opens once a month. Kendall and I've been lookin' for a way in ever since."

"Let me guess." I feel like I might sick up. "Opens on new moon."

"Ay," Kendall says. "The Jechi Hosta are good folk—kind to one another, honest, hardworking. But once a month they all gather on that plaza and worship the demon statue. Then the gate opens, and folk are marched in like sheep for the shearing."

That explains why there's no old and sick, and why there's so many empty homes. "Have you tried just marching in with 'em?"

Wonda shakes her head. "Elders pick some who're to go in advance. Give them massages and fancy baths and the best food before they're sent below. Others get picked by the high priest on the spot, and go in weeping. Crowd links hands around 'em. Reckon it's to keep folk from runnin', but no one ever does. Serves just as well to keep us out. We were scouting today for a place to hide by the gate so we could dart in when it opens and everyone's eyes are on the priest and the chosen."

It's a desperate plan. Wonda's a foot taller than me and twice as wide. I listen to her mighty heart, and the blood it pushes through her body, sensing the vibrations as it passes through muscle to her skin. She's twice my mass, at least. She can't just duck behind a plinth like I can.

"Jechi Hosta." Even I know Ruskan enough for that. "Children of the Father." Something clicks in my head, and I hear Aunt Leesha whisper her prophecy again.

The father waits below in darkness for his progeny to return.

Night.

"Ay," Kendall says. "There's a lot of them. So many they don't know every face, and it looks like the demon's added new blood over the years, so we don't stand out too much. More than a few are Hollowers carried off in the attack like Mistress Leesha and your mum."

"Really?" I ask, wondering if any of the Warded Children survived.

"Ent what you're hopin', Darin," Wonda says. "Tried talkin' to 'em. Not a one remembers anything about life before the valley, and they ent lookin' to leave."

I remember Alagai Ka out on the desert, rearranging the minds of Olive's spear brothers easy as moving chairs around for a party. Said they wouldn't even remember meeting him, and I don't reckon that's something that can be undone.

"Does . . ." I swallow the lump in my throat. "Does the demon come out, on new moon? Have you seen him?"

Kendall shakes her head. "No one has, any more than we've seen the Creator. None of these folk have ever laid eyes on a demon, or a ward, apart from the ones on the door. Whole valley's awash with magic at night, but they don't even know it's there."

"Told you our side o' things." Wonda turns a chair around and sits, leaning toward me with her forearms on the backrest. "Now it's your turn, Darin. What are you doing out here? Where's Olive? Said you wern't exactly alone. Tell me you din't bring her and Selen along."

"Is Micha with you?" Kendall blurts. There's fear and hope in her scent, and a fierce love. "Has she come for me?"

"Ay, well." I rub the back of my neck, looking from Wonda to Kendall. "There's a lot to catch you up on."

CHAPTER 44

SPORES

"WE'VE GONE TOO FAR." Rhinebeck snaps his watch shut and puts it back in his breast pocket. "We should rest here and wait for the columns to catch up."

"Rest," I laugh. "I doubt we've gone five miles."

"Five miles is a long way from the others if we get into trouble," Rhinebeck says. Used to the control of his grandmother, he is comfortable following my lead, but he isn't shy about making his feelings known when I lead somewhere unwise.

Rhinebeck and I have taken to riding ahead of the army with our personal bodyguards. It isn't responsible. *An unnecessary risk,* Mother would say. But night, I would rather be buried alive than travel the center of that monstrosity.

When the passage widens, or when multiple tunnels reach the same destination, the drillmasters and sergeants take full advantage and adjust their marching orders, but more often we pass through tunnels widened recently to the minimum width of four horses. At those times, our column stretches nearly five miles end-to-end, and takes hours to pass any given point.

I knew the pace would be slow. Fifteen miles on a good day, my generals projected. But I did not appreciate how excruciating that would be.

"What time is it?" I ask.

"Quarter hour to high sun," Rhinebeck says, "if the sun still exists."

It's easy to imagine it doesn't. That time itself has ceased to exist. We've been in complete darkness for a day and a half.

Every warrior has been issued one helm and one set of spectacles worked with symbols for wardsight. They cost more than the flamework weapons, but without them we would be blind.

For many, this is their first experience seeing magic's glow. I learned how to See in the Chamber of Shadows with Favah when I was young, but I remember how overwhelming it was in the beginning.

Before this journey, even I had never used wardsight exclusively for more than a few hours at a time. After a day and a half, I'm dizzy from all the input. My stomach is trying to decide whether it should sick up.

We have chemic lights and oil lanterns in our stores, but not enough to light five miles of column for more than a few hours. They are impossible to replace and must be used sparingly. With our eyes adjusted to the dark, lighting one for anything other than an emergency will not make you any friends. This morning one of Rhinebeck's officers struck a match for his pipe and everyone around him hissed in pain and averted their eyes.

"They will call a halt soon," Rhinebeck says. "We can enjoy the quiet."

That's welcome news at least. Three thousand cavalry horses, not to mention pack animals and carts of supply, make quite the cacophony, but it's the rhythmic stomp of eight thousand pairs of boots that resonates in the very stone, heralding my army's approach. Miles ahead of the columns, it drums in our heads.

Worse still is the smell. We're hardly fresh ourselves, but it is nothing like the miasma that precedes our army. Even this far out the air is hot and thick with it. Close up the atmosphere is moist with stink, seeping into and clinging to everything it touches. Krasian and greenlander alike wear veils now to dull the reek. Only Rhinebeck and his officers eschew them. I catch them snuffing scented powders instead to ward off the smell.

The tunnel is tight. From atop my horse, I can reach up and touch the stone above. Sometimes I think about what the miles of stone above our heads must weigh until it begins to feel like the tunnel is shrinking and I might suffocate.

I wonder if this is how Darin feels when he has one of his fits over too much sound, or smell, or crowding. I always knew it, but never truly understood. Now I do—at least in part—and realize too late that I should have been kinder.

It's not just me. Screams are common in the lines, humans and animals alike unnerved by our unnatural journey.

There is no hiding our coming anymore, but I hope the sound and stench of our approach strike fear into the black hearts of our enemies. For once, I *want* to be seen. To draw the demon king's attention from Darin and the others. Let him send his remaining drones after me, and deplete Safehold of defense.

Yet in my heart, I know it is a faint hope. Until his neo-queen lays, Alagai Ka is trapped in Safehold, strategically and physically. Even if he wanted to leave, psychic triggers she emits keep him from dissipating, or leaving her side. It will be the same with the new queen, until she is safely ensconced in the hive.

They are as vulnerable as they will ever be, and I do not think the demon king will allow his bodyguard to venture far until it is time to retake their home. But even if Alagai Ka cannot come after us personally, he will have laid defenses to weaken and hinder us on this path.

Warriors of decay, Amanvah said. *Soul drinkers. Kai'alagai.* The names run through my head as we care for the animals, but they don't mean anything more than they did when she first spoke them.

I hate the dice. Hate Asome's sticks as well. They have me jumping at every shadow, worrying at prophecies I can't understand. Do they make me more cautious, or steal my focus?

I take my ration and canteen and sit on the tunnel floor with my back to the wall. Rhinebeck joins me, and our soldiers leave us a few paces for privacy before doing the same. I can say it's our station, but I see the looks thrown our way. Rhinebeck and I are growing closer, and I'm not the only one to notice.

"Grandmother will be furious, when she hears about this," Rhiney says, tearing into his ration packet.

"If we live to tell her, it will mean we've won," I say. "It's easier to ask forgiveness when bathed in glory."

Rhiney nods. "It won't be the first time. But there's a difference between hunting demons on the surface and . . ." he waves a hand at the tunnel walls, "all this."

"Ay," I agree. "That's why you should stay close, so I can keep you safe."

"Is that why?" Rhinebeck's smile lights up his entire aura. "And here I thought you enjoyed my company."

I can't help but smile in return. I wonder if I light up like him. If he recognizes and takes as much pleasure in the sight as I do.

Lunch is a two-hour halt for the columns. Grandda Erny has a chiming clock in his wagon, and rings bells when it is time to halt for meals or rest. With no sun to guide them, most simply measure time by the halts.

Every soldier carries rations for the shorter rests, but breakfast, lunch, and supper are a different affair. Our army travels light, trusting in *dama'ting* magic to keep the army fed. Amanvah and her priestesses trace wards in great vats filled with soil, Drawing ambient magic to transform the dirt into pure water and holy couscous.

I had only heard tales of the legendary couscous, a secret guarded closely by priestesses of Everam. If done incorrectly, the food is poison, but properly Drawn, they create a food so rich a single mouthful can sustain a warrior for hours.

The tales are not exaggerated. I had never tasted anything so delicious, and felt almost rested after swallowing for the first time. It pains me that the spell is kept so secret. No doubt Mother would have teams of Warders making couscous for every hungry mouth in Thesa.

But even magical food must be distributed down the line, and soldiers need time to care for livestock, equipment, and their own necessaries. Each rest is interminable, and when the tunnel slopes down, a river of piss precedes us.

Unable to bear it, Rhinebeck and I have ranged farther and farther ahead. Despite all the time together, we haven't run out of things to talk about and stories to tell.

Rhinebeck takes off his helm with a groan of pleasure. He's blind without it, but after the chaos of wardsight, there is little more restful than staring into the darkness.

I am about to do the same when I see movement ahead and tense, snatching up my shield and reaching for my spear. The rest of our company scrambles as well, but it's only Briar and Jaavi, returning from scouting ahead.

"We have found the first *csar*," Briar says without preamble.

"Does it still stand?" I ask.

"Stand? Yes," Briar says, and the parsing of words puts me further on edge.

"What is it?" I demand.

Jaavi's lip curls in disgust. "Mushrooms."

FATHER AND MRS. BALES gave detailed accounts of their journey to the demon hive. They described an ecosystem designed to feed on magic as much as nutrients in soil or prey, with predators even the demons feared.

Few were as unnerving as the colony of fungus that infected everything it encountered, taking control of the bodies of living hosts and using them to defend the colony until they, too, were consumed.

Warriors of decay.

Rhinebeck shows me the waystation through the distance lens on his rifle. The *csar* sits in a gloriously wide cavern, its walls intact. It would be a perfect place for our forces to rest and sleep, but for the mushrooms covering the cavern floor. There's no sign of life in the *csar*, and I don't have much hope. Nearly every inch of ground is covered, and stepping on or otherwise agitating the mushrooms risks them spraying a cloud of spores that will infect us, too.

I've called a halt and sent for Erny and the *dama'ting*. We'll need magic to pass this obstacle.

We're still waiting in the tunnels when the colony attacks.

"Cave demons!" shouts Corporal Taler on watch, looking through the distance lens on his rifle.

I follow the barrel of the weapon, but it takes a moment to see what it's pointing at—three cave demons skittering along the tunnel ceiling. Their auras are . . . wrong. Powerful still, but a flat, even glow rather than the shifting rainbow that surrounds sentient creatures. I can see fungus growing between their scales.

Two of my spear brothers, Gerges and Razeel, rush to cover Taler as he raises his rifle. Too close.

"Don't shoot!" I cry too late, the word drowned in the report of his rifle as the guard fires at the lead demon, punching a hole in its armor.

Black spores burst from the wound instead of ichor, and the creature is knocked from the ceiling. It hits the ground and simply bursts, sending spores everywhere.

"Retreat!" I scream. The men turn and run as Rhinebeck and his closest riflemen take aim and pick off their pursuit at a distance. The other demons burst as well, filling the air with spores.

I pull my night veil tighter and take the lamp from my saddlebags. It takes three attempts to light it, and there are hisses as the light stings the eyes around me. I hurl the lamp at the spore cloud with more panic than I am accustomed to. I am not cowed by enemies I can stab with my spear, but this is something else entirely.

The lamp breaks on impact, igniting the cloud and filling the tunnel with fire. The flash of heat scorches my face, and I feel a breeze as the air rushes to fill the vacuum.

Black stinking smoke fills our breath, and we flee before it, praying as we taste it that the infection at least has been neutralized.

Grandda appears up ahead and we hurry past as he and his Warders take out their electrum pens. Following Erny's steady lead, they draw wards of air, gathering ambient magic to form a foul wind of our army's stench to blow the smoke away before people begin to choke.

The trick reveals the true attack, a unit of *Sharum* warriors charging from the dissipating smoke, shields up and spears leading. These haven't begun to sprout, perhaps infected more recently.

Amanvah warned of the hand of Alagai Ka, and I see it here. He cannot muster the drones to strike us while still guarding Safehold, but the demon has cultivated the mushrooms like a crop. It must have been simple to send drones to known pockets of the spores and then command them to race to favorable locations once they were infected to start—and defend—new colonies.

The control the spores exert over their hosts is clumsier, more brutal, than mind demon possession, but impressive in its own right. It has no range limit, cannot be resisted with will alone, and leaves the body with most of its skills and muscle memory until it decays beyond function.

"I do not wish to kill *Sharum* spear brothers," Menin says.

"They are no brothers of ours," I tell him. "Not anymore. They are taken by the spores, just as surely as if Alagai Ka had possessed them."

Rhiney has a line of riflemen ready, but they are holding fire. He turns to me. "Do we shoot? I don't want to release more spores, but we cannot risk fighting in close."

In that we agree. I turn to Erny. "Can you burn them?"

"We can," Erny says, "if we want to trade infection for suffocation. Better to freeze."

I nod. "That's what Mrs. Bales says they did last time."

Erny and the Warders trace cold wards in silver light, powering them effortlessly this deep underground. The attacking *Sharum* slow and stiffen in mid-stride, their skin turning a pale blue rimed with frost. One falls over and simply shatters.

I shudder, in part from horror, and in part from the steep temperature drop in the previously hot tunnel. My breath steams through my veil as I move to inspect the fallen soldiers.

They appear normal, but I dare not touch or get in close. The biting cold would kill any normal fungus, but who knows if it is enough for these magical spores.

Erny and his Warders take no chances, chilling the air until the very tunnel walls coat with rime. Normally I am not bothered by cold, or heat. A benefit of the magic that shaped me. But even I have my limits, and quickly pass them.

"We can't keep this up," I call through chattering teeth. Erny is already lowering his pen, perhaps having come to the same conclusion.

We retreat to confer, with my lieutenants coming up the line. I am grateful for the warmth of the huddle as we put our heads together to discuss.

"We can't freeze the whole chamber," I say. "We'd be killing ourselves as much as the mushrooms."

"We can't burn our way through, either," Erny says. "We'd be roasted alive, if the smoke doesn't choke us first."

"Can we just mask up and hack 'em all to pieces?" General Gared asks.

I shake my head. "I won't risk us getting infected."

For once, the general seems relieved at not having to fight. "Flamework? Liquid demonfire?"

Gatherer Roni shakes her head. "We don't have enough to set the whole chamber alight, and it would leave us with the same problems as using magical fire."

"Perhaps we can retreat?" Rhiney suggests. "Send a team to burn the place and wait out the smoke?"

I still don't like it. We're already moving so slowly, and ready to go mad from the tight tunnels and endless dark. How long do we have before these tunnels fill with demons, racing to return to their nest?

My throat is raw, and my sinuses as well. The cold wards have sucked all the moisture from the air. As I reach for my canteen, I'm reminded of the wards Mother uses in the royal gardens to pull moisture from the air to the plants that need it, or to draw moisture from saturated soil before it can drown root systems.

I look to Grandda. "Desiccation?"

"Ay, that should work." Erny beams at me, and I feel a flush of pride. This isn't Mother leading me to an answer she already knew. "We can kill the fungus and refill our freshwater supply in one stroke."

"Ay, reckon you want to drink mushroom water?" Gared asks.

"It will be quite safe," Amanvah says. "The *dama'ting* have used the spell to purify tainted water for centuries."

There is a bit of trial and error as the Warders and *dama'ting* warm the chamber up ahead and draw out the moisture as the infected corpses thaw. They direct it at a set of barrels brought forward, and they are soon close to overflowing.

I stare at the water in wardsight, but it is black, visible only for its absence against the glow of life and magic all around us. Water is a poor conductor of magic, and the desiccation process has destroyed any life that might have lived within.

The barrels are sealed and rolled back as more are brought forward. A dark road is cut through the mushroom colony, devoid of life, as Warders slowly desiccate everything in our army's path. More defenders appear, but as they draw close, the Warders and *dama'ting* turn the magic on them. I watch with horror as eyes shrivel into prunes and skin tightens and sinks in until it tears like paper and the bodies collapse into dust.

Nevertheless, none of us feel safe. We try not to breathe as we drink to replace water lost with each exhalation in the dry air.

We lose a day before the column can begin moving again, and it takes hours to pass through the cavern. The intact *csar* is tempting, and I consider taking the time to clear it completely, but this is the first of no doubt many obstacles, and we cannot afford the time.

I stay behind with an honor guard to protect Grandda and the Warders as he works tirelessly to keep the road secure. Rhiney looks like he would prefer to have ridden on, but remains unwilling to leave my side.

We've begun to feel secure when Corporal Taler raises his rifle and shoots my grandfather in the back.

Erny doesn't cry out, or thrash, simply letting out a wheeze and falling to the ground. I react on instinct, grabbing the barrel and lifting it high even as Taler chambers another round. I don't give him time to fire it, whipping the blade of my spear through his neck and sending his head tumbling through the air.

There are no spores, but in wardsight I can see fungus growing like veins in his neck. Blood that should have pumped in powerful jets simply dribbles from the wound.

I don't waste time to investigate further, rushing to my grandfather as I call for help. "Amanvah! Roni!"

Erny is still breathing when I reach him, but it is labored, and he is pale from loss of blood. I stem the flow with pressure and look up, searching for a healer. Instead I see Razeel throw his spear, taking down another Warder, even as Gerges rushes at one of the *dama'ting*, spear leading.

The woman sees him coming, and moves with the fluid grace of a *sharusahk* master. She diverts the blade and steals my spear brother's strength and momentum, flipping him to the ground. Before he can recover, she raises her *hora* wand, desiccating him.

Razeel pulls a knife, but Rhiney lifts his weapon, shooting clear through my spear brother's shield and into his body. It's a fine shot, but Razeel is unhindered, lunging in with his blade.

Rhiney flinches back and screams in fear, his aura going cold. My instinct is to rush to his aid, but doing that would mean removing the pressure that is keeping Grandda from bleeding out.

Rhiney backs away, looking around for a path to flee. It's for the best, if terror has taken him. Other defenders are closing in. But then Rhiney's aura changes, turning dark and jagged. Still screaming, he explodes into motion, knocking the blade aside with the barrel of his weapon and spinning it like a whip-staff to bring the stock down, shattering Razeel's knee.

Rhinebeck doesn't stop there, falling on my spear brother and bashing him about the head with his rifle stock, over and over until his men pull him off, still shrieking and swinging. Razeel lies lifeless, aura snuffed out, his head looking like a shattered pumpkin.

I feel Grandda's heart slowing beneath the hand I press against his wound. His breath has become the occasional slow wheeze. "Gatherer!" I bellow, and I bend to look in his eyes. "You're going to be all right, Grandda. You're a hero. Grandmum will never question it again. No one will."

A slight smile twitches at the corners of his mouth at the words, but behind his warded spectacles, his eyes have lost focus.

Amanvah reaches me, but it takes a moment for me to realize. "I can . . ."

"Peace, sister," Amanvah says quietly, pulling my hands away. "I know my craft."

Faseek is there to steady me as I get numbly to my feet. I see a flare of magic from Amanvah's hands as my spear brothers surround me protectively, but I can't bear to watch. To hope. I've witnessed this scene too many times.

Rhinebeck still shouts and thrashes. His men hold him tight, keeping him from harm as they speak soothing words. None of them seem surprised at their charming, jovial prince's sudden murderous rage.

And why should they? The stories of his uncle Prince Thamos were much the same. Full of fear until battle was upon him, and then fearless beyond reason.

There is courage in the battle rage, for what is courage, if not action in the face of fear? The greater the fear, the greater the courage of the warrior who overcomes it. Especially in defense of one's people. I can see why Mother loved Prince Thamos. He didn't seek violence, but neither did he flee from it.

I knew fighters like them in *sharaj*—fought beside them in the Maze—though the drillmasters did their best to stamp out such behavior. Action in the face of fear does a warrior honor, but those who let rage consume them were dangerous to themselves and others. Such warriors often made foolish choices, taking hits they could have avoided in exchange for a quick kill, or abandoning their position in a defensive formation. Some became unable to tell friend from foe, or halt a blow thrown in error. Their lack of discipline threatened the cohesion of the unit.

But Rhinebeck is not part of a unit. He is the leader, not a scale in a shield wall. His position allows him to be effective in dealing with outlying problems the ranks in formation can't. If the prince is called upon to fight in close, things have become dire indeed.

I go to him, pushing past my protective brothers and Rhiney's soldiers to kneel before my friend.

"Careful, Your Grace," his lieutenant cautions as I gentle his hands away, much as Amanvah did with mine. Rhinebeck tenses as I draw close, my hands still wet with Grandda's blood. I've been crying, and I let him see.

Rhinebeck lunges at me, but I catch him in my arms and hold him close. He's as big as I am, but I'm stronger. He isn't trying to hurt me in any event, just thrashing.

"It's all right," I whisper in his ear. I kiss his cheek, feeling our tears mingle. "You're all right. The fight is over."

That last is a lie. Things are only going to worsen as we progress, but I've learned to take victories when they come, and celebrate them while I can.

Rhinebeck calms, and then sobs into my shoulder. I turn from the others, wrapping my cloak around us both as I lead him away.

CHAPTER 45

SUCKERS

"*INEVERA*," Amanvah says at last, cutting off my questions. "Your grandfather will wake, or he will not, as Everam wills."

There's a finality to her tone, and I know she's right. Erny had stopped breathing when Amanvah reached him. Her spells restarted his heart and lungs, but he has not woken. Amanvah and Roni agree this is common in such cases, but every day that passes makes it more likely he will not, or will wake disabled in mind or body. In the meantime, he rests in one of the Gatherers' carts.

"What about the fungus?" Rhinebeck struggles to keep the tension from his voice. "Have you learned anything?"

"Incubation can occur in as little as twenty-four hours from exposure," Roni says, "but it's a slow process, and varies no doubt by weight and the number of spores. Based on our observations, the infected would not be ready to spore until much later. Days, perhaps even weeks. The demons who infected the men were in a later stage, still. So consumed on the inside they were little more than a flesh bag of spores, just mobile enough to travel wherever the colony wants to expand and explode."

Rhinebeck's aura takes on a tinge of green, and I share the sentiment. It's been three days, and the second waystation was just as colonized as the first. We've lost half a dozen to infection, and four more to the murderous control that forces them to defend the colony. Every Warder, *dama'ting*, and Gatherer performing desiccation has a personal bodyguard now, and it's rare the possessed can cause real harm. Amanvah's dice have led us to several of the infected before they could wreak havoc, but so far a cure eludes us.

We smell better, at least. The abundance of water from the spells has allowed us to wash and rinse away the worst of the filth as we make our way down.

Rhiney's been subdued since the first attack, something of his easy charm lost in the warrior rage. He's used to killing from a distance, or at least wounding prey to allow an easy kill in close. He is not without skill in close—Razeel could attest to that—but he's a rifleman first. Killing with your hands is harder, both in practice and emotionally. Some cannot bring themselves to do it at all. Others are haunted by memories of what they are capable of.

I want to reach out to Rhiney, to put my hand on his, to offer comfort and care. But while we've been together almost constantly, we're never alone. It would be improper, and perhaps undermine his authority.

Tarisa was Prince Thamos' nanny before she was mine, and she would speak of him like he was her own son, voice full of love. In those descriptions, I see so much of Rhiney. A good man and a good leader, wanting nothing more than to do right by everyone, even if it means his own life.

Araine was strict, but it was always to the benefit of her duchy. Angiers was in ruins when she took power, and she taught her grandson that their privilege came with duty. To be the voice of reason. To protect his people. Like his grandmother, Rhinebeck tries to be the voice of reason, mediating and guiding, though in his inexperience he lacks much of her wisdom.

The tunnel gets closer as we make a steep descent. I hear the groan of wagon brakes, and wonder what would happen if a cart of ammunition were to begin rolling out of control. The ceiling lowers to the point where we have to dismount and lead the increasingly nervous animals.

I am beginning to think bringing them was a mistake when suddenly the tunnel opens up to a massive gorge, bigger than anything I've ever seen on the surface. So wide it stretches even the limits of wardsight. Down on the canyon floor, I can see the third *csar,* and it looks intact.

Perhaps some ancient river carved this underground canyon, but if so, the water is long gone. Too dry, it seems, even for the mushroom colonies. There is no sign of them, but I know better than to relax our guard.

The remains of an ancient bridge are scaffolded and under repair, but with years of work yet to be done before they can span the distance to the far side of the gorge.

Long steps have been cut into the canyon walls in the meantime, leading down to the *csar* that housed the construction crews. There's a lift, as well, and after our engineers test it, we begin using it to expedite movement of the heavier supply.

"Surely we should take the lift down," Rhinebeck says, "so you can take command of the *csar.*"

It's a thin excuse. Gared has already put Hollowers on the packed soil walls of the *csar* and raised my banner. But the steps down are back to standard Krasian width, made smaller by animals and foot soldiers shying away from the edge. It will take hours to get down, and the better part of a day for our entire column, the first of whom are reaching the floor now.

"I think you're right," I say, and the two of us take the next lift, along with Amanvah and Kriva. The view is spectacular as weighted lines slowly lower us down.

"It is good to be reminded that the world is bigger than we know." Rhinebeck might have been speaking to anyone, but he stands close to me. Closer than any Krasian man would stand to another man. So close I can feel the heat of him, and the suede of his jacket when it brushes against my arm. Again I resist an urge to take his hand.

Instead I take a deep breath, enjoying the sense of freedom outside the cramped and claustrophobic tunnels. The breath quickly kills the mood. The air reeks, a smell that worsens the farther we descend. When we reach the bottom, I see the ground is covered in some kind of excrement, rich with bacteria that glow softly in wardsight.

"Predators?" Rhinebeck asks. "Something must have killed whoever was living here."

I look around, but there is no sign of sentient life among the stalagmite mounds. Still, I drop my shield onto my arm.

Briar and Jaavi are waiting at the bottom for us, along with my Princes Unit and Rhinebeck's personal guard.

Kriva squats as she gets off the lift, putting a finger in the filth and sniffing it. Her large eyes glow in the darkness as she looks up to the stalactite-covered cavern ceiling far above. "*Minoc*." The word sounds similar to the Krasian for "mosquito."

"Insects?" I slap my arm, miming killing a bug. I already know it's impossible, looking at the volume of waste.

Kriva confirms my fears with a shake of her head. "Big." She holds her hands perhaps eighteen inches apart, and I get that sick feeling in my stomach that comes right before a fight.

Jaavi raises a fist with a single finger extended. This he stabs into his own chest. "Blood drinkers."

"Prince Rhinebeck . . ." I say.

"On it." Rhiney is already moving. His sergeant raises a whistle and blows a series of notes, gathering anyone with a flamework weapon and directing them to the *csar's* walltop. The rest of us follow quickly after, getting into the relative safety of the *csar*.

We don't have to wait long. As if guided by some intelligence, the creatures wait until our entire force is committed to the descent, then they drop from hidden roosts amid the stalactites above.

Those on the wall are the first hit. The *minoc* dive, long proboscises leading like spears. Warriors raise warded shields, but these are not corelings, and the magic does not respond as it should. Victims are knocked onto their backs as the creatures drive their suckers into flesh and begin to drink.

The result is horrifying. I can see the auras of the victims dimming as those of the hunters brighten. Soul drinkers, the *alagai hora* called them, and as it always is with the dice, too late I understand.

Fighters rush to defend their siblings in arms, *Sharum* spearing any sucker that stays in place too long as Cutters hack them apart with axes. The creatures are not large enough to carry off their prey like wind demons, but they knock victims from the wall, feeding on them where they fall.

A flight of the creatures descends on us, but here, Rhinebeck is in his element once more. The prince opens fire, dropping the winged terrors from the sky as easily as clay discs. His corps do the same, but there are thousands of *minoc* in the swarm, and they are moving fast. Hollowers fire into the cloud, sometimes hitting as much by luck as aim, but it isn't enough to halt the attack.

Some of the Hollowers fire their flamework weapons at the creatures attacking the wall. They score some kills, but it comes at a cost. I hear screams of pain from allies struck by friendly fire.

"Fools!" Rhinebeck barks. "Don't shoot at the wall!" He's right to be frustrated. *Know what's behind your target* was one of the first—and most repeated—lessons he and his instructors taught when they began drilling my soldiers.

The sounds draw more of the *minoc* from all over the gorge. We have their attention now, and a swarm comes our way. "Princes!" I cry. "Guard the Flamework Corps!"

My spear brothers lift their shields as the creatures dive in, faster than the Flamework Corps can chamber and fire. Rhinebeck continues to shoot as I cover him with my shield. His hands are a blur, from belt to chamber to the bolt and trigger and back again, over and over.

But there are too many. I see them crash into *Sharum* shields, and am stunned when their proboscises punch clear through the steel-banded wood and hit targets, knocking them from the wall and draining their auras.

Three of the soul drinkers dive at us. Rhinebeck kills two, and I put up my shield against the last. Even this creature's enchanted snout cannot pierce warded glass, but the impact still takes me clear off my feet. I scramble to regain footing, but there's only air as I fall twenty feet from the wall, landing hard on my back.

The *minoc* is unfazed by the impact, bobbing like a woodpecker as it searches for a weakness in my Tazhan armor. Before I can recover, it finds one, stabbing its sucker between the links and driving it into my shoulder.

I've been stabbed before. Shot with arrows. Impaled on *alagai* talons. Nothing ever hurt like this. I feel the creature begin to suck, see not just my blood pumping up its proboscis, but my very life-force, my aura, sucked up with it. I scream, grabbing the appendage with both hands and hauling it, inch by excruciating inch, out of my body.

Six slender segmented legs stab at me like tiny spears. I ignore them, trusting in my armor to hold long enough for me to pull the sucker free. The moment it's out of my body, I use the energy of the *minoc's* next thrash to turn the proboscis aside as I reverse the pin and smash it against the stone of the courtyard floor.

The soul drinker pops like any other insect, its exoskeleton shattering and exploding with foul goo.

There's fighting all around me as I stagger to my feet. Another of the *minoc* dives at me, but I have something akin to Rhinebeck's battle rage now, and I swing my shield, smashing it in midair.

"They're just bugs!" I activate the sound wards on Micha's choker and roar the words for all to hear as I hold up my gore-covered shield. "Smash them!"

"You heard the duch!" Gared booms from somewhere in the melee. "Scape 'em off your boots!"

Wards on my armor come to life, absorbing the magic from the creature's innards just like they would demon ichor. Whatever I lost is returned to me with interest, and my muscles surge with strength borne of outrage. I look up and see Rhiney still fighting, shifting targets in all directions.

Minoc drop from the sky with his every shot, and he ignores his own advice, firing with precision into the melees in and out of the *csar* walls, picking off soul drinkers that have warriors pinned.

I get a running start and leap, landing atop the twenty-foot wall beside Rhinebeck with such force my feet drive inches deep into the packed soil.

A cheer goes up at the sight. I am always reluctant to display my true strength in front of others. Mother drilled that into me before I had any understanding of why. But here, in the chaos of battle, it's good for our fighters to see their leader has power.

"Ignore the ones that come for you," I tell Rhinebeck. He doesn't posture like a *Sharum* might, or doubt my ability to defend him. He simply nods and turns his distance lens back down to the yard, aiding those in close combat as only he can. The weapon belches smoke, another *minoc* destroyed mid-feed.

There isn't a lot of time between puncture and death. Less than it would take to drain sufficient blood to kill. The *minoc* may drink a bit of blood, but it is the magic they want. They leave a victim as soon as it snuffs. Rhinebeck wields his rifle like a *dama'ting* scalpel, slicing them off their prey before they reach the point of no return.

The soul drinkers see it, targeting Rhiney and the others with flamework weapons, trying to knock them from the wall like they did to me.

But my spear brothers and I are ready for them now. Every man or woman with a flamework weapon has an honor guard now. The chaos of battle has forced our warriors to mix, with *Sharum* and Cutters and the Royal Angierian Flamework Corps fighting side by side in trust.

I find rhythm in it, the sprung readiness of my center exploding into motion as I skewer or shield bash any soul drinker that comes at my prince. I create a bubble of safety around him that lets him focus fully on his task.

Together, we are devastating.

By the time their personal ammunition runs out, the Flamework Corps have turned the tide, giving our fighters the time they needed to regroup and adapt to the new threat. Hollow Soldiers with crank bows target the brightly glowing soul drinkers rushing to escape after feeding, and the Warders find another use for the desiccation wards they have practiced endlessly the last few days.

We'll need the water to wash off all the bug guts.

THE *CSAR* CANNOT house everyone, but there is space in its walls for those most in need. Food and water are abundant thanks to the spells of the warders and *dama'ting*. We post guards everywhere while those who saw combat are tended to.

The rest of my forces, safely down from the caldera steps, circle the *csar* to keep its protective walls at their back as they make camp.

For the first time in days, I have a roof over my head that isn't a natural cavern ceiling. The chambers for visitors of rank are small in the canyon *csar*, but in the dark below, any private chamber is a luxury. Even better is the small tub that lets me scrub off the greasy remains of smashed *minoc*.

Rhinebeck and I are able to have dinner together as we did on the surface, smelling like something close to our usual selves. We start with talk of wounded and our plans for the climb back out of the canyon, but there is little that hasn't already been discussed with our lieutenants.

"I should have taken out that one that knocked you from the wall," Rhiney says, when the other talk has been exhausted. "I'm sorry."

I reach across the table, putting my hand over his. "You shouldn't have needed to. I was there to protect *you*."

Rhinebeck turns his palm up, and our fingers wrap around each other's, sharing warmth and the bond of spear brothers. "We can protect each other."

I feel pulled in at the words, leaning closer until my lips nearly touch his. "Always."

Rhinebeck freezes for a moment, his aura flashing cold like it did when Razeel came at him with the knife. I feel a sheen of fear sweat build between our palms and I start to pull back, but Rhiney moves suddenly, kissing me before the moment has a chance to evaporate.

It's not like Chadan's kisses. Or Lanna's. *Every kiss is different,* Selen used to say, and I'm beginning to understand. It used to be Selen going around kissing everyone she met to try them on for size, and I was jealous. Now I'm becoming just like her.

Yet Selen always seemed to shrug those encounters off, while each one has been a seismic blow to my emotions. Am I really kissing Prince Rhinebeck? Rhiney? Who used to write me terrible poetry, and hated his astronomy tutor?

I worry it's a terrible mistake, but I don't want it to end.

When it is over, both of us are breathless. There's a knock at the door, and we pull apart quickly, putting our royal masks back on.

Rhinebeck swallows. "Olive, I . . ."

I try to think of what Selen would say. "I did that because I wanted to. And I enjoyed it. But it is not a promise between us, or our duchies."

"Of course," Rhinebeck agrees, though I don't know if either of us believes it.

"Come in," I call, hoping the delay was not too great. Gared and Amanvah enter as Rhinebeck, blushing, takes his leave to get some sleep.

Gared raises an eyebrow. "You kids need a chaperone?"

"Tsst." Amanvah's hiss is low.

"You may be old enough to be my parents, but you are not them," I remind, perhaps more tartly than I would like. "I will decide for myself who I kiss, or not."

"I do not care who you kiss, sister," Amanvah says, "but the prince of Angiers is not worthy of you."

That lights a fire under me. "Well that's the night calling it dark. Didn't folk say the same about you and Rojer Halfgrip?"

Gared snorts. "Ent no one in favor of that match at first, but they made it work."

"Indeed," Amanvah says. "But my husband was spoken to by Everam. Prince Rhinebeck . . ."

I put my hands on my hips. "Prince Rhinebeck what? Have your dice divulged some secret?"

Amanvah shakes her head. "Not the dice. But I have seen many men in my life. When it is put to the test, that one's courage will fail."

I scowl, wanting to shout at her. I'm sick of predictions and sick of being underestimated. I open my mouth, knowing it's unwise, but then Gared clears his throat.

"Your grandda is awake."

ERNY'S RECOVERY IS a relief, but Amanvah's words keep with me as we resume our trek. How dare she speak of Rhiney so? After he's left safe Angiers to be with me—with us—on this dangerous journey? Perhaps he is afraid, but that only makes his glory greater.

We find the fourth *csar* consumed by mushrooms, this at the edge of an underground lake. A newly built bridge spans the distance. We feared it might be destroyed, but it appears Alagai Ka did not have the resources for that.

The waters are dark, almost magic-dead. There are no signs of demons, but there are tubelike shells growing from the bridge supports like barnacles. Worms appear from the tubes, drawn to our magic. They will drain it just like *minoc* if they manage to touch us.

Everything in this underground world seems to feed on magic as much as any nutrient. Father wrote of the worms in his accounts, and we know how to counter them. *Sharum* clad only in their bidos cut them from the supports with long spears, dropping them into the water where they cannot reach us.

There are other obstacles. A Hollow Soldier is killed by a group of *Sharum*, and it nearly tears our alliance apart before the *dama'ting* discover the fungus in his veins.

Everyone begins eyeing one another with mistrust after that, worried the person next to them is infected, or they themselves are. Guns are pointed at friends rather than the enemy, and more than one fight breaks out between paranoid warriors.

"Can't you suck the water out of us, make sure we're not infected?" Gared asks.

"If we wanted to kill everyone, I suppose." Erny's voice is calm. A gentle reminder, not an admonishment. Gared only grunts.

The sixth *csar* and its environs are free of mushrooms, but infected instead with a caustic slime that dissolves everything it touches, absorbing magic and multiplying. The slime has eaten inhabitants and fortress alike, leaving a fetid ruin amid a cavern covered in great patches of slime.

This, too, Father wrote of, and I heard the tale firsthand from Mrs. Bales.

"The slime must have eaten their wards like sugar," Rhinebeck says.

The moment we draw near, the ooze senses our magic and comes to life, dipping and cresting like the surface of a lake. Slowly, like pouring molasses, it reaches toward us.

Fortunately, even magic slime needs water to survive. We desiccate the chamber as we did the fungal colonies, but a few soldiers and horses are lost to fresh slime dripping down from the stalactites above.

Flame and unwarded canvas ultimately prove the best protection. With no magic to feed on, the slime dissolves the fibers more slowly, giving those beneath time to kill it with fire. We break into our precious stores of torches and lamps, traveling in the light for the first time in weeks.

We're drawing close to the final waystation when Rhiney and I move from a narrow tunnel into a widening cavern and find a wall of our bodyguards blocking the way. My Princes have shields set and spears drawn, interspersed with the Royal Angierian Flamework Corps officers, rifles fixed on something ahead.

I stand up in my stirrups and see Briar and Jaavi encircled by a pack of ghostly shadows that look like great hounds, eyes glowing and talons clacking on the stone floor.

Gwilji. The dogs of darkness who ate *alagai* flesh and turned on their masters three thousand years ago.

But the dogs do not attack. They growl and pace, keeping our scouts trapped in a web of tooth and claw.

Behind them, I see the reason. Hundreds of *alamen fae* warriors fill the passage, spears in hand. Their large eyes shine eerily in the darkness.

CHAPTER 46

THE CROWN

I SEE NOW why Kriva had to come. The *alamen fae* in the front ranks present as male, broad with muscle under thick carpets of hair. They pace and beat their chests, trying to goad our disciplined warriors into dominance games.

The *gwilji* heel the *fae* like hounds do their masters, but the warriors seem unwilling or unable to negotiate, refusing to release Jaavi and Briar—if they understand us at all.

Then ancient Kriva makes it to the front of our ranks and pushes through. Immediately the warriors lower their weapons and take a more respectful posture.

Their ranks open and an older female comes forward. She is not as old as Kriva, but her ceremonial staff is hung with bottles and pouches full of cures. The two put their heads together, and a moment later Briar and Jaavi rejoin our ranks.

"Amanvah, Roni, Olive." Kriva's voice takes on an air of command as she beckons us forward. We are in her place of power now. This is a summons, not an invitation.

I step forward, eyeing the *alamen fae* warriors with their crude weapons less than the dogs of darkness at their heels. *Gwilji* look like ghosts because their bodies have all but dissipated. Weapons are said to pass right through them, and obstacles hinder them about as much as Darin

Bales. Only their jaws and claws remain solid, and must be cut away to destroy them.

The tale of how *gwilji* nearly killed my father and his companions is legendary. He was forced to draw upon the full magic of the Spear of Ala to defeat the demon dogs, yet somehow, the *fae* have brought them to heel.

"Havell." Kriva points her staff at the leader of the *fae*.

"Well meeting you." Havell's accent is thick, but her words are clear. I open my mouth to reply, but she turns back to Kriva, speaking once more in the language of the deep.

It's hard to look regal and engaged for long periods of time when the debate is in a language you don't understand. Amanvah takes on the neutral serenity *dama'ting* are known for. I settle for imposing, standing at attention and watching closely, trying to pick out Krasian words or recognizable gestures.

Their auras tell me more than my other senses can learn. There is no animosity between these leaders. The *fae* are not our enemy.

"*Doveen,*" Kriva says. The other *fae* matriarch turns to me. Her glowing eyes seem to look right through me. "*Kinser ah Erram.*"

Child of Everam.

THE *FAE* OPEN their ranks and guide us to the final *csar,* still under their control, but cut off from the others. I see modern *Sharum* patrolling the walls, and *dama* at the gates, watching our approach. At the far end of the cavern is another narrow tunnel, this one sealed with a warded gate.

"The Spear lies on the other side," Briar advises. "In your father's time this passage was underwater, but his engineers diverted the flow and cut a tunnel of standard length."

"Why is it sealed?" Rhiney sounds like he doesn't really want to know.

"*Alagai,*" Havell confirms.

"She says the gates of the Spear opened of their own accord one day," Kriva says.

Havell grunts her agreement. "Nothing in our power could close them again. Denizens of the dark flooded the streets. The *alagai* could not enter Sharik Hora, but *minoc*, cave weavers, *gwilji*, and other creatures could."

"*Gwilji?*" I ask, looking pointedly at a smoky cluster of black, filled with glowing eyes.

"For every *gwil* the *fae* have trained, there are half a dozen still in the wild," Briar says. "They will hunt and kill anything they can."

"Do any remain in the Spear of Ala?" I ask. The fortress stands in the center of a cavern where countless tunnels intersect. Any path from the surface to the hive passes through that cavern. Kaji built the *csar* to defend and control the choke point.

When Alagai Ka and his new queen return to the hive, they will bring all their hordes with them. Our only hope of stopping them is to control the Spear.

"Some, perhaps," Havell says, "if they are still hidden. Most retreated here, to the last *csar*."

"And you say the *alagai* were working together with other creatures?" I ask.

Havell nods. "They send the *minoc* and *gwilji* in to shock and weaken, driving us into their ambushes. The *alagai* have new generals, larger than the others, and wise. Thousands were lost, and many of our wounded will not recover."

"*Kai'alagai*." I turn at Amanvah's words, and see her holding the crown again, this time for all to see.

"It is time to decide, Princes. Who you trust. Who you are. Who you are meant to be. The *csar's* gate stands open to the abyss, and only the crown can close it."

I hesitate, a cold weight in my stomach, pinning me in place. My eyes rest on the blood lock's strap below the electrum crown. What will happen when it closes, sealed with my blood?

I rub my fingers together, but I know Amanvah is right. There can be no more putting it off. I reach out to take the crown, but there is a shout from the *Sharum* ranks, and one of the *kai'Sharum* steps forward.

My eyes narrow. Now. Of course, now. Asome's sticks were true, after all. The last assassin was under my nose all along, but I was too spun about by Rhinebeck to see it.

But who? Which of my brothers came all the way from Anoch Dahl in secret to challenge me when the hour is darkest?

"Name yourself, if you have any honor!" I shout.

In response, he strips off his black *Sharum* robe to stand bare-chested in white pantaloons, chest and arms thick with muscle. Even before he removes his veil, I know him from the scarred wards cut into his skin.

Asome himself, come to offer my third and final challenge.

"PUT IT ON!" Amanvah's whisper is harsh as she thrusts the crown at me. "It is not meant for him!"

But in my heart I know I cannot. In my pride before the Skull Throne, I set the dice spinning, and they will not stop until this is done. I turn away from her to face my brother as he approaches.

Asome nods. "You are wise, little sibling. You know that crown does not belong to you. It was mine, before Mother took it and worked it with her spells and demonbone. My son Kaji was to have it! That was the pact. That was the peace. Instead, Mother has given it to *you,* and that, I cannot allow."

He holds his hand out to Amanvah. "I offer you this one chance, to undo what she has wrought. Give me the crown, or I will take it from you."

"And the Spear of Ala?" I ask. "The fate of Sharak Ka?"

"Once I have the crown, the Spear will answer to me," Asome says. "I have foreseen it. Let the demons come. We will destroy them."

For a moment, I consider letting him have it. I was just questioning my own right to the crown. I do not want it, and my brother does. Perhaps he is right, and the *csar* will answer to him. Perhaps he can hold it while I take Hollow's army to the hive itself.

But it is clear that Sharak Ka will always come second to Asome's ambition. I step between him and Amanvah. "I cannot allow that, brother."

Asome offers me a warrior's bow. "Know it is not my wish to kill you, little sibling. There will be no dishonor in your death."

My brother was not born with magic like I was, but it does not matter. I can see in wardsight how the wards scarred into his muscles Draw ambient power. He will be fast, and strong. Perhaps stronger than I am. Asome is a *sharusahk* grandmaster in the prime of his life. I have my victories, but I am under no illusion I am his equal.

"You would put your pride above Sharak Ka?" I say loudly. "Did not your interference cost us enough the last time?"

There are nods and sounds of agreement, not just from Hollowers but also from more than a few of the assembling *Sharum,* who have broken rank and discipline to surround my brother and me.

"Better we lay the fate of the First War on a half-*chin* child, who has carried a spear less than a year?" Asome's voice is incredulous, and there is agreement in the sounds and auras of many of the assembled warriors. "Shar'Dama Ka could have killed me long ago when I took the throne, but said I had a part yet to play. For years I pondered his meaning, and now I know it to be true."

I see Gared and Ashia in the tightening ring around us, and plenty of Hollow Soldiers, but it's hard to tell friend from foe in the *Sharum* ranks. Rhinebeck's men have their flamework weapons to hand, and in my mind's eye, I see how quickly this could escalate into a bloody battle that could doom us all.

"Go, sister," I murmur to Amanvah. "This is no place for you."

I step forward. "Lower your weapons!" I do not wish to harm my brother, but neither will I retreat or stand aside, and all can see it in my flat aura and defiant posture. "I offered my brothers a chance to challenge me, and I will not be forsworn."

"The half-blood son of Ahmann speaks true!" Asome calls to the *Sharum* around us. "This is *Domin Sharum*! If Olive am'Paper kills me this day and dons the crown, you are honor-bound to follow your new Shar'Dama Ka!"

Domin Sharum. Literally "two warriors." It means a fight to the death, often over a blood debt or leadership position.

Asome turns a derisive eye to me. "Will you say the same, sibling?"

It's a trap, and it isn't. The idea of Asome murdering me and my people following him is abhorrent, and I don't know if they would, no matter what I command.

But they must, if the world is to live. No matter what happens here, the demon queen is coming. If we are not unified when she does . . .

"I have no interest in killing you, brother," I reply. "I am sworn to spend my life on *alagai* talons, and if you were a true Evejan, you would say the same. Your exile has not taught you honor, or humility, as I once thought."

Something ripples in Asome's placid aura at that. I know I have gotten to him, but I don't know if the anger will make him careless, or if I have only worsened my defeat.

Before he can respond, I break eye contact, turning a full circle to take in the crowd. "The Father of Demons is coming! Even my brother has foreseen it! He will ride atop a new demon queen, escorted by every *alagai* that remains, from mountain to the sea! I have faced him firsthand, and know it to be true!"

I clash my spear against my shield, the boom echoing off the cavern walls. "No matter what happens this day, when he comes, you must stand united! All the world depends on it!"

Jaavi shouts something in the language of the deep and clashes his own weapons. In response, the *alamen fae* do the same. The *Sharum* are quick to do the same, but Gared is staring hard at me, shaking his head just a little.

I face him and clash my spear and shield again, louder. "Sharak Ka is bigger than our pride! Hollow leaves no one to the demons!"

Gared turns red in the face, even as his aura goes a sickly purple, turning in on itself. I think he will shame us both by arguing, but instead he bangs his mighty two-headed axe against the huge machete that has hacked away coreling limbs by the hundred.

That's it, really. There's no great ceremony to *Domin Sharum*. The combatants state their grievances before witnesses, and then they fight.

Asome approaches me unarmed and shirtless, but there is no rule that requires I meet him on the same terms. Indeed, the drillmasters would call a boy a fool for suggesting he give up advantage in a fight.

I eye my spear and shield. *Are* they an advantage? Asome will be light and inhumanly fast. The shield offers cover, but in close my brother will be able to turn its straps against me. My spear offers reach, but if Asome can seize the shaft, he'll be able to redirect my strength momentum. My Tazhan armor will absorb his punches and kicks, but its weight will be to his advantage in a pin, and the collar can be used to choke.

Sharusahk teaches nothing, if not ways to choke.

But what is my alternative? Drop my weapons and strip down to the binding on my breasts, giving up the fighting styles in which I am most practiced to pit my *sharusahk* against a grandmaster?

Sharak Ka is bigger than pride. I stride forward, weapons in hand.

Asome's aura has returned to its cold focus. I can feel him trying to Read me, to predict what I will do and prepare counters that will bring the fight to a swift conclusion. That is what a grandmaster does.

But I am no *sharusahk* master. My training came in the Maze, where *sharusahk* was no art, it was a constant struggle against death. Things happen, and you react. If you are fast enough, strong enough, you get to live. I don't know what I will do until Asome attacks. Maybe, just maybe, my reaction will surprise him.

We begin to circle, but Asome rushes in suddenly, throwing a high kick. I raise my shield to block and whip my spear in behind to sweep his other leg. The rising shield crosses my field of vision for little more than the blink of an eye, but in that moment, Asome seems to disappear.

My spear strikes only air, and then Asome's arm hooks my shield from below. His other hand appears at the top, and he twists to roll the shield across his back, using my momentum to power the throw.

Exactly as I feared. I slip my arm from the straps and roll the other way. I escape the throw, but as if it was all part of a choreographed dance, Asome completes his spin and hurls the shield at me like a discus. I get my spear up in time to deflect it, but lose track of Asome again in that momentary distraction.

I turn with my guard up just in time. Asome comes in fast with a push-kick that breaks the wooden shaft of my spear in half and connects solidly with my chest. It might have broken ribs, but my *alagai*-scale ripples outward from the blow as the force is absorbed and distributed.

Still, the kick knocks me from my feet. I grip the halves of my spear, swinging them wildly at Asome's dancing legs, keeping him back while I roll to my feet.

Again there is no hesitation as Asome comes in. Perhaps he expects me to meet him in *sharusahk* at last, but we spent hours and hours learning Majah stick fighting in *sharaj*. I beat the broken shafts at him like sticks to a drum, constantly changing the angle of attack, moving faster and faster as I find my footing at last.

Both sides are cheering now. Asome moves like a snake, his spine impossibly limber as he avoids most of the strikes and picks the remainder off with flat hands. I wait for him to grasp one. I will be ready this time when he tries to turn my strength against me.

He doesn't take the bait, instead hooking my arm and leaping to wrap his legs around my throat. It happens so fast I don't have time to stop him, and he whips his body, using his own weight in an attempt to snap my neck.

It's his first mistake. Asome may be Drawing power to enhance his strength, but he isn't used to it. Planted on the ground, Asome can likely match me muscle for muscle, but off the ground, he has only his weight and momentum, and I'm stronger than that. My neck holds where another would have broken, and I rise to my full height, turning in sync with the throw as I bash the bottom shaft of my spear into his head.

"Ay, that's how you do it!" Gared roars.

Charged as he is, Asome is spared a cracked skull, but he opens his legs, relinquishing the hold to roll away and regroup.

I don't give him the time, charging in as he did, pressing the attack with my broken spear halves. I batter him with the club end and stab with the blade, but again Asome's skill comes to tell. The long blade at the end of my spear comes close enough to shave, but never does so much as cut his skin.

Then, with a sudden catch and twist, Asome has the blade end, and I'm on the defensive. Before I can adjust, he's in close again, this time keeping his feet firmly planted as he trips me to the ground.

My brother goes down with me, but he's always in control, threading his arms through my defenses like Darin Bales when he's slippery, until he finds a hold.

And because a master presses every advantage, that hold is the collar of my armor.

Tazhan *alagai*-scale is incredibly flexible when accepting blunt force, or conforming to my movements, but it's hard as warded glass against a spearpoint or talon. Asome has worked around behind me, pulling the collar taut with one hand and pressing my throat into it with the other.

It's terribly effective, which is why the drillmasters and *dama* put such emphasis on it. Most every *sharusahk* battle ends up with submission or unconsciousness. I catch one last breath, but Asome isn't just stealing my breath, he's stealing my blood, crushing the artery that supplies my brain.

Already I am feeling the effect, as Asome easily wraps his legs around mine, keeping me from getting leverage. He's caught my right arm in his hold, and my left isn't in a position to strike at him. I pull at his arm, but here on the *ala,* my brother is as strong as I am. Things start to go cloudy at the edge of my vision.

It's Asome's second mistake, and it will be his last. He calls me sibling, but like so many, he sees only a *Sharum.* A prince who is a threat to his succession. He doesn't know about my *hanzhar,* or the endless forms I practiced under Favah, secrets no man has ever been taught.

I heave, and Asome allows it, no doubt thinking it my last, desperate effort to break his unbreakable hold. Like a bull rider at a Solstice Festival, he lets himself be thrown up, knowing his grip is secure.

But the move was just a cover so I could thrust my left hand across my body and into a seam in my armor to grasp the handle of my *hanzhar.* Thick veins stand out on my brother's arm, targets calling to its edge. He's reached the apex of my heave, and when he comes down I will . . .

There's a bang, and a soft, wet thump. Asome's grip weakens, and he falls away, blood coming from his mouth and spurting from the hole just above his collarbone.

"No!" I scream, looking back to see Rhinebeck lowering his smoking rifle with shaking hands, his eyes wide with fear.

When it is put to the test, Amanvah said, *that one's courage will fail.*

CHAPTER 47

SPEAR OF ALA

For a moment, no one does anything.

Then, with a primal cry of outrage, a group of *Sharum* raise their spears and charge Rhinebeck.

It's hard to blame them. I'm ready to punch him myself. I could have won that fight. Taken the crown with honor and left my brother alive as our united force marched on the great *csar*.

Instead, we are shattered. Better Asome had killed me and taken the crown for himself, than this.

The Royal Angierian Flamework Corps are ready to defend their prince, and their weapons fill the air with fury. Bullets punch through *Sharum* shields, dropping warriors in mid-stride, but there are more where that came from. *Domin Sharum* is one of the Evejah's most sacred rituals, and the Krasians are outraged at the violation.

I want to put a stop to it, but Asome is bleeding out in front of me. I was ready to kill him myself if need be, but I cannot allow it now. I reach into my herb pouch, pulling out gauze I press into the wound, trying to slow the bleeding.

"Gatherer!" I scream. "Amanvah!"

Gared and the Cutters are in the scrum now, pressing in to surround me and Asome, even as I hear sounds of pitched battle outside the protective ring. With every second, it is spreading.

Again and again those awful flamework weapons smoke and boom, and I curse myself for ever seeking their power. Mother was right. It is power without discipline. Without mercy. Many Krasians believe to kill from afar is to kill without honor, to you or the foe.

If the budding Hollow Flamework Corps follows suit, it will be a slaughter.

Amanvah appears, pulling my hands away. She pushes a cloth into my hands. "Clean your hands. You cannot risk having Asome's blood on you when the lock activates."

"The lock . . . ?" I look up and see Amanvah holding out the crown again.

I swat it away. "The crown can wait. Asome is bleeding—"

"It cannot wait!" Amanvah snaps. "None of this would have happened if you had simply taken it when it was offered! Now your army is tearing itself apart and you are the only one who can stop it!"

I look at the crown doubtfully. The Krasians will never accept me wearing it now, even if the betrayal isn't mine.

Still Amanvah thrusts it at me. "Put it on, before it is too late."

I can hear Asome choking on his own blood. He thrashes on the ground. "He's your brother!" I cry. "Save him!"

Amanvah lifts her veil and spits. "My brothers have done nothing but vex the throne and undermine Sharak Ka since they took their first steps. Asome's greed and pride have brought him to this end."

She shoves the crown at me a third time, and this time I grasp her wrist and keep her from rolling away as I slap her across the face. I take the crown and let her fall away, stunned. Her cheek is already reddening, and I worry I may have hit too hard, but it cannot be helped.

"*Dama'ting* understand many things," I say, "but honor is not one of them. If Asome dies, the *Sharum* will never truly follow me. Save him for Sharak Ka, if a sister's love is not enough."

Amanvah glares. Has anyone ever dared strike this woman, since she put on the white? I wonder if I've gone too far, but I'm too angry to care. She touches her warded choker, hissing words that glide to my ears alone. "Put it on and I will save him, though you are a fool and will regret the choice."

In response, I pull off my helm and put the crown on my head, piercing my finger on the sharp point of the blood lock before latching it under my chin.

The world went dark when I removed my helm and its wards of sight, but the moment the lock clicks, my vision ignites like one of Mother's festival flamework displays. Wardsight fills the vision with color, but this . . . this is colors I did not know existed.

Amanvah's aura is so clear to me now, and I ache at its purity. Visions dance around her—her past, her present, her hopes of the future. I see her childhood fear of Asome, and his ultimate betrayal. The tear bottles she filled, night after night, when she heard Mother was missing.

I watch her scream at the Damajah and storm out of the palace to race to Anoch Dahl. The second most powerful woman in Krasia, and she walked away from everything to be at my side in the dark.

I see her standing beside me at the front of a grand army, my crown ablaze like the sun as we face down the demon queen and her horde.

Amanvah believes in me. My sister desperately wants, *needs* me to succeed.

My sister loves me.

I want to cry. To beg her forgiveness. I have heaped such distrust upon her . . .

Again the flamework weapons roar, returning me to the present. I look up at the wall of warriors surrounding us and find I can see right through them to the melee without on the other side. Ambient magic rushes toward me from every direction, filling me with strength, knowledge, and power. I look at Asome, his aura fading fast, and realize I don't need Amanvah at all. I push her aside and trace healing wards over his wound, powering them with the magic flowing into me. Immediately, the hole stops bleeding, then begins to knit itself closed.

Even his aura, so unreadable moments ago, is open to me now. His desperate ambition. His belief he was destined by Everam for greatness that those around him sought to deny. Even I believe it, seeing the measure of power in his aura.

But I see, too, what Father must have seen. Asome would be a strict ruler, but he would be fair, and clever, and stand fast against the *alagai*.

"If only you had been patient, brother," I say as the fog clears from his eyes. "The crown would have come to you on its own."

I worry he might reach out while I am bent close—try to take the crown one last time—but as I can see the power in his aura, so, too, can he see mine. I am beyond him now. Instead, Asome's face takes on a look of anguish. He knows I am right.

"Help me end this," I say. "We will have a reckoning, you and I, but not here. Not now."

Asome just looks at me blankly. "You had a weapon."

"Ay?" I ask instinctively, but I can already see his meaning. Asome felt me reach for the *hanzhar,* and knew he could not defend in time. An image hovers in his aura, me, knife in hand, standing triumphant over his bloody body.

Even now, I can see he would have preferred that. Preferred death to the dishonor of living with his failure.

I get to my feet. "What is the greater dishonor, brother? The shame of defeat, or of living with the knowledge that Sharak Ka was lost by your selfishness?" I reach a hand down to him. "It's not too late to stop this. It's not too late to play a part in victory."

Asome stares for just a few seconds, but it feels like an eternity as outside the ring people die and the conflict deepens. Then he reaches back, and I pull him to his feet. Together, we stride into the circle of my bodyguard. Cutters take one look at my face and fall over themselves to make way.

"ENOUGH!" The crown responds to my will, blazing bright with power and activating a ward of sound that turns my voice into a thunderclap that carries above the boom of flamework weapons and the screams of the wounded.

"I COULDN'T JUST STAND BY—!" Rhinebeck protests, when we are finally alone inside the *csar.*

"You could and you should!" I shout back. "It was *Domin Sharum*!"

Rhinebeck spits on the floor. "To the core with the sand rats' barbarous rituals, if it means I have to stand by and watch someone kill you!"

He means it. I can see it dancing in his aura. Rhinebeck loves me. He always has, even when we were just children writing letters. Standing by and watching me die was too much for him.

Was it fair to ask? Of him? Of Gared? Of anyone who loves anyone? Would I stand by and watch Selen or Darin die for the sake of honor? I don't know. But there is one thing I do know.

"Forty-seven *Sharum* are dead from Angierian flamework," I growl. "Hundreds more injured, and the rest with a blood debt against you."

Rhinebeck crosses his arms. "My men and I can protect ourselves."

"Stop thinking of yourself, you arrogant son of the core!" Again the crown responds without my conscious command, turning the shout into something that shatters Rhinebeck's brave façade.

I suck in a breath, trying to calm myself. I didn't mean to do that. Until I can better understand the crown, I cannot risk losing control.

"We're weeks of travel from the surface," I say as calmly as I can. "Without our alliance, none of us is likely to ever see the sun again. We cannot fight among ourselves, and our task is greater than any one life. Even mine. Even yours."

The words sting his aura like the bite of a spear, but they have to be said. Even now, he doesn't understand. Not really. In his heart the lives lost mean nothing compared to mine, and now that I have the crown, it was all worth it.

I want to shake him. To shout again, or speak some quiet wisdom to reshape his worldview, like my father was said to have done, time and again. But I have no great wisdom about love and duty to share, and there isn't time to coddle him.

"The crown is speaking to me," I say. "I can sense everything. Not just the magic all around us, but something bigger, more powerful, and very, very close. The Spear of Ala is calling."

THE *ALAMEN FAE* are amazing to look at in crownsight. Their auras are brighter and vastly different from those of surface folk. Like other denizens of the dark, their bodies can instinctively Draw and hold a bit of magic. Like me, they are unnaturally strong, slow to tire, and quick to heal.

The differences do not end there. The *fae* have senses I barely have words to describe, even as the senses given me by the crown defy description. Their eyes can see in any illumination no matter how dim, and their sensitive skin can detect the heat creatures radiate. Subtle vibrations resonate in their bones, telling them the presence of objects around them.

There is fear in them as we approach the gates to the tunnel that leads to the Spear of Ala. For thousands of years, the *fae* were little more than livestock for the demons, and I can see demons right on the other side, ready to strike.

But when the doors swing wide and the *alagai* charge, they run headlong into the crown's sphere of protection. My spear brothers are ready, striking while they are fetched up against the field like a bird flown into a window. Their spears pass through my magic effortlessly, and ichor sprays the tunnel floor. Quickly, demon bodies pile, threatening to choke off the tunnel we need to advance.

I concentrate on the sphere of protection, seeing it surround me like a bubble. The dead *alagai* are still rich with magic, but their auras are flat now, lifeless. I adjust the field to ignore them, then thrust the power into the tunnel with force. The remaining demons are pushed back, allowing my army to advance once the bodies are clear.

Amanvah was right. Had I taken the crown when it was offered, Asome would not have dared challenge me. If I had worn it on our journey, I could have desiccated whole mushroom colonies myself. Vaporized *minoc* in midair. Cleared our army's path like a force of nature.

Asome's downfall was wanting the crown too much, but my own could easily have been not wanting it enough.

The tunnel is only a mile, but my head aches from keeping my will focused on the narrow area. I'm relieved when we finally push out into the main cavern, but the feeling is short-lived.

Demons are quick to surround us, clawing at the edges of the crown's forbidding. I do not know what forces Alagai Ka holds in reserve in Safehold, but there are thousands of *alagai* in the chamber.

Rock demons thrice my height boom with every step. Wind demons smaller than *minoc* swarm in great clouds. The cavern floor is alive with flame demons and snow demons and chittering, spiderlike cave demons. Some I have encountered before, and many I have only read about in bestiaries. Some are entirely new.

But the *alagai* are pale shadows before the Spear of Ala. Still miles away, the great subterranean *csar* of Kaji shines in crownsight like the sun itself. Its walls form a gigantic greatward that Draws and holds an incredible amount of raw magic, but that is only the beginning. I can sense the faith of thousands, of *millions* of warriors who gave their lives defending it in the time of the first Deliverer. That belief, that unity of purpose, binds a different kind of magic to the first, the pure gold light of Sharik Hora, the Temple of Heroes' Bones.

The Spear's light sings to me, and I can feel my crown responding. The Damajah really did it. Her replica crown is keyed to this city like a blood lock. If I can get inside, I will be able to Draw on its power like a god.

But we are not inside yet, and the great gates stand open, just as Elder Havell warned.

I start slowly, expanding the forbidding as I move into the cavern until I find the upper limit of the crown's power, a dome nearly half a mile in diameter. I keep one end over the mouth of the tunnel as Lord Commander Gamon rides out with his cavalry, in their element, at last. They patrol the border of my forbidding as Rhinebeck leads the Flamework Corps out to give them cover, followed by Gared and Ashia, each with a thousand of their best fighters.

Even this elite and mobile force takes over an hour to assemble. I feared holding the forbidding would exhaust me, but I find it is effortless. And why not? The Crown of Kaji was designed for this very purpose—allowing the first Deliverer to protect an entire army on the field.

Still, my anxiety grows as the minutes pass, eager to face this next test, now that it is upon me. The demons are strangely quiet, having drifted back out of range of cavalry spears. Demon drones are driven by their endless hunger and instinct to kill. The sight of us should be driving them to frenzied clawing at the forbidding, but these keep their distance and bide their time.

The Flamework weapons stay blessedly silent. They have orders not to fire without my direct command, and Rhinebeck knows my patience for reckless decisions is at an end.

When all are in position I begin moving forward, surrounded by a mass of warriors forming a giant pincushion of spears and bayonets as my forbidding slowly clears a path through the cavern to the *csar*.

There is a keening sound, and I catch sight of a demon much larger than the rest, drifting at the edge of my sight. Another call sounds from a different direction, and again I glimpse a demon whose glow of power outshines the others. Then a third. A warning, perhaps. Or a command. Indeed, the demons retreat farther, out of range of even the flamework weapons.

Then the *gwilji* attack, in numbers vastly greater than those domesticated by the *alamen fae*.

The dogs of darkness are nearly invisible, even to me. They kept their glowing eyes and mouths pinched tight as they stalked in under the cover of the demon horde. Now their claws loudly clatter and scrape grooves in the stone as they race forward and spring.

Again the Flamework Corps fire without waiting for an order, though it's hard to blame them with the enemy bearing down.

Their bullets pass harmlessly through the *gwilji*, hindering them not at all. Some leap upon the horses, their talons piercing warded wooden armor like heavy nails. Others race past, tearing into the Flamework Corps.

Gared and his Cutters race to defend them, but the *Sharum* infantry hesitates. Just two days ago, the Krasians would have leapt to protect the Flamework Corps, but despite the truce I forced, the slaughter at the last *csar* has not been forgotten.

The Cutters have no such qualms, locking shields and hacking at the talons, the only way to kill a *gwil*. Their claws are what bind the ghostly creatures to this world, and as they are severed, I watch as the creatures dissipate fully and are pulled down into the Core.

There are cries from above, and *minoc* join the battle, diving down, their sharp proboscises leading.

Ashia bangs shield and spear together, activating the wards on her choker to amplify her voice. "The *alagai* send hounds of the abyss against our siblings in the night, and we let greenlanders take the glory?!" she demands in Krasian. "Follow me, if you wish to find Heaven at the end of the lonely path!"

She leaps into the fray, and a thousand shamed warriors clatter spears and follow, again throwing shields over their Angierian allies and fighting as one.

We keep moving steadily toward the *csar*, and I trust in my warriors and Warders to hold the defense as I try to make sense of the *csar's* web of power. It reaches for me like plants reach for the sun, connecting us with lines of magic than intensify as I approach, all of it pulsing in unison.

But there is disharmony in its song. The invasive creatures within, the open gate preventing the greatward from activating fully, and another signal, this one coming from afar.

The lines of power drift through the cavern, invisible to the others, but unmistakable in crownsight, nearly identical to those binding me to the *csar*.

As Inevera feared, there can only be one source of such power.

"What is it?" Asome asks, ignoring a tsst! from Amanvah.

"Father's crown," I say. "The true Crown of Kaji is holding open the gates." The signal cannot be anything else. But what does it mean? It is said the Crown of Kaji will only grant its full power to those of the Deliverer's blood. Is that overstated? Has Alagai Ka killed him and found a way to access the crown's power?

Or does Father wait in the caverns below? A prisoner, perhaps, or a slave, his will broken by Alagai Ka.

"Can you command them to close?" Asome asks.

I shake my head. "I don't know how."

"How do you move your arm?" Asome asks. "Imagine their weight, their power. Bind yourself to them until they feel an extension of your very body."

"Why are you listening to him?" Rhinebeck demands. "Why is he even here?"

"Because I am not an honorless *chin* who strikes from afar to try to cheat Everam's will," Asome says. "Because I am the only other man alive who has worn the crown. A better question is why *you* are here."

"Enough," I growl, reaching out toward the *csar*. It's a meaningless gesture, but it helps me focus as I cast my own lines of magic back at the *csar*, gripping the gates as if in a tug-of-war.

The power holding them is strong. Stronger than mine. But it is distant, reaching out over many many miles to command the *csar's* defenses down. I concentrate, willing the gates to move, but they are stubbornly still.

"I can't close them alone," I say. "I can interrupt the signal somewhat, but we'll need muscle to make up the difference."

"That, we got in plenty," Gared says. We press forward, but, limited by beats of a marching drummer, progress is excruciatingly slow.

Even with the gates open, the golden magic of heroes' bones is enough to keep demons out of the city. *Gwilji* and other subterranean terrors prowl the streets, however. They come at us as we reach the gates and enter the city, but we have the foe's measure now, and they are no match for our forces.

The gates are warded to open at the crown's command, but there are conventional cranks and counterweights for when the *csar's* master is not on-site. We lash horses the horses to the cables, and they pull with all their strength as I concentrate, trying to cancel the insidious command from afar.

More and more warriors bend their backs to the task, until I fear the great woven steel cables will snap, but then, with a great groan, the gates begin to move.

Slowly, painfully, they gain momentum, moving faster and faster until they swing the last few feet in a great rush, closing with a resounding boom.

THE MOMENT THE GATES CLOSE, I feel a circuit close and the *csar's* greatward activates, blazing with power that floods me until I fear I will drown in it.

It flows out into the cavern like ripples in a pond from a great stone. The *alagai* shriek and flee, driven like livestock out of the cavern as they scamper into the surrounding tunnels.

If the *csar* sang to me before, now it is Minister Arther, whispering secret tallies in my ear. I can sense the survivors hiding inside, who and where they are, if they are in good health or poor.

I sense, too, the invaders. Not true *alagai,* the wards and forbidding have no hold on these subterranean denizens, but they can kill just as easily as demons.

One of the most spectacular stories of my father is how he called every spear in the *csar* to be his army, spinning about him and his companions in a protective storm of blades that sent *gwilji* to the abyss in droves. I can sense those spears even now, waiting for my call.

But do I need them, with such power coursing through me? I close my eyes, letting the *csar* become an extension of my body as Asome said. I sense the invaders, and focus my anger upon them.

That is all the *csar's* magic needs to respond, flaring like festival lights as it vaporizes the enemy one by one.

Just like that, the Spear of Ala is ours, a bottleneck against the coming of the demon queen.

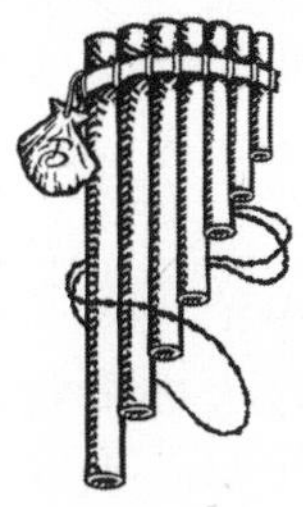

CHAPTER 48

SQUEEZING OUT THE PAIN

JECHI HOSTA DOMICILES are cut straight into the caldera, with rooms running wagon train deeper and deeper into the rock face. Arick and I are up front, watching Wonda and Selen thump around, practicing trips and throws. Olive gave Selen Wonda's old position as captain of the house guard, but Wonda was her teacher, and it din't take long for them to fall into old grooves.

Used to think no one could beat Wonda Cutter at wrestling, but Selen's older now, larger and more experienced. Wonda still has a few tricks, but I can sense her mounting worry, and her pride. Some teachers don't like being shown up by a student, but Wonda's the sort to want nothing more than for her students to reach higher than she did.

Arick leans in, watching every move. It would have my attention, too, but mostly I'm focused to the back room.

Rojvah and Kendall have retreated there for privacy as my promised collects Kendall's tears over Micha's death, but my senses have a way of takin' me places I ent invited.

It's Rojvah's place to do it. Collecting tears is women's business in Krasia, and Kendall was the apprentice of Rojer Halfgrip, Rojvah's father. That's good as family, and of course, Kendall Demonsong's a famed Jongleur in her own right—something Rojvah has always aspired to be.

I try to ignore it at first, but I can't help but hear every sob and sniffle. The scrape of the tear bottle's sharp lip against Kendall's skin. The way Kendall's heart races, how each sob racks her body like the crack of a whip.

She's breathing hard when it's done. Even her skin is activated. She takes a moment to recover, and then it's Rojvah's turn.

She doesn't need to fake it. We all cried over Nanny Micha, and the wound's still fresh. Even I had to go find a secret spot to fall apart, and I hate cryin'. Always have.

Their grief is a miasma that fills my senses. I feel the shock wave of every sob and shudder like it was my own body. The high-pitched cries stab my eardrums. Anguish fills my nostrils. If pain has a taste, I taste it now.

I hate cryin', but I'm jealous how Krasian women help each other through it. How they find a harmony in shared sorrow, and that eases it for both. When the bottles are full, they hold each other as their hearts and breath return to normal.

But I ent got anyone to hold me, or share the pain. Don't always like to be touched, but right now I feel like I might explode without someone to put their arms around me. My whole body hurts and I need it crushed out of me, but instead I got to set here and pretend to care about a wrestlin' match.

Arick's in on it now, attempting a move from Wonda's personal *sharusahk* style. All three of them got plenty of hurts, but fighting types don't like to talk about 'em when they can wrassle instead.

"This belongs to you." A click as Rojvah unfastens Micha's earring.

"Keep it." Kendall's fingers slide over Rojvah's, closing them around the jewel. "If your da hadn't died, I'd have married him, too. Your mother had already blessed it. Now that we've found each other, I don't want to risk losing you, too."

"Thank you." The ring clicks back into place, flicking against her earlobe, and they embrace again. There is no more sobbing, but I can taste their tears.

I EXCUSE MYSELF when I can, going out of the house and across the step to set on the wall, legs dangling over the side of the caldera. Come sunup there'll be plenty of traffic, but this late it's all peace.

I'd play my pipes, but the music that hides me from demons will only draw unwanted attention here. Instead I do Mam's breathing exercises, sucking in fresh air and trying to regulate my body.

Still, I know Rojvah's come up behind me before she speaks. "Even you need to rest, Intended."

"Time for that come sunup." I don't turn around. Don't want her to see my face right now. "Better we keep out of sight during the day until we've got a plan."

Rojvah isn't convinced, coming up and sliding a warm hand up my back to rest on my shoulder, ostensibly to steady her as she sets on the wall beside me. She snuggles in close, warm and soft, and lays her head into the hollow at the base of my neck.

I can smell the invitation, but I'm too scared to move until her left arm snakes behind her back and finds mine, pulling it around her. "I am sorry you had to bear that, Intended."

"'Sall right." The words threaten to make me cry again. I swallow hard to keep it down. "Bear both our pain, if I could."

"Oh, Intended," Rojvah said. "Pain is not meant to be hoarded deep. We share to make it too shallow to drown in."

Her hand slides up my neck to my face, feeling the wetness on my cheek. She turns to me, taking my face in her hands and kissing the tears off my cheeks as easily as if they were scraped with a bottle. The she moves lower, pressing her soft lips to mine and stealing my breath away.

"I . . ." I need a moment to collect myself when we finally part. "Thought we weren't meant to do that on this trip."

Rojvah spits over the side of the mountain. It's an act so unlike her it takes me by surprise.

"I spent the night collecting the tears of a woman whose love is lost forever," she says. "I will kiss who I wish, when I wish, and propriety be damned."

Her hand closes over mine, squeezing. "I love you, Intended. I did not truly understand what that meant when we made our vow, but I understand it now."

I turn to her in surprise. Rojvah, perfect, beautiful, brilliant, talented, royal Rojvah, loves me? My mouth falls open uselessly as I search for a response, but only one comes to mind.

"Why?"

"EVERAM'S BEARD, I don't even like women, and I understand them better than you!" Arick laughs, after Rojvah storms off to the back room where the other women have already settled in to get some sleep. "She wanted you to say it back."

"Say what back?" I ask.

"That you love her, you camel's backside!" Arick swats at me, and for once I'm not quick enough to slip aside. I take the thump to the head, knowing I deserve it.

"Say it back?" I can't believe it. "Can't she tell? Can't everyone tell?"

"Perhaps," Arick says, "but women need to hear it."

I shake my head. "You think she thinks I don't?" The idea is ludicrous. "How could anyone not be in love with Rojvah?"

Arick snorts. "More easily than you think. You see a side of my sister few others do. When she's protecting you, she's hissing at the rest of us."

"Night." I feel like I'm going to be sick, but I get to my feet. "I need to apologize."

"You need to grovel." Arick smells of amusement. "But it will need to wait until tomorrow, unless you want the other women judging your performance."

I sit back down. "Think I'd rather sneak into the demon's gate alone than have Captain Wonda, Selen Cutter, and Kendall Demonsong staring at me over crossed arms while I fumble through an apology I barely understand."

"Perhaps there is hope for you, then." All amusement left Arick's scent at the mention of the gate. Now it's fear, anxiety, and self-loathing.

"Don't have to go in, you don't want to," I say.

Arick looks down his nose at me. "Do you *want* to go in?"

When I don't answer, Arick nods as if I have. "Don't do that."

Arick can say what he likes about women, but men can be just as confusing. "Don't do what?"

"Read me." Arick flicks a hand my way. "Sniff my backside and listen to my heart and use it to get inside my head."

"Can't help it, Arick," I say.

"You can help by keeping your guesses about what I'm thinking to yourself," Arick says. "You're no better than Alagai Ka."

"Oh, ay?" I ask. "I ever make you shove someone off a ledge?"

I immediately know I've pushed it too far. There's deep anger in Arick. Always was. Seen it come out when he's fightin', making him lose track of everythin' but the next kill. I feel it rise up across a dozen indicators on his body, and in the flare of his aura.

Arick gets to his feet, striding my way, and it's an effort to keep from turnin' slippery and running for my life. But he ent comin' for me. He heads for the door and across the step, puttin' a foot up on the wall and pushing down till he stands atop it, looking out at the valley floor far below.

Arick is agile for someone his size, and I wouldn't think twice about standing on that wall, but something in his scent frightens me.

"Push me, cousin," he says. "Then my debt to you will be paid."

"Night, are you crazy?" I grab at Arick's belt, but he swats my hand away.

"It will be better this way," Arick says. "I cannot betray you again, if I am dead."

He means it, and I feel a chill in the warm night air. I don't know what to say when a girl says she loves me, but I'm supposed to know what to say now? I want to shout for the others, but if he wants to, Arick can jump long before they come.

"Nothin's better without you, Arick." I say. "You din't betray anyone. Demon got in your head."

"And if he's still in there?" Arick asks. "I've read the Deliverer's accounts. The Father of Lies broke the will of better men than me, and made them his agents in the day."

Arick's bigger and stronger than me, but he's slow. I could run up and grab him if he tries to jump. Trip his legs and throw my weight back, knock us onto the step.

But that won't stop him later, when I'm sleepin' away the sun. Or tomorrow.

I jump up on the wall beside him, but out of reach. "You're downwind." I keep my eyes on the far side of the valley, and take a bit of wax from my belt pouch, softening it with my fingers and sticking it in my ears and nostrils. "This is about the best I can do to stay out of your head."

Arick sighs. "It's not you I'm angry with, cousin."

Angry at yourself. I bite my lip to keep from sayin' it. "Who are you angry with?"

Arick shrugs, but my feet can feel the vibration in the stone. He's shaking. "My mother died before I was born, did you know?"

Takes a moment for that to sink in. "How's that?"

"Her wounds from defending Docktown against the *alagai* were so great, her spirit fled on the lonely path. Her body would have followed, but the Damajah used her spells to keep her heart and lungs pumping for months afterward."

"Because of you," I whisper, as the horror of it washes over me.

"Perhaps she would have carried me on the lonely path, had the Damajah let me die as well." There's a crack in Arick's deep voice at that. "Fallen in battle together, Everam would not have denied us Heaven."

"Ay, maybe," I say. "But your life would have been over before it began."

"Life?!" Arick demands. "What life? A disappointment to my stepmother and a dishonor to my father's memory. Denied the right to love as I wish. Denied the spear. And when I lifted the spear in spite of them, the Father of Lies took it from me and turned it on my friends."

I hear him choke, feel the change in pressure as he lifts a foot off the wall. "Better to have died unborn, than continue this 'life.' "

Arick doesn't cry like his sister. She's free with her sobs and wails, unashamed of her grief. Not a lie, but a performance to honor her pain to others, and anyone watchin' from above.

Arick's face scrunches and the tears flow, but he chokes back most of it, tensing his muscles to stand fast against it like a test of manhood.

Wish I could just take a bottle to his cheek and scrape away the tears. Hold him and cry together. Somethin', anythin', to lessen the pain just a little. But I'm scared anythin' I do will make him take that last step.

But I can't just do nothin'.

Slowly, deliberately, I sidestep without turning his way, sliding closer. Close enough to touch. I don't try to wrap him in my arms, just move my arm a little at a time, like a mouse poking its nose out of a hole, until our littlest fingers touch.

I freeze, waiting, but when Arick doesn't react, I move a little more. And more still, sliding my fingers over his and giving him all the time in the world to pull away. I gently close my hand over his, and for a moment he still doesn't react.

"My da died before I was born, too," I say quietly. "I'd come out five minutes sooner, I'd have met him." A knot forms in my throat, and I squeeze my eyes shut as I swallow it down. "Don't reckon he's got a lot to be proud of, either."

Arick doesn't respond with words, but his fingers close over mine and begin to squeeze so hard it hurts. This time I don't have the urge to go slippery. Instead I squeeze back with everything I've got, holding on to my cousin for his life, as he holds on for mine. The pain just makes it real, and I welcome it.

I WAKE UP with a jump, casting about with my senses for Arick. I don't smell him in the domicile at all.

I sniff again. Don't smell anyone.

I go to the front, but the setting sun is so bright it blinds me. I throw up a hand and stumble back. Must have slept later than I thought. On this side of the caldera, morning comes late. I kept watch until the women woke up and I could find a dark spot in the back.

Tried talkin' to Rojvah then, but she put her nose up and pretended she couldn't hear me. Selen took notice, and I made a quick retreat.

Still got flashes in my eyes, so I shut them tight and focus on my hearing. Selen's voice ent hard to pick out. They must have gone out when I was asleep. She's two tiers down, tellin' someone that she's Kendall's sister.

Selen speaks better Ruskan than me, but she's got the Jechi Hosta accent all wrong. It's painful to listen to, and I worry she's givin' us away. Folk sound real friendly, but nosy, too. Kendall speaks up then, and her accent is flawless.

Everyone looks the part when they get back. "Got a job," Selen says.

"Ay?" I ask.

"We found a stablemaster to put up the horses in exchange for us cutting him a new back room," Arick explains.

"You speak Ruskan?" I ask.

Arick laughs. "Not even a little. Selen tells them I am her husband who doesn't speak."

"Strong as an ox, dim as a doorknob!" Selen punches him on the shoulder.

"Better the silent one than the one stumbling through a conversation like a braying camel," Arick says.

"Didn't you learn to read Ruskan at Gatherers' University?" I ask Selen.

"Read?" she asks. "Ay. Speak? I can ask where the library is, or the privy. Count to a hundred, maybe chat about the weather, but it ent like I blend in."

"We fixing to be around so long we need to find work?" I ask.

"New moon's a week and a half away," Wonda says. "Best we lay low till then."

"And then what?" I ask. It's nice to have grown-ups around for once. To not have to be the one making decisions and taking all the responsibility.

"Then the gate opens," Wonda says, "and you sneak inside and . . ." She waggles her fingers at me.

Not havin' all the responsibility was nice while it lasted.

"I NEED A BIT OF AIR," Rojvah announces after supper, stepping out of the domicile to stare at the lights flickering in windows across the caldera. I watch her glumly, wondering how I can fix things, or if it's too late.

Arick raises his eyebrows at me, nodding for the door. "Go, fool."

"I was beginning to think you were not coming," Rojvah says as I come up behind her.

"I love you," I blurt, unable to hold it back anymore.

Rojvah does not seem impressed. She turns to regard me, arms crossed in front of her. "Took the day to think about it, did you?"

"Din't need to think," I say. "Din't think it needed sayin' it at all, 'cause 'course I do. How could I not? What is there about Rojvah vah Rojer am'Inn am'Kaji that ent perfect? Your voice, your mind, your heart. Pretty as a sunset and with all the knacks I ent got."

Rojvah's expression softens at that. She opens her mouth to reply, but now that I'm talkin' I can't seem to stop. "Asked why you loved me, 'cause why would you? How could someone so amazing ever settle for . . . for . . ."

Hurts too much to even finish the thought. My eyes fill with tears and I choke on the words. Night, what is it with me and cryin' these days?

But then Rojvah is holding me, and kissing me, and tellin' me everythin's gonna be all right.

CHAPTER 49

THE PRIEST

I SCRATCH THE MATCH along the wall, watching it spark and sizzle and flare to life in the darkness.

Not supposed to waste matches. Ent got many left, and each one is precious, but just this once, I reckon I can spare one. I hold it up before my eye, getting lost in the flames as I try to think of a wish.

I hear Selen come outside and blow it out quick, not sure if she saw.

"Think we all forgot your born day?" Selen asks quietly.

"Ent much to celebrate," I say.

"Core with that," Selen says. "We found Safehold. Found Wonda and Kendall, and maybe in a couple days, we'll find Leesha and your mum."

"Maybe," I agree. Every time I try to think that far ahead, I get so scared I can't see straight.

"Don't tell Rojvah I told you," Selen warns, "but she's been collecting ingredients to make you a cake."

My mouth waters at the thought of Krasian yellow cake, though Creator only knows what Rojvah will be able to make with Jechi Hosta flour.

Selen comes to lean on the wall beside me. "Don't like Wonda's plan. You shouldn't be going in there alone."

I put my hands in my pockets before she can notice them shaking.

"Ay, how's it any different than you sending me down to sneak around Safehold?"

"Because Safehold's a big open valley, with plenty of places for you to run and hide," Selen says. "Klats to suns there's a trap on the other side of that gate, and once it's shut, we won't be able to get to you."

"Got a better plan, now's the time for it," I say. "Don't like this one any more'n you."

"Don't know." Selen spreads her hands. "But there's got to be something better than sending you in there alone."

"If there is, no one's mentioned." I suck in a deep breath, trying to calm a heart beating like a hummingbird's wings. "Maybe I just need to sack up for once. Might be everything would be different, I hadn't been too scared to just go on my own from the start."

"Ay, what's that supposed to mean?" Selen asks.

"That first night Olive was taken," I say. "We were losing ground. They were getting away."

"Because of me," Selen puts her hands on her hips. "Sack up and say it, if that's what you mean."

"What do you want from me, Sel?" I shrug. "I'm faster than you. Ent a criticism, it's a fact. If I'd gone on alone . . ."

"Not this again." Selen rolls her eyes. "What would you have done if you'd caught them? Three Krasian Watchers that took down Micha and Olive? Love you like a brother, Darin Bales, but you're not a fighter, and you ent got the stomach for killin' folk in their sleep."

"That's just my point." Selen's lookin' for a fight, but I don't have one to give. "Ent got the stomach for anythin'. Just so corespawned scared all the time, I'll do anything not to feel alone."

"Darin, that's nonsense," Selen says. "You're one of the bravest people I've ever met."

It's so ridiculous I can't help but laugh, but it ent the kind of laugh that makes you feel good. "I was brave, I'd've just *gone,* Sel. Reckon I'd have figured somethin' out. Freed Micha, maybe, or run off their horses so they couldn't get Olive away in time. Left a trail for your da to follow. *Somethin'*."

"So that's your plan?" Selen demands. "Just creep into that gate like a mouse and hope you figure something out before Alagai Ka gets you?"

I hold up my palms. "Hopin' what I figure out is how to open that gate from the inside, and then we all go sneakin' together."

"Ay," Selen says. "I hope so, too."

Turns out Hosta corn flour is perfect for Krasian yellow cake. Maybe it's that I ent had a proper meal in months, but Rojvah's is the best thing I've ever tasted. Better'n my aunt Selia's butter cookies, and that's sayin' something.

She cut me a big piece and waited for me to have a bite before serving the others. I was tasting the cake before it even reached my tongue, but when I closed my mouth and felt its spongy texture and my taste buds exploded, I let out a little moan of pleasure.

Rojvah smelled so happy after that. She was stingy with slices for the others, and stood watch by the leftovers, but I can't complain. She gave me a piece every day until Waning.

Only now the cake's gone and new moon is here.

You can see it all over town. People puttin' on their Seventhday best like they're goin' to services, carrying tribute for the mountain god.

Thought about stowin' away with the offerings. Most are baskets of food, small enough to be carried by one or two people. Even I'd have trouble hiding in those. There are some barrels, too, but those are empty—I can hear it in the roll. Folk would have to be idiots not to notice a change if someone was scrunched up inside.

I'm already in my hiding spot when the crowd arrives in force at sunset. Too much traffic to hide behind one of the plinths, so I'm squeezed into a little nook behind one of the stone horns of the gigantic demon's skull carved above the gate.

Got a good view of the crowd in the meantime. Selen and the others hang back, trying not to draw attention to themselves as the Jechi Hosta gather and begin singing a sunset prayer. Song's got a nice tune, but the words are somethin' about welcoming the night, and I don't like the sound of that. All I know, Alagai Ka's right on the other side of that gate, waitin' to come on out.

Ent long to wait. The sun sets, and the only light comes from the big braziers illuminating the gate, and a scattering of oil lamps on poles in the crowd.

I feel gears turning below me, tumblers clacking into place. A physical lock. But then there is a tingle of magic and the giant doors swing open of their own accord, revealing a lone man. He lowers a hand, as if he just touched something on the inside to trigger the effect. Maybe I can trigger it, too.

"Cavivat," some of the Jechi Hosta chant. Ruskan for "priest." There is wonder at the word, and fear.

The priest ent like any I've ever seen. Tenders of the Creator wear plain brown robes, but in my experience clergy's a job for tidy folk. Those plain brown robes were clean and pressed, as were the bodies beneath. Hair always cropped in close.

Dama take pride in their long beards, but they're nothin' if not fastidious. Cavivat's robes are grubby and worn. His long hair and beard are knotted and wild, fingernails overgrown and filthy, and he stinks like a demon's outhouse.

But his aura is something else. Bright as Olive Paper's when she's full of fire, it pulses and pulls at a tether of magic seeping up from below.

Cavivat strides forward, wavin' his staff and shouting in the Jechi Hosta dialect. I don't catch much of it, but I can sense the crowd's attention on him. Ent caught a whiff of Alagai Ka, but just inside the gate there's a residual scent in the air. Drones were there just moments ago.

But they ent there now.

No one notices as I spider-crawl out of hiding and skitter under the lip of the gate.

It's an entry hall of sorts, with another smaller gate on the far side. Walls and floor are cut with an artisan's hand, and soaring supports around the room house statue nooks between. Squint and it might look like any other fancy hall, except the statues are all of demons.

Supports all meet in the center of the high ceiling, giving me plenty of places to hide as I have a look around.

The hall is packed with baskets and barrels, just like those the Jechi Hosta brought forth with their offerings. These are stuffed with gifts from the deep. Baskets of the meaty cave crabs Jechi Hosta favor in their cooking. Iron and other minerals for their forges. Barrels of oil for their lamps.

"Feed the mountain, and the mountain feeds you!" Cavivat shouts. He's been shouting a lot, but I can't follow most of it.

It all makes sense. How has this place stayed isolated for so long? With help from below. The villagers with gifts line up, each delivering a barrel or a basket, taking one in return and hurrying off smellin' like they just won the horseshoe toss at the fair.

Cavivat watches everyone, and I know it would be foolish for the others to try to sneak in this way. Even if they managed to squat behind a barrel and the priest didn't notice, the door on the far side is still shut, and I don't reckon things stay friendly once it's open.

"I have seen the mountain god in the Sight," the grubby priest cries. "He is a numinous being, far greater than we mere mortals. It is an honor to serve Him. Who else is prepared to meet His gaze?"

I crawl down the wall until I can peek out of the gates. Villagers are brought forward, most with gray hair and wrinkled skin, but others that look sickly or weak. One is missing a foot, the bandages still fresh.

The Jechi Hosta volunteer the ones that slow them down, but there are no tears, save those of joy. Folk really think they're off to live in Heaven?

Cavivat ent satisfied. He starts pacing the edge of the crowd, Drawing magic through the Jechi Hosta and into himself, to Read their lives like the rings in a tree stump. Occasionally he stops, tapping folk with his staff and sending a pulse of magic through them and those around.

Obediently, those chosen step forward, marching toward the gate, still singing. A girl who couldn't be more than eight. A handsome man with arms like a blacksmith. A young mother, serenely walking right into the demon's mouth with a babe still suckling at her breast.

I wonder if the babe's meant to be an appetizer, and feel like I might sick up.

But then Cavivat shouts something I don't understand, and waves begin rippling through the crowd, pushing forward until I see my friends shoved before the grubby priest.

He reaches out with his staff, tapping Rojvah and sending out another pulse of magic, but whatever the spell is, it dun't work on my friends. Harder to charm someone when they're wise to it.

The crowd opens and tries to push Rojvah forward, but Arick steps in, tripping and shoving anyone that puts a hand near his sister.

The crowd turns ugly at that. I hear cries of "Unbelievers!" and "Strangers!" as the Jechi Hosta surge forward. Wonda and Selen join the fight, blacking eyes and breaking bones. Even Kendall puts herself between Rojvah and the crowd. But there ent much they can do against thousands of angry villagers. They're quickly overpowered and hauled inside with the other sacrifices.

Cavivat follows, and the villagers who forced my friends into the hall are quick to exit before the grubby priest touches a symbol, and the great demon gate slams shut.

HERE I WAS worryin' about how to sneak my friends inside, and instead the villagers did it for me.

I crawl along the ceiling, watching. For a moment my friends are alone with Cavivat. Arick, Selen, and Wonda are lying on the ground, badly beaten but still conscious. All are trying to get shaky limbs under them.

Rojvah offered less resistance to the crowd, but as soon as the gates close, she slips her hero's bone *hanzhar* out of its hidden sheath and darts at the priest, blade leading.

Ent a good idea. Cavivat's back is turned until the last minute, but when he moves, he moves fast. Catches her wrist and twists the blade from her hand as he bashes her head with his staff. She falls to the ground, blood pooling around her.

The priest hisses, dropping the holy weapon like a hot frying pan. I can smell the burn where it touched his skin. I use the distraction to move until I'm directly above Cavivat, ready to pounce.

The inner gate groans and opens before I can let go. Cave demons come out in a swarm, moving quick on eight legs. Met their kind before out on the desert, and heard of them in Mam's stories. They can spin webs that are magic-dead and nearly invisible, yet strong as steel cable.

I want to get to Rojvah, to make sure she's all right. I want to help my friends. Mam wouldn't hesitate, but Mam can rip a demon's arm off and beat them to death with it. I have her knife, and maybe I could kill a cave demon with it, but there's dozens of them.

The demons avoid Rojvah's knife; the hero's bone relic's magic is anathema to them. One squirts a glop of webbing onto it to insulate its magic.

The Jechi Hosta finally realize they're not marching into Heaven and start screaming. The cave demons pounce and snatch them up in their forelegs, spinning them around as thick strands of silk bind their limbs to their bodies.

But the demons ent killing anyone. Ent even hurting 'em. Didn't know demons could be gentle, but they ent biting or stabbing with those long, pointed limbs, and they're careful not to web up anyone's mouth or nose.

Then they carry them through the second gate. Cavivat strolls after like he's walking in the garden. I move quick to the doors, but they don't close as the grubby priest and his demons exit. Instead, smaller worker drones come out and begin collecting the baskets of food.

Something to keep the sacrifices fed until the demons get hungry.

I spy Arick's kamanj case where a cave demon cast it aside. I let go of the ceiling and turn slippery, quietly absorbing the impact as I hit the floor. I keep my Cloak of Unsight wrapped tight around me as I collect Rojvah's *hanzhar* and the kamanj.

Then I suck in, my body becoming smaller and tougher as I move among the worker drones, trusting in Mam's cloak to hide me. Sucking in dulls my scent as well. I tiptoe quieter than a cat stalking a bird as I head for the gates.

And into the demon's web.

TRAIL ENT HARD to follow. Cavivat's stink leaves a trail like a demon with runny bowels.

Got to take special care. Made the mistake the last time I went into one of Alagai Ka's lairs of thinkin' I was invisible because of my cloak and pipes. And I was—to the demons. Even King Coreling himself.

But I wasn't invisible to folk the demon corrupted. They could see me plain as day in my magic cloak, and my pipes couldn't affect them the way they do demons. If anything, the music gave me away.

So I sneak the regular way. Selen and Wonda ent wrong that it's what I'm best at. I crawl the walls and ceilings with bare hands and feet, going slippery into crevices and then filling them to stick like a spider.

Even without the stink, all I need to do is follow the worker drones carrying food down into the hive, presumably to feed the prisoners. Six-limbed and low to the ground with reticulated spines, the demons can balance and carry huge loads on their backs.

They ent smart, though. Auras are flat as they go about their business, more like ants than farm hounds. Not worried they'll spot me, or even that they'll attack right away if they see me. Got to assume every demon in the hive could be eyes for Alagai Ka, though. If he tells them to, I bet the drones can turn from ants to wasps right quick.

The tunnel slopes steeply down, branching several times. Still don't smell Alagai Ka anywhere. Reckon he doesn't sully himself in the larder any more than royals slop their own pigs. That's good news if I want to get everyone out alive.

I pull up short, freezing in place as Cavivat comes back down the tunnel. He doesn't so much as glance upward, or acknowledge the drones filing past, save to snatch a couple baskets for himself.

I hesitate. Should I follow the priest, or the drones presumably heading toward my friends? I choose the latter, knowing the grubby priest's stench will linger in the air like a signpost for hours to come.

The drones lead me to a deep pit holding several dozen people, including my friends. They look relatively unharmed, though the Jechi Hosta are holding one another and weeping, understanding at last that they ent going to live in paradise with the mountain gods.

I see ugly whorls of pain in my friends' auras, but nothing looks broken. Everyone is conscious, cut free of the webs that bound them. Rojvah has her electrum pen in hand, and I know she can heal anything serious.

The drones line up, emptying the baskets into the pit, one after another. Food tumbles down to land battered and filthy on the floor, but the prisoners stampede blindly in the dark to fall on it like animals.

Reckon I could get my friends out. Maybe. Could sneak in easy enough, give Arick back his kamanj, turn us invisible to the demons while we find a rope or something to climb out of the pit.

But then there'll be six of us tryin' to sneak around, and the others can't crawl on the ceiling or slip into crevices too small for demons.

Long as they're okay, maybe I should sneak a bit more on my own. Find what we came for, or a way out.

Sack up, for once.

CHAPTER 50

JAILBREAK

Easy enough to find Cavivat. Leaves a trail of stink anyone could follow. Don't know what life is like for a human drone, but apparently bathin' ent part of it.

But I want to know what he's doin' with those other baskets. Ent for him. I can smell everything he's et in the last few days, and it sure ent fruits, vegetables, and bread. His diet is baser things, creatures that live in darkness, soaked in magic.

Like me.

We travel through a maze of tunnels. For once I stop holding back, letting my senses expand to their limits. Nothing is solid anymore, even the walls around us. All a mix of scent trails that travel anywhere there's air. Vibrations in the stone beneath my feet. The bounce of sounds and their resonance on objects. And most of all the magic, flowing through and around everything.

Tunnel walls become just a cloudy glass I can look through. I can see other tunnels, and the precision of their shape. I'm creepin' through a greatward.

Can't follow the grubby priest too close or he'll see me. I keep just a turn or two behind, advancing as he does until he comes to a stop in a place closer to the center of the ward.

There's a chamber there, but it's opaque at this distance. Need to get closer.

The priest ent paying any mind my way. He's opened a chamber on one of the stone walls, and is busy emptying one of the baskets into it. Then he locks it tight and works a lever. The food tumbles down a chute and into the chamber.

The walls are thick.

Cavivat moves on immediately, but I linger close to that chamber, reaching out with my senses.

The whole thing is a wardnet—walls, ceiling, and floor.

It's a Drain. A net made to suck magic, like a skeeter sucks blood. Even up the tunnel, I feel it tugging at the magic in my blood and suck in, toughening myself against the pull.

I inch closer, listening. Smelling. Tasting. Feeling.

There's someone inside. Knew that, of course, since the priest dropped in food, but I'm starting to make them out as I get closer. A silhouette setting crisscross on the floor, chin up high, sucked in like me to keep the drain from suckin' her dry.

A silhouette I'd recognize anywhere.

Mam!

Want to run up to the chamber. To pound on the walls. To hack at them with my knife. Her knife.

I ent stupid. This is like the Bunker, where the Warded Children would put those that et demon meat and got too drunk on magic to act responsible.

Closer I get, though, the more I see it ent working. Mam's aura is fuzzing a little at the edges where the Draw is greatest, but at its center it is bright, and serene. Running across the surface like a reflection on water, I can see the wards tattooed just under her skin in electrum ink.

Then I take one step too close, and she turns her head, seeing me like I do her.

Instantly the serenity in her aura is gone, and it is a wash of emotion as she leaps to her feet and goes to the wall closest to me, pounding it with her fists.

Mam really can punch through rock, but not this rock, which sucks at her own magic to make itself stronger. I can see she's shouting something at me, but I can't make it out. I get even closer, reaching out to touch the wall. Maybe if I can feel the vibrations, I can hear . . .

Suddenly Mam stops and starts frantically waving me off. I freeze, my fingers so close to the wall I can sense its crevices. Mam whisks her hand at me, and I can almost hear her shouting, "Shoo!"

I pull my hand back, trying to make something out of her gestures. Mam seems to come to the same conclusion, putting her hands on her hips as she considers the problem.

At last she comes to a decision. Pointing at me in an exaggerated gesture.

You.

She makes the shooing motion again.

Go.

She taps her nose.

Sniff. Smell?

She ent wearing skirts, but she reaches for an imaginary one, sweeping it about as she puts her nose in the air and struts about in perfect posture, pointing at things she does not deign to look at.

I snicker in spite of the circumstances. That's the easiest one.

Aunt Leesha.

Go sniff out Aunt Leesha.

It's an easy enough request, and the smart thing to do. Out of my depth in here, and Aunt Leesha always knows what to do.

But I don't want to leave Mam now that I've found her at last.

I stare a long moment, trying to think of something to say. I see pain and sadness in Mam's aura as she watches me. She points to herself, then to her heart, and then to me.

I love you.

This time I've learned my lesson, and say it right back. We stare at each other a moment longer, and then she claps her hands at me, and makes the *shoo!* motion again.

CAVIVAT'S TRAIL IS as easy to pick up as before. Need to hide when he doubles back, empty baskets in hand, but I breathe a little easier as his sounds recede. I keep my cloak pulled close around me, but I don't sense any corelings nearby.

The next prison is nothing like Mam's. Ent even got a wardnet. Just stone walls and a thick wood door. It's so unspecial it feels like a trap, and I creep up cautiously, reaching out with all my senses.

The woman inside ent setting serene like Mam was, and she ent struttin' around with her nose in the air. She's crawling on her hands and knees, feeling around for food that's right in front of her on the floor.

I can sense it through a wall, but without her crown and warded jewelry, Aunt Leesha's blind as the Jechi Hosta here in the darkness.

Stinks, too. Makes Cavivat smell rosy. Usin' one side of the room as a privy, but I doubt the demons care to clean it, or give her something to wipe with or wash up.

She's dehydrated. Smells like she ent fed often, maybe just an offering basket once a month. I watch her aura through the wall, meticulously sorting the contents of the basket and laying them out in a precise row, with things that spoil quick on one side and things that last on the other. Don't know how that pile could last anyone a month.

Even lookin' close, don't think her prison's anything more than it appears. Magic's always been a part of me, same as Olive. Came to Mam later in life, but now that it has it ent something she can just get rid of, or have taken away.

But Aunt Leesha ent got tattoos or *alagai* blood. She can't draw wards without her wand. Can't tell the future without her dice. Can't even see without her crown. Why bother with a Bunker to hold her?

Olive said the demon wanted to feed the magic-rich blood of his enemies to the new hive queen. Something of a demon tradition. But Aunt Leesha ent magic-rich. Demon's keeping her for the queen to feast on out of spite. Out of hate.

And that's a lot scarier.

Aunt Leesha lets herself eat a single, small tomato. She groans in pleasure as she savors it in her mouth, swallowing only reluctantly. Then she gets up and walks right toward me like Mam did. Like she knows I'm right there on the other side of the door.

Only she doesn't. She kneels and raises her arm very precisely, tracing an impact ward on the door with the tip of her fingernail, over and over in the exact same spot. I smell dried blood, and wonder how long she's been at this. Long as she's been in this cell, I reckon.

I can sense the groove she's worn. The ward has taken on substance, but there is nothing to power it with. Without magic, it's just some squiggly lines, and the hive ward regulates almost all the ambient magic in these tunnels. The bit that's left would take years to charge a ward big enough for a jailbreak.

I go right up to the door. "Aunt Leesha."

On the other side, she stiffens, turning her ear to the door like she's not sure she heard.

"It's me, Darin Bales," I say as loud as I dare. "Step back. Gonna slide under the door."

She moves back so fast she stumbles, landing on her bottom with a thump. Her heart and breath quicken into the beginnings of a full-on panic.

I let myself go slippery, squeezing under the door easy as a mouse. I drop to one knee beside her, reaching out to take her arms. She's shaking, and so very thin.

"Darin?" She croaks my name, and I hear the skin splitting on her cracked lips.

"Ay, it's me."

She lets out an awful sound that hurts my ears, and throws her arms around me, squeezing tight as she shakes and weeps, even if she's too dried out for actual tears.

Hate cryin'. Hate hugs most of the time, too. Never used to mind them from Aunt Leesha, though she never used to smell like a demon ate her and shat her back out.

But I'm so glad I found her, so glad she's okay, I hold my breath and squeeze back until I feel her wince. She hasn't atrophied, but her muscle tone is gone. She's all skin and sinew and bones, like old Favah.

I pull back and press my waterskin into her hands. "Drink. Breathe. Gonna figure out a way to get you out of here."

She's so dehydrated I expect her to throw her head back and empty the skin, but she takes just one sip, swishing it around and swallowing. "Do you have charcoal? And a clean cloth?"

"Ay, ma'am." I produce a cloth and a charcoal writing stick. Leesha takes a moment to gather her wild, tangled mass of hair and wind it together, tying it off with a bit of string. Then she wets the cloth and starts washing her face like a cat.

"Maybe I should . . ." I begin.

Aunt Leesha holds up a finger. "Patience, Darin."

That's the Aunt Leesha I remember, and something inside me unclenches as I wait. Wouldn't call her face clean when she's done, but she's gotten off most of the muck and grime. She takes the bit of charcoal and quick as if she was signing her own name, draws sight wards around her eyes.

She closes her eyes and breathes a moment, then reaches out, feeling around until she finds my hand. Slowly, she lifts it until my fingers just barely brush against the symbols.

It's enough for them to Draw a bit of my magic, and instead of sucking in, I let it happen. The wards begin to glow, and Aunt Leesha inhales like she's just been kissed. She opens her eyes and looks around, seeing the chamber she's been trapped in all these months for the first time.

"That's better." Something of the duchess' old tone of voice returns as she takes another sip from the waterskin. "I'll need tools. Do you have any demonbone? Electrum? A warding kit?"

All business, Aunt Leesha. Not so much as a *How d'you do?* or a *What in the core are you doing here?* Might be why I've always liked her. Don't have to do a dance to get to the point.

"Ent got any of that," I say.

Leesha sighs. "Your father would have."

Starting to understand why Mam doesn't much like her. "Ay, well. Ent my da."

Aunt Leesha tilts her head and it's like she can see right through me. "Oh, sweet Darin. I'm sorry. I didn't mean it like that."

She lays a hand on my arm, and it's hard to stay shady at her. But then she reaches down, pulling the pipes off my belt. "What's this? You said you didn't have any electrum."

She means the tiny electrum shell Inevera made me, to amplify the sound of my pipes. I snatch them back before she knows I've moved. "Pipes are mine. You can't have them."

Leesha frowns and I can see her readying a lecture, but I ignore it, reaching into my jacket. "But you can have this."

I hold out a fountain pen. Leesha takes it eagerly, but her emotions ent changed. She thinks she needs that shell more than I do.

"And this."

I hold out Mam's knife, and that pulls her up short. Mam's knife is a legend in Hollow. A foot of razor-sharp warded steel with a bone handle that runs deep with emotional resonance. Ent made of *hora,* but it glows with power anyway, and Aunt Leesha can see it. She takes the weapon reverently, running a finger along its edge and shivering.

"Oh, yes," she breathes. "Yes, this will do nicely."

I'M EAGER TO move on, but Aunt Leesha takes her sweet time, as Mam would say.

"Tell me everything," she says.

Getting good at this part. Hary says every time you tell a story it gets smoother, easier, better. I've been tellin' this one a lot. I start with Olive's disappearance, and quickly run through everything up until now, leaving out the part about where Olive is now, just in case the demon's been inside her head. Only say Olive's duch of Hollow, and building an army.

Aunt Leesha listens to it all rigidly, her emotions in check as she absorbs the information. While I talk she cuts away her sleeves and wipes her arms clean, then goes at them with the pen, covering her arms in sleeves of interlocking wardwork, then penning more on her hands and feet.

Can't follow what it all does, but I see the net activate and start Drawing power. Ent much in the air around us in the cell, but they'll charge quicker in the tunnels, restoring her strength, at least for a while.

She's careful not to Draw directly from Mam's knife. It has more than enough power to restore her, but the magic in Mam's knife ent the happy kind. Full of hate and pain, shame and anger. Reckon Drawing its power inward would be like experiencing all that pain like you lived it yourself. Mam might call Leesha a busybody, but it seems she doesn't want a peek inward the dark parts of Mam's life any more than I do.

I expect Aunt Leesha to use the knife to power the ward she scratched into the door. Blow it right off the wall. Instead she walks up to it and fits the blade into the seam of the doorframe. The cutting wards along the blade glow as she presses it right through the hinges and bolt like they were blocks of cheese.

"Be a dear and slip outside," she tells me, "then suck in and brace yourself. Pushing the door over onto you will cushion the impact, so we don't make too much noise."

I look at the big heavy wooden door, banded with steel. "Won't that squash me?"

"Nonsense," Leesha says. "You can withstand far more pressure than that when you're sucked in."

I cock my head at her. "How do you know my powers better than I do?"

Leesha sniffs, and there's the duchess again. "I've been observing you and Olive since you were born."

"Like we're some kind of experiment." Startin' to understand how Olive feels about her mam.

"Life is an experiment, Darin," Leesha says. "Observing. Learning. Evolving. That is how we survive. It doesn't mean I loved either of you less than any mum."

She means it, and if I'm to tell honest word, she's making a lot of sense. I think again of my missed moment with Rojvah. "Love you, too, Aunt Leesha."

I hold my breath as she hugs me again, then turn slippery and slide under the door. I brace my back against it and suck in. "Ready."

"Now," Leesha says. I hear the knife swish through the air, and the impact ward activates with a *thump!* I try to brace the door and let it down slowly, but it's too heavy and the impact too sudden. Door weighs a couple hundred pounds and comes down on me hard, but like she said, it ent heavy enough to harm me.

I turn slippery again, sliding out from under as Leesha steps from her cell.

I GIVE AUNT LEESHA my cloak. She made it for my da a long time ago, and I can see she feels safer with it around her shoulders.

"What about you, Darin?" she asks.

I hold up my pipes. "Got this."

I begin to play, using the magic shell to limit the music to just the hall around us. Occasionally we pass cave demon guards patrolling the ceilings, or worker drones going about their tasks, but they take no notice of us, even as they instinctively move out of our path.

Leesha looks at me when she thinks I don't notice, and under all the layers of stink, she smells nostalgic.

It doesn't take Aunt Leesha long to figure out how Mam's prison is warded up. 'Course it doesn't. This is why Mam sent me to fetch her first.

Even the door to Mam's prison is a bare slab of stone fitted into grooves in the wall. Would take a rock demon to lift it.

It's too thick for Leesha to cut through with the knife, and the Bunker might drain the knife's power if she tried. Instead she uses the charcoal to draw a large ward circle on the door.

"How are you going to power it?" I ask.

"I'm not." Leesha never takes her eyes off her work. "I'm going to tap into the Drain and use its own magic to power the circle."

As she draws the final shape, the circle lights up with magic. Then it seems to start spinnin'. Don't know if the circle is really rotating, or if it's an illusion of the magic streaking faster and faster around the wardnet.

The wards get hotter and hotter, brighter and brighter. I can smell the stone beginning to melt, the air starting to burn. I turn away from the light and put my attention back on my music.

Nothing to see here, my song says. *Everything's normal.*

The light and smell get so strong, accompanied by a loud hissing that dulls my music. I'm startin' to worry I won't be able to hide it from our captors when there's a final flare and I feel air from within the prison.

I turn and see a perfectly round window burned into the door slab.

Inside, Mam gets a running start, then dives through, landing in a roll that would do any Jongleur proud.

She's on me before I can reorient, wrapping her arms around me and hugging me harder than the falling door. "Darin Bales, you're just as reckless and brave as your da ever was."

"Ent," I say. "Just doin' what needs to be done."

Mam only squeezes tighter. "Ay, that's exactly what he would've said."

I squeeze her back, burying my face in her hair. Mam don't stink like Aunt Leesha. Benefit of being able to turn slippery is dirt and grime slide right off. She just smells like Mam, and for the first time in nearly a year, I feel like everythin's going to be all right.

"You all right, Leesha?" Mam asks over my shoulder. Two of them never much liked each other, but there's no sign of it, now.

"I've been better," Leesha admits.

Mam lets go of me, walking over and extending her hands. Aunt Leesha takes them, and gasps as Mam pulls in a bit of her aura, Reading it.

"Rude!" Leesha's brows tighten and she focuses her will, Drawing back stronger than you'd expect from someone it don't come naturally to. She gets a bit of Mam's power in return, lighting up the fountain pen wards on her skin. Her aura brightens. Already I can see the magic at work on her body, healing and strengthening.

"Sorry, Leesha." Mam lets go and takes a step back. "Had to be sure he din't get inside your head."

Leesha crosses her arms. "And?"

Mam shakes her head. "You're clean. Think messing around in someone's mind makes the brains taste awful, and he's lookin' forward to eating ours."

"Sunny." Leesha holds up Mam's knife. "I suppose you'll want this back?"

Mam's eyes widen, and there's a flare of fear in her, quickly burned away in anger. "Where did you get that?!"

"Darin gave it to me," Leesha says. "I couldn't have freed you without it. But I wasn't *rude* about it."

Mam calms at that. She turns to me, and I smell sadness, and regret.

"Knife's heavy, Darin. Must've been hard, carrying it around all this time."

We both know she don't mean the weight. Dark memories embedded in that bone handle. Could feel 'em, even if like Aunt Leesha I resisted the urge to pry. "A bit. But needed to get it back to you, din't I?"

Mam smiles and lays a hand on my shoulder before turning back to Leesha. "Keep it for now."

"All right, Darin," Leesha says. "Take us to where they're keeping the others."

Mam turns to me in surprise. "Others?!"

CHAPTER 51

THE HEIR

THE *ALAMEN FAE* are all calling me Erram now, even Kriva and Havell. The *fae* can't sense magic as I can in crownsight, but they see the *csar* responding to me as it once did my father, and it seems that is enough.

I don't entirely know if Erram is an honorific, like Duch; if it's a religious title, like Deliverer; or if they truly think I am Everam the Creator, walking among them.

Crownsight lets me gaze into their hearts, and I think it's on the latter end of the spectrum. I see utter, fanatical devotion, but also a deep and abiding fear of offending me. It makes me profoundly uncomfortable, but I don't even know how to begin addressing something I "see in their hearts" while trying to convince them I am not a god.

Even the *dama* are bowing and scraping now, and whatever resentments lingered among the Sharum over Rhinebeck's interference in *Domin Sharum* have been subsumed by the call to glory. Before we were marching toward an abstraction. Now the reality of defending the holy *csar* has set in, and their devotion moves me.

Sharik Hora pulses at the center of the *csar,* resonating in the crown like it's calling me. I allow myself to be drawn there, learning more and more about the *csar* and my new powers with every step. The crown was potent before, but here on the greatward it is nearly overwhelming.

Grandda Erny leans on a cane beside me, and I see not only the pain in his aura, but how it is outweighed by his love and concern. He will follow me without complaint until he collapses.

I lay a hand on his back, pulling a bit of the greatward's magic into him. It's effortless, and the power goes to work quickly, not simply healing his injuries, but sloughing off years like a dry scab. I give him back a decade as easily as I might massage his shoulders.

Perhaps the *alamen fae* are right to be afraid of me. I'm beginning to scare myself.

I am not the greatest believer, but as we approach Sharik Hora, the ancient Temple of Heroes' Bones does not question my piety. It senses the crown, and my purpose, and responds. Doors open and portcullises lift seemingly of their own accord as I walk at speed to the heart of the *csar.*

I've never seen a map of the temple, but it's as if I've known these halls all my life. I can sense every inch of stone, *hora,* and the people within. I can gaze into their hearts like looking off my terrace onto Mother's garden.

As I go, I delegate officers to secure the streets and position flamework weapons along the walltops. To search for survivors and find billeting. To guard the temple doors.

The great doors of Sharik Hora's prayer hall swing silently open at my approach. Within, nearly everything is made from human remains. The canvas of paintings is stretched human skin. Even the dyes and oils in the paint contain the remains of heroes. Rugs and tapestries woven of human hair. Oil and candles made from rendered human fat, unburned for thousands of years. I know instinctively their light and smoke would be anathema to the *alagai.*

There are pews to seat thousands, all made from human bone, polished and carved. Chandeliers made of rib cages and skulls that stare down in judgment.

Everyone is struck by the power and wonder of the place, but in the hearts of the Evejans it is overwhelming. Their knees weaken as they enter, and if not for the need to keep pace with my steady stride forward, they would fall to them in supplication.

But there is no time. On the altar there is a dais much like that in

Everam's Bounty, with a Skull Throne and a Pillow Throne beside. The Skull Throne is coated in electrum, and along its back are set seven fist-sized gems that pulse and throb in sync with the much smaller gems in my crown. I can see in crownsight how the Damajah removed them in turn, cutting away the chips that power the duplicate crown I wear.

But if this crown that has me brimming with power is the lesser version, what must Father's be like? I can see the flows of magic that connect each gem to its sibling at my brow. The flows split as they leave the throne, one ribbon connecting to me, and another to that other crown, wherever it is.

Could it really be the Crown of Kaji? Or has Alagai Ka found a way to mimic its power? It seems impossible. The gems are not power in and of themselves, they are a gateway, a connection, to the power of the *csar*. Some of that is raw core magic shaped by the greatward, but it is mingled with the holy magic of Sharik Hora, a magic born of faith that exists only to destroy the *alagai*. No demon, even the father of them all, could touch such power and hope to survive.

So the crown is likely real. That doesn't mean my father is wearing it. The demons could have killed him and taken it somehow. But the crown's power is keyed to heirs of Kaji. Inevera suspected Alagai Ka had meant Iraven to wear it, but my Majah brother is dead. One of my other brothers could use it, perhaps, but the holy family is ensconced in Everam's Bounty, as far from the demon's reach as Hollow.

The father waits below in darkness for his progeny to return.

That was Mother's prophecy for Darin Bales, but now it feels meant for me, even as he and the others—I pray—approach the mountain Safehold foretold in Mother's prophecy for me.

I can see the pain in Asome's heart as I ascend the seven steps to the Skull Throne. He truly believed it would be him, and because of Rhinebeck's interference, we will never truly know for sure he was wrong. He does not attempt to stop me as I turn and sit.

I am suffused with power, until I feel I must be consumed by it. There is no pain, just the roaring embrace of a hurricane, with me in the eye. I feel the storm bending itself to my will as my mind floods with knowledge and understanding that makes the wardcraft I learned in the Chamber of Shadows seem primitive by comparison.

The ribbons connecting me to the throne are gone. I *am* the throne. But still I see the others flowing through the air. I could follow them like a spool of yarn in a maze, a path leading to my father and, unless I am a fool, the demon hive. We thought it dormant, but it seems *alagai* have returned to ready the place for the return of its king and queen.

But what do I do now? Even the Damajah did not have much of a plan, once I reclaimed the *csar*. From here we can control the cavern, perhaps preventing the queen from physically entering the hive. But with the other crown still at large, will that be enough? Or will the fortress turn on us when we need it most?

Alagai Ka has laid a trap, and now it is sprung. I cannot leave the *csar* without yielding our advantage, but unless I do, we may yet be undone.

I look up, only to find everyone, even Amanvah and Asome, on their knees. The Krasians have their hands on the floor. Hollowers and Angierians keep their backs straight, even though they cast their eyes down. Only Rhinebeck rests on a single knee, looking up at me with love and awe in equal measure.

"Rise." I sweep a hand upward, and everyone gets back to their feet. What need do I have for such shows of supplication when I can see into hearts as easily as looking through a clear window? "We have won a great victory today, but it is not the war."

"We are strong," Ashia says. "We have the *csar*. The *alagai* will not get by."

I nod. "I am glad you feel that way. You will be in command until I return."

Everyone's aura goes cold at the words. Only Rhinebeck dares break the stunned silence that follows. "Your Grace?"

"My father is out there." I flick a hand into the distance. "The *alagai* have found a way to pervert the power of his crown, and until it is secured, our position remains tenuous."

"So it's a rescue." Gared is satisfied. "Your da and I ent exactly friends, but he saved the rippin' world. Ent gonna be left to the corelings while I'm around."

Mother used to say the general vexed her, but she always felt safer when he was close. Like Faseek, there is only loyalty in his heart.

"Ahmann Jardir is my uncle," Ashia begins. "I should . . ."

I hold up a hand. "Someone has to take command and hold these walls."

Ashia nods. "And that should be you, Olive asu Ahmann. Allow me to go in your stead and we will bring back my uncle."

"If this . . . other crown is trying to force open the gates," Rhinebeck asks, "what happens if you leave?"

"I can close them behind me," I say. "We can seal them with physical locks to keep the magic from forcing them open."

"And if they open before you return?" Rhinebeck asks, though he knows full well.

"Then they will stay open," I admit.

"And the greatward will deactivate," Rhinebeck notes, "and we will be infested again."

"They will stay closed until I return, then," I say.

"And if you don't return?" Rhinebeck presses. "How can we hold the cavern if the demons attack and our forces cannot sally forth from safety?"

He's deliberately poking holes in my plan, and I can't blame him. It's hardly airtight. But it's more than that. I can see it in his heart.

"Have you considered that this might be a trap?" Rhiney asks. "A trick to lure you from your place of power?" He looks around for support, but there is little to be had. This isn't helping his reputation among the *Sharum*.

"So long as the demon king has a connection to the fortress," I say, "it will never truly be secure. We have to break that connection, one way or another."

I leave unsaid the possibility we may need to kill my father. I don't want to believe it, myself.

"Perhaps there is another way," Asome suggests. I don't need to ask what he means. It's written all over his aura. He wants me to give him the crown and leave him in command of the *csar.* I can see hope of it swelling in him. He believes the desire is virtue, but I can peel his emotions away like layers of an onion, and know that if he blood-locks the crown to his head, he will never remove it willingly.

"I will need the crown to enter the hive." I don't look at him directly, but he takes my meaning and does not argue further.

"If the *chin* coward does not have the courage to go," Asome says, "he can stay here with the *Sharum'ting*. I will go."

"Ay," Rhinebeck sneers, "and look for another chance to kill Olive and take the crown."

Asome turns to face him, and immediately Rhinebeck's bodyguards raise their flamework weapons. My brother is fast, but not faster than bullets.

"Enough," I growl, and unbidden the *csar's* magic responds, snatching the weapons from soldiers' hands and dangling them in midair, just out of reach.

"Everyone except Rhinebeck get out," I say, and the others are quick to comply.

I come down from the dais to stand eye-to-eye with Rhinebeck. The anger I felt for him has dissipated, but it has not rekindled what we had just a short while ago.

"You lied about why you wanted the weapons," Rhinebeck says, "but I convinced Mother to give them to you. You lied about where we were going, but still I followed, even down into this night that never ends. Now we've done what we set out to do, and still you change the deal."

"He's my father," I say.

"Your father killed thousands when he invaded," Rhinebeck reminds me. "Because of your father, my whole family is dead. Angiers brought to the brink of ruin. We are still recovering, even now. I've followed you all this way, but I won't take my corps into the ripping hive to save the demon of the desert."

It's a common name in Thesa, used by those who suffered losses in my father's war. But his goal was always to save us all, no matter the cost.

It is my goal now, too.

"Then stay." I'm surprised how much the words hurt me. How much I want him to come. Like Gared did for Mother, I feel safer when Rhinebeck is around, however much he vexes me.

"Either way, you gamble our lives," Rhinebeck says. "Whether we follow you into the Core, or sit here, trapped within the *csar,* hoping you survive as we wait for a horde to descend upon us."

The prince of Angiers is not worthy of you. Amanvah's words come back to me again. Not a prophecy, she said, but it has the feeling of one. Rhinebeck is frightened, and out of his depth.

I kiss him, but it is a cold thing, mouths closed, bereft of warmth or passion. An apology. A goodbye.

CHAPTER 52

THE FATHER

When my father and Mr. and Mrs. Bales went down to the hive, they needed Alagai Ka, chained and shamed, to guide them through the maze of tunnels connecting to the cavern where the Spear of Ala sits.

That humiliation, much as anything, is why the demon hungers for revenge.

But I don't need the Father of Lies to guide us through the endless branches, twists, turns, slopes, and climbs to and through the demon hive. I follow the strands of power to the Crown of Kaji like Darin follows a scent.

I've kept the group small, but powerful. Twenty of my spear brothers. General Gared and ten of his best Cutters, along with the ten steadiest guns in the budding Hollow Flamework Corps. Asome, Amanvah, and twenty *Sharum*. I have looked into their hearts and trust them in this endeavor. Even my treacherous half brother.

Asome has shed his *kai'Sharum* disguise, dressed once more in *dama* white. At his belt is an alagai tail—the barbed whip of Krasian clerics whose bite I know well. He carries a flexible whip-staff, banded at the ends with electrum. Both are warded, and glow brightly, powered by potent demonbone cores.

The *alagai* are on alert the moment the gates of the *csar* open, but our group is small enough for me to comfortably protect with the crown. I extend the crown's dome of forbidding around us like the glass of a snow globe, and we ride through the massing demons unhindered as they claw helplessly at the barrier.

Those in front of us are shunted to the sides as we move, like water flowing around a boat. Wind demons circle above, and the Flamework Corps take aim.

"Hold your fire," I command. "Don't waste ammunition unless they're a threat."

It doesn't take long before they become one, carrying in stones to drop from above, even as the demons around us part to clear space for rock demons with boulders of their own.

"Hold," I say again, and concentrate. I am still getting used to the crown's abilities, but Kaji's dome of forbidding is legendary. Like throwing a punch, I quickly extend it outward, bowling the rock demons over and slapping wind demons from the air, then pull it back in.

My warriors do not break stride, but when stunned demons draw close to our lines, they are quick to take advantage and strike. We put on speed, but the exit from the great cavern is blocked by cave demon webs—sticky as tar, strong as steel cable, and magic-dead. Even in crownsight, they are visible only as shadows.

Outside the *csar,* much of my powers have faded. I can no longer heal with a touch or incinerate my enemies with a thought. The cavern floor does not respond as if part of my body. But the crown can tap into the ambient magic of the eternal dark around us, and bend it to my will. I raise a finger and focus, tracing a heat ward in the air and feeding it power.

The webs flash like lightning, blinding us with visible light even as they vaporize.

"Have a care, sibling," Asome notes with the casual air of discussing the weather, "or you may lose us in a puff of smoke as well."

"You must learn your own power, sister," Amanvah agrees.

Easy for them to say. I didn't want this power. Didn't ask for it. But this, too, Mother worked to prepare me for. I won't fail. I cannot.

"Incoming!" Gorvan shouts. I whirl to see a huge stone arcing through the air toward us. The dome acts as a barrier to the *alagai,* but like the magic-dead webbing, stones can pass unhindered.

Asome steps forward. "Observe." He performs an advanced whip-staff *sharukin,* but in crownsight, I see the power he is Drawing from the *hora* beneath the electrum cap, and the impact ward he traces in the air with its tip. With a final swipe he completes the ward and flicks the spell at the stone.

There's no explosion, only a *thump!* as the ward expends its power, knocking the stone off course to smash down amid the *alagai* gathered around us.

Then Asome touches his staff back to the ground, and I see it pulling at the ambient magic to refill its reserve. The lesson in restraint is well taken, but I can't help wondering how much power he could call upon if he opened the well completely.

He wonders the same about my crown. Images dance in his aura of him with it at his brow, incinerating demons by the thousand.

Purposely, I turn my back on him and continue.

Demons pack the smaller tunnels, where it is harder for the forbidding to push them aside. It gets harder for me to move while maintaining the dome, until I am brought to a halt.

"Clear a path," I say, and the warriors set to work, advancing to the edge of the forbidding and thrusting spears into the packed bodies.

Even in death, *alagai* cannot pass the forbidding, and their corpses fill the tunnel. I am forced to pull the dome in close, withdrawing its protection from my escort.

But this is what we've all trained for. My greatest power had been effectively neutralized, but it frees me, as well. I join my spear brothers on the front line, calling commands while spearing corelings like I'm back in the Maze.

Tight spaces normally favor the defender against greater numbers, but I can still use the crown to stop the *alagai* in their tracks anytime we need to catch our breath. The limited space means the demons do not have room to hurl projectiles, and we carve through them in droves. The few injuries the demons inflict in return are quickly healed by bodies charged with feedback magic.

Up ahead, the tunnel widens into another cavern, and we push forward into it. I'm about to activate the dome once more when something strikes me about the face and shoulders, blinding me. It feels like slime at first, but when I try to move, I find myself stuck fast as it thickens into fiber.

Even as I flex my arms in an attempt to break free, I am hauled off the ground and up toward the stalactite ceiling. The effort sets me to swinging, losing much of the expended force. I can feel the vibration as the creature uses four legs to rapidly reel in its catch. There are shouts of alarm below, but there is little any of them can do. They're more likely to kill me with magic and projectiles than whatever lurks above.

My stomach seems to fall away as I ascend. Even if I kill the demon, can I survive the fall? Tales say my father could fly, but in all the paintings he did it with the Spear of Kaji held in both hands, pulled along by its power. I don't think that can help me now.

But none of that matters if I become a cave demon's meal. My hands are still free, and I snatch my *hanzhar,* slashing through the strands that bind my upper arms. Then I pray for control as I squeeze my eyes shut and lift a finger of my free hand to draw a desiccation ward in front of my face. Too much power, and this will be magic-assisted suicide, but I draw just a touch, not from the powerful but unpredictable flows around me, but the crown's more stable reserve.

I hear a crackle as the adhesives dry out, and punch myself hard in the face, shattering the web and clawing it away from my eyes.

It's almost too late. My first sight is the gaping maw of the largest cave demon I have ever seen. There are no teeth, but its fangs drip with venom, and the sharp ridges of its huge chelicerae threaten to mash and masticate as I am pulled inside.

I raise the crown's forbidding, but the demon is . . . altered. Looking down its mouth I can see powerful magic, but its exoskeleton is as magic-dead as its webs, and the barrier has no effect.

I trust in my armor to protect me as the fangs come in, but even the Tazhan masters did not account for *alagai* so powerful. The demon's fangs punch through my *alagai*-scale armor like nails into wood.

I scream as I feel them pump venom into my body. I've seen cave demons eat, and it is horrible. They dissolve prey on the inside with their venom, then suck the foul remains from the husk.

I slash instinctively with my *hanzhar*, cutting off the fangs before the demon has a chance to withdraw them. Not my wisest move. The cave demon lets out a high-pitched chittering as ichor and venom pump from the wound. It throws its head back to toss me between its chelicerae as they open and slam shut over and over with crushing force.

The sharp ridges do not penetrate my Tazhan armor as the fangs did, but I am battered and bruised, struggling to get my bearings. While this cave demon's webs and exoskeleton are too mundane for the crown to affect, its venom relies heavily on magic to do what nature does with chemics and enzymes.

It takes only a thought for the crown to absorb the magic, neutralizing the venom enough for my body to handle the rest. Already I am healing, flesh knitting and working to push the fangs out. They fall to the cavern floor, far below, where my bodyguards no doubt fight for their lives against an overwhelming foe.

The next time the chelicerae open I curl up, and when they move to close again I heave with all my strength, hearing a satisfying snap as one of the appendages loses all strength. I'm still caught by its web, but with my feet dangling in midair I stab my *hanzhar* into the exoskeleton to hold on to as it thrashes.

Those long, magic-dead forelegs come stabbing in, and I twist, kick, and parry with my free hand, trying to keep them all at bay. One slips through, and again the sharp point breaks through my armor and impales me.

I see the demon's many eyes staring at me, mirrors into its aura, and I gaze into them with crownsight. This is no natural demon. It has emotions. Intelligence. A body designed to pierce defenses, both magical and mundane.

I can see Alagai Ka's hand in it, taking a baser coreling and working it with magic, reshaping it into a weapon, a lieutenant.

A *kai'alagai*.

I am surrounded by countless stalactites, but echoing through them I can hear cave demons skittering our way, come to defend their *kai*.

With no time to experiment with wardings I take a direct approach, balling a fist and punching between the rows of the demon's eyes. The thin strip of carapace shatters and I thrust my hand into the wet, ichorous opening. Here at last I can reach the creature's magic, and I use the crown's power to activate a Draw, sucking it out like a *minoc*.

I am flooded with power, but after sitting on the Skull Throne in the Spear of Ala, it is not enough to overwhelm me. Even as the *kai's* aura is extinguished, I redirect the power to the crown's forbidding, thrust the barrier as far as it will go.

And then I am falling, along with dozens of cave demons I knocked from their perches on the cavern ceiling. Still flush with power, I wonder if perhaps I can survive the fall, but I am not eager to find out. I draw a wind ward as the floor comes rushing toward me, and the blast of air arrests my momentum, even pushing me back up for a moment.

I fall the remaining thirty feet, but there's time to twist to my side, and the impact does little more than knock the air from my lungs. The other cave demons aren't so lucky, their exoskeletons shattering against the stone as they fall like raindrops from the sky.

My bodyguards have retreated into the narrower tunnel to limit the area they must defend, but they are hard-pressed on both sides, even with my brother and sister invoking considerable magic to hold the line.

"To me!" I call, again raising the dome. My spear brothers give a cheer, and throw up a shield wall as they advance to join me and we resume our progress. I wrap Mother's Cloak of Unsight about myself now, knowing the demons will seek me out in particular, if they can.

I SENSE A CHANGE in the flows of the ambient magic when we enter the hive. The power is Drawn into the hive ward, but without Alagai Ka or a queen at the center of the warding the power lies dormant, and we move unhindered by it.

If anything, the regularity of it makes it easier to sense deep into the tunnels as I follow the ever-strengthening call of my father's crown.

The *kai'alagai* come in different types. One is a sand demon as big as a horse. Its sand and clay demon minions tunnel under our path, and the forbidding is no protection when the floor collapses beneath us.

Against anyone else, the move would have been devastating. Countless sand demons wait in the tunnels for us to fall, surprised and disoriented, into their trap. But the crown holds them back as we collect ourselves and set to killing.

Next is an altered flame demon, who with its brethren tries to smoke us out, setting fires that choke the tunnels with non-magical smoke. My wind wards are enough to clear the worst of it, as Amanvah and Asome reverse desiccation wards, drawing moisture from the air to douse the fires and any flame demons that do not flee quickly enough.

There are no false turns as the train leads us unerringly to the prison, a three-dimensional greatward like the hive itself, but solid, as if poured into a mold, rather than made of the negative space of the tunnels. It stands before us like some twisted tree, branches growing wild in every direction.

But in crownsight, I can see how the greatward pulls magic from its center and perverts it, sending out the ribbons of power that command the *csar's* defenses to stand down.

I peel away the layers of stone in crownsight and see a human aura within, trapped in a space no larger than a coffin. There are holes in the stone, just large enough to allow for a pocket of air inside, but so small I doubt even Darin could slip through.

"Father!" I call. "Father, can you hear me?" There's no reply. He could be bound, or unconscious.

Or it could be a trap.

But I've come too far, fought too hard, to walk away now. If it's a trap, time it was sprung.

"Break it."

Gared and the Cutters step up, carrying heavy warded mattocks. The tools were designed more for wood than stone, but years of feedback magic have strengthened them beyond mere wood and steel.

While the *Sharum* stand guard, Amanvah, Asome, and I point to different branches of the twisted ward, and the Cutters break them off like cutting limbs from a tree before chopping it down.

The signal to the *csar* changes with each branch we remove, until it stops entirely. Only then do the Cutters put their mighty arms to work breaking the stone around the coffin-like chamber at the center.

Cracks start to form, but the men take their time, careful not to harm whoever is inside.

They needn't have bothered. As the ward lost power, the aura inside strengthened, becoming brighter and brighter. The cracks begin to glow, and the Cutters scatter just in time as the stone explodes outward, revealing Ahmann Jardir, my father.

FOR A MOMENT I am stunned, unable to believe it's really him, that he's really here. For all the time he's been trapped, he doesn't seem to have lost weight, or muscle. Has he been drawing on the power of the crown all this time to stay alive?

His face is a mask of rage, and the power that burns around him is terrifying to behold. The others tense, worried Alagai Ka may have corrupted him, but I don't believe it. The Crown of Kaji is still blood-locked to his chin. Even unconscious, demons could not touch it, could not remove it.

His eyes fix on me, and something softens. He tilts his head. "Olive?"

It's not my face or form he recognizes—Father hasn't seen me since I was a babe. He's seeing something deeper as he peers at me in Crownsight.

I nod, and he eases his stance, drawing the power crackling all around him back into the crown—the real crown.

Suddenly I feel foolish, standing here in what I see now is only a pale replica. *I* am a pale replica, a child clomping around in Father's enormous boots. We stare at each other in lengthening silence. For sixteen summers I've dreamed of what I might say upon meeting this man, yet now that the moment is here, none of it is adequate. *Where were you?* doesn't seem a fair question for someone who has just escaped a coffin of stone.

"Father." Amanvah steps forward as she breaks the silence. Our father turns to her, and I can't help but feel a twinge of jealousy as he recognizes her face and opens his arms without hesitation.

Father's aura is unreadable to me, but images dance around Amanvah, and I see how familiar even their embrace is. Father hasn't held me since I was in swaddling, but he has held Amanvah, his firstborn daughter, countless times.

She senses it, too, turning to draw attention back to me. "Mother sent us to secure the Spear of Ala, but it was Olive who . . . sensed you close by, and insisted we come to your aid."

He reaches for me, and I take an instinctive step back. I don't know why I do it, but Father inclines his head, and I realize I do not have his skill at masking my aura. He looks into my heart as easily as I have been doing to others.

"You are right," he says after a moment. "You had a right to know me. All my children do. Ever I was a warrior first, a ruler second, and a father last."

My throat catches as he steps forward again. This time I hold my ground, allowing him to put his hands on my shoulders. "But know, child, that I am proud of you. I see the glory in your spirit, and it is boundless."

"Father." Asome does not speak in the confident voice he uses with others, but something much more vulnerable. Still speechless myself, I understand.

Father looks at him as if noticing him and the others around us for the first time. His eyes take on the faraway look of crownsight, like he's looking right through his son and into infinity.

"After all these years, my son," Father shakes his head sadly, "still blinded by your own pride to the glory you could achieve."

Even though it doesn't touch his face, the effect of the words on Asome's aura is devastating. There was no accusation in the words, no punishment. It reminds me of Mother's *I'm disappointed in you* look, which always hurt worse than the rare occasions when she got fed up enough to shout.

Father's aura is unreadable, apart from my sense of his power. Decades of practice have taught him control over what others can see. But now that I have tasted crownsight, I know he sees the impact of his words on his son as clearly as I do. If he had struck Asome to the ground, it would have done less harm.

I find my voice at last. "Your absence shaped us as much as your presence, Father. I expect you visited the Tower of Nothing as often as you did Hollow."

I can barely believe it. All my life I have dreamed of this moment. Of Father holding me and telling me he was proud, and now that I have it, I would rather defend a brother who tried to kill me.

To everyone's relief, General Gared clears his throat. "Ay, maybe the family reunion can wait until we're out of this rippin' hornet's nest and back in the fort?"

Just like that, the moment is shattered. A regal air of command comes over Father, and he turns to Gared. "You are correct, son of Steave. Report."

"We're in the outskirts of the demon hive," I say. "It took us two days to get here from the Spear. Your prison was a greatward that twisted the signal of the Crown of Kaji into opening the gates of the *csar,* which was overrun. The Damajah's crown," I touch the circlet, "allowed us to close them again. We have a force of ten thousand at the walls, but an assault is coming. A new demon queen is hatching, if she has not already, and they will need to cross through the *csar's* cavern to take possession of the hive."

"Which we cannot allow," Father agrees. "We must get back to the *csar.*"

"Father, what happened to your spear?" Asome asks.

"Lost," Father says. "The Father of Demons laid a trap for me, and in my arrogance, I flew right into it. Separating me from the Spear of Kaji was the first part. Perhaps the first Deliverer's weapon remains where it fell, or perhaps the enemy found a way to destroy it."

He speaks of losing one of the greatest artifacts of the first Deliverer like he would a hammer forgotten on a worksite.

Father looks at Asome, but it is as if he can read my thoughts. "It is just a thing, my son. Our people, Sharak Ka, they are what is important. The spear and crown are linked. If I am meant to find it again, I will. If not . . ." He shrugs. "*Inevera.*"

CHAPTER 53

HATCHLING

DON'T NEED MY pipes now that Mam's leading the way. She's got unsight wards tattooed all over her, and feeds them steady power to surround us all in a cloak even Cavivat can't penetrate.

Feels so good to just do as I'm told and trust the adults. Hate feelin' like everything's on me all the time.

"Proud of you, Darin," Mam says when I've caught her up on the basics of what's happened since she's been gone. Her scent is honest and there's nothing sunnier she could ever say to me, but it dun't feel right.

"Ent told you everythin'," I say. "Might still have a thing or two to holler about."

"Won't lie and say you ent been reckless, comin' here and bringin' the other kids," Mam says. "But it'd have to really be somethin' to get me to holler after this. Din't put out the sun, did you?"

"I kind of . . . got promised," I say.

That stops Mam short, and I nearly walk right into her. I expect Aunt Leesha to complain, but I see she's pulled up at the words, too.

"Selen Cutter?" Mam asks, a smile twitching at the corner of her mouth.

"No." Disappointment in both their scents.

"Ami Rice?" Mam guesses. "She always shined on you."

Ami Rice shined on me? Me, the weird kid who skipped school and hid from the sun in Soggy Marsh? That don't make a lick of sense, but I ent got time to think about it.

"Ent been back to the Brook since we left." I start walking again. "It's a long story."

Not *that* long, as it turns out. Mam leaves us in a safe spot while she fetches the others out of the demon's livestock pit. All it takes is one look as I give Rojvah back her sacred bone *hanzhar* and she throws both of us into a hug. We tense up, but Mam keeps a warm, even hold until all three of us relax.

"Does this mean we have your blessing?" Rojvah whispers.

"Ay." Mam sobs a little. "All the blessin's in the world. You and Arick were already family. Now it's just official."

Everyone starts huggin', then, and I do my best to stay out of it. Rojvah holds out the electrum pen when she and Aunt Leesha have their turn. "Your Grace, your father made a gift of this to me, but I think you will make better use of it."

Aunt Leesha keeps eye contact with Rojvah, but she *wants* that pen. So much it scares me a little. She keeps her hands at her sides, that regal and aloof way she has, but aura, scent, and muscle are focused on that pen like a cat fixin' to pounce.

And why not? No one in the world better able to use one of those things. They were invented in Hollow. And havin' a rope from your da appear when you're stuck in a hole . . . know how that can overwhelm a body. Aunt Leesha's been helpless a long time, and even more than Mam's knife, that pen can help her get somethin' back of who she was before all this.

"Thank you." Aunt Leesha gives Rojvah a kiss on the cheek as she graciously accepts the gift, but she ent the same once she's got it in her hands.

She takes the sheath with Mam's knife from her waist and offers it back. "I won't be needing this anymore, Renna, thank you."

A weight seems to lift off her with the words. Mam used to say owin' Aunt Leesha a favor felt like wearin' an itchy sweater, and she couldn't wait to pay them back. Reckon the feelin' was always mutual.

Can smell Mam's relief when she takes it back. Reckon it's how Leesha felt about the pen. How I'd feel, if someone had my pipes. Know it's right for it to be back in Mam's hands, but not sure I would have survived the last year without Mam's knife. Harder than I thought, giving it up.

Mam catches me lookin'. "Ent been keepin' secrets, Darin." Her voice drops, too low for the others to hear. We used to do this all the time, havin' conversations no one else could catch. "Was only waitin' till you were old enough."

"Old enough now?" I have to ask, but part of me hopes she'll say no.

"That was your grandda's knife," Mam says, "and Harl Tanner was as mean a son of the Core as you'll ever meet. Put hurts on folk just to forget his own, includin' his own kith and kin. But Creator as my witness, Dar, no one was fool enough to try fightin' him twice. There's anger in this." She pats the sheath. "And hate. And pain. But when you're in a scrap for your life, there ent an armor in the world that's a match for it."

Thought I might find some comfort in the secret, but instead there's a new chill in my bones. Know what she means. Felt the pain imprinted on the bone, even if I didn't understand it. There's more she's not tellin', but I've got all I can handle just now.

Arick ent doing much better. He's wound up like a noose, and I can smell his panic. Can't blame him. These tunnels feel a lot like the hive ward out in the desert, where Alagai Ka got in his head and turned him on his friends.

"All right, Arick?" I ask as I go to him.

"What do you think?" Arick whispers. "I don't suppose you've brought my spear?"

I shake my head, pulling his kamanj case off my back. "You can do more with this, anyway."

I can tell he's too knotted to believe me, but Rojvah still has her choker, and I've my pipes. The three of us have power even in this place, if we can work together. Selen's got her warded rings, Wonda's arms are covered in sleeves of tattooed wardwork, and Kendall still has her fiddle case, not to mention a few bits and bobs of warded jewelry. Maybe we're in over our heads, but we ent helpless.

Not that it matters much, with Mam around. Anything she can't handle is apt to be too much for us, too.

"We need to get out of here before they notice we've escaped," Leesha says.

"Ay, you do," Mam agrees. "Take the kids and head out quick. Don't look back."

Aunt Leesha dun't like that answer, and neither do I. "What about you?"

"Be along once I've finished up some old business," Mam says.

"Renna Bales, don't be an idiot," Leesha snaps, and it's all I can do not to go slippery. No one gets to talk to Mam like that.

Mam throws a glare that would make Alagai Ka shit his scales, but Leesha don't back down. "He took us both together, Renna, with an army and the Warded Children besides."

"Ay," Mam agrees. "And he's going to pay for it, and for taking a swipe at my boy."

"Yes!" Leesha agrees. "But not here, in his place of power."

"Did it once, when the queen was big as a house," Mam says. "Ent got any problem makin' an omelet out of this one before she hatches."

"You didn't do that alone," Leesha reminds her.

Mam mashes her lips. "Got a better plan?"

"We run," Aunt Leesha says. "We get back to Hollow, where Olive is already building an army. We call Inevera, and raise the greatest army in history to go to the Spear of Ala and destroy the hive for good."

I stiffen at the name, glancing at Selen. She, Rojvah, and Arick all do the same.

Din't tell Mam and Aunt Leesha about Olive and the Spear. Din't want them to worry, I guess, and Olive made me promise not to tell anyone who din't need to know. Truer is, anyone, Wonda, Kendall, Leesha, even Mam, could be working for the demon king and not even know it.

But Mam and Leesha both see the change in our auras, and the looks we all exchange.

"What was that?" Mam demands.

"Ay, well . . ." I rub the back of my neck where it clenches up at her tone. "Said I din't tell you everything . . ."

Mam puts her fists on her hips, and I know the smell when she ent got any patience left. "Out with it, Darin Bales."

"There's already an army at the Spear of Ala, or one was headed there." I swallow hard. "Olive's leadin' it."

Mam's eyes narrow, and I know she's mad as spit. "And you din't think it worth mentioning?"

Used to sensing Mam's anger. It's always there, like a knife on her hip even when she's calm as trees. Aunt Leesha don't get angry, though. Frustrated? Sure. Irritated? Plenty. But angry? Ready to kill somethin' angry? Never.

Until now. "Darin Bales . . ."

I'm suddenly glad she gave back the knife. She takes two steps my way and instantly Selen Cutter is standin' between us, ballin' a fist. "Take a breath, Leesha."

"Olive is my *child*." Leesha blows out the word in a harsh and shaky breath as she takes another step forward. She ent holdin' her electrum pen, but she could snatch it quick.

"Ay, what of it?" Selen doesn't budge. "She's my niece and best friend since we were playing in the same crib. Spent more hours with Olive than you ever did, Leesha Paper. Don't you tell me I don't understand. Olive made us all swear not to tell anyone."

"It is true, Your Grace," Rojvah says, coming to stand next to Selen.

"Even me?" Leesha demands.

Arick steps in next, and Leesha is forced to stop her advance. "You have been prisoners of Alagai Ka." He says the words as if to a child. "Even now, how can we truly trust you, in the lair of the Father of Lies?"

Leesha inhales, calming at that. She's more of a thinker than a feeler, and I can smell her making her calculations. Arick's got a point, and he should know.

"Point is," I say into the tense quiet, "Olive's right where the demons need to go, if that queen hatches."

Now the anger's back. Leesha puts her hand on the electrum pen. "So we kill her, and the demon king, once and for all."

"Ay, that's the spirit." Mam puts a hand on her knife. "You and me, just like old times."

Leesha snorts. Truer is the two of them never got along.

"Ent the two of you," Selen says. "It's all of us."

"It most certainly is not," Aunt Leesha snaps.

Selen ent impressed. "You're my sister, Leesha, not my mum. And I don't listen to her, either."

Aunt Leesha draws herself up at that. "I am your duchess."

Selen laughs. "Not anymore. Hollow thinks you're dead. We all went to Olive's coronation."

There's that anger again. "Wonda, please escort . . ."

Wonda clears her throat loudly, interrupting. Aunt Leesha turns to look at her, smelling of shock and surprise. Don't think this has ever happened before.

"Sorry, mistress," Wonda cuts in, "but I'm with them on this one. Ent losin' you again, no matter what you say."

"Either we all run," I say, "or we all stay. And if we run, don't reckon we'll get another chance, and everything comes down to Olive."

"Won't be able to look after you kids in there, Darin," Mam says. "Going to need you to look after yourselves."

I swallow. So much for settin' back and lettin' the adults take charge. "Came all this way to get you. Ent runnin' off while you go in deeper."

AUNT LEESHA LOOKS stronger and stronger as we go down into the ward. Still smells like Grandda's outhouse that time the fish stew went bad, but she's been working on herself with the electrum pen, steadily suckin' on magic like a calf at the udder. Hidden by her Cloak of Unsight, her aura is bright, and her thin, toneless muscles have grown thick and taut. She still smells angry.

"We break the greatward first," she's tellin' Mam. "Then we storm the center. Darin and the children can hang back with their instruments. I—"

"Ent interested in practicin' a dance with you, Leesha," Mam cuts in. "Can't plan a fight. You'd know that, you ever been in one. Moment the demon senses us, all plans are out the window and it's kill or be killed. You ready for that?"

"Oh, I'm ready," Aunt Leesha growls, and again I'm glad she's on our side.

Hive wards are great cave systems meant to collect and reshape magic venting from the Core. Even if we can't see the whole thing, it's easy to follow the flows to the center, where the lines converge. Find the right spot and cause a cave-in, the whole thing might snuff out like a candle.

But then what? Ent even sure what the ward does. The greatward in Hollow keeps demons out, but this one doesn't seem to affect us at all. Where's all that power going? What's it for?

I'm a little light-headed, reaching out with all my senses to look for trouble. Keep expectin' to find a pack of demons standin' guard. I can smell them everywhere, as well as Cavivat and other, more faded human scents, tinged with fear.

Suppers past.

But there's nothing. We get to a convergence point, and Aunt Leesha and Mam stop together. They look up at the ceiling where we've just passed, eyeing it like a target. Bringing it down might take away some of the demons' power, but it will also trap us in with them.

Like we ent trapped already.

"Steady, Intended." Rojvah's hand slips into mine, and I squeeze it gratefully.

But somethin' ent right. Alagai Ka ent fool enough to let a spot like this sit without a guard. Is this even the right spot? I can see the walls around us guiding the flows of magic, but the scents and sounds are all wrong. It reminds me of the cliffs on the road to Safehold.

Slipping my hand from Rojvah's I pick up my pipes, improvising a tune to follow around the walls with my senses. The vibrations at my feet, the echoes in my ears, the air on my skin.

"It's a trap," I say as I pierce the illusion and realize we're not alone.

"Clever as your sire," Cavivat laughs, and the veil drops, letting the others see what I've just discovered.

We're deeper than we thought, at the center of the ward. It's a great wide chamber, and behind Cavivat at its center is a well of magic so strong it's like a pit dug halfway to the Core. Beyond that are other tunnels, teeming with corelings. Cave and sand and clay demons, mostly, but there's a little of everything. They know we're here. I can tell.

Alagai Ka himself stands rigid by the well in the center of the chamber, the magic passing through him and into the mimic queen like blood through an umbilicus. The little dangle between his legs has grown, standin' up like he's got wood in the mornin'. Still ent much next to the queen, who's big as a barn, but I reckon it ent for her. Magic has Alagai Ka stuck, waitin' on the new queen to hatch so they can mate.

Then somethin' inside the mimic queen moves, and I notice the ichor pooling on the floor, full of demon stink but drained of magic. A seam appears in the queen's belly, opening in a flap. A head pokes free, covered in ichor. Rows of sharp teeth are stuck with meat as the hatchling consumes the mimic queen from the inside.

The new queen slithers out of her mam, covered in gore and blazing with magic. She looks at us with giant, unknowable eyes, and a chill runs through me.

"Did you think you could hide?" Cavivat sneers. "I knew you were coming before you did. We have been watching since you pierced the outer veil. You arrive just in time for the queen to feed."

THOUGHT I WAS used to seein' Mam angry. Thought Aunt Leesha was scarier. Turns out, never seen Mam angry. Least, not really. Not like now.

"Ent dinner, yet," is all she says, but magic starts buildin' up in her, fixin' to burst.

Cavivat laughs again. "You actually thought you were coming to fight! Delightful! The breaking of hope will make your minds delicious."

"Bold talk," Mam is lookin' at the demon, not the priest, "with you too horned up to move. What's to stop me coming over and crackin' open that big head of yours?"

"The queen is far more powerful than I," Cavivat says, "but she is hungry. Already she has stung and feasted upon her dam, but it is not enough. For a young queen, it is never enough. Your bodies are magic-rich, and will nourish her well, even as they prove what her Consort can do to her enemies. We will mate, and swarm. After millennia, we will destroy the fortress of Kavri and consume the new Unifier, if it is not already done."

Master always spins ale stories where the villain brags out their plan. Never made much sense to me, so I asked about it.

Pride is what separates villains from heroes, Hary said. *It is not enough for a villain to* be *great. Everyone must be forced to* acknowledge *their greatness.*

But Alagai Ka dropped a clue in his bragging. Maybe he knows where Olive went, but he doesn't know any more than we do what's happening there. Probably hasn't left this chamber in months.

Maybe he's right and she's dead anyway, but like with Mam, I just can't believe it. Olive Paper ent one to die easy. Maybe she's found the *csar.* Maybe she's found her da. Maybe . . .

I give a little shake, tryin' to snap out of it. What's the point of maybes? Dun't change anything here. Can't look to Olive to save us. If Alagai Ka and that new queen mate and get back to the hive, she'll start spitting out eggs, and threaten to undo everything my da died for.

Ent the only one to see it. Even before Mam explodes, Aunt Leesha raises her pen, writing a series of cutting wards quick as I can sign my name, sending them streaking toward the queen with enough power to cut through a city's wardwall.

The queen just buzzes her wings, dissolving the spell into raw magic and absorbing it. The queen has rows of segmented legs to support her abdomen. The mimic's is large and distended, armored exoskeleton holding its shape even as the hatchling hollowed it out.

Queen's is round, but still sleek and light. She tamps down and leaps, flying across the room at Aunt Leesha. Six wings pump rapidly, multiplying her speed. Her reticulated tail is bent over her head like a scorpion, stinger poised to strike.

Aunt Leesha responds by drawing a queen ward in the air like it was written in silver fire. Queen bounces off it, but she ent hurt. Most wards work by stealing corelings' own magic and throwin' it back at them, but the queen ent givin' anything up. All the power's comin' from Leesha's pen, and that has its limits.

The queen stabs at the forbidding with the clawed ends of her forelegs. First two bounce off, but the third punches a few inches through, sending a shower of sparks like a log poked on the fire.

Mam tackles the queen away before she can strike again. She cries out as the queens' wings cut at her, and I smell blood, but she works her way in between them, where neither wing nor leg can reach her. Her arm moves so fast even I can barely keep up, stabbing into the thorax again and again. Like the forbidding, the first few skitter off, but Mam was right about that blade, and soon even the queen's armor begins to crack.

The stinger comes for her, but Mam is ready for it, collapsing into mist and re-forming atop the reticulated tail as the stinger strikes the cracked armor, punching through.

It looks like a kill, but it ent. Queen stabs herself, but she doesn't pump any venom, and before the stinger is in too far, the tail flicks back hard, smashin' Mam into the stone.

"Renna!" Aunt Leesha cries, drawing another queen ward to knock the demon away from Mam.

Cavivat charges her, staff raised like a club, but he's intercepted by Wonda and Selen. Arick looks ready to help them, but the demons around the room, frozen a moment ago, start to move for us.

I have my pipes to my lips before the others can react, using all the power in the little warded shell to fill the room with my song. No point tryin' to hide. That many demons will trample us flat whether they see us or not.

Instead I sow confusion, driving them back and into one another with sharp, stabbing notes. Corelings are creature of vicious instinct, and not too particular about who they scrap with. Happy to lash out at one another when they stumble together.

Another clue. If Alagai Ka was controlling them directly, there would be greater discipline in the demon horde. But he's still frozen in place, the queen sucking magic from the well through him like water through a straw. She's gettin' stronger by the moment, and even if Mam kills her, that will just free him to destroy us.

Key is to get to him, first.

Rojvah lifts her voice to join me and Kendall's bow touches string, but I'm in the lead, feeding the chaos with our song as I work out the plan. Can't get the corelings to attack Alagai Ka. Don't think they could intentionally lift a claw to him even if they wanted.

But we can drive them his way, and an accidental trampling is just as good as one on purpose.

Arick appears beside me, and I feel the rightness of it. This is what we've spent all those hours training for. We got this. Soon as he's got his kamanj set, we'll finish my da's work once and for all.

But then Arick slaps the pipes from my hand, and punches me right in the nose.

CHAPTER 54

THE WELL

"ARICK!" KENDALL SHOUTS, but she and Rojvah dare not cease their song. It falters a moment without me to lead, but Kendall's fiddle smoothly slips in to guide them, keeping the demon horde at bay a little longer.

"I'm sorry, cousin!" Arick cries as I try to shake off the festival flamework detonating inside my head. Nose is scrunched and bloody. Can't smell a thing.

Arick sounds sincere. Not angry, even as he punches me in the head, reigniting the explosions. If anythin' he sounds scared.

"It's not me!" he shouts.

Vision's still blurry, but I think I see him spin and I suck in just in time as his heel connects with my chest, throwing me onto my back. That kick would have broken ribs, but sucked in and tough, it's probably worse on his foot than on me.

Arick doesn't seem hindered as he attempts to pin me, but I go slippery and pop out from under him. "It's not you then cut it out!"

"I can't!" Arick tries to sweep my feet out from under me, but I quickstep back.

"Why in the core not?!" I've got my bearings now, even if I still can't smell. I stay slippery, letting Arick's punches and kicks slide off me as I get in close.

"You were going to stampede the demons," Arick says. "Can't let you hurt him."

Suddenly it all makes sense. Alagai Ka might not have scrambled Arick's brains entirely, but he left a little trigger, 'case he was ever threatened.

Arick lunges, attempting to grapple, but I'm slipperier than a fish flopping in the mud. I slide around him easy, getting behind his back and catching his head and one armpit in a hold. Then I suck in.

"You should have let me jump!" Arick's words come in a choked gurgle as he struggles, smashing me into the floor, a wall, a stalagmite. But I'm tough when I suck in, and the bumps don't keep me from tightening the hold. This move worked on Olive Paper, and she's a lot stronger'n Arick.

"Core with that talk!" I snap at him. "Said yourself it ent you!"

"Kill me," Arick growls, even as he pulls at my arm with all his strength.

Means it. See it in his aura, and it breaks my heart. How many people I love gotta die, before this is done? Well not this one. No, ma'am.

"Ent you we need to kill to fix this, Arick." In close, I can read Arick's body like it's my own. Feel his pulse, his breath, I can sense right down to the oxygen in his blood. Moment Arick passes out, I ease up and wait for him to unconsciously take a breath. Drag him over to Rojvah and Kendall, laying him between them and covering him with his motley cloak. Won't be but a few minutes before he wakes up, but by then this should be over, one way or another.

I yank my nose straight, pressing my nostrils one at a time to blow out the blood. Hurts like the core, but I can smell again. Should heal quick enough. Nose might end up lookin' different, but it'll do its job.

Mam and the demon queen are still fightin'. Mam's got cuts all over, but her aura is bright, and there's hot ichor sizzling on her knife. She's cut off one of the queen's legs, using it to bat away the deadly tail stinger. Both of them are already healing, but the queen's missing leg doesn't grow back.

I catch a whiff of Selen's blood, and turn to see her lying on the ground spewing a stream of cusses as she tries to set her own broken leg. Wonda lies next to her, facedown with blood pooling around her head. Her aura is dimming, but she ent dead yet, for what that's worth.

I can smell the blood spattered on the knob end of Cavivat's staff. The grubby priest is strong as a wood demon, quick as a flame. He's drawin' wards in the air with his staff, blasting Aunt Leesha with heat, wind, and bolts of lightning. This ent like Arick, or even the demons in the chamber. Either Alagai Ka's controlling his priest direct, or as good as.

But Aunt Leesha's still angry and stands her ground. Wards on her arms and legs are so charged she's moving as fast as me, drawing siphon wards to dissolve and absorb Cavivat's spells same as the queen did by flappin' her wings.

Aunt Leesha scribbles offensive wards of her own in between defenses, using indirect attacks that are harder to siphon. Impact wards explode the stone at his feet, sending him stumbling back onto a patch of black ice from her cold wards.

Cavivat's feet go out from under him, but he's quick enough to keep from falling. His staff flares with magic, and he slams it down, sending a shock wave that sets Aunt Leesha stumbling in return.

It's Mam I'm really worried about. Most of the time growin' up, she went out of her way to hide her power. Folk could sense it, though. Never say it, but she made them uneasy, just like I did.

Now she's shining like the sun, but it's just a fraction of what the queen's holdin', with more comin' every second through the tether to Alagai Ka. I can actually see the queen growing, even as she and Mam try to rip each other's throats out.

Want to help, but what can I do but get in the way? Mam's misting keeps her from being stung, but she needs to get in close if she's going to finish the job. Already her knife is looking tiny in comparison with the demon queen. How's she going to stab deep enough to do damage beyond the queen's ability to heal?

I can see Mam knows it, too, but it doesn't stop her going in close for another pass. The queen meets her head-on, but at the last second Mam stops and draws a queen ward, stopping her cold. Like Leesha's, it doesn't have power to hold her more than a second, but that's time enough for Mam to thrust her knife, all the way to the length of her arm, into one of the queen's giant, lidless eyes.

The queen shrieks and rears, taking Mam with her as she thrashes back and forth trying to shake her off. Mam's feet kick wildly, trying to keep away from the queen's snapping teeth as she twists the knife and tries to drive it deeper. Sharp, clawed legs puncture her body, but she lets it happen, not misting until the tail strike comes.

She stumbles when she rematerializes, and I notice she ent got the knife anymore. Looking back, I can see why. Queen's clawing her own eye, tryin' to dig it out. Mam draws queen wards in the air to hold her back while the weapon does its work, pumping killing magic into the queen's brain.

Kendall and Rojvah are doing brilliantly, but the demons are in a frenzy, and getting closer and closer. I spot my pipes on the ground where Arick kicked them. Not too late to stampede them toward Alagai Ka. I go for them.

"Darin." There's something off about Mam's voice. I turn and see her skin blackening around a scratch the queen's stinger left on her shoulder. It was only a little thing, but it's spreading, the poison eating Mam's magic and using it to make more poison. Already her arm hangs limp.

"Mam!" I run to her, getting under her shoulder as she stumbles. "Mam, tell me what to do!"

"Steer clear of that wound," Mam says. "Ent no cure for queen venom."

All the chaos and noise around us seems to quiet at that. All I can see is Mam. All I can think is this is how Da died.

"Been thinking a lot about how he did it," Mam says, like she read my mind. "Think maybe I can do it, too. Maybe get to see him again, on the other side."

Her words are slurring. She's delirious. "He's gone, Mam. Burned away."

"Oh, Darin." She gently touches my face with her good hand, but it's weak, shaking. "Now who doesn't believe?"

The tears are cold on my cheeks. "No. Wait. Please. You can't just . . ."

"Got to." Mam turns to look at the queen just as she digs the knife from her ruined eye, sending it clattering across the ground. I can sense her anger, her hate, as she moves to claw down Mam's wards.

"Love you, Darin Bales," Mam says. "Proud of you. Don't you ever forget that. And when I see your da, gonna tell him, too." She sobs, putting her forehead against mine. "Gonna say, *Look up at our boy, ent he perfect?*"

I choke, my face twisting so much it hurts.

"See you there, too, when it's your turn," Mam whispers, kissing just above my broken nose.

"How?" I cling harder as she starts to let go. "Can't dissipate like you."

"Oh, Darin," Mam says. "'Course you can. Just like swimmin'. First lesson is stop bein' scared of the water."

I scream, clutching at her as she starts to go slippery. I go slippery with her, and somehow it lets me hold on, like when I melt my fingertips into crevices on a wall. She dissipates further, but I hold on with sheer will.

A sound fills my ears, thrumming, piercing, deafening. It makes me feel like my head is going to split open, but I can't block it out, because I am the one making it. I won't lose her. Not after all this. I can't.

Sometimes Mam would grab hold of me and force me to dissipate, dragging me along with her as she rode currents of magic at the speed of thought. Ent nothin' in the world scared me more, but this ent like that. She's tryin' to cut me off, to leave me behind, but I ent lettin'go. Forcin' her to stay corporeal.

But Mam's stronger'n me. Pull as hard as I can, but I feel her . . . stretching. Thinning, until the bonds tethering her to the physical world begin to tear.

Her arm falls to the ground, dead and lifeless, along with a big infected chunk of collar and chest. I wonder if she could even survive if she re-formed, but the true Mam, the aura at her center, breaks free of that dying material form.

Somehow, I'm still holdin' on. Feel myself stretching, pulling apart just like she did. Terrified I won't be able to suck back together if I do. I can stop it anytime. All I have to do is let go.

I hold on tighter, if that word even means anything anymore. It's a choice.

Can't live my whole life too scared to go in the water.

Just like goin' slippery, but I don't stop, letting my very cells rend apart, then the molecules themselves, first from each other, and then from their own particles until nothing physical of me remains. There's a flash of intense pain, like walkin' through fire, but then I'm on the other side, a being of pure energy, of magic itself.

Still me. I can think and feel. Aware of everything around me, but no longer a prisoner to my senses. Any other time, it might feel . . . nice.

Immediately, I feel the pull of the well. The room, the hive ward itself, is designed to Draw and store ambient magic in the well, the central connecting line of the greatward. The only output is the line through Alagai Ka himself to the demon queen.

The moment we misted, it started suckin' us in. Feels like it's happenin' slow, but I think it's the other way round. Everything around us seems frozen in place as the well drags us like water to a drain.

Darin, let go! Still connected, auras touching, Mam can speak to me like she's in my head. I know everything she's thinking, everything she's feeling.

Mam is frantic. Desperate.

No! I holler back, even though I ent got a voice. I know what she's going to do. I felt it in our link.

Can't let them come back, Darin, Mam says, and I know she means it. *Not for anythin'. Not even for you. Go. Get the others and you* run.

She gathers her will and breaks my hold, flinging me upstream before she turns and dives into the well.

Immediately, I feel the change as Mam diffuses into the well of power, becoming a part of it, and imposing one last wish on the near-limitless power.

Then she detonates, and takes the whole thing with her.

STILL CAUGHT IN its current, I feel the explosion like a bucket of hot water to the face. Reflexively I turn and flee.

Mam was right. Moving as mist is a bit like swimming, but also a bit like dreaming. I have to navigate currents and push against resistance, but it's all done by will, not arms and legs.

Pullin' myself back together ent as hard as I feared. Got incentive, with the currents of magic burning like lamp oil. I suck in, and suddenly my feet are back on solid ground, and I'm screaming with my throat and lungs and not just my thoughts.

The ground shakes violently, cracks appearing in the stone. They run up the walls, and chunks of stone start raining down. I look at the well as it begins to collapse, its spent magic shattering the tunnels below. Mam kept the worst of it away from us, but that don't mean we can't be squashed by a falling stalactite or fall into a fissure.

The queen shrieks as the tether to the well breaks and she's no longer drawing power. Ent as big as the mimic queen was, but she's forty feet long if she's an inch, and she clears the chamber in a single bound.

She pounces on Alagai Ka, still frozen with that ugly tree sticking out from between his legs. The queen mounts him in a quick, violent motion even as she encloses him protectively in her folded legs. Reckon she's lost interest in fightin' with the place falling apart all around us. She spreads her wings and takes flight with her consort, mating even as she flees through a tunnel high above us.

As one, the demons around us flee into the tunnels as well, swarming after their queen.

Ent hard to guess where they're headed, but I got other lookouts right now. Cavivat's fighting by himself now, but he ent letting up, even as the chamber rattles like it's about to come down around our ears. Aunt Leesha's staggering, and the others ent in a position to help.

It's easier this time, dissolving into mist. I cross the distance before the priest knows I've moved, re-forming inside his guard with a choke hold that's less gentle than the one I used on Arick. He stumbles to one knee, and Aunt Leesha knocks his staff away with a flick of her pen and an impact ward. Then she sucks the excess magic out of him and Cavivat hits the end of his strength, collapsing.

Aunt Leesha is already using her pen to tend to Selen and Wonda. Rojvah and Kendall are supporting Arick as they come to join us. I spot my pipes and Mam's knife lying forgotten amid the dust. I snatch them up as I hurry over to help my friends stumble into the smaller tunnel we came from. No stalactites to fall there, and the floors are more stable.

By the time they're safe, Selen limps in, followed by Leesha carrying Wonda in her arms like a baby.

"Oh, Intended!" Rojvah throws her arms around me. After being scared I might never be solid again, it's the best feeling in the world. I inhale her scent and hold tight, knowing it might be my last chance.

"Your mother?" Rojvah asks.

All I can do is shake my head. Ent ready to talk about it. Can't even let myself think about it. Not now, when there's still work to be done.

"We need to get out of here," Leesha says. "Darin, can you guide us . . . ?"

I'm already shaking my head. "You can do it. Reckon it's night outside if you can make it to the gate, but there ent any demons to stop you."

Aunt Leesha's eyes narrow. "And what will you be doing?"

I squeeze tight one more time, putting my mouth close to Rojvah's ear. "Love you, Rojvah Inn. Honored to be promised to you."

Then I let go and step back. "Demons can't mist while the queen is vulnerable. Swarm's headed straight for Olive, and someone's got to warn her."

I expect Aunt Leesha to try to stop me. To tell me I'm being foolish or it's too dangerous. But we're past that now. She's as determined as Mam was, and Olive's her own child. "Tell Olive I love her, and I'm proud of her. And for the Creator's sake, be careful."

I nod, casting a last look at the others. Arick meets my eyes and gives no more than a tilt of his head, but I can smell all the many meanings hidden behind it. He's barely holdin' it together after that happened.

"Ent your fault, Arick. Goin' to make sure you're free once and for all." I turn to Selen, not knowin' what to say, but I don't need to say anything. She throws me into a hug, squeezing the breath out of me. "Make a necklace out of his teeth, Dar."

I squeeze once in return before I melt away.

There are currents of magic everywhere. With the greatward broken, the flows are in chaos. Deep below, I can sense the Core, beautiful and terrible as the sun, callin' to me like a supper bell. Da's there, and maybe Mam, too. I could be with them, if Mam was speakin' honest word.

But first, as always, there's chores.

Vents of magic flow up from the Core tryin' to find their way to the surface. I plunge into one, going down, down into the surface of the world, far below Safehold. There I find flows heading upward in the direction I want to go, and pick one, following it to the surface in less time than it takes to blink an eye.

Ent an exact science. Mam used to do this all the time, and even she needed a few extra hops when she was goin' someplace new. I end up in the mountains, but looking at the settin' sun, they ent the mountains I just left. Up near Miln, I reckon.

I look around for the highest peak and mist up there. Clear night, and I get a good lookabout. Can see for hundreds of miles, watching the flows of magic venting up from the Core.

Don't really know where I'm going, even if I was born there, and saw a bit of Bloodfather's maps. But I know more or less where the Mouth of the Abyss is, and after starin' in that direction a bit, it's easy enough to spot the glow of that giant vent.

Fastest way is to go back down, try to find a vent that gets me closer. But I ent eager to risk another mistake. Instead I try a trick I seen Mam play, misting just enough to be lighter than air. Then I hold my breath and take a flyin' leap, willing myself toward the vent.

Slower than ridin' currents, I guess, but still faster'n I've ever gone. I'm so insubstantial I barely feel the wind, speedin' frictionless through the night at the speed of thought.

Hard to keep time when you're moving fast in the night sky. Might be a couple hours or just a few minutes before I make it to the demon's mouth cave. Don't know how fast the queen can fly, or her demons run, but it ent this fast. I can get to the fortress first, but speed ent much if I can't find the rippin' place.

There's guards, and a sealed gate, but I dissolve into mist and they don't see me as I slip past. Once I'm through, I Draw in some of the magic venting up from the Core, and Read it.

Waystations reveal themselves down below like torches in the darkness, leading a path all the way to the Spear of Ala. It shines like a Solstice bonfire as I slip into the current, swimmin' upstream.

And just like that, I'm drifting before the walls of the great *csar* of Kaji, and it's even more amazing than in Mam's ale stories. Gates are sealed so tight even I can't mist or slip through, but that ent a problem.

Weightless, I rise above the walltops. Ent a demon, and the greatward does nothin' to stop me as I cross over and drop down the other side.

When I'm misting, none of my regular senses work. All I can sense is magic, but it tells me more than the other five ever did. Like the hive ward, the Spear of Ala is full of controlled flows of magic. Wardwork scrolls along the walls and streets, doing everything from securing the walls to purifying the air.

But it's all comin' from one place, and it's simple to just slip into the wardwork and follow it back to the source. Olive's there, in the throne room, and she ent alone.

Ever since we were kids, one of my favorite games was to sneak up on Olive and Selen, settin' down beside them and waitin' for them to notice me. Don't even think about it as I do it now, materializing atop the dais beside Olive, standing at my bloodfather's right hand as he sits the Skull Throne.

CHAPTER 55

THE SPARE

THE *CSAR* FEELS DIFFERENT, with my father returned. For a brief moment, I was absolute ruler here. The very stones of the fortress answered to me.

But the Spear of Ala knows its true master. My replica crown is only a shadow of my father's, as is my skill at using it. I can still sense the *csar*, call its power, but I can no longer peer into the hearts of everyone inside or Draw too much without my father's sufferance.

Father keeps his royal family close, but it is unclear if we are advisors, gatekeepers, or simply bodyguards. The moment we are inside the *csar's* walls, he begins touring the defenses. Ashia leads our bodyguard in the front while I walk at Father's right and Amanvah, his left. Asome brings up the rear.

I try not to think too much about my brother standing so close to my back. I can only hope that if he turns to treachery again, I will sense the change in his aura in time to act. Father seems unconcerned.

And why should he be concerned? The *Sharum*, even my Majah spear brothers, worship Ahmann Jardir like a god. Steel-eyed warriors, killers of killers, fall to their knees at his passage, pressing foreheads to the ground in utter submission.

The Hollow Soldiers—many of whose families were refugees of Father's invasion of the green lands—have good reasons to mistrust, but

Krasia was an ally against the demons in the war, and our borders have been peaceful and prosperous in the years since. They take their cues from the general and me, accepting this change of command with military stoicism.

Even Gared calls my father sir as often as not, and defers to him without question. I can look into individual hearts still, though it is no great mystery that Gared is happy to have the adults back in charge. He resents my father for his invasion all those years ago, but they have shed blood together in the night, and the general holds my father in more than a little awe.

"Folk sometimes say they feel safer when I'm around," Gared told me when I asked him about it, "like no matter what happens, I got it handled."

He wasn't bragging. I grew up feeling that way about him myself.

"Ent a lot of men make me feel like that," he went on. "Just Darin's da, and yours. If Ahmann Jardir's on our side, we're going to win."

He really believes that. They all do. Everyone who knows my father is afraid of him, awed by him. But if he is so powerful, why did he need our rescue? Is it disrespectful to see him as a man, albeit a powerful one?

Certainly Ahmann Jardir exudes regal power. His bearing, his gestures, his voice, all masterfully perform the art of statecraft Mother tried so hard to instill in me. He inspires and heartens everyone around him, bringing new unity to our tired and divided forces as he reviews the defenses I have positioned around the *csar.*

Father's experience as a military commander is legendary. I can't help but feel anxious, my stomach churning like it would when Mother would unexpectedly begin quizzing me on my studies. I've learned a bit at the head of an army these last months, but most of my training was on the unit level, defending set portions of the Maze. Thankfully, I had Ashia to advise me.

Rhinebeck is drilling the Flamework Corps when we inspect the walltops. Like me, Rhinebeck doesn't really know my father. To him Ahmann Jardir is the infamous warlord who murdered and displaced tens of thousands of people in his conquest of the south, not to mention killing Rhinebeck's father and uncles. He is stone-faced as I introduce him to Father, and he falls, uninvited, into line behind us as Father continues his tour.

"Flamework is best at shorter range," Father says. "Why position them at the walltops?"

My guts clench, but I keep the anxiety from my voice. "The demons have driven other subterranean creatures to attack us, including *minoc* . . ."

"Who are unhindered by the greatward," Father says, nodding. "The Flamework Corps keeps the walltops clear for the scorpion teams. Wisely done."

As much as I tell myself he's only a man, childish giddiness washes over me at his approval. I fall into my breath, embracing the feeling and letting it go. Now more than ever, I cannot let the others see weakness in me.

Father has more questions, but again I know the answers, feeling less and less a fraud, even as I realize how much I have to learn. The places where he repositions our troops, he is right to do so.

The replica crown feels heavier than it did before. I never really wanted it. Now with my father in command it feels almost wrong to continue wearing it.

But my father does not suggest I remove it. Indeed, I stand at his right hand, a clear sign to the Krasians and *alamen fae* that I am his heir. The power of the replica crown is exhilarating, addictive, and we are about to face the greatest threat of our lives. It is not something I am willing to give up just to ease my own discomfort. Blood-locked to my chin, it cannot be taken from me if I do not wish it.

Am I more like Asome than I think? I do not covet power, but neither will I relinquish it.

"Olive will stand atop the dais, right of the Skull Throne," Father says as we approach the seven steps on the altar of Sharik Hora. Again I suppress a girlish thrill at Father's esteem. Here, most of all, I must never lose composure.

"Amanvah." Father gestures to the Pillow Throne on the dais of the sixth step.

My sister puts her hands together, bowing even as we walk. "Yes, Father."

"Ashia, the base of the steps," he says. The traditional place of the First Warrior. "General Gared, opposite."

"Your will, Shar'Dama Ka." Ashia punches a fist to her chest.

"Ay," Gared says simply, but he, too, pushes down a little thrill at having earned his place.

Father's face is serene, eyes closed as he ascends the steps. I remember the feeling. He is becoming one with the *csar* and everyone in it. When he sits the throne and the connection is direct, he will feel he *is* the *csar*, and every sacrifice made to build it from heroes' bone. It is glory and ecstasy and three thousand years of pain, mixed with the sum of the current inhabitants' hopes and fears.

Caught in the throes of it, I do not know if he is aware of Asome following us up the steps, or if his thoughts are sweeping across millennia like stacks in a library. Either way, he does not protest as his eldest living son takes his place unbidden at Father's left hand on the sixth step, on par with his sister and only a step from me. I remember how fast he was when we fought. How deadly.

As the right hand, it falls to me to protest my brother's presence, but I dare not interrupt Father as the glowing lines of magic connecting his crown and the throne shine brighter and brighter until they become one aura of light with him inside.

My siblings and I take our places, regal as we look down at the other leaders standing like penitents. Rhinebeck and my grandfather, Briar and the *alamen fae*. Gatherer Roni, Gorvan and Faseek. I stand stone-faced, waiting for Father to speak.

Then Darin Bales appears and scares the core out of me.

I'm moving before I've realized it's him, hooking his arm and locking it tight as I put my *hanzhar* to his throat. Only then do I recognize my friend. He smirks, turning to mist and slipping my hold.

"Corespawn it, Darin Bales!" No matter how many demons and monsters I kill, how many troops I command, Darin Bales can still make me feel like I only have ten summers to my name.

"Son of Arlen!" Father is on his feet immediately, showing far more enthusiasm for the son of his friend than for his own children. He tries to sweep Darin into a hug, but again Darin collapses, misting a couple steps to the side and forming up again.

Father only chuckles. "Now you remind me of your sire."

It's the wrong thing to say to Darin. He hates being compared to his da all the time. I wish I could say it serves him right for sneaking up, but I don't want anyone to feel that way.

I cross my arms. "You *have* learned some new tricks."

Darin shrugs, a little chastened. No doubt he smells my irritation and didn't really mean to step in it like he did. "Still gettin' used to it, myself. Your mam says she loves you and she's proud of you."

"She's alive?!" The words hit me like a kick in the chest, again breaking my careful composure. "Is she all right?"

"Ay," Darin says. "We found them, Olive. Mam and Aunt Leesha, even Wonda and Kendall."

Relief floods me, but Father seems tenser than ever. "If you found your mother, why isn't Renna am'Bales here with you now?"

Darin chews his lip. I know that gesture. It means there's something he doesn't want to talk about because he's scared of getting emotional, but this is too big to keep to himself. "New demon queen's already hatched. Mam fought her off, but she got stung."

It's all he needs to say. There is nothing more deadly than a demon queen's venom. Mrs. Bales, who used to sing me to sleep and delight us with her ale stories, is gone.

I feel his pain like it's my own. "Oh, Darin." Gared lets out a grief-stricken moan, but it's Darin I keep focus on. His mother and father, both taken from him the same way, sixteen years apart. I can see the pain inside him, shriveled up in the center of his aura like a black prune, kept under pressure by his immense will. I fear what will happen when he can no longer keep it contained.

I want to throw my arms around him. To call Amanvah for tear bottles and weep together, lancing and draining some of that pain away, but Darin is not me. I know my friend and know what he needs. I lay a hand on his arm instead, squeezing gently but firmly, giving him a pressure to focus on without the suffocation of a hug.

Darin seems to draw strength from the gesture, and I am grateful. "Queen grabbed Alagai Ka and fled. Got thousands of drones, and I'll bet the pot they're headed straight here."

Father nods with unnatural calm, as if Darin had simply warned of a coming rain shower. "How long do we have?"

Darin shrugs again. "Queen can't mist, and the rest of them are staying solid to keep her surrounded. Headed here on foot, and they left maybe . . . four hours ago? Six? How long does it take a horde of demons to run a thousand miles?"

Father shakes his head. "Not long enough."

"OLIVE, YOU WILL sit the throne when I go out to meet Alagai'ting Ka."

Father has taken one of Ashia's glass spears, laced with electrum. I've watched him knead magic into it like dough as he meets with his commanders and sets them to task. By the time he gets to me, the weapon is alight with power. If any weapon other than the Spear of Kaji can kill a demon queen, it is that one.

I'm getting better at reading hearts, now, especially those close to me. I sense the wounded pride in Asome's aura without even looking at him, but my brother says nothing as I punch my fist to my chest. "Yes, Father."

"Two thrones, now?" Darin asks as we exit the audience. "Startin' a collection? Maybe the Damajah was right to worry."

"I don't want any of them," I say, perhaps a little too vehemently.

"Ent turnin' 'em down," Darin notes.

"Never been given much choice in the matter," I say. "Lord Arther told me Hollow's whole economy might crash if I didn't put a crown on my head. You think I want to be stuck sitting on a pile of skulls while my warriors take the field under Father's command?"

"Ay, just tweakin' your nose," Darin says. "We don't do that anymore?"

Darin's aura is unique. Hard to read. Some of it's the power. Magic he was born with, like me, because our parents were full of it when we were conceived and in the womb. But it's more than that.

Darin's emotions are organized differently than others I've observed. Most are a constantly shifting spectrum, coexisting with one another on a level the person isn't even aware of. Others, like clerics and elite warriors, have learned techniques to suppress emotions when they threaten to overwhelm, but they are not truly under control. A crowd of prisoners rattling their bars.

But Darin's emotions are all kept separate, like the way he keeps different foods on the same plate separate when he eats. Some folk think Darin doesn't have emotions at all. His face seldom shows them unless he's mumming. But he does. He's just got them on a tighter leash, second to his logic as he studies things and works them out.

"We're not kids anymore, Darin," I say. "You can't just spook me in front of everyone like we've only got ten summers, chasing around Mum's keep. Things are serious, and people are looking to us. We need to back each other up, not pop bubbles for fun."

Darin takes it in and nods. "Ay, I know. Just . . . a little scared to feel serious right now, that makes any sense."

"It makes a lot of sense, Darin. I'm scared, too. I want to fight, but the *csar's* magic is strongest with someone atop the throne to direct it. Father is the only one among us with the strength to fight the queen directly. He cannot stay behind."

"Well he got me runnin' messages," Darin says, "so you'll be seein' me a lot, 'less I get into trouble."

"I should be there to keep you out of trouble," I say. "It's my job."

"Used to be," Darin says sadly. "Right we ent kids anymore, Olive. Can't keep hidin' behind your skirts. 'Specially since you stopped wearing 'em."

That gets a chuckle from me. "Dresses aren't terribly practical on horseback. But if we live to see peace again . . ." I shrug.

"Speakin' of life after this," Darin says, "your boyfriend's waitin' for you outside the doors at the end of the hall."

"He isn't—" I begin, but Darin cuts me off by tapping his nose.

"Sure it's complicated," he says. "Ent lookin' to argue. But whatever it is, I can smell it on you both. See how you avoid lookin' at him, too."

I fall into my breath. "Never could get anything past that nose of yours."

"Do you want him to be?" Darin asks. "Because he stinks of it. *Honest suitor*, Mam would say."

I focus on breathing. "You tell me."

Darin turns and I see his nostrils flare, but in crownsight I can see him reaching for me with all five senses, and some I don't even have a name for. A shower of information comes back for him to sort, so much I can't understand how he processes it all.

I remember all the times he couldn't—the fits he'd go into, with me and Selen having to carry him sometimes to get away from a crowd or cacophony. For just a second, I understand what it's like to be Darin, and I marvel at my friend. He's so much stronger than I knew.

"Don't know what you want," Darin says at last.

I cluck my tongue. "I was hoping you knew more than I did."

Darin reaches out again, this time fixed down the hall as he sucks a breath through his nose. "He smells guilty. Like he's lookin' to patch things up. What'd he do?"

I fill Darin in quickly, but he doesn't have any answers.

"Core if I know how courtin' works," he says. "Only reason I'm with Rojvah is because she or Selen or someone always explains what I should do, and I do it."

"So explain it," I say. "He's waiting to talk and I don't want to. I'm not ready to. What do I say?"

Darin considers. "Said it yourself, I guess. We ent got ten summers anymore. Things are serious. Whatever it is he's lookin' to resolve can wait until we know we're going to live through the week. 'Specially if you're still raw about what happened."

"Maybe I'll get lucky and the demons will eat me first," I say. Darin laughs, but it's the fake laugh he does when he doesn't get the joke but wants to be polite. The black knot of pain in his chest is still there, and growing.

"I know you're hurting," I say.

Darin nods. "Know that. Thank you. Reckon there will be plenty of time to fall to pieces, we live to see next week."

"Next week's calendar is really filling quickly." That one gets a genuine laugh out of Darin.

"Going to find Briar," Darin says. "Give you some peace to talk to your prince." I reach for him, wanting to offer comfort, but he's already insubstantial, and then he's gone.

Rhiney is waiting right where Darin said he would be. His heart is an open book in crownsight, and every bit as sincere as Darin warned. He wants to make peace, to get back to where we were just a week ago, but that seems an impossible divide. Twice now, he has failed me when I needed him most. I understand his reasons, but it doesn't make the betrayals sting any less.

"Olive." He reaches for my hand, but I move it just out of his grasp.

I see the hurt in him at the simple act, like a puppy denied a scratch behind the ears. These sorts of things endeared me to him once, but now they only push us further apart.

"Are you afraid your father will see us together?" Rhinebeck asks.

I pinch the bridge of my nose. "That has nothing to do with it." Perhaps it does, a little. "Father can see into the hearts of everyone in this *csar.* He already knows."

"Then what is it?" Rhinebeck asks. "That I did not watch you die? That I did not want to rescue the man who . . ."

"It's that I can't trust you!" I snap, and he jumps back as if struck. "Two times I needed you, and two times you weren't there."

"And that negates all the times I was?" Rhinebeck demands. "Would you have even made it this far, without me?"

"You're right," I say. "Your support has been essential. I don't know if I could have done this without you. But I don't owe you kisses, or a promise for it. Did you come all this way for me, or because it was the right thing to do?"

"For a while," Rhinebeck says, "they were one and the same."

"And now?" I ask. "With all the forces of darkness assembling?"

"I'm not a coward," Rhinebeck says. "I will do my duty, fight—die, if need be—to defend this *csar,* even if half its occupants are enemies of my people. What more do you want?"

"Time," I say. "Questions of you and me can be answered under the sun."

"And if we never see the sun again?" he asks.

"Then the answer doesn't matter."

CHAPTER 56

SACRIFICE

SEVEN HUNDRED AND SEVENTY-SEVEN STEPS, a sacred number, brings one atop the great dome of Sharik Hora, the highest point in the city. There stands Sharik Vonn—hero's gaze—a great observation deck affording a 360-degree view of the great cavern in which the *csar* sits.

Father strides to the center of the stairwell, lifts his gaze, and simply rises. He is beyond such things as steps.

Gared looks up the spiraling stair and lets out a low whistle. "Reckon the rest of us have to do it the hard way."

"Speak for yourself." Darin winks and dissipates, following Father directly to the roof.

Everyone else hesitates, and I realize all of them are waiting for me to lead the climb.

But I'm not ready to give up. I don't understand Darin's magic, but this time I paid close attention to Father's. He simply bound himself to the *csar's* magic and willed it upward.

I still feel the power of the *csar,* like Mother's credit account when I went shopping. There was no limit to what vendors would extend me, but Mother could cut it off with a wave.

Here, too, I can tap into seemingly limitless power, so long as Father allows it, and I need to set an example, and to give heart to our people by reminding them that we, too, are strong.

I stride to the center of the well, Drawing the *csar's* power and wrapping it around me like a blanket. Then I look up, and simply will myself to rise.

And I do. Slowly at first, then faster as I grow more confident, flights of steps blurring past.

The last thing I sense from the floor is another flare of injured pride in Asome's aura. Then I am standing beside Father and Darin, staring out at the cavern and the hundreds of tunnels that exit into it from every direction.

"We're in trouble," Darin says.

"Courage, son of Arlen." Father lays a hand on Darin's shoulder, and, amazingly, Darin allows it. Memories flash in Darin's aura, other times they have stood thus when Darin was young. Ahmann Jardir was more father to Darin than he ever was to me.

I have right to resent that, but am surprised to discover I don't. Arlen Bales was Father's *ajin'pal.* His blood brother. I touch my Tazhan armor. Chadan's armor. I know the pain of losing your *ajin'pal.*

If anyone in the world needs a da, it's Darin Bales. Ahmann Jardir wasn't there for me, but I feel better knowing Darin had someone he could always turn to.

Footsteps, and the moment is broken. Darin slides away as the others, legs strong from weeks of marching, join us on Sharik Vonn.

"The *alagai* have us surrounded." Asome states the obvious, but someone needed to say it aloud.

There are too many tunnels to easily count, but all of them shine bright as stars to my crownsight, teeming with demons clustered right at the edge of the *csar's* forbidding. Some are around the cavern floor, others high on the wall or ceiling. All of them alive with scales and talons.

"Which one is the queen comin' through?" Gared asks.

All of us look to Darin, but he only shrugs. "Core if I know."

Darin has a way about him. He'll answer questions to the letter, but won't volunteer anything, as if the spirit of the question never occurred to him.

I lay a gentle hand on his arm and move my eyes into his field of vision. "A lot of people are going to die if we can't narrow it down, Darin. We need more than a shrug."

Darin nods, looking around again. "Queen's already big as a ranch house, not counting her wings. Ent a lot of tunnels she'd fit through. Reckon I'll hear 'em comin' when they get closer. These ones are just clustered all around so there's no bottleneck when she gets here."

"Father," I say. "The *alagai* are vulnerable, clustered so close to the forbidding without cover. With your permission, I will lead sallies to thin their numbers before the queen arrives."

"And when she does?" Ashia asks. "What will the *alagai* do, in the presence of their queen? Will the greatward not still hold them at bay?"

"Queen eats magic like sugar," Darin says, oblivious to how his words dampen morale. "Forbidding is just a hard candy shell to crack."

"Olive, lead your sallies to thin the *alagai* numbers," Father says. "We must seize every advantage."

I come to attention, punching a fist to my chest. "Yes, Father."

RHINEBECK IS MOUNTED with the Royal Angierian Flamework Corps when I reach the stables. At times bringing horses this far underground seemed a horrible mistake, but now the advantage of mobility makes up for weeks of difficulty.

I mount my own horse and ride over to him, close enough so the others cannot hear. "Your orders were to keep position atop the walls."

He crosses his arms at me, and the indignance in his aura takes me aback. "Is that how it is now, Olive? Banished from your presence? All my loyalty and sacrifice forgotten? We will both be needed in the *csar* when the true attack comes. Until then, I will do what I came to do."

He leaves the last bit unspoken, but I can see it clearly written on his heart. Rhinebeck came on this journey to protect *me*, and for no other reason. His loyalty and sense of duty outweigh his hurt feelings. Even now, he would die for me.

And I for him. Isn't that the very definition of a spear brother?

"I'm sorry," I say quietly. "I am glad to have you along."

Darin Bales, easily running to pace my horse, is less pleased to have Rhiney along, as are the demons. He dissolves into mist as soon as the flamework weapons begin barking fire, sending a withering barrage into the demons gathered at the edge of the forbidding.

As the creatures fall shrieking to the cavern floor, I use my crown to put up a bubble of forbidding around the injured creatures as we trample them under warded hooves and cavalry spears before the Cutters march in on foot to make sure they stay down.

It doesn't seem to make a difference. More demons cluster behind those we fell, and more behind those. The Flamework Corps are already rationing ammunition, and I am hesitant to expend too much.

I call them back and send in the fighters, making sure to keep them covered with the crown as they charge. The forbidding does not hinder them as they smash into the foe with *Sharum* spear walls, Cutter axe mattocks, and the warded clubs of the *alamen fae*.

We strike wherever we can, felling hundreds of *alagai*, but it doesn't seem to make a difference as more press forward to take their place.

"Like slappin' at the rain," Darin says, but then his head tilts. "Trouble's on its way."

"Where?" I ask. "How long do we have?"

Darin turns, pointing to one of the largest tunnels, this one near the cavern ceiling. Impossible to guard. "Movin' fast. We need to go."

I close my eyes, using one of my crown's gems as a resonance stone. "Father."

"I sense it, child." Father's voice hangs in the air around us. "Return to the *csar* and reposition the Flamework Corps atop the wall."

Rhiney catches my eye and winks before giving his horse a kick and riding back toward the *csar*.

Darin rides behind me in the saddle as we gallop ahead of the foot soldiers. It isn't fast enough. There's a shrill cry as the queen appears high above.

"Night," Darin whispers. "She's . . . bigger."

Even at a distance, the queen is massive. Still sleek and agile, but I'd guess closer to one hundred feet long than Darin's reported forty.

I focus my crownsight on the demon queen, peering deep. The power contained in her is terrifying, so bright I have to squint and adjust before I can see more than glare. Clutched in her limbs, I find the true enemy.

"The queen is on the field," I tell Father. "She has the Father of Demons clutched to her chest. He is weak, but alive. I believe the mating is done."

My eyes drift to her abdomen, and my stomach knots painfully. Thousands of fertilized eggs, all drinking that rich power, and growing. A first laying of many to come, but already enough to throw the surface lands into another bloody demon war.

"I will deal with Alagai'ting Ka as soon as you return to take the throne." Again, Father speaks for all to hear from the resonance gemstone.

I do not understand what even he can do alone against this creature, but I put my faith in my father's reputation. "We are coming."

Magic skitters across the forbidding as the queen lands upon it like a bee atop a flower. Her wings buzz frantically as she thrusts her mouth against the wardnet and begins drinking its power like nectar.

The queen pulses and swells larger. At the same time, I see the forbidding contract, exposing the foot soldiers trailing our fierce gallop toward the *csar.* The demons massed against the wardnet surge forward. In seconds our forces will be overrun.

"Olive." Father says only my name, but his meaning is clear in the link between us. He feeds fresh power to my crown, until I think I might burst with it.

"Rhinebeck!" The crown amplifies my voice for all to hear. "Take your men back to the walls! The rest of you, cover the retreat!"

They have barely a moment to cast curious looks my way before I snatch my spear from its harness and slip my feet from the stirrups. Darin skitters back as I put my feet on the saddle. I sense the waves of magic flowing from the *csar* to power the forbidding and wrap myself up in one as I spring.

It isn't flying, precisely, but it's no less impressive. The wave's arc carries me across hundreds of yards in a single bound. I roll the shield off my shoulder and onto my arm, charging its wards to their limits. I smash into the center of the wave of demons bearing down on my warriors, scattering them like leaves.

"Prince Olive's a miser!" Gorvan cries, part of a chant the Princes Unit used to shout before battle. "It is time to haggle for our lives!" They clash their spears against shields, and turn to face the tide with me.

I'd rather they continue their retreat, but I cannot bring myself to deny their glory as my warriors, Hollower and *Sharum* alike, charge the foe.

I raise my bubble of protection, but the lines have broken and blurred into open melee. I can keep the tide from overwhelming us, but we'll have to deal with the ones in close the traditional way.

My spear is a thing of fire in my hands. After seeing Father do it, it's easy to feed some of the *csar's* magic directly through my body and into the weapon. Charged until they overflow with power, the piercing and cutting wards penetrate the hardest *alagai* armor as easily as soft flesh.

I skewer a stone demon, picking it clear up off the ground. I swing my spear like a hammer with the demon as its head, bashing lesser demons into pulp. I've always been strong, but Drawing on the *csar's* power through the crown I am orders of magnitude stronger. I fling the stone demon into a charging web of cave demons, knocking them over like tenpins.

I leap again, feeling unstoppable as I ride another line of magic to smash into a reap of field demons charging the Hollow Soldiers. I feed power to the field demon wards on my shield, practically incinerating them on the spot. They fall as burned-out husks, but I am already turning to draw an impact ward in the air with the tip of my spear. The weapon is holding so much power the resulting blast crushes another group of cave demons beyond hope of healing.

My warriors do the rest, their glory boundless as they shed ichor.

It is glory enough. We cannot win the field. "Back to the *csar*!" I command. "Quickly!"

Flush with power, I steal another glance at the queen, wondering if I can end this myself.

My sudden wild confidence bleeds away at the sight. She's grown again, as the forbidding continues to shrink. Even if I rode a current that high and managed to pierce her armor, against a creature that size, my spear is little more than a needle. She'd drain me of magic before I did her any harm.

She's getting closer to the *csar,* and her demons with her. *Minoc* exit tunnels in the ceiling, swarming the walltops. I see Rhinebeck there, leading the Flamework Corps in shooting them down while the stinger teams prepare for the demons coming into range on the ground.

I keep our retreating ranks under my crown's bubble, but *gwilji* penetrate the field, harrying our forces as we flee to the *csar.* One leaps onto a Hollow Soldier's back, but Darin materializes atop it, cutting free its claws with his mother's knife.

"Hurry." I hear the strain in Father's voice, feel it in our connection. "I do not know how much longer I can maintain the forbidding outside the *csar.*"

I keep to the field until everyone else is inside. The moment the gates slam shut, Father draws the forbidding back to the *csar* walls. The queen stumbles in midair, wings buzzing as the net she was sucking on disappears.

I catch a wave of magic, riding it to the walltop to watch in fear. With the cavern's forbidding down, there is nothing to stop the queen and her drones from fleeing to repopulate their hive. If they do, we've lost. Everything that happened this past year would be for nothing. All those deaths, all that pain, and the demons still win in the end.

But the queen is hungry, and she hasn't finished her meal. She flies in close, hovering outside the forbidding as she resumes her drain. The golden magic of heroes' bones, of sacrifice, seems to give her pause. She does not cease to feed, but slows as she struggles to corrupt something so pure.

It's only a matter of time before she succeeds.

Spears fly from every open door and window, the weapons of ancient warriors called back into service by Father's will. Soldiers draw wards in the air as the spears fly past in a spinning, buzzing cloud. They stream toward the queen, only to shatter against her armor.

Rhinebeck orders the flamework teams to open fire, but the bullets have no more effect than the spears, little more than an irritation to the massive creature as she keeps focus on her meal.

"Attend me," Father commands.

I LISTEN TO the sound of artillery fire, but the wardwalls appear to be holding against the demons on the ground. I can feel the *csar's* enormous power, but it grows steadily weaker. How long can we hold out before the queen consumes us all?

Father sits rigid on the Skull Throne, slid back until his crown is touching the sacred bones. His hands, white-knuckled, clutch the arms of the holy seat. His eyes are far away and unblinking. He looks like a statue of some ancient warrior king.

But Father isn't dead. His aura is bright as a star, fused almost completely with the power of the *csar.* He is it, and it is him. Every bit of masonry has become a resonance stone, and his voice is everywhere, commanding the defense as our enemies mount.

I can see the truth of it, though. More and more of Father's concentration is going toward simply powering the forbidding that keeps the demon queen at bay.

"I have consulted the Damajah." Father's voice fills the air around us, even though his lips have not moved. "She has put forth a plan, but its weight does not fall to me."

I feel the tension in my belly at the mention of the Damajah. I had thought us free of her manipulations, but it seems she still has a part to play.

"The replica crown has an open channel to the *csar's* power," Inevera's voice joins Father's in the empty air around us, "but it is not as . . . durable as the Crown of Kaji."

"What does that mean?" I ask.

"It means Mother is dissembling," Asome says. "She is saying that if Father feeds the crown too much power, it will explode."

"Along with whoever wears it," Amanvah agrees.

"Core it will," Gared growls.

"Outrageous!" Rhiney shouts.

It takes me a moment to understand what they're upset about, but then I see it clearly. For us to win, I have to die.

I look around the room. At my friends and my family, at the *alamen fae,* my spear brothers and my citizens.

"The crown does not mean power," Mother told me once. "It means sacrifice."

I don't want to die, but I was taught in *sharaj* to envision it. To imagine the honor of spending my life on *alagai* talons, a hero's death. Of having my bones bleached and added to Sharik Hora to protect generations to come.

The drillmasters taught us to imagine every death, from the glorious to the shameful. A flame demon's spit. Being cast from a great height. Stabbed in the back. Stoned for immorality.

Death is the only certainty of life, and what greater glory could there be than to take the Mother of Demons with me, so my people may live?

I look up at the throne, punching a fist to my chest and offering a bow. "I'll do it."

I GIVE NO one time to protest, and myself no time to reconsider. I Draw power, wrapping myself up in the *csar's* magic and willing myself to fly into the stairwell and up to Sharik Vonn.

Darin's already waiting for me up there, of course. "Came all this way to save you, Olive, not watch you die."

That black little seed of pain inside him is growing now, as fast as the queen sucking at our wards, but it's only in my power to stop one of them. "I'm sorry, Darin. You're the brother I never had, and I love you. But this is my destiny."

"Perhaps not," a voice behind us says. I turn to see Asome, holding tight to his warded staff. He's bound it to a wave of magic and let it pull him up the stairwell.

"Sibling." I take a step back as Asome's feet touch the platform.

Asome puts up his hands, bending without taking his eyes off me to lay down his staff. He follows suit, kneeling with his hands on the floor. "I am not here to fight. I will come no closer. I only ask you listen."

My eyes flick to the demon queen. She has grown enormous, still hungrily trying to claw through the forbidding. I look back at Asome and cross my arms. "Be quick."

"When Father spared my life all those years ago, he said it was because I still had a part to play. A path to redemption. All these years, I have sought it. First in my heart, then in my sticks, and then in the stars."

"And that, brother, is why I can never trust you," I say. "This is not about your redemption, it is about the survival of our people."

"Can they not be one and the same?" Asome asks. "Every time I try to live for Sharak Ka, I bring ruin and strife. I see now, it is because I was meant to die for it."

"Your sticks and stars told you that?" I ask.

"The *dama'ting* say it is a curse to predict your own death, but I had nothing to lose," Asome says, and I can see the truth of it in his aura. "I pondered my own for many years, but of course I did not understand. I knew I would die here, in the endless night below, at a convergence point."

Favah taught me of convergences in the Chamber of Shadows. The future is woven out of choices, each casting us down a different path. Some choices, like what to have for breakfast, cause little variation. Others can shape the world. Those points can cloud a seer's ability to look beyond.

"I did not know if I would die on the journey," Asome continues, "or in challenging you, or in Sharak Ka. But I knew, I know, I will not return. This is my death."

He leans forward, pressing his forehead to the floor between his hands. "I beg you, sibling. Let it be the one death that can bring balance to the evil I have done."

He means it, as much as I can tell. Against my better judgment, I again feel sympathy for my brother. "I have barely learned to control the crown with a week to practice. How can you hope to master it in time?"

There's a change in Asome's aura, something of the old haughtiness returning. "The replica of Father's crown I made when I took the throne? The Damajah enhanced its powers, but I daresay I know them better than you."

He's right, though it is strange to think of. Why shouldn't it burn him to see me wear it?

I walk over to where my brother kneels, laying a hand on his shoulder. I am willing to die, but I don't want to. For Asome, it is all he wants. A final glory to weigh against his soul on Everam's scales.

I don't believe in a literal Heaven, but it doesn't matter what I believe, it matters what he does.

I press the meat of my thumb into the spiked ward of the crown's chin strap, undoing the blood lock with a click. Asome doesn't look up, but he removes his turban and the helm beneath, holding it out. My vision goes black as I remove the crown, cutting me off not only from the *csar* and its power, but even from wardsight, itself.

I take Asome's helm and slip it on. The fit is disconcertingly comfortable, and the world once again lights up with magic's glow. I fall into my breath, setting the crown on Asome's head and fastening the strap, letting him press his thumb into the blood lock and activate the crown's power.

Asome gasps as magic suffuses him, but he does not falter, getting to his feet. "Father. I am ready."

"Oh, my son." Father's voice resonates in the stone around us. "It is only now you see. But there is still time to embrace glory."

Magic begins flowing into Asome at a frightening rate. Not the raw magic of the Core, but the pure golden fire of Sharik Hora, of the sacrifice of heroes.

Asome is suffused with power, filling the crown, his staff, his very body. Still it flows, the wards cut into his skin flaring so hot they burn through his robes. Darin and I both step back as the heat of it flushes our faces.

Then Asome crouches, whirling the golden fire around himself like a cyclone as he launches toward the demon queen.

THE FORBIDDING FLICKERS as Father summons all the power at his command, funneling it into my brother through the crown. He smashes into the queen so hard her legs flail, dropping her precious charge, the weakened Alagai Ka.

And he *is* weak. If he had any strength, the Father of Demons would never do something so mundane as to fall. But fall he does, skittering off the forbidding and riding its curve down to the ground with a streak of wardlight.

"There!" Darin points, already dissipating.

"Don't go alone!" I shout, but I know it isn't enough. Without the crown I can no longer fly or ride waves of magic like a bird on the wind. Darin can be there before I get down the steps.

I leap the railing instead, sliding down the great dome of Sharik Hora. When I get to the bottom I leap, taking off much of my momentum as I land on one of the lesser domes and slide from there to a terrace, where I pick a path down that has me swinging from masonry, statues, and banner poles until I can drop to the street.

I ignore the sting of impact, not knowing if Darin is with me or already gone. I take off at a mad run through the streets toward the section of wall where Alagai Ka fell.

Darin is waiting at the nearest small gate, little more than a thick door just large enough to admit warriors one at a time. The guards fall over themselves to open it and get out of our way.

I look up as we exit the *csar,* but the light from above is blinding. Next to the massive demon queen, my brother is little more than an insect, but he shines like the sun, and even the magic-hungry queen cannot withstand the glare. Her shrieks are echoed by the demonic multitudes clawing at the forbidding.

One group of demons ignores the barrier, circling inward. I don't need to guess around what as I put on speed. My weapons and armor are still hot with magic, and I am prepared to smash through as many *alagai* as necessary to get to their king.

Darin paces me, raising his pipes. Sharp, discordant sounds drive the demons out of our path like a shepherd's switch, revealing Alagai Ka, lying limp on the ground.

The Father of Demons is emaciated compared to when I last saw him, just knobbed charcoal flesh sunken over a tiny skeleton. His aura is dim, barely alive, and I can see lines of magic still tethering him to the queen. I grip my short spear, stalking in. Even Darin has his knife in hand.

I hear a whine in the air, rising in tension until there is a shattering sound and the eternal night of the cavern turns to day as my brother's crown—and my brother—are consumed. Momentarily blinded, I hold my killing blow for a clearer strike.

My eyes flick upward. Already the light of Asome's sacrifice has faded, but the queen herself is burning, her thorax blown open and hollowed as she drops to the ground.

I flick my eyes back, finding Alagai Ka right where he was before. I lunge.

I am tackled by a field demon, knocked from his path. I catch the impact on my shield and drive home a killing blow in seconds, but it's all the time the demon king needs, now that his tether to the queen is broken.

The *alagai* have stopped responding to Darin's pipes. They're moving with direction now, encircling us, cutting us off from Alagai Ka.

Not this time. Darin turns to mist, passing through the other demons to materialize on the other side, knife leading.

I take a less subtle approach, locking my shoulder against my shield and bulling right through. It's reckless, but we have only seconds before . . .

Just as our blades come in range, the demon king dissipates, and we strike only the stone where he lay.

The demon horde perks up then, as if in answer to some distant call. As one, they stampede for the tunnels leading to the hive.

CHAPTER 57

DRAGGING

No. No no no. Can't end like this. Not again.

Olive looks at me in horror. I reach out, taking her arm in a tight grip. "We have to go after him. Now."

"How?" Olive demands.

I take it as consent, Drawing power through her as effortlessly as I pull in a breath. I feel our auras connect, an invasion of privacy neither of us would normally allow, but there's no time for blushing at secrets. Olive trusts me, letting down her defenses as I probe.

Olive's magic ent the same as mine. My parents et demon meat, and it became a part of them. It's why they could do magic tricks other folk couldn't, and how it got passed on to me.

Olive's parents din't eat demon meat, but they were using a lot of magic when she was conceived. There's rippin' paintings in every Holy House in Hollow of Duchess Leesha casting her spells against the demons, belly round with child.

She can't dissipate, but Olive's got magic in her, just like me. She soaks it like a sponge, suffusing her aura and manifesting in physical ways. She heals quick as a demon. Bones like iron and muscles like steel cable.

I Know her now, and reach for the center of her aura, tugging experimentally with my will.

Then I blow us apart.

Dragging, I called it, when Mam used to do it to me. Name's apt. I pull Olive along, feeling her screams more than I hear them as her mind is subjected to the madness of skating, riding through an endless network of magic streams flowing from the Core.

I'd never have found the right one on my own, but I can follow Alagai Ka's tainted spoor through streams of magic as easily as I track a scent.

Olive said mating with the mimic queen nearly killed Alagai Ka. That a queen takes everything for her young, leaving her mate close to death, if he survives at all.

It's all we got goin' for us as we materialize in the center of the hive ward where a well larger than Safehold's lies dormant. Demon ent expectin' us, and isn't quick enough as Olive punches her spear through his abdomen, pinnin' him to the ground.

He claws at her, but he's slow. I hack off the arm with Mam's knife. Before he can recover, Olive stabs him in the chest with her *hanzhar*, over and over.

Should have hit him in the head. Demon don't need his limbs to trigger dissipation. He melts away from our weapons and makes another break for it. Doesn't run away this time. Not with all that power beneath our feet. He reaches out a tendril like a straw, drinking in the magic. Growin' strong again.

No way to stop him like this, but facin' the demon's will alone in the mists scares the core out of me.

Lucky I ent alone. I grab Olive again, linking auras as I dissolve us into mist and reach for the well. Alagai Ka senses us and attacks, will against will, but he is still weak and disoriented, no match for the sum of our determination. He forms a connection, but he does not control it.

I use the connection to pull close, trying grab him like when I turn sticky, like I did with Mam. I ent the angry sort. Never seemed to serve much purpose or make things better. Hate feeling that way.

But I got a hurt deep inside me, and I don't mind sharing it with the monster that caused it.

Ent gettin' away this time, I growl in the demon's mind. *Ent a dozen people will miss me when I'm gone, but the whole world's better off without you.*

What? Olive's voice sounds in the darkness.

You were right, I tell her. *Mam was right. Da, too. This is bigger'n us.*

I try to peel her off me like Mam did as I reach for the well. Just one more sacrifice, and it's over. Won't need to live with the pain of losing Mam. Won't have to live with anythin'. And maybe, just maybe, we'll all find each other in the Core.

I touch the dormant power, lying in wait of a will to command it. Limitless potential, enough to grant me one wish. One infinite act, and then oblivion.

Olive is still clutching at my aura. She understands what I mean to do. Wants me to do it. But she ent lettin' go. Friends to the end.

Together, she whispers in my mind.

Alagai Ka doesn't understand. Not at all. Sacrificing oneself for others? That is the design of lesser creatures, drones and prey and livestock. But he doesn't have to understand the act to know it will prove his undoing.

Demon sends us visions, reminders of what we got to lose. The shady spot by the swimming hole in Soggy Marsh. Grandda Jeph's farm. Rojvah's kisses. Selen's embrace.

And Olive. Funeral processions at her loss, her mother weeping, clad ever more in black. The wailing across Hollow, the breaking of Prince Rhinebeck's heart. That bouncy girl she kissed at Solstice, cryin' her eyes out.

I hesitate for only a moment, but the demon senses it and flexes the last of his will, breaking our hold. He casts his senses deep into the pathways of magic flowing from the hive, until he finds the one he's looking for. One he has never dared explore.

There's a queen there. He senses her, even from so far away. The thought fills him with fear, but not as much as the oblivion he faces here, as Olive and I put the collective spark of our anger into the well of power.

Before the magic ignites, Alagai Ka binds himself to the deep pathway and lets it carry him away.

It is a desperate leap. If he survives at all, he will materialize weak, crippled, and vulnerable in foreign lands. If this new hive has any strength to it, they will destroy him on sight.

Olive and I are of one mind as we follow, escaping the hive even as the tremors begin. Alagai Ka will find no solace here ever again.

Already the path is growing cold, but I give over to instinct, diving deeper than Mam ever dragged me. Deeper than anyone in their right mind would dare.

We're so close to the Core. I hear it callin', but it's the sound of a cliff callin' you to leap off. A fire callin' you to stick in your hand. Always thought it would be more than I can resist, but it's easier than I expect to say no, finding the powerful upward current Alagai Ka used and shooting for the surface like a geyser.

We're spat out like water in a fountain, landing face-first in the sand.

Are we back in the desert? Did I make a mistake? Lead us to the wrong place?

Then water splashes us, thick and salty, and both of us cough and choke on it, staggering to our feet.

There's stone overhead, and for a moment I think we're still underground. Then I see moonlight reflecting off the water, and I see we're in some sort of grotto. Behind us, the caves run deep, but we stumble, coughing and choking, for the open air.

"Look out!" I call as I hear the swell. Olive sees the rising wave and grabs on to me, setting her feet as it crashes over us. With a grip on the back of my coat, she hauls us both to shore.

Olive spits salt water onto the beach. "Where are we?"

I shrug. "Across the sea."

"That isn't terribly helpful," Olive says, looking around. "I don't see the demon."

"Me either," I admit. "But he's been here. He's weak, wounded, and can't travel much farther until he gets his strength back. Came here because he sensed a queen. We find her, we find him."

"You make it sound simple," Olive says.

"Is," I say. "Demon thought he's been huntin' us all this time.

"Now we're huntin' him."

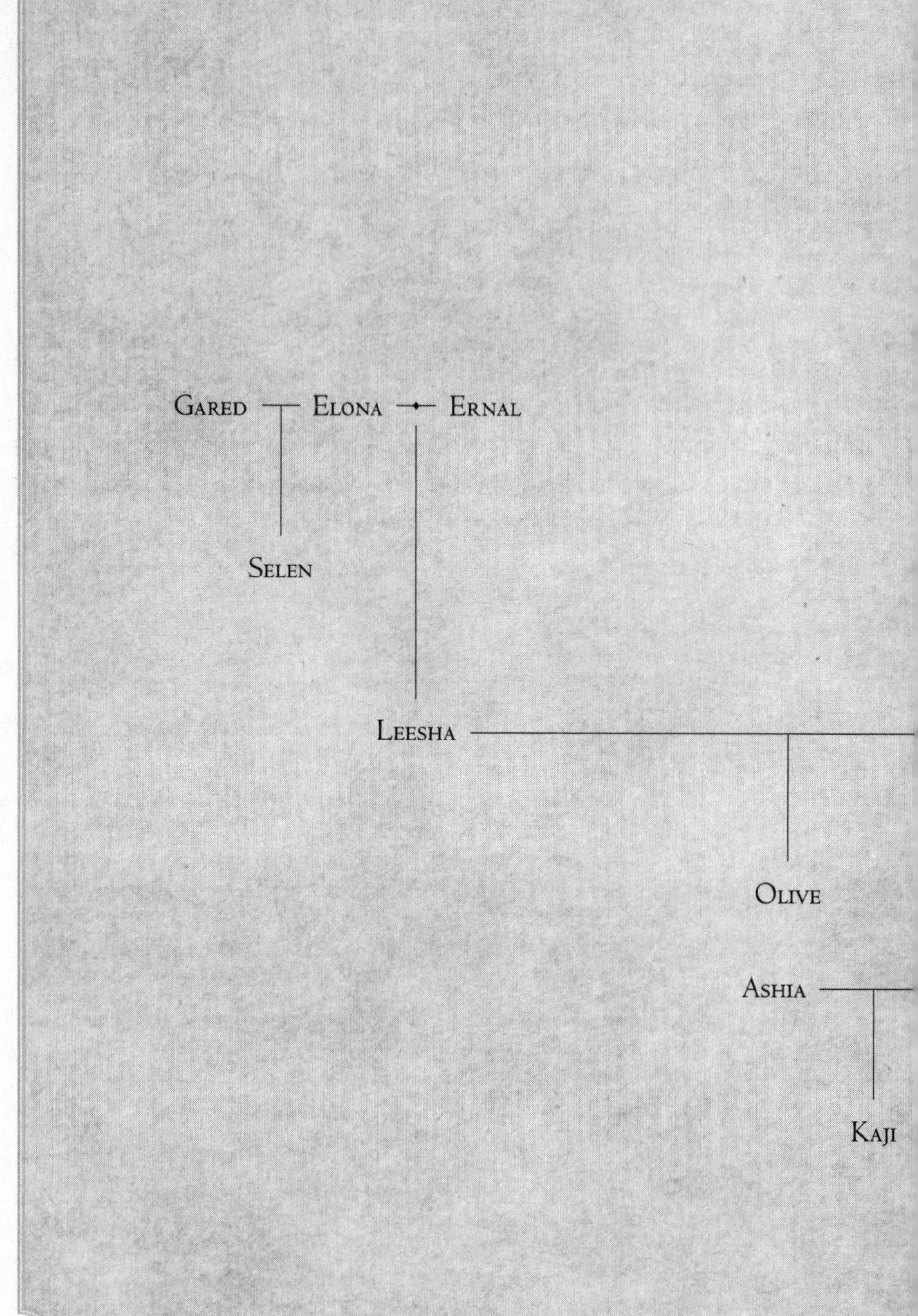
Gared
Elona
Ernal
Selen
Leesha
Olive
Ashia
Kaji

FAMILY TREE

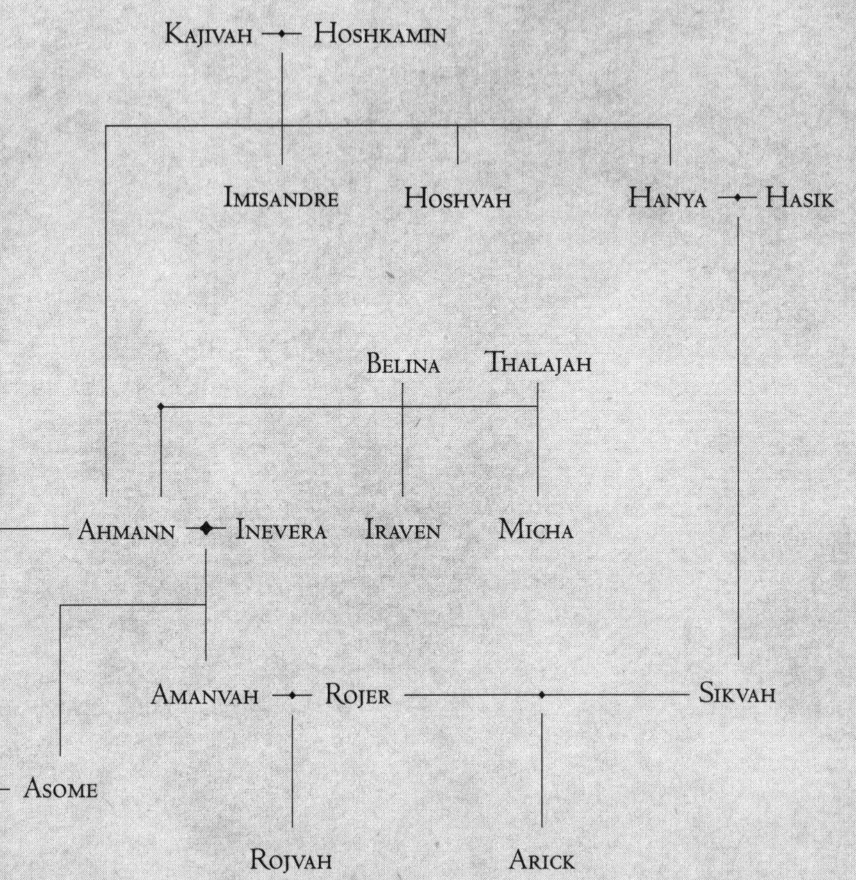

Kajivah
Hoshkamin
Imisandre
Hoshvah
Hanya
Hasik
Belina
Thalajah
Ahmann
Inevera
Iraven
Micha
Amanvah
Rojer
Sikvah
Asome
Rojvah
Arick

KRASIAN DICTIONARY

Ajin'pal/ajin'pan: Blood brother/blood sister. Name for the bond that forms between a mentor and a young warrior fighting their first *alagai'sharak*. An *ajin'pal* or *pan* is considered a blood relative thereafter.

Ajin'pel: Blooded to many. A warrior of such renown that they have blooded many an *ajin'pal* over the years. *Ajin'pel* are very influential among the *Sharum*.

Ala: (1) The perfect world created by Everam, corrupted by Nie. (2) Dirt, soil, clay, et cetera.

Alagai: Corelings (demons). Direct translation is "plague of Ala."

Alagai hora: Demonbones used to create magic items, such as the warded dice *dama'ting* use to tell the future. *Alagai hora* burst into flame if exposed to direct sunlight.

Alagai Ka: The mind demon, Consort to Alagai'ting Ka, the Mother of Demons. Also known as Father of Demons, the Father of Lies, and the demon king. Alagai Ka and his sons were said to be the most powerful of the demon lords—generals and captains of Nie's forces.

Alagai-scale: Special Majah armor technique guarded by the powerful Tazhan family.

Alagai'sharak: Holy war against demonkind.

Alagai tail: A whip consisting of three strips of leather braided with sharp barbs to cut into a victim's flesh. Used by *dama* as an instrument of punishment.

Alagai'ting Ka: The Mother of Demons of Krasian myth, also known as the Mother of Evil and the demon queen.

Alomom: Powder that Watchers use to hide the scent of their sweat.

Arms of Everam: Guards of the Holy City in Desert Spear. They wear white sleeves with their *Sharum* blacks, symbolizing their arms in service to the *dama.*

Asu: "Son" or "son of," often used as a suffix or prefix in a boy's name.

Baba: Grandfather (informal term of affection).

Bido: Loincloth worn by both men and women under their robes. A youth who has not yet earned vocational robes is referred to as "still in their bido."

Bloodfather: Godparent, used most often for *ajin'pal* of a deceased father.

Chin: Outsider/infidel. Anyone who is not at least half-blood Krasian. *Chin* is derogatory, synonymous with coward.

Chi'Sharum: Greenbloods who go through *Hannu Pash* and are raised to warrior status with all of its rights and privileges. Their caste remains below that of the Krasian-blood *dal'Sharum.*

Couzi: A harsh, illegal liquor filtered with cinnamon. Because of its potency, couzi is served in tiny cups meant to be taken in one swallow.

Dal: Prefix meaning "honored."

Dal'Sharum: The Krasian warrior caste, which includes the vast majority of the men. *Dal'Sharum* are broken into smaller units answerable to individual *kai'Sharum*. *Dal'Sharum* dress in black armored robes with a black turban helm and night veil. All are trained in hand-to-hand combat (*sharusahk*), as well as spear fighting and shield formations.

Dama: Clerical caste, which is above warrior. *Dama* are both religious and secular leaders. They wear white robes and eschew the spear in favor of alagai tail whips. All *dama* are masters of *sharusahk*, the Krasian hand-to-hand martial art, including secret techniques not given to the *Sharum*.

Damajah: Singular title for Inevera, the First Wife of Ahmann Jardir, the Shar'Dama Ka. The Damajah is both spiritual and secular leader of every woman in New Krasia.

Damaji: Male religious and secular leader of one of the twelve tribes of Krasia.

Damaji'ting: Female religious and secular leader of a tribe with dominion over its women.

Dama'ting: Female clerical caste, holy women who also serve as healers and midwives. *Dama'ting* hold the secrets of *hora* magic, including the power to foretell the future, and are held in fear and awe. Harming a *dama'ting* or hindering her in any way is punishable by death.

Desert Spear: Known in the North as Fort Krasia, an enormous fortress city built around the oasis and ancient Holy City of Sharik Hora.

Draki: Krasian unit of currency.

Drillmasters: Elite warriors who train *nie'Sharum*. Drillmasters wear standard *dal'Sharum* blacks, but their night veils are red.

Evejah, the: The holy book of Everam, written by Kaji, the first Deliverer, some three millennia past. The Evejah is separated into sections called Dunes. Each *dama* pens a copy of the Evejah in his own blood during his clerical training.

Evejan: Name of the Krasian religion, "those who follow the Evejah."

Evejan law: Militant religious law imposed on general citizenry.

Everam: The Creator.

Everam's Bounty: Formerly the Free City of Fort Rizon, it was conquered in 333 AR with its vast farmland and became the capital of New Krasia in the green lands.

Ginjaz: Turncoat, traitor.

Greenlander: One from the green lands. A less derogatory term than *chin.*

Green lands: Krasian name for Thesa (the lands north of the Krasian desert), a large swath of which has become New Krasia.

Hannu Pash: Literally "life's path," this represents both a ceremony and a period of training and religious indoctrination to determine a young Krasian's vocation.

Hava: Spice to flavor and preserve food. Hava is foundational in Krasian cooking.

Heasah: Prostitute.

Hora magic: Any magic using demon body parts (bones, ichor, et cetera) as a battery to power spells.

Horn of Sharak: Ceremonial horn blown to begin and end *alagai'sharak*.

Inevera: (1) Krasian word meaning "Everam's will" or "Everam willing." (2) A common name for women in the Kaji tribe.

Jiwah/jiwan: Wife/husband.

Jiwah Ka: First Wife. The *Jiwah Ka* is the first and most honored of a Krasian man's wives. She has veto power over subsequent marriages, and can command her sister-wives.

Jiwah Sen: Lesser wives, subservient to a man's *Jiwah Ka.*

Jiwah'Sharum: Literally "wives of warriors," these are women who live in *Sharum* harems during their fertile years. It is considered a great honor to serve. All warriors have access to their tribe's *Jiwah'Sharum,* and are expected to keep them continually with child, adding warriors to the tribe.

Kai'Sharum: Krasian military captains. *Kai'Sharum* receive special training in Sharik Hora and lead individual units in *alagai'sharak. Kai'Sharum* wear *dal'Sharum* blacks, but their night veils are white.

Kaji: The name of the original Deliverer and patriarch of the Kaji tribe, also known as Shar'Dama Ka. More than three thousand years ago, Kaji united the known world in a war against the demons, ushering in millennia of peace.

Kamanj: A bowed string instrument similar to a fiddle that ends in a spike planted on the ground or a player's leg to steady it.

Khaffit: Lowest male caste in Krasian society. Expelled from *sharaj, khaffit* are forced to dress in the tan clothes of children and shave their cheeks as a sign that they are not true men.

Lonely path: Krasian term for death. All warriors must walk the mist-shrouded road to Heaven, with temptations on the path to test their spirit and ensure that only the worthy stand before Everam to be judged. Spirits who venture off the path are lost.

Nie: (1) The name of the Uncreator, feminine opposite to Everam, and the goddess of night and demonkind. (2) Nothing, none, void, no, not. (3) Prefix for trainees in line for a vocation.

Nie'dama: Nie'Sharum selected for *dama* training.

Nie'dama'ting: Dama'ting-in-training. Also known as Betrothed, they are promised Brides of Everam. For a man to lay hands on them is punishable by death or loss of the offending limb.

Nie Ka: Literally "first of none," a term for the head boy of a *nie'Sharum* class, who commands the other boys as sergeant to the *dal'Sharum* drillmasters.

Nie's abyss: Also known as the Core. In Evejan scripture, it is the seven-layered underworld where *alagai* hide from the sun. Each layer is populated with a different breed of demon.

Nie'Sharum: Warriors-in-training.

Night veil: Veil worn by *Sharum* during *alagai'sharak* to hide their identities, showing that all men are equal allies in the night.

Oot: *Dal'Sharum* signal for "beware" or "demon approaching."

Princes Unit: Olive and Chadan's *Sharum* unit, composed of *nie'Sharum* of various castes blooded young due to crisis. Derided by older warriors as the "Princess" Unit, they top the kill counts almost every night, taking on the most dangerous missions.

Push'ting: Literal translation "false woman." While Queer relationships are common in Krasia, Evejan law commands all those who are able to add people to the tribe. *Push'ting* is most commonly used in a derogatory sense toward those who refuse even a symbolic marriage for the purpose of children, but can be used affectionately between loved ones.

Scorpion: A giant crossbow using springs instead of a bowstring. It shoots thick spears with heavy heads (stingers) and can kill sand and wind demons outright at a thousand feet, even without wards.

Sharaj: Barracks for young boys in *Hannu Pash,* much like a military boarding school. The *sharaji* are organized by blood. Full blood for the sons and daughters of pure-blooded Majah warrior families. Half blood for the sons of *dal'Sharum* and *chin* women. Coward's blood for the sons of *khaffit*. Green blood for the sons of *chin*.

Sharak Ka: The First War. The final battle of *alagai'sharak,* when the Deliverer will lead Everam's armies to victory or defeat.

Sharak Sun: The Daylight War, during which humanity must be conquered and united into Everam's army for Sharak Ka.

Shar'dama: Dama who fight *alagai'sharak* in defiance of Evejan law.

Shar'Dama Ka: First Warrior–Cleric. The Krasian term for the Deliverer, who will come to free mankind from the *alagai.*

Sharik Hora: The great temple in Krasia made out of the bones of fallen warriors. Having their bones lacquered and added to the temple is the highest honor that warriors can attain.

Sharukin: Warrior poses. Practiced series of movements for *sharusahk.*

Sharum: Warrior. The *Sharum* dress in black robes inlaid with pockets for fired clay armor plates.

Sharum Ka: First Warrior. A title for the secular leader of *alagai'sharak.* The Sharum Ka is appointed by the occupant of the Skull Throne, and all *Sharum* answer to him and him only from dusk until dawn. The Sharum Ka has his own palace at the head of the training grounds and sits on the Spear Throne. He wears *dal'Sharum* blacks, but his turban and night veil are white.

Sharum'ting: Female warriors, mostly serving as personal guards to the *dama'ting*.

Sharusahk: The Krasian art of unarmed combat. There are various schools of *sharusahk* depending on caste and tribe, but all consist of brutal, efficient moves designed to turn an opponent's strength against them to stun, cripple, and kill.

Shield team: Small teams of two to five warriors subdividing *Sharum* units.

Skull Throne: The traditional seat of power for Krasia's leader. Since the split with the Majah tribe, there are now two Skull Thrones. The one in New Krasia is the original—made from the skulls of deceased Sharum Ka and coated in electrum, the throne is powered by the skull of a mind demon, casting a forbiddance that prevents demons from entering the inner city of Everam's Bounty. The one in old Krasia is newly made from the skulls of fallen warriors and sits in the holy temple of Sharik Hora.

Spears of the Desert: Sharum Ka Iraven's elite bodyguard unit.

Spear Throne: The throne of the Sharum Ka, made from the broken spears of previous Sharum Kas.

Stinger: The ammunition for the scorpion ballistae. Stingers are giant spears with heavy iron heads that can punch through demon armor on a parabolic shot.

Tikka: Grandmother (informal term of affection).

'ting: Suffix meaning "woman."

Tribes: Reference to the twelve tribes of Krasia—Anjha, Bajin, Halvas, Jama, Kaji, Khanjin, Krevakh, Majah, Mehnding, Nanji, Sharach, Shunjin.

Undercity: Huge honeycomb of warded caverns beneath Desert Spear where women, children, and *khaffit* are locked at night to keep them safe from demons while the men fight.

Vah: "Daughter" or "daughter of." Often used as a suffix or prefix in a girl's name.

Waning: Three-day monthly religious observance for Evejans occurring on the days directly before, on, and after the new moon. Attendance at Sharik Hora is mandatory, and families spend the days together, even pulling sons out of *sharaj*. Demons are said to be more powerful on Waning, when it is said Alagai Ka walks the surface.

Wardwork: Scrollwork on clothing or items consisting of ward patterns with real potency.

Watchers: *Dal'Sharum*, primarily of the Krevakh and Nanji tribes, trained in special weapons and tactics. They serve as scouts, spies, and assassins. Watchers carry and fight with iron-shod ladders six feet long as well as smaller, close-combat weapons. The ladders have interconnecting ends so they can be joined together. Watchers are so proficient they can run straight up a ladder without bracing it and balance at the top.

WARD GRIMOIRE

PROTECTION WARDS

Protection (defensive) wards Draw magic to form a barrier (forbiddance) through which demon corelings cannot pass. Wards are strongest when used against the specific demon type to which they are assigned, and are most commonly used in conjunction with other wards in circles of protection. When a circle activates, all coreflesh is forcibly banished from its line. A mixed group of demons is referred to as a host.

BANK DEMON

Description: Also called frog demons or froggies, these demons look much like common fly frogs, but they are large enough to swallow humans whole. They lie in wait in shallow water, springing only when prey comes within range. They lash out with long, powerful tongues, catching victims and dragging them into their wide maws. Bank demons will then return to the water, drowning their struggling prey. A group of bank demons is called an army.

CAVE DEMON

Description: Cave demons, also known as tunnel or spider demons, have eight segmented legs and can run at great speed. Cave demons excrete a sticky silk that is magic-dead—invisible to wardsight and immune to wards of protection. They will prepare traps and lie in wait for the unwary. These demons seldom rise to the surface unless summoned by a mind; they are more commonly found in deep caves and the tunnels of a demon hive. A group of cave demons is called a clutter.

CLAY DEMON

Description: Clay demons are native to the hard clay flats on the outskirts of the Krasian desert. They are perhaps three feet long, but heavy with compact muscle and thick, overlapping armor plates. Their short, hard talons allow them to cling to most any rock face, even hanging upside down. Their orange-brown armor can blend invisibly into an adobe wall or clay bed. The blunt head of a clay demon can smash through nearly anything, cracking stone and denting steel. A group of clay demons is known as a shattering.

FIELD DEMON

Description: Sleek and low to the ground, with long, powerful limbs and retractable claws, field demons are the fastest thing on four legs when they have open ground to run and can leap great distances. Tough scales on their limbs and back can turn aside most weapons, but their underbelly—if exposed—is more vulnerable. A group of field demons, also known as fieldies, is called a reap.

FLAME DEMON

Description: Flame demons have eyes, nostrils, and mouths that glow with a smoky orange light. They are the smallest demons, no larger than a cat. Like all demons, they have long, hooked claws and rows of razor-sharp teeth. Their armor consists of small, overlapping scales, sharp and hard. Flame demons can spit fire in brief bursts. Their sticky firespit burns intensely on contact with air and can set almost any substance alight, even metal and stone. A group of flame demons is known as a blaze.

LIGHTNING DEMON

Description: Though lightning demons are nearly indistinguishable from their wind demon cousins, their spit is charged with electricity that can paralyze a victim. They spit as they dive, snatching up their helpless victims to devour them alive. A group of lightning demons is known as a thundercloud.

MIMIC DEMON

Description: Mimics are the elite bodyguards to mind demons. Less vulnerable to light than their masters and more intelligent than the lesser breeds, mimics serve as lieutenants and are able to summon and exert their will upon coreling drones. Their natural form is unknown, but they are able to assume the form of nearly anything they encounter, from inanimate objects to creatures, clothing, and equipment. One of their favorite tricks is to learn the names of their prey and take the form of a friend, feigning distress and calling to their victims to convince them to leave the safety of their wards. A gathering of mimic demons is known as a troupe.

MIND DEMON

Description: Also known as coreling princes, mind demons are the generals of demonkind. The only male-sexed caste among demonkind, minds are physically weak and have little in the way of the natural defenses of the other corelings, but they have vast mental and magical powers. They can read and control minds, communicate telepathically, and implant permanent suggestions. They can draw wards in the air and power them with their own innate magic. Coreling drones follow their every mental command without hesitation, and will give their lives to protect them. Sensitive to even moonlight, mind demons only rise on the three-night period of the new moon cycle, in the hours when night is darkest. A gathering of mind demons is known as a court.

ROCK DEMON

Description: The largest of the coreling breeds, rock demons, also known as rockies, can range in height from six to twenty feet. Hulking masses of sinew and sharp edges, they have thick carapaces knobbed with bony protrusions, and their spiked tails can shatter stone. They stand hunched on two clawed feet, with long, gnarled arms ending in talons the size of butcher knives, and multiple rows of bladelike teeth. No known physical force can harm a rock demon. A group of rock demons is called a quake.

SAND DEMON

Description: Cousins to rock demons, sand demons are smaller and more nimble, but still among the strongest and best armored of the coreling breeds. They have small, sharp scales that are a dirty yellow almost indistinguishable from gritty sand. They run on all fours but can rise to two legs in combat. Their short snouts have rows of sharp teeth, with nostril slits just below large, lidless eyes. Thick horns curve upward and back, cutting through the scales. Sand demons hunt in packs known as storms.

SNOW DEMON

Description: Similar to flame demons in size and build, snow demons are native to frozen Northern climates and high mountain elevations. Their scales are such pure white, they scintillate with color if caught in the light. Snow demons are nearly invisible in the snow, and spit a liquid so cold it instantly freezes anything it touches. Steel struck with coldspit can become brittle enough to shatter. A group of snow demons is called a blizzard.

STONE DEMON

Description: Smaller cousins of rock demons—who form through faces of pure rock—stone demons feature armor with the mottled appearance of conglomerate rock. They tend to be squat and slow, but are among the strongest and most indestructible of demons. Requiring less specialized environments to rise, stone demons are more common than rock demons. A group of stone demons is called a conglomerate.

SUCCOR

Description: The succor ward is a general ward of protection taught to children. Not as powerful as wards keyed to individual breeds, succor wards create a general field of discomfort that is enough to drive most corelings away unless prey is in sight. Very large or powerful wards can form a forbiddance. The ward is used in the Thesan dice game Succor, as well as its Krasian variation, Sharak.

SWAMP DEMON

Description: Swamp demons are native to swamps and marshy areas, an amphibious form of wood demon at home both in the water and in the trees. Swamp demons are blotched green and brown to blend into their surroundings, and will often hide in trees, mud, or shallow water to spring on prey. They spit a thick, sticky slime that rots any organic material it comes in contact with. A group of swamp demons is called a muck.

WATER DEMON

Description: Water demons are seldom seen. They come in various forms and sizes. Some are man-sized, sleek and scaly, with webbed hands and feet, tipped with sharp talons. Others are large enough to pull ships beneath the surface with their thick, horned tentacles. Others are bigger still, leviathans able to leap above the water and splash down to create tremendous waves. Water demons can only breathe underwater, though they can surface for a short time. A group of water demons is called a wave.

WIND DEMON

Description: Wind demons stand as tall as humans at the shoulder, but have head fins that rise much higher, topping eight or nine feet. Their sharp-edged beaks hide rows of teeth. Their skin is a tough, flexible armor that can turn most any spearpoint or arrowhead. It stretches out from their sides and along the underside of their arms to form the tough membrane of their wings, which can span three times their height. Clumsy and slow on land, wind demons have tremendous power in the sky. The thin wing bones are jointed with wicked hooked talons. Their preferred attack is a silent dive, opening their wings with a great snap just before impact, severing a victim's head before grabbing the body in their hind talons and flying off. A group of wind demons is called a flight.

WOOD DEMON

Description: Wood demons, also called woodies, are native to forests. Next to rock demons, they are the largest and most powerful demons, averaging from five to fifteen feet tall when standing on their hind legs, the smallest sometimes referred to as stump demons. Wood demons have short, powerful hindquarters and long, sinewy arms, perfect for climbing trees and leaping from branch to branch. Their claws are short, hard points, designed for gripping trees. Wood demons' armor is barklike in color and texture, and they have large black eyes. Wood demons cannot be harmed by normal fire, but will burn readily if brought into contact with hotter fires, such as firespit or liquid demonfire. Wood demons will kill flame demons on sight, and hunt in groups called copses.

COMBAT WARDS

Combat wards repurpose magic for offensive effects. Some Draw power directly from the demon they strike, while others are powered by batteries such as demonbone, also known as *hora*.

COLD

Description: Cold wards reduce thermal energy, rapidly dropping the temperature of their target area to below freezing. Powerful cold wards can shatter steel or even rock demon armor.

CUTTING

Description: Cutting wards, when etched along the length of a blade, siphon power from demons as they strike, weakening armor, strengthening the weapon, and sharpening the blade down to a near-molecular level, allowing the weapon to cut through even coreling armor and flesh.

FIRESPIT/COLDSPIT

Description: These wards are used as defense against flame demons, turning their firespit into a cool breeze. When drawn in reverse, they turn the coldspit of a snow demon into a warm breeze.

GLASS

Description: When etched on glass and charged with magic, these wards effect a permanent change, making glass harder than diamond and stronger than steel without changing its weight or appearance. Warded glass is widely used to create near-indestructible windows, vials, weapons, and armor.

HEAT

Description: Heat wards increase thermal energy, converting magic directly to heat. Objects painted with heat wards are consumed when the wards activate unless highly resistant to extreme temperatures.

IMPACT

Description: These wards turn magic into concussive force. They can be used alone, or to augment the blow of a blunt weapon. When used to strike a demon, they siphon magic like cutting wards, weakening armor even as they multiply force. The stronger the original impact, the more power is generated.

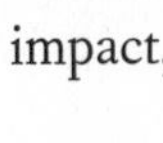

LECTRIC

Description: These wards convert magic directly into electricity that can be directed at an object or creature. The wards can also be linked to form circuits.

MAGNETIC

Description: Magnetic wards charge their target area, drawing ferrous materials like a powerful magnet. They are sometimes used to increase the accuracy of iron cannonballs.

MOISTURE

Description: Moisture wards attract moisture from the air or nearby bodies of water. They can be used to ensure that plants get the necessary water without human care, to fill a small reservoir, or to quench a flame demon. Powerful moisture wards can drown or, if reversed, dehydrate a victim.

PIERCING

Description: Piercing wards Draw from the point of impact on a demon's body, weakening coreling armor even as they focus magic into a weapon's point for maximum penetrative power.

PRESSURE

Description: Pressure wards exert a crushing force that builds in heat and intensity the longer they remain in contact with a demon.

PERCEPTION WARDS

Perception wards create magical effects that can alter the senses of demons and sometimes humans.

BLENDING

Description: Blending wards pull from their surroundings to camouflage their target area. Unlike unsight wards, which only work on demons, blending wards can hide things from human senses, as well. Sudden or quick movement can negate a blending ward's power.

CONFUSION

Description: Confusion wards radiate a field of disorientation that can cause creatures to become dizzy and lose their sense of direction. Unless prey is in sight, affected coreling drones will often forget what they are doing, wandering away harmlessly.

LIGHT

Description: Light wards convert magic to pure white light. Depending on the power source, the light can be anything from a soft glow to a blinding glare.

PROPHECY

Description: Carved into the *alagai hora* of the *dama'ting*, prophecy wards read the currents of magic to make predictions about the future. Their magic pulls the demonbone dice out of their natural trajectories to answer questions spoken in prayer to Everam. The processes used both to make the dice and to read them are closely guarded secrets of the Krasian priestesses—it is death to share them with outsiders.

RESONANCE

Description: Resonance wards can affect the flow of soundwaves, disrupting them to create areas of silence, or strengthening them to amplify sound. A demonbone broken into two pieces and carved with wards of resonance can effect communication over great distances.

UNSIGHT

Description: Wards of unsight can make objects invisible to demons, provided those objects keep relatively still. Wards of unsight in conjunction with wards of confusion are used to make Cloaks of Unsight that protect humans in the naked night.

WARDSIGHT

Description: When worn around the eyes and charged, these wards can allow surface creatures to see in the magical spectrum. Creatures with wardsight can see in complete darkness as easily as clear day, watch the flow of ambient magic, judge the relative power of wardings, and see the auras given off by all living things. A skilled practitioner can Read these auras to tell what others are feeling or thinking, and sometimes to gain a sense of their past or even their future.

ACKNOWLEDGMENTS

The Hidden Queen is my seventh novel. Did I think, when I first published *The Warded Man,* that I would still be in the game fifteen years later? Reader, I did not.

I make it sound like it was all me, but the book in your hands wouldn't be there without vast support. Phoenix, who read it first and inspired more than a little. Lauren, my rock of stability. Sirena, my agent of chaos. Mom and Dad, for liking every post and reminding me not to swear so much.

I want to thank Tricia Narwani for the lion's share of editing and project management, and Natasha Bardon for reading and offering thoughts even while on leave. Thanks to my publishing friends, Lauren Panepinto, Naomi Novik, Katherine Arden, Wesley Chu, and Jay Franco, who offered endless advice and trails of breadcrumbs in the dark forest. My beloved copy editor Laura Jorstad, who reminds me when I spell my own made-up words wrong and makes every book better. Martina Fačková, for stepping in mid-series with an unforgettable cover. Rachel Winterbottom, Claire Ward, and the rest of the Voyager team for taking up the burden while my editor was away, and the amazing team at Del Rey Books, who I am eternally proud to work with. Dominik Broniek and Larry Rostant, who have been illustrating my work for more than a decade. Editorial, production, marketing, and publicity teams at my publishers all over the world.

I want to thank my beloved translators, who work so hard to find the spirit behind the words, and the distributors and booksellers who put it in your hands/devices.

Most of all, and always, always, always, thank you to my readers, fan artists, cosplayers, tattoo artists, reviewers, and folk who just reach out to say they enjoyed the books. You keep me going when it's tough.

ABOUT THE AUTHOR

PETER V. BRETT is the internationally bestselling author of the Demon Cycle series, which has sold more than four million copies in twenty-seven languages worldwide. Novels include *The Warded Man*, *The Desert Spear*, *The Daylight War*, *The Skull Throne*, *The Core*, and *The Desert Prince*. He lives in Brooklyn.

petervbrett.com

@pvbrett

ABOUT THE TYPE

This book was set in Fournier, a typeface named for Pierre-Simon Fournier (1712–68), the youngest son of a French printing family. He started out engraving woodblocks and large capitals, then moved on to fonts of type. In 1736 he began his own foundry and made several important contributions in the field of type design; he is said to have cut 147 alphabets of his own creation. Fournier is probably best remembered as the designer of St. Augustine Ordinaire, a face that served as the model for the Monotype Corporation's Fournier, which was released in 1925.